Penguin Books
Last and First Men *and*
Last Men in London

William Olaf Stapledon was born in 1886 and educated at Abbotsholme School, Balliol College, Oxford, and Liverpool University. After spending eighteen months with a shipping office in Liverpool and Port Said, he lectured extramurally for Liverpool University in English literature and industrial history. He served in France with the Friends' Ambulance Unit from 1915 to 1919. He subsequently lectured again, extramurally, for Liverpool University, in psychology and philosophy. He died in 1950. His books include *A Modern Theory of Ethics, Odd John* (1935), *Star Maker* (1937), *Sirius* (1944), and *A Man Divided* (1950).

Olaf Stapledon

Last and First Men *and*
Last Men in London

Penguin Books

Penguin Books Ltd, Harmondsworth,
Middlesex, England
Penguin Books Inc., 7110 Ambassador Road,
Baltimore, Maryland 21207, U.S.A.
Penguin Books Australia Ltd, Ringwood,
Victoria, Australia

Last and First Men first published by Methuen 1930
Published in Pelican Books 1937, reissued in Penguin Books 1963
Last Men in London first published by Methuen 1932
Published together in one volume in Penguin Books 1972
Reprinted 1973

Made and printed in Great Britain by
Cox & Wyman Ltd, London, Reading and Fakenham
Set in Monotype Times

This book is sold subject to the condition that
it shall not, by way of trade or otherwise, be lent,
re-sold, hired out, or otherwise circulated without
the publisher's prior consent in any form of
binding or cover other than that in which it is
published and without a similar condition
including this condition being imposed on the
subsequent purchaser

Last and First Men

Contents

Contents

Contents

Preface

THIS is a work of fiction. I have tried to invent a story which may seem a possible, or at least not wholly impossible, account of the future of man; and I have tried to make that story relevant to the change that is taking place today in man's outlook.

To romance of the future may seem to be indulgence in ungoverned speculation for the sake of the marvellous. Yet controlled imagination in this sphere can be a very valuable exercise for minds bewildered about the present and its potentialities. Today we should welcome, and even study, every serious attempt to envisage the future of our race; not merely in order to grasp the very diverse and often tragic possibilities that confront us, but also that we may familiarize ourselves with the certainty that many of our most cherished ideals would seem puerile to more developed minds. To romance of the far future, then, is to attempt to see the human race in its cosmic setting, and to mould our hearts to entertain new values.

But if such imaginative construction of possible futures is to be at all potent, our imagination must be strictly disciplined. We must endeavour not to go beyond the bounds of possibility set by the particular state of culture within which we live. The merely fantastic has only minor power. Not that we should seek actually to prophesy what will as a matter of fact occur; for in our present state such prophecy is certainly futile, save in the simplest matters. We are not set up as historians attempting to look ahead instead of backwards. We can only select a certain thread out of the tangle of many equally valid possibilities. But we must select with a purpose. The activity that we are undertaking is not science, but art; and the effect that it should have on the reader is the effect that art should have.

Yet our aim is not merely to create aesthetically admirable fiction. We must achieve neither mere history, nor mere fiction, but myth. A true myth is one which, within the universe of a certain culture (living or dead), expresses richly, and often perhaps tragically, the highest admirations possible within that culture. A false myth is one which either violently transgresses the limits of credibility set by its own cultural matrix, or expresses admirations less developed than those of

11

Preface

its culture's best vision. This book can no more claim to be true myth than true prophecy. But it is an essay in myth creation.

The kind of future which is here imagined, should not, I think, seem wholly fantastic, or at any rate not so fantastic as to be without significance, to modern western individuals who are familiar with the outlines of contemporary thought. Had I chosen matter in which there was nothing whatever of the fantastic, its very plausibility would have rendered it unplausible. For one thing at least is almost certain about the future, namely, that very much of it will be such as we should call incredible. In one important respect, indeed, I may perhaps seem to have strayed into barren extravagance. I have supposed an inhabitant of the remote future to be communicating with us of today. I have pretended that he has the power of partially controlling the operations of minds now living, and that this book is the product of such influence. Yet even this fiction is perhaps not wholly excluded by our thought. I might, of course, easily have omitted it without more than superficial alteration of the theme. But its introduction was more than a convenience. Only by some such radical and bewildering device could I embody the possibility that there may be more in time's nature than is revealed to us. Indeed, only by some such trick could I do justice to the conviction that our whole present mentality is but a confused and halting first experiment.

If ever this book should happen to be discovered by some future individual, for instance by a member of the next generation sorting out the rubbish of his predecessors, it will certainly raise a smile; for very much is bound to happen of which no hint is yet discoverable. And indeed even in our generation circumstances may well change so unexpectedly and so radically that this book may very soon look ridiculous. But no matter. We of today must conceive our relation to the rest of the universe as best we can; and even if our images must seem fantastic to future men, they may none the less serve their purpose today.

Some readers, taking my story to be an attempt at prophecy, may deem it unwarrantably pessimistic. But it is not prophecy; it is myth, or an essay in myth. We all desire the future to turn out more happily than I have figured it. In particular we desire our present civilization to advance steadily toward some kind of Utopia. The thought that it may decay and collapse, and that all its spiritual treasure may be lost irrevocably, is repugnant to us. Yet this must be faced as at least a possibility. And this kind of tragedy, the tragedy of a race, must, I think, be admitted in any adequate myth.

And so, while gladly recognizing that in our time there are strong seeds of hope as well as of despair, I have imagined for aesthetic pur-

12

poses that our race will destroy itself. There is today a very earnest movement for peace and international unity; and surely with good fortune and intelligent management it may triumph. Most earnestly we must hope that it will. But I have figured things out in this book in such a manner that this great movement fails. I suppose it incapable of preventing a succession of national wars; and I permit it only to achieve the goal of unity and peace after the mentality of the race has been undermined. May this not happen! May the League of Nations, or some more strictly cosmopolitan authority, win through before it is too late! Yet let us find room in our minds and in our hearts for the thought that the whole enterprise of our race may be after all but a minor and unsuccessful episode in a vaster drama, which also perhaps may be tragic.

American readers, if ever there are any, may feel that their great nation is given a somewhat unattractive part in the story. I have imagined the triumph of the cruder sort of Americanism over all that is best and most promising in American culture. May this not occur in the real world! Americans themselves, however, admit the possibility of such an issue, and will, I hope, forgive me for emphasizing it, and using it as an early turning-point in the long drama of Man.

Any attempt to conceive such a drama must take into account whatever contemporary science has to say about man's own nature and his physical environment. I have tried to supplement my own slight knowledge of natural science by pestering my scientific friends. In particular, I have been very greatly helped by conversation with Professors P. G. H. Boswell, J. Johnstone, and J. Rice, of Liverpool. But they must not be held responsible for the many deliberate extravagances which, though they serve a purpose in the design, may jar upon the scientific ear.

To Dr L. A. Reid I am much indebted for general comments, and to Mr E. V. Rieu for many very valuable suggestions. To Professor and Mrs L. C. Martin, who read the whole book in manuscript, I cannot properly express my gratitude for constant encouragement and criticism. To my wife's devastating sanity I owe far more than she supposes.

Before closing this preface I would remind the reader that throughout the following pages the speaker, the first person singular, is supposed to be, not the actual writer, but an individual living in the extremely distant future.

O. S.

WEST KIRBY
July 1930

Introduction

By One of the Last Men

THIS book has two authors, one contemporary with its readers, the other an inhabitant of an age which they would call the distant future. The brain that conceives and writes these sentences lives in the time of Einstein. Yet I, the true inspirer of this book, I who have begotten it upon that brain, I who influence that primitive being's conception, inhabit an age which, for Einstein, lies in the very remote future.

The actual writer thinks he is merely contriving a work of fiction. Though he seeks to tell a plausible story, he neither believes it himself, nor expects others to believe it. Yet the story is true. A being whom you would call a future man has seized the docile but scarcely adequate brain of your contemporary, and is trying to direct its familiar processes for an alien purpose. Thus a future epoch makes contact with your age. Listen patiently; for we who are the Last Men earnestly desire to communicate with you, who are members of the First Human Species. We can help you, and we need your help.

You cannot believe it. Your acquaintance with time is very imperfect, and so your understanding of it is defeated. But no matter. Do not perplex yourselves about this truth, so difficult to you, so familiar to us of a later aeon. Do but entertain, merely as a fiction, the idea that the thought and will of individuals future to you may intrude, rarely and with difficulty, into the mental processes of some of your contemporaries. Pretend that you believe this, and that the following chronicle is an authentic message from the Last Men. Imagine the consequences of such a belief. Otherwise I cannot give life to the great history which it is my task to tell.

When your writers romance of the future, they too easily imagine a progress toward some kind of Utopia, in which beings like themselves live in unmitigated bliss among circumstances perfectly suited to a fixed human nature. I shall not describe any such paradise. Instead, I shall record huge fluctuations of joy and woe, the results of changes not only in man's environment but in his fluid nature. And I must tell how, in my own age, having at last achieved spiritual maturity and the philosophic mind, man is forced by an unexpected crisis to embark on an enterprise both repugnant and desperate.

Introduction

I invite you, then, to travel in imagination through the aeons that lie between your age and mine. I ask you to watch such a history of change, grief, hope, and unforeseen catastrophe, as has nowhere else occurred, within the girdle of the Milky Way. But first, it is well to contemplate for a few moments the mere magnitudes of cosmical events. For, compressed as it must necessarily be, the narrative that I have to tell may seem to present a sequence of adventures and disasters crowded together, with no intervening peace. But in fact man's career has been less like a mountain torrent hurtling from rock to rock, than a great sluggish river, broken very seldom by rapids. Ages of quiescence, often of actual stagnation, filled with the monotonous problems and toils of countless almost identical lives, have been punctuated by rare moments of racial adventure. Nay, even these few seemingly rapid events themselves were in fact often long-drawn-out and tedious. They acquire a mere illusion of speed from the speed of the narrative.

The receding depths of time and space, though they can indeed be haltingly conceived even by primitive minds, cannot be imaged save by beings of a more ample nature. A panorama of mountains appears to naïve vision almost as a flat picture, and the starry void is a roof pricked with light. Yet in reality, while the immediate terrain could be spanned in an hour's walking, the sky-line of peaks holds within it plain beyond plain. Similarly with time. While the near past and the new future display within them depth beyond depth, time's remote immensities are foreshortened into flatness. It is almost inconceivable to simple minds that man's whole history should be but a moment in the life of the stars, and that remote events should embrace within themselves aeon upon aeon.

In your day you have learnt to calculate something of the magnitudes of time and space. But to grasp my theme in its true proportions, it is necessary to do more than calculate. It is necessary to brood upon these magnitudes, to draw out the mind toward them, to feel the littleness of your here and now, and of the moment of civilization which you call history. You cannot hope to image, as we do, such vast proportions as one in a thousand million, because your sense-organs, and therefore your perceptions, are too coarse-grained to discriminate so small a fraction of their total field. But you may at least, by mere contemplation, grasp more constantly and firmly the significance of your calculations.

Men of your day, when they look back into the history of their planet, remark not only the length of time but also the bewildering acceleration of life's progress. Almost stationary in the earliest period of the earth's career, in your moment it seems headlong. Mind in you, it is said, not merely stands higher than ever before in respect of percipience, know-ledge, insight, delicacy of admiration, and sanity of will, but also it moves upward century by century ever more swiftly. What next? Surely, you think, there will come a time when there will be no further heights to conquer.

This view is mistaken. You underestimate even the foothills that stand in front of you, and never suspect that far above them, hidden by cloud, rise precipices and snow-fields. The mental and spiritual advances which, in your day, mind in the solar system has still to attempt, are overwhelmingly more complex, more precarious and dangerous, than those which have already been achieved. And though in certain humble respects you have attained full development, the loftier potencies of the spirit in you have not yet even begun to put forth buds.

Somehow, then, I must help you to feel not only the vastness of time and space, but also the vast diversity of mind's possible modes. But this I can only hint to you, since so much lies wholly beyond the range of your imagination.

Historians living in your day need grapple only with one moment of the flux of time. But I have to present in one book the essence not of centuries but of aeons. Clearly we cannot walk at leisure through such a tract, in which a million terrestrial years are but as a year is to your historians. We must fly. We must travel as you do in your aeroplanes, observing only the broad features of the continent. But since the flier sees nothing of the minute inhabitants below him, and since it is they who make history, we must also punctuate our flight with many descents, skimming as it were over the house-tops, and even alighting at critical points to speak face to face with individuals. And as the plane's journey must begin with a slow ascent from the intricate pedestrian view to wider horizons, so we must begin with a somewhat close inspection of that little period which includes the culmination and collapse of your own primitive civilization.

The Chronicle

I *Balkan Europe*

1. THE EUROPEAN WAR AND AFTER

OBSERVE now your own epoch of history as it appears to the Last Men.

Long before the human spirit awoke to clear cognizance of the world and itself, it sometimes stirred in its sleep, opened bewildered eyes, and slept again. One of these moments of precocious experience embraces the whole struggle of the First Men from savagery towards civilization. Within that moment, you stand almost in the very instant when the species attains its zenith. Scarcely at all beyond your own day is this early culture to be seen progressing, and already in your time the mentality of the race shows signs of decline.

The first, and some would say the greatest, achievement of your own 'Western' culture was the conceiving of two ideals of conduct, both essential to the spirit's well-being. Socrates, delighting in the truth for its own sake and not merely for practical ends, glorified unbiased thinking, honesty of mind and speech. Jesus, delighting in the actual human persons around him, and in that flavour of divinity which, for him, pervaded the world, stood for unselfish love of neighbours and of God. Socrates woke to the ideal of dispassionate intelligence, Jesus to the ideal of passionate yet self-oblivious worship. Socrates urged intellectual integrity, Jesus integrity of will. Each, of course, though starting with a different emphasis, involved the other.

Unfortunately both these ideals demanded of the human brain a degree of vitality and coherence of which the nervous system of the First Men was never really capable. For many centuries these twin stars enticed the more precociously human of human animals, in vain. And the failure to put these ideals in practice helped to engender in the race a cynical lassitude which was one cause of its decay.

There were other causes. The peoples from whom sprang

21

Socrates and Jesus were also among the first to conceive admiration for Fate. In Greek tragic art and Hebrew worship of divine law, as also in the Indian resignation, man experienced, at first very obscurely, that vision of an alien and supernal beauty, which was to exalt and perplex him again and again throughout his whole career. The conflict between this worship and the intransigent loyalty to Life, embattled against Death, proved insoluble. And though few individuals were ever clearly conscious of the issue, the first human species was again and again unwittingly hampered in its spiritual development by this supreme perplexity.

While man was being whipped and enticed by these precocious experiences, the actual social constitution of his world kept changing so rapidly through increased mastery over physical energy, that his primitive nature could no longer cope with the complexity of his environment. Animals that were fashioned for hunting and fighting in the wild were suddenly called upon to be citizens, and moreover citizens of a world-community. At the same time they found themselves possessed of certain very dangerous powers which their petty minds were not fit to use. Man struggled; but, as you shall hear, he broke under the strain.

The European War, called at the time the War to End War, was the first and least destructive of those world conflicts which display so tragically the incompetence of the First Men to control their own nature. At the outset a tangle of motives, some honourable and some disreputable, ignited a conflict for which both antagonists were all too well prepared, though neither seriously intended it. A real difference of temperament between Latin-France and Nordic Germany combined with a superficial rivalry between Germany and England, and a number of stupidly brutal gestures on the part of the German Government and military command, to divide the world into two camps; yet in such a manner that it is impossible to find any difference of principle between them. During the struggle each party was convinced that it alone stood for civilization. But in fact both succumbed now and again to impulses of sheer brutality, and both achieved acts not merely of heroism, but of generosity unusual among the First Men. For conduct which to clearer minds seems merely sane, was in those days to be performed only by rare vision and self-mastery.

As the months of agony advanced, there was bred in the warring peoples a genuine and even passionate will for peace and a united world. Out of the conflict of the tribes arose, at least for a while, a spirit loftier than tribalism. But this fervour lacked as yet clear guidance, lacked even the courage of conviction. The peace which followed the European War is one of the most significant moments of ancient history; for it epitomizes both the dawning vision and the incurable blindness, both the impulse toward a higher loyalty and the compulsive tribalism of a race which was, after all, but superficially human.

2. THE ANGLO-FRENCH WAR

One brief but tragic incident, which occurred within a century after the European War, may be said to have sealed the fate of the First Men. During this century the will for peace and sanity was already becoming a serious factor in history. Save for a number of most untoward accidents, to be recorded in due course, the party of peace might have dominated Europe during its most dangerous period; and, through Europe, the world. With either a little less bad luck or a fraction more of vision and self-control at this critical time, there might never have occurred that aeon of darkness, in which the First Men were presently to be submerged. For had victory been gained before the general level of mentality had seriously begun to decline, the attainment of the world state might have been regarded, not as an end, but as the first step towards true civilization. But this was not to be.

After the European War the defeated nation, formerly no less militaristic than the others, now became the most pacific, and a stronghold of enlightenment. Almost everywhere, indeed, there had occurred a profound change of heart, but chiefly in Germany. The victors on the other hand, in spite of their real craving to be human and generous, and to found a new world, were led partly by their own timidity, partly by their governors' blind diplomacy, into all the vices against which they believed themselves to have been crusading. After a brief period in which they desperately affected amity for one another they began to indulge once more in physical conflicts. Of these conflicts, two must be observed.

The first outbreak, and the less disastrous for Europe, was a short and grotesque struggle between France and Italy. Since the fall of ancient Rome, the Italians had excelled more in art and literature than in martial achievement. But the heroic liberation of Italy in the nineteenth Christian century had made Italians peculiarly sensitive to national prestige; and since among Western peoples national vigour was measured in terms of military glory, the Italians were fired, by their success against a rickety foreign domination, to vindicate themselves more thoroughly against the charge of mediocrity in warfare. After the European War, however, Italy passed through a phase of social disorder and self-distrust. Subsequently a flamboyant but sincere national party gained control of the State, and afforded the Italians a new self-respect, based on reform of the social services, and on militaristic policy. Trains became punctual, streets clean, morals puritanical. Aviation records were won for Italy. The young, dressed up and taught to play at soldiers with real fire-arms, were persuaded to regard themselves as saviours of the nation, encouraged to shed blood, and used to enforce the will of the Government. The whole movement was engineered chiefly by a man whose genius in action combined with his rhetoric and crudity of thought to make him a very successful dictator. Almost miraculously he drilled the Italian nation into efficiency. At the same time, with great emotional effect and incredible lack of humour he trumpeted Italy's self-importance, and her will to 'expand'. And since Italians were slow to learn the necessity of restricting their population, 'expansion' was a real need.

Thus it came about that Italy, hungry for French territory in Africa, jealous of French leadership of the Latin races, indignant at the protection afforded to Italian 'traitors' in France, became increasingly prone to quarrel with the most assertive of her late allies. It was a frontier incident, a fancied 'insult to the Italian flag', which at last caused an unauthorized raid upon French territory by a small party of Italian militia. The raiders were captured, but French blood was shed. The consequent demand for apology and reparation was calm, but subtly offensive to

Italian dignity. Italian patriots worked themselves into short-sighted fury. The Dictator, far from daring to apologize, was forced to require the release of the captive militia-men, and finally to declare war. After a single sharp engagement the relentless armies of France pressed into North Italy. Resistance, at first heroic, soon became chaotic. In consternation the Italians woke from their dream of military glory. The populace turned against the Dictator whom they themselves had forced to declare war. In a theatrical but gallant attempt to dominate the Roman mob, he failed, and was killed. The new government made a hasty peace, ceding to France a frontier territory which she had already annexed for 'security'.

Thenceforth Italians were less concerned to outshine the glory of Garibaldi than to emulate the greater glory of Dante, Giotto, and Galileo.

France had now complete mastery of the continent of Europe; but having much to lose, she behaved arrogantly and nervously. It was not long before peace was once more disturbed.

Scarcely had the last veterans of the European War ceased from wearying their juniors with reminiscence, when the long rivalry between France and England culminated in a dispute between their respective Governments over a case of sexual outrage said to have been committed by a French African soldier upon an Englishwoman. In this quarrel, the British Government happened to be definitely in the wrong, and was probably confused by its own sexual repressions. The outrage had never been committed. The facts which gave rise to the rumour were, that an idle and neurotic Englishwoman in the south of France, craving the embrace of a 'cave man', had seduced a Senegalese corporal in her own apartments. When, later, he had shown signs of boredom, she took revenge by declaring that he had attacked her indecently in the woods above the town. This rumour was such that the English were all too prone to savour and believe. At the same time, the magnates of the English Press could not resist this opportunity of trading upon the public's sexuality, tribalism, and self-righteousness. There followed an epidemic of abuse, and occasional violence, against French subjects in England; and thus the party of fear and militarism in France was given the oppor-

tunity it had long sought. For the real cause of this war was connected with air power. France had persuaded the League of
Nations (in one of its less intelligent moments) to restrict the size
of military aeroplanes in such a manner that, while London lay
within easy striking distance of the French coast, Paris could only
with difficulty be touched by England. This state of affairs
obviously could not last long. Britain was agitating more and
more insistently for the removal of the restriction. On the other
hand, there was an increasing demand for complete aerial disarmament in Europe; and so strong was the party of sanity in
France, that the scheme would almost certainly have been accepted by the French Government. On both counts, therefore, the
militarists of France were eager to strike while yet there was
opportunity.

In an instant, the whole fruit of this effort for disarmament was
destroyed. That subtle difference of mentality which had ever
made it impossible for these two nations to understand one another, was suddenly exaggerated by this provocative incident into
an apparently insoluble discord. England reverted to her conviction that all Frenchmen were sensualists, while to France the
English appeared, as often before, the most offensive of hypo-
crites. In vain did the saner minds in each country insist on the
fundamental humanity of both. In vain did the chastened Germans seek to mediate. In vain did the League, which by now had
very great prestige and authority, threaten both parties with ex-
pulsion, even with chastisement. Rumour got about in Paris that
England, breaking all her international pledges, was now feverish-
ly building giant planes which would wreck France from Calais to
Marseilles. And indeed the rumour was not wholly a slander, for,
when the struggle began, the British air force was found to have a
range of intensive action far wider than was expected. Yet the
actual outbreak of war took England by surprise. While the London papers were selling out upon the news that war was declared,
enemy planes appeared over the city. In a couple of hours a third
of London was in ruins, and half her population lay poisoned in
the streets. One bomb, falling beside the British Museum, turned
the whole of Bloomsbury into a crater, wherein fragments of
mummies, statues, and manuscripts were mingled with the con-

tents of shops, and morsels of salesmen and the intelligentsia. Thus in a moment was destroyed a large proportion of England's most precious relics and most fertile brains.

Then occurred one of those microscopic, yet supremely potent incidents which sometimes mould the course of events for centuries. During the bombardment a special meeting of the British Cabinet was held in a cellar in Downing Street. The party in power at the time was progressive, mildly pacifist, and timorously cosmopolitan. It had got itself involved in the French quarrel quite unintentionally. At this Cabinet meeting an idealistic member urged upon his colleagues the need for a supreme gesture of heroism and generosity on the part of Britain. Raising his voice with difficulty above the bark of English guns and the volcanic crash of French bombs, he suggested sending by radio the following message. 'From the people of England to the people of France. Catastrophe has fallen on us at your hands. In this hour of agony, all hate and anger have left us. Our eyes are opened. No longer can we think of ourselves as merely English, and you as merely French; all of us are, before all else, civilized beings. Do not imagine that we are defeated, and that this message is a cry for mercy. Our armament is intact, and our resources still very great. Yet, because of the revelation which has come to us today, we will not fight. No plane, no ship, no soldier of Britain shall commit any further act of hostility. Do what you will. It would be better even that a great people should be destroyed than that the whole race should be thrown into turmoil. But you will not strike again. As our own eyes have been opened by agony, yours now will be opened by our act of brotherhood. The spirit of France and the spirit of England differ. They differ deeply; but only as the eye differs from the hand. Without you, we should be barbarians. And without us, even the bright spirit of France would be but half expressed. For the spirit of France lives again in our culture and in our very speech; and the spirit of England is that which strikes from you your most distinctive brilliance.'

At no earlier stage of man's history could such a message have been considered seriously by any government. Had it been suggested during the previous war, its author would have been ridiculed, execrated, perhaps even murdered. But since those days much had happened. Increased communication, increased cultural intercourse, and a prolonged vigorous campaign for cosmopolitanism, had changed the mentality of Europe. Even so, when, after a brief discussion, the Government ordered this unique message to be sent, its members were awed by their own act. As one of them expressed it, they were uncertain whether it was the devil or the deity that had possessed them, but possessed they certainly were.

That night the people of London (those who were left) experienced an exaltation of spirit. Disorganization of the city's life, overwhelming physical suffering and compassion, the consciousness of an unprecedented spiritual act in which each individual felt himself to have somehow participated – these influences combined to produce, even in the bustle and confusion of a wrecked metropolis, a certain restrained fervour, and a deep peace of mind, wholly unfamiliar to Londoners.

Meanwhile the undamaged North knew not whether to regard the Government's sudden pacificism as a piece of cowardice or as a superbly courageous gesture. Very soon, however, they began to make a virtue of necessity, and incline to the latter view. Paris itself was divided by the message into a vocal party of triumph and a silent party of bewilderment. But as the hours advanced, and the former urged a policy of aggression, the latter found voice for the cry, '*Vive l'Angleterre, vive l'humanité*'. And so strong by now was the will for cosmopolitanism that the upshot would almost certainly have been a triumph of sanity, had there not occurred in England an accident which tilted the whole precarious course of events in the opposite direction.

The bombardment had occurred on a Friday night. On Saturday the repercussions of England's great message were echoing throughout the nations. That evening, as a wet and foggy day was achieving its pallid sunset, a French plane was seen over the western outskirts of London. It gradually descended, and was regarded by onlookers as a messenger of peace. Lower and lower it came. Something was seen to part from it and fall. In a few seconds an immense explosion occurred in the neighbourhood of a great school and a royal palace. There was hideous destruction in the school. The palace escaped. But, chief disaster for the cause of peace, a beautiful and extravagantly popular young princess was caught by the explosion. Her body, obscenely mutilated, but still recognizable to every student of the illustrated papers, was impaled upon some high park-railings beside the main thoroughfare towards the city. Immediately after the explosion the enemy plane crashed, burst into flame, and was destroyed with its occupants.

A moment's cool thinking would have convinced all onlookers that this disaster was an accident, that the plane was a belated straggler in distress, and no messenger of hate. But, confronted with the mangled bodies of schoolboys, and harrowed by cries of agony and terror, the populace was in no state for ratiocination. Moreover there was the princess, an overwhelmingly potent sexual symbol and emblem of tribalism, slaughtered and exposed before the eyes of her adorers.

The news was flashed over the country, and distorted of course in such a manner as to admit no doubt that this act was the crowning devilry of sexual fiends beyond the Channel. In an hour the mood of London was changed, and the whole population of England succumbed to a paroxysm of primitive hate far more extravagant than any that had occurred even in the war against Germany. The British air force, all too well equipped and prepared, was ordered to Paris.

Meanwhile in France the militaristic government had fallen, and the party of peace was now in control. While the streets were still thronged by its vociferous supporters, the first bomb fell. By Monday morning Paris was obliterated. There followed a few days of strife between the opposing armaments, and of butchery committed upon the civilian populations. In spite of French gallantry, the superior organization, mechanical efficiency, and more cautious courage of the British Air Force soon made it impossible for a French plane to leave the ground. But if France was broken, England was too crippled to pursue her advantage. Every city of the two countries was completely disorganized. Famine, riot, looting, and above all the rapidly accelerating and quite uncontrollable spread of disease, disintegrated both States, and brought war to a standstill.

Indeed, not only did hostilities cease, but also both nations were too shattered even to continue hating one another. The energies of each were for a while wholly occupied in trying to prevent complete annihilation by famine and pestilence. In the work of reconstruction they had to depend very largely on help from outside. The management of each country was taken over, for the time, by the League of Nations.

It is significant to compare the mood of Europe at this time with that which followed the European War. Formerly, though there had been a real effort toward unity, hate and suspicion continued to find expression in national policies. There was much wrangling about indemnities, reparations, securities; and the division of the whole continent into two hostile camps persisted, though by then it was purely artificial and sentimental. But after the Anglo-French war, a very different mood prevailed. There was no mention of reparations, no possibility of seeking security by alliances. Patriotism simply faded out, for the time, under the influence of extreme disaster. The two enemy peoples cooperated with the League in the work of reconstructing not only each one itself, but each one the other. This change of heart was due partly to the temporary collapse of the whole national organization, partly to the speedy dominance of each nation by pacifist and anti-nationalist Labour, partly to the fact that the League was powerful enough to inquire into and publish the whole story of the origins of the war, and expose each combatant to itself and to the world in a sorry light.

We have now observed in some detail the incident which stands out in man's history as perhaps the most dramatic example of petty cause and mighty effect. For consider. Through some miscalculation, or a mere defect in his instruments, a French airman went astray, and came to grief in London after the sending of the peace message. Had this not happened, England and France would not have been wrecked. And, had the war been nipped at the outset, as it almost was, the party of sanity throughout the world would have been very greatly strengthened; the precarious will to unity would have gained the conviction which it lacked, would have dominated man not merely during the terrified revulsion after each spasm of national strife, but as a permanent policy based on mutual trust. Indeed so delicately balanced were man's primitive and developed impulses at this time, that, but for this trivial accident, the movement which was started by

England's peace message might have proceeded steadily and rapidly toward the unification of the race. It might, that is, have attained its goal, before, instead of after, the period of mental deterioration, which in fact resulted from a long epidemic of wars. And so the first Dark Age might never have occurred.

3. EUROPE AFTER THE ANGLO-FRENCH WAR

A subtle change now began to affect the whole mental climate of the planet. This is remarkable, since, viewed for instance from America or China, this war was, after all, but a petty disturbance, scarcely more than a brawl between quarrelsome statelets, an episode in the decline of a senile civilization. Expressed in dollars, the damage was not impressive to the wealthy West and the potentially wealthy East. The British Empire, indeed, that unique banyan tree of peoples, was henceforward less effective in world diplomacy; but since the bond that held it together was by now wholly a bond of sentiment, the Empire was not disintegrated by the misfortune of its parent trunk. Indeed, a common fear of American economic imperialism was already helping the colonies to remain loyal.

Yet this petty brawl was in fact an irreparable and far-reaching disaster. For in spite of those differences of temperament which had forced the English and French into conflict, they had cooperated, though often unwittingly, in tempering and clarifying the mentality of Europe. Though their faults played a great part in wrecking Western civilization, the virtues from which these vices sprang were needed for the salvation of a world prone to uncritical romance. In spite of the inveterate blindness and meanness of France in international policy, and the even more disastrous timidity of England, their influence on culture had been salutary, and was at this moment sorely needed. For, poles asunder in tastes and ideals, these two peoples were yet alike in being on the whole more sceptical, and in their finest individuals more capable of dispassionate yet creative intelligence than any other Western people. This very character produced their distinctive faults, namely, in the English a caution that amounted often to moral cowardice,

31

and in the French a certain myopic complacency and cunning, which masqueraded as realism. Within each nation there was, of course, great variety. English minds were of many types. But most were to some extent distinctively English; and hence the special character of England's influence in the world. Relatively detached, sceptical, cautious, practical, more tolerant than others, because more complacent and less prone to fervour, the typical Englishman was capable both of generosity and of spite, both of heroism and of timorous or cynical abandonment of ends proclaimed as vital to the race. French and English alike might sin against humanity, but in different manners. The French sinned blindly, through a strange inability to regard France dispassionately. The English sinned through faintheartedness, and with open eyes. Among all nations they excelled in the union of common sense and vision. But also among all nations they were most ready to betray their visions in the name of common sense. Hence their reputation for perfidy.

Differences of national character and patriotic sentiment were not the most fundamental distinctions between men at this time. Although in each nation a common tradition or cultural environment imposed a certain uniformity on all its members, yet in each nation every mental type was present, though in different proportions. The most significant of all cultural differences between men, namely, the difference between the tribalists and the cosmopolitans, traversed the national boundaries. For throughout the world something like a new, cosmopolitan 'nation' with a new all-embracing patriotism was beginning to appear. In every land there was by now a salting of awakened minds who, whatever their temperament and politics and formal faith, were at one in respect of their allegiance to humanity as a race or as an adventuring spirit. Unfortunately this new loyalty was still entangled with old prejudices. In some minds the defence of the human spirit was sincerely identified with the defence of a particular nation, conceived as the home of all enlightenment. In others, social injustice kindled a militant proletarian loyalty, which, though at heart cosmopolitan, infected alike its champions and its enemies with sectarian passions.

Another sentiment, less definite and conscious than cosmopolitanism, also played some part in the minds of men, namely loyalty toward the dispassionate intelligence and perplexed admiration of the world which was beginning to be revealed, a world august, immense, subtle, in which, seemingly, man was doomed to play a part minute but tragic. In many races there had, no doubt, long existed some fidelity toward the dispassionate intelligence. But it was England and France that excelled in this respect. On the other hand, even in these two nations there was much that was opposed to this allegiance. These, like all peoples of the age, were liable to bouts of insane emotionalism. Indeed the French mind, in general so clear sighted, so realistic, so contemptuous of ambiguity and mist, so detached in all its final valuations, was yet so obsessed with the idea 'France' as to be wholly incapable of generosity in international affairs. But it was France, with England, that had chiefly inspired the intellectual integrity which was the rarest and brightest thread of Western culture, not only within the territories of these two nations, but throughout Europe and America. In the seventeenth and eighteenth Christian centuries, the French and English had conceived, more clearly than other peoples, an interest in the objective world for its own sake, had founded physical science, and had fashioned out of scepticism the most brilliantly constructive of mental instruments. At a later stage it was largely the French and English who, by means of this instrument, had revealed man and the physical universe in something like their true proportions; and it was chiefly the elect of these two peoples that had been able to exult in this bracing discovery.

With the eclipse of France and England this great tradition of dispassionate cognizance began to wane. Europe was now led by Germany. And the Germans, in spite of their practical genius, their scholarly contributions to history, their brilliant science and austere philosophy, were at heart romantic. This inclination was both their strength and their weakness. Thereby they had been inspired to their finest art and their most profound metaphysical speculation. But thereby they were also often rendered un-self-critical and pompous. More eager than other Western minds to solve the mystery of existence, less sceptical of the power of human reason, and therefore more inclined to ignore or argue away recalcitrant facts, the Germans were courageous systematizers. In this direction they had achieved great things. Without them, European thought would have been chaotic. But their passion for order and for a systematic reality behind the disorderly appearances, rendered their reasoning all too often biased. Upon shifty foundations they balanced ingenious ladders to reach the stars. Thus, without constant ribald criticism from across the Rhine and the North Sea, the Teutonic soul could not achieve full self-expression. A vague uneasiness about its own sentimentalism and lack of detachment did indeed persuade this great people to assert its virility now and again by ludicrous acts of brutality, and to compensate for its dream life by ceaseless hard-driven and brilliantly successful commerce; but what was needed was a far more radical self-criticism.

Beyond Germany, Russia. Here was a people whose genius needed, even more than that of the Germans, discipline under the critical intelligence. Since the Bolshevik revolution, there had risen in the scattered towns of this immense tract of corn and forest, and still more in the metropolis, an original mode of art and thought, in which were blended a passion for iconoclasm, a vivid sensuousness, and yet also a very remarkable and essentially mystical or intuitive power of detachment from all private cravings. America and Western Europe were interested first in the individual human life, and only secondarily in the social whole. For these peoples loyalty involved a reluctant self-sacrifice, and the ideal was ever a person, excelling in prowess of various kinds. Society was but the necessary matrix of this jewel. But the Russians, whether by an innate gift, or through the influence of age-long political tyranny, religious devotion, and a truly social revolution, were prone to self-contemptuous interest in groups, prone, indeed, to a spontaneous worship of whatever was conceived as loftier than the individual man whether society, or God, or the blind forces of nature. Western Europe could reach by way of the intellect a precise conception of man's littleness and irrelevance when regarded as an alien among the stars; could even glimpse from this standpoint the cosmic theme in which all human striving is but one contributory factor. But the Russian mind, whether orthodox or Tolstoyan or fanatically materialist, could attain much the same conviction intuitively, by direct perception, instead of after an arduous intellectual pilgrimage; and, reaching it, could rejoice in it. But because of this independence of intellect, the experience was confused, erratic, frequently misinterpreted; and its effect on conduct was rather explosive than directive. Great indeed was the need that the West and East of Europe should strengthen and temper one another.

After the Bolshevik revolution a new element appeared in Russian culture, and one which had not been known before in any modern state. The old regime was displaced by a real proletarian government, which, though an oligarchy, and sometimes bloody and fanatical, abolished the old tyranny of class, and encouraged the humblest citizen to be proud of his partnership in the great community. Still more important, the native Russian disposition not to take material possessions very seriously cooperated with the political revolution, and brought about such a freedom from the snobbery of wealth as was quite foreign to the West. Attention which elsewhere was absorbed in the amassing or display of money was in Russia largely devoted either to spontaneous instinctive enjoyments or to cultural activity.

In fact, it was among the Russian townsfolk, less cramped by tradition than other city-dwellers, that the spirit of the First Men was beginning to achieve a fresh and sincere readjustment to the facts of its changing world. And from the townsfolk something of the new way of life was spreading even to the peasants; while in the depths of Asia a hardy and ever-growing population looked increasingly to Russia, not only for machinery, but for ideas. There were times when it seemed that Russia might transform the almost universal autumn of the race into a new spring.

After the Bolshevik revolution the new Russia had been boycotted by the West, and had therefore passed through a stage of self-conscious extravagance. Communism and naïve materialism became the dogmas of a new crusading atheist church. All criticism was suppressed, even more rigorously than was the opposite criticism in other countries; and Russians were taught to think of themselves as saviours of mankind. Later, however, as economic isolation began to hamper the Bolshevik state, the new culture was mellowed and broadened. Bit by bit, economic intercourse with the West was restored, and with it cultural intercourse increased.

The intuitive mystical detachment of Russia began to define itself, and so consolidate itself, in terms of the intellectual detachment of the best thought of the West. Iconoclasm was harnessed. The life of the senses and of impulse was tempered by a new critical movement. Fanatical materialism, whose fire had been derived from a misinterpreted, but intense, mystical intuition of dispassionate Reality, began to assimilate itself to the far more rational stoicism which was the rare flower of the West. At the same time, through intercourse with peasant culture and with the peoples of Asia, the new Russia began to grasp in one unifying act of apprehension both the grave disillusion of France and England and the ecstasy of the East.

The harmonizing of these two moods was now the chief spiritual need of mankind. Failure to integrate them into an all-dominant sentiment could not but lead to racial insanity. And so in due course it befell. Meanwhile this task of integration was coming to seem more and more urgent to the best minds of Russia, and might have been finally accomplished had they been longer illumined by the cold light of the West.

But this was not to be. The intellectual confidence of France and England, already shaken through progressive economic eclipse at the hands of America and Germany, was now undermined. For many decades England had watched these newcomers capture her markets. The loss had smothered her with a swarm of domestic problems, such as could never be solved save by drastic surgery; and this was a course which demanded more courage and energy than was possible to a people without hope. Then came the war with France, and harrowing disintegration. No delirium seized her, such as occurred in France; yet her whole mentality was changed, and her sobering influence in Europe was lessened.

As for France, her cultural life was now grievously reduced. It might, indeed, have recovered from the final blow, had it not already been slowly poisoned by gluttonous nationalism. For love of France was the undoing of the French. They prized the truly admirable spirit of France so extravagantly that they regarded all other nations as barbarians.

Thus it befell that in Russia the doctrines of communism and materialism, products of German systematists, survived uncriticized. On the other hand, the practice of communism was gradually undermined. For the Russian state came increasingly under the influence of Western, and especially American, finance. The materialism of the official creed also became a farce, for it was foreign to the Russian mind. Thus between practice and theory there was, in both respects, a profound inconsistency. What was once a vital and promising culture became insincere.

4. THE RUSSO-GERMAN WAR

The discrepancy between communist theory and individualist practice in Russia was one cause of the next disaster which befell Europe. Between Russia and Germany there should have been close partnership, based on interchange of machinery and corn. But the theory of communism stood in the way, and in a strange manner. Russian industrial organization had proved impossible without American capital; and little by little this influence had transformed the communistic system. From the Baltic to the Himalayas and the Bering Straits, pasture, timberlands, machine-tilled corn-lands, oil-fields, and a spreading rash of industrial towns, were increasingly dependent on American finance and organization. Yet not America but the far less individualistic Germany had become in the Russian mind the symbol of capitalism. Self-righteous hate of Germany compensated Russia for her own betrayal of the communistic ideal. This perverse antagonism was encouraged by the Americans; who, strong in their own individualism and prosperity, and by now contemptuously tolerant of Russian doctrines, were concerned only to keep Russian finance to themselves. In truth, of course, it was America that had helped Russia's self-betrayal; and it was the spirit of America that was most alien to the Russian spirit. But American wealth was by now indispensable to Russia; so the hate due to America had to be borne vicariously by Germany.

The Germans, for their part, were aggrieved that the Americans had ousted them from a most profitable field of enterprise, and in particular from the exploitation of Russian Asiatic oil. The economic life of the human race for for some time been based on coal, but latterly oil had been found a far more convenient source of power, and as the oil store of the planet was much smaller than its coal store, and the expenditure of oil had of course been wholly uncontrolled and wasteful, a shortage was already being felt. Thus the national ownership of the remaining oil fields had become a main factor in politics and a fertile source of wars. America, having used up most of her own supplies, was now anxious to compete with the still prolific sources under Chinese control, by forestalling Germany in Russia. No wonder the Germans were aggrieved. But the fault was their own. In the days when Russian communism had been seeking to convert the world, Germany had taken over England's leadership of individualistic Europe. While greedy for trade with Russia, she had been at the same time frightened of contamination by Russian social doctrine, the more so because communism had at first made some headway among the German workers. Later, even when sane industrial reorganization in Germany had deprived communism of its appeal to the workers, and thus had rendered it impotent, the habit of anti-communist vituperation persisted.

Thus the peace of Europe was in constant danger from the bickerings of two peoples who differed rather in ideals than in practice. For the one, in theory communistic, had been forced to belegate many of the community's rights to enterprising individuals; while the other, in theory organized on a basis of private business, was becoming ever more socialized.

Neither party desired war. Neither was interested in military glory, for militarism as an end was no longer reputable. Neither was professedly nationalistic, for nationalism, though still potent, was no longer vaunted. Each claimed to stand for internationalism and peace, but accused the other of narrow patriotism. Thus Europe, though more pacific than ever before, was doomed to war.

Like most wars, the Anglo-French War had increased the desire for peace, yet made peace less secure. Distrust, not merely the old distrust of nation for nation, but a devastating distrust of human nature, gripped men like the dread of insanity. Individuals who thought of themselves as wholehearted Europeans, feared that at any moment they might succumb to some ridiculous epidemic of patriotism, and participate in the further crippling of Europe.

This dread was one cause of the formation of a European Confederacy, in which all the nations of Europe, save Russia, surrendered their sovereignty to a common authority and actually pooled their armaments. Ostensibly the motive of this act was peace; but America interpreted it as directed against herself, and withdrew from the League of Nations. China, the 'natural enemy' of America, remained within the League, hoping to use it against her rival.

From without, indeed, the Confederacy at first appeared as a close-knit whole: but from within it was known to be insecure, and in every serious crisis it broke. There is no need to follow the many minor wars of this period, though their cumulative effect was serious, both economically and psychologically. Europe did at last, however, become something like a single nation in sentiment, though this unity was brought about less by a common loyalty than by a common fear of America.

Final consolidation was the fruit of the Russo-German War, the cause of which was partly economic and partly sentimental. All the peoples of Europe had long watched with horror the financial conquest of Russia by the United States, and they dreaded that they also must presently succumb to the same tyrant. To attack Russia, it was thought, would be to wound America in her only vulnerable spot. But the actual occasion of the war was sentimental. Half a century after the Anglo-French War, a second-rate German author published a typically German book of the baser sort. For as each nation had its characteristic virtues, so also each was prone to characteristic follies. This book was one of those brilliant but extravagant works in which the whole diversity of existence is interpreted under a single formula, with extreme detail and plausibility, yet with amazing *naïveté*. Highly astute within its own artificial universe, it was none the less in wider regard quite uncritical. In two large volumes the author claimed that the cosmos was a dualism in which a heroic and obviously Nordic spirit ruled by divine right over an un-self-disciplined, yet servile and obviously Slavonic spirit. The whole of history, and of evolution, was interpreted on this principle; and of the contem-

porary world it was said that the Slavonic element was poisoning
Europe. One phrase in particular caused fury in Moscow, 'the
anthropoid face of the Russian sub-man'.

Moscow demanded apology and suppression of the book.
Berlin regretted the insult but with its tongue in its cheek; and
insisted on the freedom of the press. Followed a crescendo of
radio hate, and war.

The details of this war do not matter to one intent upon the
history of mind in the Solar System, but its result was important.
Moscow, Leningrad and Berlin were shattered from the air. The
whole West of Russia was flooded with the latest and deadliest
poison gas, so that not only was all animal and vegetable life
destroyed, but also the soil between the Black Sea and the Baltic
was rendered infertile and uninhabitable for many years. Within a
week the war was over, for the reason that the combatants were
separated by an immense territory in which life could not exist.
But the effects of the war were lasting. The Germans had set going
a process which they could not stop. Whiffs of the poison continued to be blown by fickle winds into every country of Europe
and Western Asia. It was spring-time; but save in the Atlantic
coast-lands the spring flowers shrivelled in the bud, and every
young leaf had a withered rim. Humanity also suffered; though,
save in the regions near the seat of war, it was in general only the
children and the old people who suffered greatly. The poison
spread across the Continent in huge blown tresses, broad as
principalities, swinging with each change of wind. And wherever
it strayed, young eyes, throats, and lungs were blighted like the
leaves.

America, after much debate, had at last decided to defend her
interests in Russia by a punitive expedition against Europe. China
began to mobilize her forces. But long before America was ready
to strike, news of the widespread poisoning changed her policy.
Instead of punishment, help was given. This was a fine gesture of
good will. But also, as was observed in Europe, instead of being
costly, it was profitable; for inevitably it brought more of Europe
under American financial control.

The upshot of the Russo-German war, then, was that Europe
was unified in sentiment by hatred of America, and that European

mentality definitely deteriorated. This was due in part to the emotional influence of the war itself, partly to the socially damaging effects of the poison. A proportion of the rising generation had been rendered sickly for life. During the thirty years which intervened before the Euro-American war, Europe was burdened with an exceptional weight of invalids. First-class intelligence was on the whole rarer than before, and was more strictly concentrated on the practical work of reconstruction.

Even more disastrous for the human race was the fact that the recent Russian cultural enterprise of harmonizing Western intellectualism and Eastern mysticism was now wrecked.

II *Europe's Downfall*

1. EUROPE AND AMERICA

OVER the heads of the European tribes two mightier peoples regarded each other with increasing dislike. Well might they; for the one cherished the most ancient and refined of all surviving cultures, while the other, youngest and most self-confident of the great nations, proclaimed her novel spirit as the spirit of the future.

In the Far East, China, already half American, though largely Russian and wholly Eastern, patiently improved her rice lands, pushed forward her railways, organized her industries, and spoke fair to all the world. Long ago, during her attainment of unity and independence, China had learnt much from militant Bolshevism. And after the collapse of the Russian state it was in the East that Russian culture continued to live. Its mysticism influenced India. Its social ideal influenced China. Not indeed that China took over the theory, still less the practice of communism; but she learnt to entrust herself increasingly to a vigorous, devoted, and despotic party, and to feel in terms of the social whole rather than individualistically. Yet she was honeycombed with individualism, and in spite of her rulers she had precipitated a submerged and desperate class of wage slaves.

In the Far West, the United States of America openly claimed to be custodians of the whole planet. Universally feared and envied, universally respected for their enterprise, yet for their complacency very widely despised, the Americans were rapidly changing the whole character of man's existence. By this time every human being throughout the planet made use of American products, and there was no region where American capital did not support local labour. Moreover the American press, gramophone, radio, cinematograph, and televisor ceaselessly drenched the planet with American thought. Year by year the ether reverberated with echoes of New York's pleasures and the religious fervours of the

the great cultural difference between the East and West; but both the negotiants seemed anxious to believe that this was only a minor matter which need not be allowed to trouble a business discussion.

At this point occurred one of those incidents which, minute in themselves, have disproportionately great effects. The unstable nature of the First Men made them peculiarly liable to suffer from such accidents, and especially so in their decline.

The talk was interrupted by the appearance of a human figure swimming round a promontory into the little bay. In the shallows she arose, and walked out of the water towards the creators of the World State. A bronze young smiling woman, completely nude, with breasts heaving after her long swim, she stood before them, hesitating. The relation between the two men was instantly changed, though neither was at first aware of it.

'Delicious daughter of Ocean,' said the Chinese, in that somewhat archaic and deliberately un-American English which the Asians now affected in communication with foreigners, 'what is there that these two despicable land animals can do for you? For my friend, I cannot answer, but I at least am henceforth your slave.' His eyes roamed caressingly, yet as it were with perfect politeness, all over her body. And she, with that added grace which haloes women when they feel the kiss of an admiring gaze, pressed the sea from her hair and stood at the point of speech.

But the American protested, 'Whoever you are, please do not interrupt us. We are really very busy discussing a matter of great importance, and we have no time to spare. Please go. Your nudity is offensive to one accustomed to civilized manners. In a modern country you would not be allowed to bathe without a costume. We are growing very sensitive on this point.'

A distressful but enhancing blush spread under the wet bronze, and the intruder made as if to go. But the Chinese cried, 'Stay! We have almost finished our business talk. Refresh us with your presence. Bring the realities back into our discussion by permitting us to contemplate for a while the perfect vase line of your waist and thigh. Who are you? Of what race are you? My anthropological studies fail to place you. Your skin is fairer than is native here, though rich with sun. Your breasts are Grecian.

69

Your lips are chiselled with a memory of Egypt. Your hair, night though it was, is drying with a most bewildering hint of gold. And your eyes, let me observe them. Long, subtle, as my country-women's, unfathomable as the mind of India, they yet reveal themselves to your new slave as not wholly black, but violet as the zenith before dawn. Indeed this exquisite unity of incompatibles conquers both my heart and my understanding.'

During this harangue her composure was restored, though she glanced now and then at the American, who kept ever removing his gaze from her.

She answered in much the same diction as the other; but, surprisingly, with an old-time English accent, 'I am certainly a mongrel. You might call me, not daughter of Ocean, but daughter of Man; for wanderers of every race have scattered their seed on this island. My body, I know, betrays its diverse ancestry in a rather queer blend of characters. My mind is perhaps unusual too, for I have never left this island. And though it is actually less than a quarter of a century since I was born, a past century has perhaps had more meaning for me than the obscure events of today. A hermit taught me. Two hundred years ago he lived actively in Europe; but towards the end of his long life he retreated to this island. As an old man he loved me. And day by day he gave me insight into the great spirit of the past; but of this age he gave me nothing. Now that he is dead, I struggle to familiarize myself with the present, but I continue to see everything from the angle of another age. And so,' (turning to the American) 'if I have offended against modern customs, it is because my insular mind has never been taught to regard nakedness as indecent. I am very ignorant, truly a savage. If only I could gain experience of your great world! If ever this war ends, I must travel.'

'Delectable,' said the Chinese, 'exquisitely proportioned, exquisitely civilized savage! Come with me for a holiday in modern China. There you can bathe without a costume, so long as you are beautiful.'

She ignored this invitation, and seemed to have fallen into a reverie. Then absently she continued, 'Perhaps I should not suffer from this restlessness, this craving to experience the world, if only I were to experience motherhood instead. Many of the islanders from time to time have enriched me with their embraces. But with none of them could I permit myself to conceive. They are dear; but not one of them is at heart more than a child.'

The American became restless. But again the Mongol intervened, with lowered and deepened voice. 'I,' he said, 'I, the Vice-President of the World Finance Directorate, shall be honoured to afford you the opportunity of motherhood.'

She regarded him gravely, then smiled as on a child who asks more than it is reasonable to give. But the American rose hastily. Addressing the silken Mongol, he said, 'You probably know that the American Government is in the act of sending a second poison fleet to turn your whole population insane, more insane than you are already. You cannot defend yourselves against this new weapon; and if I am to save you, I must not trifle any longer. Nor must you, for we must act simultaneously. We have settled all that matters for the moment. But before I leave, I must say that your behaviour towards this woman has very forcibly reminded me that there is something wrong with the Chinese way of thought and life. In my anxiety for peace, I overlooked my duty in this respect. I now give you notice that when the Directorate is established, we Americans must induce you to reform these abuses, for the world's sake and your own.'

The Chinese rose and answered, 'This matter must be settled locally. We do not expect you to accept our standards, so do not you expect us to accept yours.' He moved towards the woman, smiling. And the smile outraged the American.

We need not follow the wrangle which now ensued between the two representatives, each of whom, though in a manner cosmopolitan in sentiment, was heartily contemptuous of the other's values. Suffice it that the American became increasingly earnest and dictatorial, the other increasingly careless and ironical. Finally the American raised his voice and presented an ultimatum. 'Our treaty of world-union,' he said, 'will remain unsigned unless you add a clause promising drastic reforms, which, as a matter of fact, my colleagues had already proposed as a condition of cooperation. I had decided to withhold them, in case they should wreck our treaty; but now I see they are essential. You must educate your people out of their lascivious and idle ways, and

71

give them modern scientific religion. Teachers in your schools and universities must pledge themselves to the modern fundamentalized physics, and behaviourism, and must enforce worship of the Divine Mover. The change will be difficult, but we will help you. You will need a strong order of Inquisitors, responsible to the Directorate. They will see also to the reform of your people's sexual frivolity in which you squander so much of the Divine Energy. Unless you agree to this, I cannot stop the war. The law of God must be kept, and those who know it must enforce it.'

The woman interrupted him. 'Tell me, what is this "God" of yours? The Europeans worshipped love, not energy. What do you mean by energy? Is it merely to make engines go fast, and to agitate the ether?'

He answered flatly, as if repeating a lesson, 'God is the all-pervading spirit of movement which seeks to actualize itself wherever it is latent. God has appointed the great American people to mechanize the universe.' He paused, contemplating the clean lines of his sea-plane. Then he continued with emphasis, 'But come! Time is precious. Either you work for God, or we trample you out of God's way.'

The woman approached him, saying, 'There is certainly something great in this enthusiasm. But somehow, though my heart says you are right, my head is doubting still. There must be a mistake somewhere.'

'Mistake!' he laughed, overhanging her with his mask of power. 'When a man's soul is action, how can he be mistaken that action is divine? I have served the great God, Energy, all my life, from garage boy to World President. Has not the whole American people proved its faith by its success?'

With rapture, but still in perplexity, she gazed at him. 'There's something terribly wrong-headed about you Americans,' she said, 'but certainly you are great.' She looked him in the eyes. Then suddenly she laid a hand on him, and said with conviction, 'Being what you are, you are probably right. Anyhow you are a man, a real man. Take me. Be the father of my boy. Take me to the dangerous cities of America to work with you.'

The President was surprised with sudden hunger for her body, and she saw it; but he turned to the Vice-President and said, 'She has seen where the truth lies. And you? War, or cooperation in God's work?'

'The death of our bodies, or the death of our minds,' said the Chinese, but with a bitterness that lacked conviction; for he was no fanatic. 'Well, since the soul is only the harmoniousness of the body's behaviour, and since, in spite of this little dispute, we are agreed that the coordination of activity is the chief need of the planet today, and since in respect of our differences of temperament this lady has judged in favour of America, and moreover since, if there is any virtue in our Asian way of life, it will not succumb to a little propaganda, but rather will be strengthened by opposition – since all these matters are so, I accept your terms. But it would be undignified in China to let this great change be imposed upon her externally. You must give me time to form in Asia a native and spontaneous party of Energists, who will themselves propagate your gospel, and perhaps give it an elegance which, if I may say so, it has not yet. Even this we will do to secure the cosmopolitan control of Antarctica.'

Thereupon the treaty was signed; but a new and secret codicil was drawn up and signed also, and both were witnessed by the Daughter of Man, in a clear, round, old-fashioned script.

Then, taking a hand of each, she said, 'And so at last the world is united. For how long, I wonder. I seem to hear my old master's voice scolding, as though I had been rather stupid. But he failed me, and I have chosen a new master, Master of the World.'

She released the hand of the Asian, and made as if to draw the American away with her. And he, though he was a strict monogamist with a better half waiting for him in New York, longed to crush her sun-clad body to his Puritan cloth. She drew him away among the palm trees.

The Vice-President of the World sat down once more, lit a cigarette, and meditated, smiling.

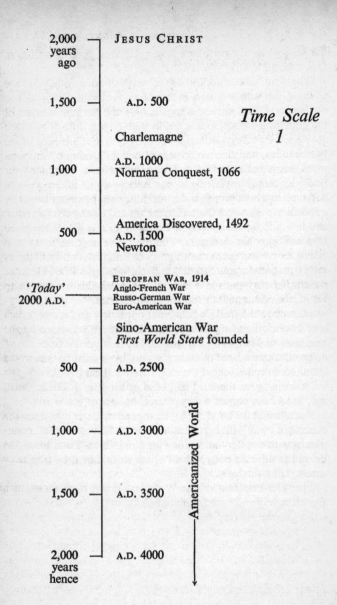

2,000 years ago	JESUS CHRIST
1,500	A.D. 500
	Charlemagne
1,000	A.D. 1000 Norman Conquest, 1066
500	America Discovered, 1492 A.D. 1500 Newton
'Today' 2000 A.D.	EUROPEAN WAR, 1914 Anglo-French War Russo-German War Euro-American War
	Sino-American War *First World State* founded
500	A.D. 2500
1,000	A.D. 3000
1,500	A.D. 3500
2,000 years hence	A.D. 4000

Time Scale
1

Americanized World

IV *An Americanized Planet*

1. THE FOUNDATION OF THE FIRST WORLD STATE

WE have now reached that point in the history of the First Men when, some three hundred and eighty terrestrial years after the European War, the goal of world unity was at last achieved – not, however, before the mind of the race had been seriously crippled.

There is no need to recount in detail the transition from rival national sovereignties to unitary control by the World Financial Directorate. Suffice it that by concerted action in America and China the military governments found themselves hamstrung by the passive resistance of cosmopolitan big business. In China this process was almost instantaneous and bloodless; in America there was serious disorder for a few weeks, while the bewildered government attempted to reduce its rebels by martial law. But the population was by now eager for peace; and, although a few business magnates were shot, and a crowd of workers here and there mown down, the opposition was irresistible. Very soon the governing clique collapsed.

The new order consisted of a vast system akin to guild socialism, yet at bottom individualistic. Each industry was in theory democratically governed by all its members, but in practice was controlled by its dominant individuals. Coordination of all industries was effected by a World Industrial Council, whereon the leaders of each industry discussed the affairs of the planet as a whole. The status of each industry on the Council was determined partly by its economic power in the world, partly by public esteem. For already the activities of men were beginning to be regarded as either 'noble' or 'ignoble'; and the noble were not necessarily the most powerful economically. Thus upon the Council appeared an inner ring of noble 'industries,' which were, in approximate order of prestige, Finance, Flying, Engineering, Surface Locomotion, Chemical Industry, and Professional Athletics. But the real seat of power was not the Council, not even the inner ring of the Council, but the Financial Directorate. This consisted of a dozen million-aires, with the American President and the Chinese Vice-President at their head.

Within this august committee internal dissensions were inevit-able. Shortly after the system had been inaugurated the Vice-President sought to overthrow the President by publishing his connexion with the coloured woman who now styled herself the Daughter of Man. This piece of scandal was expected to enrage the virtuous American public against their hero. But by a stroke of genius the President saved both himself and the unity of the world. Far from denying the charge, he gloried in it. In that moment of sexual triumph, he said, a great truth had been re-vealed to him. Without this daring sacrifice of his private purity, he would never have been really fit to be President of the World; he would have remained simply an American. In this lady's veins flowed the blood of all races, and in her mind all cultures mingled. His union with her, confirmed by many subsequent visits, had taught him to enter into the spirit of the East, and had given him a broad human sympathy such as his high office demanded. As a private individual, he insisted, he remained a monogamist with a wife in New York; and, as a private individual, he had sinned, and must suffer for ever the pangs of conscience. But as President of the World, it was incumbent upon him to espouse the World. And since nothing could be said to be real without a physical basis, this spiritual union had to be embodied and symbolized by his physical union with the Daughter of Man. In tones of grave emotion he described through the microphone how, in the presence of that mystical woman, he had suddenly triumphed over his private moral scruples; and how, in a sudden access of the divine energy, he had consummated his marriage with the World in the shade of a banana tree.

The lovely form of the Daughter of Man (decently clad) was transmitted by television to every receiver in the world. Her face, blended of Asia and the West, became a most potent symbol of human unity. Every man on the planet became in imagination her lover. Every woman identified herself with this supreme woman.

Undoubtedly there was some truth in the plea that the Daughter of Man had enlarged the President's mind, for his policy had been unexpectedly tactful towards the East. Often he had moderated the American demand for the immediate Americanization of China. Often he had persuaded the Chinese to welcome some policy which at first they had regarded with suspicion.

The President's explanation of his conduct enhanced his prestige both in American and Asia. America was hypnotized by the romantic religiosity of the story. Very soon it became fashionable to be a strict monogamist with one domestic wife, and one 'symbolical' wife in the East, or in another town, or a neighbouring street, or with several such in various localities. In China the cold tolerance with which the President was at first treated was warmed by this incident into something like affection. And it was partly through his tact, or the influence of his symbolical wife, that the speeding up of China's Americanization was effected without disorder.

For some months after the foundation of the World State, China had been wholly occupied in coping with the plague of insanity, called 'the American madness,' with which her former enemy had poisoned her. The coast region of North China had been completely disorganized. Industry, agriculture, transport, were at a standstill. Huge mobs, demented and starving, staggered about the country devouring every kind of vegetable matter and wrangling over the flesh of their own dead. It was long before the disease was brought under control; and indeed for years afterwards an occasional outbreak would occur, and cause panic throughout the land.

To some of the more old-fashioned Chinese it appeared as though the whole population had been mildly affected by the germ; for throughout China a new sect, apparently a spontaneous native growth, calling themselves Energists, began to preach a new interpretation of Buddhism in terms of the sanctity of action. And, strange to say, this gospel throve to such an extent that in a few years the whole educational system was captured by its adherents, though not without a struggle with the reactionary members of the older universities. Curiously enough, however, in spite of this general acceptance of the New Way, in spite of the fact that the young of China were now taught to admire movement in all its forms, in spite of a much increased wage-scale,

which put all workers in possession of private mechanical locomotion, the masses of China continued at heart to regard action
as a mere means towards rest. And when at last a native physicist
pointed out that the supreme expression of energy was the tense
balance of forces within the atom, the Chinese applied the doctrine to themselves, and claimed that in them quiescence was the
perfect balance of mighty forces. Thus did the East contribute to
the religion of this age. The worship of activity was made to
include the worship of inactivity. And both were founded on the
principles of natural science.

2. THE DOMINANCE OF SCIENCE

Science now held a position of unique honour among the First
Men. This was not so much because it was in this field that the
race long ago during its high noon had thought most rigorously,
nor because it was through science that men had gained some
insight into the nature of the physical world, but rather because
the application of scientific principles had revolutionized their
material circumstances. The once fluid doctrines of science had
by now begun to crystallize into a fixed and intricate dogma; but
inventive scientific intelligence still exercised itself brilliantly in
improving the technique of industry, and thus completely dominated the imagination of a race in which the pure intellectual curiosity had waned. The scientist was regarded as an embodiment,
not merely of knowledge, but of power; and no legends of the
potency of science seemed too fantastic to be believed.

A century after the founding of the first World State a rumour
began to be heard in China about the supreme secret of scientific
religion, the awful mystery of Gordelpus, by means of which it
should be possible to utilize the energy locked up in the opposition of proton and electron. Long ago discovered by a Chinese
physicist and saint, this invaluable knowledge was now reputed
to have been preserved ever since among the *élite* of science, and
to be ready for publication as soon as the world seemed fit to
possess it. The new sect of Energists claimed that the young Discoverer was himself an incarnation of Buddha, and that, since

the world was still unfit for the supreme revelation, he had entrusted his secret to the Scientists. On the side of Christianity a very similar legend was concerned with the same individual. The Regenerate Christian Brotherhood, by now overwhelmingly the most powerful of the Western Churches, regarded the Discoverer as the Son of God, who, in this his Second Coming, had proposed to bring about the millennium by publishing the secret of divine power; but, finding the peoples still unable to put in practice even the more primitive gospel of love which was announced at his First Coming, he had suffered martyrdom for man's sake, and had entrusted his secret to the Scientists.

The scientific workers of the world had long ago organized themselves as a close corporation. Entrance to the International College of Science was to be obtained only by examination and the payment of high fees. Membership conferred the title of 'Scientist,' and the right to perform experiments. It was also an essential qualification for many lucrative posts. Moreover, there were said to be certain technical secrets which members were pledged not to reveal. Rumour had it that in at least one case of minor blabbing the traitor had shortly afterwards mysteriously died.

Science itself, the actual corpus of natural knowledge, had by now become so complex that only a tiny fraction of it could be mastered by one brain. Thus students of one branch of science knew practically nothing of the work of others in kindred branches Especially was this the case with the huge science called Sub-atomic Physics. Within this were contained a dozen studies, any one of which was as complex as the whole of the physics of the Nineteenth Christian Century. This growing complexity had rendered students in one field ever more reluctant to criticize, or even to try to understand, the principles of other fields. Each petty department, jealous of its own preserves, was meticulously respectful of the preserves of others. In an earlier period the sciences had been coordinated and criticized philosophically by their own leaders and by the technical philosophers. But philosophy, as a rigorous technical discipline, no longer existed. There was, of course, a vague framework of ideas, or assumptions, based on science, and common to all men, a popular pseudoscience, constructed by the journalists from striking phrases current among scientists. But actual scientific workers prided themselves on the rejection of this ramshackle structure, even while they themselves were unwittingly assuming it. And each insisted that his own special subject must inevitably remain unintelligible even to most of his brother scientists.

Under these circumstances, when rumour declared that the mystery of Gordelpus was known to the physicists, each department of sub-atomic physics was both reluctant to deny the charge explicitly in its own case, and ready to believe that some other department really did possess the secret. Consequently, the conduct of the scientists as a body strengthened the general belief that they knew and would not tell.

About two centuries after the formation of the first World State, the President of the World declared that the time was ripe for a formal union of science and religion, and called a conference of the leaders of these two great disciplines. Upon that island in the Pacific which had become the Mecca of cosmopolitan sentiment, and was by now one vast many-storied and cloud-capped Temple of Peace, the heads of Buddhism, Mohammedanism, Hinduism, the Regenerate Christian Brotherhood, and the Modern Catholic Church in South America, agreed that their differences were but differences of expression. One and all were worshippers of the Divine Energy, whether expressed in activity, or in tense stillness. One and all recognized the saintly Discoverer as either the last and greatest of the prophets or an actual incarnation of divine Movement. And these two concepts were easily shown, in the light of modern science, to be identical.

In an earlier age it had been the custom to single out heresy and extirpate it with fire and sword. But now the craving for uniformity was fulfilled by explaining away differences, amid universal applause.

When the Conference had registered the unity of the religions, it went on to establish the unity of religion and science. All knew, said the President, that some of the scientists were in possession of the supreme secret, though, wisely, they would not definitely admit it. It was time, then, that the organizations of Science and Religion should be merged, for the better guidance of men. He, therefore, called upon the International College of Science to nominate from amongst themselves a select body, which should be sanctified by the Church, and called the Sacred Order of Scientists. These custodians of the supreme secret were to be kept at public expense. They were to devote themselves wholly to the service of science, and in particular to research into the most scientific manner of worshipping the Divine Gordelpus.

Of the scientists present, some few looked distinctly uncomfortable, but the majority scarcely concealed their delight under dignified and thoughtful hesitation. Amongst the priests also two expressions were visible; but on the whole it was felt that the Church must gain by thus gathering into herself the unique prestige of science. And so it was that the Order was founded which was destined to become the dominant force in human affairs until the downfall of the first world civilization.

3. MATERIAL ACHIEVEMENT

Save for occasional minor local conflicts, easily quelled by the World Police, the race was now a single social unit for some four thousand years. During the first of these millennia material progress at least was rapid, but subsequently there was little change until the final disintegration. The whole energy of man was concentrated on maintaining at a constant pitch the furious routine of his civilization, until, after another three thousand years of lavish expenditure, certain essential sources of power were suddenly exhausted. Nowhere was there the mental agility to cope with this novel crisis. The whole social order collapsed.

We may pass over the earlier stages of this fantastic civilization, and examine it as it stood before the fatal change began to be felt.

The material circumstances of the race at this time would have amazed all its predecessors, even those who were in the true sense far more civilized beings. But to us, the Last Men, there is an extreme pathos and even comicality, not only in this most thorough confusion of material development with civilization, but also in the actual paucity of the vaunted material development itself, compared with that of our own society.

All the continents, indeed, were by now minutely artificialized. Save for the many wild reserves which were cherished as museums and playgrounds, not a square mile of territory was left in a natural state. Nor was there any longer a distinction between agricultural and industrial areas. All the continents were urbanized, not of course in the manner of the congested industrial cities of an earlier age, but none the less urbanized. Industry and agriculture interpenetrated everywhere. This was possible partly through the great development of aerial communication, partly through a no less remarkable improvement of architecture. Great advances in artificial materials had enabled the erection of buildings in the form of slender pylons which, rising often to a height of three miles, or even more, and founded a quarter of a mile beneath the ground, might yet occupy a ground plan of less than half a mile across. In section these structures were often cruciform; and on each floor, the centre of the long-armed cross consisted of an aerial landing, providing direct access from the air for the dwarf private aeroplanes which were by now essential to the life of every adult. These gigantic pillars of architecture, prophetic of the still mightier structures of an age to come, were scattered over every continent in varying density. Very rarely were they permitted to approach one another by a distance less than their height; on the other hand, save in the arctic, they were very seldom separated by more than twenty miles. The general appearance of every country was thus rather like an open forest of lopped tree-trunks, gigantic in stature. Clouds often encircled the middle heights of these artificial peaks, or blotted out all but the lower stories. Dwellers in the summits were familiar with the spectacle of a dazzling ocean of cloud, dotted on all sides with steep islands of architecture. Such was the altitude of the upper floors that it was sometimes necessary to maintain in them, not merely artificial heating, but artificial air pressure and oxygen supply.

Between these columns of habitation and industry, the land was everywhere green or brown with the seasonal variations of agriculture, park, and wild reserve. Broad grey thoroughfares for heavy freight traffic netted every continent; but lighter transport and the passenger services were wholly aerial. Over all the more populous districts the air was ever aswarm with planes up to a height of five miles, where the giant air-liners plied between the continents.

The enterprise of an already distant past had brought every land under civilization. The Sahara was a lake district, crowded with sun-proud holiday resorts. The arctic islands of Canada, ingeniously warmed by directed tropical currents, were the homes of vigorous northerners. The coasts of Antarctica, thawed in the same manner, were permanently inhabited by those engaged in exploiting the mineral wealth of the hinterland.

Much of the power needed to keep this civilization in being was drawn from the buried remains of prehistoric vegetation, in the form of coal. Although after the foundation of the World State the fuel of Antarctica had been very carefully husbanded, the new supply of oil had given out in less than three centuries, and men were forced to drive their aeroplanes by electricity generated from coal. It soon became evident, however, that even the unexpectedly rich coal-fields of Antarctica would not last for ever. The cessation of oil had taught men a much needed lesson, had made them feel the reality of the power problem. At the same time the cosmopolitan spirit, which was learning to regard the whole race as compatriots, was also beginning to take a broader view temporally, and to see things with the eyes of remote generations. During the first and sanest thousand years of the World State, there was a widespread determination not to incur the blame of the future by wasting power. Thus not only was there serious economy (the first large-scale cosmopolitan enterprise), but also efforts were made to utilize more permanent sources of power. Wind was used extensively. On every building swarms of windmills generated electricity, and every mountain range was similarly decorated, while every considerable fall of water forced its way through turbines. More important still was the utilization of power derived from volcanos and from borings into the subterranean heat. This, it had been hoped, would solve the whole problem of power, once and for all. But even in the earlier and more intelligent period of the World State inventive genius was not what it had been, and no really satisfactory method was found. Consequently at no stage of this civilization did volcanic sources do more than supplement the amazingly rich coal seams of Antarctica. In this region coal was preserved at far greater depth than elsewhere, because, by some accident, the earth's central heat was not here fierce enough (as it was elsewhere) to turn the deeper beds into graphite. Another possible source of power was known to exist in the ocean tides; but the use of this was forbidden by the S.O.S. because, since tidal motion was so obviously astronomical in origin, it had come to be regarded as sacred.

Perhaps the greatest physical achievement of the First World State in its earlier and more vital phase had been in preventive medicine. Though the biological sciences had long ago become stereotyped in respect of fundamental theories, they continued to produce many practical benefits. No longer did men and women have to dread for themselves or those dear to them such afflictions as cancer, tuberculosis, angina pectoris, the rheumatic diseases, and the terrible disorders of the nervous system. No longer were there sudden microbic devastations. No longer was child-birth an ordeal, and womanhood itself a source of suffering. There were no more chronic invalids, no more life-long cripples. Only senility remained; and even this could be repeatedly alleviated by physiological rejuvenation. The removal of all these ancient sources of weakness and misery, which formerly had lamed the race and haunted so many individuals either with definite terrors or vague and scarcely conscious despond, brought about now a pervading buoyancy and optimism impossible to earlier peoples.

4. THE CULTURE OF THE FIRST WORLD STATE

Such was the physical achievement of this civilization. Nothing half so artificial and intricate and prosperous had ever before existed. An earlier age, indeed, had held before itself some such ideal as this; but its nationalistic mania prevented it from attaining the necessary economic unity. This latter-day civilization, however, had wholly outgrown nationalism, and had spent many centuries of peace in consolidating itself. But to what end? The terrors of destitution and ill-health having been abolished, man's spirit was freed from a crippling burden, and might have dared great adventures. But unfortunately his intelligence had by now seriously declined. And so this age, far more than the notorious 'nineteenth century', was the great age of barren complacency.

Every individual was a well-fed and physically healthy human animal. He was also economically independent. His working day was never more than six hours, often only four. He enjoyed a fair share of the products of industry; and in his long holidays he was free to wander in his own aeroplane all over the planet. With good luck he might find himself rich, even for those days, at forty; and if fortune had not favoured him, he might yet expect affluence before he was eighty, when he could still look forward to a century of active life.

But in spite of this material prosperity he was a slave. His work and his leisure consisted of feverish activity, punctuated by moments of listless idleness which he regarded as both sinful and unpleasant. Unless he was one of the furiously successful minority, he was apt to be haunted by moments of brooding, too formless to be called meditation, and of yearning, too blind to be called desire. For he and all his contemporaries were ruled by certain ideas which prevented them from living a fully human life.

Of these ideas one was the ideal of progress. For the individual, the goal imposed by his religious teaching was continuous advance in aeronautical prowess, legal sexual freedom, and millionaire-ship. For the race also the ideal was progress, and progress of the same unintelligent type. Ever more brilliant and extensive aviation, ever more extensive legal sexual intercourse, ever more gigantic manufacture and consumption, were to be coordinated in an ever more intricately organized social system. For the last three thousand years, indeed, progress even of this rude kind had been minute; but this was a source of pride rather than of regret. It implied that the goal was already almost attained, the perfection which should justify the release of the secret of divine power, and the inauguration of an era of incomparably mightier activity.

For the all-pervading idea which tyrannized over the race was the fanatical worship of movement. Gordelpus, the Prime Mover, demanded of his human embodiments swift and intricate activity, and the individual's prospect of eternal life depended on the fulfilment of this obligation. Curiously, though science had long ago destroyed the belief in personal immortality as an intrinsic attribute of man, a complementary belief had grown up to the effect that those who justified themselves in action were preserved eternally, by special miracle, in the swift spirit of Gordelpus. Thus from childhood to death the individual's conduct was determined by the obligation to produce as much motion as possible, whether by his own muscular activity or by the control of natural forces. In the hierarchy of industry three occupations were honoured almost as much as the Sacred Order of Scientists, namely flying, dancing, and athletics. Every one practised all three of these crafts to some extent, for they were imposed by religion; but the professional fliers and aeronautical engineers, and the professional dancers and athletes, were a privileged class.

Several causes had raised flying to a position of unique honour. As a means of communication it was of extreme practical importance; and as the swiftest locomotion it constituted the supreme act of worship. The accident that the form of the aeroplane was reminiscent of the main symbol of the ancient Christian religion lent flying an additional mystical significance. For though the spirit of Christianity was lost, many of its symbols had been preserved in the new faith. A more important source of the dominance of flying was that, since warfare had long ceased to exist, aviation of a gratuitously dangerous kind was the main outlet for the innate adventurousness of the human animal. Young men and women risked their lives fervently for the glory of Gordelpus and their own salvation, while their seniors took vicarious satisfaction in this endless festival of youthful prowess. Indeed, apart from the thrills of devotional aerial acrobatics, it is unlikely that the race would so long have preserved its peace and its unity. On each of the frequent Days of Sacred Flight special rituals of communal and solo aviation were performed at every religious centre. On these occasions the whole sky would be intricately patterned with thousands of planes, wheeling, tumbling, soaring, plunging, in perfect order and at various altitudes, the dance at one level being subtly complementary to the dance at others. It was as though the spontaneous evolutions of many distinct flocks of redshank and dunlin were multiplied a thousand-fold in complexity, and subordinated to a single ever-developing terpsichorean theme. Then suddenly the whole would burst asunder to the horizon, leaving the sky open for the quartets, duets, and solos of the most brilliant stars of flight. At night also, regiments of planes bearing coloured lights would inscribe on the zenith ever-changing and symbolical patterns of fire. Besides these aerial dances, there had existed for eight hundred years a custom of spelling out periodically in a dense flight of planes six thousand miles long the sacred rubrics of the gospel of Gordelpus, so that the living word might be visible to other planets.

In the life of every individual, flying played a great part. Immediately after birth he was taken up by a priestess of flight and dropped, clinging to a parachute, to be deftly caught upon the wings of his father's plane. This ritual served as a substitute for contraception (forbidden as an interference with the divine energy); for since in many infants the old simian grasping-instinct was atrophied, a large proportion of the new-born let go and were smashed upon the paternal wings. At adolescence the individual (male or female) took charge of a plane for the first time, and his life was subsequently punctuated by severe aeronautical tests. From middle age onwards, namely as a centenarian, when he could no longer hope to rise in the hierarchy of active flight, he continued to fly daily for practical purposes.

The two other forms of ritual activity, dancing and athletics, were scarcely less important. Nor were they confined wholly to the ground. For certain rites were celebrated by dances upon the wings of a plane in mid air.

Dancing was especially associated with the Negro race, which occupied a very peculiar position in the world at this time. As a matter of fact the great colour distinctions of mankind were now beginning to fade. Increased aerial communication had caused the black, brown, yellow and white stocks so to mingle that everywhere there was by now a large majority of the racially indistinguishable. Nowhere was there any great number of persons of marked racial character. But each of the ancient types was liable to crop up now and again in isolated individuals, especially in its ancient homeland. These 'throw-backs' were customarily treated in special and historically appropriate manners. Thus, for instance, it was to 'sports' of definite Negro character that the most sacred dancing was entrusted.

In the days of the nations, the descendants of emancipated African slaves in North America had greatly influenced the artistic and religious life of the white population, and had inspired a cult of negroid dancing which survived till the end of the First Men. This was partly due to the sexual and primitive character of Negro dancing, sorely needed in a nation ridden by sexual taboos. But it had also a deeper source. The American nation had acquired its slaves by capture, and had long continued to spurn their descendants. Later it unconsciously compensated for its guilt by a cult of the Negro spirit. Thus when American culture dominated the planet, the pure Negroes became a sacred cast. Forbidden many of the rights of citizenship, they were regarded as the private servants of Gordelpus. They were both sacred and outcast. This dual role was epitomized in an extravagant ritual which took place once a year in each of the great national parks. A white woman and Negro, both chosen for their prowess in dance, performed a long and symbolical ballet, which culminated in a ritual act of sexual violation, performed in full view of the maddened spectators. This over, the Negro knifed his victim, and fled through the forest pursued by an exultant mob. If he reached sanctuary, he became a peculiarly sacred object for the rest of his life. But if he was caught, he was torn to pieces, or drenched with inflammable spirit and burned. Such was the superstition of the First Men at this time that the participants in this ceremony were seldom reluctant; for it was firmly believed that both were assured of eternal life in Gordelpus. In America this Sacred Lynching was the most popular of all festivals; for it was both sexual and bloody, and afforded a fierce joy to the masses whose sex-life was restricted and secret. In India and Africa the violator was always an 'Englishman,' when such a rare creature could be found. In China the whole character of the ceremony was altered; for the violation became a kiss, and the murder a touch with a fan.

One other race, the Jews, were treated with a similar combination of honour and contempt, but for very different reasons. In ancient days their general intelligence, and in particular their financial talent, had cooperated with their homelessness to make them outcasts; and now, in the decline of the First Men, they retained the fiction, if not strictly the fact, of racial integrity. They were still outcasts, though indispensable and powerful. Almost the only kind of intelligent activity which the First Men could still respect was financial operation, whether private or cosmopolitan. The Jews had made themselves invaluable in the financial organization of the world state, having far outstripped the other races because they alone had preserved a furtive respect for pure intelligence. And so, long after intelligence had come to be regarded as disreputable in ordinary men and women, it was expected of the Jews. In them it was called satanic cunning, and they were held to be embodiments of the powers of evil, harnessed in the service of Gordelpus. Thus in time the Jews had made something like 'a corner' in intelligence. This precious commodity they used largely for their own purposes; for two thousand years of persecution had long ago rendered them permanently tribalistic, subconsciously if not consciously. Thus when they had gained control of the few remaining operations which demanded originality rather than routine, they used this advantage chiefly to strengthen their own position in the world. For, though relatively bright, they had suffered much of the general coarsening and limitation which had beset the whole world. Though capable to some extent of criticizing the practical means by which ends should be realized, they were by now wholly incapable of criticizing the major ends which had dominated their race for thousands of years. In them intelligence had become utterly subservient to tribalism. There was thus some excuse for the universal hate and even physical repulsion with which they were regarded; for they alone had failed to make the one great advance, from tribalism to a cosmopolitanism which in other races was no longer merely theoretical. There was good reason also for the respect which they received, since they retained and used somewhat ruthlessly a certain degree of the most distinctively human attribute, intelligence.

In primitive times the intelligence and sanity of the race had been preserved by the inability of its unwholesome members to survive. When humanitarianism came into vogue, and the unsound were tended at public expense, this natural selection ceased. And since these unfortunates were incapable alike of prudence and of social responsibility, they procreated without restraint, and threatened to infect the whole species with their rottenness. During the zenith of Western Civilization, therefore, the sub-normal were sterilized. But the latter-day worshippers of Gordelpus regarded both sterilization and contraception as a wicked interference with the divine potency. Consequently the only restriction on population was the suspension of the newborn from aeroplanes, a process which, though it eliminated weaklings, favoured among healthy infants rather the primitive than the highly developed. Thus the intelligence of the race steadily declined. And no one regretted it.

The general revulsion from intelligence was a corollary of the adoration of instinct, and this in turn was an aspect of the worship of activity. Since the unconscious source of human vigour was the divine energy, spontaneous impulse must so far as possible never be thwarted. Reasoning was indeed permitted to the individual within the sphere of his official work, but never beyond. And not even specialists might indulge in reasoning and experiment without obtaining a licence for the particular research. The licence was expensive, and was only granted if the goal in view could be shown to be an increase of world activity. In old times certain persons of morbid curiosity had dared to criticize the time-honoured methods of doing things, and had suggested 'better' methods not convenient to the Sacred Order of Scientists. This had to be stopped. By the fourth millennium of the World State the operations of civilization had become so intricately stereotyped that novel situations of a major order never occurred.

One kind of intellectual pursuit in addition to finance was, indeed, honoured, namely mathematical calculation. All ritual movements, all the motions of industrial machinery, all observable natural phenomena, had to be minutely described in mathematical formulae. The records were filed in the sacred archives of the S.O.S. And there they remained. This vast enterprise of mathematical description was the main work of the scientists, and was said to be the only means by which the evanescent thing, movement, could be passed into the eternal being of Gordelpus.

The cult of instinct did not result simply in a life of ungoverned impulse. Far from it. For the fundamental instinct, it was said, was the instinct to worship Gordelpus in action, and this should rule all the other instincts. Of these, the most important and sacred was the sexual impulse, which the First Men had ever tended to regard as both divine and obscene. Sex, therefore, was now very strictly controlled. Reference to sexuality, save by circumlocution, was forbidden by law. Persons who remarked on the obvious sexual significance of the religious dances were severely punished. No sexual activity and no sex knowledge were permitted to the individual until he had won his (or her) wings. Much information, of a distorted and perverted nature could, indeed, be gained meanwhile by observation of the religious writings and practices; but officially these sacred matters were all given a metaphysical, not a sexual interpretation. And though legal maturity, the Wing-Winning, might occur as early as the age of fifteen, sometimes it was not attained till forty. If at that age the individual still failed in the test, he or she was forbidden sexual intercourse and information for ever.

In China and India this extravagant sexual taboo was some-what mitigated. Many easy-going persons had come to feel that the imparting of sex knowledge to the 'immature' was only wrong when the medium of communication was the sacred American language. They therefore made use of the local patois. Similarly, sexual activity of the 'immature' was permissible so long as it was performed solely in the wild reserves, and without American speech. These subterfuges, however, were condemned by the orthodox, even in Asia.

When a man had won his wings, he was formally initiated into the mystery of sex and all its 'biologico-religious' significance. He was also allowed to take a 'domestic wife,' and after a much more severe aviation test, any number of 'symbolical' wives. Similarly with the woman. These two kinds of partnership differed greatly. The 'domestic' husband and wife appeared in public together, and their union was indissoluble. The 'symbolic' union, on the other hand, could be dissolved by either party. Also it was too sacred ever to be revealed, or even mentioned, in public.

A very large number of persons never passed the test which sanctioned sexuality. These either remained virgin, or indulged in sexual relations which were not only illegal but sacrilegious. The successful, on the other hand, were apt to consummate sexually every casual acquaintance.

Under these circumstances it was natural that there should exist among the sexually submerged part of the population certain secret cults which sought escape from harsh reality into worlds of fantasy. Of these illicit sects, two were most widespread. One was a perversion of the ancient Christian faith in a God of Love. All love, it was said, is sexual; therefore in worship, private or public, the individual must seek a direct sexual relation with God. Hence arose a grossly phallic cult, very contemptible to those more fortunate persons who had no need of it.

The other great heresy was derived partly from the energy of repressed intellective impulses, and was practised by persons of natural curiosity, who nevertheless, shared the universal paucity of intelligence. These pathetic devotees of intellect were inspired by Socrates. That great primitive had insisted that clear thought is impossible without clear definition of terms, and that without clear thinking man misses fullness of being. These his last disciples were scarcely less fervent admirers of truth than their master, yet they missed his spirit completely. Only by knowing the truth, they said, can the individual attain immortality; only by defining can he know the truth. Therefore, meeting together in secret, and in constant danger of arrest for illicit intellection, they disputed endlessly about the definition of things. But the things which they were concerned to define were not the basic concepts of human thought; for these, they affirmed, had been settled once for all by Socrates and his immediate followers. Therefore, accepting these as true, and grossly misunderstanding them, the ultimate Socratics undertook to define all the processes of the world state and the ritual of the established religion, all the emotions of men and women, all the shapes of noses, mouths, buildings, mountains, clouds, and in fact the whole superficies of their world. Thus they believed that they emancipated themselves from the philistinism of their age, and secured comradeship with Socrates in the hereafter.

5. DOWNFALL

The collapse of this first world-civilization was due to the sudden failure of the supplies of coal. All the original fields had been sapped centuries earlier, and it should have been obvious that those more recently discovered could not last for ever. For some thousands of years the main supply had come from Antarctica. So prolific was this continent that latterly a superstition had arisen in the clouded minds of the world-citizens that it was in some mysterious manner inexhaustible. Thus when at last, in spite of strict censorship, the news began to leak out that even the deepest possible borings had failed to reveal further vegetable deposits of any kind, the world was at first incredulous.

The sane policy would have been to abolish the huge expense of power on ritual flying, which used more of the community's resources than the whole of productive industry. But to believers in Gordelpus such a course was almost unthinkable. Moreover it would have undermined the flying aristocracy. This powerful class now declared that the time had come for the release of the secret of divine power, and called on the S.O.S. to inaugurate the new era. Vociferous agitation in all lands put the scientists in an awkward plight. They gained time by declaring that, though the moment of revelation was approaching, it had not yet arrived; for they had received a divine intimation that this failure of coal was imposed as a supreme test of man's faith. The service of Gordelpus in ritual flight must be rather increased than reduced. Spending a bare minimum of its power on secular matters, the race must concentrate upon religion. When Gordelpus had evidence of their devotion and trust, he would permit the scientists to save them.

Such was the prestige of science that at first this explanation was universally accepted. The ritual flights were maintained. All luxury trades were abolished, and even vital services were reduced to a minimum. Workers thus thrown out of employment were turned over to agricultural labour; for it was felt that the use of mechanical power in mere tillage must be as soon as possible abolished. These changes demanded far more organizing ability than was left in the race. Confusion was widespread, save here and there where serious organization was attempted by certain Jews.

93

The first result of this great movement of economy and self-denial was to cause something of a spiritual awakening among many who had formerly lived a life of bored ease. This was augmented by the widespread sense of crisis and impending marvels. Religion, which, in spite of its universal authority in this age, had become a matter of ritual rather than of inward experience, began to stir in many hearts – not indeed as a moment of true worship, but rather as a vague awe, not unmixed with self-importance.

But as the novelty of this enthusiasm dwindled, and life became increasingly uncomfortable, even the most zealous began to notice with horror that in moments of inactivity they were prone to doubts too shocking to confess. And as the situation worsened, even a life of ceaseless action could not suppress these wicked fantasies.

For the race was now entering upon an unprecedented psychological crisis, brought about by the impact of the economic disaster upon a permanently unwholesome mentality. Each individual, it must be remembered, had once been a questioning child, but had been taught to shun curiosity as the breath of Satan. Consequently the whole race was suffering from a kind of inverted repression, a repression of the intellective impulses. The sudden economic change, which affected all classes throughout the planet, thrust into the focus of attention a shocking curiosity, an obsessive scepticism, which had hitherto been buried in the deepest recesses of the mind.

It is not easy to conceive the strange mental disorder that now afflicted the whole race, symbolizing itself in some cases by fits of actual physical vertigo. After centuries of prosperity, of routine, of orthodoxy, men were suddenly possessed by a doubt which they regarded as diabolical. No one said a word of it; but in each man's own mind the fiend raised a whispering head, and each was haunted by the troubled eyes of his fellows. Indeed the whole changed circumstances of his life jibed at his credulity.

Earlier in the career of the race, this world crisis might have served to wake men into sanity. Under the first pressure of distress they might have abandoned the extravagances of their culture. But by now the ancient way of life was too deeply rooted.

Consequently, we observe the fantastic spectacle of a world engaged, devotedly and even heroically, on squandering its resources in vast aeronautical displays, not through single-minded faith in their rightness and efficacy, but solely in a kind of desperate automatism. Like those little rodents whose migration became barred by an encroachment of the sea, so that annually they drowned themselves in thousands, the First Men helplessly continued in their ritualistic behaviour; but unlike the lemmings, they were human enough to be at the same time oppressed by unbelief, an unbelief which, moreover, they dared not recognize.

Meanwhile the scientists were earnestly and secretly delving in the ancient literature of their science, in hope of discovering the forgotten talisman. They undertook also clandestine experiments, but upon a false trail laid by the wily English contemporary of the Discoverer. The main results were, that several researchers were poisoned or electrocuted, and a great college was blown up. This event impressed the populace, who supposed the accident to be due to an over-daring exercise of the divine potency. The misunderstanding inspired the desperate scientists to rig further impressive 'miracles', and moreover to use them to dispel the increasing restlessness of hungry industrial workers. Thus when a deputation arrived outside the offices of Cosmopolitan Agriculture to demand more flour for industrialists Gordelpus miraculously blew up the ground on which they stood, and flung their bodies among the onlookers. When the agriculturists of China struck to obtain a reasonable allowance of electric power for their tillage, Gordelpus affected them with an evil atmosphere, so that they choked and died in thousands. Stimulated in this manner by direct divine intervention, the doubting and disloyal elements of the world population recovered their faith and their docility. And so the world jogged on for a while, as nearly as possible as it had done for the last four thousand years, save for a general increase of hunger and ill health.

But inevitably, as the conditions of life became more and more severe, docility gave place to desperation. Daring spirits began publicly to question the wisdom, and even the piety, of so vast an expenditure of power upon ritual flight, when prime necessities

95

such as food and clothing were becoming so scarce. Did not this
helpless devotion merely ridicule them in the divine eyes? God
helps him who helps himself. Already the death rate had risen
alarmingly. Emaciated and ragged persons were beginning to beg
in public places. In certain districts whole populations were
starving, and the Directorate did nothing for them. Yet, elsewhere, harvests were being wasted for lack of power to reap
them. In all lands an angry clamour arose for the inauguration of
the new era.

The scientists were by now panic-stricken. Nothing had come
of their researches, and it was evident that in future all wind- and
water-power must be devoted to the primary industries. Even so,
there was starvation ahead for many. The President of the
Physical Society suggested to the Directorate that ritual flying
should at once be reduced by half, as a compromise with Gordelpus. Immediately the hideous truth, which few hitherto had
dared to admit even to themselves, was blurted out upon the
ether by a prominent Jew: the whole hoary legend of the divine
secret was a lie, else why were the physicists temporizing? Dismay
and rage spread over the planet. Everywhere the people rose
against the scientists, and against the governing authority which
they controlled. Massacres and measures of retaliation soon
developed into civil wars. China and India declared themselves
free national states, but could not achieve internal unity. In
America, ever a stronghold of science and religion, the Government maintained its authority for a while; but as its seat became
less secure, its methods became more ruthless. Finally it made the
mistake of using not merely poison gas, but microbes; and such
was the decayed state of medical science that no one could invent
a means of restraining their ravages. The whole American continent succumbed to a plague of pulmonary and nervous diseases.
The ancient 'American Madness', which long ago had been used
against China, now devastated America. The great stations of
water-power and wind-power were wrecked by lunatic mobs who
sought vengeance upon anything associated with authority. Whole
populations vanished in an orgy of cannibalism.

In Asia and Africa, some semblance of order was maintained
for a while. Presently, however, the American Madness spread to

these continents also, and very soon all living traces of their civilization vanished.

Only in the most naturally fertile areas of the world could the diseased remnant of a population now scrape a living from the soil. Elsewhere, utter desolation. With easy strides the jungle came back into its own.

V *The Fall of the First Men*

1. THE FIRST DARK AGE

WE have reached a period in man's history rather less than five thousand years after the life of Newton. In this chapter we must cover about one hundred and fifteen thousand years, and in the next chapter another ten million years. That will bring us to a point as remotely future from the First World State as the earliest anthropoids were remotely past. During the first tenth of the first million years after the fall of the World State, during a hundred thousand years, man remained in complete eclipse. Not till the close of this span, which we will call the First Dark Age, did he struggle once more from savagery through barbarism into civilization. And then his renaissance was relatively brief. From its earliest beginnings to its end, it covered only fifteen thousand years; and in its final agony the planet was so seriously damaged that mind lay henceforth in deep slumber for ten more millions of years. This was the Second Dark Age. Such is the field which we must observe in this and the following chapter.

It might have been expected that, after the downfall of the First World State, recovery would have occurred within a few generations. Historians have, indeed, often puzzled over the cause of this surprisingly complete and lasting degradation. Innate human nature was roughly the same immediately after as immediately before the crisis; yet minds that had easily maintained a world-civilization in being, proved quite incapable of building a new order on the ruins of the old. Far from recovering, man's estate rapidly deteriorated till it had sunk into abject savagery.

Many causes contributed to this result, some relatively superficial and temporary, some profound and lasting. It is as though Fate, directing events toward an allotted end, had availed herself of many diverse instruments, none of which would have sufficed alone, though all worked together irresistibly in the same sense. The immediate cause of the helplessness of the race during the actual crisis of the World State was of course the vast epidemic of insanity and still more widespread deterioration of intelligence, which resulted from the use of microbes. This momentary seizure made it impossible for man to check his downfall during its earliest and least unmanageable stage. Later, when the epidemic was spent, even though civilization was already in ruins, a concerted effort of devotion might yet have rebuilt it on a more modest plan. But among the First Men only a minority had ever been capable of wholehearted devotion. The great majority were by nature too much obsessed by private impulses. And in this black period, such was the depth of disillusion and fatigue that even normal resolution was impossible. Not only man's social structure but the structure of the universe itself, it seemed, had failed. The only reaction was supine despair. Four thousand years of routine had deprived human nature of all its suppleness. To expect these beings to refashion their whole behaviour, were scarcely less unreasonable than to expect ants, when their nest was flooded, to assume the habits of water beetles.

But a far more profound and lasting cause doomed the First Men to lie prone for a long while, once they had fallen. A subtle physiological change, which it is tempting to call 'general senescence of the species', was undermining the human body and mind. The chemical equilibrium of each individual was becoming more unstable, so that, little by little, man's unique gift of prolonged youth was being lost. Far more rapidly than of old, his tissues failed to compensate for the wear and tear of living. This disaster was by no means inevitable; but it was brought on by influences peculiar to the make-up of the species, and aggravated artificially. For during some thousands of years man had been living at too high a pressure in a biologically unnatural environment, and had found no means of compensating his nature for the strain thus put upon it.

Conceive, then, that after the fall of the First World State, the generations slid rapidly through dusk into night. To inhabit those centuries was to live in the conviction of universal decay, and under the legend of a mighty past. The population was derived almost wholly from the agriculturists of the old order, and since agriculture had been considered a sluggish and base occupation, fit only for sluggish natures, the planet was now peopled with yokels. Deprived of power, machinery, and chemical fertilizers, these bumpkins were hard put to it to keep themselves alive. And indeed only a tenth of their number survived the great disaster. The second generation knew civilization only as a legend. Their days were filled with ceaseless tillage, and in banding together to fight marauders. Women became once more sexual and domestic chattels. The family, or tribe of families, became the largest social whole. Endless brawls and feuds sprang up between valley and valley, and between the tillers and the brigand swarms. Small military tyrants rose and fell; but no permanent unity of control could be maintained over a wide region. There was no surplus wealth to spend on such luxuries as governments and trained armies.

Thus without appreciable change the millennia dragged on in squalid drudgery. For these latter-day barbarians were hampered by living in a used planet. Not only were coal and oil no more, but almost no mineral wealth of any kind remained within reach of their feeble instruments and wits. In particular the minor metals, needed for so many of the multifarious activities of developed material civilization, had long ago disappeared from the more accessible depths of the earth's crust. Tillage moreover was hampered by the fact that iron itself, which was no longer to be had without mechanical mining, was now inaccessible. Men had been forced to resort once more to stone implements, as their first human ancestors had done. But they lacked both the skill and the persistence of the ancients. Not for them the delicate flaking of the Paleoliths nor the smooth symmetry of the Neoliths. Their tools were but broken pebbles, chipped improvements upon natural stones. On almost every one they engraved the same pathetic symbol, the Swastika or cross, which had been used by the First Men as a sacred emblem throughout their existence, though with varying significance. In this instance it had originally been the figure of an aeroplane diving to destruction, and had been used by the rebels to symbolize the downfall of Gordelpus and the State. But subsequent generations reinterpreted the emblem as the sign manual of a divine ancestor, and as a memento of the golden age from which they were destined to decline for ever, or until the gods should intervene. Almost one might say

The Fall of the First Men

that in its persistent use of this symbol the first human species unwittingly epitomized its own dual and self-thwarting nature.

The idea of irresistible decay obsessed the race at this time. The generation which brought about the downfall of the World State oppressed its juniors with stories of past amenities and marvels, and hugged to itself the knowledge that the young men had not the wit to rebuild such complexity. Generation by generation, as the circumstances of actual life became more squalid, the legend of past glory became more extravagant. The whole mass of scientific knowledge was rapidly lost, save for a few shreds which were of practical service even in savage life. Fragments of the old culture were indeed preserved in the tangle of folk lore that meshed the globe, but they were distorted beyond recognition. Thus there was a wide-spread belief that the world had begun as fire, and that life had evolved out of the fire. After the apes had appeared, evolution ceased (so it was said), until divine spirits came down and possessed the female apes, thereby generating human beings. Thus had arisen the golden age of the divine ancestors. But unfortunately after a while the beast in man had triumphed over the god, so that progress had given place to age-long decay. And indeed decay was now unavoidable, until such time as the gods should see fit to come down to cohabit with women and fire the race once more. This faith in the second coming of the gods persisted here and there throughout the First Dark Age, and consoled men for their vague conviction of degeneracy.

Even at the close of the First Dark Age the ruins of the ancient residential pylons still characterized every landscape, often with an effect of senile domination over the hovels of latter-day savages. For the living races dwelt beneath these relics like puny grandchildren playing around the feet of their fathers' once mightier fathers. So well had the past built, and with such durable materials, that even after a hundred millennia the ruins were still recognizably artifacts. Though for the most part they were of course by now little more than pyramids of debris overgrown with grass and brushwood, most of them retained some stretch of standing wall, and here and there a favoured specimen still reared from its rubble-encumbered base a hundred foot or so of cliff, punctured with windows. Fantastic legends now clustered round these relics. In one myth the men of old had made for themselves huge palaces which could fly. For a thousand years (an aeon to these savages) men had dwelt in unity, and in reverence of the gods; but at last they had become puffed up with their own glory, and had undertaken to fly to the sun and moon and the field of stars, to oust the gods from their bright home. But the gods sowed discord among them, so that they fell a-fighting one another in the upper air, and their swift palaces crashed down to the earth in thousands, to be monuments of man's folly for ever after. In yet another saga it was the men themselves who were winged. They inhabited dovecots of masonry, with summits over-topping the stars and outraging the gods; who therefore destroyed them. Thus in one form or another, this theme of the downfall of the mighty fliers of old tyrannized over these abject peoples. Their crude tillage, their hunting, their defence against the reviving carnivora, were hampered at every turn by fear of offending the gods by any innovation.

2. THE RISE OF PATAGONIA

As the centuries piled up, the human species had inevitably diverged once more into many races in the various geographical areas. And each race consisted of a swarm of tribes, each ignorant of all but its immediate neighbours. After many millennia this vast diversification of stocks and cultures made it possible for fresh biological transfusions and revivifications to occur. At last, after many racial copulations, a people arose in whom the ancient dignity of humanity was somewhat restored. Once more there was a real distinction between the progressive and the backward regions, between 'primitive' and relatively enlightened cultures.

This rebirth occurred in the Southern Hemisphere. Complex climatic changes had rendered the southern part of South America a fit nursery for civilization. Further, an immense warping of the earth's crust to the east and south of Patagonia had turned what was once a relatively shallow region of the ocean into a vast new land connecting America with Antarctica by way of the former

Falkland Islands and South Georgia, and stretching thence east and north-east into the heart of the Atlantic.

It happened also that in South America the racial conditions were more favourable than elsewhere. After the fall of the First World State the European element in this region had dwindled, and the ancient 'Indian' and Peruvian stock had come into dominance. Many thousands of years earlier, this race had achieved a primitive civilization of its own. After its ruin at the hands of the Spaniards, it had seemed a broken and negligible thing; yet it had ever kept itself curiously aloof in spirit from its conquerors. Though the two stocks had mingled inextricably, there remained ever in the remoter parts of this continent a way of life which was foreign to the dominant Americanism. Superficially Americanized, it remained fundamentally 'Indian' and unintelligible to the rest of the world. Throughout the former civilization this spirit had lain dormant like a seed in winter; but with the return of barbarism it had sprouted, and quietly spread in all directions. From the interaction of this ancient primitive culture and the many other racial elements left over in the continent from the old cosmopolitan civilization, civil life was to begin once more. Thus in a manner the Incas were at last to triumph over their conquerors.

Various causes, then, combined in South America, and especially in the new and virgin plains of Patagonia, to bring the First Dark Age to an end. The great theme of mind began to repeat itself. But in a minor key. For a grave disability hampered the Patagonians. They began to grow old before their adolescence was completed. In the days of Einstein, an individual's youth lasted some twenty-five years, and under the World State it had been artificially doubled. After the downfall of civilization the increasing natural brevity of the individual life was no longer concealed by artifice, and at the end of the First Dark Age a boy of fifteen was already settling into middle age. Patagonian civilization at its height afforded considerable ease and security of life, and enabled man to live to seventy or even eighty; but the period of sensitive and supple youth remained at the very best little more than a decade and a half. Thus the truly young were never able to contribute to culture before they were already at heart middle-aged. At fifteen their bones were definitely becoming brittle, their hair

103

grizzled, their faces lined. Their joints and muscles were stiffening, their brains were no longer quick to learn new adjustments, their fervour was evaporating.

It may seem strange that under these circumstances any kind of civilization could be achieved by the race, that any generation should ever have been able to do more than learn the tricks of its elders. Yet in fact, though progress was never swift, it was steady. For though these beings lacked much of the vigour of youth, they were compensated somewhat by escaping much of youth's fevers and distractions. The First Men, in fact, were now a race whose wild oats had been sown; and though their youthful escapades had somewhat crippled them, they had now the advantage of sobriety and singleness of purpose. Though doomed by lassitude, and a certain fear of extravagance, to fall short of the highest achievements of their predecessors, they avoided much of the wasteful incoherence and mental conflict which had tortured the earlier civilization at its height, though not in its decline. Moreover, because their animal nature was somewhat subdued, the Patagonians were more capable of dispassionate cognition, and more inclined toward intellectualism. They were a people in whom rational behaviour was less often subverted by passion, though more liable to fail through mere indolence or faint-heartedness. Though they found detachment relatively easy, theirs was the detachment of mere lassitude, not the leap from the prison of life's cravings into a more spacious world.

One source of the special character of the Patagonian mind was that in it the sexual impulses was relatively weak. Many obscure causes had helped to temper that lavish sexuality in respect of which the first human species differed from all other animals, even the continuously sexual apes. These causes were diverse, but they combined to produce in the last phase of the life of the species a general curtailment of excess energy. In the Dark Ages the severity of the struggle for existence had thrust the sexual interest back almost into the subordinate place which it occupies in the animal mind. Coitus became a luxury only occasionally desired, while self-preservation had become once more an urgent and ever-present necessity. When at last life began to be easier, sexuality remained in partial eclipse, for the forces of racial 'senescence' were at work. Thus the Patagonian culture differed in mood from all the earlier cultures of the First Men. Hitherto it had been the clash of sexuality and social taboo that had generated half the fervour and half the delusions of the race. The excess energy of a victorious species, directed by circumstance into the great river of sex, and damned by social convention, had been canalized for a thousand labours. And though often it would break loose and lay all waste before it, in the main it had been turned to good account. At all times indeed, it had been prone to escape in all directions and carve out channels for itself, as a lopped tree stump sends forth not one but a score of shoots. Hence the richness, diversity, incoherence, violent and uncomprehended cravings and enthusiasms, of the earlier peoples. In the Patagonians there was no such luxuriance. That they were not highly sexual was not in itself a weakness. What mattered was that the springs of energy which formerly happened to flood into the channel of sex were themselves impoverished.

Conceive, then, a small and curiously sober people established east of the ancient Bahia Blanca, and advancing century by century over the plains and up the valleys. In time it reached and encircled the heights which were once the island of South Georgia, while to the north and west it spread into the Brazilian highlands and over the Andes. Definitely of higher type than any of their neighbours, definitely more vigorous and acute, the Patagonians were without serious rivals. And since by temperament they were peaceable and conciliatory, their cultural progress was little delayed, either by military imperialism or internal strife. Like their predecessors in the northern hemisphere, they passed through phases of disruption and union, retrogression and regeneration; but their career was on the whole more steadily progressive, and less dramatic, than anything that had occurred before. Earlier peoples had leapt from barbarism to civil life and collapsed again within a thousand years. The slow march of the Patagonians took ten times as long to pass from a tribal to a civic organization.

Eventually they comprised a vast and highly organized community of autonomous provinces, whose political and cultural centre lay upon the new coast north-east of the ancient Falkland Islands, while its barbarian outskirts included much of Brazil

and Peru. The absence of serious strife between the various parts
of this 'empire' was due partly to an innately pacific disposition,
partly to a genius for organization. These influences were
strengthened by a curiously potent tradition of cosmopolitanism,
or human unity, which had been born in the agony of disunion
before the days of the World State, and was so burnt into men's
hearts that it survived as an element of myth even through the
Dark Age. So powerful was this tradition, that even when the
sailing ships of Patagonia had founded colonies in remote Africa
and Australia, these new communities remained at heart one
with the mother country. Even when the almost Nordic culture of
the new and temperate Antarctic coasts had outshone the ancient
centre, the political harmony of the race was never in danger.

3. THE CULT OF YOUTH

The Patagonians passed through all the spiritual phases that
earlier races had experienced, but in a distinctive manner. They
had their primitive tribal religion, derived from the dark past, and
based on the fear of natural forces. They had their monotheistic
impersonation of Power as a vindictive Creator. Their most
adored racial hero was a god-man who abolished the old religion
of fear. They had their phases, also, of devout ritual and their
phases of rationalism, and again their phases of empirical
curiosity.

Most significant for the historian who would understand their
special mentality is the theme of the god-man; so curiously did it
resemble, yet differ from, similar themes in earlier cultures of the
first human species. He was conceived as eternally adolescent,
and as mystically the son of all men and women. Far from being
the Elder Brother, he was the Favourite Child; and indeed he
epitomises that youthful energy and enthusiasm which the race
now guessed was slipping away from it. Though the sexual interest
of this people was weak, the parental interest was curiously strong.
But the worship of the Favourite Son was not merely parental; it
expressed also both the individual's craving for his own lost youth,
and his obscure sense that the race itself was senescent.

It was believed that the prophet had actually lived a century as a fresh adolescent. He was designated the Boy who Refused to Grow up. And this vigour of will was possible to him, it was said, because in him the feeble vitality of the race was concentrated many millionfold. For he was the fruit of all parental passion that ever was and would be; and as such he was divine. Primarily he was the Son of Man, but also he was God. For God, in this religion, was no prime Creator but the fruit of man's endeavour. The Creator was brute power, which had quite inadvertently begotten a being nobler than itself. God, the adorable, was the eternal outcome of man's labour in time, the eternally realized promise of what man himself should become. Yet though this cult was based on the will for a young-hearted future, it was also overhung by a dread, almost at times a certainty, that in fact such a future would never be, that the race was doomed to grow old and die, that spirit could never conquer the corruptible flesh, but must fade and vanish. Only by taking to heart the message of the Divine Boy, it was said, could man hope to escape this doom.

Such was the legend. It is instructive to examine the reality. The actual individual, in whom this myth of the Favourite Son was founded, was indeed remarkable. Born of shepherd parents among the Southern Andes, he had first become famous as the leader of a romantic 'youth movement'; and it was this early stage of his career that won him followers. He urged the young to set an example to the old, to live their own life undaunted by conventions, to enjoy, to work hard but briefly, to be loyal comrades. Above all, he preached the religious duty of remaining young in spirit. No one, he said, need grow old, if he willed earnestly not to do so, if he would but keep his soul from falling asleep, his heart open to all rejuvenating influences and shut to every breath of senility. The delight of soul in soul, he said, was the great rejuvenator; it re-created both lover and beloved. If Patagonians would only appreciate each other's beauty without jealousy, the race would grow young again. And the mission of his ever-increasing Band of Youth was nothing less than the rejuvenation of man.

The propagation of this attractive gospel was favoured by a seeming miracle. The prophet turned out to be biologically unique among Patagonians. When many of his coevals were showing signs of senescence, he remained physically young. Also he possessed a sexual vigour which to the Patagonians seemed miraculous. And since sexual taboo was unknown, he exercised himself so heartily in love-making, that he had paramours in every village, and presently his offspring were numbered in hundreds. In this respect his followers strove hard to live up to him, though with small success. But it was not only physically that the prophet remained young. He preserved also a strikingly youthful agility of mind. His sexual prodigality, though startling to his contemporaries, was in him a temperate overflow of surplus energy. Far from exhausting him, it refreshed him. Presently, however, this exuberance gave place to a more sober life of work and meditation. It was in this period that he began to differentiate himself mentally from his fellows. For at twenty-five, when most Patagonians were deeply settled into a mental groove, he was still battling with successive waves of ideas, and striking out into the unknown. Not till he was forty, and still physically in earliest prime, did he gather his strength and deliver himself of his mature gospel. This, his considered view of existence, turned out to be almost unintelligible to Patagonians. Though in a sense it was an expression of their own culture, it was an expression upon a plane of vitality to which very few of them could ever reach.

The climax came when, during a ceremony in the supreme temple of the capital city, while the worshippers were all prostrated before the hideous image of the Creator, the ageless prophet strode up to the altar, regarded first the congregation and then the god, burst into a hearty peal of laughter, slapped the image resoundingly, and cried, 'Ugly, I salute you! Not as almighty, but as the greatest of all jokers. To have such a face, and yet to be admired for it! To be so empty, and yet so feared!' Instantly there was hubbub. But such was the young iconoclast's god-like radiance, confidence, unexpectedness, and such his reputation as the miraculous Boy, that when he turned upon the crowd, they fell silent, and listened to his scolding.

'Fools!' he cried. 'Senile infants! If God really likes your adulation, and all this hugger-mugger, it is because he enjoys the joke against you, and against himself, too. You are too serious, yet not serious enough; too solemn, and all for puerile ends. You are so eager for life, that you cannot live. You cherish your youth so much that it flies from you. When I was a boy, I said, "Let us keep young"; and you applauded, and went about hugging your toys and refusing to grow up. What I said was not bad for a boy, but it was not enough. Now I am a man; and I say, "For God's sake, grow up!" Of course we must keep young; but it is useless to keep young if we do not also grow up, and never stop growing up. To keep young, surely, is just to keep supple and keen; and to grow up is not at all a mere sinking into stiffness and into disillusion, but a rising into ever finer skill in all the actions of the game of living. There is something else, too, which is a part of growing up – to see that life is really, after all, a game; a terribly serious game, no doubt, but none the less a game. When we play a game, as it should be played, we strain every muscle to win; but all the while we are less for winning than for the game. And we play the better for it. When barbarians play against a Patagonian team, they forget that it is a game, and go mad for victory. And then how we despise them! If they find themselves losing, they turn savage; if winning, blatant. Either way, the game is murdered, and they cannot see that they are slaughtering a lovely thing. How they pester and curse the umpire, too! I have done that myself, of course, before now; not in games but in life. I have actually cursed the umpire of life. Better so, anyhow, than to insult him with presents, in the hope of being favoured; which is what you are doing here, with your salaams and your vows. I never did that. I merely hated him. Then later I learned to laugh at him, or rather at the thing you set up in his place. But now at last I see him clearly, and laugh with him, at myself, for having missed the spirit of the game. But as for you! Coming here to fawn and whine and cadge favours of the umpire!'

At this point the people rushed toward him to seize him. But he checked them with a young laugh that made them love while they hated. He spoke again.

'I want to tell you how I came to learn my lesson. I have a queer love for clambering about the high mountains; and once when I was up among the snow-fields and precipices of Aconcagua, I was caught in a blizzard. Perhaps some of you may know what storms can be like in the mountains. The air became a hurtling flood of snow. I was swallowed up and carried away. After many hours of floundering, I fell into a snow-drift. I tried to rise, but fell again and again, till my head was buried. The thought of death enraged me, for there was still so much that I wanted to do. I struggled frantically, vainly. Then suddenly – how can I put it? – I saw the game that I was losing, and it was good. Good, no less to lose than to win. For it was the game, now, not victory, that mattered. Hitherto I had been blindfold, and a slave to victory; suddenly I was free, and with sight. For now I saw myself, and all of us, through the eyes of the umpire. It was as though a play-actor were to see the whole play, with his own part in it, through the author's eyes, from the auditorium. Here was I, acting the part of a rather fine man who had come to grief through his own carelessness before his work was done. For me, a character in the play, the situation was hideous; yet for me, the spectator, it had become excellent within a wider excellence. I saw that it was equally so with all of us, and with all the worlds. For I seemed to see a thousand worlds taking part with us in the great show. And I saw everything through the calm eyes, the exultant, almost derisive, yet not unkindly, eyes of the playwright.

'Well, it had seemed that my exit had come; but no, there was still a cue for me. Somehow I was so strengthened by this new view of things that I struggled out of the snow-drift. And here I am once more. But I am a new man. My spirit is free. While I was a boy, I said, "Grow more alive"; but in those days I never guessed that there was an aliveness far intenser than youth's flicker, a kind of still incandescence. Is there no one here who knows what I mean? No one who at least *desires* this keener living? The first step is to outgrow this adulation of life itself, and this cadging obsequiousness toward Power. Come! Put it away! Break the ridiculous image in your hearts, as I now smash this idol.'

So saying he picked up a great candlestick and shattered the image. Once more there was an uproar, and the temple authorities had him arrested. Not long afterwards he was tried for sacrilege and executed. For this final extravagance was but the climax of many indiscretions, and those in power were glad to have so obvious a pretext for extinguishing this brilliant but dangerous lunatic.

But the cult of the Divine Boy had already become very popular, for the earlier teaching of the prophet expressed the fundamental craving of the Patagonians. Even his last and perplexing message was accepted by his followers, though without real understanding. Emphasis was laid upon the act of iconoclasm, rather than upon the spirit of his exhortation.

Century by century the new religion, for such it was, spread over the civilized world. And the race seemed to have been spiritually rejuvenated to some extent by widespread fervour. Physically also a certain rejuvenation took place; for before his death this unique biological 'sport', or throw-back to an earlier vitality, produced some thousands of sons and daughters; and they in turn propagated the good seed far and wide. Undoubtedly it was this new strain that brought about the golden age of Patagonia, greatly improving the material conditions of the race, carrying civilization into the northern continents, and attacking problems of science and philosophy with renewed ardour.

But the revival was not permanent. The descendants of the prophet prided themselves too much on violent living. Physically, sexually, mentally, they over-reached themselves and became enfeebled. Moreover, little by little the potent strain was diluted and overwhelmed by intercourse with the greater volume of the innately 'senile'; so that, after a few centuries, the race returned to its middle-aged mood. At the same time the vision of the Divine Boy was gradually distorted. At first it had been youth's ideal of what youth should be, a pattern woven of fanatical loyalty, irresponsible gaiety, comradeship, physical gusto, and not a little pure devilry. But insensibly it became a pattern of that which was expected of youth by sad maturity. The violent young hero was sentimentalized into the senior's vision of childhood, naïve and docile. All that had been violent was forgotten; and what was left became a whimsical and appealing stimulus to the parental impulses. At the same time this phantom was credited with all the sobriety and caution which are so easily appreciated by the middle-aged.

Inevitably this distorted image of youth became an incubus

111

upon the actual young men and women of the race. It was held up as the model of social virtue; but it was a model to which they could never conform without doing violence to their best nature, since it was not any longer an expression of youth at all. Just as, in an earlier age, woman had been idealized and at the same time hobbled, so now youth.

Some few, indeed, throughout the history of Patagonia, attained a clearer vision of the prophet. Fewer still were able to enter into the spirit of his final message, in which his enduring youthfulness raised him to a maturity alien to Patagonia. For the tragedy of this people was not so much their 'senescence' as their arrested growth. Feeling themselves old, they yearned to be young again. But, through fixed immaturity of mind, they could never recognize that the true, though unlooked-for, fulfilment of youth's passionate craving is not the mere achievement of the ends of youth itself, but an advance into a more awake and far-seeing vitality.

4. THE CATASTROPHE

It was in these latter days that the Patagonians discovered the civilization that had preceded them. In rejecting the ancient religion of fear, they had abandoned also the legend of a remote magnificence, and had come to regard themselves as pioneers of the mind. In the new continent which was their homeland there were, of course, no relics of the ancient order; and the ruins that besprinkled the older regions had been explained as mere freaks of nature. But latterly, with the advance of natural knowledge, archaeologists had reconstructed something of the forgotten world. And the crisis came when, in the basement of a shattered pylon in China, they found a store of metal plates (constructed of an immensely durable artificial element), on which were embossed crowded lines of writing. These objects were, in fact, blocks from which books were printed a thousand centuries earlier. Other deposits were soon discovered, and bit by bit the dead language was deciphered. Within three centuries the outline of the ancient culture was laid bare; and presently the whole history of man's rise and ruin fell upon this latter-day civilization with crushing effect, as though an ancient pylon were to have fallen on a village of wigwams at its foot. The pioneers discovered that all the ground which they had so painfully won from the wild had been conquered long ago, and lost; that on the material side their glory was nothing beside the glory of the past; and that in the sphere of mind they had established only a few scattered settlements where formerly was an empire. The Patagonian system of natural knowledge had been scarcely further advanced than that of pre-Newtonian Europe. They had done little more than conceive the scientific spirit and unlearn a few superstitions. And now suddenly they came into a vast inheritance of thought.

This in itself was a gravely disturbing experience for a people of strong intellectual interest. But even more overwhelming was the discovery, borne in on them in the course of their research, that the past had been not only brilliant but crazy, and that in the long run the crazy element had completely triumphed. For the Patagonian mind was by now too sane and empirical to accept the ancient knowledge without testing it. The findings of the archaeologists were handed over to the physicists and other scientists, and the firm thought and valuation of Europe and America at their zenith were soon distinguished from the degenerate products of the World State.

The upshot of this impact with a more developed civilization was dramatic and tragic. It divided the Patagonians into loyalists and rebels, into those who clung to the view that the new learning was a satanic lie, and those who faced the facts. To the former party the facts were thoroughly depressing; the latter, though overawed, found in them a compelling majesty, and also a hope. That the earth was a mote among the starclouds was the least subversive of the new doctrines, for the Patagonians had already abandoned the geocentric view. What was so distressing to the reactionaries was the theory that an earlier race had long ago possessed and spent the vitality that they themselves so craved. The party of progress, on the other hand, urged that this vast new knowledge must be used; and that, thus equipped, Patagonia might compensate for lack of youthfulness by superior sanity.

This divergence of will resulted in a physical conflict such as

113

had never before occurred in the Patagonian world. Something like nationalism emerged. The more vigorous Antarctic coasts became modern, while Patagonia itself clung to the older culture. There were several wars, but as physics and chemistry advanced in Antarctica, the Southerners were able to devise engines of war which the Northerners could not resist. In a couple of centuries the new 'culture' had triumphed. The world was once more unified.

Hitherto Patagonian civilization had been of a medieval type. Under the influence of physics and chemistry it began to change. Wind- and water-power began to be used for the generation of electricity. Vast mining operations were undertaken in search of the metals and other minerals which no longer occurred at easy depths. Architecture began to make use of steel. Electrically driven aeroplanes were made, but without real success. And this failure was symptomatic; for the Patagonians were not sufficiently foolhardy to master aviation, even had their planes been more efficient. They themselves naturally attributed their failure wholly to lack of a convenient source of power, such as the ancient petrol. Indeed this lack of oil and coal hampered them at every turn. Volcanic power, of course, was available; but, never having been really mastered by the more resourceful ancients, it defeated the Patagonians completely.

As a matter of fact, in wind and water they had all that was needed. The resources of the whole planet were available, and the world population was less than a hundred million. With this source alone they could never, indeed, have competed in luxury with the earlier World State, but they might well have achieved something like Utopia.

But this was not to be. Industrialism, though accompanied by only a slow increase of population, produced in time most of the social discords which had almost ruined their predecessors. To them it appeared that all their troubles would be solved if only their material power were far ampler. The strong and scarcely rational conviction was a symptom of their ruling obsession, the craving for increased vitality.

Under these circumstances it was natural that one event and one strand of ancient history should fascinate them. The secret of limitless material power had once been known and lost. Why should not Patagonians rediscover it, and use it, with their superior sanity, to bring heaven on earth? The ancients, no doubt, did well to forego this dangerous source of power; but the Patagonians, level-headed and single-minded, need have no fear. Some, indeed, considered it less important to seek power than to find a means of checking biological senescence; but, unfortunately, though physical science had advanced so rapidly, the more subtle biological sciences had remained backward, largely because among the ancients themselves little more had been done than to prepare their way. Thus it happened that the most brilliant minds of Patagonia, fascinated by the prize at stake, concentrated upon the problem of matter. The state encouraged this research by founding and endowing laboratories whose avowed end was this sole work.

The problem was difficult, and the Patagonian scientists, though intelligent, were somewhat lacking in grit. Only after some five hundred years of intermittent research was the secret discovered, or partially so. It was found possible, by means of a huge initial expenditure of energy, to annihilate the positive and negative electric charges in one not very common kind of atom. But this limitation mattered not at all; the human race now possessed an inexhaustible source of power which could be easily manipulated and easily controlled. But though controllable, the new gift was not fool-proof; and there was no guarantee that those who used it might not use it foolishly, or inadvertently let it get out of hand.

Unfortunately, at the time when the new source of energy was discovered, the Patagonians were more divided than of old. Industrialism, combined with the innate docility of the race, had gradually brought about a class cleavage more extreme even than that of the ancient world, though a cleavage of a curiously different kind. The strongly parental disposition of the average Patagonian prevented the dominant class from such brutal exploitation as had formerly occurred. Save during the first century of industrialism, there was no serious physical suffering among the proletariat. A paternal government saw to it that all Patagonians were at least properly fed and clothed, that all had ample leisure and opportunities of amusement. At the same time they saw to it also that the populace became more and more regimented. As in the First World State, civil authority was once more in the hands of a small group of masters of industry, but with a difference. Formerly the dominant motive of big business had been an almost mystical passion for the creation of activity; now the ruling minority regarded themselves as standing towards the populace *in loco parentis*, and aimed at creating 'a young-hearted people, simple, gay, vigorous, and loyal'. Their ideal of the state was something between a preparatory school under a sympathetic but strict adult staff, and a joint-stock company, in which the shareholders retained only one function, to delegate their powers thankfully to a set of brilliant directors.

That the system had worked so well and survived so long was due not only to innate Patagonian docility, but also to the principle by which the governing class recruited itself. One lesson at least had been learnt from the bad example of the earlier civilization, namely respect for intelligence. By a system of careful testing the brightest children were selected from all classes and trained to be governors. Even the children of the governors themselves were subjected to the same examination, and only those who qualified were sent to the 'schools for young governors'. Some corruption no doubt existed, but in the main this system worked. The children thus selected were very carefully trained in theory and practice, as organizers, scientists, priests, and logicians.

The less brilliant children of the race were educated very differently from the young governors. It was impressed on them that they were less able than the others. They were taught to respect the governors as superior beings, who were called upon to serve the community in specially skilled and arduous work, simply because of their ability. It would not be true to say that the less intelligent were educated merely to be slaves; rather they were expected to be the docile, diligent, and happy sons and daughters of the fatherland. They were taught to be loyal and optimistic. They were given vocational training for their various occupations, and encouraged to use their intelligence as much as possible upon the plane suited to it; but the affairs of the state and the problems of religion and theoretical science were strictly forbidden. The official doctrine of the beauty of youth was fundamental in their education. They were taught all the conventional virtues of youth, and in particular modesty and simplicity. As a class they were extremely healthy, for physical training was a very important part of education in Patagonia. Moreover, the universal practice of sun-bathing, which was a religious rite, was especially encouraged among the proletariat, as it was believed to keep the body 'young' and the mind placid. The leisure of the governed class was devoted mostly to athletics and other sport, physical and mental. Music and other forms of art were also practised, for these were considered fit occupations for juveniles. The government exercised a censorship over artistic products, but it was seldom enforced; for the common folk of Patagonia were mostly too phlegmatic and too busy to conceive anything but the most obvious and respectable art. They were fully occupied with work and pleasure. They suffered no sexual restraints. Their impersonal interests were satisfied with the official religion of youth-worship and loyalty to the community.

This placid condition lasted for some four hundred years after the first century of industrialism. But as time passed the mental difference between the two classes increased. Superior intelligence became rarer and rarer among the proletariat; the governors were recruited more and more from their own offspring, until finally they became an hereditary caste. The gulf widened. The governors began to lose all mental contact with the governed. They made a mistake which could never have been committed had their psychology kept pace with their other sciences. Ever confronted with the workers' lack of intelligence, they came to treat them more and more as children, and forgot that, though simple, they were grown men and women who needed to feel themselves as free partners in a great human enterprise. Formerly this illusion of responsibility had been sedulously encouraged. But as the gulf widened the proletarians were treated rather as infants than as adolescents, rather as well-cared-for domestic animals than as human beings. Their lives became more and more minutely, though benevolently, systematized for them. At the same time less care was taken to educate them up to an understanding and appreciation of the common human enterprise. Under these circumstances the temper of the people changed. Though their

117

material condition was better than had ever been known before, save under the first World State, they became listless, discontented, mischievous, ungrateful to their superiors.

Such was the state of affairs when the new source of energy was discovered. The world community consisted of two very different elements, first a small, highly intellectual caste, passionately devoted to the state and to the advancement of culture amongst themselves; and, second, a much more numerous population of rather obtuse, physically well-cared-for, and spiritually starved industrialists. A serious clash between the two classes had already occurred over the use of a certain drug, favoured by the people for the bliss it produced, forbidden by the governors for its evil after-effects. The drug was abolished; but the motive was misinterpreted by the proletariat. This incident brought to the surface a hate that had for long been gathering strength in the popular mind, though unwittingly.

When rumour got afoot that in future mechanical power would be unlimited, the people expected a millennium. Every one would have his own limitless source of energy. Work would cease. Pleasure would be increased to infinity. Unfortunately the first use made of the new power was extensive mining at unheard-of depths in search of metals and other minerals which had long ago ceased to be available near the surface. This involved difficult and dangerous work for the miners. There were casualties. Riots occurred. The new power was used upon the rioters with murderous effect, the governors declaring that, though their paternal hearts bled for their foolish children, this chastisement was necessary to prevent worse evils. The workers were urged to face their troubles with that detachment which the Divine Boy had preached in his final phase; but this advice was greeted with the derision which it deserved. Further strikes, riots, assassinations. The proletariat had scarcely more power against their masters than sheep against the shepherd, for they had not the brains for large-scale organization. But it was through one of these pathetically futile rebellions that Patagonia was at last destroyed.

A petty dispute had occurred in one of the new mines. The management refused to allow miners to teach their trade to their sons; for vocational education, it was said, should be carried on professionally. Indignation against this interference with parental authority caused a sudden flash of the old rage. A power unit was seized, and after a bout of insane monkeying with the machinery, the mischief-makers inadvertently got things into such a state that at last the awful djinn of physical energy was able to wrench off his fetters and rage over the planet. The first explosion was enough to blow up the mountain range above the mine. In those mountains were huge tracts of the critical element, and these were detonated by rays from the initial explosion. This sufficed to set in action still more remote tracts of the element. An incandescent hurricane spread over the whole of Patagonia, reinforcing itself with fresh atomic fury wherever it went. It raged along the line of the Andes and the Rockies, scorching both continents with its heat. It undermined and blew up the Bering Straits, spread like a brood of gigantic fiery serpents into Asia, Europe, and Africa. Martians, already watching the earth as a cat a bird beyond its spring, noted that the brilliance of the neighbour planet was suddenly enhanced. Presently the oceans began to boil here and there with submarine commotion. Tidal waves mangled the coasts and floundered up the valleys. But in time the general sea level sank considerably through evaporation and the opening of chasms in the ocean floor. All volcanic regions became fantastically active. The polar caps began to melt, but prevented the arctic regions from being calcined like the rest of the planet. The atmosphere was a continuous dense cloud of moisture, fumes, and dust, churned in ceaseless hurricanes. As the fury of the electromagnetic collapse proceeded, the surface temperature of the planet steadily increased, till only in the Arctic and a few favoured corners of the sub-Arctic could life persist.

Patagonia's death agony was brief. In Africa and Europe a few remote settlements escaped the actual track of the eruptions, but succumbed in a few weeks to hurricanes of steam. Of the two hundred million members of the human race, all were burnt or roasted or suffocated within three months – all but thirty-five, who happened to be in the neighbourhood of the North Pole.

VI *Transition*

1. THE FIRST MEN AT BAY

BY one of those rare tricks of fortune, which are as often favourable as hostile to humanity, an Arctic exploration ship had
recently been embedded in the pack-ice for a long drift across the
Polar sea. She was provisioned for four years, and when the
catastrophe occurred she had already been at sea for six months.
She was a sailing vessel; the expedition had been launched before
it was practicable to make use of the new source of power. The
crew consisted of twenty-eight men and seven women. Individuals
of an earlier and more sexual race, proportioned thus, in such
close proximity and isolation, would almost certainly have fallen
foul of one another sooner or later. But to Patagonians the
arrangement was not intolerable. Besides managing the whole
domestic side of the expedition, the seven women were able to
provide moderate sexual delight for all, for in this people the
female sexuality was much less reduced than the male. There
were, indeed, occasional jealousies and feuds in the little community, but these were subordinated to a strong *esprit de corps*.
The whole company had, of course, been very carefully chosen
for comradeship, loyalty, and health, as well as for technical skill.
All claimed descent from the Divine Boy. All were of the governing class. One quaint expression of the strongly parental Patagonian temperament was that a pair of diminutive pet monkeys was
taken with the expedition.

The crew's first intimation of the catastrophe was a furious hot
wind that melted the surface of the ice. The sky turned black. The
Arctic summer became a weird and sultry night, torn by fantastic
thunderstorms. Rain crashed on the ship's deck in a continuous
waterfall. Clouds of pungent smoke and dust irritated the eyes
and nose. Submarine earthquakes buckled the pack-ice.

A year after the explosion, the ship was labouring in tempestuous
and berg-strewn water near the Pole. The bewildered little com-

pany now began to feel its way south; but, as they proceeded, the air became more fiercely hot and pungent, storms more savage. Another twelve months were spent in beating about the Polar sea, ever and again retreating north from the impossible southern weather. But at length conditions improved slightly, and with great difficulty these few survivors of the human race approached their original objective in Norway, to find that the lowlands were a scorched and lifeless desert, while on the heights the valley vegetation was already struggling to establish itself, in patches of sickly green. Their base town had been flattened by a hurricane, and the skeletons of its population still lay in the streets. They coasted further south. Everywhere the same desolation. Hoping that the disturbance might be merely local, they headed round the British Isles and doubled back on France. But France turned out to be an appalling chaos of volcanoes. With a change of wind, the sea around them was infuriated with falling debris, often red hot. Miraculously they got away and fled north again. After creeping along the Siberian coast they were at last able to find a tolerable resting-place at the mouth of one of the great rivers. The ship was brought to anchor, and the crew rested. They were a diminished company, for six men and two women had been lost on the voyage.

Conditions even here must recently have been far more severe, since much of the vegetation had been scorched, and dead animals were frequent. But evidently the first fury of the vast explosion was now abating.

By this time the voyagers were beginning to realize the truth. They remembered the half jocular prophecies that the new power would sooner or later wreck the planet, prophecies which had evidently been all too well founded. There had been a world-wide disaster; and they themselves had been saved only by their remoteness and the Arctic ice from a fate that had probably overwhelmed all their fellow-men.

So desperate was the outlook for a handful of exhausted persons on a devastated planet, that some urged suicide. All dallied with the idea, save a woman, who had unexpectedly become pregnant. In her the strong parental disposition of her race was now awakened, and she implored the party to make a fight for the sake of her child. Reminded that the baby would only be born into a life of hardship, she reiterated with more persistence than reason, 'My baby must live'.

The men shrugged their shoulders. But as their tired bodies recovered after the recent struggle, they began to realize the solemnity of their position. It was one of the biologists who expressed a thought which was already present to all. There was at least a chance of survival, and if ever men and women had a sacred duty, surely these had. For they were now the sole trustees of the human spirit. At whatever cost of toil and misery they must people the earth again.

This common purpose now began to exalt them, and brought them all into a rare intimacy. 'We are ordinary folk,' said the biologist, 'but somehow we must become great.' And they were, indeed, in a manner made great by their unique position. In generous minds a common purpose and common suffering breed a deep passion of comradeship, expressed perhaps not in words but in acts of devotion. These, in their loneliness and their sense of obligation, experienced not only comradeship, but a vivid communion with one another as instruments of a sacred cause.

The party now began to build a settlement beside the river. Though the whole area had, of course, been devastated, vegetation had soon revived, from roots and seeds, buried or windborne. The countryside was now green with those plants that had been able to adjust themselves to the new climate. Animals had suffered far more seriously. Save for the Arctic fox, a few small rodents, and one herd of reindeer, none were left but the dwellers in the actual Arctic seas, the Polar bear, various cetaceans, and seals. Of fish there were plenty. Birds in great numbers had crowded out of the south, and had died off in thousands through lack of food, but certain species were already adjusting themselves to the new environment. Indeed, the whole remaining fauna and flora of the planet was passing through a phase of rapid and very painful readjustment. Many well-established species had wholly failed to get a footing in the new world, while certain hitherto insignificant types were able to forge ahead.

The party found it possible to grow maize and even rice from seed brought from a ruined store in Norway. But the great heat, frequent torrential rain, and lack of sunlight made agriculture laborious and precarious. Moreover, the atmosphere had become seriously impure, and the human organism had not yet succeeded in adapting itself. Consequently the party were permanently tired and liable to disease.

The pregnant woman had died in child-birth, but her baby lived. It became the party's most sacred object, for it kindled in every mind the strong parental disposition so characteristic of Patagonians.

Little by little the numbers of the settlement were reduced by sickness, hurricanes, and volcanic gases. But in time they achieved a kind of equilibrium with their environment, and even a certain strenuous amenity of life. As their prosperity increased, however, their unity diminished. Differences of temperament began to be dangerous. Among the men two leaders had emerged, or rather one leader and a critic. The original head of the expedition had proved quite incapable of dealing with the new situation, and had at last committed suicide. The company had then chosen the second navigating officer as their chief and had chosen him unanimously. The other born leader of the party was a junior biologist, a man of very different type. The relations of these two did much to determine the future history of man, and are worthy of study in themselves; but here we can only glance at them. In all times of stress the navigator's authority was absolute, for everything depended on his initiative and heroic example. But in less arduous periods, murmurs arose against him for exacting discipline when discipline seemed unnecessary. Between him and the young biologist there grew up a strange blend of hostility and affection; for the latter, though critical, loved and admired the other, and declared that the survival of the party depended on this one man's practical genius.

Three years after their landing, the community, though reduced in numbers and in vitality, was well established in a routine of hunting, agriculture, and building. Three fairly healthy infants rejoiced and exasperated their elders. With security, the navigator's genius for action found less scope, while the knowledge of the scientists became more valuable. Plant and poultry-breeding were beyond the range of the heroic leader, and in prospecting for minerals he was equally helpless. Inevitably as time passed he and the other navigators grew restless and irritable; and at last, when the leader decreed that the party should take to the ship and explore for better land, a serious dispute occurred. All the sea-farers applauded; but the scientists, partly through clearer understanding of the calamity that had befallen the planet, partly through repugnance at the hardship involved, refused to go.

Violent emotions were aroused; but both sides restrained themselves through well-tried mutual respect and loyalty to the community. Then suddenly sexual passion set a light to the tinder. The woman who, by general consent, had come to be queen of the settlement, and was regarded as sacred to the leader, asserted her independence by sleeping with one of the scientists. The leader surprised them, and in sudden rage killed the young man. The little community at once fell into two armed factions, and more blood was shed. Very soon, however, the folly and sacrilege of this brawl became evident to these few survivors of a civilized race, and after a parley a grave decision was made.

The company was to be divided. One party, consisting of five men and two women, under the young biologist, was to remain in the settlement. The leader himself, with the remaining nine men and two women, was to navigate the ship toward Europe, in search of a better land. They promised to send word, if possible, during the following year.

With this decision taken the two parties once more became amicable. All worked to equip the pioneers. When at last it was the time of departure, there was a solemn leave-taking. Every one was relieved at the cessation of a painful incompatibility; but more poignant than relief was the distressed affection of those who had so long been comrades in a sacred enterprise.

It was a parting even more momentous than was supposed. For from this act arose at length two distinct human species.

Those who stayed behind heard no more of the wanderers, and finally concluded that they had come to grief. But in fact they were driven west and south-west past Iceland, now a cluster of volcanoes, to Labrador. On this voyage through fantastic storms and oceanic convulsions they lost nearly half their number, and were at last unable to work the ship. When finally they were wrecked on a rocky coast, only the carpenter's mate, two women, and the pair of monkeys succeeded in clambering ashore.

These found themselves in a climate far more sultry than Siberia; but like Siberia, Labrador contained uplands of luxuriant vegetation. The man and his two women had at first great difficulty in finding food, but in time they adapted themselves to a diet of berries and roots. As the years passed, however, the climate undermined their mentality, and their descendants sank into abject savagery, finally degenerating into a type that was human only in respect of its ancestry.

The little Siberian settlement was now hard-pressed but single-minded. Calculation had convinced the scientists that the planet would not return to its normal state for some millions of years; for though the first and superficial fury of the disaster had already ceased, the immense pent-up energy of the central explosions would take millions of years to leak out through volcanic vents. The leader of the party, by rare luck a man of genius, conceived their situation thus. For millions of years the planet would be uninhabitable save for a fringe of Siberian coast. The human race was doomed for ages to a very restricted and uncongenial environment. All that could be hoped for was the persistence of a mere remnant of civilized humanity, which should be able to lie dormant until a more favourable epoch. With this end in view the party must propagate itself, and make some possibility of cultured life for its offspring. Above all it must record in some permanent form as much as it could remember of Patagonian culture. 'We are the germ,' he said. 'We must play for safety, mark time, preserve man's inheritance. The chances against us are almost overwhelming, but just possibly we shall win through.'

And so in fact they did. Several times almost exterminated at the outset, these few harassed individuals preserved their spark of humanity. A close inspection of their lives would reveal an intense personal drama; for, in spite of the sacred purpose which united them, almost as muscles in one limb, they were individuals of different temperaments. The children, moreover, caused jealousy between their parentally hungry elders. There was ever a subdued, and sometimes an open, rivalry to gain the affection of these young things, these few and precious buds on the human stem. Also there was sharp disagreement about their education. For though all the elders adored them simply for their childishness, one at least, the visionary leader of the party, thought of them chiefly as potential vessels of the human spirit, to be moulded strictly for their great function. In this perpetual subdued antagonism of aims and temperaments the little society lived from day to day, much as a limb functions in the antagonism of its muscles.

The adults of the party devoted much of their leisure during the long winters to the heroic labour of recording the outline of man's whole knowledge. This task was very dear to the leader, but the others often grew weary of it. To each person a certain sphere of culture was assigned; and after he or she had thought out a section and scribbled it down on slate, it was submitted to the company for criticism, and finally engraved deeply on tablets of hard stone. Many thousands of such tablets were produced in the course of years, and were stored in a cave which was carefully prepared for them. Thus was recorded something of the history of the earth and of man, the outlines of physics, chemistry, biology, psychology, and geometry. Each scribe set down also in some detail a summary of his own special study, and added a personal manifesto of his own views about existence. Much ingenuity was spent in devising a vast pictorial dictionary and grammar, with which, it was hoped, the remote future might interpret the whole library.

Years passed while this immense registration of human thought was still in progress. The founders of the settlement grew feebler while the eldest of the next generation were still adolescent. Of the two women, one had died and the other was almost a cripple, both martyrs to the task of motherhood. A youth, an infant boy, and four girls of various ages – on these the future of man now depended. Unfortunately these precious beings had suffered from their very preciousness. Their education had been bungled. They had been both pampered and oppressed. Nothing was thought too good for them, but they were overwhelmed with cherishing and teaching. Thus they came to hold the elders at arm's length, and to weary of the ideals imposed on them. Brought into a ruined world without their own consent, they refused to accept the crushing obligation toward an improbable future. Hunting, and the daily struggle of a pioneering age, afforded their spirits full exercise in courage, mutual loyalty, and interest in one another's personality. They would live for the present only, and for the tangible reality, not for a culture which they knew only by hearsay. In particular, they loathed the hardship of engraving endless verbiage upon granitic slabs.

The crisis came when the eldest girl had crossed the threshold of physical maturity. The leader told her that it was her duty to begin bearing children at once, and ordered her to have intercourse with her half-brother, his own son. Having herself assisted at the last birth, which had destroyed her mother, she refused; and when pressed she dropped her graving tool and fled. This was the first serious act of rebellion. In a few years the older generation was deposed from authority. A new way of life, more active, more dangerous, zestful, and careless, resulted in a lowering of the community's standard of comfort and organization, but also in greater health and vitality. Experiments in plant and stock-breeding were neglected, buildings went out of repair; but great feats of hunting and exploration were undertaken. Leisure was given over to games of hazard and calculation, to dancing, singing, and romantic story-telling. Music and romance, indeed, were now the main expression of the finer nature of these beings, and became the vehicles of obscure religious experience. The intellectualism of the elders was ridiculed. What could their poor sciences tell of reality, of the many-faced, never-for-a-moment-the-same, superbly inconsequent, and ever-living Real? Man's intelligence was all right for hunting and tillage in the world of common sense; but if he rode it further afield, he would find himself in a desert, and his soul would starve. Let him live as nature prompted. Let him keep the young god in his heart alive. Let him give free play to the struggling, irrational, dark vitality that sought to realize itself in him not as logic but as beauty.

The tablets were now engraved only by the aged.

But one day, after the infant boy had reached the early Patagonian adolescence, his curiosity was roused by the tail-like hind

limbs of a seal. The old people timidly encouraged him. He made
other biological observations, and was led on to envisage the
whole drama of life on the planet, and to conceive loyalty to the
cause which they had served.

Meanwhile, sexual and parental nature had triumphed where
schooling had failed. The young things inevitably fell in love with
each other, and in time several infants appeared.

Thus, generation by generation, the little settlement maintained
itself with varying success, varying zestfulness, and varying
loyalty toward the future. With changing conditions the population fluctuated, sinking as low as two men and one woman, but
increasing gradually up to a few thousand, the limit set by the
food capacity of their strip of coast. In the long run, though
circumstances did not prevent material survival, they made for
mental decline. For the Siberian coast remained a tropical land,
bounded on the south by a forest of volcanoes; and consequently
in the long run the generations declined in mental vigour and
subtlety. This result was perhaps due in part to too intensive in-
breeding; but this factor had also one good effect. Though mental
vigour waned, certain desirable characteristics were consolidated.
The founders of the group represented the best remaining stock
of the first human species. They had been chosen for their hardi-
hood and courage, their native loyalty, their strong cognitive
interest. Consequently, in spite of phases of depression, the race
not only survived but retained its curiosity and its group feeling.
Even while the ability of men decreased, their will to understand,
and their sense of racial unity, remained. Though their conception
of man and the universe gradually sank into crude myth, they
preserved a strong unreasoning loyalty towards the future, and
toward the now sacred stone library which was rapidly becoming
unintelligible to them. For thousands and even millions of years,
after the species had materially changed its nature, there remained
a vague admiration for mental prowess, a confused tradition of a
noble past, and pathetic loyalty toward a still nobler future.
Above all, internecine strife was so rare that it served only to
strengthen the clear will to preserve the unity and harmony of
the race.

2. THE SECOND DARK AGE

We must now pass rapidly over the Second Dark Age, observing merely those influences which were to affect the future of humanity.

Century by century the pent energy of the vast explosion dispersed itself; but not till many hundred thousand years had passed did the swarms of upstart volcanoes begin to die, and not till after millions of years did the bulk of the planet become once more a possible home for life.

During this period many changes took place. The atmosphere became clearer, purer, and less turbulent. With the fall of temperature, frost and snow appeared occasionally in the Arctic regions, and in due course the Polar caps were formed again. Meanwhile, ordinary geological processes, augmented by the strains to which the planet was subjected by increased internal pressure, began to change the continents. South America mostly collapsed into the hollows blasted beneath it, but a new land rose to join Brazil with West Africa. The East Indies and Australia became a continuous continent. The huge mass of Tibet sank deeply into its disturbed foundations, lunged West, and buckled Afghanistan into a range of peaks nearly forty thousand feet above the sea. Europe sank under the Atlantic. Rivers writhed shiftingly hither and thither upon the continents, like tortured worms. New alluvial areas were formed. New strata were laid upon one another under new oceans. New animals and plants developed from the few surviving Arctic species, and spread south through Asia and America. In the new forests and grass-lands appeared various specialized descendants of the reindeer, and swarms of rodents. Upon these preyed the large and small descendants of the Arctic fox, of which one species, a gigantic wolf-like creature, rapidly became the 'King of Beasts' in the new order, and remained so, until it was ousted by the more slowly-modified offspring of the polar bears. A certain genus of seals, reverting to the ancient terrestrial habit, had developed a slender snake-like body and an almost swift, and very serpentine, mode of locomotion among the coastal sand-dunes. There it was wont to stalk its rodent prey, and even follow them into their burrows. Everywhere there were birds. Many of the places left vacant by the destruction of the ancient fauna were now filled by birds which had discarded flight and developed pedestrian habits. Insects, almost exterminated by the great conflagration, had afterwards increased so rapidly, and had refashioned their types with such versatility, that they soon reached almost to their ancient profusion. Even more rapid was the establishment of the new micro-organisms. In general, among all the beasts and plants of the earth there was a great change of habit, and a consequent over-laying of old body-forms with new forms adapted to a new way of life.

The two human settlements had fared very differently. That of Labrador, oppressed by a more sweltering climate, and unsupported by the Siberian will to preserve human culture, sank into animality; but ultimately it peopled the whole West with swarming tribes. The human beings in Asia remained a mere handful throughout the ten million years of the Second Dark Age. An incursion of the sea cut them off from the south. The old Taimyr Peninsula, where their settlements clustered, became the northern promontory of an island whose coasts were the ancient valley-edges of the Yenessi, the Lower Tunguska, and the Lena. As the climate became less oppressive, the families spread towards the southern coast of the island, but there the sea checked them. Temperate conditions enabled them to regain a certain degree of culture. But they had no longer the capacity to profit much from the new clemency of nature, for the previous ages of tropical conditions had undermined them. Moreover, towards the end of the ten million years of the Second Dark Age, the Arctic climate spread south into their island. The crops failed, the rodents that formed their chief cattle dwindled, their few herds of deer faded out through lack of food. Little by little this scanty human race degenerated into a mere remnant of Arctic savages. And so they remained for a million years. Psychologically they were so crippled that they had almost completely lost the power of innovation. When their sacred quarries in the hills were covered with ice, they had not the wit to use stone from the valleys, but were reduced to making implements of bone. Their language degenerated into a few grunts to signify important acts, and a more complex system of emotional expressions. For emotionally these creatures still preserved a certain refinement. Moreover, though they had almost wholly lost the power of intelligent innovation, their instinctive responses were often such as a more enlightened intelligence would justify. They were strongly social, deeply respectful of the individual human life, deeply parental, and often terribly earnest in their religion.

Not till long after the rest of the planet was once more covered with life, not till nearly ten million years after the Patagonian disaster, did a group of these savages, adrift on an iceberg, get blown southward across the sea to the mainland of Asia. Luckily, for Arctic conditions were increasing, and in time the islanders were extinguished.

The survivors settled in the new land and spread, century by century, into the heart of Asia. Their increase was very slow for they were an infertile and inflexible race. But conditions were now extremely favourable. The climate was temperate; for Russia and Europe were now a shallow sea warmed by currents from the Atlantic. There were no dangerous animals save the small grey bears, an offshoot from the polar species, and the large wolf-like foxes. Various kinds of rodents and deer provided meat in plenty. There were birds of all sizes and habits. Timber, fruit, wild grains, and other nourishing plants throve on the well-watered volcanic soil. The prolonged eruptions, moreover, had once more enriched the upper layers of the rocky crust with metals.

A few hundred thousand years in this new world sufficed for the human species to increase from a handful of individuals to a swarm of races. It was in the conflict and interfusion of these races, and also through the absorption of certain chemicals from the new volcanic soil, that humanity at last recovered its vitality.

VII *The Rise of the Second Men*

1. THE APPEARANCE OF A NEW SPECIES

IT was some ten million years after the Patagonian disaster that the first elements of a new human species appeared, in an epidemic of biological variations, many of which were extremely valuable. Upon this raw material the new and stimulating environment worked for some hundred thousand years until at last there appeared the Second Man.

Though of greater stature and more roomy cranium, these beings were not wholly unlike their predecessors in general proportions. Their heads, indeed, were large even for their bodies, and their necks massive. Their hands were huge, but finely moulded. Their almost titanic size entailed a seemingly excessive strength of support; their legs were stouter, even proportionately, than the legs of the earlier species. Their feet had lost the separate toes, and, by a strengthening and growing together of the internal bones, had become more efficient instruments of locomotion. During the Siberian exile the First Men had acquired a thick hairy covering, and most races of the Second Man retained something of this blonde hirsute appearance throughout their career. Their eyes were large, and often jade green, their features firm as carved granite, yet mobile and lucent. Of the second human species one might say that Nature had at last repeated and far excelled the noble but unfortunate type which she had achieved once, long ago, with the first species, in certain prehistoric cave-dwelling hunters and artists.

Inwardly the Second Men differed from the earlier species in that they had shed most of those primitive relics which had hampered the First Men more than was realized. Not only were they free of appendix, tonsils, and other useless excrescences, but also their whole structure was more firmly knit into unity. Their chemical organization was such that their tissues were kept in

200,000 years ago	Palaeolithic Culture well established 'Heidelberg' Man
150,000	*Time Scale* **2**
100,000	One hundred times the preceding scale Doubtless extremely inaccurate
50,000	ICE AGE (most recent) Mousterian Culture 'Neanderthal' Man
'Today' 2000 A.D.	Late Palaeolithic Neolithic Egyptian Pyramids Jesus Christ Fall of the FIRST WORLD STATE
50,000	First Men in Eclipse
100,000	Rise of *Patagonia* Fall of Patagonia
150,000	First Men in Eclipse
200,000 years hence	↓

better repair. Their teeth, though proportionately small and few, were almost completely immune from caries. Such was their glandular equipment that puberty did not begin till twenty; and not till they were fifty did they reach maturity. At about one hundred and ninety their powers began to fail, and after a few years of contemplative retirement they almost invariably died before true senility could begin. It was as though, when a man's work was finished, and he had meditated in peace upon his whole career, there were nothing further to hold his attention and prevent him from falling asleep. Mothers carried the foetus for three years, suckled the infant for five years, and were sterile during this period and for another seven years. Their climacteric was reached at about a hundred and sixty. Architecturally massive like their mates, they would have seemed to the First Men very formidable titanesses; but even those early half-human beings would have admired the women of the second species both for their superb vitality and for their brilliantly human expression.

In temperament the Second Men were curiously different from the earlier species. The same factors were present, but in different proportions, and in far greater subordination to the considered will of the individual. Sexual vigour had returned. But sexual interest was strangely altered. Around the ancient core of delight in physical and mental contact with the opposite sex there now appeared a kind of innately sublimated, and no less poignant, appreciation of the unique physical and mental forms of all kinds of live things. It is difficult for less ample natures to imagine this expansion of the innate sexual interest; for to them it is not apparent that the lusty admiration which at first directs itself solely on the opposite sex is the appropriate attitude to all the beauties of flesh and spirit in beast and bird and plant. Parental interest also was strong in the new species, but it too was universalized. It had become a strong innate interest in, and a devotion to, all beings that were conceived as in need of help. In the earlier species this passionate spontaneous altruism occurred only in exceptional persons. In the new species, however, all normal men and women experienced altruism as a passion. And yet at the same time primitive parenthood had become tempered to a less possessive and more objective love, which among the First Men was less common than they themselves were pleased to believe. Assertiveness had also greatly changed. Formerly very much of a man's energy had been devoted to the assertion of himself as a private individual over against other individuals; and very much of his generosity had been at bottom selfish. But in the Second Men this competitive self-assertion, this championship of the most intimately known animal against all others, was greatly tempered. Formerly the major enterprises of society would never have been carried through had they not been able to annex to themselves the egoism of their champions. But in the Second Men the parts were reversed. Few individuals could ever trouble to exert themselves to the last ounce for merely private ends, save when those ends borrowed interest or import from some public enterprise. It was only his vision of a world-wide community of persons, and of his own function therein, that could rouse the fighting spirit in a man. Thus it was inwardly, rather than in outward physical characters, that the Second Men differed from the First. And in nothing did they differ more than in their native aptitude for cosmopolitanism. They had their tribes and nations. War was not quite unknown amongst them. But even in primitive times a man's most serious loyalty was directed toward the race as a whole; and wars were so hampered by impulses of kindliness towards the enemy that they were apt to degenerate into rather violent athletic contests, leading to an orgy of fraternization.

It would not be true to say that the strongest interest of these beings was social. They were never prone to exalt the abstraction called the state, or the nation, or even the world-commonwealth. For their most characteristic factor was not mere gregariousness but something novel, namely an innate interest in personality, both in the actual diversity of persons and in the ideal of personal development. They had a remarkable power of vividly intuiting their fellows as unique persons with special needs. Individuals of the earlier species had suffered from an almost insurmountable spiritual isolation from one another. Not even lovers, and scarcely even the geniuses with special insight into personality, ever had anything like accurate vision of one another. But the Second Men, more intensely and accurately self-conscious, were also more intensely and accurately conscious of one another. This they achieved by no unique faculty, but solely by a more ready interest in each other, a finer insight, and a more active imagination.

They had also a remarkable innate interest in the higher kinds of mental activity, or rather in the subtle objects of these activities. Even children were instinctively inclined towards a genuinely aesthetic interest in their world and their own behaviour, and also towards scientific inquiry and generalization. Small boys, for instance, would delight in collecting not merely such things as eggs or crystals, but mathematical formulae expressive of the different shapes of eggs and crystals, or of the innumerable rhythms of shells, fronds, leaflets, grass-nodes. And there was a wealth of traditional fairy-stories whose appeal was grounded in philosophical puzzles. Little children delighted to hear how the poor things called Illusions were banished from the Country of the Real, how one-dimensional Mr Line woke up in a two-dimensional world, and how a brave young tune slew cacophonous beasts and won a melodious bride in that strange country where the landscape is all of sound and all living things are music. The First Men had attained to interest in science, mathematics, philosophy, only after arduous schooling, but in the Second Men there was a natural propensity for these activities, no less vigorous than the primitive instincts. Not, of course, that they were absolved from learning; but they had the same zest and facility in these matters as their predecessors had enjoyed only in humbler spheres.

In the earlier species, indeed, the nervous system had maintained only a very precarious unity, and was all too liable to derangement by the rebellion of one of its subordinate parts. But in the second species the highest centres maintained an almost absolute harmony among the lower. Thus the moral conflict between momentary impulse and considered will, and again between private and public interest, played a very subordinate part among the Second Men.

In actual cognitive powers, also, this favoured species far outstripped its predecessor. For instance, vision had greatly developed. The Second Men distinguished in the spectrum a new primary colour between green and blue; and beyond blue they saw, not a reddish blue, but again a new primary colour, which faded with increasing ruddiness far into the old ultra-violet. These two new primary colours were complementary to one another. At the other end of the spectrum they saw the infra-red as a peculiar purple. Further, owing to the very great size of their retinae, and the multiplication of rods and cones, they discriminated much smaller fractions of their field of vision.

Improved discrimination combined with a wonderful fertility of mental imagery to produce a greatly increased power of insight into the character of novel situations. Whereas among the First Men, native intelligence had increased only up to the age of fourteen, among the Second Men it progressed up to forty. Thus an average adult was capable of immediate insight into problems which even the most brilliant of the First Men could only solve by prolonged reasoning. This superb clarity of mind enabled the second species to avoid most of those age-long confusions and superstitions which had crippled its predecessor. And along with great intelligence went a remarkable flexibility of will. In fact the Second Men were far more able than the First to break habits that were seen to be no longer justified.

To sum the matter, circumstance had thrown up a very noble species. Essentially it was of the same type as the earlier species, but it had undergone extensive improvements. Much that the First Men could only achieve by long schooling and self-discipline the Second Men performed with effortless fluency and delight. In particular, two capacities which for the First Men had been unattainable ideals were now realized in every normal individual, namely the power of wholly dispassionate cognition, and the power of loving one's neighbour as oneself, without reservation. Indeed, in this respect the Second Men might be called 'Natural Christians', so readily and constantly did they love one another in the manner of Jesus, and infuse their whole social policy with loving-kindness. Early in their career they conceived the religion of love, and they were possessed by it again and again, in diverse forms, until their end. On the other hand, their gift of dispassionate cognition helped them to pass speedily to the admiration of fate. And being by nature rigorous thinkers, they were peculiarly liable to be disturbed by the conflict between their religion of love and their loyalty to fate.

Well might it seem that the stage was now set for a triumphant and rapid progress of the human spirit. But though the second human species constituted a real improvement on the first, it lacked certain faculties without which the next great mental advance could not be made.

Moreover its very excellence involved one novel defect from which the First Men were almost wholly free. In the lives of humble individuals there are many occasions when nothing but an heroic effort can wrest their private fortunates from stagnation or decline, and set them pioneering in new spheres. Among the First Men this effort was often called forth by passionate regard for self. And it was upon the tidal wave of innumerable egoisms, blindly surging in one direction, that the first species was carried forward. But, to repeat, in the Second Men self-regard was never an over-mastering motive. Only at the call of social loyalty or personal love would a man spur himself to desperate efforts. Whenever the stake appeared to be mere private advancement, he was apt to prefer peace to enterprise, the delights of sport, companionship, art or intellect, to the slavery of self-regard. And so in the long run, though the Second Men were fortunate in their almost complete immunity from the lust of power and personal ostentation (which cursed the earlier species with industrialism and militarism), and though they enjoyed long ages of idyllic peace, often upon a high cultural plane, their progress towards full self-conscious mastery of the planet was curiously slow.

2. THE INTERCOURSE OF THREE SPECIES

In a few thousand years the new species filled the region from Afghanistan to the China Sea, overran India, and penetrated far into the new Australasian continent. Its advance was less military than cultural. The remaining tribes of the First Men, with whom the new species could not normally interbreed, were unable to live up to the higher culture that flooded round them and over them. They faded out.

For some further thousands of years the Second Men remained as noble savages, then passed rapidly through the pastoral into the agricultural stage. In this era they sent an expedition across the new and gigantic Hindu Kush to explore Africa. Here it was that they came upon the subhuman descendants of the ship's crew that had sailed from Siberia millions of years earlier. These animals had spread south through America and across the new Atlantic Isthmus into Africa.

Dwarfed almost to the knees of the superior species, bent so that as often as not they used their arms as aids to locomotion, flat-headed and curiously long-snouted, these creatures were by now more baboon-like than human. Yet in the wild state they maintained a very complicated organization into castes, based on the sense of smell. Their powers of scent, indeed, had developed at the expense of their intelligence. Certain odours, which had become sacred through their very repulsiveness, were given off only by individuals having certain diseases. Such individuals were treated with respect by their fellows; and though, in fact, they were debilitated by their disease, they were so feared that no healthy individual dared resist them. The characteristic odours were themselves graded in nobility, so that those individuals who bore only the less repulsive perfume, owed respect to those in whom a widespread rotting of the body occasioned the most nauseating stench. These plagues had the special effect of stimulating repro-ductive activity; and this fact was one cause both of the respect felt for them, and of the immense fertility of the species, such a fertility that, in spite of plagues and obtuseness, it had flooded two continents. For though the plagues were fatal, they were slow to develop. Further, though individuals far advanced in disease were often incapable of feeding themselves, they profited by the devotion of the healthy, who were well-pleased if they also became infected.

But the most startling fact about these creatures was that many of them had become enslaved to another species. When the Second Men had penetrated further into Africa they came to a forest region where companies of diminutive monkeys resisted their intrusion. It was soon evident that any interference with the imbecile and passive subhumans in this district was resented by the monkeys. And as the latter made use of a primitive kind of bow and poisoned arrows, their opposition was seriously inconvenient to the invaders. The use of weapons and other tools, and a remarkable coordination in warfare, made it clear that in intelligence this simian species had far outstripped all creatures save man. Indeed, the Second Men were now face to face with the only terrestrial species which ever evolved so far as to compete with man in versatility and practical shrewdness.

As the invaders advanced, the monkeys were seen to round up whole flocks of the submen and drive them out of reach. It was noticed also that these domesticated submen were wholly free from the diseases that infected their wild kinsfolk, who on this account greatly despised the healthy drudges. Later it transpired that the submen were trained as beasts of burden by the monkeys and that their flesh was a much relished article of diet. An arboreal city of woven branches was discovered, and was apparently in course of construction, for the submen were dragging timber and hauling it aloft, goaded by the boneheaded spears of the monkeys. It was evident also that the authority of the monkeys was maintained less by force than by intimidation. They anointed themselves with the juice of a rare aromatic plant, which struck terror into their poor cattle, and reduced them to abject docility.

Now the invaders were only a handful of pioneers. They had come over the mountains in search of metals, which had been brought to the earth's surface during the volcanic era. An amiable race, they felt no hostility toward the monkeys, but rather amusement at their habits and ingenuity. But the monkeys resented the mere presence of these mightier beings; and, presently collecting in the tree-tops in thousands, they annihilated the party with their poisoned arrows. One man alone escaped into Asia. In a couple of years he returned, with a host. Yet this was no punitive expedition, for the bland Second Men were strangely lacking in resentment. Establishing themselves on the outskirts of the forest region, they contrived to communicate and barter with the little people of the trees, so that after a while they were allowed to enter the territory unmolested, and begin their great metallurgical survey.

A close study of the relations of these very different intelligences would be enlightening, but we have no time for it. Within their own sphere the monkeys showed perhaps a quicker wit than the men; but only within very narrow limits did their intelligence work at all. They were deft at finding new means for the better satisfaction of their appetites. But they wholly lacked self-criticism. Upon a normal outfit of instinctive needs they had developed many acquired, traditional cravings, most of which were fantastic and harmful. The Second Men, on the other hand, though often momentarily outwitted by the monkeys, were in the long run incomparably more able and more sane.

The difference between the two species is seen clearly in their reaction to metals. The Second Men sought metal solely for the carrying on of an already well-advanced civilization. But the monkeys, when for the first time they saw the bright ingots, were fascinated. They had already begun to hate the invaders for their native superiority and their material wealth; and now this jealousy combined with primitive acquisitiveness to make the slabs of copper and tin become in their eyes symbols of power. In order to remain unmolested in their work, the invaders had paid a toll of the wares of their own country, of baskets, pottery, and various specially designed miniature tools. But at the sight of the crude metal, the monkeys demanded a share of this noblest product of their own land. This was readily granted, since it did away with the need of bringing goods from Asia. But the monkeys had no real use for metal. They merely hoarded it, and became increasingly avaricious. No one had respect among them who did not laboriously carry a great ingot about with him wherever he went. And after a while it came to be considered actually indecent to be seen without a slab of metal. In conversation between the sexes this symbol of refinement was always held so as to conceal the genitals.

The more metal the monkeys acquired the more they craved. Blood was often shed in disputes over the possession of hoards. But this internecine strife gave place at length to a concerted movement to prevent the whole export of metal from their land. Some even suggested that the ingots in their possession should be used for making more effective weapons, with which to expel the invaders. This policy was rejected, not merely because there were none who could work up the crude metal, but because it was generally agreed that to put such a sacred material to any kind of service would be base.

The will to be rid of the invader was augmented by a dispute about the submen. These abject beings were treated very harshly by their masters. Not only were they overworked, but also they were tortured in cold blood, not precisely through lust in cruelty, but through a queer sense of humour, or delight in the incongruous. For instance, it afforded the monkeys a strangely innocent and extravagant pleasure to compel these cattle to carry on their work in an erect posture, which was by now quite unnatural to them, or to eat their own excrement or even their own young. If ever these tortures roused some exceptional subman to rebel, the monkeys flared into contemptuous rage at such a lack of humour, so incapable were they of realizing the subjective processes of others. To one another they could, indeed, be kindly and generous; but even among themselves the imp of humour would sometimes run riot. In any matter in which an individual was misunderstood by his fellows, he was sure to be gleefully baited, and often harried to death. But in the main it was only the slave-species that suffered.

The invaders were outraged by this cruel imbecility, and ventured to protest. To the monkeys the protest was unintelligible. What were cattle for, but to be used in the service of superior beings? Evidently, the monkeys thought, the invaders were after all lacking in the finer capacities of mind, since they failed to appreciate the beauty of the fantastic.

This and other causes of friction finally led the monkeys to conceive a means of freeing themselves for ever. The Second Men had proved to be terribly liable to the diseases of their wretched subhuman kinsfolk. Only by very rigorous quarantine had they stamped out the epidemic that had revealed this fact. Now partly for revenge, but partly also through malicious delight in the topsy-turvy, the monkeys determined to make use of this human weakness. There was a certain nut, very palatable to both men and monkeys, which grew in a remote part of the country. The monkeys had already begun to barter this nut for extra metal;

and the pioneering Second Men were arranging to send caravans laden with nuts into their own country. In this situation the monkeys found their opportunity. They carefully infected large quantities of nuts with the plagues rampant among those herds of submen which had not been domesticated. Very soon caravans of infected nuts were scattered over Asia. The effect upon a race wholly fresh to these microbes was disastrous. Not only were the pioneering settlements wiped out, but the bulk of the species also. The submen themselves had become adjusted to the microbes, and even reproduced more rapidly because of them. Not so the more delicately organized species. They died off like autumn leaves. Civilization fell to pieces. In a few generations Asia was peopled only by a handful of scattered savages, all diseased and mostly crippled.

But in spite of this disaster the species remained potentially the same. Within a few centuries it had thrown off the infection and had begun once more the ascent towards civilization. After another thousand years, pioneers again crossed the mountain and entered Africa. They met with no opposition. The precarious flicker of simian intelligence had long ago ceased. The monkeys had so burdened their bodies with metal and their minds with the obsession of metal, that at length the herds of subhuman cattle were able to rebel and devour their masters.

3. THE ZENITH OF THE SECOND MEN

For nearly a quarter of a million years the Second Men passed through successive phases of prosperity and decline. Their advance to developed culture was not nearly so steady and triumphal as might have been expected from a race of such brilliance. As with individuals, so with species, accidents are all too likely to defeat even the most cautious expectations. For instance, the Second Men were for a long time seriously hampered by a 'glacial epoch' which at its height imposed Arctic conditions even as far south as India. Little by little the encroaching ice crowded their tribes into the extremity of that peninsula, and reduced their culture to the level of the Esquimaux. In time, of

143

course, they recovered, but only to suffer other scourges, of which the most devastating were epidemics of bacteria. The more recently developed and highly organized tissues of this species were peculiarly susceptible to disease, and not once but many times a promising barbarian culture or 'medieval' civilization was wiped out by plagues.

But of all the natural disasters which befell the Second Men, the worst was due to a spontaneous change in their own physical constitution. Just as the fangs of the ancient sabre-toothed tiger had finally grown so large that the beast could not eat, so the brain of the second human species threatened to outgrow the rest of its body. In a cranium that was originally roomy enough, this rare product of nature was now increasingly cramped; while a circulatory system, that was formerly quite adequate, was becoming more and more liable to fail in pumping blood through so cramped a structure. These two causes at last began to take serious effect. Congenital imbecility became increasingly common, along with all manner of acquired mental diseases. For some thousands of years the race remained in a most precarious condition, now almost dying out, now rapidly attaining an extravagant kind of culture in some region where physical nature happened to be peculiarly favourable. One of these precarious flashes of spirit occurred in the Yang-tze valley as a sudden and brief effulgence of city states peopled by neurotics, geniuses and imbeciles. The lasting upshot of this civilization was a brilliant literature of despair, dominated by a sense of the difference between the actual and the potential in man and the universe. Later, when the race had attained its noontide glory, it was wont to brood upon this tragic voice from the past in order to remind itself of the underlying horror of existence.

Meanwhile, brains became more and more overgrown, and the race more and more disorganized. There is no doubt that it would have gone the way of the sabre-toothed tiger, simply through the fatal direction of its own physiological evolution, had not a more stable variety of this second human species at last appeared. It was in North America, into which, by way of Africa, the Second Men had long ago spread, that the roomier-skulled and stronger-hearted type first occurred. By great good fortune this new variety

proved to be a dominant Mendelian character. And as it inter-
bred freely with the older variety, a superbly healthy race soon
peopled America. The species was saved.

But another hundred thousand years were to pass before the
Second Men could reach their zenith. I must not dwell on this
movement of the human symphony, though it is one of great
richness. Inevitably many themes are now repeated from the
career of the earlier species, but with special features, and transposed, so to speak, from the minor to the major key. Once more
primitive cultures succeed one another, or pass into civilization,
barbarian or 'medieval'; and in turn these fall or are transformed.
Twice, indeed, the planet became the home of a single world-wide
community which endured for many thousands of years, until
misfortune wrecked it. The collapse is not altogether surprising,
for unlike the earlier species, the Second Men had no coal and oil.
In both these early world societies of the Second Men there was a
complete lack of mechanical power. Consequently, though world-
wide and intricate, they were in a manner 'medieval'. In every
continent intensive and highly skilled agriculture crept from the
valleys up the mountain sides and over the irrigated deserts. In
the rambling garden-cities each citizen took his share of drudgery,
practised also some fine handicraft, and yet had leisure for gaiety
and contemplation. Intercourse within and between the five great
continental communities had to be maintained by coaches,
caravans, and sailing ships. Sail, indeed, now came back into its
own, and far surpassed its previous achievements. On every sea,
fleets of great populous red-sailed clippers, wooden, with carved
poops and prows, but with the sleek flanks of the dolphin, carried
the produce of every land, and the many travellers who delighted
to spend a sabbatical year among foreigners.

So much, in the fullness of time, could be achieved, even
without mechanical power, by a species gifted with high intelligence and immune from anti-social self-regard. But inevitably there
came an end. A virus, whose subtle derangement of the glandular
system was never suspected by a race still innocent of physiology,
propagated throughout the world a mysterious fatigue. Century
by century, agriculture withdrew from the hills and deserts,
craftsmanship deteriorated, thought became stereotyped. And the

vast lethargy produced a vast despond. At length the nations lost touch with one another, forgot one another, forgot their culture, crumbled into savage tribes. Once more Earth slept.

Many thousand years later, long after the disease was spent, several great peoples developed in isolation. When at last they made contact, they were so alien that in each there had to occur a difficult cultural revolution, not unaccompanied by bloodshed, before the world could once more feel as one. But this second world order endured only a few centuries, for profound subconscious differences now made it impossible for the races to keep whole-heartedly loyal to each other. Religion finally severed the unity which all willed but none could trust. An heroic nation of monotheists sought to impose its faith on a vaguely pantheist world. For the first and last time the Second Men stumbled into a world-wide civil war; and just because the war was religious it developed a brutality hitherto unknown. With crude artillery, but with fanaticism, the two groups of citizen armies harried one another. The fields were laid waste, the cities burned, the rivers, and finally the winds, were poisoned. Long after that pitch of horror had been passed, at which an inferior species would have lost heart, these heroic madmen continued to organize destruction. And when at last the inevitable breakdown came, it was the more complete. In a sensitive species the devastating enlightenment which at last began to invade every mind, the overwhelming sense of treason against the human spirit, the tragic comicality of the whole struggle, sapped all energy. Not for thousands of years did the Second Men achieve once more a world-community. But they had learnt their lesson.

The third and most enduring civilization of the Second Men repeated the glorified medievalism of the first, and passed beyond it into a phase of brilliant natural science. Chemical fertilizers increased the crops, and therefore the world population. Wind- and water-power was converted into electricity to supplement human and animal labour. At length, after many failures, it became possible to use volcanic and subterranean energy to drive dynamos. In a few years the whole physical character of civilization was transformed. Yet in this headlong passage into industrialism the Second Men escaped the errors of ancient Europe,

America, and Patagonia. This was due partly to their greater gift of sympathy, which, save during the one great aberration of the religious war, made them all in a very vivid manner members one of another. But partly also it was due to their combination of a practical commonsense that was more than British, with a more than Russian immunity from the glamour of wealth, and a passion for the life of the mind that even Greece had never known. Mining and manufacture, even with plentiful electric power, were occupations scarcely less arduous than of old; but since each individual was implicated by vivid sympathy in the lives of all persons within his ken, there was little or no obsession with private economic power. The will to avoid industrial evils was effective, because sincere.

At its height, the culture of the Second Men was dominated by respect for the individual human personality. Yet contemporary individuals were regarded both as end and as means, as a stage towards far ampler individuals in the remote future. For, although they themselves were more long-lived than their predecessors, the Second Men were oppressed by the brevity of human life, and the pettiness of the individual's achievement in comparison with the infinity round about him which awaited apprehension and admiration. Therefore they were determined to produce a race endowed with much greater natural longevity. Again, though they participated in one another far more than their predecessors, they themselves were dogged by despair at the distortion and error which spoiled every mind's apprehension of others. Like their predecessors, they had passed through all the more naïve phases of self-consciousness and other-consciousness, and through idealizations of various modes of personality. They had admired the barbarian hero, the romantical, the sensitive-subtle, the bluff and hearty, the decadent, the bland, the severe. And they had concluded that each person, while being himself an expression of some one mode of personality, should seek to be also sensitive to every other mode. They even conceived that the ideal community should be knit into one mind by each unique individual's direct telepathic apprehension of the experience of all his fellows. And the fact that this ideal seemed utterly unattainable wove through their whole culture a thread of darkness, a yearning for spiritual union, a horror of loneliness, which never seriously troubled their far more insulated predecessors.

This craving for union influenced the sexual life of the species. In the first place, so closely was the mental related to the physiological in their composition, that when there was no true union of minds, the sexual act failed to give conception. Casual sexual relations thus came to be regarded very differently from those which expressed a deeper intimacy. They were treated as a delightful embroidery on life, affording opportunity of much elegance, light-hearted tenderness, banter, and of course physical inebriation; but they were deemed to signify nothing more than the delight of friend in friend. Where there was a marriage of minds, but then only during the actual passion of communion, sexual intercourse almost always resulted in conception. Under these circumstances, intimate persons had often to practise contraception, but acquaintances never. And one of the most beneficial inventions of the psychologists was a technique of auto-suggestion, which, at will, either facilitated conception, or prevented it, surely, harmlessly, and without inaesthetic accompaniments.

The sexual morality of the Second Men passed through all the phases known to the First Men; but by the time that they had established a single world-culture it had a form not known before. Not only were both men and women encouraged to have as much casual sexual intercourse as they needed for their enrichment, but also, on the higher plane of spiritual union, strict monogamy was deprecated. For in sexual union of this higher kind they saw a symbol of that communion of minds which they longed to make universal. Thus the most precious gift that a lover could bring to the beloved was not virginity but sexual experience. The union, it was felt, was the more pregnant the more each party could contribute from previous sexual and spiritual intimacy with others. Yet, though as a principle monogamy was not applauded, the higher kind of union would in practice sometimes result in a life-long partnership. But since the average life was so much longer than among the First Men, such fortuitously perennial unions were often deliberately interrupted for a while, by a change of partners, and then restored with their vitality renewed. Sometimes, on the other hand, a group of persons of both sexes

148

would maintain a composite and permanent marriage together. Sometimes such a group would exchange a member, or members, with another group, or disperse itself completely among other groups, to come together again years afterwards with enriched experience. In one form or another, this 'marriage of groups' was much prized, as an extension of the vivid sexual participation into an ampler sphere. Among the First Men the brevity of life made these novel forms of union impossible; for obviously no sexual, and no spiritual, relation can be developed with any richness in less than thirty years of close intimacy. It would be interesting to examine the social institutions of the Second Men at their zenith; but we have not time to spare for this subject, nor even for the brilliant intellectual achievements in which the species so far outstripped its predecessor. Obviously any account of the natural science and the philosophy of the Second Men would be unintelligible to readers of this book. Suffice it that they avoided the errors which had led the First Men into false abstraction, and into metaphysical theories which were at once sophisticated and naïve.

Not until after they had passed beyond the best work of the First Men in science and philosophy did the Second Men discover the remains of the great stone library in Siberia. A party of engineers happened upon it while they were preparing to sink a shaft for subterranean energy. The tablets were broken, disordered, weathered. Little by little, however, they were reconstructed and interpreted, with the aid of the pictorial dictionary. The finds were of extreme interest to the Second Men, but not in the manner which the Siberian party had intended, not as a store of scientific and philosophic truth, but as a vivid historical document. The view of the universe which the tablets recorded was both too naïve and too artificial; but the insight which they afforded into the mind of the earlier species was invaluable. So little of the old world had survived the volcanic epoch that the Second Men had failed hitherto to get a clear picture of their predecessors.

One item alone in this archaeological treasure had more than historical interest. The biologist leader of the little party in Siberia had recorded much of the sacred text of the Life of the Divine Boy. At the end of the record came the prophet's last words,

149

which had so baffled Patagonia. This theme was full of meaning for the Second Men, as indeed it would have been even for the First Men in their prime. But whereas for the First Men the dispassionate ecstasy which the Boy had preached was rather an ideal than a fact of experience, the Second Men recognized in the prophet's words an intuition familiar to themselves. Long ago the tortured geniuses of the Yang-tze cities had expressed this same intuition. Subsequently also it had often been experienced by the more healthy generations, but always with a certain shame. For it had become associated with morbid mentality. But now with growing conviction that it was wholesome, the Second Men had begun to grope for a wholesome expression of it. In the life and the last words of the remote apostle of youth they found an expression which was not wholly inadequate. The species was presently to be in sore need of this gospel.

The world community reached at length a certain relative perfection and equilibrium. There was a long summer of social harmony, prosperity, and cultural embellishment. Almost all that could be done by mind in the stage to which it had then reached seemed to have been done. Generations of long-lived, eager, and mutually delightful beings succeeded one another. There was a widespread feeling that the time had come for man to gather all his strength for a flight into some new sphere of mentality. The present type of human being, it was recognized, was but a rough and incoherent natural product. It was time for man to take control of himself and remake himself upon a nobler pattern. With this end in view, two great works were set afoot, research into the ideal of human nature, and research into practical means of remaking human nature. Individuals in all lands, living their private lives, delighting in each other, keeping the tissue of society alive and vigorous, were deeply moved by the thought that their world-community was at last engaged upon this heroic task.

But elsewhere in the solar system life of a very different kind was seeking, in its own strange manner, ends incomprehensible to man, yet at bottom identical with his own ends. And presently the two were to come together, not in cooperation.

VIII *The Martians*

1. THE FIRST MARTIAN INVASION

UPON the foot-hills of the new and titanic mountains that were once the Hindu Kush, were many holiday centres, whence the young men and women of Asia were wont to seek Alpine dangers and hardships for their souls' refreshment. It was in this district, and shortly after a summer dawn, that the Martians were first seen by men. Early walkers noticed that the sky had an unaccountably greenish tinge, and that the climbing sun, though free from cloud, was wan. Observers were presently surprised to see the green concentrate itself into a thousand tiny cloudlets, with clear blue between. Field-glasses revealed within each fleck of green some faint hint of a ruddy nucleus, and shifting strands of an infrared colour, which would have been invisible to the earlier human race. These extraordinary specks of cloud were all of about the same size, the largest of them appearing smaller than the moon's disc; but in form they varied greatly, and were seen to be changing their shapes more rapidly than the natural cirrus which they slightly resembled. In fact, though there was much that was cloud-like in their form and motion, there was also something definite about them, both in their features and behaviour, which suggested life. Indeed they were strongly reminiscent of primitive amoeboid organisms seen through a microscope.

The whole sky was strewn with them, here and there in concentrations of unbroken green, elsewhere more sparsely. And they were observed to be moving. A general drift of the whole celestial population was setting toward one of the snowy peaks that dominated the landscape. Presently the foremost individuals reached the mountain's crest, and were seen to be creeping down the rock-face with a very slow amoeboid action.

Meanwhile a couple of aeroplanes, electrically driven, had climbed the sky to investigate the strange phenomenon at close quarters. They passed among the drifting cloudlets, and actually

151

through many of them, without hindrance, and almost without being obscured from view.

On the mountain a vast swarm of the cloudlets was collecting, and creeping down the precipices and snowfields into a high glacier valley. At a certain point, where the glacier dropped steeply to a lower level, the advance guard slowed down and stopped, while hosts of their fellows continued to pack in on them from behind. In half an hour the whole sky was once more clear, save for normal clouds; but upon the glacier lay what might almost have been an exceptionally dark solid-looking thundercloud, save for its green tinge and seething motion. For some minutes this strange object was seen to concentrate itself into a somewhat smaller bulk and become darker. Then it moved forward again, and passed over the cliffy end of the glacier into the pine-clad valley. An intervening ridge now hid it from its first observers.

Lower down the valley there was a village. Many of the inhabitants, when they saw the mysterious dense fume advancing upon them, took to their mechanical vehicles and fled; but some waited out of curiosity. They were swallowed up in a murky olive-brown fog, shot here and there with queer shimmering streaks of a ruddier tint. Presently there was complete darkness. Artificial lights were blotted out almost at arm's length. Breathing became difficult. Throats and lungs were irritated. Every one was seized with a violent attack of sneezing and coughing. The cloud streamed through the village, and seemed to exercise irregular pressures upon objects, not always in the general direction of movement but sometimes in the opposite direction, as though it were getting a purchase upon human bodies and walls, and actually elbowing its way along. Within a few minutes the fog lightened; and presently it left the village behind it, save for a few strands and whiffs of its smoke-like substance, which had become entangled in side-streets and isolated. Very soon, however, these seemed to get themselves clear and hurry to overtake the main body.

When the gasping villagers had somewhat recovered, they sent a radio message to the little town lower down the valley, urging temporary evacuation. The message was not broadcast, but transmitted on a slender beam of rays. It so happened that the beam had to be directed through the noxious matter itself. While the message was being given, the cloud's progress ceased, and its outlines became vague and ragged. Fragments of it actually drifted away on the wind and dissipated themselves. Almost as soon as the message was completed, the cloud began to define itself again, and lay for a quarter of an hour at rest. A dozen bold young men from the town now approached the dark mass out of curiosity. No sooner did they come face to face with it, round a bend in the valley, than the cloud rapidly contracted, till it was no bigger than a house. Looking now something between a dense, opaque fume and an actual jelly, it lay still until the party had ventured within a few yards. Evidently their courage failed, for they were seen to turn. But before they had retreated three paces, a long proboscis shot out of the main mass with the speed of a chameleon's tongue, and enveloped them. Slowly it withdrew; but the young men had been gathered in with it. The cloud, or jelly, churned itself violently for some seconds, then ejected the bodies in a single chewed lump.

The murderous thing now elbowed itself along the road towards the town, leaned against the first house, crushed it, and proceeded to wander hither and thither, pushing everything down before it, as though it were a lava-stream. The inhabitants took to their heels, but several were licked up and slaughtered.

Powerful beam radiation was now poured into the cloud from all the neighbouring installations. Its destructive activity slackened, and once more it began to disintegrate and expand. Presently it streamed upwards as a huge column of smoke; and, at a great altitude, it dissipated itself again into a swarm of the original green cloudlets, noticeably reduced in numbers. These again faded into a uniform greenish tinge, which gradually vanished.

Thus ended the first invasion of the Earth from Mars.

2. LIFE ON MARS

Our concern is with humanity, and with the Martians only in relation to men. But in order to understand the tragic intercourse of the two planets, it is necessary to glance at conditions on Mars, and conceive something of those fantastically different yet fundamentally similar beings, who were now seeking to possess man's home.

To describe the biology, psychology, and history of a whole world in a few pages is as difficult as it would be to give the Martians themselves in the same compass a true idea of man. Encyclopaedias, libraries, would be needed in either case. Yet, somehow, I must contrive to suggest the alien sufferings and delights, and the many aeons of struggle, which went to the making of these strange non-human intelligences, in some ways so inferior yet in others definitely superior to the human species which they encountered.

Mars was a world whose mass was about one-tenth that of the earth. Gravity therefore had played a less tyrannical part in Martian than in terrestrial history. The weakness of Martian gravity combined with the paucity of the planet's air envelope to make the general atmospheric pressure far lighter than on earth. Oxygen was far less plentiful. Water also was comparatively rare. There were no oceans or seas, but only shallow lakes and marshes, many of which dried up in summer. The climate of the planet was in general very dry, and yet very cold. Being without cloud, it was perennially bright with the feeble rays of a distant sun.

Earlier in the history of Mars, when there were more air, more water, and a higher temperature from internal heat, life had appeared in the coastal waters of the seas, and evolution had proceeded in much the same manner as on earth. Primitive life was differentiated into the fundamental animal and vegetable types. Multicellular structures appeared, and specialized themselves in diverse manners to suit diverse environments. A great variety of plant forms clothed the lands, often with forests of gigantic and slender-stemmed plumes. Mollusc-like and insect-like animals crept or swam, or shot themselves hither and thither in fantastic jumps. Huge spidery creatures of a type not wholly unlike crustaceans, or gigantic grasshoppers, bounded after their prey, and developed a versatility and cunning which enabled them to dominate the planet almost as, at a much later date, early man was to dominate the terrestrial wild.

But meanwhile a rapid loss of atmosphere, and especially of water-vapour, was changing Martian conditions beyond the limits of adaptability of this early fauna and flora. At the same time a very different kind of vital organization was beginning to profit by the change. On Mars, as on the Earth, life had arisen from one of many 'subvital' forms. The new type of life on Mars evolved from another of these subvital kinds of molecular organization, one which had hitherto failed to evolve at all, and had played an insignificant part, save occasionally as a rare virus in the respiratory organs of animals. These fundamental subvital units of organization were ultra-microscopic, and indeed far smaller than the terrestrial bacteria, or even the terrestrial viruses. They originally occurred in the marshy ponds, which dried up every spring, and became depressions of baked mud and dust. Certain of their species, borne into the air upon dust-particles, developed an extremely dry habit of life. They maintained themselves by absorbing chemicals from the wind-borne dust, and a very slight amount of moisture from the air. Also they absorbed sunlight by a photo-synthesis almost identical with that of the plants.

To this extent they were similar to the other living things, but they had also certain capacities which the other stock had lost at the very outset of its evolutionary career. Terrestrial organisms, and Martian organisms of the terrestrial type, maintained themselves as vital unities by means of nervous systems, or other forms of material contact between parts. In the most developed forms, an immensely complicated neural 'telephone' system connected every part of the body with a vast central exchange, the brain. Thus on the earth a single organism was without exception a continuous system of matter, which maintained a certain constancy of form. But from the distinctively Martian subvital unit there evolved at length a very different kind of complex organism, in which material contact of parts was not necessary either to coordination of behaviour or unity of consciousness. These ends were achieved upon a very different physical basis. The ultra-microscopic subvital members were sensitive to all kinds of aetherial vibrations, directly sensitive, in a manner impossible to terrestrial life; and they could also initiate vibrations. Upon this basis Martian life developed at length the capacity of maintaining vital organization as a single conscious individual without continuity of living matter. Thus the typical Martian organism was a cloudlet, a group of free-moving members dominated by a 'group-mind'. But in one species individuality came to inhere, for certain purposes, not in distinct cloudlets only, but in a great fluid system of cloudlets. Such was the single-minded Martian host which invaded the Earth.

The Martian organism depended, so to speak, not on 'telephone' wires, but on an immense crowd of mobile 'wireless stations', transmitting and receiving different wave-lengths according to their function. The radiation of a single unit was of course very feeble; but a great system of units could maintain contact with its wandering parts over a considerable distance.

One other important characteristic distinguished the dominant form of life on Mars. Just as a cell, in the terrestrial form of life, has often the power of altering its shape (whence the whole mechanism of muscular activity), so in the Martian form the free-floating ultra-microscopic unit might be specialized for generating around itself a magnetic field, and so either repelling or attracting its neighbours. Thus a system of materially disconnected units had a certain cohesion. Its consistency was something between a smoke-cloud and a very tenuous jelly. It had a definite though ever-changing contour and resistant surface. By massed mutual repulsions of its constituent units it could exercise pressure on surrounding objects; and in its most concentrated form the Martian cloud-jelly could bring to bear immense forces which could also be controlled for very delicate manipulation. Magnetic forces were also responsible for the mollusc-like motion of the cloud as a whole over the ground, and again for the transport of lifeless material and living units from region to region within the cloud.

The magnetic field of repulsion and attraction generated by a subvital unit was much more restricted than its field of 'wireless' communication. Similarly with organized systems of units. Thus each of the cloudlets which the Second Men saw in their sky was an independent motor unit; but also it was in a kind of 'telepathic' communication with all its fellows. Indeed in every public enterprise, such as the terrestrial campaigns, almost perfect unity of consciousness was maintained within the limits of a huge field of radiation. Yet only when the whole population concentrated itself into a small and relatively dense cloud-jelly, did it become a single magnetic motor unit. The Martians, it should be noted, had three possible forms, or formations, namely: first, an 'open order' of independent and very tenuous cloudlets in 'telephathic' communication, and often in strict unity as a group mind; second, a more concentrated and less vulnerable corporate cloud; and third, an extremely concentrated and formidable cloud-jelly.

Save for these very remarkable characteristics, there was no really fundamental difference between the distinctively Martian and the distinctively terrestrial forms of life. The chemical basis of the former was somewhat more complicated than that of the latter; and selenium played a part in it, to which nothing corresponded in terrestrial life. The Martian organism, moreover, was unique in that it fulfilled within itself the functions of both animal and vegetable. But, save for these peculiarities, the two types of life were biochemically much the same. Both needed material from the ground, both needed sunlight. Each lived in the chemical changes occurring in its own 'flesh'. Each, of course, tended to maintain itself as an organic unity. There was a certain difference, indeed, in respect of reproduction; for the Martian subvital units retained the power of growth and subdivision. Thus the birth of a Martian cloud arose from the subdivision of myriads of units within the parent cloud, followed by their ejection as a new individual. And, as the units were highly specialized for different functions, representatives of many types had to pass into the new cloud.

In the earliest stages of evolution on Mars the units had become independent of each other as soon as they parted in reproduction. But later the hitherto useless and rudimentary power of emitting radiation was specialized, so that, after reproduction, free individuals came to maintain radiant contact with one another, and to behave with ever-increasing coordination. Still later, these organized groups themselves maintained radiant contact with groups of their offspring, thus constituting larger individuals with specialized members. With each advance in complexity the sphere of radiant influence increased; until, at the zenith of Martian evolution, the whole planet (save for the remaining animal and vegetable representatives of the other and unsuccessful kind of life) constituted sometimes a single biological and psychological individual. But this occurred as a rule only in respect of matters which concerned the species as a whole. At most times the Martian individual was a cloudlet, such as those which first astonished the Second Men. But in great public crises each cloudlet would suddenly wake up to find himself the mind of the whole race, sensing through many individuals, and interpreting his sensations in the light of the experience of the whole race.

The life which dominated Mars was thus something between an extremely well-disciplined army of specialized units, and a body possessed by one mind. Like an army, it could take any form without destroying its organic unity. Like an army it was sometimes a crowd of free-wandering units, yet at other times also it disposed itself in very special orders to fulfil special functions. Like an army it was composed of free, experiencing individuals who voluntarily submitted themselves to discipline. On the other hand, unlike an army, it woke occasionally into unified consciousness.

The same fluctuation between individuality and multiplicity which characterized the race as a whole, characterized also each of the cloudlets themselves. Each was sometimes an individual, sometimes a swarm of more primitive individuals. But while the race rather seldom rose to full individuality, the cloudlets declined from it only in very special circumstances. Each cloudlet was an organization of specialized groups formed of minor specialized groups, which in turn were composed of the fundamental specialized varieties of subvital units. Each free-roving group of free-roving units constituted a special organ, fulfilling some particular function in the whole. Thus some were specialized for attraction and repulsion, some for chemical operations, some for storing the sun's energy, some for emitting radiation, some for absorbing and storing water, some for special sensitivities, such as awareness of mechanical pressure and vibration, or temperature changes, or light rays. Others again were specialized to fulfil the function of the brain of man; but in a peculiar manner. The whole volume of the cloudlet vibrated with innumerable 'wireless' messages in very many wave-lengths from the different 'organs'. It was the function of the 'brain' units to receive, and correlate, and interpret these messages in the light of past experience, and to initiate responses in the wave-lengths appropriate to the organs concerned.

All these subvital units, save a few types that were too highly specialized, were capable of independent life as air-borne bacteria or viruses. And whenever they lost touch with the radiation of the whole system, they continued to live their own simple lives until they were once more controlled. All were free-floating units, but normally they were under the influence of the cloudlet's system of electro-magnetic fields, and were directed hither and thither for their special functions. And under this influence some of them might be held rigidly in position in relation to one another. Such was the case of the organs of sight. In early stages of evolution, some of the units had specialized for carrying minute globules of water. Later, much larger droplets were carried, millions of units holding between them a still microscopic globule of life's most precious fluid. Ultimately this function was turned to good account in vision. Aqueous lenses as large as the eye of an ox were supported by a scaffolding of units; while, at focal length from the lens, a rigid retina of units was held in position. Thus the Martian could produce eyes of every variety whenever he wanted them, and telescopes and microscopes too. This production and manipulation of visual organs was of course largely subconscious, like the focussing mechanism in man. But latterly the Martians had greatly increased their conscious control of physiological processes; and it was this achievement which facilitated their remarkable optical triumphs.

One other physiological function we must note before considering the Martian psychology. The fully evolved, but as yet uncivilized, Martian had long ago ceased to depend for his chemicals on wind-borne volcanic dust. Instead, he rested at night on the ground, like a knee-high mist on terrestrial meadows, and projected specialized tubular groups of units into the soil, like rootlets. Part of the day also had to be occupied in this manner. Somewhat later this process was supplemented by devouring the declining plant-life of the planet. But the final civilized Martians had greatly improved their methods of exploiting the ground and the sunlight, both by mechanical means and by artificial specialization of their own organs. Even so, however, as their activities increased, these vegetable functions became an ever more serious problem for them. They practised agriculture; but only a very small area of the arid planet could be induced to bear. It was terrestrial water and terrestrial vegetation that finally determined them to make the great voyage.

3. THE MARTIAN MIND

The Martian mind was of a very different type from the terrestrial, different, yet at bottom identical. In so strange a body, the mind was inevitably equipped with alien cravings, and alien manners of apprehending its environment. And with so different a history, it was confused by prejudices very unlike those of man. Yet it was none the less mind, concerned in the last resort with the maintenance and advancement of life, and the exercise of vital capacities. Fundamentally the Martian was like all other living beings, in that he delighted in the free working of his body and his mind. Yet superficially, he was as unlike man in mind as in body.

The most distinctive feature of the Martian, compared with man, was that his individuality was both far more liable to disruption, and at the same time immeasurably more capable of direct participation in the minds of other individuals. The human mind in its solid body maintained its unity and its dominance over its members in all normal circumstances. Only in disease was man liable to mental or physical dissociation. On the other hand, he was incapable of direct contact with other individuals, and the emergence of a 'super-mind' in a group of individuals was quite impossible. The Martian cloudlet, however, though he fell to pieces physically, and also mentally, far more readily than a man, might also at any moment wake up to be the intelligent mind of his race, might begin to perceive with the sense-organs of all other individuals, and experience thoughts and desires which were, so to speak, the resultant of all individual thoughts and desires upon some matter of general interest. But unfortunately, as I shall tell, the common mind of the Martians never woke into any order of mentality higher than that of the individual.

These differences between the Martian and the human psyche entailed characteristic advantages and disadvantages. The Martian, immune from man's inveterate selfishness and spiritual isolation from his fellows, lacked the mental coherence, the concentrated attention and far-reaching analysis and synthesis, and again the vivid self-consciousness and relentless self-criticism, which even the First Men, at their best, had attained in some degree, and which in the Second Men were still more developed. The Martians, moreover, were hampered by being almost identical in character. They possessed perfect harmony; but only through being almost wholly in temperamental unison. They were all hobbled by their sameness to one another. They were without that rich diversity of personal character, which enabled the human spirit to cover so wide a field of mentality. This infinite variety of human nature entailed, indeed, endless wasteful and cruel personal conflicts in the first, and even to some extent in the second, species of man; but also it enabled every individual of developed sympathy to enrich his spirit by intercourse with individuals whose temperament, thought, and ideals differed from his own. And while the Martians were little troubled by internecine strife and the passion of hate, they were also almost wholly devoid of the passion of love. The Martians individual could admire, and be utterly faithful to, the object of his loyalty; but his admiration was given, not to concrete and uniquely charactered persons of the same order as himself, but at best to the vaguely conceived 'spirit of the race'. Individuals like himself he regarded merely as instruments or organs of the 'super-mind'.

This would not have been amiss, had the mind of the race, into which he so frequently awoke under the influence of the general radiation, been indeed a mind of higher rank than his own. But it was not. It was but a pooling of the percipience and thought and will of the cloudlets. Thus it was that the superb loyalty of the Martians was squandered upon something which was not greater than themselves in mental calibre, but only in mere bulk.

The Martian cloudlet, like the human animal, had a complex instinctive nature. By night and day, respectively, he was impelled to perform the vegetative functions of absorbing chemicals from the ground and energy from the sunlight. Air and water he also craved, though he dealt with them, of course, in his own manner. He had also his own characteristic instinctive impulses to move his 'body', both for locomotion and manipulation. Martian civilization provided an outlet for these cravings, both in the practice of agriculture and in intricate and wonderfully beautiful cloud-dances and gymnastics. For these perfectly supple beings rejoiced in executing aerial evolutions, flinging out wild rhythmical streamers, intertwining with one another in spirals, concentrating into opaque spheres, cubes, cones, and all sorts of fantastical volumes. Many of these movements and shapes had intense emotional significance for them in relation to the operations of their life, and were executed with a religious fervour and solemnity.

The Martian had also his impulses of fear and pugnacity. In the remote past these had often been directed against hostile members of his own species; but since the race had become unified, they found exercise only upon other types of life and upon inanimate nature. Instinctive gregariousness was, of course, extremely developed in the Martian at the expense of instinctive self-assertion. Sexuality the Martian had not; there were not partners in reproduction. But his impulse to merge physically and mentally with other individuals, and wake up as the supermind, had in it much that was characteristic of sex in man. Parental impulses, of a kind, he knew; but they were scarcely worthy of the name. He cared only to eject excessive living matter from his system, and to keep *en rapport* with the new individual thus formed, as he would with any other individual. He knew no more of the human devotion to children as budding personalities than of the subtle intercourse of male and female temperaments. By the time of the first invasion, however, reproduction had been greatly restricted; for the planet was fully populated, and each individual cloudlet was potentially immortal. Among the Martians there was no 'natural death', no spontaneous death through mere senility. Normally the cloudlet's members kept themselves in repair indefinitely by the reproduction of their constituent units. Diseases, indeed, were often fatal. And chief among them was a plague, corresponding to terrestrial cancer, in which the subvital units lost their sensitivity to radiation, so that they proceeded to live as primitive organisms and reproduce without restraint. As they also became parasitic on the unaffected units, the cloudlet inevitably died.

Like the higher kinds of terrestrial mammal, the Martians had strong impulses of curiosity. Having also many practical needs to fulfil as a result of their civilization, and being extremely well equipped by nature for physical experiment and microscopy, they had gone far in the natural sciences. In physics, astronomy, chemistry, and even in the chemistry of life, man had nothing to teach them.

The vast corpus of Martian knowledge had taken many thousands of years to grow. All its stages, and its current achievements, were recorded on immense scrolls of paper made from vegetable pulp, and stored in libraries of stone. For the Martians, curiously enough, had become great masons, and had covered much of their planet with buildings of feathery and toppling design, such as would have been quite impossible on earth. They had no need of buildings for habitation, save in the arctic regions; but as workshops, granaries, and store rooms of all sorts, buildings had become very necessary to the Martians. Moreover these extremely tenuous creatures took a peculiar joy in manipulating solids. Even their most utilitarian architecture blossomed with a sort of gothic or arabesque ornateness and fantasy, wherein the ethereal seemed to torture the substance of solid rock into its own likeness.

At the time of the invasion, the Martians were still advancing intellectually; and, indeed, it was through an achievement in theoretical physics that they were able to leave their planet. They had long known that minute particles at the upper limit of the atmosphere might be borne into space by the pressure of the sun's rays at dawn and sunset. And at length they discovered how to use this pressure as the wind is used in sailing. Dissipating themselves into their ultra-microscopic units, they contrived to get a purchase on the gravitational fields of the solar system, as a boat's keel and rudder get a purchase on the water. Thus they were able to tack across to the earth as an armada of ultra-microscopic vessels. Arrived in the terrestrial sky, they re-formed themselves as cloudlets, swam through the dense air to the alpine summit, and climbed downwards, as a swimmer may climb down a ladder under water.

This achievement involved very intricate calculations and chemical inventions, especially for the preservation of life in transit and on an alien planet. It could never have been done save by beings with far-reaching and accurate knowledge of the physical world. But though in respect of 'natural knowledge' the Martians were so well advanced, they were extremely backward in all those spheres which may be called 'spiritual knowledge'. They had little understanding of their own mentality, and less of the place of mind in the cosmos. Though in a sense a highly intelligent species, they were at the same time wholly lacking in philosophical interest. They scarcely conceived, still less tackled, the problems which even the First Men had faced so often, though so vainly. For the Martians there was no mystery in the distinction between reality and appearance or in the relation of the one and the many, or in the status of good and evil. Nor were they ever critical of their own ideals. They aimed wholeheartedly at the advancement of the Martian super-individual. But what should constitute individuality, and its advancement, they never seriously considered. And the idea that they were under obligation also towards beings not included in the Martian system of radiation, proved wholly beyond them. For, though so clever, they were the most naïve of self-deceivers, and had no insight to see what it is that is truly desirable.

4. DELUSIONS OF THE MARTIANS

To understand how the Martians tricked themselves, and how they were finally undone by their own insane will, we must glance at their history.

The civilized Martians constituted the sole remaining variety of a species. That species itself, in the remote past, had competed with, and exterminated, many other species of the same general type. Aided by the changing climate, it had also exterminated almost all the species of the more terrestrial kind of fauna, and had thereby much reduced the vegetation which it was subsequently to need and foster so carefully. This victory of the species had been due partly to its versatility and intelligence, partly to a remarkable zest in ferocity, partly to its unique powers of radiation and sensitivity to radiation, which enabled it to act with a Coordination impossible even to the most gregarious of animals. But, as with other species in biological history, the capacity by which it triumphed became at length a source of weakness. When the species reached a stage corresponding to primitive human culture, one of its races, achieving a still higher degree of radiant intercourse and physical unity, was able to behave as a single vital unit; and so it succeeded in exterminating all its rivals. Racial conflict had persisted for many thousands of years, but as soon as the favoured race had developed this almost absolute solidarity of will, its victory was sweeping, and was clinched by joyous massacre of the enemy.

But ever afterwards the Martians suffered from the psychological effects of their victory at the close of the epoch of racial wars. The extreme brutality with which the other races had been exterminated conflicted with the generous impulses which civilization had begun to foster, and left a scar upon the conscience of the victors. In self-defence they persuaded themselves that since they were so much more admirable than the rest, the extermination was actually a sacred duty. And their unique value, they said, consisted in their unique radiational development. Hence arose a gravely insincere tradition and culture, which finally ruined the species. They had long believed that the physical basis of consciousness must necessarily be a system of units directly sensitive to etherial vibrations, and that organisms dependent on the physical contact of their parts were too gross to have any experience whatever. After the age of the racial massacres they sought to persuade themselves that the excellence, or ethical worth, of any organism depended upon the degree of complexity and unity of its radiation. Century by century they strengthened their faith in this vulgar doctrine, and developed also a system of quite irrational delusions and obsessions based upon an obsessive and passionate lust in radiation.

It would take too long to tell of all these subsidiary fantasies, and of the ingenious ways in which they were reconciled with the main body of sane knowledge. But one at least must be mentioned, because of the part it played in the struggle with man. The Martians knew, of course, that 'solid matter' was solid by virtue of the interlocking of the minute electro-magnetic systems called atoms. Now rigidity had for them somewhat the same significance and prestige that air, breath, spirit, had for early man. It was in the quasi-solid form that Martians were physically most potent; and the maintenance of this form was exhausting and difficult. These facts combined in the Martian consciousness with the knowledge that rigidity was after all the outcome of interlocked electro-magnetic systems. Rigidity was thus endowed with a peculiar sanctity. The superstition was gradually consolidated, by a series of psychological accidents, into a fanatical admiration of all very rigid materials, but especially of hard crystals, and above all of diamonds. For diamonds were extravagantly resistant; and at the same time, as the Martians themselves put it, diamonds were superb jugglers with the ethereal radiation called light. Every diamond was therefore a supreme embodiment of the tense energy and eternal equilibrium of the cosmos, and must be treated with reverence. In Mars, all known diamonds were exposed to sunlight on the pinnacles of sacred buildings; and the thought that on the neighbour planet might be diamonds which were not properly treated, was one motive of the invasion.

Thus did the Martian mind, unwittingly side-tracked from its true development, fall sick, and strive ever more fanatically towards mere phantoms of its goal. In the early stages of the disorder, radiation was merely regarded as an infallible *sign* of mentality, and radiative complexity was taken as an infallible *measure*, merely, of spiritual worth. But little by little, radiation and mentality failed to be distinguished, and radiative organization was actually mistaken for spiritual worth.

In this obsession the Martians resembled somewhat the First Men during their degenerate phase of servitude to the idea of movement; but with a difference. For the Martian intelligence was still active, though its products were severely censored in the name of the 'spirit of the race'. Every Martian was a case of dual personality. Not merely was he sometimes a private consciousness, sometimes the consciousness of the race, but further, even as a private individual he was in a manner divided against himself. Though his practical allegiance to the super-individual was absolute, so that he condemned or ignored all thoughts and impulses that could not be assimilated to the public consciousness, he did in fact have such thoughts and impulses, as it were in the deepest recesses of his being. He very seldom noticed that he was having them, and whenever he did notice it, he was shocked and terrified; yet he did have them. They constituted an intermittent, sometimes almost a continuous, critical commentary on all his more reputable experience.

This was the great tragedy of the spirit on Mars. The Martians were in many ways extremely well equipped for mental progress and for true spiritual adventure, but through a trick of fortune which had persuaded them to prize above all else unity and uniformity, they were driven to thwart their own struggling spirits at every turn.

Far from being superior to the private mind, the public mind which obsessed every Martian was in many ways actually inferior. It had come into dominance in a crisis which demanded severe military coordination; and though, since that remote age, it had made great intellectual progress, it remained at heart a military mind. Its disposition was something between that of a field-marshal and the God of the ancient Hebrews. A certain English philosopher once described and praised the fictitious corporate personality of the state, and named it 'Leviathan'. The Martian super-individual was Leviathan endowed with consciousness. In this consciousness there was nothing but what was easily assimilated and in accord with tradition. Thus the public mind was always intellectually and culturally behind the times. Only in respect of practical social organization did it keep abreast of its own individuals. Intellectual progress had always been initiated by private individuals, and had only penetrated the public mind when the mass of individuals had been privately infected by intercourse with the pioneers. The public consciousness itself initiated progress only in the sphere of social, military, and economic organization.

The novel circumstances which were encountered on the earth put the mentality of the Martians to a supreme test. For the unique enterprise of tackling a new world demanded the extremes of both public and private activity, and so led to agonizing conflicts within each private mind. For, while the undertaking was essentially social and even military, and necessitated very strict coordination and unity of action, the extreme novelty of the new environment demanded all the resources of the untrammelled private consciousness. Moreover the Martians encountered much on the earth which made nonsense of their fundamental assumptions. And in their brightest moment of private consciousness they sometimes recognized this fact.

IX *Earth and Mars*

1. THE SECOND MEN AT BAY

SUCH were the beings that invaded the earth when the Second Men were gathering their strength for a great venture in artificial evolution. The motives of the invasion were both economic and religious. The Martians sought water and vegetable matter; but they came also in a crusading spirit, to 'liberate' the terrestrial diamonds.

Conditions on the earth were very unfavourable to the invaders. Excessive gravitation troubled them less than might have been expected. Only in their most concentrated form did they find it oppressive. More harmful was the density of the terrestrial atmosphere, which constricted the tenuous animate cloudlets very painfully, hindering their vital processes, and deadening all their movements. In their native atmosphere they swam hither and thither with ease and considerable speed; but the treacly air of the earth hampered them as a bird's wings are hampered under water. Moreover, owing to their extreme buoyancy as individual cloudlets, they were scarcely able to dive down so far as the mountain-tops. Excessive oxygen was also a source of distress; it tended to put them into a violent fever, which they had only been able to guard against very imperfectly. Even more damaging was the excessive moisture of the atmosphere, both through its solvent effect upon certain factors in the subvital units, and because heavy rain interfered with the physiological processes of the cloudlets and washed many of their materials to the ground.

The invaders had also to cope with the tissue of 'radio' messages that constantly enveloped the planet, and tended to interfere with their own organic systems of radiation. They were prepared for this to some extent; but 'beam wireless' at close range surprised, bewildered, tortured, and finally routed them; so that they fled back to Mars, leaving many of their number disintegrated in the terrestrial air.

169

But the pioneering army (or individual, for throughout the adventure it maintained unity of consciousness) had much to report at home. As was expected, there was rich vegetation, and water was even too abundant. There were solid animals, of the type of the prehistoric Martian fauna, but mostly two-legged and erect. Experiment had shown that these creatures died when they were pulled to pieces, and that though the sun's rays affected them by setting up chemical action in their visual organs, they had no really direct sensitivity to radiation. Obviously, therefore, they must be unconscious. On the other hand, the terrestrial atmosphere was permanently alive with radiation of a violent and incoherent type. It was still uncertain whether these crude ethereal agitations were natural phenomena, mere careless offshoots of the cosmic mind, or whether they were emitted by a terrestrial organism. There was reason to suppose this last to be the case, and that the solid organisms were used by some hidden terrestrial intelligence as instruments; for there were buildings, and many of the bipeds were found within the buildings. Moreover, the sudden violent concentration of beam radiation upon the Martian cloud suggested purposeful and hostile behaviour. Punitive action had therefore been taken, and many buildings and bipeds had been destroyed. The physical basis of such a terrestrial intelligence was still to be discovered. It was certainly not in the terrestrial clouds, for these had turned out to be insensitive to radiation. Anyhow, it was obviously an intelligence of very low order, for its radiation was scarcely at all systematic, and was indeed excessively crude. One or two unfortunate diamonds had been found in a building. There was no sign that they were properly venerated.

The Terrestrials, on their side, were left in complete bewilderment by the extraordinary events of that day. Some had jokingly suggested that since the strange substance had behaved in a manner obviously vindictive, it must have been alive and conscious; but no one took the suggestion seriously. Clearly, however, the thing had been dissipated by beam radiation. That at least was an important piece of practical knowledge. But theoretical knowledge about the real nature of the clouds, and their place in the order of the universe, was for the present wholly lacking. To a race of strong cognitive interest and splendid scientific achievement, this ignorance was violently disturbing. It seemed to shake the foundations of the great structure of knowledge. Many frankly hoped, in spite of the loss of life in the first invasion, that there would soon be another opportunity for studying these amazing objects, which were not quite gaseous and not quite solid, not (apparently) organic, yet capable of behaving in a manner suggestive of life. An opportunity was soon afforded.

Some years after the first invasion, the Martians appeared again, and in far greater force. This time, moreover, they were almost immune from man's offensive radiation. Operating simultaneously from all the alpine regions of the earth, they began to dry up the great rivers at their sources; and, venturing further afield, they spread over jungle and agricultural land, and stripped off every leaf. Valley after valley was devastated as though by endless swarms of locusts, so that in whole countries there was not a green blade left. The booty was carried off to Mars. Myriads of the subvital units, specialized for transport of water and food materials, were loaded each with a few molecules of the treasure, and dispatched to the home planet. The traffic continued indefinitely. Meanwhile the main body of the Martians proceeded to explore and loot. They were irresistible. For the absorption of water and leafage, they spread over the countryside as an impalpable mist which man had no means to dispel. For the destruction of civilization, they became armies of gigantic cloud-jellies, far bigger than the brute which had formed itself during the earlier invasion. Cities were knocked down and flattened, human beings masticated into pulp. Man tried weapon after weapon in vain.

Presently the Martians discovered the sources of terrestrial radiation in the innumerable wireless transmitting stations. Here at last was the physical basis of the terrestrial intelligence! But what a lowly creature! What a caricature of life! Obviously in respect of complexity and delicacy of organization these wretched immobile systems of glass, metal, and vegetable compounds were not to be compared with the Martian cloud. Their only feat seemed to be that they had managed to get control of the unconscious bipeds who tended them.

In the course of their explorations the Martians also discovered

a few more diamonds. The second human species had outgrown
the barbaric lust for jewellery; but they recognized the beauty of
gems and precious metals, and used them as badges of office.
Unfortunately, the Martians, in sacking a town, came upon a
woman who was wearing a large diamond between her breasts;
for she was mayor of the town, and in charge of the evacuation.
That the sacred stone should be used thus, apparently for the mere
identification of cattle, shocked the invaders even more than the
discovery of fragments of diamonds in certain cutting-instru-
ments. The war now began to be waged with all the heroism and
brutality of a crusade. Long after a rich booty of water and
vegetable matter had been secured, long after the Terrestrials had
developed an effective means of attack, and were slaughtering the
Martian clouds with high-tension electricity in the form of artificial lightning flashes, the misguided fanatics stayed on to rescue
the diamonds and carry them away to the mountain tops, where,
years afterwards, climbers discovered them, arranged along the
rock-edges in glittering files, like sea-bird's eggs. Thither the
dying remnant of the Martian host had transported them with its
last strength, scorning to save itself before the diamonds were
borne into the pure mountain air, to be lodged with dignity.
When the Second Men learned of this great hoard of diamonds,
they began to be seriously persuaded that they had been dealing,
not with a freak of physical nature, nor yet (as some said) with
swarms of bacteria, but with organisms of a higher order. For how
could the jewels have been singled out, freed from their metallic
settings, and so carefully regimented on the rocks, save by conscious purpose? The murderous clouds must have had at least the
pilfering mentality of jackdaws, since evidently they had been
fascinated by the treasure. But the very action which revealed
their consciousness suggested also that they were no more intelligent than the merely instinctive animals. There was no opportunity
of correcting this error, since all the clouds had been destroyed.

The struggle had lasted only a few months. Its material effects
on Man were serious but not insurmountable. Its immediate
psychological effect was invigorating. The Second Men had long
been accustomed to a security and prosperity that were almost
utopian. Suddenly they were overwhelmed by a calamity which

was quite unintelligible in terms of their own systematic knowledge. Their predecessors, in such a situation, would have behaved with their own characteristic vacillation between the human and the subhuman. They would have contracted a fever of romantic loyalty, and have performed many random acts of secretly self-regarding self-sacrifice. They would have sought profit out of the public disaster, and howled at all who were more fortunate than themselves. They would have cursed their gods, and looked for more useful ones. But also, in an incoherent manner, they would sometimes have behaved reasonably, and would even have risen now and again to the standards of the Second Men. Wholly unused to large-scale human bloodshed, these more developed beings suffered an agony of pity for their mangled fellows. But they said nothing about their pity, and scarcely noticed their own generous grief; for they were busy with the work of rescue. Suddenly confronted with the need of extreme loyalty and courage, they exulted in complying, and experienced that added keenness of spirit which comes when danger is well faced. But it did not occur to them that they were bearing themselves heroically; for they thought they were merely behaving reasonably, showing common sense. And if any one failed in a tight place, they did not call him coward, but gave him a drug to clear his head; or, if that failed, they put him under a doctor. No doubt, among the First Men such a policy would not have been justified, for these bewildered beings had not the clear and commanding vision which kept all sane members of the second species constant in loyalty.

The immediate psychological effect of the disaster was that it afforded this very noble race healthful exercise for its great reserves of loyalty and heroism. Quite apart from this immediate invigoration, however, the first agony, and those many others which were to follow, influenced the Second Men for good and ill in a train of effects which may be called spiritual. They had long known very well that the universe was one in which there could be not only private but also great public tragedies; and their philosophy did not seek to conceal this fact. Private tragedy they were able to face with a bland fortitude, and even an ecstasy of acceptance, such as the earlier species had but rarely attained.

Public tragedy, even world-tragedy, they declared should be faced in the same spirit. But to know world-tragedy in the abstract, is very different from the direct acquaintance with it. And now the Second Men, even while they held their attention earnestly fixed upon the practical work of defence, were determined to absorb this tragedy into the very depths of their being, to scrutinize it fearlessly, savour it, digest it, so that its fierce potency should henceforth be added to them. Therefore they did not curse their gods, nor supplicate them. They said to themselves, 'Thus, and and thus, and thus, is the world. Seeing the depth we shall see also the height; and we shall praise both.'

But their schooling was yet scarcely begun. The Martian invaders were all dead, but their subvital units were dispersed over the planet as a virulent ultra-microscopic dust. For, though as members of the living cloud they could enter the human body without doing permanent harm, now that they were freed from their functions within the higher organic system, they became a predatory virus. Breathed into man's lungs, they soon adapted themselves to the new environment, and threw his tissues into disorder. Each cell that they entered overthrew its own constitution, like a state which the enemy has successfully infected with lethal propaganda through a mere handful of agents. Thus, though man was temporarily victor over the Martian superindividual, his own vital units were poisoned and destroyed by the subvital remains of his dead enemy. A race whose physique had been as utopian as its body politic, was reduced to timid invalidity. And it was left in possession of a devastated planet. The loss of water proved negligible; but the destruction of vegetation in all the war areas produced for a while a world famine such as the Second Men had never known. And the material fabric of civilization had been so broken that many decades would have to be spent in rebuilding it.

But the physical damage proved far less serious than the physiological. Earnest research discovered, indeed, a means of checking the infection; and, after a few years of rigorous purging the atmosphere and man's flesh were clean once more. But the generations that had been stricken never recovered; their tissues had been too seriously corroded. Little by little, of course, there arose a fresh population of undamaged men and women. But it was a small population; for the fertility of the stricken had been much reduced. Thus the earth was now occupied by a small number of healthy persons below middle age and a very large number of ageing invalids. For many years these cripples had contrived to carry on the work of the world in spite of their frailty, but gradually they began to fail both in endurance and competence. For they were rapidly losing their grip on life, and sinking into a long-drawn-out senility, from which the Second Men had never before suffered; and at the same time the young, forced to take up work for which they were not equipped, committed all manner of blunders and crudities of which their elders would never have been guilty. But such was the general standard of mentality in the second human species, that what might have been an occasion for recrimination produced an unparalleled example of human loyalty at its best. The stricken generations decided almost unanimously that whenever an individual was declared by his generation to have outlived his competence, he should commit suicide. The younger generations, partly through affection, partly through dread of their own incompetence, were at first earnestly opposed to this policy. 'Our elders', one young man said, 'may have declined in vigour, but they are still beloved, and still wise. We dare not carry on without them.' But the elders maintained their point. Many members of the rising generation were no longer juveniles. And, if the body politic was to survive the economic crisis, it must now ruthlessly cut out all its damaged tissues. Accordingly the decision was carried out. One by one, as occasion demanded, the stricken 'chose the peace of annihilation,' leaving a scanty, inexperienced, but vigorous, population to rebuild what had been destroyed.

Four centuries passed, and then again the Martian clouds appeared in the sky. Once more devastation and slaughter. Once more a complete failure of the two mentalities to conceive one another. Once more the Martians were destroyed. Once more the pulmonary plague, the slow purging, a crippled population, and generous suicide.

Again, and again they appeared, at irregular intervals for fifty thousand years. On each occasion the Martians came irresistibly

175

fortified against whatever weapon humanity had last used against them. And so, by degrees, men began to recognize that the enemy was no merely instinctive brute, but intelligent. They there-fore made attempts to get in touch with these alien minds, and make overtures for a peaceful settlement. But since obviously the negotiations had to be performed by human beings, and since the Martians always regarded human beings as the mere cattle of the terrestrial intelligence, the envoys were always either ignored or destroyed.

During each invasion the Martians contrived to dispatch a considerable bulk of water to Mars. And every time, not satisfied with this material gain, they stayed too long crusading, until man had found a weapon to circumvent their new defences; and then they were routed. After each invasion man's recovery was slower and less complete, while Mars, in spite of the loss of a large proportion of its population, was in the long run invigorated with the extra water.

2. THE RUIN OF TWO WORLDS

Rather more than fifty thousand years after their first appearance, the Martians secured a permanent footing on the Antarctic table-land and over-ran Australasia and South Africa. For many centuries they remained in possession of a large part of the earth's surface, practising a kind of agriculture, studying terrestrial con-ditions, and spending much energy on the 'liberation' of diamonds.

During the considerable period before their settlement their mentality had scarcely changed; but actual habitation of the earth now began to undermine their self-complacency and their unity. It was borne in upon certain exploring Martians that the terrestrial bipeds, though insensitive to radiation, were actually the intelli-gences of the planet. At first this fact was studiously shunned, but little by little it gripped the attention of all terrestrial Martians. At the same time they began to realize that the whole work of research into terrestrial conditions, and even the social construc-tion of their colony, depended, not on the public mind, but on private individuals, acting in their private capacity. The colonial super-individual inspired only the diamond crusade, and the attempt to extirpate the terrestrial intelligence, or radiation. These various novel acts of insight woke the Martian colonists from an age-long dream. They saw that their revered super-individual was scarcely more than the least common measure of themselves, a bundle of atavistic fantasies and cravings, knit into one mind and gifted with a certain practical cunning. A rapid and bewildering spiritual renascence now came over the whole Martian colony. The central doctrine of it was that what was valuable in the Martian species was not radiation but mentality. These two utterly different things had been confused, and even identified, since the dawn of Martian civilization. At last they were clearly distinguished. A fumbling but sincere study of mind now began; and distinction was even made between the humbler and loftier mental activities.

There is no telling whither this renascence might have led, had it run its course. Possibly in time the Martians might have recognized worth even in minds other than Martian minds. But such a leap was at first far beyond them. Though they now understood that human animals were conscious and intelligent, they regarded them with no sympathy, rather indeed, with increased hostility. They still rendered allegiance to the Martian race, or brotherhood, just because it was in a sense one flesh, and, indeed, one mind. For they were concerned not to abolish but to recreate the public mind of the colony, and even that of Mars itself.

But the colonial public mind still largely dominated them in their more somnolent periods, and actually sent some of those who, in their private phases, were revolutionaries across to Mars for help against the revolutionary movement. The home planet was quite untouched by the new ideas. Its citizens cooperated whole-heartedly in an attempt to bring the colonists to their senses. But in vain. The colonial public mind itself changed its character as the centuries passed, until it became seriously alienated from Martian orthodoxy. Presently, indeed, it began to undergo a very strange and thorough metamorphosis, from which, conceivably, it might have emerged as the noblest inhabitant of the solar system. Little by little it fell into a kind of hypnotic trance. That is to say, it ceased to possess the attention of its private members, yet remained as a unity of their subconscious, or unnoticed mentality. Radiational unity of the colony was maintained, but only in this subconscious manner; and it was at that depth that the great metamorphosis began to take place under the fertilizing influence of the new ideas; which, so to speak, were generated in the tempest of the fully conscious mental revolution, and kept on spreading down into the oceanic depth of the sub-consciousness. Such a condition was likely to produce in time the emergence of a qualitatively new and finer mentality, and to waken at last into a fully conscious super-individual of higher order than its own members. But meanwhile this trance of the public consciousness incapacitated the colony for that prompt and co-ordinated action which had been the most successful faculty of Martian life. The public mind of the home planet easily destroyed its disorderly offspring, and set about re-colonizing the earth.

Several times during the next three hundred thousand years this process repeated itself. The changeless and terribly efficient super-individual of Mars extirpated its own offspring on the earth, before it could emerge from the chrysalis. And the tragedy might have been repeated indefinitely, but for certain changes that took place in humanity.

The first few centuries after the foundation of the Martian colony had been spent in ceaseless war. But at last, with terribly reduced resources, the Second Men had reconciled themselves to the fact that they must live in the same world with their mysterious enemy. Moreover, constant observation of the Martians began to restore somewhat man's shattered self-confidence. For during the fifty thousand years before the Martian colony was founded his opinion of himself had been undermined. He had formerly been used to regarding himself as the sun's ablest child. Then suddenly a stupendous new phenomenon had defeated his intelligence. Slowly he had learned that he was at grips with a determined and versatile rival, and that this rival hailed from a despised planet. Slowly he had been forced to suspect that he himself was outclassed, outshone, by a race whose very physique was incomprehensible to man. But after the Martians had established a permanent colony, human scientists began to discover the real physiological nature of the Martian organism, and were comforted to find that it did not make nonsense of human science. Man also learned that the Martians, though very able in certain spheres, were not really of a high mental type. These discoveries restored human self-confidence. Man settled down to make the best of the situation. Impassable barriers of high-power electric current were devised to keep the Martians out of human territory, and men began patiently to rebuild their ruined homes as best they could. At first there was little respite from the crusading zeal of the Martians, but in the second millennium this began to abate, and the two races left one another alone, save for occasional revivals of Martian fervour. Human civilization was at last reconstructed and consolidated, though upon a modest scale. Once more, though interrupted now and again by decades of agony, human beings lived in peace and relative prosperity. Life was somewhat harder than formerly, and the physique of the race was definitely less reliable than of old; but men and women still enjoyed conditions which most nations of the earlier species would have envied. The age of ceaseless personal sacrifice in service of the stricken community had ended at last. Once more a wonderful diversity of untrammelled personalities was put forth. Once more the minds of men and women were devoted without hindrance to the joy of skilled work, and all the subtleties of personal intercourse. Once more the passionate interest in one's fellows, which had for so long been hushed under the all-dominating public calamity, refreshed and enlarged the mind. Once more there was music, sweet, and backward-hearkening towards a golden past. Once more a wealth of literature, and of the visual arts. Once more intellectual exploration into the nature of the physical world and the potentiality of mind. And once more the religious experience, which had for so long been coarsened and obscured by all the violent distractions and inevitable self-deceptions of war, seemed to be refining itself under the influence of re-awakened culture.

In such circumstances the earlier and less sensitive human species might well have prospered indefinitely. Not so the Second Men. For their very refinement of sensibility made them incapable of shunning an ever-present conviction that in spite of all their prosperity they were undermined. Though superficially they seemed to be making a slow but heroic recovery they were at the same time suffering from a still slower and far more profound spiritual decline. Generation succeeded generation. Society became almost perfected, within its limited territory and its limitations of material wealth. The capacities of personality were developed with extreme subtlety and richness. At last the race proposed to itself once more its ancient project of re-making human nature upon a loftier plane. But somehow it had no longer the courage and self-respect for such work. And so, though there was much talk, nothing was done. Epoch succeeded epoch, and everything human remained apparently the same. Like a twig that has been broken but not broken off, man settled down to retain his life and culture, but could make no progress.

It is almost impossible to describe in a few words the subtle malady of the spirit that was undermining the Second Men. To say that they were suffering from an inferiority complex, would not be wholly false, but it would be a misleading vulgarization of the truth. To say that they had lost faith, both in themselves and in the universe, would be almost as inadequate. Crudely stated, their trouble was that, as a species, they had attempted a certain spiritual feat beyond the scope of their still-primitive nature. Spiritually they had over-reached themselves, broken every muscle (so to speak) and incapacitated themselves for any further effort. For they had determined to see their own racial tragedy as a thing of beauty, and they had failed. It was the obscure sense of this defeat that had poisoned them. For, being in many respects a very noble species, they could not simply turn their backs upon their failure and pursue the old way of life with the accustomed zest and thoroughness.

During the earliest Martian raids, the spiritual leaders of humanity had preached that the disaster must be an occasion for a supreme religious experience. While striving mightily to save their civilization, men must yet (so it was said) learn not merely to endure, but to admire, even the sternest issue. 'Thus and thus is the world. Seeing the depth, we shall see also the height, and praise both.' The whole population had accepted this advice. At first they had seemed to succeed. Many noble literary expressions were given forth, which seemed to define and elaborate, and even actually to create in men's hearts, this supreme experience. But as the centuries passed and the disasters were repeated, men began to fear that their forefathers had deceived themselves. Those remote generations had earnestly longed to feel the racial tragedy as a factor in the cosmic beauty; and at last they had persuaded themselves that this experience had actually befallen them. But their descendants were slowly coming to suspect that no such experience had ever occurred, that it would never occur to any man, and that there was in fact no such cosmic beauty to be experienced. The First Men would probably, in such a situation, have swung violently either into spiritual nihilism, or else into some comforting religious myth. At any rate, they were of too coarse-grained a nature to be ruined by a trouble so impalpable. Not so the Second Men. For they realized all too clearly that they were faced with the supreme crux of existence. And so, age after age the generations clung desperately to the hope that, if only they could endure a little longer, the light would break in on them. Even after the Martian colony had been three times established and destroyed by the orthodox race in Mars, the supreme preoccupation of the human species was with this religious crux. But afterwards, and very gradually, they lost heart. For it was borne in on them that either they themselves were by nature too obtuse to perceive this ultimate excellence of things (an excellence which they had strong reason to believe in intellectually, although they could not actually experience it), or the human race had utterly deceived itself, and the course of cosmic events after all was not significant, but a meaningless rigmarole.

It was this dilemma that poisoned them. Had they been still physically in their prime, they might have found fortitude to accept it, and proceed to the patient exfoliation of such very real excellences as they were still capable of creating. But they had lost the vitality which alone could perform such acts of spiritual abnegation. All the wealth of personality, all the intricacies of personal relationship, all the complex enterprise of a very great community, all art, all intellectual research, had lost their savour. It is remarkable that a purely religious disaster should have warped even the delight of lovers in one another's bodies, actually taken the flavour out of food, and drawn a veil between the sun-bather and the sun. But individuals of this species, unlike their predecessors, were so closely integrated, that none of their functions could remain healthy while the highest was disordered. Moreover, the general slight failure of physique, which was the legacy of age-long war, had resulted in a recurrence of those shattering brain disorders which had dogged the earliest races of their species. The very horror of the prospect of racial insanity increased their aberration from reasonableness. Little by little, shocking perversions of desire began to terrify them. Masochistic and sadistic orgies alternated with phases of extravagant and ghastly revelry. Acts of treason against the community, hitherto almost unknown, at last necessitated a strict police system. Local groups organized predatory raids against one another. Nations appeared, and all the phobias that make up nationalism.

The Martian colonists, when they observed man's disorganization, prepared, at the instigation of the home planet, a very great offensive. It so happened that at this time the colony was going through its phase of enlightenment, which had always hitherto been followed sooner or later by chastisement from Mars. Many individuals were at the moment actually toying with the idea of seeking harmony with man, rather than war. But the public mind of Mars, outraged by this treason, sought to overwhelm it by instituting a new crusade. Man's disunion offered a great opportunity.

The first attack produced a remarkable change in the human race. Their madness seemed suddenly to leave them. Within a few weeks the national governments had surrendered their sovereignty to a central authority. Disorders, debauchery, perversions, wholly ceased. The treachery and self-seeking and corruption, which had by now been customary for many centuries, suddenly gave place to universal and perfect devotion to the social cause. The species was apparently once more in its right mind. Everywhere, in spite of the war's horrors, there was gay brotherliness, combined with a heroism, which clothed itself in an odd extravagance of jocularity.

The war went ill for man. The general mood changed to cold resolution. And still victory was with the Martians. Under the influence of the huge fanatical armies which were poured in from the home planet, the colonists had shed their tentative pacifism, and sought to vindicate their loyalty by ruthlessness. In reply the human race deserted its sanity, and succumbed to an uncontrollable lust for destruction. It was at this stage that a human bacteriologist announced that he had bred a virus of peculiar deadliness and transmissibility, with which it would be possible to infect the enemy, but at the cost of annihilating also the human race. It is significant of the insane condition of the human population at this time that, when these facts were announced and broadcast, there was no discussion of the desirability of using this weapon. It was immediately put in action, the whole human race applauding.

Within a few months the Martian colony had vanished, their home planet itself had received the infection, and its population was already aware that nothing could save it. Man's constitution was tougher than that of the animate clouds, and he appeared to be doomed to a somewhat more lingering death. He made no effort to save himself, either from the disease which he himself had propagated, or from the pulmonary plague which was caused by the disintegrated substance of the dead Martian colony. All the public processes of civilization began to fall to pieces; for the community was paralysed by disillusion, and by the expectation of death. Like a bee-hive that has no queen, the whole population of the earth sank into apathy. Men and women stayed in their homes, idling, eating whatever food they could procure, sleeping far into the mornings, and, when at last they rose, listlessly avoiding one another. Only the children could still be gay, and even they were oppressed by their elders' gloom. Meanwhile the disease was spreading. Household after household was stricken, and was left unaided by its neighbours. But the pain in each individual's flesh was strangely numbed by his more poignant distress in the spiritual defeat of the race. For such was the high development of this species, that even physical agony could not distract it from the racial failure. No one wanted to save himself; and each knew that his neighbours desired not his aid. Only the children, when the disease crippled them, were plunged into agony and terror. Tenderly, yet listlessly, their elders would then give them the last sleep. Meanwhile the unburied dead spread corruption among the dying. Cities fell still and silent. The corn was not harvested.

3. THE THIRD DARK AGE

So contagious and so lethal was the new bacterium, that its authors expected the human race to be wiped out as completely as the Martian colony. Each dying remnant of humanity, isolated from its fellows by the breakdown of communications, imagined its own last moments to be the last of man. But by accident, almost one might say by miracle, a spark of human life was once more preserved, to hand on the sacred fire. A certain stock or strain of the race, promiscuously scattered throughout the continents, proved less susceptible than the majority. And, as the bacterium was less vigorous in a hot climate, a few of these favoured individuals, who happened to be in the tropical jungle, recovered from the infection. And of these few a minority recovered also from the pulmonary plague which, as usual, was propagated from the dead Martians.

It might have been expected that from this human germ a new civilized community would have soon arisen. With such brilliant beings as the Second Men, surely a few generations, or at the most a few thousand years, should have sufficed to make up the lost ground.

But no. Once more it was in a manner the very excellence of the species that prevented its recovery, and flung the spirit of Earth into a trance which lasted longer than the whole previous career of mammals. Again and again, some thirty million times, the seasons were repeated; and throughout this period man remained as fixed in bodily and mental character as, formerly, the platypus. Members of the earlier human species must find it difficult to understand this prolonged impotence of a race far more developed than themselves. For here apparently were both the requisites of progressive culture, namely a world rich and unpossessed, and a race exceptionally able. Yet nothing was done.

When the plagues, and all the immense consequent putrefactions, had worked themselves off, the few isolated groups of human survivors settled down to an increasingly indolent tropical life. The fruits of past learning were not imparted to the young, who therefore grew up in extreme ignorance of almost everything beyond their immediate experience. At the same time the elder generation cowed their juniors with vague suggestions of racial

defeat and universal futility. This would not have mattered, had
the young themselves been normal; they would have reacted with
fervent optimism. But they themselves were now by nature incapable of any enthusiasm. For, in a species in which the lower
functions were so strictly disciplined under the higher, the long-
drawn-out spiritual disaster had actually begun to take effect
upon the germ-plasm; so that individuals were doomed before
birth to lassitude, and to mentality in a minor key. The First Men,
long ago, had fallen into a kind of racial senility through a combination of vulgar errors and indulgences. But the second species,
like a boy whose mind has been too soon burdened with grave
experience, lived henceforth in a sleep-walk.

As the generations passed, all the lore of civilization was shed,
save the routine of tropical agriculture and hunting. Not that
intelligence itself had waned. Not that the race had sunk into
mere savagery. Lassitude did not prevent it from readjusting itself
to suit its new circumstances. These sleep-walkers soon invented
convenient ways of making, in the home and by hand, much that
had hitherto been made in factories and by mechanical power.
Almost without mental effort they designed and fashioned tolerable instruments out of wood and flint and bone. But though still
intelligent, they had become by disposition, supine, indifferent.
They would exert themselves only under the pressure of urgent
primitive need. No man seemed capable of putting forth the full
energy of a man. Even suffering had lost its poignancy. And no
ends seemed worth pursuing that could not be realized speedily.
The sting had gone out of experience. The soul was calloused
against every goad. Men and women worked and played, loved
and suffered; but always in a kind of rapt absent-mindedness. It
was as though they were ever trying to remember something
important which escaped them. The affairs of daily life seemed
too trivial to be taken seriously. Yet that other, and supremely
important thing, which alone deserved consideration, was so
obscure that no one had any idea what it was. Nor indeed was
anyone aware of this hypnotic subjection, any more than a
sleeper is aware of being asleep.

The minimum of necessary work was performed, and there
was even a certain dreamy zest in the performance, but nothing

which would entail extra toil ever seemed worth while. And so, when adjustment to the new circumstances of the world had been achieved, complete stagnation set in. Practical intelligence was easily able to cope with a slowly changing environment, and even with sudden natural upheavals such as floods, earthquakes, and disease epidemics. Man remained in a sense master of his world, but he had no idea what to do with his mastery. It was everywhere assumed that the sane end of living was to spend as many days as possible in indolence, lying in the shade. Unfortunately human beings had, of course, many needs which were irksome if not appeased, and so a good deal of hard work had to be done. Hunger and thirst had to be satisfied. Other individuals beside oneself had to be cared for, since man was cursed with sympathy and with a sentiment for the welfare of his group. The only fully rational behaviour, it was thought, would be general suicide, but irrational impulses made this impossible. Beatific drugs offered a temporary heaven. But, far as the Second Men had fallen, they were still too clear-sighted to forget that such beatitude is outweighed by subsequent misery.

Century by century, epoch by epoch, man glided on in this seemingly precarious, yet actually unshakable equilibrium. Nothing that happened to him could disturb his easy dominance over the beasts and over physical nature; nothing could shock him out of his racial sleep. Long-drawn-out climatic changes made desert, jungle, and grass-land fluctuate like the clouds. As the years advanced by millions, ordinary geological processes, greatly accentuated by the immense strains set up by the Patagonian upheaval, remodelled the surface of the planet. Continents were submerged, or lifted out of the sea, till presently there was little of the old configuration. And along with these geological changes went changes in the fauna and flora. The bacterium which had almost exterminated man had also wrought havoc amongst other mammals. Once more the planet had to be re-stocked, this time from the few surviving tropical species. Once more there was a great re-making of old types, only less revolutionary than that which had followed the Patagonian disaster. And since the human race remained minute, through the effects of its spiritual fatigue, other species were favoured. Especially the ruminants and the large carnivora increased and diversified themselves into many habits and forms.

But the most remarkable of all the biological trains of events in this period was the history of the Martian subvital units that had been disseminated by the slaughter of the Martian colony, and had then tormented men and animals with pulmonary diseases. As the ages passed, certain species of mammals so readjusted themselves that the Martian virus became not only harmless but necessary to their well-being. A relationship which was originally that of parasite and host became in time a true symbiosis, a co-operative partnership, in which the terrestrial animals gained something of the unique attributes of the vanished Martian organisms. The time was to come when Man himself should look with envy on these creatures, and finally make use of the Martian 'virus' for his own enrichment.

But meanwhile, and for many million years, almost all kinds of life were on the move, save Man. Like a ship-wrecked sailor, he lay exhausted and asleep on his raft, long after the storm had abated.

But his stagnation was not absolute. Imperceptibly, he was drifting on the oceanic currents of life, and in a direction far out of his original course. Little by little, his habit was becoming simpler, less artificial, more animal. Agriculture faded out, since it was no longer necessary in the luxuriant garden where man lived. Weapons of defence and of the chase became more precisely adapted to their restricted purposes, but at the same time less diversified and more stereotyped. Speech almost vanished; for there was no novelty left in experience. Familiar facts and familiar emotions were conveyed increasingly by gestures which were mostly unwitting. Physically, the species had changed little. Though the natural period of life was greatly reduced, this was due less to physiological change than to a strange and fatal increase of absent-mindedness in middle-age. The individual gradually ceased to react to his enviroment; so that even if he escaped a violent death, he died of starvation.

Yet in spite of this great change, the species remained essentially human. There was no bestialization, such as had formerly produced a race of submen. These tranced remnants of the second human species were not beasts but innocents, simples, children of nature, perfectly adjusted to their simple life. In many ways their state was idyllic and enviable. But such was their dimmed mentality that they were never clearly aware even of the blessings they had, still less, of course, of the loftier experiences which had kindled and tortured their ancestors.

X *The Third Men in the Wilderness*

1. THE THIRD HUMAN SPECIES

WE have now followed man's career during some forty million years. The whole period to be covered by this chronicle is about two thousand million. In this chapter, and the next, therefore, we must accomplish a swift flight at great altitude over a tract of time more than three times as long as that which we have hitherto observed. This great expanse is no desert, but a continent teeming with variegated life, and many successive and very diverse civilizations. The myriads of human beings who inhabit it far outnumber the First and Second Men combined. And the content of each one of these lives is a universe, rich and poignant as that of any reader of this book.

In spite of the great diversity of this span of man's history, it is a single movement within the whole symphony, just as the careers of the First and of the Second Men are each a single movement. Not only is it a period dominated by a single natural human species and the artificial human species into which the natural species at length transformed itself; but, also, in spite of innumerable digressions, a single theme, a single mood of the human will, informs the whole duration. For now at last man's main energy is devoted to remaking his own physical and mental nature. Throughout the rise and fall of many successive cultures this purpose is progressively clarifying itself, and expressing itself in many tragic and even devastating experiments; until, towards the close of this immense period, it seems almost to achieve its end.

When the Second Men had remained in their strange racial trance for about thirty million years, the obscure forces that make for advancement began to stir in them once more. This reawakening was favoured by geological accident. An incursion of the sea gradually isolated some of their number in an island continent, which was once part of the North Atlantic ocean-bed. The climate of this island gradually cooled from sub-tropical to temperate and

189

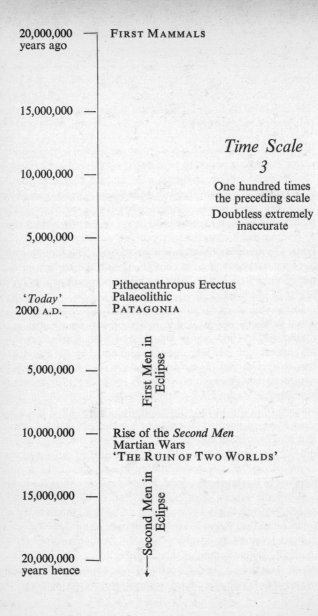

20,000,000 years ago	FIRST MAMMALS
15,000,000	
10,000,000	
5,000,000	
'Today' 2000 A.D.	Pithecanthropus Erectus Palaeolithic PATAGONIA
5,000,000	First Men in Eclipse
10,000,000	Rise of the Second Men Martian Wars 'THE RUIN OF TWO WORLDS'
15,000,000	Second Men in Eclipse
20,000,000 years hence	

Time Scale
3

One hundred times
the preceding scale

Doubtless extremely
inaccurate

sub-arctic. The vast change of conditions caused in the imprisoned race a subtle chemical re-arrangement of the germ-plasm, such that there ensued an epidemic of biological variation. Many new types appeared, but in the long run one, more vigorous and better adapted than the rest, crowded out all competitors and slowly consolidated itself as a new species, the Third Men.

Scarcely more than half the stature of their predecessors, these beings were proportionately slight and lithe. Their skin was of a sunny brown, covered with a luminous halo of red-gold hairs, which on the head became a russet mop. Their golden eyes, reminiscent of the snake, were more enigmatic than profound. Their faces were compact as cat's muzzles, their lips full, but subtle at the corners. Their ears, objects of personal pride and of sexual admiration, were extremely variable both in individuals and races. These surprising organs, which would have seemed merely ludicrous to the First Men, were expressive both of temperament and passing mood. They were immense, delicately involuted, of a silken texture, and very mobile. They gave an almost bat-like character to the otherwise somewhat feline heads. But the most distinctive feature of the Third Men was their great lean hands, on which were six versatile fingers, six antennae of living steel.

Unlike their predecessors, the Third Men were short-lived. They had a brief childhood and a brief maturity, followed (in the natural course) by a decade of senility, and death at about sixty. But such was their abhorrence of decrepitude, that they seldom allowed themselves to grow old. They preferred to kill themselves when their mental and physical agility began to decline. Thus, save in exceptional epochs of their history, very few lived to be fifty.

But though in some respects the third human species fell short of the high standard of its predecessor, especially in certain of the finer mental capacities, it was by no means simply degenerate. The admirable sensory equipment of the second species was retained, and even improved. Vision was no less ample and precise and colourful. Touch was far more discriminate, especially in the delicately pointed sixth finger-tip. Hearing was so developed that a man could run through wooded country blindfold without colliding with the trees. Moreover the great range of sounds and rhythms had acquired an extremely subtle gamut of emotional significance. Music was therefore one of the main preoccupations of the civilizations of this species.

Mentally the Third Men were indeed very unlike their predecessors. Their intelligence was in some ways no less agile; but it was more cunning than intellectual, more practical than theoretical. They were interested more in the world of sense-experience than in the world of abstract reason, and again far more in living things than in the lifeless. They excelled in certain kinds of art, and indeed also in some fields of science. But they were led into science more through practical, aesthetic, or religious needs than through intellectual curiosity. In mathematics, for instance (helped greatly by the duo-decimal system, which resulted from their having twelve fingers), they became wonderful calculators; yet they never had the curiosity to inquire into the essential nature of number. Nor, in physics, were they ever led to discover the more obscure properties of space. They were, indeed, strangely devoid of curiosity. Hence, though sometimes capable of a penetrating mystical intuition, they never seriously disciplined themselves under philosophy, nor tried to relate their mystical intuitions with the rest of their experience.

In their primitive phases the Third Men were keen hunters; but also, owing to their strong parental impulses, they were much addicted to making pets of captured animals. Throughout their career they displayed what earlier races would have called an uncanny sympathy with, and understanding of, all kinds of animals and plants. This intuitive insight into the nature of living things, and this untiring interest in the diversity of vital behaviour, constituted the dominating impulse throughout the whole career of the third human species. At the outset they excelled not only as hunters but as herdsmen and domesticators. By nature they were very apt in every kind of manipulation, but especially in the manipulation of living things. As a species they were also greatly addicted to play of all kinds, but especially to manipulative play, and above all to the playful manipulation of organisms. From the first they performed great feats of riding on the moose-like deer which they had domesticated. They tamed also a certain gregarious coursing beast. The pedigree of this great leonine wolf led, through the tropical survivors of the Martian plague, back to those descendants of the arctic fox which had over-run the world after the Patagonian disaster. This animal the Third Men trained not only to help them in shepherding and in the chase, but also to play intricate hunting games. Between this hound and its master or mistress there frequently arose a very special relation, a kind of psychical symbiosis, a dumb intuitive mutual insight, a genuine love, based on economic cooperation, but strongly toned also, in a manner peculiar to the third human species, with religious symbolism and frankly sexual intimacy.

As herdsmen and shepherds the Third Men very early practised selective breeding; and increasingly they became absorbed in the perfecting and enriching of all types of animals and plants. It was the boast of every local chieftain not only that the men of his tribe were more manly and the women more beautiful than all others, but also that the bears in his territory were the noblest and most bear-like of all bears, that the birds built more perfect nests and were more skilful fliers and singers than birds elsewhere. And so on, through all the animal and vegetable races.

This biological control was achieved at first by simple breeding experiments, but later and increasingly by crude physiological manipulation of the young animal, the foetus and (later, still) the germ-plasm. Hence arose a perennial conflict, which often caused wars of a truly religious bitterness, between the tender-hearted, who shrank from the infliction of pain, and the passionately manipulative, who willed to create at whatever cost. This conflict, indeed, was waged not only between individuals but within each mind; for all were innately hunters and manipulators, but also all had intuitive sympathy even with the quarry which they torment-ed. The trouble was increased by a strain of sheer cruelty which occurred even in the most tender-hearted. This sadism was at bottom an expression of an almost mystical reverence for sensory experience. Physical pain, being the most intense of all sensed qualities, was apt to be thought the most excellent. It might be expected that this would lead rather to self-torture than to cruelty. Sometimes it did. But in general those who could not appreciate pain in their own flesh were yet able to persuade themselves that in inflicting pain on lower animals they were creating vivid psychic

193

reality, and therefore high excellence. It was just the intense reality of pain, they said, that made it intolerable to men and animals. Seen with the detachment of the divine mind, it appeared in its true beauty. And even man, they declared, could appreciate its excellence when it occurred not in men but in animals.

Though the Third Men lacked interest in systematic thought, their minds were often concerned with matters outside the fields of private and social economy. They experienced not only aesthetic but mystical cravings. And though they were without any appreciation of those finer beauties of human personality, which their predecessors had admired as the highest attainment of life on the planet, the Third Men themselves, in their own way, sought to make the best of human nature, and indeed of animal nature. Man they regarded in two aspects. In the first place he was the noblest of all animals, gifted with unique aptitudes. He was, as was sometimes said, God's chief work of art. But secondly, since his special virtues were his insight into the nature of all living things and his manipulative capacity, he was himself God's eye and God's hand. These convictions were expressed over and over again in the religions of the Third Men by the image of the deity as a composite animal, with wings of the albatross, jaws of the great wolf-fox, feet of the deer, and so on. For the human element was represented in this deity by the hands, the eyes, and the sexual organs of man. And between the divine hands lay the world, with all its diverse population. Often the world was represented as being the fruit of God's primitive potency, but also as in process of being drastically altered and tortured into perfection by the hands.

Most of the cultures of the Third Men were dominated by this obscure worship of Life as an all-pervading spirit, expressing itself in myriad diverse individuals. And at the same time the intuitive loyalty to living things and to a vaguely conceived life-force was often complicated by sadism. For in the first place it was recognized, of course, that what is valued by higher beings may be intolerable to lower; and, as has been said, pain itself was thought to be a superior excellence of this kind. And again in a second manner sadism expressed itself. The worship of Life, as agent or subject, was complemented by worship of environment, as object to life's subjectivity, as that which remains ever foreign to life, thwarting its enterprises, torturing it, yet making it possible, and, by its very resistance, goading it into nobler expressions. Pain, it was said, was the most vivid apprehension of the sacred and universal Object.

The thought of the third human species was never systematic. But in some such manner as the foregoing it strove to rationalize its obscure intuition of the beauty which includes at once Life's victory and defeat.

2. DIGRESSIONS OF THE THIRD MEN

Such, in brief, was the physical and mental nature of the third human species. In spite of innumerable distractions, the spirit of the Third Men kept on returning to follow up the thread of biological interest through a thousand variegated cultures. Again and again folk after folk would clamber out of savagery and barbarism into relative enlightenment; and mostly, though not always, the main theme of this enlightenment was some special mood either of biological creativeness or of sadism, or of both. To a man born into such a society, no dominant characteristic would be apparent. He would be impressed rather by the many-sidedness of human activities in his time. He would note a wealth of personal intercourse, of social organization and industrial invention, of art and speculation, all set in that universal matrix, the private struggle to preserve or express the self. Yet the historian may often see in a society, over and above this multifarious proliferation, some one controlling theme.

Again and again, then, at intervals of a few thousand or a few hundred thousand years, man's whim was imposed upon the fauna and flora of the earth, and at length directed to the task of remaking man himself. Again and again, through a diversity of causes, the effort collapsed, and the species sank once more into chaos. Sometimes indeed there was an interlude of culture in some quite different key. Once, early in the history of the species, and before its nature had become fixed, there occurred a non-industrial civilization of a genuinely intellectual kind, almost like that of

Greece. Sometimes, but not often, the third human species fooled itself into an extravagantly industrial world civilization, in the manner of the Americanized First Men. In general its interest was too much concerned with other matters to become entangled with mechanical devices. But on three occasions at least it succumbed. Of these civilizations one derived its main power from wind and falling water, one from the tides, one from the earth's internal heat. The first, saved from the worst evils of industrialism by the limitations of its power, lasted some hundred thousand years in barren equilibrium, until it was destroyed by an obscure bacterium. The second was fortunately brief; but its fifty thousand years of unbridled waste of tidal energy was enough to interfere appreciably with the orbit of the moon. This world-order collapsed at length in a series of industrial wars. The third endured a quarter of a million years as a brilliantly sane and efficient world organization. Throughout most of its existence there was almost complete social harmony with scarcely as much internal strife as occurs in a bee-hive. But once more civilization came at length to grief, this time through the misguided effort to breed special human types for specialized industrial pursuits.

Industrialism, however, was never more than a digression, a lengthy and disastrous irrelevance in the life of this species. There were other digressions. There were for instance cultures, enduring sometimes for several thousand years, which were predominantly musical. This could never have occurred among the First Men; but, as was said, the third species was peculiarly developed in hearing, and in emotional sensitivity to sound and rhythm. Consequently, just as the First Men at their height were led into the wilderness by an irrational obsession with mechanical contrivances, just as the Third Men themselves were many times undone by their own interest in biological control, so, now and again, it was their musical gift that hypnotized them.

Of these predominantly musical cultures the most remarkable was one in which music and religion combined to form a tyranny no less rigid than that of religion and science in the remote past. It is worth while to dwell on one of these episodes for a few moments.

The Third Men were very subject to a craving for personal immortality. Their lives were brief, their love of life intense. It seemed to them a tragic flaw in the nature of existence that the melody of the individual life must either fade into a dreary senility or be cut short, never to be repeated. Now, music had a special significance for this race. So intense was their experience of it, that they were ready to regard it as in some manner the underlying reality of all things. In leisure hours, snatched from a toilful and often tragic life, groups of peasants would seek to conjure about them by song or pipe or viol a universe more beautiful, more real, than that of daily labour. Concentrating their sensitive hearing upon the inexhaustible diversity of tone and rhythm, they would seem to themselves to be possessed by the living presence of music, and to be transported thereby into a lovelier world. No wonder they believed that every melody was a spirit, leading a life of its own within the universe of music. No wonder they imagined that a symphony or chorus was itself a single spirit inhering in all its members. No wonder it seemed to them that when men and women listened to great music, the barriers of their individuality were broken down, so that they became one soul through communion with the music.

The prophet was born in a highland village where the native faith in music was intense, though quite unformulated. In time he learnt to raise his peasant audiences to the most extravagant joy and the most delicious sorrow. Then at last he began to think, and to expound his thoughts with the authority of a great bard. Easily he persuaded men that music was the reality, and all else illusion, that the living spirit of the universe was pure music, and that each individual animal and man, though he had a body that must die and vanish for ever, had also a soul that was music and eternal. A melody, he said, is the most fleeting of things. It happens and ceases. The great silence devours it, and seemingly annihilates it. Passage is essential to its being. Yet though for a melody, to halt is to die a violent death, all music, the prophet affirmed, has also eternal life. After silence it may occur again, with all its freshness and aliveness. Time cannot age it; for its home is in a country outside time. And that country, thus the young musician earnestly preached, is also the home land of every man and woman, nay of every living thing that has any gift of music. Those who seek immortality, must strive to waken their tranced souls into melody

197

and harmony. And according to their degree of musical originality and proficiency will be their standing in the eternal life.

The doctrine, and the impassioned melodies of the prophet, spread like fire. Instrumental and vocal music sounded from every pasture and corn plot. The government tried to suppress it, partly because it was thought to interfere with agricultural productivity, largely because its passionate significance reverberated even in the hearts of courtly ladies, and threatened to undo the refinement of centuries. Nay, the social order itself began to crumble. For many began openly to declare that what mattered was not aristocratic birth, nor even proficiency in the time-honoured musical forms (so much prized by the leisured), but the gift of spontaneous emotional expression in rhythm and harmony. Persecution strengthened the new faith with a glorious company of martyrs who, it was affirmed, sang triumphantly even in the flames.

One day the sacred monarch himself, hitherto a prisoner within the conventions, declared half sincerely, half by policy, that he was converted to his people's faith. Bureaucracy gave place to an enlightened dictatorship, the monarch assumed the title of Supreme Melody, and the whole social order was refashioned, more to the taste of the peasants. The subtle prince, backed by the crusading zeal of his people, and favoured by the rapid spontaneous spread of the faith in all lands, conquered the whole world, and founded the universal Church of Harmony. The prophet himself, meanwhile, dismayed by his own too facile success, had retired into the mountains to perfect his art under the influence of their great quiet, or the music of wind, thunder, and waterfall. Presently, however, the silence of the fells was shattered by the blare of military bands and ecclesiastical choirs, which the emperor had sent to salute him and conduct him to the metropolis. He was secured, though not without a scrimmage, and lodged in the High Temple of Music. There he was kept a prisoner, dubbed God's Big Noise, and used by the world-government as an oracle needing interpretation. In a few years the official music of the temple, and of deputations from all over the world, drove him into raving madness; in which state he was the more useful to the authorities.

Thus was founded the Holy Empire of Music, which gave order and purpose to the species for a thousand years. The sayings of the prophet, interpreted by a series of able rulers, became the foundation of a great system of law which gradually supplanted all local codes by virtue of its divine authority. Its root was madness; but its final expression was intricate common sense, decorated with harmless and precious flowers of folly. Throughout, the individual was wisely, but tacitly, regarded as a biological organism having definite needs or rights and definite social obligations; but the language in which this principle was expressed and elaborated was a jargon based on the fiction that every human being was a melody, demanding completion within a greater musical theme of society.

Toward the close of this millennium of order a schism occurred among the devout. A new and fervent sect declared that the true spirit of the musical religion had been stifled by ecclesiasticism. The founder of the religion had preached salvation by individual musical experience, by an intensely emotional communion with the Divine Music. But little by little, so it was said, the church had lost sight of this central truth, and had substituted a barren interest in the objective forms and principles of melody and counterpoint. Salvation, in the official view, was not to be had by subjective experience, but by keeping the rules of an obscure musical technique. And what was this technique? Instead of making the social order a practical expression of the divine law of music, churchmen and statesmen had misinterpreted these divine laws to suit mere social convenience, until the true spirit of music had been lost. Meanwhile on the other side a counter-revival took place. The self-centred and soul-saving mood of the rebels was ridiculed. Men were urged to care rather for the divine and exquisitely ordered forms of music itself than for their own emotion.

It was amongst the rebel peoples that the biological interest of the race, hitherto subordinate, came into its own. Mating, at least among the more devout sort of women, began to be influenced by the desire to have children who should be of outstanding musical brilliance and sensitivity. Biological sciences were rudimentary, but the general principle of selective breeding was known. Within a century this policy of breeding for music, or breeding 'soul', developed from a private idiosyncrasy into a racial obsession. It was so far successful that after a while a new type became common, and thrived upon the approbation and devotion of ordinary persons. These new beings were indeed extravagantly sensitive to music, so much so that the song of a skylark caused them serious torture by its banality, and in response to any human music of the kind which they approved, they invariably fell into a trance. Under the stimulus of music which was not to their taste they were apt to run amok and murder the performers.

We need not pause to trace the stages by which an infatuated race gradually submitted itself to the whims of these creatures of human folly, until for a brief period they became the tyrannical ruling caste of a musical theocracy. Nor need we observe how they reduced society to chaos; and how at length an age of confusion and murder brought mankind once more to its senses, but also into so bitter a disillusionment that the effort to re-orientate the whole direction of its endeavour lacked determination. Civilization fell to pieces and was not rebuilt till after the race had lain fallow for some thousands of years.

So ended perhaps the most pathetic of racial delusions. Born of a genuine and potent aesthetic experience, it retained a certain crazy nobility even to the end.

Many scores of other cultures occurred, separated often by long ages of barbarism, but they must be ignored in this brief chronicle. The great majority of them were mainly biological in spirit. Thus one was dominated by an obsessive interest in flight, and therefore in birds, another by the concept of metabolism, several by sexual creativity, and very many by some general but mostly unenlightened policy of eugenics. All these we must pass over, so that we may descend to watch the greatest of all the races of the third species torture itself into a new form.

3. THE VITAL ART

It was after an unusually long period of eclipse that the spirit of the third human species attained its greatest brilliance. We need not watch the stages by which this enlightenment was reached. Suffice it that the upshot was a very remarkable civilization, if such a word can be applied to an order in which agglomerations of architecture were unknown, clothing was used only when needed for warmth, and such industrial development as occurred was wholly subordinated to other activities.

Early in the history of this culture the requirements of hunting and agriculture, and the spontaneous impulse to manipulate live things, gave rise to a primitive but serviceable system of biological knowledge. Not until the culture had unified the whole planet, did biology itself give rise to chemistry and physics. At the same time a well-controlled industrialism, based first on wind and water, and later on subterranean heat, afforded the race all the material luxuries it desired, and much leisure from the business of keeping itself in existence. Had there not already existed a more powerful and all-dominating interest, industrialism itself would probably have hypnotized the race, as it had so many others. But in this race the interest in live things, which characterized the whole species, was dominant before industrialism began. Egotism among the Third Men could not be satisfied by the exercise of economic power, nor by the mere ostentation of wealth. Not that the race was immune from egotism. On the contrary, it had lost almost all that spontaneous altruism which had distinguished the Second Men. But in most periods the only kind of personal ostentation which appealed to the Third Men was directly connected with the primitive interest in 'pecunia'. To own many and noble beasts, whether they were economically productive or not, was ever the mark of respectability. The vulgar, indeed, were content with mere numbers, or at most with the convential virtues of the recognized breeds. But the more refined pursued, and flaunted, certain very exact principles of aesthetic excellence in their control of living forms.

In fact, as the race gained biological insight, it developed a very remarkable new art, which we may call 'plastic vital art'. This was to become the chief vehicle of expression of the new culture. It was practised universally, and with religious fervour; for it was very closely connected with the belief in a life-god. The canons of this art, and the precepts of this religion, fluctuated from age to age, but in general certain basic principles were accepted. Or rather, though there was almost always universal agreement that the practice of vital art was the supreme goal, and should not be treated in a utilitarian spirit, there were two conflicting sets of principles which were favoured by opposed sects. One mode of vital art sought to evoke the full potentiality of each natural type as a harmonious and perfected nature, or to produce new types equally harmonious. The other prided itself on producing monsters. Sometimes a single capacity was developed at the expense of the harmony and welfare of the organism as a whole. Thus a bird was produced which could fly faster than any other bird; but it could neither reproduce nor even feed, and therefore had to be maintained artificially. Sometimes, on the other hand, certain characters incompatible in nature were forced upon a single organism, and maintained in precarious and torturing equilibrium. To give examples, one much-talked-of feat was the production of a carnivorous mammal in which the fore limbs had assumed the structure of a bird's wings, complete with feathers. This creature could not fly, since its body was wrongly proportioned. Its only mode of locomotion was a staggering run with outstretched wings. Other examples of monstrosity were an eagle with twin heads, and a deer in which, with incredible ingenuity, the artists had induced the tail to develop as a head, with brain, sense organs, and jaws. In this monstrous art, interest in living things was infected with sadism through the preoccupation with fate, especially internal fate, as the divinity that shapes our ends. In its more vulgar forms, of course, it was a crude expression of egotistical lust in power.

This *motif* of the monstrous and the self-discrepant was less prominent than the other, the *motif* of harmonious perfection; but at all times it was apt to exercise at least a sub-conscious influence. The supreme aim of the dominant, perfection-seeking movement was to embellish the planet with a very diverse fauna and flora, with the human race as at once the crown and the instrument of terrestrial life. Each species, and each variety, was to have its place and fulfil its part in the great cycle of living types. Each was to be internally perfected to its function. It must have no harmful relics of a past manner of life; and its capacities must be in true accord with one another. But, to repeat, the supreme aim was not concerned merely with individual types, but with the whole vital economy of the planet. Thus, though there were to be types of every order from the most humble bacterium up to man, it was contrary to the canon of orthodox sacred art that any type should thrive by the destruction of a type higher than itself. In the sadistic mode of the art, however, a peculiarly exquisite tragic beauty was said to inhere in situations in which a lowly type exterminated a higher. There were occasions in the history of the race when the two sects indulged in bloody conflict because the sadists kept devising parasites to undermine the noble products of the orthodox.

Of those who practised vital art, and all did so to some extent, a few, though they deliberately rejected the orthodox principles, gained notoriety and even fame by their grotesques; while others, less fortunate, were ready to accept ostracism and even martyrdom, declaring that what they had produced was a significant symbol of the universal tragedy of vital nature. The great majority, however, accepted the sacred canon. They had therefore to choose one or other of certain recognized modes of expression. For instance, they might seek to enhance some extant type of organism, both by perfecting its capacities and by eliminating from it all that was harmful or useless. Or else, a more original and precarious work, they might set about creating a new type to fill a niche in the world, which had not yet been occupied. For this end they would select a suitable organism, and seek to remake it upon a new plan, striving to produce a creature of perfectly harmonious nature precisely adapted to the new way of life. In this kind of work sundry strict aesthetic principles must be observed. Thus it was considered bad art to reduce a higher type to a lower, or in any manner to waste the capacities of a type. And further, since the true end of art was not the production of individual types, but the production of a worldwide and perfectly systematic fauna and flora, it was inadmissible to harm even accidentally any type higher than that which it was intended to produce. For the practice of orthodox vital art was regarded as a cooperative enterprise. The ultimate artist, under God, was mankind as a whole; the ultimate work of art must be an ever more subtle garment of living forms for the adornment of the planet, and the delight of the supreme Artist, in relation to whom man was both creature and instrument.

Little was achieved, of course, until the applied biological sciences had advanced far beyond the high-water mark attained long ago during the career of the Second Men. Much more was needed than the rule-of-thumb principles of earlier breeders. It took this brightest of all the races of the third species many thousands of years of research to discover the more delicate principles of heredity, and to devise a technique by which the actual hereditary factors in the germ could be manipulated. It was this increasing penetration of biology itself that opened up the deeper regions of chemistry and physics. And owing to this historical sequence the latter sciences were conceived in a biological manner, with the electron as the basic organism, and the cosmos as an organic whole.

Imagine, then, a planet organized almost as a vast system of botanical and zoological gardens, or wild parks, interspersed with agriculture and industry. In every great centre of communications occurred annual and monthly shows. The latest creations were put through their paces, judged by the high priests of vital art, awarded distinctions, and consecrated with religious ceremony. At these shows some of the exhibits would be utilitarian, others purely aesthetic. There might be improved grains, vegetables, cattle, some exceptionally intelligent or sturdy variety of herdsman's dog, or a new micro-organism with some special function in agriculture or in human digestion. But also there would be the latest achievements in pure vital art. Great sleek-limbed, hornless, racing deer, birds or mammals adapted to some hitherto unfulfilled role, bears intended to outclass all existing varieties in the struggle for existence, ants with specialized organs and instincts, improvements in the relations of parasite and host, so as to make a true symbiosis in which the host profited by the parasite. And so on. And everywhere there would be the little unclad ruddy faunlike beings who had created these marvels. Shy forest-dwelling folk of Gurkha physique would stand beside their antelopes, vultures, or new great cat-like prowlers. A grave young woman might cause a stir by entering the grounds followed by several gigantic bears. Crowds would perhaps press round to examine the creatures' teeth or limbs, and she might scold the meddlers away from her patient flock. For the normal relation between man and beast at this time was one of perfect amity, rising, sometimes, in the case of domesticated animals, to an exquisite, almost painful, mutual adoration. Even the wild beasts never troubled to avoid man, still less to attack him, save in the special circumstances of the hunt and the sacred gladiatorial show.

These last need special notice. The powers of combat in beasts were admired no less than other powers. Men and women alike experienced a savage joy, almost an ecstasy, in the spectacle of mortal combat. Consequently there were formal occasions when different kinds of beasts were enraged against one another and allowed to fight to the death. Not only so, but also there were sacred contests between beast and man, between man and man, between woman and woman, and, most surprising to the readers of this book, between woman and man. For in this species, woman in her prime was not physically weaker than her partner.

4. CONFLICTING POLICIES

Almost from the first, vital art had been applied to some extent to man himself, though with hesitation. Certain great improvements had been effected, but only improvements about which there could be no two opinions. The many diseases and abnormalities left over from past civilizations were patiently abolished, and various more fundamental defects were remedied. For instance, teeth, digestion, glandular equipment, and the circulatory system were greatly improved. Extreme good health and considerable physical beauty became universal. Child-bearing was made a painless and health-giving process. Senility was postponed. The standard of practical intelligence was appreciably raised. These reforms were made possible by a vast concerted effort of research and experiment supported by the world-community. But private enterprise was also effective, for the relation between the sexes was much more consciously dominated by the thought of offspring than among the First Men. Every individual knew the characteristics of his or her hereditary composition, and knew what kinds of offspring were to be expected from intercourse of different hereditary types. Thus in courtship the young man was not content to persuade his beloved that his mind was destined by nature to afford her mind joyful completion; he sought also to persuade her that with his help she might bear children of a peculiar excellence. Consequently there was at all times going on a process of selective breeding towards the conventionally ideal type. In certain respects the ideal remained constant for many thousands of years. It included health, cat-like agility, manipulative dexterity, musical sensitivity, refined perception of rightness and wrongness in the sphere of vital art, and an intuitive practical judgement in all the affairs of life. Longevity, and the abolition of senility, were also sought, and partially attained. Waves of fashion sometimes directed sexual selection toward prowess in combat, or some special type of facial expression or vocal powers. But these fleeting whims were negligible. Only the permanently desired characters were actually intensified by private selective breeding.

But at length there came a time when more ambitious aims were entertained. The world-community was now a highly organized theocratic hierarchy, strictly but on the whole benevolently ruled by a supreme council of vital priests and biologists. Each individual, down to the humblest agricultural worker, had his special niche in society, allotted him by the supreme council or its delegates, according to his known heredity and the needs of society. This system, of course, sometimes led to abuse, but mostly it worked without serious friction. Such was the precision of biological knowledge that each person's mental calibre and special aptitudes were known beyond dispute, and rebellion against his lot in society would have been rebellion against his own heredity. This fact was universally known, and accepted without regret. A man had enough scope for emulation and triumph among his peers, without indulging in vague attempts to transcend his own nature, by rising into a superior hierarchical order. This state of affairs would have been impossible had there not been universal faith in the religion of life and the truth of biological science. Also it would have been impossible had not all normal persons been active practitioners of the sacred vital art, upon a plane suited to their capacity. Every individual adult of the rather scanty world-

population regarded himself or herself as a creative artist, in
however humble a sphere. And in general he, or she, was so
fascinated by the work, that he was well content to leave social
organization and control to those who were fitted for it. Moreover,
at the back of every mind was the conception of society itself as
an organism of specialized members. The strong sentiment for
organized humanity tended, in this race, to master even its strong
egotistical impulses, though not without a struggle.

It was such a society, almost unbelievable to the First Men, that
now set about remaking human nature. Unfortunately there were
conflicting views about the goal. The orthodox desired only to
continue the work that had for long been on foot; though they proposed greater enterprise and coordination. They would perfect
man's body, but upon its present plan; they would perfect his
mind, but without seeking to introduce anything new in essence.
His physique, percipience, memory, intelligence, and emotional
nature should be improved almost beyond recognition; but they
must, it was said, remain essentially what they had always
been.

A second party, however, finally persuaded orthodox opinion
to amplify itself in one important respect. As has already been
said, the Third Men were prone to phases of preoccupation with
the ancient craving for personal immortality. This craving had
often been strong among the First Men; and even the Second Men,
in spite of their great gift of detachment, had sometimes allowed
their admiration for human personality to persuade them that
souls must live for ever. The short-lived and untheoretical Third
Men, with their passion for living things of all kinds, and all the
diversity of vital behaviour, conceived immortality in a variety of
manners. In their final culture they imagined that at death all
living things whom the Life God approved passed into another
world, much like the familiar world, but happier. There they were
said to live in the presence of the deity, serving him in untrammelled vital creativeness of sundry kinds.

Now it was believed that communication might occur between
the two worlds, and that the highest type of terrestrial life was
that which communicated most effectively, and further that the
time had now arrived for much fuller revelation of the life to

come. It was therefore proposed to breed highly specialized communicants whose office should be to guide this world by means of advice from the other. As among the First Men, this communication with the unseen world was believed to take place in the mediumistic trance. The new enterprise, then, was to breed extremely sensitive mediums, and to increase the mediumistic powers of the average individual.

There was yet another party, whose aim was very different. Man, they said, is a very noble organism. We have dealt with other organisms so as to enhance in each its noblest attributes. It is time to do the same with man. What is most distinctive in man is intelligent manipulation, brain and hand. Now hand is really outclassed by modern mechanisms, but brain will never be outclassed. Therefore we must breed strictly for brain, for intelligent coordination of behaviour. All the organic functions which can be performed by machinery, must be relegated to machinery, so that the whole vitality of the organism may be devoted to brain-building and brain-working. We must produce an organism which shall be no mere bundle of relics left over from its primitive ancestors and precariously ruled by a glimmer of intelligence. We must produce a man who is nothing but man. When we have done this we can, if we like, ask him to find out the truth about immortality. And also, we can safely surrender to him the control of all human affairs.

The governing caste were strongly opposed to this policy. They declared that, if it succeeded, it would only produce a most inharmonious being whose nature would violate all the principles of vital aesthetics. Man, they said, was essentially an animal, though uniquely gifted. His whole nature must be developed, not one faculty at the expense of others. In arguing thus, they were probably influenced partly by the fear of losing their authority; but their arguments were cogent, and the majority of the community agreed with them. Nevertheless a small group of the governors themselves were determined to carry through the enterprise in secret.

There was no need of secrecy in breeding communicants. The world state encouraged this policy and even set up institutions for its pursuit.

XI *Man Remakes Himself*

1. THE FIRST OF THE GREAT BRAINS

THOSE who sought to produce a super-brain embarked upon a great enterprise of research and experiment in a remote corner of the planet. It is unnecessary to tell in detail how they fared. Working first in secret, they later strove to persuade the world to approve of their scheme, but only succeeded in dividing mankind into two parties. The body politic was torn asunder. There were religious wars. But after a few centuries of intermittent bloodshed the two sects, those who sought to produce communicants and those who sought the super-brain, settled down in different regions to pursue their respective aims unmolested. In time each developed into a kind of nation, united by a religious faith and crusading spirit. There was little cultural intercourse between the two.

Those who desired to produce the super-brain employed four methods, namely selective breeding, manipulation of the hereditary factors in germ cells (cultivated in the laboratory), manipulation of the fertilized ovum (cultivated also in the laboratory), and manipulation of the growing body. At first they produced innumerable tragic abortions. These we need not observe. But at length, several thousand years after the earliest experiments, something was produced which seemed to promise success. A human ovum had been carefully selected, fertilized in the laboratory, and largely reorganized by artificial means. By inhibiting the growth of the embryo's body, and the lower organs of the brain itself, and at the same time greatly stimulating the growth of the cerebral hemispheres, the dauntless experimenters succeeded at last in creating an organism which consisted of a brain twelve feet across, and a body most of which was reduced to a mere vestige upon the under-surface of the brain. The only parts of the body which were allowed to attain the natural size were the arms and hands. These sinewy organs of manipulation were induced to key themselves at the shoulders into the solid masonry which formed the creature's house. Thus they were able to get a purchase for their work. The hands were the normal six-fingered hands of the Third Men, very greatly enlarged and improved. The fantastic organism was generated and matured in a building designed to house both it and the complicated machinery which was necessary to keep it alive. A self-regulating pump, electrically driven, served it as a heart. A chemical factory poured the necessary materials into its blood and removed waste products, thus taking the place of digestive organs and the normal battery of glands. Its lungs consisted of a great room full of oxidizing tubes, through which a constant wind was driven by an electric fan. The same fan forced air through the artificial organs of speech. These organs were so constructed that the natural nerve-fibres, issuing from the speech centres of the brain, could stimulate appropriate electrical controls so as to produce sounds identical with those which they would have produced from a living throat and mouth. The sensory equipment of this trunkless brain was a blend of the natural and the artificial. The optic nerves were induced to grow out along two flexible proboscies, five feet long, each of which bore a huge eye at the end. But by a very ingenious alteration of the structure of the eye, the natural lens could be moved aside at will, so that the retina could be applied to any of a great diversity of optical instruments. The ears also could be projected upon stalks, and were so arranged that the actual nerve endings could be brought into contact with artificial resonators of various kinds, or could listen directly to the microscopic rhythms of the most minute organisms. Scent and taste were developed as a chemical sense, which could distinguish almost all compounds and elements by their flavour. Pressure, warmth, and cold were detected only by the fingers, but there with great subtlety. Sensory pain was to have been eliminated from the organism altogether; but this end was not achieved.

The creature was successfully launched upon life, and was actually kept alive for four years. But though at first all went well, in his second year the unfortunate child, if such he may be called, began to suffer severe pain, and to show symptoms of mental derangement. In spite of all that his devoted foster-parents could do, he gradually sank into insanity and died. He had succumbed to his own brain weight and to certain failures in the chemical regulation of his blood.

We may overlook the next four hundred years, during which sundry vain attempts were made to repeat the great experiment more successfully. Let us pass on to the first true individual of the fourth human species. He was produced in the same artificial manner as his forerunners, and was designed upon the same general plan. His mechanical and chemical machinery, however, was far more efficient; and his makers expected that, owing to careful adjustments of the mechanisms of growth and decay, he would prove to be immortal. His general plan, also, was changed in one important respect. His makers built a large circular 'brain turret' which they divided with many partitions, radiating from a central space, and covered everywhere with pigeon-holes. By a technique which took centuries to develop, they induced the cells of the growing embryonic brain to spread outwards, not as normal hemispheres of convolutions, but into the pigeon-holes which had been prepared for them. Thus the artificial 'cranium' had to be a roomy turret of ferro-concrete some forty feet in diameter. A door and a passage led from the outer world into the centre of the turret, and thence other passages radiated between tiers of little cupboards. Innumerable tubes of glass, metal, and a kind of vulcanite conveyed blood and chemicals over the whole system. Electric radiators preserved an even warmth in every cupboard, and throughout the innumerable carefully protected channels of the nerve fibres. Thermometers, dials, pressure gauges, indicators of all sorts, informed the attendants of every physical change in this strange half-natural, half-artificial system, this preposterous factory of mind.

Eight years after its inception the organism had filled its brain room, and attained the mentality of a new-born infant. His advance to maturity seemed to his foster-parents dishearteningly slow. Not till almost at the end of his fifth decade could he be said to have reached the mental standard of a bright adolescent. But there was no real reason for disappointment. Within another decade this pioneer of the Fourth Men had learned all that the Third Men could teach him, and had also seen that a great part of their

211

wisdom was folly. In manual dexterity he could already vie with the best; but though manipulation afforded him intense delight, he used his hands almost wholly in service of his tireless curiosity. In fact, it was evident that curiosity was his main characteristic. He was a huge bump of curiosity equipped with most cunning hands. A department of state had been created to look after his nurture and education. An army of learned persons was kept in readiness to answer his impatient questions and assist him in his own scientific experiments. Now that he had attained maturity these unfortunate pundits found themselves hopelessly outclassed, and reduced to mere clerks, bottle-washers, and errand-boys. Hundreds of his servants were for ever scurrying into every corner of the planet to seek information and specimens; and the significance of their errands was by now often quite beyond the range of their own intelligence. They were careful, however, not to let their ignorance appear to the public. On the contrary, they succeeded in gaining much prestige from the mere mysteriousness of their errands.

The great brain was wholly lacking in all normal instinctive responses, save curiosity and constructiveness. Instinctive fear he knew not, though of course he was capable of cold caution in any circumstances which threatened to damage him and hinder his passionate research. Anger he knew not, but only an adamantine firmness in the face of opposition. Normal hunger and thirst he knew not, but only an experience of faintness when his blood was not properly supplied with nutriment. Sex was wholly absent from his mentality. Instinctive tenderness and instinctive group-feeling were not possible to him, for he was without the bowels of mercy. The heroic devotion of his most intimate servants called forth no gratitude, but only cold approval.

At first he interested himself not at all in the affairs of the society which maintained him, served his every whim, and adored him. But in time he began to take pleasure in suggesting brilliant solutions of all the current problems of social organization. His advice was increasingly sought and accepted. He became autocrat of the state. His own intelligence and complete detachment combined with the people's superstitious reverence to establish him far more securely than any ordinary tyrant. He cared nothing for the petty troubles of his people, but he was determined to be served by a harmonious, healthy, and potent race. And as relaxation from the more serious excitement of research in physics and astronomy, the study of human nature was not without attractions. It may seem strange that one so completely devoid of human sympathy could have the tact to govern a race of the emotional Third Men. But he had built up for himself a very accurate behaviouristic psychology; and like the skilful master of animals, he knew unerringly how much could be expected of his people, even though their emotions were almost wholly foreign to him. Thus, for instance, while he thoroughly despised their admiration of animals and plants, and their religion of life, he soon learned not to seem hostile to these obsessions, but rather to use them for his own ends. He himself was interested in animals only as material for experiments. In this respect his people readily helped him, partly because he assured them that his goal was the further improvement of all types, partly because they were fascinated by his complete disregard, in his experimentation, of the common techniques for preventing pain. The orgy of vicarious suffering awakened in his people the long-suppressed lust in cruelty which, in spite of their intuitive insight into animal nature, was so strong a factor in the third human species.

Little by little the great brain probed the material universe and the universe of mentality. He mastered the principles of biological evolution, and constructed for his own delight a detailed history of life on earth. He learned, by marvellous archaeological technique, the story of all the earlier human peoples, and of the Martian episode, matters which had remained hidden from the Third Men. He discovered the principles of relativity and the quantum theory, the nature of the atom as a complex system of wave trains. He measured the cosmos; and with his delicate instruments he counted the planetary systems in much of the remote universe. He casually solved, to his own satisfaction at least, the ancient problems of good and evil, of mind and its object, of the one and the many, and of truth and error. He created many new departments of state for the purpose of recording his discoveries in an artificial language which he devised for the purpose. Each department consisted of many colleges of carefully

213

bred and educated specialists who could understand the subject of their own department to some extent. But the coordination of all, and true insight into each, lay with the great brain alone.

2. THE TRAGEDY OF THE FOURTH MEN

When some three thousand years had passed since his beginning, the unique individual determined to create others of his kind. Not that he suffered from loneliness. Not that he yearned for love, or even for intellectual companionship. But solely for the undertaking of more profound research, he needed the cooperation of beings of his own mental stature. He therefore designed, and had built in various regions of the planet, turrets and factories like his own, though greatly improved. Into each he sent, by his servants, a cell of his own vestigial body, and directed how it should be cultivated so as to produce a new individual. At the same time he caused far-reaching operations to be performed upon himself, so that he should be remade upon a more ample plan. Of the new capacities which he inculcated in himself and his progeny the most important was direct sensitivity to radiation. This was achieved by incorporating in each brain-tissue a specially bred strain of Martian parasites. These henceforth were to live in the great brain as integral members of each one of its cells. Each brain was also equipped with a powerful wireless transmitting apparatus. Thus should the widely scattered sessile population maintain direct 'telepathic' contact with one another.

The undertaking was successfully accomplished. Some ten thousand of these new individuals, each specialized for his particular locality and office, now constituted the Fourth Men. On the highest mountains were super-astronomers with vast observatories, whose instruments were partly artificial, partly natural excrescences of their own brains. In the very entrails of the planet others, specially adapted to heat, studied the subterranean forces, and were kept in 'telepathic' union with the astronomers. In the tropics, in the Arctic, in the forests, the deserts, and on the ocean floor, the Fourth Men indulged their immense curiosity; and in the homeland, around the father of the race, a group of great buildings housed a hundred individuals. In the service of this world-wide population, those races of Third Men which had originally cooperated to produce the new human species tilled the land, tended the cattle, manufactured the immense material requisites of the new civilization, and satisfied their spirits with an ever more stereotyped ritual of their vital art. This degradation of the whole race to a menial position had occurred slowly, imperceptibly. But the result was none the less irksome. Occasionally there were sparks of rebellion, but they always failed to kindle serious trouble; for the prestige and persuasiveness of the Fourth Men were irresistible.

At length, however, a crisis occurred. For some three thousand years the Fourth Men had pursued their research with constant success, but latterly progress had been slow. It was becoming increasingly difficult to devise new lines of research. True, there was still much detail to be filled in, even in their knowledge of their own planet, and very much in their knowledge of the stars. But there was no prospect of opening up entirely new fields which might throw some light on the essential nature of things. Indeed, it began to dawn on them that they had scarcely plumbed a surface ripple of the ocean of mystery. Their knowledge seemed to them perfectly systematic, yet wholly enigmatic. They had a growing sense that though in a manner they knew almost everything, they really knew nothing.

The normal mind, when it experiences intellectual frustration, can seek recreation in companionship, or physical exercise, or art. But for the Fourth Men there was no such escape. These activities were impossible and meaningless to them. The Great Brains were whole-heartedly interested in the objective world, but solely as a vast stimulus to intellection, never for its own sake. They admired only the intellective process itself and the interpretative formulae and principles which it devised. They cared no more for men and women than for material in a test-tube, no more for one another than for mechanical calculators. Nay, of each one of them it might almost be said that he cared ever for himself solely as an instrument of knowing. Many of the species had actually sacrificed their sanity, even in some cases their lives, to the obsessive lust of intellection.

As the sense of frustration became more and more oppressive, the Fourth Men suffered more and more from the onesidedness of their nature. Though so completely dispassionate while their intellectual life proceeded smoothly, now that it was thwarted they began to be confused by foolish whims and cravings which they disguised from themselves under a cloak of excuses. Sessile and incapable of affection, they continually witnessed the free movement, the group life, the love-making of their menials. Such activities became an offence to them, and filled them with a cold jealousy, which it was altogether beneath their dignity to notice. The affairs of the serf-population began to be conducted by their masters with less than the accustomed justice. Serious grievances arose.

The climax occurred in connexion with a great revival of research, which, it was said, would break down the impalpable barriers and set knowledge in progress again. The Great Brains were to be multiplied a thousand fold, and the resources of the whole planet were to be devoted far more strictly than before to the crusade of intellection. The menial Third Men would therefore have to put up with more work and less pleasure. Formerly they would willingly have accepted this fate for the glory of serving the superhuman brains. But the days of their blind devotion were past. It was murmured among them that the great experiment of their forefathers had proved a great disaster, and that the Fourth Men, the Great Brains, in spite of their devilish cunning, were mere abortions.

Matters came to a head when the tyrants announced that all useless animals must be slaughtered, since their upkeep was too great an economic burden upon the world-community. The vital art, moreover, was to be practised in future only by the Great Brains themselves. This announcement threw the Third Men into violent excitement, and divided them into two parties. Many of those whose lives were spent in direct service of the Great Brains favoured implicit obedience, though even these were deeply distressed. The majority, on the other hand, absolutely refused to permit the impious slaughter, or even to surrender their privileges as vital artists. For, they said, to kill off the fauna of the planet would be to violate the fair form of the universe by blotting out many of its most beautiful features. It would be an outrage to the Life God, and he would surely avenge it. They therefore urged that the time was come for all true human beings to stand together and depose the tyrants. And this, they pointed out, could easily be done. It was only necessary to cut a few electric cables, connecting the Great Brains with the subterranean generating stations. The electric pumps would then cease to supply the brain-turrets with aerated blood. Or, in the few cases in which the Great Brains were so located that they could control their own source of power in wind or water, it was necessary merely to refrain from transporting food to their digestion laboratories.

The personal attendants of the Great Brains shrank from such action; for their whole lives had been devoted, proudly and even in a manner lovingly, to service of the revered beings. But the agriculturists determined to withhold supplies. The Great Brains, therefore, armed their servitors with a diversity of ingenious weapons. Immense destruction was done; but since the rebels were decimated, there were not enough hands to work the fields. Some of the Great Brains, and many of their servants, actually died of starvation. And as hardship increased, the servants themselves began to drift over to the rebels. It now seemed certain to the Third Men that the Great Brains would very soon be impotent, and the plant once more under the control of natural beings. But the tyrants were not to be so easily defeated. Already for some centuries they had been secretly experimenting with a means of gaining a far more thorough dominion over the natural species. At the eleventh hour they succeeded.

In this undertaking they had been favoured by the results which a section of the natural species itself had produced long ago in the effort to breed specialized communicants to keep in touch with the unseen world. That sect, or theocratic nation, which had striven for many centuries toward this goal, had finally attained what they regarded as success. There came into existence an hereditary caste of communicants. Now, though these beings were subject to mediumistic trances in which they apparently conversed with denizens of the other world and received instructions about the ordering of matters terrestrial, they were in fact merely abnormally suggestible. Trained from childhood in the lore of the unseen world, their minds, during the trance, were amazingly fertile in developing fantasies based on that lore. Left to themselves, they were merely folk who were abnormally lacking in initiative and intelligence. Indeed, so naïve were they, and so sluggish, that they were mentally more like cattle than human beings. Yet under the influence of suggestion they became both intelligent and vigorous. Their intelligence, however, operating strictly in service of the suggestion, was wholly incapable of criticizing the suggestion itself.

There is no need to revert to the downfall of this theocratic society, beyond saying that, since both private and public affairs were regulated by reference to the sayings of the communicants, inevitably the state fell into chaos. The other community of the Third Men, that which was engaged upon breeding the Great Brains, gradually dominated the whole planet. The mediumistic stock, however, remained in existence, and was treated with a half-contemptuous reverence. The mediums were still generally regarded as in some manner specially gifted with the divine spirit, but they were now thought to be too holy for their sayings to have any relation to mundane affairs.

It was by means of this mediumistic stock that the Great Brains had intended to consolidate their position. Their earlier efforts may be passed over. But in the end they produced a race of living and even intelligent machines whose will they could control absolutely, even at a great distance. For the new variety of Third Men was 'telepathically' united with its masters. Martian units had been incorporated in its nervous system.

At the last moment the Great Brains were able to put into the field an army of these perfect slaves, which they equipped with the most efficient lethal weapons. The remnant of original servants discovered too late that they had been helping to produce their supplanters. They joined the rebels, only to share in the general destruction. In a few months all the Third Men, save the new docile variety, were destroyed; except for a few specimens which were preserved in cages for experimental purposes. And in a few years every type of animal that was not known to be directly or indirectly necessary to human life had been exterminated. None were preserved even as specimens, for the Great Brains had already studied them through and through.

But though the Great Brains were now absolute possessors of the Earth, they were after all no nearer their goal than before. The actual struggle with the natural species had provided them with an aim; but now that the struggle was over, they began to be obsessed once more with their intellectual failure. With painful clarity they realized that, in spite of their vast weight of neural tissue, in spite of their immense knowledge and cunning, they were practically no nearer the ultimate truth than their predecessors had been. Both were infinitely far from it.

For the Fourth Men, the Great Brains, there was no possible life but the life of intellect; and the life of intellect had become barren. Evidently something more than mere bulk of brain was needed for the solving of the deeper intellectual problems. They must, therefore, somehow create a new brain-quality, or organic formation of brain, capable of a mode of vision or insight impossible in their present state. They must learn somehow to remake their own brain-tissues upon a new plan. With this aim, and partly through unwitting jealousy of the natural and more balanced species which had created them, they began to use their captive specimens of that species for a great new enterprise of research into the nature of human brain-tissue. It was hoped thus to find some hint of the direction in which the new evolutionary leap should take place. The unfortunate specimens were therefore submitted to a thousand ingenious physiological and psychological tortures. Some were kept alive with their brains spread out permanently on a laboratory table, for microscopic observation during their diverse psychological reactions. Others were put into fantastic states of mental abnormality. Others were maintained in perfect health of body and mind, only to be felled at last by some ingeniously contrived tragic experience. New types were produced which, it was hoped, might show evidence of emergence into a qualitatively higher mode of mentality; but in fact they succeeded only in ranging through the whole gamut of insanity.

The research continued for some thousands of years, but gradually slackened, so utterly barren did it prove to be. As this frustration became more and more evident, a change began to come over the minds of the Fourth Men.

They knew, of course, that the natural species valued many things and activities which they themselves did not appreciate at all. Hitherto this had seemed a symptom merely of the low mental development of the natural species. But the behaviour of the unfortunate specimens upon whom they had been experimenting had gradually given the Fourth Men a greater insight into the likings and admirations of the natural species, so that they had learned to distinguish between those desires which were fundamental and those merely accidental cravings which clear thinking would have dismissed. In fact, they came to see that certain activities and certain objects were appreciated by these beings with the same clear-sighted conviction as they themselves appreciated knowledge. For instance, the natural human beings valued one another, and were sometimes capable of sacrificing themselves for the sake of others. They also valued love itself. And again they valued very seriously their artistic activities; and the activities of their bodies and of animal bodies appeared to them to have intrinsic excellence.

Little by little the Fourth Men began to realize that what was wrong with themselves was not merely their intellectual limitation, but, far more seriously, the limitation of their insight into values. And this weakness, they saw, was the result, not of paucity of intellective brain, but of paucity of body and lower brain tissues. This defect they could not remedy. It was obviously impossible to remake themselves so radically that they should become of a more normal type. Should they concentrate their efforts upon the production of new individuals more harmonious than themselves? Such a work, it might be supposed, would have seemed unattractive to them. But no. They argued thus. 'It is our nature to care most for knowing. Full knowledge is to be attained only by minds both more penetrating and more broadly based than ours. Let us, therefore, waste no more time in seeking to achieve the goal in ourselves. Let us seek rather to produce a kind of being, free from our limitations, in whom we may attain the goal of perfect knowledge vicariously. The producing of such a being will exercise all our powers, and will afford the highest

kind of fulfilment possible to us. To refrain from this work would
be irrational.'

Thus it came about that the artificial Fourth Men began to
work in a new spirit upon the surviving specimens of the Third
Men to produce their own supplanters.

3. THE FIFTH MEN

The plan of the proposed new human being was worked out in
great detail before any attempt was made to produce an actual
individual. Essentially he was to be a normal human organism,
with all the bodily functions of the natural type; but he was to be
perfected through and through. Care must be taken to give him
the greatest possible bulk of brain compatible with such a general
plan, but no more. Very carefully his creators calculated the
dimensions and internal proportions which their creature must
have. His brain could not be nearly as large as their own, since
he would have to carry it about with him, and maintain it with
his own physiological machinery. On the other hand, if it was to
be at all larger than the natural brain, the rest of the organism
must be proportionately sturdy. Like the Second Men, the new
species must be titanic. Indeed, it must be such as to dwarf even
those natural giants. The body, however, must not be so huge as
to be seriously hampered by its own weight, and by the necessity
of having bones so massive as to be unmanageable.

In working out the general proportions of the new man, his
makers took into account the possibility of devising more efficient
bone and muscle. After some centuries of patient experiment they
did actually invent a means of inducing in germ cells a tendency
toward far stronger bone-tissues and far more powerful muscle.
At the same time they devised nerve-tissues more highly specialized
for their particular functions. And in the new brain, so minute
compared with their own, smallness was to be compensated for
by efficiency of design, both in the individual cells and in their
organization.

Further, it was found possible to economize somewhat in bulk
and vital energy by improvements in the digestive system. Certain

new models of micro-organisms were produced, which, living symbiotically in the human gut, should render the whole process of digestion easier, more rapid, and less erratic.

Special attention was given to the system of self-repair in all tissues, especially in those which had hitherto been the earliest to wear out. And at the same time the mechanism regulating growth and general senescence was so designed that the new man should reach maturity at the age of two hundred years, and should remain in full vigour for at least three thousand years, when, with the first serious symptom of decay, his heart should suddenly cease functioning. There had been some dispute whether the new being should be endowed with perennial life, like his makers. But in the end it had been decided that, since he was intended only as a transitional type, it would be safer to allow him only a finite, though a prolonged lifetime. There must be no possibility that he should be tempted to regard himself as life's final expression.

In sensory equipment, the new man was to have all the advantages of the Second and Third Men, and, in addition a still wider range and finer discrimination in every sense organ. More important was the incorporation of Martian units in the new model of germ cell. As the organism developed, these should propagate themselves and congregate in the cells of the brain, so that every brain area might be sensitive to ethereal vibrations, and the whole might emit a strong system of radiation. But care was taken so that this 'telephathic' faculty of the new species should remain subordinate. There must be no danger that the individual should become a mere resonator of the herd.

Long drawn out chemical research enabled the Fourth Men to design also far-reaching improvements in the secretions of the new man, so that he should maintain both a perfect physiological equilibrium, and a well-balanced temperament. For they were determined that though he should experience all the range of emotional life, his passions should not run into disastrous excess; nor should he be prone to some one emotion in season and out of season. It was necessary also to revise in great detail the whole system of natural reflexes, abolishing some, modifying others, and again strengthening others. All the more complex, 'instinctive' responses, which had persisted in man since the days of Pithecanthropus Erectus, had also to be meticulously revised, both in respect of the form of the activity and the objects upon which they should be instinctively directed. Anger, fear, curiosity, humour, tenderness, egoism, sexual passion, and sociality must all be possible, but never uncontrollable. In fact, as with the Second Men, but more emphatically, the new type was to have an innate aptitude for, and inclination toward, all those higher activities and objects which, in the First Men, were only achieved after laborious discipline. Thus, while the design included self-regard, it also involved a disposition to prize the self chiefly as a social and intellectual being, rather than as a primeval savage. And while it included strong sociality, the group upon which instinctive interest was to be primarily directed was to be nothing less than the organized community of all minds. And again, while it included vigorous primitive sexuality and parenthood, it provided also those innate 'sublimations' which had occurred in the second species; for instance, the native aptitude for altruistic love of individual spirits of every kind, and for art and religion. Only by a miracle of pure intellectual skill could the cold-natured Great Brains, who were themselves doomed never to have actual experience of such activities, contrive, merely by study of the Third Men, to see their importance, and to design an organism splendidly capable of them. It was much as though a blind race, after studying physics, should invent organs of sight.

It was recognized, of course, that in a race in which the average life-span should be counted in thousands of years, procreation must be very rare. Yet it was also recognized that, for full development of mind, not only sexual intercourse but parenthood was necessary in both sexes. This difficulty was overcome partly by designing a very prolonged infancy and childhood; which, necessary in themselves for the proper mental and physical growth of these complicated organisms, provided also a longer exercise of parenthood for the mature. At the same time the actual process of childbirth was designed to be as easy as among the Third Men. And it was expected that with its greatly improved physiological organization the infant would not need that anxious and absorbing care which had so seriously hobbled most mothers among the earlier races.

The mere sketching out of these preliminary specifications of an improved human being involved many centuries of research and calculation which taxed even the ingenuity of the Great Brains. Then followed a lengthy period of tentative experiment in the actual production of such a type. For some thousands of years little was done but to show that many promising lines of attack were after all barren. And several times during this period the whole work was held up by disagreements among the Great Brains themselves as to the policy to be adopted. Once, indeed, they took to violence, one party attacking the other with chemicals, microbes, and armies of human automata.

In short it was only after many failures, and after many barren epochs during which, for a variety of reasons, the enterprise was neglected, that the Fourth Men did at length fashion two individuals almost precisely of the type they had originally designed. These were produced from a single fertilized ovum, in laboratory conditions. Identical twins, but of opposite sexes, they became the Adam and Eve of a new and glorious human species, the Fifth Men.

It may fittingly be said of the Fifth Men that they were the first to attain true human proportions of body and mind. On the average they were more than twice as tall as the First Men, and much taller than the Second Men. Their lower limbs had therefore to be extremely massive compared with the torso which they had to support. Thus, upon the ample pedestal of their feet, they stood like columns of masonry. Yet though their proportions were in a manner elephantine, there was a remarkable precision and even delicacy in the volumes that composed them. Their great arms and shoulders, dwarfed somewhat by their still mightier legs, were instruments not only of power but also of fine adjustment. Their hands also were fashioned both for power and for minute control; for, while the thumb and forefinger constituted a formidable vice, the delicate sixth finger had been induced to divide its tip into two Lilliputian fingers and a corresponding thumb. The contours of the limbs were sharply visible, for the body bore no hair, save for a close, thick skullcap which, in the original stock, was of ruddy brown. The well-marked eyebrows, when drawn down, shaded the sensitive eyes from the sun. Elsewhere there was no need of hair, for the brown skin had been so ingeniously contrived that it maintained an even temperature alike in tropical and sub-Arctic climates, with no aid either from hair or clothes. Compared with the great body, the head was not large, though the brain capacity was twice that of the Second Men. In the original pair of individuals the immense eyes were of a deep violet, the features strongly moulded and mobile. These facial characters had not been specially designed, for they seemed unimportant to the Fourth Men; but the play of biological forces resulted in a face not unlike that of the Second Men, though with an added and indescribable expression which no human face had hitherto attained.

How from this pair of individuals the new population gradually arose; how at first it was earnestly fostered by its creators; how it subsequently asserted its independence and took control of its own destiny; how the Great Brains failed piteously to understand and sympathize with the mentality of their creatures, and tried to tyrannize over them; how for a while the planet was divided into two mutually intolerant communities, and was at last drenched with man's blood, until the human automata were exterminated, the Great Brains starved or blown to pieces, and the Fifth Men themselves decimated; how, as a result of these events, a dense fog of barbarism settled once more upon the planet, so that the Fifth Men, like so many other races, had after all to start rebuilding civilization and culture from its very foundations; how all these things befell we must not in detail observe.

4. THE CULTURE OF THE FIFTH MEN

It is not possible to recount the stages by which the Fifth Men advanced toward their greatest civilization and culture; for it is that fully developed culture itself which concerns us. And even of their highest achievement, which persisted for so many millions of years, I can say but little, not merely because I must hasten to the end of my story, but also because so much of that achievement lies wholly beyond the comprehension of those for whom this book is intended. For I have at last reached that period in the history of man when he first began to reorganize his whole mentality to cope with matters whose very existence had been hitherto almost completely hidden from him. The old aims persist, and are progressively realized as never before; but also they become increasingly subordinate to the requirements of new aims which are more and more insistently forced upon him by his deepening experience. Just as the interests and ideals of the First Men lie beyond the grasp of their ape contemporaries, so the interests and ideals of the Fifth Men in their full development lie beyond the grasp of the First Men. On the other hand, just as, in the life of primitive man, there is much which would be meaningful even to the ape, so in the life of the Fifth Men much remains which is meaningful even to the First Men.

Conceive a world-society developed materially far beyond the wildest dreams of America. Unlimited power, derived partly from the artificial disintegration of atoms, partly from the actual annihilation of matter through the union of electrons and protons to form radiation, completely abolished the whole grotesque burden of drudgery which hitherto had seemed the inescapable price of civilization, nay of life itself. The vast economic routine of the world-community was carried on by the mere touching of appropriate buttons. Transport, mining, manufacture, and even agriculture, were performed in this manner. And indeed in most cases the systematic coordination of these activities was itself the work of self-regulating machinery. Thus, not only was there no longer need for any human beings to spend their lives in unskilled monotonous labour, but further, much that earlier races would have regarded as highly skilled though stereotyped work was now carried on by machinery. Only the pioneering of industry, the endless exhilarating research, invention, design, and re-organization, which is incurred by an ever-changing society, still engaged the minds of men and women. And though this work was of course immense, it could not occupy the whole attention of a great world-community. Thus very much of the energy of the race was free to occupy itself with other no less difficult and exacting matters, or to seek recreation in its many admirable sports and arts. Materially every individual was a multi-millionaire, in that he had at his beck and call a great diversity of powerful mechanisms; but also he was a penniless friar, for he had no vestige of economic control over any other human being. He could fly through the upper air to the ends of the earth in an hour, or hang idle among the clouds all day long. His flying machine was no cumbersome aeroplane, but either a wingless aerial boat, or a mere suit of overalls in which he could disport himself with the freedom of a bird. Not only in the air, but in the sea also, he was free. He could stroll about the ocean bed, or gambol with the deep sea fishes. And for habitation he could make his home, as he willed, either in a shack in the wilderness or in one of the great pylons which dwarfed the architecture even of the American age. He could possess this huge palace in loneliness and fill it with his possessions, to be automatically cared for without human service; or he could join with others and create a hive of social life. All these amenities he took for granted as the savage takes for granted the air which he breathes. And because they were as universally available as air, no one craved them in excess, and no one grudged another the use of them.

Yet the population of the earth was now very numerous. Some ten thousand million persons had their homes in the snow-capped pylons which covered the continents with an open forest of architecture. Between these great obelisks lay corn-land, park, and wilderness. For there were very many areas of hill-country and forest which were preserved as playgrounds. And indeed one whole continent, stretching from the Tropical to the Arctic, was kept as nearly as possible in its natural state. This region was chosen mainly for its mountains; for since most of the Alpine tracts had by now been worn into insignificance by water and frost, mountains were much prized. Into this Wild Continent individuals of all ages repaired to spend many years at a time in living the life of primitive man without any aid whatever for civilization. For it was recognized that a highly sophisticated race, devoted almost wholly to art and science, must take special measures to preserve its contact with the primitive. Thus in the Wild Continent was to be found at any time a sparse population of 'savages', armed with flint and bone, or more rarely with iron, which they or their friends had wrested from the earth. These voluntary primitives were intent chiefly upon hunting and simple agriculture. Their scanty leisure was devoted to art, and meditation, and to savouring fully all the primeval human values. Indeed it was a hard life and a dangerous one that these intellectuals periodically imposed on themselves. And though of course they had zest in it, they often dreaded its hardship and the uncertainty that they would ever return from it. For the danger was very real. The Fifth Men had compensated for the Fourth Men's foolish destruction of the animals by creating a whole system of new types, which they set at large in the Wild Continent; and some of these creatures were extremely formidable carnivora, which man himself, armed only with primitive weapons, had very good reason to fear. In the Wild Continent there was inevitably a high death-rate. Many promising lives were tragically cut short. But it was recognized that from the point of view of the race this sacrifice was worth while, for the spiritual effects of the institution of periodic savagery were very real. Beings whose natural span was three thousand years, given over almost wholly to civilized pursuits, were greatly invigorated and enlightened by an occasional decade in the wild.

The culture of the Fifth Men was influenced in many respects by their 'telepathic' communication with one another. The obvious advantages of this capacity were now secured without its dangers. Each individual could isolate himself at will from the radiation of his fellows, either wholly or in respect of particular elements of his mental process; and thus he was in no danger of losing his individuality. But, on the other hand, he was immeasurably more able to participate in the experience of others than were beings for whom the only possible communication was symbolic. The result was that, though conflict of wills was still possible, it was far more easily resolved by mutual understanding than had ever been the case in earlier species. Thus there were no lasting and no radical conflicts, either of thought or desire. It was universally recognized that every discrepancy of opinion and of aim could be abolished by telepathic discussion. Sometimes the process would be easy and rapid; sometimes it could not be achieved without a patient and detailed 'laying of mind to mind', so as to bring to light the point where the difference originated.

One result of the general 'telepathic' facility of the species was that speech was no longer necessary. It was still preserved and prized, but only as a medium of art, not as a means of communication. Thinking, of course, was still carried on largely by means of words; but in communication there was no more need actually to speak the words than in thinking in private. Written language remained essential for the recording and storing of thought. Both language and the written expression of it had become far more complex and accurate than they had ever been, more faithful instruments for the expression and creation of thought and emotion.

'Telepathy' combined with longevity and the extremely subtle brain-structure of the species to afford each individual an immense number of intimate friendships, and some slight acquaintance actually with the whole race. This, I fear, must seem incredible to my readers, unless they can be persuaded to regard it as a symptom of the high mental development of the species. However that may be, it is a fact that each person was aware of every other, at least as a face, or a name, or the holder of a certain office. It is impossible to exaggerate the effects of this facility of personal intercourse. It meant that the species constituted at any moment, if not strictly a community of friends, at least a vast club or college. Further, since each individual saw his own mind reflected, as it were, in very many other minds, and since there was great variety of psychological types, the upshot in each individual was a very accurate self-consciousness.

In the Martians, 'telepathic' intercourse had resulted in a true group-mind, a single psychical process embodied in the electromagnetic radiation of the whole race; but this group-mind was inferior in calibre to the individual minds. All that was distinctive of an individual at his best failed to contribute to the group-mind. But in the fifth human species 'telepathy' was only a means of intercourse between individuals; there was no true group-mind. On the other hand, telepathic intercourse occurred even on the highest planes of experience. It was by 'telepathic' intercourse in respect of art, science, philosophy, and the appreciation of personalities, that the public mind, or rather the public culture, of the Fifth Men had being. With the Martians, 'telepathic' union took place chiefly by elimination of the differences between individuals; with the Fifth Men 'telephathic' communication was, as it were, a kind of spiritual multiplication of mental diversity, by which each mind was enriched with the wealth of ten thousand million. Consequently each individual was, in a very real sense, the cultured mind of the species; but there were as many such minds as there were individuals. There was no additional racial mind over and above the minds of the individuals. Each individual himself was a conscious centre which participated in, and contributed to, the experience of all other centres.

This state of affairs would not have been possible had not the world-community been able to direct so much of its interest and energy into the higher mental activities. The whole structure of society was fashioned in relation to its best culture. It is almost impossible to give even an inkling of the nature and aims of this culture, and to make it believable that a huge population should have spent scores of millions of years not wholly, not even chiefly, on industrial advancement, but almost entirely on art, science, and philosophy, without ever repeating itself or falling into ennui I can only point out that, the higher a mind's development, the more it discovers in the universe to occupy it.

Needless to say, the Fifth Men had early mastered all those paradoxes of physical science which had so perplexed the First Men. Needless to say, they had a very complete knowledge of the geography of the cosmos and of the atom. But again and again the very foundations of their science were shattered by some new discovery, so that they had patiently to reconstruct the whole upon an entirely new plan. At length, however, with the clear formulation of the principles of psycho-physics, in which the older psychology and the older physics were held, so to speak, in chemical combination, they seemed to have built upon the rock. In this science, the fundamental concepts of psychology were given a physical meaning, and the fundamental concepts of physics were stated in a psychological manner. Further, the most fundamental relations of the physical universe were found to be of the same nature as the fundamental principles of art. But, and herein lay mystery and horror even for the Fifth Men, there was no shred of evidence that this aesthetically admirable cosmos was the work of a conscious artist, nor yet that any mind would ever develop so greatly as to be able to appreciate the Whole in all its detail and unity.

Since art seemed to the Fifth Men to be in some sense basic to the cosmos, they were naturally very much preoccupied with artistic creation. Consequently, all those who were not social or economic organizers, or scientific researchers, or pure philosophers, were by profession creative artists or handicraftsmen. That is to say, they were engaged on the production of material objects of various kinds, whose form should be aesthetically significant to the receiver. In some cases the material object was a pattern of spoken words, in others pure music, in others moving coloured shapes, in others a complex of steel cubes and bars, in others some translation of the human figure into a particular medium, and so on. But also the aesthetic impulse expressed itself in the production, by hand, of innumerable common utensils, indulging sometimes in lavish decoration, trusting at other times to the beauty of function. Every medium of art that had ever been employed was employed by the Fifth Men, and innumerable new vehicles were also used. They prized on the whole more highly those kinds of art which were not static, but involved time as well as space, for as a race they were peculiarly fascinated by time.

These innumerable artists held that they were doing something of great importance. The cosmos was to be regarded as an aesthetic unity in four dimensions, and of inconceivable complexity. Human works of pure art were thought of as instruments through which man might behold and admire some aspect of the cosmic beauty. They were said to focus together features of the cosmos too vast and elusive for man otherwise to apprehend their form. The work of art was sometimes likened to a compendious mathematical formula expressive of some immense and apparently chaotic field of facts. But in the case of art, it was said, the unity which the artistic object elicited was one in which factors of vital nature and of mind itself were essential members.

The race thus deemed itself to be engaged upon a great enterprise both of discovery and creation in which each individual was both an originator of some unique contribution, and an appraiser of all.

231

Now, as the years advanced in millions and in decades of millions, it began to be noticed that the movement of world culture was in a manner spiral. There would be an age during which the interest of the race was directed almost wholly upon certain tracts or aspects of existence; and then, after perhaps a hundred thousand years, these would seem to have been fully cultivated, and would be left fallow. During the next epoch attention would be in the main directed to other spheres, and then afterwards to yet others, and again others. But at length a return would be made to the fields that had been deserted, and it would be discovered that they could now miraculously bear a million-fold the former crop. Thus, in both science and art man kept recurring again and again to the ancient themes, to work over them once more in meticulous detail and strike from them new truth and new beauty, such as, in the earlier epoch, he could never have conceived. Thus it was that, though science gathered to itself unfalteringly an ever wider and more detailed view of existence, it periodically discovered some revolutionary general principle in terms of which its whole content had to be given a new significance. And in art there would appear in one age works superficially almost identical with works of another age, yet to the discerning eye incomparably more significant. Similarly, in respect of human personality itself, those men and women who lived at the close of the aeon of the Fifth Men could often discover in the remote beginning of their own race beings curiously like themselves, yet, as it were, expressed in fewer dimensions than their own many-dimensional natures. As a map is like the mountainous land, or the picture like the landscape, or indeed as the point and the circle are like the sphere, so, and only so, the earlier Fifth Men resembled the flower of the species.

Such statements would be in a manner true of any period of steady cultural progress. But in the present instance they have a peculiar significance which I must now somehow contrive to suggest.

XII *The Last Terrestrials*

1. THE CULT OF EVANESCENCE

THE Fifth Men had not been endowed with that potential immortality which their makers themselves possessed. And from the fact that they were mortal and yet long-lived, their culture drew its chief brilliance and poignancy. Beings for whom the natural span was three thousand years, and ultimately as much as fifty thousand, were peculiarly troubled by the prospect of death, and by the loss of those dear to them. The more ephemeral kind of spirit, that comes into being and then almost immediately ceases, before it has entered at all deeply into consciousness of itself, can face its end with a courage that is half unwitting. Even its smart in the loss of other beings with whom it has been intimate is but a vague and dream-like suffering. For the ephemeral spirit has no time to grow fully awake, or fully intimate with another, before it must lose its beloved, and itself once more fade into unconsciousness. But with the long-lived yet not immortal Fifth Men the case was different. Gathering to themselves experience of the cosmos, acquiring an ever more precise and vivid insight and appreciation, they knew that very soon all this wealth of the soul must cease to be. And in love, though they might be fully intimate not merely with one but with very many persons, the death of one of these dear spirits seemed an irrevocable tragedy, an utter annihilation of the most resplendent kind of glory, an impoverishment of the cosmos for evermore.

In their brief primitive phase, the Fifth Men, like so many other races, sought to console themselves by unreasoning faith in a life after death. They conceived, for instance, that at death terrestrial beings embarked upon a career continuous with earthly life, but far more ample, either in some remote planetary system, or in some wholly distinct orb of space-time. But though such theories were never disproved in the primitive era, they

233

gradually began to seem not merely improbable but ignoble. For it came to be recognized that the resplendent glories of personality, even in that degree of beauty which now for the first time was attained, were not after all the extreme of glory. It was seen with pain, but also with exultation, that even love's demand that the beloved should have immortal life is a betrayal of man's paramount allegiance. And little by little it became evident that those who used great gifts, and even genius, to establish the truth of the after life, or to seek contact with their beloved dead, suffered from a strange blindness, an obtuseness of the spirit. Though the love which had misled them was itself a very lovely thing, yet they were misled. Like children, searching for lost toys, they wandered. Like adolescents seeking to recapture delight in the things of childhood, they shunned those more difficult admirations which are proper to the grown mind.

And so it became a constant aim of the Fifth Men to school themselves to admire chiefly even in the very crisis of bereavement, not persons, but that great music of innumerable personal lives, which is the life of the race. And quite early in their career they discovered an unexpected beauty in the very fact that the individual must die. So that, when they had actually come into possession of the means to make themselves immortal, they refrained, choosing rather merely to increase the life-span of succeeding generations to fifty thousand years. Such a period seemed to be demanded for the full exercise of human capacity; but immortality, they held, would lead to spiritual disaster.

Now as their science advanced they saw that there had been a time, before the stars were formed, when there was no possible footing for minds in the cosmos; and that there would come a time when mentality would be driven out of existence. Earlier human species had not needed to trouble about mind's ultimate fate; but for the long-lived Fifth Men the end, though remote, did not seem infinitely distant. The prospect distressed them. They had schooled themselves to live not for the individual but for the race; and now the life of the race itself was seen to be a mere instant between the endless void of the past and the endless void of the future. Nothing within their ken was more worthy of admiration than the organized progressive mentality of mankind; and the conviction that this most admired thing must soon cease filled many of their less ample minds with horror and indignation. But in time the Fifth Men, like the Second Men long before them, came to suspect that even in this tragic brevity of mind's course there was a quality of beauty, more difficult than the familiar beauty, but also more exquisite. Even thus imprisoned in an instant, the spirit of man might yet plumb the whole extent of space, and also the whole past and the whole future; and so, from behind his prison bars, he might render the universe that intelligent worship which, they felt, it demanded of him. Better so, they said, than that he should fret himself with puny efforts to escape. He is dignified by his very weakness, and the cosmos by its very indifference to him.

For aeons they remained in this faith. And they schooled their hearts to acquiesce in it, saying, if it is so, it is best, and somehow we must learn to see that it is best. But what they meant by 'best' was not what their predecessors would have meant. They did not, for instance, deceive themselves by pretending that after all they themselves actually preferred life to be evanescent. On the contrary, they continued to long that it might be otherwise. But having discovered, both behind the physical order and behind the desires of minds, a fundamental principle whose essence was aesthetic, they were faithful to the conviction that whatever was fact must somehow in the universal view be fitting, right, beautiful, integral to the form of the cosmos. And so they accepted as right a state of affairs which in their own hearts they still felt grievously wrong.

This conviction of the irrevocability of the past and of the evanescence of mind induced in them a great tenderness for all beings that had lived and ceased. Deeming themselves to be near the crest of life's achievement, blessed also with longevity and philosophic detachment, they were often smitten with pity for those humbler, briefer, and less free spirits whose lot had fallen in the past. Moreover, themselves extremely complex, subtle, conscious, they conceived a generous admiration for all simple minds, for the early men, and for the beasts. Very strongly they condemned the action of their predecessors in destroying so many

235

joyous and delectable creatures. Earnestly they sought to reconstruct in imagination all those beings that blind intellectualism had murdered. Earnestly they delved in the near and the remote past so as to recover as much as possible of the history of life on the planet. With meticulous love they would figure out the life stories of extinct types, such as the brontosaurus, the hippopotamus, the chimpanzee, the Englishman, the American, as also of the still extant amoeba. And while they could not but relish the comicality of these remote beings, their amusement was the outgrowth of affectionate insight into simple natures, and was but the obverse of their recognition that the primitive is essentially tragic, because blind. And so, while they saw that the main work of man must have regard to the future, they felt that he owed also a duty toward the past. He must preserve it in his own mind, if not actually in life at least in being. In the future lay glory, joy, brilliance of the spirit. The future needed service, not pity, not piety; but in the past lay darkness, confusion, waste, and all the cramped primitive minds, bewildered, torturing one another in their stupidity, yet one and all in some unique manner beautiful.

The reconstruction of the past, not merely as abstract history but with the intimacy of the novel, thus became one of the main preoccupations of the Fifth Men. Many devoted themselves to this work, each individual specializing very minutely in some particular episode of human or animal history, and transmitting his work into the culture of the race. Thus increasingly the individual felt himself to be a single flicker between the teeming gulf of the never-more and the boundless void of the not-yet. Himself a member of a very noble and fortunate race, his zest in existence was tempered, deepened, by a sense of the presence, the ghostly presence, of the myriad less fortunate beings in the past. Sometimes, and especially in epochs when the contemporary world seemed most satisfactory and promising, this piety toward the primitive and the past became the dominant activity of the race, giving rise to alternating phases of rebellion against the tyrannical nature of the cosmos, and faith that in the universal view, after all, this horror must be right. In this latter mood it was held that the very irrevocability of the past dignified all past existence, and dignified the cosmos, as a work of tragic art is dignified by the irrevocability of disaster. It was this mood of acquiescence and faith which in the end became the characteristic attitude of the Fifth Men for many millions of years.

But a bewildering discovery was in store for the Fifth Men, a discovery which was to change their whole attitude toward existence. Certain obscure biological facts began to make them suspect, on purely empirical grounds, that past events were not after all simply non-existent, that though no longer existent in the temporal manner, they had eternal existence in some other manner. The effect of this increasing suspicion about the past was that a once harmonious race was divided for a while into two parties, those who insisted that the formal beauty of the universe demanded the tragic evanescence of all things, and those who determined to show that living minds could actually reach back into past events in all their pastness.

The readers of this book are not in a position to realize the poignancy of the conflict which now threatened to wreck humanity. They cannot approach it from the point of view of a race whose culture had consisted of an age-long schooling in admiration of an ever-vanishing cosmos. To the orthodox it seemed that the new view was iconoclastic, impertinent, vulgar. Their opponents, on the other hand, insisted that the matter must be decided dispassionately, according to the evidence. They were also able to point out that this devotion to evanescence was after all but the outcome of the conviction that the cosmos must be supremely noble. No one, it was said, really had direct vision of evanescence as in itself an excellence. So heartfelt was the dispute that the orthodox party actually broke off all 'telepathic' communication with the rebels, and even went so far as to plan their destruction. There can be no doubt that if violence had actually been used the human race would have succumbed; for in a species of such high mental development internecine war would have been a gross violation of its nature. It would never have been able to live down so shameful a spiritual disaster. Fortunately, however, at the eleventh hour, commonsense prevailed. The iconoclasts were permitted to carry on their research, and the whole race awaited the result.

2. EXPLORATION OF TIME

This first attack upon the nature of time involved an immense cooperative work, both theoretical and practical. It was from biology that the first hint had come that the past persisted. And it would be necessary to restate the whole of biology and the physical sciences in terms of the new idea. On the practical side it was necessary to undertake a great campaign of experiment, physiological and psychological. We cannot stay to watch this work. Millions of years passed by. Sometimes, for thousands of years at a spell, temporal research was the main preoccupation of the race; sometimes it was thrust into the background, or completely ignored, during epochs which were dominated by other interests. Age after age passed, and always the effort of man in this sphere remained barren. Then at last there was a real success.

A child had been selected from among those produced by an age-long breeding enterprise, directed towards the mastery of time. From infancy this child's brain had been very carefully controlled physiologically. Psychologically also he had been subjected to a severe treatment, that he might be properly schooled for his strange task. In the presence of several scientists and historians he was put into a kind of trance, and brought out of it again, half an hour later. He was then asked to give an account 'telepathically' of his experiences during the trance. Unfortunately he was now so shattered that his evidence was almost unintelligible. After some months of rest he was questioned again, and was able to describe a curious episode which turned out to be a terrifying incident in the girlhood of his dead mother. He seemed to have seen the incident through her eyes, and to have been aware of all her thoughts. This alone proved nothing, for he might have received the information from some living mind. Once more, therefore, and in spite of his entreaties, he was put into the peculiar trance. On waking he told a rambling story of 'little red people living in a squat white tower'. It was clear that he was referring to the Great Brains and their attendants. But once more, this proved nothing; and before the account was finished the child died.

Another child was chosen, but was not put to the test until

late in adolescence. After an hour of the trance, he woke and became terribly agitated, but forced himself to describe an episode which the historians assigned to the age of the Martian invasions. The importance of this incident lay in his account of a certain house with a carved granite portico, situated at the head of a waterfall in a mountain valley. He said he had found himself to be an old woman, and that he, or she, was being hurriedly helped out of the house by the other inmates. They watched a formless monster creep down the valley, destroy their house, and mangle two persons who failed to get away in time. Now this house was not at all typical of the Second Men, but must have expressed the whim of some freakish individual. From evidence derived from the boy himself, it proved possible to locate the valley with reference to a former mountain, known to history. No valley survived in that spot; but deep excavations revealed the ancient slopes, the fault that had occasioned the waterfall, and the broken pillars.

This and many similar incidents confirmed the Fifth Men in their new view of time. There followed an age in which the technique of direct inspection of the past was gradually improved, but not without tragedy. In the early stages it was found impossible to keep the 'medium' alive for more than a few weeks after his venture into the past. The experience seemed to set up a progressive mental disintegration which produced first insanity, then paralysis, and, within a few months, death. This difficulty was at last overcome. By one means and another a type of brain was produced capable of undergoing the strain of supra-temporal experience without fatal results. An increasingly large proportion of the rising generation had now direct access to the past, and were engaged upon a great re-statement of history in relation to their first-hand experience; but their excursions into the past were uncontrollable. They could not go where they wanted to go, but only where fate flung them. Nor could they go of their own will, but only through a very complicated technique, and with the cooperation of experts. After a time the process was made much easier, in fact, too easy. The unfortunate medium might slip so easily into the trance that his days were eaten up by the past. He might suddenly fall to the ground, and lie rapt, inert, dependent on artificial feeding, for weeks, months, even for years. Or a dozen times in the same day he might be flung into a dozen different epochs of history. Or, still more distressing, his experience of past events might not keep pace with the actual rhythm of those events themselves. Thus he might behold the events of a month, or even a lifetime, fantastically accelerated so as to occupy a trance of no more than a day's duration. Or, worse, he might find himself sliding backwards down the vista of the hours and experiencing events in an order the reverse of the natural order. Even the magnificent brains of the Fifth Men could not stand this. The result was maniacal behaviour, followed by death. Another trouble also beset these first experimenters. Supra-temporal experience proved to be like a dangerous and habit-forming drug. Those who ventured into the past might become so intoxicated that they would try to spend every moment of their natural lives in roaming among past events. Thus gradually they would lose touch with the present, live in absentminded brooding, fail to react normally to their environment, turn socially worthless, and often come actually to physical disaster through inability to look after themselves.

Many more thousands of years passed before these difficulties and dangers were overcome. At length, however, the technique of supra-temporal experience was so perfected that every individual could at will practise it with safety, and could, within limits, project his vision into any locality of space-time which he desired to inspect. It was only possible, however, to see past events through the mind of some past organism, no longer living. And in practice only human minds, and to some extent the minds of the higher mammals, could be entered. The explorer retained throughout his adventure his own personality and system of memory. While experiencing the past individual's perceptions, memories, thoughts, desires, and in fact the whole process and content of the past mind, the explorer continued to be himself, and to react in terms of his own character, now condemning, now sympathizing, now critically enjoying the spectacle.

The task of explaining the mechanism of this new faculty occupied the scientists and philosophers of the species for a very long period. The final account, of course, cannot be presented save by parable; for it was found necessary to recast many fundamental concepts in order to interpret the facts coherently. The only hint that I can give of the explanation is in saying, metaphorically of course, that the living brain had access to the past, not by way of some mysterious kind of racial memory, nor by some equally impossible journey up the stream of time, but by a partial awakening, as it were, into eternity, and into inspection of a minute tract of space-time through some temporal mind in the past, as though through an optical instrument. In the early experiments the fantastic speeding, slowing, and reversal of the temporal process resulted from disorderly inspection. As a reader may either skim the pages of a book, or read at a comfortable pace, or dwell upon one word, or spell the sentence backwards, so, unintentionally, the novice in eternity might read or misread the mind that was presented to him.

This new mode of experience, it should be noted, was the activity of living brains, though brains of a novel kind. Hence what was to be discovered 'through the medium of eternity' was limited by the particular exploring brain's capacity of understanding what was presented to it. And, further, though the actual supra-temporal contact with past events occupied no time in the brain's natural life, the assimilating of that moment of vision, the reduction of it to normal temporal memory in the normal brain structures, took time, and had to be done during the period of the trance. To expect the neural structure to record the experience instantaneously would be to expect a complicated machine to effect a complicated readjustment without a process of readjusting.

The new access to the past had, of course, far-reaching effects upon the culture of the Fifth Men. Not only did it give them an incomparably more accurate knowledge of past events, and insight into the motives of historical personages, and into large-scale cultural movements, but also it effected a subtle change in their estimate of the importance of things. Though intellectually they had, of course, realized both the vastness and the richness of the past, now they realized it with an overwhelming vividness. Matters that had been known hitherto only historically, schematically, were now available to be lived through by intimate acquaintance. The only limit to such acquaintance was set by the limitations of the explorer's own brain-capacity. Consequently the remote past came to enter into a man and shape his mind in a manner in which only the recent past, through memory, had shaped him hitherto. Even before the new kind of experience was first acquired, this race had been, as was said, peculiarly under the spell of the past; but now it was infinitely more so. Hitherto the Fifth Men had been like stay-at-home folk who had read minutely of foreign parts, but had never travelled; now they had become travellers experienced in all the continents of human time. The presences that had hitherto been ghostly were now presences of flesh and blood seen in broad daylight. And so the moving instant called the present appeared no longer as the only, and infinitesimal, real, but as the growing surface of an everlasting tree of existence. It was now the past that seemed most real, while the future still seemed void, and the present merely the impalpable becomingness of the indestructible past.

The discovery that past events were after all persistent, and accessible, was of course for the Fifth Men a source of deep joy; but also it caused them a new distress. While the past was thought of as a mere gulf of non-existence, the inconceivably great pain, misery, baseness, that had fallen into that gulf, could be dismissed as done with; and the will could be concentrated wholly on preventing such horrors from occurring in the future. But now, along with past joy, past distress was found to be everlasting. And those who, in the course of their voyaging in the past, encountered regions of eternal agony, came back distraught. It was easy to remind these harrowed explorers that if pain was eternal, so also was joy. Those who had endured travel in the tragic past were apt to dismiss such assurances with contempt, affirming that all the delights of the whole population of time could not compensate for the agony of one tortured individual. And anyhow, they declared, it was obvious that there had been no preponderance of joy over pain. Indeed, save in the modern age, pain had been overwhelmingly in excess.

So seriously did these convictions prey upon the minds of the Fifth Men, that in spite of their own almost perfect social order, in which suffering had actually to be sought out as a tonic, they fell into despair. At all times, in all pursuits, the presence of the tragic past haunted them, poisoning their lives, sapping their strength. Lovers were ashamed of the delight in one another. As in the far-off days of sexual taboo, guilt crept between them, and held their spirits apart even while their bodies were united.

3. VOYAGING IN SPACE

It was while they were struggling in the grip of this vast social melancholy, and anxiously craving some new vision by which to reinterpret or transcend the agony of the past, that the Fifth Men were confronted with a most unexpected physical crisis. It was discovered that something queer was happening to the moon; in fact, that the orbit of the satellite was narrowing in upon the earth in a manner contrary to all the calculations of the scientists.

The Fifth Men had long ago fashioned for themselves an all-embracing and minutely coherent system of natural sciences, every factor in which had been put to the test a thousand times and had never been shaken. Imagine, then, their bewilderment at this extraordinary discovery. In ages when science was still fragmentary, a subversive discovery entailed merely a reorganization of some one department of science; but by now, such was the coherence of knowledge, that any minute discrepancy of fact and theory must throw man into a state of complete intellectual vertigo.

The evolution of the lunar orbit had, of course, been studied from time immemorial. Even the First Men had learned that the moon must first withdraw from and subsequently once more approach the earth, till it should reach a critical proximity and begin to break up into a swarm of fragments like the rings of Saturn. This view had been very thoroughly confirmed by the Fifth Men themselves. The satellite should have continued to withdraw for yet many hundreds of millions of years; but in fact it was now observed that not only had the withdrawal ceased, but a comparatively rapid approach had begun.

Observations and calculations were repeated, and ingenious theoretical explanations were suggested; but the truth remained completely hidden. It was left to a future and more brilliant species to discover the connexion between a planet's gravitation and its cultural development. Meanwhile, the Fifth Men knew only that the distance between the earth and the moon was becoming smaller with ever-increasing rapidity.

This discovery was a tonic to a melancholy race, Men turned from the tragic past to the bewildering present and the uncertain future.

For it was evident that, if the present acceleration of approach were to be maintained, the moon would enter the critical zone and disintegrate in less than ten million years; and, further, that the fragments would not maintain themselves as a ring, but would soon crash upon the earth. Heat generated by their impact would make the surface of the earth impossible as the home of life. A short-lived and short-sighted species might well have considered ten million years as equivalent to eternity. Not so the Fifth Men. Thinking primarily in terms of the race, they recognized at once that their whole social policy must now be dominated by this future catastrophe. Some there were indeed who at first refused to take the matter seriously, saying that there was no reason to believe that the moon's odd behaviour would continue indefinitely. But as the years advanced, this view became increasingly improbable. Some of those who had spent much of their lives in exploration of the past now sought to explore the future also, hoping to prove that human civilization would always be discoverable on the earth in no matter how remote a future. But the attempt to unveil the future by direct inspection failed completely. It was surmised, erroneously, that future events, unlike past events, must be strictly non-existent until their creation by the advancing present.

Clearly humanity must leave its native planet. Research was therefore concentrated on the possibility of flight through empty space, and the suitability of neighbouring worlds. The only alternatives were Mars and Venus. The former was by now without water and without atmosphere. The latter had a dense moist atmosphere, but one which lacked oxygen. The surface of Venus, moreover, was known to be almost completely covered with a shallow ocean. Further the planet was so hot by day that, even at the poles, man in his present state would scarcely survive.

It did not take the Fifth Men many centuries to devise a tolerable means of voyaging in interplanetary space. Immense rockets were constructed, the motive power of which was derived from the annihilation of matter. The vehicle was propelled simply by the terrific pressure of radiation thus produced. 'Fuel' for a voyage of many months, or even years, could, of course, easily be carried, since the annihilation of a minute amount of matter produced a vast wealth of energy. Moreover, when once the vessel had emerged from the earth's atmosphere, and had attained full speed, she would, of course, maintain it without the use of power from the rocket apparatus. The task of rendering the 'ether-ship' properly manageable and decently habitable proved difficult, but not insurmountable. The first vessel to take the ether was a cigar-shaped hull some three thousand feet long, and built of metals whose artificial atoms were incomparably more rigid than anything hitherto known. Batteries of 'rocket' apparatus at various points on the hull enabled the ship not only to travel forward, but to reverse, turn in any direction, or side-step. Windows of an artificial transparent element, scarcely less strong than the metal of the hull, enabled the voyagers to look around them. Within there was ample accommodation for a hundred persons and their provisions for three years. Air for the same period was manufactured in transit from protons and electrons stored under pressure comparable to that in the interior of a star. Heat was, of course, provided by the annihilation of matter. Powerful refrigeration would permit the vessel to approach the sun almost to the orbit of Mercury. An 'artificial gravity' system, based on the properties of the electro-magnetic field, could be turned on and regulated at will, so as to maintain a more or less normal environment for the human organism.

This pioneer ship was manned with a navigating crew and a company of scientists, and was successfully dispatched upon a trial trip. The intention was to approach close to the surface of the moon, possibly to circumnavigate it at an altitude of ten thousand feet, and to return without landing. For many days those on earth received radio messages from the vessel's powerful installation, reporting that all was going well. But suddenly the messages ceased, and no more was ever heard of the vessel.

Almost at the moment of the last message, telescopes had revealed a sudden flash of light at a point on the vessel's course. It was therefore surmised that she had collided with a meteor and fused with the heat of the impact.

Other vessels were built and dispatched on trial voyages. Many failed to return. Some got out of control, and reported that they were heading for outer space or plunging towards the sun, their hopeless messages continuing until the last of the crew succumbed to suffocation. Other vessels returned successfully, but with crews haggard and distraught from long confinement in bad atmosphere. One, venturing to land on the moon, broke her back, so that the air rushed out of her, and her people died. After her last message was received, she was detected from the earth, as an added speck on the stippled surface of a lunar 'sea'.

As time passed, however, accidents became rarer; indeed, so rare that trips in the void began to be a popular form of amusement. Literature of the period reverberates with the novelty of such experiences, with the sense that man had at last learned true flight, and acquired the freedom of the solar system. Writers dwelt upon the shock of seeing, as the vessel soared and accelerated, the landscape dwindle to a mere illuminated disc or crescent, surrounded by constellations. They remarked also the awful remoteness and mystery which travellers experienced on these early voyages, with dazzling sunlight on one side of the vessel and dazzlingly bespangled night on the other. They described how the intense sun spread his corona against a black and star-crowded sky. They expatiated also on the overwhelming interest of approaching another planet; of inspecting from the sky the still visible remains of Martian civilization; of groping through the cloud banks of Venus to discover islands in her almost coastless ocean; of daring an approach to Mercury, till the heat became insupportable in spite of the best refrigerating mechanism; of feeling a way across the belt of the asteroids and onwards toward Jupiter, till shortage of air and provisions forced a return.

But though the mere navigation of space was thus easily accomplished, the major task was still untouched. It was necessary either to remake man's nature to suit another planet, or to modify conditions upon another planet to suit man's nature. The former alternative was repugnant to the Fifth Men. Obviously it would entail an almost complete refashioning of the human organism. No existing individual could possibly be so altered as to live in the present conditions of Mars or Venus. And it would probably prove impossible to create a new being, adapted to these conditions, without sacrificing the brilliant and harmonious constitution of the extant species.

On the other hand, Mars could not be made habitable without first being stocked, with air and water; and such an undertaking seemed impossible. There was nothing for it, then, but to attack Venus. The polar surfaces of that planet, shielded by impenetrable depths of cloud, proved after all not unendurably hot. Subsequent generations might perhaps be modified so as to withstand even the sub-arctic and 'temperate' climates. Oxygen was plentiful, but it was all tied up in chemical combination. Inevitably so, since oxygen combines very readily, and on Venus there was no vegetable life to exhale the free gas and replenish the ever-vanishing supply. It was necessary, then, to equip Venus with an appropriate vegetation, which in the course of ages should render the planet's atmosphere hospitable to man. The chemical and physical conditions on Venus had therefore to be studied in great detail, so that it might be possible to design a kind of life which would have a chance of flourishing. This research had to be carried out from within the ether-ships, or with gas helmets, since no human being could live in the natural atmosphere of the planet.

We must not dwell upon the age of heroic research and adventure which now began. Observations of the lunar orbit were showing that ten million years was too long an estimate of the future habitability of the earth; and it was soon realized that Venus could not be made ready soon enough unless some more rapid change was set on foot. It was therefore decided to split up some of the ocean of the planet into hydrogen and oxygen by a vast process of electrolysis. This would have been a more difficult task, had not the ocean been relatively free from salt, owing to the fact that there was so little dry land to be denuded of salts by rain and river. The oxygen thus formed by electrolysis would be allowed to mix with the atmosphere. The hydrogen had to be got rid of somehow, and an ingenious method was devised by which it should be ejected beyond the limits of the atmosphere at so great a speed that it would never return. Once sufficient free oxygen had been produced, the new vegetation would replenish the loss due to oxidation. This work was duly set on foot. Great automatic electrolysing stations were founded on several of the islands; and biological research produced at length a whole flora of specialized vegetable types to cover the land surface of the planet. It was hoped that in less than a million years Venus would be fit to receive the human race, and the race fit to live on Venus.

Meanwhile a careful survey of the planet had been undertaken. Its land surface, scarcely more than a thousandth that of the earth, consisted of an unevenly distributed archipelago of mountainous islands. The planet had evidently not long ago been through a mountain-forming era, for soundings proved its whole surface to be extravagantly corrugated. The ocean was subject to terrific storms and currents; for since the planet took several weeks to rotate, there was a great difference of temperature and atmospheric pressure between the almost Arctic hemisphere of night and the sweltering hemisphere of day. So great was the evaporation, that open sky was almost never visible from any part of the planet's surface; and indeed the average day-time weather was a succession of thick fogs and fantastic thunderstorms. Rain in the evening was a continuous torrent. Yet before night was over the waves clattered with fragments of ice.

Man looked upon his future home with loathing, and on his birthplace with an affection which became passionate. With its blue sky, its incomparable starry nights, its temperate and varied continents, its ample spaces of agriculture, wilderness, and park, its well-known beasts and plants, and all the material fabric of the most enduring of terrestrial civilizations, it seemed to the men and women who were planning flight almost a living thing imploring them not to desert it. They looked often with hate at the quiet moon, now visibly larger than the moon of history. They revised again and again their astronomical and physical theories, hoping for some flaw which should render the moon's observed behaviour less mysterious, less terrifying. But they found nothing.

It was as though a fiend out of some ancient myth had come to life in the modern world, to interfere with the laws of nature for man's undoing.

4. PREPARING A NEW WORLD

Another trouble now occurred. Several electrolysis stations on Venus were wrecked, apparently by submarine eruption. Also, a number of ether-ships, engaged in surveying the ocean, mysteriously exploded. The explanation was found when one of these vessels, though damaged, was able to return to the earth. The commander reported that, when the sounding line was drawn up, a large spherical object was seen to be attached to it. Closer inspection showed that this object was fastened to the sounding apparatus by a hook, and was indeed unmistakably artificial, a structure of small metal plates riveted together. While preparations were being made to bring the object within the ship, it happened to bump against the hull, and then it exploded.

Evidently there must be intelligent life somewhere in the ocean of Venus. Evidently the marine Venerians resented the steady depletion of their aqueous world, and were determined to stop it. The terrestrials had assumed that water in which no free oxygen was dissolved could not support life. But observation soon revealed that in this world-wide ocean there were many living species, some sessile, others free-swimming, some microscopic, others as large as whales. The basis of life in these creatures lay not in photosynthesis and chemical combination, but in the controlled disintegration of radio-active atoms. Venus was particularly rich in these atoms, and still contained certain elements which had long ago ceased to exist on the earth. The oceanic fauna subsisted in the destruction of minute quantities of radio-active atoms throughout its tissues.

Several of the Venerian species had attained considerable mastery over their physical environment, and were able to destroy one another very competently with various mechanical contrivances. Many types were indeed definitely intelligent and versatile within certain limits. And of these intelligent types, one had come to dominate all the others by virtue of its superior intelligence, and had constructed a genuine civilization on the basis of radio-active power. These most developed of all the Venerian creatures were beings of about the size and shape of a swordfish. They had three manipulative organs, normally sheathed within the long 'sword', but capable of extension beyond its point, as three branched muscular tentacles. They swam with a curious screw-like motion of their bodies and triple tails. Three fins enabled them to steer. They had also organs of phosphorescence, vision, touch, and something analogous to hearing. They appeared to reproduce asexually, laying eggs in the ooze of the ocean bed. They had no need of nutrition in the ordinary sense; but in infancy they seemed to gather enough radio-active matter to keep them alive for many years. Each individual, when his stock was running out and he began to be feeble, was either destroyed by his juniors or buried in a radio-active mine, to rise from this living death in a few months completely rejuvenated.

At the bottom of the Venerian ocean these creatures thronged in cities of proliferated coral-like buildings, equipped with many complex articles, which must have constituted the necessities and luxuries of their civilization. So much was ascertained by the Terrestrials in the course of their submarine exploration. But the mental life of the Venerians remained hidden. It was clear, indeed, that like all living things, they were concerned with self-maintenance and the exercise of their capacities; but of the nature of these capacities little was discoverable. Clearly they used some kind of symbolic language, based on mechanical vibrations set up in the water by the snapping claws of their tentacles. But their more complex activities were quite unintelligible. All that could be recorded with certainty was that they were much addicted to warfare, even to warfare between groups of one species; and that even in the stress of military disaster they maintained a feverish production of material articles of all sorts, which they proceeded to destroy and neglect.

One activity was observed which was peculiarly mysterious. At certain seasons three individuals, suddenly developing unusual luminosity, would approach one another with rhythmic swayings and tremors, and would then rise on their tails and press their bodies together. Sometimes at this stage an excited crowd would collect, whirling around the three like driven snow. The chief performers would now furiously tear one another to pieces with their crab-like pincers, till nothing was left but tangled shreds of flesh, the great swords, and the still twitching claws. The Terrestrials, observing these matters with difficulty, at first suspected some kind of sexual intercourse; but no reproduction was ever traced to this source. Possibly the behaviour had once served a biological end, and had now become a useless ritual. Possibly it was a kind of voluntary religious sacrifice. More probably it was of a quite different nature, unintelligible to the human mind.

As man's activities on Venus became more extensive, the Venerians became more energetic in seeking to destroy him. They could not come out of the ocean to grapple with him, for they were deep-sea organisms. Deprived of oceanic pressure, they would have burst. But they contrived to hurl high explosives into the centres of the islands, or to undermine them from tunnels. The work of electrolysis was thus very seriously hampered. And as all efforts to parley with the Venerians failed completely, it was impossible to effect a compromise. The Fifth Men were thus faced with a grave moral problem. What right had man to interfere in a world already possessed by beings who were obviously intelligent, even though their mental life was incomprehensible to man? Long ago man himself had suffered at the hands of Martian invaders, who doubtless regarded themselves as more noble than the human race. And now man was committing a similar crime. On the other hand, either the migration to Venus must go forward, or humanity must be destroyed; for it seemed quite certain by now that the moon would fall, and at no very distant date. And though man's understanding of the Venerians was so incomplete, what he did know of them strongly suggested that they were definitely inferior to himself in mental range. This judgement might, of course, be mistaken; the Venerians might after all be so superior to man that man could not get an inkling of their superiority. But this argument would apply equally to jelly-fish and micro-organisms. Judgement had to be passed according to the evidence available. So far as man could judge at all in the matter, he was definitely the higher type.

There was another fact to be taken into account. The life of the Venerian organism depended on the existence of radioactive atoms. Since those atoms are subject to disintegration, they must become rarer. Venus was far better supplied than the earth in this respect, but there must inevitably come a time when there would be no more radio-active matter in Venus. Now submarine research showed that the Venerian fauna had once been much more extensive, and that the increasing difficulty of procuring radio-active matter was already the great limiting factor of civilization. Thus the Venerians were doomed, and man would merely hasten their destruction.

It was hoped, of course, that in colonizing Venus mankind would be able to accommodate itself without seriously interfering with the native population. But this proved impossible for two reasons. In the first place, the natives seemed determined to destroy the invader even if they should destroy themselves in the process. Titanic explosions were engineered, which caused the invaders serious damage, but also strewed the ocean surface with thousands of dead Venerians. Secondly, it was found that, as electrolysis poured more and more free oxygen into the atmosphere, the ocean absorbed some of the potent element back into itself by solution; and this dissolved oxygen had a disastrous effect upon the oceanic organisms. Their tissues began to oxidize. They were burnt up, internally and externally, by a slow fire. Man dared not stop the process of electrolysis until the atmosphere had become as rich in oxygen as his native air. Long before this state was reached, it was already clear that the Venerians were beginning to feel the effects of the poison, and that in a few thousand years, at most, they would be exterminated. It was therefore determined to put them out of their misery as quickly as possible. Men could by now walk abroad on the islands of Venus, and indeed the first settlements were already being founded. They were thus able to build a fleet of powerful submarine vessels to scour the ocean and destroy the whole native fauna.

This vast slaughter influenced the mind of the fifth human species in two opposite directions, now flinging it into despair, now rousing it to grave elation. For on the one hand the horror of the slaughter produced a haunting guiltiness in all men's minds, an unreasoning disgust with humanity for having been driven to murder in order to save itself. And this guiltiness combined with the purely intellectual loss of self-confidence which had been produced by the failure of science to account for the moon's approach. It reawakened, also, that other quite irrational sense of guilt which had been bred of sympathy with the everlasting distress of the past. Together, these three influences tended toward racial neurosis.

On the other hand a very different mood sometimes sprang from the same three sources. After all, the failure of science was a challenge to be gladly accepted; it opened up a wealth of possibilities hitherto unimagined. Even the unalterable distress of the past constituted a challenge; for in some strange manner the present and future, it was said, must transfigure the past. As for the murder of Venerian life, it was, indeed, terrible, but right. It had been committed without hate; indeed, rather in love. For as the navy proceeded with its relentless work, it had gathered much insight into the life of the natives, and had learned to admire, even in a sense to love, while it killed. This mood, of inexorable yet not ruthless will, intensified the spiritual sensibility of the species, refined, so to speak, its spiritual hearing, and revealed to it tones and themes in the universal music which were hitherto obscure.

Which of these two moods, despair or courage, would triumph? All depended on the skill of the species to maintain a high degree of vitality in untoward circumstances.

Man now busied himself in preparing his new home. Many kinds of plant life, derived from the terrestrial stock, but bred for the Venerian environment, now began to swarm on the islands and in the sea. For so restricted was the land surface, that great areas of ocean had to be given over to specially designed marine plants, which now formed immense floating continents of vegetable matter. On the least torrid islands appeared habitable pylons, forming an architectural forest, with vegetation on every acre of free ground. Even so, it would be impossible for Venus ever to support the huge population of the earth. Steps had therefore been taken to ensure that the birth-rate should fall far short of the death-rate; so that, when the time should come, the race might emigrate without leaving any living members behind. No more than a hundred million, it was reckoned, could live tolerably on Venus. The population had therefore to be reduced to a hundredth of its former size. And since, in the terrestrial community, with its vast social and cultural activity, every individual had fulfilled some definite function in society, it was obvious that the new community must be not merely small but mentally impoverished. Hitherto, each individual had been enriched by intercourse with a far more intricate and diverse social environment that would be possible on Venus.

Such was the prospect when at length it was judged advisable to leave the earth to its fate. The moon was now so huge that it periodically turned day into night, and night into a ghastly day. Prodigious tides and distressful weather conditions had already spoilt the amenities of the earth, and done great damage to the fabric of civilization. And so at length humanity reluctantly took flight. Some centuries passed before the migration was completed, before Venus had received, not only the whole remaining human population, but also representatives of many other species of organisms, and all the most precious treasure of man's culture.

XIII *Humanity on Venus*

1. TAKING ROOT AGAIN

MAN'S sojourn on Venus lasted somewhat longer than his whole career on the Earth. From the days of Pithecanthropus to the final evacuation of his native planet he passed, as we have seen, through a bewildering diversity of form and circumstance. On Venus, though the human type was somewhat more constant biologically, it was scarcely less variegated in culture.

To give an account of this period, even on the minute scale that has been adopted hitherto, would entail another volume. I can only sketch its bare outline. The sapling, humanity, transplanted into foreign soil, withers at first almost to the root, slowly readjusts itself, grows into strength and a certain permanence of form, burgeons, season by season, with leaf and flower of many successive civilizations and cultures, sleeps winter by winter, through many ages of reduced vitality, but at length (to force the metaphor), avoids this recurrent defeat by attaining an evergreen constitution and a continuous efflorescence. Then once more, through the whim of Fate, it is plucked up by the roots and cast upon another world.

The first human settlers on Venus knew well that life would be a sorry business. They had done their best to alter the planet to suit human nature, but they could not make Venus into another Earth. The land surface was minute. The climate was almost unendurable. The extreme difference of temperature between the protracted day and night produced incredible storms, rain like a thousand contiguous waterfalls, terrifying electrical disturbances, and fogs in which a man could not see his own feet. To make matters worse, the oxygen supply was as yet barely enough to render the air breathable. Worse still, the liberated hydrogen was not always successfully ejected from the atmosphere. It would sometimes mingle with the air to form an explosive mixture, and sooner or later there would occur a vast atmospheric flash.

Recurrent disasters of this sort destroyed the architecture and the human inhabitants of many islands, and further reduced the oxygen supply. In time, however, the increasing vegetation made it possible to put an end to the dangerous process of electrolysis.

Meanwhile, these atmospheric explosions crippled the race so seriously that it was unable to cope with a more mysterious trouble which beset it some time after the migration. A new and inexplicable decay of the digestive organs, which first occurred as a rare disease, threatened within a few centuries to destroy mankind. The physical effects of this plague were scarcely more disastrous than the psychological effects of the complete failure to master it; for, what with the mystery of the moon's vagaries and the deep-seated, unreasoning sense of guilt produced by the extermination of the Venerians, man's self-confidence was already seriously shaken, and his highly organized mentality began to show symptoms of derangement. The new plague was, indeed, finally traced to something in the Venerian water, and was supposed to be due to certain molecular groupings, formerly rare, but subsequently fostered by the presence of terrestrial organic matter in the ocean. No cure was discovered.

And now another plague seized upon the enfeebled race. Human tissues had never perfectly assimilated the Martian units which were the means of 'telepathic' communication. The universal ill-health now favoured a kind of 'cancer' of the nervous system, which was due to the ungoverned proliferation of these units. The harrowing results of this disease may be left unmentioned. Century by century it increased; and even those who did not actually contract the sickness lived in constant terror of madness.

These troubles were aggravated by the devastating heat. The hope that, as the generations passed, human nature would adapt itself even to the more sultry regions, seemed to be unfounded. Far otherwise, within a thousand years the once-populous arctic and antarctic islands were almost deserted. Out of each hundred of the great pylons, scarcely more than two were inhabited, and these only by a few plague-stricken and broken-spirited human relics. These alone were left to turn their telescopes upon the

256

earth and watch the unexpectedly delayed bombardment of their native world by the fragments of the moon.

Population decreased still further. Each brief generation was slightly less well developed than its parents. Intelligence declined. Education became superficial and restricted. Contact with the past was no longer possible. Art lost its significance, and philosophy its dominion over the minds of men. Even applied science began to be too difficult. Unskilled control of the subatomic sources of power led to a number of disasters, which finally gave rise to a superstition that all 'tampering with nature' was wicked, and all the ancient wisdom a snare of Man's Enemy. Books, instruments, all the treasures of human culture, were therefore burnt. Only the perdurable buildings resisted destruction. Of the incomparable world-order of the Fifth Men nothing was left but a few island tribes cut off from one another by the ocean, and from the rest of space-time by the depths of their own ignorance.

After many thousands of years human nature did begin to adapt itself to the climate and to the poisoned water without which life was impossible. At the same time a new variety of the fifth species now began to appear, in which the Martian units were not included. Thus at last the race regained a certain mental stability, at the expense of its faculty of 'telepathy', which man was not to regain until almost the last phase of his career. Meanwhile, though he had recovered somewhat from the effects of an alien world, the glory that had been was no more. Let us therefore hurry through the ages that passed before noteworthy events again occurred.

In early days on Venus men had gathered their foodstuff from the great floating islands of vegetable matter which had been artificially produced before the migration. But as the oceans became populous with modifications of the terrestrial fauna, the human tribes turned more and more to fishing. Under the influence of its marine environment, one branch of the species assumed such an aquatic habit that in time it actually began to develop biological adaptations for marine life. It is perhaps surprising that man was still capable of spontaneous variation; but the fifth human species was artificial, and had always been prone to epidemics of mutation. After some millions of years of variation

257

and selection there appeared a very successful species of seal-like submen. The whole body was moulded to stream-lines. The lung capacity was greatly developed. The spine had elongated, and increased in flexibility. The legs were shrunken, grown together, and flattened into a horizontal rudder. The arms also were diminutive and fin-like, though they still retained the manipulative forefinger and thumb. The head had sunk into the body and looked forward in the direction of swimming. Strong carnivorous teeth, emphatic gregariousness, and a new, almost human, cunning in the chase, combined to make these seal-men lords of the ocean. And so they remained for many million years, until a more human race, annoyed at their piscatorial successes, harpooned them out of existence.

For another branch of the degenerated fifth species had retained a more terrestrial habit and the ancient human form. Sadly reduced in stature and in brain, these abject beings were so unlike the original invaders that they are rightly considered a new species, and may therefore be called the Sixth Men. Age after age they gained a precarious livelihood by grubbing roots upon the forest-clad islands, trapping the innumerable birds, and catching fish in the tidal inlets with ground bait. Not infrequently they devoured, or were devoured by, their seal-like relatives. So restricted and and constant was the environment of these human remnants, that they remained biologically and culturally stagnant for some millions of years.

At length, however, geological events afforded man's nature once more the opportunity of change. A mighty warping of the planet's crust produced an island almost as large as Australia. In time this was peopled, and from the clash of tribes a new and versatile race emerged. Once more there was methodical tillage, craftsmanship, complex social organization, and adventure in the realm of thought.

During the next two hundred million years all the main phases of man's life on earth were many times repeated on Venus with characteristic differences. Theocratic empires; free and intellectualistic island cities; insecure overlordships of feudal archipelagos; rivalries of high priest and emperor; religious feuds over the interpretation of sacred scriptures; recurrent fluctuations of thought from naïve animism, through polytheism, conflicting monotheisms, and all the desperate 'isms' by which mind seeks to blur the severe outline of truth; recurrent fashions of comfort-seeking fantasy and cold intelligence; social disorders through the misuse of volcanic or wind power in industry; business empires and pseudo-communistic empires – all these forms flitted over the changing substance of mankind again and again, as in an enduring hearth-fire there appear and vanish the infinitely diverse forms of flame and smoke. But all the while the brief spirits, in whose massed configurations these forms inhered, were intent chiefly on the primitive needs of food, shelter, companionship, crowd-lust, love-making, the two-edged relationship of parent and child, the exercise of muscle and intelligence in facile sport. Very seldom, only in rare moments of clarity, only after ages of misapprehension, did a few of them, here and there, now and again, begin to have the deeper insight into the world's nature and man's. And no sooner had this precious insight begun to propagate itself, than it would be blotted out by some small or great disaster, by epidemic disease, by the spontaneous disruption of society, by an access of racial imbecility, by a prolonged bombardment of meteorites, or by the mere cowardice and vertigo that dared not look down the precipice of the fact.

2. THE FLYING MEN

We need not dwell upon these multitudinous reiterations of culture, but must glance for a moment at the last phase of this sixth human species, so that we may pass on to the artificial species which it produced.

Throughout their career the Sixth Men had often been fascinated by the idea of flight. The bird was again and again their most sacred symbol. Their monotheism was apt to be worship not of a god-man, but of a god-bird, conceived now as the divine sea eagle, winged with power, now as the giant swift, winged with mercy, now as a disembodied spirit of air, and once as the bird-god that became man to endow the human race with flight, physical and spiritual.

259

It was inevitable that flight should obsess man on Venus, for the planet afforded but a cramping home for groundlings; and the riotous efflorescence of avian species shamed man's pedestrian habit. When in due course the Sixth Men attained knowledge and power comparable to that of the First Men at their height, they invented flying machines of various types. Many times, indeed, mechanical flight was rediscovered and lost again with the downfall of civilization. But at its best it was regarded only as a make-shift. And when at length, with the advance of the biological sciences, the Sixth Men were in a position to influence the human organism itself, they determined to produce a true flying man. Many civilizations strove vainly for this result, sometimes half-heartedly, sometimes with religious earnestness. Finally the most enduring and brilliant of all the civilizations of the Sixth Men actually attained the goal.

The Seventh Men were pigmies, scarcely heavier than the largest of terrestrial flying birds. Through and through they were organized for flight. A leathery membrane spread from the foot to the tip of the immensely elongated and strengthened 'middle finger'. The three 'outer' fingers, equally elongated, served as ribs to the membrane; while the index and thumb remained free for manipulation. The body assumed the stream-lines of a bird, and was covered with a deep quilt of feathery wool. This, and the silken down of the flight-membranes, varied greatly from individual to individual in colouring and texture. On the ground the Seventh Men walked much as other human beings, for the flight-membranes were folded close to the legs and body, and hung from the arms like exaggerated sleeves. In flight the legs were held extended as a flattened tail, with the feet locked together by the big toes. The breastbone was greatly developed as a keel, and as a base for the muscles of flight. The other bones were hollow, for lightness, and their internal surfaces were utilized as supplementary lungs. For, like the birds, these flying men had to maintain a high rate of oxidation. A state which others would regard as fever was normal to them.

Their brains were given ample tracts for the organization of prowess in flight. In fact, it was found possible to equip the species with a system of reflexes for aerial balance, and a true, though artificial, instinctive aptitude for flight, and interest in flight. Compared with their makers their brain volume was of necessity small, but their whole neural system was very carefully organized. Also it matured rapidly, and was extremely facile in the acquirement of new modes of activity. This was very desirable; for the individual's natural life period was but fifty years, and in most cases it was deliberately cut short by some impossible feat at about forty, or whenever the symptoms of old age began to be felt.

Of all human species these bat-like Flying Men, the Seventh Men, were probably the most carefree. Gifted with harmonious physique and gay temperament, they came into a social heritage well adapted to their nature. There was no occasion for them, as there had often been for some others, to regard the world as fundamentally hostile to life, or themselves as essentially deformed. Of quick intelligence in respect of daily personal affairs and social organization, they were untroubled by the insatiable lust of understanding. Not that they were an unintellectual race, for they soon formulated a beautifully systematic account of experience. They clearly perceived, however, that the perfect sphere of their thought was but a bubble adrift in chaos. Yet it was an elegant bubble. And the system was true, in its own gay and frankly insincere manner, true as significant metaphor, not literally true. What more, it was asked, could be expected of human intellect? Adolescents were encouraged to study the ancient problems of philosophy, for no reason but to convince themselves of the futility of probing beyond the limits of the orthodox system. 'Prick the bubble of thought at any point', it was said, 'and you shatter the whole of it. And since thought is one of the necessities of human life, it must be preserved.'

Natural science was taken over from the earlier species with half-contemptuous gratitude, as a necessary means of sane adjustment to the environment. Its practical applications were valued as the ground of the social order; but as the millenia advanced, and society approached that remarkable perfection and stability which was to endure for many million years, scientific inventiveness became less and less needful, and science itself

261

was relegated to the infant schools. History also was given in out-line during childhood, and subsequently ignored.

This curiously sincere intellectual insincerity was due to the fact that the Seventh Men were chiefly concerned with matters other than abstract thought. It is difficult to give to members of the first human species an inkling of the great preoccupation of these Flying Men. To say that it was flight would be true, yet far less than the truth. To say that they sought to live dangerously and vividly, to crowd as much experience as possible into each moment, would again be a caricature of the truth. On the physical plane, indeed, 'the universe of flight', with all the variety of peril and skill afforded by a tempestuous atmosphere, was every individual's chief medium of self-expression. Yet it was not flight itself, but the spiritual aspect of flight which obsessed the species.

In the air and on the ground the Seventh Men were different beings. Whenever they exercised themselves in flight they suffered a remarkable change of spirit. Much of their time had to be spent on the ground, since most of the work upon which civilization rested was impossible in the air. Moreover, life in the air was life at high pressure, and necessitated spells of recuperation on the ground. In their pedestrian phase the Seventh Men were sober folk, mildly bored, yet in the main cheerful, humorously impatient of the drabness and irk of pedestrian affairs, but ever supported by memory and anticipation of the vivid life of the air. Often they were tired, after the strain of that other life, but seldom were they despondent or lazy. Indeed, in the routine of agriculture and industry they were industrious as the wingless ants. Yet they worked in a strange mood of attentive absentmindedness; for their hearts were ever in the air. So long as they could have frequent periods of aviation, they remained bland even on the ground. But if for any reason such as illness they were confined to the ground for a long period, they pined, developed acute melancholia, and died. Their makers had so contrived them that with the onset of any very great pain or misery their hearts should stop. Thus they were to avoid all serious distress. But, in fact, this merciful device worked only on the ground. In the air they assumed a very different and more heroic nature, which their makers had not foreseen, though indeed it was a natural consequence of their design.

In the air the flying man's heart beat more powerfully. His temperature rose. His sensation became more vivid and more discriminate, his intelligence more agile and penetrating. He experienced a more intense pleasure or pain in all that happened to him. It would not be true to say that he became more emotional; rather the reverse, if by emotionality is meant enslavement to the emotions. For the most remarkable feature of the aerial phase was that this enhanced power of appreciation was dispassionate. So long as the individual was in the air, whether in lonely struggle with the storm, or in the ceremonial ballet with sky-darkening hosts of his fellows; whether in the ecstatic love dance with a sexual partner, or in solitary and meditative circlings far above the world; whether his enterprise was fortunate, or he found himself dismembered by the hurricane, and crashing to death; always the gay and the tragic fortunes of his own person were regarded equally with detached aesthetic delight. Even when his dearest companion was mutilated or destroyed by some aerial disaster, he exulted; though also he would give his own life in the hope of effecting a rescue. But very soon after he had returned to the ground he would be overwhelmed with grief, would strive vainly to recapture the lost vision, and would perhaps die of heart failure.

Even when, as happened occasionally in the wild climate of Venus, a whole aerial population was destroyed by some worldwide atmospheric tumult, the few broken survivors, so long as they could remain in the air, exulted. And actually while at length they sank exhausted towards the ground, towards certain disillusionment and death, they laughed inwardly. Yet an hour after they had alighted, their constitution would be changed, their vision lost. They would remember only the horror of the disaster, and the memory would kill them.

No wonder the Seventh Men grudged every moment that was passed on the ground. While they were in the air, of course, the prospect of a pedestrian interlude, or indeed of endless pedestrianism, though in a manner repugnant, would be accepted with unswerving gaiety; but while they were on the ground, they grudged bitterly to be there. Early in the career of the species the proportion of aerial to terrestrial hours was increased by a biological invention. A minute food-plant was produced which spent the winter rooted in the ground, and the summer adrift in the sunlit upper air, engaged solely in photosynthesis. Henceforth the populations of the Flying Men were able to browse upon the bright pastures of the sky, like swallows. As the ages passed, material civilization became more and more simplified. Needs which could not be satisfied without terrestrial labour tended to be outgrown. Manufactured articles became increasingly rare. Books were no longer written or read. In the main, indeed, they were no longer necessary; but to some extent their place was taken by verbal tradition and discussion, in the upper air. Of the arts, music, spoken lyric and epic verse, and the supreme art of winged dance, were constantly practised. The rest vanished. Many of the sciences inevitably faded into tradition; yet the true scientific spirit was preserved in a very exact meteorology, a sufficient biology, and a human psychology surpassed only by the second and fifth species at their height. None of these sciences, however, was taken very seriously, save in its practical applications. For instance, psychology explained the ecstasy of flight very neatly as a febrile and 'irrational' beatitude. But no one was disconcerted by this theory; for every one, while on the wing, felt it to be merely an amusing half-truth.

The social order of the Seventh Men was in essence neither utilitarian, nor humanistic, nor religious, but aesthetic. Every act and every institution were to be justified as contributing to the perfect form of the community. Even social prosperity was conceived as merely the medium in which beauty should be embodied, the beauty, namely, of vivid individual lives harmoniously related. Yet not only for the individual, but even for the race itself (so the wise insisted), death on the wing was more excellent than prolonged life on the ground. Better, far better, would be racial suicide than a future of pedestrianism. Yet though both the individual and the race were conceived as instrumental to objective beauty, there was nothing religious, in any ordinary sense, in this conviction. The Seventh Men were completely without interest in the universal and the unseen. The beauty which they sought to create was ephemeral and very largely sensuous. And they were well content that it should be so. Personal immortality, said a dying sage, would be as tedious as an endless song. Equally so with the race. The lovely flame, of which we all are members, must die, he said, must die; for without death she would fall short of beauty.

For close on a hundred million terrestrial years this aerial society endured with little change. On many of the islands throughout this period stood even yet a number of the ancient pylons, though repaired almost beyond recognition. In these nests the men and women of the seventh species slept through the long Venerian nights, crowded like roosting swallows. By day the same great towers were sparsely peopled with those who were serving their turn in industry, while in the fields and on the sea others laboured. But most were in the air. Many would be skimming the ocean, to plunge, gannet-like, for fish. Many, circling over land or sea, would now and again stoop like hawks upon the wild-fowl which formed the chief meat of the species. Others, forty or fifty thousand feet above the waves, where even the plentiful atmosphere of Venus was scarcely capable of supporting them, would be soaring, circling, sweeping, for pure joy of flight. Others, in the calm and sunshine of high altitudes, would be hanging effortless upon some steady up-current of air for meditation and the rapture of mere percipience. Not a few love-intoxicated pairs would be entwining their courses in aerial patterns, in spires, cascades, and true-love knots of flight, presently to embrace and drop ten thousand feet in bodily union. Some would be driving hither and thither through the green mists of vegetable particles, gathering the manna in their open mouths. Companies, circling together, would be discussing matters social or aesthetic; others would be singing together, or listening to recitative epic verse. Thousands, gathering in the sky like migratory birds, would perform massed convolutions, reminiscent of the vast mechanical aerial choreography of the First World State, but more vital and expressive, as a bird's flight is more vital than the flight of any machine. And all the while there would be some, solitary or in companies, who, either in the pursuit of fish and wildfowl, or out of pure devilment, pitted their strength and skill against the hurricane, often tragically, but never without zest, and laughter of the spirit.

It may seem to some incredible that the culture of the Seventh Men should have lasted so long. Surely it must either have decayed through mere monotony and stagnation or have advanced into richer experience. But no. Generation succeeded generation, and each was too short-lived to outlast its young delight and discover boredom. Moreover, so perfect was the adjustment of these beings to their world, that even if they had lived for centuries they would have felt no need of change. Flight provided them with intense physical exhilaration, and with the physical basis of a genuine and ecstatic, though limited, spiritual experience. In this their supreme attainment they rejoiced not only in the diversity of flight itself, but also in the perceived beauties of their variegated world, and most of all, perhaps, in the thousand lyric and epic ventures of human intercourse in an aerial community.

The end of this seemingly everlasting elysium was nevertheless involved in the very nature of the species. In the first place, as the ages lengthened into aeons, the generations preserved less and less of the ancient scientific lore. For it became insignificant to them. The aerial community had no need of it. This loss of mere information did not matter so long as their condition remained unaltered; but in due course biological changes began to undermine them. The species had always been prone to a certain biological instability. A proportion of infants, varying with circumstances, had always been misshapen; and the deformity had generally been such as to make flight impossible. The normal infant was able to fly early in its second year. If some accident prevented it from doing so, it invariably fell into a decline and died before its third year was passed. But many of the deformed types, being the result of a partial reversion to the pedestrian nature, were able to live on indefinitely without flight. According to a merciful custom these cripples had always to be destroyed. But at length, owing to the gradual exhaustion of a certain marine salt essential to the high-strung nature of the Seventh Men, infants were more often deformed than true to type. The world population declined so seriously that the organized aerial life of the community could no longer be carried on according to the time-honoured aesthetic principles. No one knew how to check this racial decay, but many felt that with greater biological knowledge it might be avoided. A disastrous policy was now adopted. It was decided to spare a carefully selected proportion of the deformed infants, those namely which, though doomed to pedestrianism, were likely to develop high intelligence. Thus it was hoped to raise a specialized group of persons whose work should be biological research untrammelled by the intoxication of flight.

The brilliant cripples that resulted from this policy looked at existence from a new angle. Deprived of the supreme experience for which their fellows lived, envious of a bliss which they knew only by report, yet contemptuous of the naïve mentality which cared for nothing (it seemed) but physical exercise, love-making, the beauty of nature, and the elegances of society, these flightless intelligences sought satisfaction almost wholly in the life of research and scientific control. At the best, however, they were a tortured and resentful race. For their natures were fashioned for the aerial life which they could not lead. Although they received from the winged folk just treatment and a certain compassionate respect, they writhed under this kindness, locked their hearts against all the orthodox values, and sought out new ideals. Within a few centuries they had rehabilitated the life of intellect, and, with the power that knowledge gives, they had made themselves masters of the world. The amiable fliers were surprised, perplexed, even pained; and yet withal amused. Even when it became evident that the pedestrians were determined to create a new world-order in which there would be no place for the beauties of natural flight, the fliers were only distressed while they were on the ground.

The islands were becoming crowded with machinery and flightless industrialists. In the air itself the winged folk found themselves outstripped by the base but effective instruments of mechanical flight. Wings became a laughing stock, and the life of natural flight was condemned as a barren luxury. It was ordained that in future every flier must serve the pedestrian world-order, or starve. And as the cultivation of wind-borne plants had been abandoned, and fishing and fowling rights were strictly controlled, this law was no empty form. At first it was impossible for the fliers to work on the ground for long hours, day after day, without incurring serious ill-health and an early death. But the pedestrian physiologists invented a drug which preserved the poor wage-slaves in something like physical health, and actually prolonged their life. No drug, however, could restore their spirit, for their normal aerial habit was reduced to a few tired hours of recreation once a week. Meanwhile, breeding experiments were undertaken to produce a wholly wingless large-brained type. And finally a law was enacted by which all winged infants must be either mutilated or destroyed. At this point the fliers made an heroic but ineffectual bid for power. They attacked the pedestrian population from the air. In reply the enemy rode them down in his great aeroplanes and blew them to pieces with high explosive.

The fighting squadrons of the natural fliers were finally driven to the ground in a remote and barren island. Thither the whole flying population, a mere remnant of its former strength, fled out of every civilized archipelago in search of freedom: the whole population – save the sick, who committed suicide, and all infants that could not yet fly. These were stifled by their mothers or next-of-kin, in obedience to a decree of the leaders. About a million men, women and children, some of whom were scarcely old enough for the prolonged flight, now gathered on the rocks, regardless that there was not food in the neighbourhood for a great company.

Their leaders, conferring together, saw clearly that the day of Flying Man was done, and that it would be more fitting for a high-souled race to die at once than to drag on in subjection to contemptuous masters. They therefore ordered the population to take part in an act of racial suicide that should at least make death a noble gesture of freedom. The people received the message while they were resting on the stony moorland. A wail of sorrow broke from them. It was checked by the speaker, who bade them strive to see, even on the ground, the beauty of the thing that was to be done. They could not see it; but they knew that if they had the strength to take wing again they would see it clearly, almost as soon as their tired muscles bore them aloft. There was no time to waste, for many were already faint with hunger, and anxious lest they should fail to rise. At the appointed signal the whole population rose into the air with a deep roar of wings. Sorrow was left behind. Even the children, when their mothers explained what was to be done, accepted their fate with zest; though, had they learned of it on the ground, they would have been terror-stricken. The company now flew steadily West, forming themselves into a double file many miles long. The cone of a volcano appeared over the horizon, and rose as they approached. The leaders pressed on towards its ruddy smoke plume; and unflinchingly, couple by couple, the whole multitude darted into its fiery breath and vanished. So ended the career of Flying Man.

3. A MINOR ASTRONOMICAL EVENT

The flightless yet still half avian race that now possessed the planet settled down to construct a society based on industry and science. After many vicissitudes of fortune and of aim, they produced a new human species, the Eighth Men. These long-headed and substantial folk were designed to be strictly pedestrian, physically and mentally. Apt for manipulation, calculation, and invention, they very soon turned Venus into an engineer's paradise. With power drawn from the planet's central heat, their huge electric ships bored steadily through the perennial monsoons and hurricanes, which also their aircraft treated with contempt. Islands were joined by tunnels and by millipede bridges. Every inch of land served some industrial or agricultural end. So successfully did the generations amass wealth that their rival races and rival castes were able to indulge, every few centuries, in vast revelries of mutual slaughter and material destruction without, as a rule, impoverishing their descendants. And so insensitive had man become that these orgies shamed him not at all. Indeed, only by the ardours of physical violence could this most philistine species wrench itself for a while out of its complacency. Strife, which to nobler beings would have been a grave spiritual disaster, was for these a tonic, almost a religious exercise. These cathartic paroxysms, it should be observed, were but the rare and brief crises which automatically punctuated ages of stolid peace. At no time did they threaten the existence of the species; seldom did they even destroy its civilization.

It was after a lengthy period of peace and scientific advancement that the Eighth Men made a startling astronomical discovery. Ever since the First Men had learned that in the life of every star there comes a critical moment when the great orb collapses, shrinking to a minute, dense grain with feeble radiation, man had periodically suspected that the sun was about to undergo this change, and become a typical 'White Dwarf'. The Eighth Men detected sure signs of the catastrophe, and predicted its date. Twenty thousand years they gave themselves before the change should begin. In another fifty thousand years, they guessed, Venus would probably be frozen and uninhabitable. The only hope was to migrate to Mercury during the great change, when that planet was already ceasing to be intolerably hot. It was necessary then to give Mercury an atmosphere, and to breed a new species which should be capable of adapting itself finally to a world of extreme cold.

This desperate operation was already on foot when a new astronomical discovery rendered it futile. Astronomers detected, some distance from the solar system, a volume of non-luminous gas. Calculation showed that this object and the sun were approaching one another at a tangent, and that they would collide. Further calculation revealed the probable results of this event. The sun would flare up and expand prodigiously. Life would be quite impossible on any of the planets save, just possibly, Uranus, and more probably Neptune. The three planets beyond Neptune would escape roasting, but were unsuitable for other reasons. The two outermost would remain glacial, and, moreover, lay beyond the range of the imperfect etherships of the Eighth Men. The innermost was practically a bald globe of iron, devoid not merely of atmosphere and water, but also of the normal covering of rock. Neptune alone might be able to support life; but how could even Neptune be populated? Not only was its atmosphere very unsuitable, and its gravitational pull such as to make man's body an intolerable burden, but also up to the time of the collision it would remain excessively cold. Not till after the collision could it support any kind of life known to man.

How these difficulties were overcome I have no time to tell, though the story of man's attack upon his final home is well worthy of recording. Nor can I tell in detail of the conflict of policy which now occurred. Some, realizing that the Eighth Men themselves could never live on Neptune, advocated an orgy of pleasure-living till the end. But at length the race excelled itself in an almost unanimous resolve to devote its remaining centuries to the production of a human being capable of carrying the torch of mentality into a new world.

Ether-vessels were able to reach that remote world and set up chemical changes for the improvement of the atmosphere. It was also possible, by means of the lately rediscovered process of automatic annihilation of matter, to produce a constant supply of energy for the warming of an area where life might hope to survive until the sun should be rejuvenated.

When at last the time for migration was approaching, a specially designed vegetation was shipped to Neptune and established in the warm area to fit it for man's use. Animals, it was decided, would be unnecessary. Subsequently a specially designed human species, the Ninth Men, was transported to man's new home. The giant Eighth Men could not themselves inhabit Neptune. The trouble was not merely that they could scarcely support their own weight, let alone walk, but that the atmospheric pressure on Neptune was unendurable. For the great planet bore a gaseous envelope thousands of miles deep. The solid globe was scarcely more than the yolk of a huge egg. The mass of the air itself combined with the mass of the solid to produce a gravitational pressure greater than that upon the Venerian ocean floor. The Eighth Men, therefore, dared not emerge from their ether-ships to tread the surface of the planet save for brief spells in steel diving suits. For them there was nothing else to do but to return to the archipelagos of Venus, and make the best of life until the end. They were not spared for long. A few centuries after the settlement of Neptune had been completed by transferring thither all the most precious material relics of humanity, the great planet itself narrowly missed collision with the dark stranger from space. Uranus and Jupiter were at the time well out of its track. Not so Saturn, which, a few years after Neptune's escape, was engulfed with all its rings and satellites. The sudden incandescence which resulted from this minor collision was but a prelude. The huge foreigner rushed on. Like a finger poked into a spider's web, it tangled up the planetary orbits. Having devoured its way through the asteroids, it missed Mars, caught Earth and Venus in its blazing hair, and leapt at the sun. Henceforth the centre of the solar system was a star nearly as wide as the old orbit of Mercury and the system was transformed.

XIV *Neptune*

1. BIRD'S-EYE VIEW

I HAVE told man's story up to a point about half-way from his origin to his annihilation. Behind lies the vast span which includes the whole Terrestrial and Venerian ages, with all their slow fluctuations of darkness and enlightenment. Ahead lies the Neptunian age, equally long, equally tragic perhaps, but more diverse, and in its last phase incomparably more brilliant. It would not be profitable to recount the history of man on Neptune on the scale of the preceding chronicle. Very much of it would be incomprehensible to terrestrials, and much of it repeats again and again, in the many Neptunian modes, themes that we have already observed in the Terrestrial or the Venerian movements of the human symphony. To appreciate fully the range and subtlety of the great living epic, we ought, no doubt, to dwell on its every movement with the same faithful care. But this is impossible to any human mind. We can but attend to significant phrases, here and there, and hope to capture some fragmentary hint of its vast intricate form. And for the readers of this book, who are themselves tremors in the opening bars of the music, it is best that I should dwell chiefly on things near to them, even at the cost of ignoring much that is in fact greater.

Before continuing our long flight let us look around us. Hitherto we have passed over time's fields at a fairly low altitude, making many detailed observations. Now we shall travel at a greater height and with speed of a new order. We must therefore orientate ourselves within the wider horizon that opens around us; we must consider things from the astronomical rather than the human point of view. I said that we were half-way from man's beginning to his end. Looking back to that remote beginning we see that the span of time which includes the whole career of the First Men from Pithecanthropus to the Patagonian disaster is an unanalysable point. Even the preceding and much longer period between the first mammal and the first man, some twenty-five millions of terrestrial years, seems now inconsiderable. The whole of it, together with the age of the First Men, may be said to lie half-way between the formation of the planets, two thousand million years earlier, and their final destruction, two thousand million years later. Taking a still wider view, we see that this aeon of four thousand million years is itself no more than a moment in comparison with the sun's age. And before the birth of the suns the stuff of this galaxy had already endured for aeons as a nebula. Yet even these aeons look brief in relation to the passage of time before the myriad great nebulae themselves, the future galaxies, condensed out of the all-pervading mist in the beginning. Thus the whole duration of humanity, with its many sequent species and its incessant downpour of generations, is but a flash in the lifetime of the cosmos.

Spatially, also, man is inconceivably minute. If in imagination we reduce this galaxy of ours to the size of an ancient terrestrial principality, we must suppose it adrift in the void with millions of other such principalities, very remote from one another. On the same scale the all-embracing cosmos would bulk as a sphere whose diameter was some twenty times greater than that of the lunar orbit in your day; and somewhere within the little wandering asteroid-like principality which is our own universe, the solar system would be an ultramicroscopic point, the greatest planet incomparably smaller.

We have watched the fortunes of eight successive human species for a thousand million years, the first half of that flicker which is the duration of man. Ten more species now succeed one another, or are contemporary, on the plains of Neptune. We, the Last Men, are the Eighteenth Men. Of the eight pre-Neptunian species, some, as we have seen, remained always primitive; many achieved at least a confused and fleeting civilization, and one, the brilliant Fifth, was already wakening into true humanity when misfortune crushed it. The ten Neptunian species show an even greater diversity. They range from the instinctive animal to modes of consciousness never before attained. The definitely sub-human degenerate types are confined mostly to the first six hundred million years of man's sojourn on Neptune. During the earlier half of this long phase of preparation, man, at first almost crushed out of existence by a hostile environment, gradually peopled the huge north; but with beasts, not men. For man, as man, no longer existed. During the latter half of the preparatory six hundred million years, the human spirit gradually awoke again, to undergo the fluctuating advance and decline characteristic of the pre-Neptunian ages. But subsequently, in the last four hundred million years of his career on Neptune, man has made an almost steady progress toward full spiritual maturity.

Let us now look rather more closely at these three great epochs of man's history.

2. DA CAPO

It was in desperate haste that the last Venerian men had designed and fashioned the new species for the colonization of Neptune. The mere remoteness of the great planet, moreover, had prevented its nature from being explored at all thoroughly, and so the new human organism was but partially adapted to its destined environment. Inevitably it was a dwarf type, limited in size by the necessity of resisting an excessive gravitation. Its brain was so cramped that everything but the bare essentials of humanity had to be omitted from it. Even so, the Ninth Men were too delicately organized to withstand the ferocity of natural forces on Neptune. This ferocity the designers had seriously underestimated; and so they were content merely to produce a miniature copy of their own type. They should have planned a hardy brute, lustily procreative, cunning in the struggle for physical existence, but above all tough, prolific, and so insensitive as to be scarcely worthy of the name man. They should have trusted that if once this crude seed could take root, natural forces themselves would in time conjure from it something more human. Instead, they produced a race cursed with the inevitable fragility of miniatures, and designed for a civilized environment which feeble spirits could not possibly maintain in a tumultuous world. For it so happened that the still youthful giant, Neptune, was slowly entering one of his phases of crustal shrinkage, and therefore of earthquake and eruption. Thus the frail colonists found themselves increasingly in danger of being swallowed in sudden fiery crevasses or buried under volcanic dust. Moreover, their squat buildings, when not actually being trampled by lava streams, or warped and cracked by their shifting foundations, were liable to be demolished by the battering-ram thrust of a turbulent and massive atmosphere. Further, the atmosphere's unwholesome composition killed all possibility of cheerfulness and courage in a race whose nature was doomed to be, even in favourable circumstances, neurotic.

Fortunately this agony could not last indefinitely. Little by little, civilization crumbled into savagery, the torturing vision of better things was lost, man's consciousness was narrowed and coarsened into brute-consciousness. By good luck the brute precariously survived.

Long after the Ninth Men had fallen from man's estate, nature herself, in her own slow and blundering manner, succeeded where man had failed. The brute descendants of this human species became at length well adapted to their world. In time there arose a wealth of sub-human forms in the many kinds of environment afforded by the lands and seas of Neptune. None of them penetrated far towards the Equator, for the swollen sun had rendered the tropics at this time far too hot to support life of any kind. Even at the pole the protracted summer put a great strain on all but the most hardy creatures.

Neptune's year was at this time about one hundred and sixty-five times the length of the old terrestrial year. The slow seasonal change had an important effect on life's own rhythms. All but the most ephemeral organisms tended to live through at least one complete year, and the higher mammals survived longer. At a much later stage this natural longevity was to play a great and beneficial part in the revival of man. But, on the other hand, the increasing sluggishness of individual growth, the length of immaturity in each generation, retarded the natural evolutionary process on Neptune, so that compared with the Terrestrial and Venerian epochs the biological story now moves at a snail's pace.

After the fall of the Ninth Men the subhuman creatures had one and all adopted a quadruped habit, the better to cope with gravity. At first they had indulged merely in occasional support from their knuckles, but in time many species of true quadrupeds had appeared. In several of the running types the fingers, like the toes, had grown together, and a hoof had developed, not on the old finger-tips, which were bent back and atrophied, but on the knuckles.

Two hundred millions years after the solar collision innumerable species of subhuman grazers with long sheep-like muzzles, ample molars, and almost ruminant digestive systems, were competing with one another on the polar continent. Upon these preyed the subhuman carnivora, of whom some were built for speed in the chase, others for stalking and a sudden spring. But since jumping was no easy matter on Neptune, the cat-like types were all minute. They preyed upon man's more rabbit-like and rat-like descendants, or on the carrion of the larger mammals, or on the lusty worms and beetles. These had sprung originally from vermin which had been transported accidentally from Venus. For of all the ancient Venerian fauna only man himself, a few insects and other invertebrates, and many kinds of microorganisms, succeeded in colonizing Neptune. Of plants, many types had been artificially bred for the new world, and from these eventually arose a host of grasses, flowering plants, thick-trunked bushes, and novel sea-weeds. On this marine flora fed certain highly developed marine worms; and of these last, some in time became vertebrate, predatory, swift, and fish-like. On these in turn man's own marine descendants preyed, whether as subhuman seals, or still more specialized sub-human porpoises. Perhaps most remarkable of these developments of the ancient human stock was that which led, through a small insectivorous bat-like glider, to a great diversity of true flying mammals, scarcely larger than humming birds, but in some cases agile as swallows.

Nowhere did the typical human form survive. There were only beasts, fitted by structure and instinct to some niche or other of their infinitely diverse and roomy world.

Certain strange vestiges of human mentality did indeed persist here and there, even as, in the fore-limbs of most species, there still remained buried the relics of man's once cunning fingers. For instance, there were certain grazers which in times of hardship would meet together and give tongue in cacophonous ululation; or, sitting on their haunches with fore-limbs pressed together, they would listen by the hour to the howls of some leader, responding intermittently with groans and whimpers, and working themselves at last into foaming madness. And there were carnivora which, in the midst of the spring-time fervour, would suddenly cease from love-making, fighting, and the daily routine of hunting, to sit alone in some high place day after day, night after night, watching, waiting; until at last hunger forced them into action.

Now in the fullness of time, about three hundred million terrestrial years after the solar collision, a certain minute, hairless, rabbit-like creature, scampering on the polar grasslands, found itself greatly persecuted by a swift hound from the south. The subhuman rabbit was relatively unspecialized, and had no effective means of defence or flight. It was almost exterminated. A few individuals, however, saved themselves by taking to the dense and thick-trunked scrub, whither the hound could not follow them. Here they had to change their diet and manner of life, deserting grass for roots, berries, and even worms and beetles. Their fore-limbs were now increasingly used for digging and climbing, and eventually for weaving nests of stick and straw. In this species the fingers had never grown together. Internally the fore-paw was like a minute clenched fist from the elongated and exposed knuckles of which separate toes protruded. And now the knuckles elongated themselves still further, becoming in time a new set of fingers. Within the palm of the new little monkey-hand there still remained traces of man's ancient fingers, bent in upon themselves.

As of old, manipulation gave rise to clearer percipience. And this, in conjunction with the necessity of frequent experiments in diet, hunting, and defence, produced at length a real versatility of behaviour and suppleness of mind. The rabbit throve, adopted an almost upright gait, continued to increase in stature and in brain. Yet, just as the new hand was not merely a resurrection of the old hand, so the new regions of the brain were no mere revival of the atrophied human cerebrum, but a new organ, which overlaid and swallowed up that ancient relic. The creature's mind, therefore, was in many respects a new mind, though moulded to the same great basic needs. Like his fore-runners, of course, he craved food, love, glory, companionship. In pursuit of these ends he devised weapons and traps, and built wicker villages. He held pow-wows. He became the Tenth Men.

3. SLOW CONQUEST

For a million terrestrial years these long-armed hairless beings were spreading their wicker huts and bone implements over the great northern continents, and for many more millions they remained in possession without making further cultural progress; for evolution, both biological and cultural, was indeed slow on Neptune. At last the Tenth Men were attacked by a micro-organism and demolished. From their ruins several primitive human species developed, and remained isolated in remote terri-tories for millions of decades, until at length chance or enterprise brought them into contact. One of these early species, crouched and tusked, was persistently trapped for its ivory by an abler type, till it was exterminated. Another, long of muzzle and large of base, habitually squatted on its haunches like the kangaroo. Shortly after this industrious and social species had discovered the use of the wheel, a more primitive but more war-like type crashed into it like a tidal wave and overwhelmed it. Erect, but literally almost as broad as they were tall, these chunkish and bloody-minded savages spread over the whole arctic and sub-arctic region and spent some millions of years in monotonous reiteration of progress and decline; until at last a slow decay of their germ-plasm almost ended man's career. But after an aeon of darkness, there appeared another thick-set, but larger brained, species. This, for the first time on Neptune, conceived the religion of love, and all those spiritual cravings and agonies which had flickered in man so often and so vainly upon Earth and Venus. There appeared again feudal empires, militant nations, economic class wars, and, not once but often, a world-state covering the whole northern hemisphere. These men it was that first crossed the equator in artificially cooled electric ships, and explored the huge south. No life of any kind was discovered in the southern hemisphere; for even in that age no living matter could have crossed the roasting tropics without artificial refrigeration. Indeed, it was only because the sun's temporary revival had already passed its zenith that even man, with all his ingenuity, could endure a long tropical voyage.

Like the First Men and so many other natural human types, these Fourteenth Men were imperfectly human. Like the First Men, they conceived ideals of conduct which their imperfectly organized nervous systems could never attain and seldom approach. Unlike the First Men, they survived with but minor biological changes for three hundred million years. But even so long a period did not enable them to transcend their imperfect spiritual nature. Again and again and again they passed from savagery to world-civilization and back to savagery. They were captive within their own nature, as a bird in a cage. And as a caged bird may fumble with nest-building materials and periodically destroy the fruit of its aimless toil, so these cramped beings destroyed their civilizations.

At length, however, this second phase of Neptunian history, this era of fluctuation, was brought to an end. At the close of the six hundred million years after the first settlement of the planet, unaided nature produced, in the Fifteenth human species, that highest form of natural man which she had produced only once before, in the Second species. And this time no Martians interfered. We must not stay to watch the struggle of this greatheaded man to overcome his one serious handicap, excessive weight of cranium and unwieldy proportions of body. Suffice it that after a long-drawn-out immaturity, including one great mechanized war between the northern and southern hemispheres, the Fifteenth Men outgrew the ailments and fantasies of youth, and consolidated themselves as a single world-community. This civilization was based economically on volcanic power, and spiritually on devotion to the fulfilment of human capacity. It was this species which, for the first time on Neptune, conceived, as an enduring racial purpose, the will to remake human nature upon an ampler scale.

Henceforth in spite of many disasters, such as another period of earthquake and eruption, sudden climatic changes, innumerable plagues and biological aberrations, human progress was relatively steady. It was not by any means swift and sure. There were still to be ages, often longer than the whole career of the First Men, in which the human spirit would rest from its pioneering to consolidate its conquests, or would actually stray into the wilderness. But never again, seemingly, was it to be routed and crushed into mere animality.

In tracing man's final advance to full humanity we can observe only the broadest features of a whole astronomical era. But in fact it is an era crowded with many thousands of long-lived generations. Myriads of individuals, each one unique, live out their lives in rapt intercourse with one another, contribute their heart's pulses to the universal music, and presently vanish, giving place to others. All this age-long sequence of private living, which is the actual tissue of humanity's flesh, I cannot describe. I can only trace, as it were, the disembodied form of its growth.

The Fifteenth Men first set themselves to abolish five great evils, namely, disease, suffocating toil, senility, misunderstanding, ill-will. The story of their devotion, their many disastrous experiments, and ultimate triumph, cannot here be told. Nor can I recount how they learned and used the secret of deriving power from the annihilation of matter, nor how they invented etherships for the exploration of neighbouring planets, nor how, after ages of experiments, they designed and produced a new species, the Sixteenth, to supersede themselves.

The new type was analogous to the ancient Fifth, which had colonized Venus. Artificial rigid atoms had been introduced into its bone tissues, so that it might support great stature and an ample brain; in which, moreover, an exceptionally fine-grained cellular structure permitted a new complexity of organization. 'Telepathy', also, was once more achieved, not by means of the Martian units, which had long ago become extinct, but by the synthesis of new molecular groups of a similar type. Partly through the immense increase of mutual understanding, which resulted from 'telepathic' rapport, partly through improved co-ordination of the nervous system, the ancient evil of selfishness was entirely and finally abolished from the normal human being.

Egoistic impulses, whenever they refused to be subordinated, were henceforth classed as symptoms of insanity. The sensory powers of the new species were, of course, greatly improved; and it was even given a pair of eyes in the back of the head. Henceforth man was to have a circular instead of a semi-circular field of vision. And such was the general intelligence of the new race that many problems formerly deemed insoluble were now solved in a single flash of insight.

Of the great practical uses to which the Sixteenth Men put their powers, one only need be mentioned as an example. They gained control of the movement of their planet. Early in their career they were able, with the unlimited energy at their disposal, to direct it into a wider orbit, so that its average climate became more temperate, and snow occasionally covered the polar regions. But as the ages advanced, and the sun became steadily less ferocious, it became necessary to reverse this process and shift the planet gradually nearer to the sun.

When they had possessed their world for nearly fifty million years, the Sixteenth Men, like the Fifth before them, learned to enter into past minds. For them this was a more exciting adventure than for their forerunners, since they were still ignorant of Terrestrial and Venerian history. Like their forerunners, so dismayed were they at the huge volume of eternal misery in the past, that for a while, in spite of their own great blessings and spontaneous gaiety, existence seemed a mockery. But in time they came to regard the past's misery as a challenge. They told themselves that the past was calling to them for help, and that somehow they must prepare a great 'crusade to liberate the past'. How this was to be done, they could not conceive; but they were determined to bear in mind this quixotic aim in the great enterprise which had by now become the chief concern of the race, namely the creation of a human type of an altogether higher order.

It had become clear that man had by now advanced in understanding and creativeness as far as was possible to the individual human brain acting in physical isolation. Yet the Sixteenth Men were oppressed by their own impotence. Though in philosophy they had delved further than had ever been possible, yet even at their deepest they found only the shifting sands of mystery. In particular they were haunted by three ancient problems, two of which were purely intellectual, namely the mystery of time and the mystery of mind's relation to the world. Their third problem was the need somehow to reconcile their confirmed loyalty to life, which they conceived as embattled against death, with their ever-strengthening impulse to rise above the battle and admire it dispassionately.

Age after age the races of the Sixteenth Men blossomed with culture after culture. The movement of thought ranged again and again through all the possible modes of the spirit, ever discovering new significance in ancient themes. Yet throughout this epoch the three great problems remained unsolved, perplexing the individual and vitiating the policy of the race.

Forced thus at length to choose between spiritual stagnation and a perilous leap in the dark, the Sixteenth Men determined to set about devising a type of brain which, by means of the mental fusion of many individuals, might waken into an altogether new mode of consciousness. Thus, it was hoped, man might gain insight into the very heart of existence, whether finally to admire or loathe. And thus the racial purpose, which had been so much confused by philosophical ignorance, might at last become clear.

Of the hundred million years which passed before the Sixteenth Men produced the new human type, I must not pause to tell. They thought they had achieved their hearts' desire; but in fact the glorious beings which they had produced were tortured by subtle imperfections beyond their makers' comprehension. Consequently, no sooner had these Seventeenth Men peopled the world and attained full cultural stature, than they also bent all their strength to the production of a new type, essentially like their own, but perfected. Thus after a brief career of a few hundred thousand years, crowded with splendour and agony, the Seventeenth gave place to the Eighteenth, and, as it turns out, the Last, human species. Since all the earlier cultures find their fulfilment in the world of the Last Men, I pass over them to enlarge somewhat upon our modern age.

XV *The Last Men*

1. INTRODUCTION TO THE LAST HUMAN SPECIES

IF one of the First Men could enter the world of the Last Men, he would find many things familiar and much that would seem strangely distorted and perverse. But nearly everything that is most distinctive of the last human species would escape him. Unless he were to be told that behind all the obvious and imposing features of civilization, behind all the social organization and personal intercourse of a great community, lay a whole other world of spiritual culture, round about him, yet beyond his ken, he would no more suspect its existence than a cat in London suspects the existence of finance or literature.

Among the familiar things that he would encounter would be creatures recognizably human yet in his view grotesque. While he himself laboured under the weight of his own body, these giants would be easily striding. He would consider them very sturdy, often thick-set, folk, but he would be compelled to allow them grace of movement and even beauty of proportion. The longer he stayed with them the more beauty he would see in them, and the less complacently would he regard his own type. Some of these fantastic men and women he would find covered with fur, hirsute, or mole-velvet, revealing the underlying muscles. Others would display bronze, yellow, or ruddy skin, and yet others a translucent ashgreen, warmed by the underflowing blood. As a species, though we are all human, we are extremely variable in body and mind, so variable that superficially we seem to be not one species but many. Some characters, of course, are common to all of us. The traveller might perhaps be surprised by the large yet sensitive hands which are universal, both in men and women. In all of us the outermost finger bears at its tip three minute organs of manipulation, rather similar to those which were first devised for the Fifth Men. These excrescences would doubtless revolt our visitor. The pair of occipital eyes, too, would shock him; so would the upward-look-

284

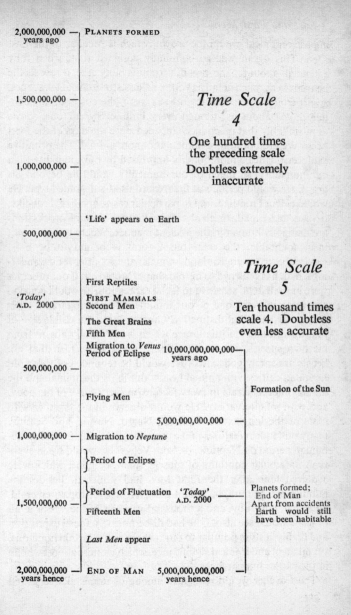

2,000,000,000 years ago —	PLANETS FORMED
1,500,000,000 —	*Time Scale* **4** One hundred times the preceding scale **Doubtless extremely inaccurate**
1,000,000,000 —	
500,000,000 —	'Life' appears on Earth
	Time Scale **5**
	First Reptiles
'Today' A.D. 2000	FIRST MAMMALS Second Men Ten thousand times scale 4. Doubtless even less accurate
	The Great Brains Fifth Men
	Migration to *Venus* Period of Eclipse 10,000,000,000,000 years ago
500,000,000 —	
	Formation of the Sun
	Flying Men
	5,000,000,000,000
1,000,000,000 —	Migration to *Neptune*
	} Period of Eclipse
	} Period of Fluctuation 'Today' A.D. 2000
1,500,000,000 —	Fifteenth Men Planets formed; End of Man Apart from accidents Earth would still have been habitable
	Last Men appear
2,000,000,000 years hence —	END OF MAN 5,000,000,000,000 years hence

ing astronomical eye on the crown, which is peculiar to the Last Men. This organ was so cunningly designed that, when fully extended, about a hand-breadth from its bony case, it reveals the heavens in as much detail as your smaller astronomical telescopes. Apart from such special features as these, there is nothing definitely novel about us; though every limb, every contour, shows unmistakably that much has happened since the days of the First Men. We are both more human and more animal. The primitive explorer might be more readily impressed by our animality than our humanity, so much of our humanity would lie beyond his grasp. He would perhaps at first regard us as a degraded type. He would call us faun-like, and in particular cases, ape-like, bear-like, ox-like, marsupial, or elephantine. Yet our general proportions are definitely human in the ancient manner. Where gravity is not insurmountable, the erect biped form is bound to be most serviceable to intelligent land animals; and so, after long wanderings, man has returned to his old shape. Moreover, if our observer were himself at all sensitive to facial expression, he would come to recognize in every one of our innumerable physiognomic types an indescribable but distinctively human look, the visible sign of that inward and spiritual grace which is not wholly absent from his own species. He would perhaps say, 'These men that are beasts are surely gods also'. He would be reminded of those old Egyptian deities with animal heads. But in us the animal and the human interpenetrate in every feature, in every curve of the body, and with infinite variety. He would observe in us, together with hints of the long-extinct Mongol, Negro, Nordic, and Semitic, many outlandish features and expressions, deriving from the sub-human period on Neptune, or from Venus. He would see in every limb unfamiliar contours of muscle, sinew, or bone, which were acquired long after the First Men had vanished. Besides the familiar eye-colours, he would discover orbs of topaz, emerald, amethyst, and ruby, and a thousand varieties of these. But in all of us he would see also, if he had discernment, a facial expression and bodily gesture peculiar to our own species, a certain luminous, yet pungent and ironical significance, which we miss almost wholly in the earlier human faces.

The traveller would recognize among us unmistakable sexual

features, both of general proportions and special organs. But it would take him long to discover that some of the most striking bodily and facial differences were due to differentiation of the two ancient sexes into many sub-sexes. Full sexual experience involves for us a complicated relationship between individuals of all these types. Of the extremely important sexual groups I shall speak again.

Our visitor would notice, by the way, that, though all persons on Neptune go habitually nude, save for a pouch or ruck-sack, clothing, often brightly coloured, and made of diverse lustrous or homely tissues unknown before our time, is worn for special purposes.

He would notice also, scattered about the green countryside, many buildings, mostly of one storey; for there is plenty of room on Neptune even for the million million of the Last Men. Here and there, however, we have great architectural pylons, cruciform or star-shaped in section, cloud-piercing, dignifying the invariable planes of Neptune. These mightiest of all buildings, which are constructed in adamantine materials formed of artificial atoms, would seem to our visitor geometrical mountains, far taller than any natural mountain could be, even on the smallest planet. In many cases the whole fabric is translucent or transparent, so that at night, with internal illumination, it appears as an edifice of light. Springing from a base twenty or more miles across, these star-seeking towers attain a height where even Neptune's atmosphere is somewhat attenuated. In their summits work the hosts of our astronomers, the essential eyes through which our community, on her little raft, peers across the ocean. Thither also all men and women repair at one time or another to contemplate this galaxy of ours and the unnumbered remoter universes. There they perform together those supreme symbolic acts for which I find no adjective in your speech but the debased word 'religious'. There also they seek the refreshment of mountain air in a world where natural mountains are unknown. And on the pinnacles and precipices of these loftiest horns many of us gratify that primeval lust of climbing which was ingrained in man before ever he was man. These buildings thus combine the functions of observatory, temple, sanatorium, and gymnasium. Some of them are almost as old as the species, some are not yet completed. They embody, therefore, many styles. The traveller would find modes which he would be tempted to call Gothic, Classical, Egyptian, Peruvian, Chinese, or American, besides a thousand architectural ideas unfamiliar to him. Each of these buildings was the work of the race as a whole at some stage in its career. None of them is a mere local product. Every successive culture has expressed itself in one or more of these supreme monuments. Once in forty thousand years or so some new architectural glory would be conceived and executed. And such is the continuity of our cultures that there has scarcely ever been need to remove the handiwork of the past.

If our visitor happened to be near enough to one of these great pylons, he would see it surrounded by a swarm of midges, which would turn out to be human fliers, wingless, but with outspread arms. The stranger might wonder how a large organism could rise from the ground in Neptune's powerful field of gravity. Yet flight is our ordinary means of locomotion. A man has but to put on a suit of overalls fitted at various points with radiation-generators. Ordinary flight thus becomes a kind of aerial swimming. Only when very high speed is desired do we make use of closed-in air-boats and liners.

At the feet of the great buildings the flat or undulating country is green, brown, golden, and strewn with houses. Our traveller would recognize that much land was under cultivation, and would see many persons at work upon it with tools or machinery. Most of our food, indeed, is produced by artificial photosynthesis on the broiling planet Jupiter, where, even now that the sun is becoming normal again, no life can exist without powerful refrigeration. As far as mere nutrition is concerned, we could do without vegetation; but agriculture and its products have played so great a part in human history that today agricultural operations and vegetable foods are very beneficial to the race psychologically. And so it comes about that vegetable matter is in great demand, not only as raw material for innumerable manufactures, but also for table delicacies. Green vegetables, fruit, and various alcoholic fruit drinks have come to have the same kind of ritual significance for us as wine has for you. Meat also, though not a part of ordinary diet, is eaten on very rare and sacred occasions. The cherished wild fauna of the planet contributes its toll to periodic symbolical banquets. And whenever a human being has chosen to die, his body is ceremoniously eaten by his friends.

Communication with the food factories of Jupiter and the agricultural polar regions of the less torrid Uranus, as also with the automatic mining stations on the glacial outer planets, is maintained by ether-ships, which, travelling much faster than the planets themselves, make the passage to the neighbour worlds in a small fraction of the Neptunian year. These vessels, of which the smallest are about a mile in length, may be seen descending on our oceans like ducks. Before they touch the water they cause a prodigious tumult with the downward pressure of their radiation; but once upon the surface, they pass quietly into harbour.

The ether-ship is in a manner symbolic of our whole community, so highly organized is it, and so minute in relation to the void which engulfs it. The ethereal navigators, because they spend so much of their time in the empty regions, beyond the range of 'telepathic' communication and sometimes even of mechanical radio, form mentally a unique class among us. They are a hardy, simple, and modest folk. And though they embody man's proud mastery of the ether, they are never tired of reminding land-lubbers, with dour jocularity, that the most daring voyages are confined within one drop of the boundless ocean of space.

Recently an exploration ship returned from a voyage into the outer tracts. Half her crew had died. The survivors were emaciated, diseased, and mentally unbalanced. To a race that thought itself so well established in sanity that nothing could disturb it, the spectacle of these unfortunates was instructive. Throughout the voyage, which was the longest ever attempted, they had encountered nothing whatever but two comets and an occasional meteor. Some of the nearer constellations were seen with altered forms. One or two stars increased slightly in brightness; and the sun was reduced to being the most brilliant of stars. The aloof and changeless presence of the constellations seems to have crazed the voyagers. When at last the ship returned and berthed, there was a scene such as is seldom witnessed in our modern world. The crew flung open the ports and staggered blubbering into the arms of the crowd. It would never have been believed that members of our species could be so far reduced from the self-possession that is normal to us. Subsequently these poor human wrecks have shown an irrational phobia of the stars, and of all that not human. They dare not go out at night. They live in an extravagant passion for the presence of others. And since all others are astronomically minded, they cannot find real companionship. They insanely refuse to participate in the mental life of the race upon the plane where all things are seen in their just proportions. They cling piteously to the sweets of individual life; and so they are led to curse the immensities. They fill their minds with human conceits, and their houses with toys. By night they draw the curtains and drown the quiet voice of the stars in revelry. But it is a joyless and a haunted revelry, desired less for itself than as a defence against reality.

2. CHILDHOOD AND MATURITY

I said that we were all astronomically minded; but we are not without 'human' interests. Our visitor from the earth would soon discover that the low buildings, sprinkled on all sides, were the homes of individuals, families, sexual groups, and bands of companions. Most of these buildings are so constructed that the roof and walls can be removed, completely or partially, for sun-bathing and for the night. Round each house is a wilderness, or a garden, or an orchard of our sturdy fruit trees. Here and there men and women may be seen at work with hoe or spade or secateurs. The buildings themselves affect many styles; and within doors our visitor would find great variety from house to house. Even within a single house he might come on rooms seemingly of different epochs. And while some rooms are crowded with articles, many of which would be incomprehensible to the stranger, others are bare, save for a table, chairs, a cupboard, and perhaps some single object of pure art. We have an immense variety of manufactured goods. But the visitor from a world obsessed with material wealth would probably remark the simplicity, even austerity, which characterizes most private houses.

He would doubtless be surprised to see no books. In every

room, however, there is a cupboard filled with minute rolls of tape, microscopically figured. Each of these rolls contains matter which could not be cramped into a score of your volumes. They are used in connexion with a pocket-instrument, the size and shape of the ancient cigarette case. When the roll is inserted, it reels itself off at any desired speed, and interferes systematically with ethereal vibrations produced by the instrument. Thus is generated a very complex flow of 'telepathic' language which permeates the brain of the reader. So delicate and direct is this medium of expression that there is scarcely any possibility of misunderstanding the author's intention. The rolls themselves, it should be said, are produced by another special instrument, which is sensitive to vibrations generated in the author's brain. Not that it produces a mere replica of his stream of consciousness; it records only those images and ideas with which he deliberately 'inscribes' it. I may mention also that, since we can at any moment communicate by direct 'telepathy' with any person on the planet, these 'books' of ours are not used for the duplication of merely ephemeral thought. Each one of them preserves only the threshed and chosen grain of some mind's harvest.

Other instruments may be observed in our houses, which I cannot pause to describe, instruments whose office is either to carry out domestic drudgery, or to minister directly in one way or another to cultured life. Near the outer door would be hanging a number of flying-suits, and in a garage attached to the house would be the private air-boats, gaily coloured torpedo-shaped objects of various sizes.

Decoration in our houses, save in those which belong to children, is everywhere simple, even severe. None the less we prize it greatly, and spend much consideration upon it. Children, indeed, often adorn their houses with splendour, which adults themselves can also enjoy through children's eyes, even as they can enter into the frolics of infants with unaffected glee.

The number of children in our world is small in relation to our immense population. Yet, seeing that every one of us is potentially immortal, it may be wondered how we can permit ourselves to have any children at all. The explanation is twofold. In the first place, our policy is to produce new individuals of higher type than ourselves, for we are very far from biologically perfect. Consequently we need a continuous supply of children. And as these successively reach maturity, they take over the functions of adults whose nature is less perfect; and these, when they are aware that they are no longer of service, elect to retire from life.

But even though every individual, sooner or later, ceases to exist, the average length of life is not much less than a quarter of a million terrestrial years. No wonder, then, that we cannot accommodate many children. But we have more than might be expected, for with us infancy and adolescence are very lengthy. The foetus is carried for twenty years. Ectogenesis was practised by our predecessors, but was abandoned by our own species, because, with greatly improved motherhood, there is no need for it. Our mothers, indeed, are both physically and mentally most vigorous during the all too rare period of pregnancy. After birth, true infancy lasts for about a century. During this period, in which the foundations of body and mind are being laid, very slowly, but so securely that they will never fail, the individual is cared for by his mother. Then follow some centuries of childhood, and a thousand years of adolescence.

Our children, of course, are very different beings from the children of the First Men. Though physically they are in many respects still childlike, they are independent persons in the community. Each has either a house of his own, or rooms in a larger building held in common by himself and his friends. Thousands of these are to be found in the neighbourhood of every educational centre. There are some children who prefer to live with their parents, or with one or other of their parents; but this is rare. Though there is often much friendly intercourse between parents and children, the generations usually fare better under separate roofs. This is inevitable in our species. For the adult's overwhelmingly greater experience reveals the world to him in very different proportions from those which are possible even to the most brilliant of children; while on the other hand with us the mind of every child is, in some potentiality or other, definitely superior to every adult mind. Consequently, while the child can never appreciate what is best in his elders, the adult, in spite of his power of direct insight into all minds not superior to himself, is doomed to incomprehension of all that is novel in his own offspring.

Six or seven hundred years after birth a child is in some respects physically equivalent to a ten-year-old of the First Men. But since his brain is destined for much higher development, it is already far more complex than any adult brain of that species. And though temperamentally he is in many ways still a child, intellectually he has already in some respects passed beyond the culture of the best adult minds of the ancient races. The traveller, encountering one of our bright boys, might sometimes be reminded of the wise simplicity of the legendary Child Christ. But also he might equally well discover a vast exuberance, boisterousness, impishness, and a complete inability to stand outside the child's own eager life and regard it dispassionately. In general our children develop intellectually beyond the level of the First Men long before they begin to develop the dispassionate will which is characteristic of our adults. When there is conflict between a child's personal needs and the need of society, he will as a rule force himself to the social course; but he does so with resentment and dramatic self-pity, thereby rendering himself in the adult view exquisitely ridiculous.

When our children attain physical adolescence, nearly a thousand years after birth, they leave the safe paths of childhood to spend another thousand years in one of the antarctic continents, known as the Land of the Young. Somewhat reminiscent of the Wild Continent of the Fifth Men, this territory is preserved as virgin bush and prairie. Sub-human grazers and carnivora abound. Volcanic eruption, hurricanes, and glacial seasons afford further attractions to the adventurous young. There is consequently a high death rate. In this land our young people live the half primitive, half sophisticated life to which their nature is fitted. They hunt, fish, tend cattle, and till the ground. They cultivate all the simple beauties of human individuality. They love and hate. They sing, paint, and carve. They devise heroic myths, and delight in fantasies of direct intercourse with a cosmic person. They organise themselves as tribes and nations. Sometimes they even indulge in warfare of a primitive but bloody type. Formerly when this happened, the adult world interfered; but we have since learned to let the fever run its course. The loss of life is regrettable; but it is a small price to pay for the insight afforded even by this restricted and juvenile warfare, into those primitive agonies and passions which, when they are experienced by the adult mind, are so transformed by philosophy that their import is wholly changed. In the Land of the Young our boys and girls experience all that is precious and all that is abject in the primitive. They live through in their own persons, century by century, all its toilsomeness and cramped meanness, all its blind cruelty and precariousness; but also they taste its glamour, its vernal and lyrical glory. They make in little all the mistakes of thought and action that men have ever made; but at last they emerge ready for the large and more difficult world of maturity.

It was expected that some day, when we should have perfected the species, there would be no need to build up successive generations, no need of children, no need of all this schooling. It was expected that the community would then consist of adults only; and that they would be immortal not merely potentially but in fact, yet also, of course, perennially in the flower of young maturity. Thus, death should never cut the string of individuality and scatter the hard-won pearls, necessitating new strings, and laborious re-gatherings. The many and very delectable beauties of childhood could still be amply enjoyed in exploration of the past.

We know now that this goal is not to be attained, since man's end is imminent.

3. A RACIAL AWAKENING

It is easy to speak of children; but how can I tell you anything significant of our adult experience, in relation to which not only the world of the First Men but the worlds of the most developed earlier species seem so naïve?

The source of the immense difference between ourselves and all other human races lies in the sexual group, which is in fact much more than a sexual group.

The designers of our species set out to produce a being that might be capable of an order of mentality higher than their own. The only possibility of doing so lay in planning a great increase of brain organization. But they knew that the brain of an individual human being could not safely be allowed to exceed a certain weight. They therefore sought to produce the new order of mentality in a system of distinct and specialized brains held in 'telepathic' unity by means of ethereal radiation. Material brains were to be capable of becoming on some occasions mere nodes in a system of radiation which itself should then constitute the physical basis of a single mind. Hitherto there had been 'telepathic' communication between many individuals, but no super-individual, or group-mind. It was known that such a unity of individual minds had never been attained before, save on Mars; and it was known how lamentably the racial mind of Mars had failed to transcend the minds of the Martians. By a combination of shrewdness and good luck the designers hit upon a policy which escaped the Martian failure. They planned as the basis of the super-individual a small multi-sexual group.

Of course the mental unity of the sexual group is not the direct outcome of the sexual intercourse of its members. Such intercourse does occur. Groups differ from one another very greatly in this respect; but in most groups all the members of the male sexes have intercourse with all the members of the female sexes. Thus sex is with us essentially social. It is impossible for me to give any idea of the great range and intensity of experience afforded by these diverse types of union. Apart from this emotional enrichment of the individuals, the importance of sexual activity in the group lies in its bringing individuals into that extreme intimacy, temperamental harmony, and complementariness, without which no emergence into higher experience would be possible.

Individuals are not necessarily confined to the same group for ever. Little by little a group may change every one of its ninety-six members, and yet it will remain the same super-individual mind, though enriched with the memories grafted into it by the new-comers. Very rarely does an individual leave a group before he has been in it for ten thousand years. In some groups the members live together in a common home. In others they live apart. Sometimes an individual will form a sort of monogamous relation with another individual of his group, homing with the chosen one for many thousands of years, or even for a lifetime. Indeed some claim that life-long monogamy is the ideal state, so deep and delicate is the intimacy which it affords. But of course, even in monogamy, each partner must be periodically refreshed by intercourse with other members of the group, not only for the spiritual health of the two partners themselves, but also that the group-mind may be maintained in full vigour. Whatever the sexual custom of the group, there is always in the mind of each member a very special loyalty towards the whole group, a peculiar sexually toned *esprit de corps*, unparalleled in any other species.

Occasionally there is a special kind of group intercourse in which, during the actual occurrence of group mentality, all the members of one group will have intercourse with those of another. Casual intercourse outside the group is not common, but not discouraged. When it occurs it comes as a symbolic act crowning a spiritual intimacy.

Unlike the physical sex-relationship, the mental unity of the group involves all the members of the group every time it occurs, and so long as it persists. During times of group experience the individual continues to perform his ordinary routine of work and recreation, save when some particular activity is demanded of him by the group-mind itself. But all that he does as a private individual is carried out in a profound absent-mindedness. In familiar situations he reacts correctly, even to the extent of executing familiar types of intellectual work or entertaining acquaintances with intelligent conversation. Yet all the while he is in fact 'far away', rapt in the process of the group-mind. Nothing short of an urgent and unfamiliar crisis can recall him; and in recalling him it usually puts an end to the group's experience.

Each member of the group is fundamentally just a highly developed human animal. He enjoys his food. He has a quick eye for sexual attraction, within or without the group. He has his personal idiosyncrasies and foibles, and is pleased to ridicule the foibles of others – and of himself. He may be one of those who abhor children, or one of those who enter into children's antics with fervour, if they will tolerate him. He may move heaven and earth to procure permission for a holiday in the Land of the Young. And if he fails, as he almost surely does, he may go walking with a friend, or boating and swimming, or playing violent games. Or he may merely potter in his garden, or refresh his mind though not his body by exploring some favourite region of the past. Recreation occupies a large part of his life. For this reason he is always glad to get back to work in due season, whether his function is to maintain some part of the material organization of our world, or to educate, or to perform scientific research, or to cooperate in the endless artistic venture of the race, or, as is more likely, to help in some of those innumerable enterprises whose nature it is impossible for me to describe.

As a human individual, then, he or she is somewhat of the same type as a member of the Fifth species. Here once more is the perfected glandular outfit and instinctive nature. Here too is the highly developed sense perception and intellection. As in the Fifth species, so in the Eighteenth, each individual has his own private needs, which he heartily craves to fulfil; but also, in both species, he subordinates these private cravings to the good of the race absolutely and without struggle. The only kind of conflict which ever occurs between individuals is not the irreconcilable conflict of wills, but the conflict due to misunderstanding, to imperfect knowledge of the matter under dispute; and this can always be abolished by patient telepathic explication.

In addition to the brain organization necessary to this perfection of individual human nature, each member of a sexual group has in his own brain a special organ which, useless by itself, can cooperate 'telepathically' with the special organs of other members of the group to produce a single electromagnetic system, the physical basis of the group-mind. In each sub-sex this organ has a peculiar form and function; and only by the simultaneous operation of the whole ninety-six does the group attain unified mental life. These organs do not merely enable each member to share the experience of all; for this is already provided in the sensitivity to radiation which is characteristic of all brain tissue in our species. By means of the harmonious activity of the special organs a true group-mind emerges, with experience far beyond the range of the individuals in isolation.

This would not be possible did not the temperament and capacity of each sub-sex differ appropriately from those of the others. I can only hint at these differences by analogy. Among the First Men there are many temperamental types whose essential natures the psychologists of that species never fully analysed. I may mention, however, as superficial designations of these types, the meditative, the active, the mystical, the intellectual, the artistic, the theoretical, the concrete, the placid, the highly-strung. Now our sub-sexes differ from one another temperamentally in some such manners as these, but with a far greater range and diversity. These differences of temperament are utilized for the enrichment of a group self, such as could never have been attained by the First Men, even if they had been capable of 'telepathic' communication and electromagnetic unity; for they had not the range of specialized brain form.

For all the daily business of life, then, each of us is mentally a distinct individual, though his ordinary means of communication with others is 'telepathic'. But frequently he wakes up to be a group-mind. Apart from this 'waking of individuals together', if I may so call it, the group-mind has no existence; for its being is solely the being of the individuals comprehended together. When this communal awakening occurs, each individual experiences all the bodies of the group as 'his own multiple body', and perceives the world equally from all those bodies. This awakening happens to all the individuals at the same time. But over and above this simple enlargement of the experienced field is the awakening into new kinds of experience. Of this obviously I can tell you nothing, save that it differs from the lowlier state more radically than the infant mind differs from the mind of the individual adult, and that it consists of insight into many unsuspected and previously inconceivable features of the familiar world of men and things. Hence, in our group mode, most, but not all, of the perennial philosophical puzzles, especially those connected with the nature of personality, can be so lucidly restated that they cease to be puzzles.

Upon this higher plane of mentality the sexual groups, and

therefore the individuals participating in them, have social intercourse with one another as super-individuals. Thus they form
together a community of minded communities. For each group is
a person differing from other groups in character and experience
somewhat as individuals differ. The groups themselves are not
allocated to different works, in such a manner that one group
should be wholly engaged in industry, another in astronomy,
and so on. Only the individuals are thus allocated. In each group
there will be members of many professions. The function of the
group itself is purely some special manner of insight and mode of
appreciation; in relation to which, of course, the work of the
individuals is constantly controlled, not only while they are
actually supporting the group-self, but also when they have each
fallen once more into the limited experience which is ordinary
individual selfhood. For though, as individuals, they cannot retain
clear insight into the high matters which they so recently experienced, they do remember so much as is not beyond the range of
individual mentality; and in particular they remember the bearing
of the group experience upon their own conduct as individuals.

Recently another and far more penetrating kind of experience
has been attained, partly by good fortune, partly through research
directed by the group-minds. For these have specialized themselves for particular functions in the mental life of the race, as
previously the individuals were specialized for functions within
the mind of a group. Very rarely and precariously has this
supreme experience been achieved. In it the individual passes
beyond his group experience, and becomes the mind of the race.
At all times, of course, he can communicate 'telepathically' with
other individuals anywhere upon the planet; and frequently the
whole race 'listens in' while one individual addresses the world.
But in the true racial experience the situation is different. The
system of radiation which embraces the whole planet, and includes
the million million brains of the race, becomes the physical basis
of a racial self. The individual discovers himself to be embodied
in all the bodies of the race. He savours in a single intuition all
bodily contacts, including the mutual embraces of all lovers.
Through the myriad feet of all men and women he enfolds his
world in a single grasp. He sees with all eyes, and comprehends

in a single vision all visual fields. Thus he perceives at once and as a continuous, variegated sphere, the whole surface of the planet. But not only so. He now stands above the group-minds as they above the individuals. He regards them as a man may regard his own vital tissues, with mingled contempt, sympathy, reverence, and dispassion. He watches them as one might study the living cells of his own brain; but also with the aloof interest of one observing an ant hill; and yet again as one enthralled by the strange and diverse ways of his fellow-men; and further as one who, from above the battle, watches himself and his comrades agonizing in some desperate venture; yet chiefly as the artist who has no thought but for his vision and its embodiment. In the racial mode a man apprehends all things astronomically. Through all eyes and all observatories, he beholds his voyaging world, and peers outward into space. Thus he merges in one view, as it were, the views of deck-hand, captain, stoker, and the man in the crow's-nest. Regarding the solar system simultaneously from both limbs of Neptune, he perceives the planets and the sun stereoscopically, as though in binocular vision. Further, his perceived 'now' embraces not a moment but a vast age. Thus, observing the galaxy from every point in succession along Neptune's wide orbit, and watching the nearer stars shift hither and thither, he actually perceives some of the constellations in three dimensions. Nay, with the aid of our most recent instruments the whole galaxy appears stereoscopically. But the great nebulae and remote universes remain mere marks upon the flat sky; and in contemplation of their remoteness man, even as the racial self of the mightiest of all human races, realizes his own minuteness and impotence.

But chiefly the racial mind transcends the minds of groups and individuals in philosophical insight into the true nature of space and time, mind and its objects, cosmical striving and cosmical perfection. Some hints of this great elucidation must presently be given; but in the main it cannot be communicated. Indeed such insight is beyond the reach of ourselves as isolated individuals, and even beyond the group-minds. When we have declined from the racial mentality, we cannot clearly remember what it was that we experienced.

In particular we have one very perplexing recollection about our racial experience, one which involves a seeming impossibility. In the racial mind our experience was enlarged not only spatially but temporarily in a very strange manner. In respect of temporal perception, of course, minds may differ in two ways, in the length of the span which they can comprehend as 'now', and the minuteness of the successive events which they can discriminate within the 'now'. As individuals we can hold within one 'now' a duration equal to the old terrestrial day; and within that duration, we can, if we will, discriminate rapid pulsations such as commonly we hear together as a high musical tone. As the race-mind we perceived as 'now' the whole period since the birth of the oldest living individuals, and the whole past of the species appeared as personal memory, stretching back into the mist of infancy. Yet we could, if we willed, discriminate within the 'now' one light-vibration from the next. In this mere increased breadth and precision of temporal perception there is no contradiction. But how, we ask ourselves, could the race-mind experience as 'now' a vast period in which it had no existence whatever? Our first experience of racial mentality lasted only as long as Neptune's moon takes to complete one circuit. Before that period, then, the race-mind was not. Yet during the month of its existence it regarded the whole previous career of the race as 'present'.

Indeed, the racial experience has greatly perplexed us as individuals, and we can scarcely be said to remember more of it than that it was of extreme subtlety and extreme beauty. At the same time we often have of it an impression of unspeakable horror. We who, in our familiar individual sphere are able to regard all conceivable tragedy not merely with fortitude but with exultation, are obscurely conscious that as the racial mind we have looked into an abyss of evil such as we cannot now conceive, and could not endure to conceive. Yet even this hell we know to have been acceptable as an organic member in the austere form of the cosmos. We remember obscurely, and yet with a strange conviction, that all the age-long striving of the human spirit, no less than the petty cravings of individuals, was seen as a fair component in something far more admirable than itself; and that man

301

ultimately defeated, no less than man for a while triumphant, contributes to this higher excellence.

How colourless these words! How unworthy of that wholly satisfying beauty of all things, which in our awakened racial mode we see face to face. Every human being, of whatever species, may occasionally glimpse some fragment or aspect of existence transfigured thus with the cold beauty which normally he cannot see. Even the First Men, in their respect for tragic art, had something of this experience. The Second, and still more surely the Fifth, sought it deliberately. The winged Seventh happened upon it while they were in the air. But their minds were cramped; and all that they could appreciate was their own small world and their own tragic story. We, the Last Men, have all their zest in private and in racial life, whether it fares well or ill. We have it at all times, and we have it in respect of matters inconceivable to lesser minds. We have it, moreover, intelligently. Knowing well how strange it is to admire evil along with good, we see clearly the subversiveness of this experience. Even we, as mere individuals, cannot reconcile our loyalty to the striving spirit of man with our own divine aloofness. And so, if we were mere individuals, there would remain conflict in each of us. But in the racial mode each one of us has now experienced the great elucidation of intellect and of feeling. And though, as individuals once more, we can never recapture that far-seeing vision, the obscure memory of it masters us always, and controls all our policies. Among yourselves, the artist, after his phase of creative insight is passed, and he is once more a partisan in the struggle for existance, may carry out in detail the design conceived in his brief period of clarity. He remembers, but no longer sees the vision. He tries to fashion some perceptible embodiment of the vanished splendour. So we, living our individual lives, delighting in the contacts of flesh, the relations of minds, and all the delicate activities of human culture, cooperating and conflicting in a thousand individual undertakings and performing each his office in the material maintenance of our society, see all things as though transfused with light from a source which is itself no longer revealed.

I have tried to tell you something of the most distinctive

characteristics of our species. You can imagine that the frequent occasions of group mentality, and even more the rare occasions of race mentality, have a far-reaching effect on every individual mind, and therefore on our whole social order. Ours is in fact a society dominated, as no previous society, by a single racial purpose which is in a sense religious. Not that the individual's private efflorescence is at all thwarted by the racial purpose. Indeed, far otherwise; for that purpose demands as the first condition of its fulfilment a wealth of individual fulfilment, physical and mental. But in each mind of man or woman the racial purpose presides absolutely; and hence it is the unquestioned motive of all social policy.

I must not stay to describe in detail this society of ours, in which a million million citizens, grouped in over a thousand nations, live in perfect accord without the aid of armies or even a police force. I must not tell of our much prized social organization which assigns a unique function to each citizen, controls the procreation of new citizens of every type in relation to social need, and yet provides an endless supply of originality. We have no government and no laws, if by law is meant a stereotyped convention supported by force, and not to be altered without the aid of cumbersome machinery. Yet, though our society is in this sense an anarchy, it lives by means of a very intricate system of customs, some of which are so ancient as to have become spontaneous taboos, rather than deliberate conventions. It is the business of those among us who correspond to your lawyers and politicians to study these customs and suggest improvements. Those suggestions are submitted to no representative body, but to the whole world-population in 'telepathic' conference. Ours is thus in a sense the most democratic of all societies. Yet in another sense it is extremely bureaucratic, since it is already some millions of terrestrial years since any suggestion put forward by the College of Organizers was rejected or even seriously criticized, so thoroughly do these social engineers study their material. The only serious possibility of conflict lies now between the world population as individuals and the same individuals as group minds or racial mind. But though in these respects there have formerly occurred serious conflicts, peculiarly distressing to the individuals who experienced them, such conflicts are now extremely rare. For, even as mere individuals, we are learning to trust more and more to the judgement and dictates of our own super-individual experience.

It is time to grapple with the most difficult part of my whole task. Somehow, and very briefly, I must give you an idea of that outlook upon existence which has determined our racial purpose, making it essentially a religious purpose. This outlook has come to us partly through the work of individuals in scientific research and philosophic thought, partly through the influence of our group and racial experiences. You can imagine that it is not easy to describe this modern vision of the nature of things in any manner intelligible to those who have not our advantages. There is much in this vision which will remind you of your mystics; yet between them and us there is far more difference than similarity, in respect both of the matter and the manner of our thought. For while they are confident that the cosmos is perfect, we are sure only that it is very beautiful. While they pass to their conclusion without the aid of intellect, we have used that staff every step of the way. Thus, even when in respect of conclusions we agree with your mystics rather than your plodding intellectuals, in respect of method we applaud most your intellectuals; for they scorned to deceive themselves with comfortable fantasies.

4. COSMOLOGY

We find ourselves living in a vast and boundless, yet finite, order of spatio-temporal events. And each of us, as the racial mind, has learned that there are other such orders, other and incommensurable spheres of events, related to our own neither spatially nor temporally but in another mode of eternal being. Of the contents of those alien spheres we know almost nothing but that they are incomprehensible to us, even in our racial mentality.

Within this spatio-temporal sphere of ours we remark what we call the Beginning and what we call the End. In the Beginning there came into existence, we know not how, that all-pervading and unimaginably tenuous gas which was the parent of all material and spiritual existence within time's known span. It was in fact a very multitudinous yet precisely numbered host. From the crowding together of this great population into many swarms, arose in time the nebulae, each of which in its turn condenses as a galaxy, a universe of stars. The stars have their beginnings and their ends; and for a few moments somewhere in between their beginnings and their ends a few, very few, may support mind. But in due course will come the universal End, when all the wreckage of the galaxies will have drifted together as a single, barren, and seemingly changeless ash, in the midst of a chaos of unavailing energy.

But the cosmic events which we call the Beginning and the End are final only in relation to our ignorance of the events which lie beyond them. We know, and as the racial mind we have apprehended as a clear necessity, that not only space but time also is boundless, though finite. For in a sense time is cyclic. After the End, events unknowable will continue to happen during a period much longer than that which will have passed since the Beginning; but at length there will recur the identical event which was itself also the Beginning.

Yet though time is cyclic, it is not repetitive; there is no other time within which it can repeat itself. For time is but an abstraction from the successiveness of events that pass; and since all events whatsoever form together a cycle of successiveness, there is nothing constant in relation to which there can be repetition. And so the succession of events is cyclic, yet not repetitive. The birth of the all-pervading gas in the so-called Beginning is not merely *similar* to another such birth which will occur long after us and long after the cosmic End, so-called; the past Beginning *is* the future Beginning.

From the Beginning to the End is but the span from one spoke to the next on time's great wheel. There is a vaster span, stretching beyond the End and round to the Beginning. Of the events therein we know nothing, save that there must be such events.

Everywhere within time's cycle there is endless passage of events. In a continuous flux, they occur and vanish, yielding to their successors. Yet each one of them is eternal. Though passage is of their very nature, and without passage they are nothing, yet they have eternal being. But their passage is no illusion. They have eternal being, yet eternally they exist with passage. In our racial mode we see clearly that this is so; but in our individual mode it remains a mystery. Yet even in our individual mode we must accept both sides of this mysterious antinomy, as a fiction needed for the rationalizing of our experience.

The Beginning precedes the End by some hundred million million terrestrial years, and succeeds it by a period at least nine times longer. In the middle of the smaller span lies the still shorter period within which alone the living worlds can occur. And they are very few. One by one they dawn into mentality and die, successive blooms in life's short summer. Before that season and after it, even to the Beginning and to the End, and even before the Beginning and after the End, sleep, utter oblivion. Not before there are stars, and not after the stars are chilled, can there be life. And then, rarely.

In our own galaxy there have occurred hitherto some twenty thousand worlds that have conceived life. And of these a few score have attained or surpassed the mentality of the First Men. But of those that have reached this development, man has now outstripped the rest, and today man alone survives.

There are the millions of other galaxies, for instance the Andromedan island. We have some reason to surmise that in that favoured universe mind may have attained to insight and power incomparably greater than our own. But all that we know for certain is that it contains four worlds of high order.

Of the host of other universes that lie within range of our mind-detecting instruments, none have produced anything comparable with man. But there are many universes too remote to be estimated.

You may wonder how we have come to detect these remote lives and intelligences. I can say only that the occurrence of mentality produces certain minute astronomical effects, to which our instruments are sensitive even at great distances. These effects increase slightly with the mere mass of living matter on any astronomical body, but far more with its mental and spiritual development. Long ago it was the spiritual development of the world-community of the Fifth Men that dragged the moon from its orbit. And in our own case, so numerous is our society today, and so greatly developed in mental and spiritual activities, that only by continuous expense of physical energy can we preserve the solar system from confusion.

We have another means of detecting minds remote from us in space. We can, of course, enter into past minds wherever they are, so long as they are intelligible to us; and we have tried to use this power for the discovery of remote minded worlds. But in general the experience of such minds is too different in fibre from our own for us to be able even to detect its existence. And so our knowledge of minds in other worlds is almost wholly derived from their physical effects.

We cannot say that nowhere save on those rare bodies called planets does life ever occur. For we have evidence that in a few of the younger stars there is life, and even intelligence. How it persists in an incandescent environment we know not, nor whether it is perhaps the life of the star as a whole, as a single organism, or the life of many flame-like inhabitants of the star. All that we know is that no star in its prime has life, and therefore that the lives of the younger ones are probably doomed.

Again, we know that mind occurs, though very seldom, on a few extremely old stars, no longer incandescent. What the future of these minds will be, we cannot tell. Perhaps it is with them, and not with man, that the hope of the cosmos lies. But at present they are all primitive.

Today nothing anywhere in this galaxy of ours can compare with man in respect of vision and mental creativeness.

We have, therefore, come to regard our community as of some importance. Especially so in the light of our metaphysics; but I can only hint at our metaphysical vision of things by means of metaphors which will convey at best a caricature of that vision.

In the Beginning there was great potency, but little form. And the spirit slept as the multitude of discrete primordial existents. Thenceforth there has been a long and fluctuating adventure towards harmonious complexity of form, and towards the awakening of the spirit into unity, knowledge, delight, and self-expression. And this is the goal of all living, that the cosmos may be known, and admired, and that it may be crowned with further beauties.

Nowhere and at no time, so far as we can tell, at least within our own galaxy, has the adventure reached further than in ourselves. And in us, what has been achieved is but a minute beginning. But it is a real beginning. Man in our day has gained some depth of insight, some breadth of knowledge, some power of creation, some faculty of worship. We have looked far afield. We have probed not altogether superficially into the nature of existence, and have found it very beautiful, though also terrible. We have created a not inconsiderable community; and we have wakened together to be the unique spirit of that community. We had proposed to ourselves a very long and arduous future, which should culminate, at some time before the End, in the complete achievement of the spirit's ideal. But now we know that disaster is already near at hand.

When we are in full possession of our faculties, we are not distressed by this fate. For we know that though our fair community must cease, it has also indestructible being. We have at least carved into one region of the eternal real a form which has beauty of no mean order. The great company of diverse and most lovely men and women in all their subtle relationships, striving with a single purpose towards the goal which is mind's final goal; the community and super-individuality of that great host; the beginnings of further insight and creativeness upon the higher plane – these surely are real achievements – even though, in the larger view, they are minute achievements.

Yet though we are not at all dismayed by our own extinction, we cannot but wonder whether or not in the far future some other spirit will fulfil the cosmic ideal, or whether we ourselves are the modest crown of existence. Unfortunately, though we can explore the past wherever there are intelligible minds, we cannot enter into the future. And so in vain we ask, will ever any spirit awake to gather all spirits into itself, to elicit from the stars their full flower of beauty, to know all things together, and admire all things justly.

If in the far future this end will be achieved, it is really achieved even now; for whenever it occurs, its being is eternal. But on the other hand if it is indeed achieved eternally, this achievement must be the work of spirits or a spirit not wholly unlike ourselves, though infinitely greater. And the physical location of that spirit must lie in the far future.

But if no future spirit will achieve this end before it dies, then, though the cosmos is indeed very beautiful, it is not perfect.

I said that we regard the cosmos as very beautiful. Yet it is also very terrible. For ourselves, it is easy to look forward with equanimity to our end, and even to the end of our admired community; for what we prize most is the excellent beauty of the cosmos. But there are the myriads of spirits who have never entered into that vision. They have suffered, and they were not permitted that consolation. There are, first, the incalculable hosts of lowly creatures scattered over all the ages in all the minded worlds. Theirs was only a dream life, and their misery not often poignant; but none the less they are to be pitied for having missed the more poignant experience in which alone spirit can find fulfilment. Then there are the intelligent beings, human and otherwise; the many minded worlds throughout the galaxies, that have struggled into cognizance, striven for they knew not what, tasted brief delights and lived in the shadow of pain and death, until at last their life has been crushed out by careless fate. In our solar system there are the Martians, insanely and miserably obsessed; the native Venerians, imprisoned in their ocean and murdered for man's sake; and all the hosts of the forerunning human species. A few individuals no doubt in every period, and many in certain favoured races, have lived on the whole happily. And a few have even known something of the supreme beatitude. But for most, until our modern epoch, thwarting has outweighed fulfilment; and if actual grief has not preponderated over joy, it is because, mercifully, the fulfilment that is wholly missed cannot be conceived.

Our predecessors of the Sixteenth species, oppressed by this vast horror, undertook a forlorn and seemingly irrational crusade for the rescue of the tragic past. We see now clearly that their enterprise, though desperate, was not quite fantastic. For, if ever the cosmic ideal should be realized, even though for a moment only, then in that time the awakened Soul of All will embrace within itself all spirits whatever throughout the whole of time's wide circuit. And so to each one of them, even to the least, it will seem that he has awakened and discovered himself to be the Soul of All, knowing all things and rejoicing in all things. And though afterwards, through the inevitable decay of the stars, this most glorious vision must be lost, suddenly or in the long-drawn-out defeat of life, yet would the awakened Soul of All have eternal being, and in it each martyred spirit would have beatitude eternally, though unknown to itself in its own temporal mode.

It may be that this is the case. If not, then eternally the martyred spirits are martyred only, and not blest.

We cannot tell which of these possibilities is fact. As individuals we earnestly desire that the eternal being of things may include this supreme awakening. This, nothing less than this, has been the remote but ever-present goal of our practical religious life and of our social policy.

In our racial mode also we have greatly desired this end, but differently.

Even as individuals, all our desires are tempered by that relentless admiration of fate which we recognize as the spirit's highest achievement. Even as individuals, we exult in the issue whether our enterprises succeed or fail. The pioneer defeated, the lover bereaved and overwhelmed, can find in his disaster the supreme experience, the dispassionate ecstasy which salutes the Real as it is and would not change one jot of it. Even as individuals, we can regard the impending extinction of mankind as a thing superb though tragic. Strong in the knowledge that the human spirit has already inscribed the cosmos with indestructible beauty, and that inevitably, whether sooner or later, man's career must end, we face this too sudden end with laughter in our hearts, and peace.

But there is the one thought by which, in our individual state, we are still dismayed, namely that the cosmic enterprise itself may fail; that the full potentiality of the Real may never find expression; that never, in any stage of time, the multitudinous and conflicting existents should be organized as the universal harmonious living body; that the spirit's eternal nature, therefore, should be discordant, miserably tranced; that the indestructible beauties of this our sphere of space and time should remain imperfect, and remain, too, not adequately worshipped.

But in the racial mind this ultimate dread has no place. On those few occasions when we have awakened racially, we have come to regard with piety even the possibility of cosmical defeat. For as the racial mind, though in a manner we earnestly desired the fulfilment of the cosmical ideal, yet we were no more enslaved to this desire than, as individuals, we are enslaved to our private desires. For though the racial mind wills this supreme achievement, yet in the same act it holds itself aloof from it, and from all desire, and all emotion, save the ecstasy which admires the real as it is, and accepts its dark-bright form with joy.

As individuals, therefore, we try to regard the whole cosmic adventure as a symphony now in progress, which may or may not some day achieve its just conclusion. Like music, however, the vast biography of the stars is to be judged not in respect of its final moment merely, but in respect of the perfection of its whole form; and whether its form as a whole is perfect or not, we cannot know. Actual music is a pattern of intertwining themes which evolve and die; and these again are woven of simpler members, which again are spun of chords and unitary tones. But the music of the spheres is of a complexity almost infinitely more subtle, and its themes rank above and below one another in hierarchy beyond hierarchy. None but a God, none but a mind subtle as the music itself, could hear the whole in all its detail, and grasp in one act its close-knit individuality, if such it has. Not for any human mind to say authoritatively, 'This is music, wholly', or to say, 'This is mere noise, flecked now and then by shreds of significance'.

The music of the spheres is unlike other music not only in respect of its richness, but also in the nature of its medium. It is a music not merely of sounds but of souls. Each of its minor themes, each of its chords, each single tone of it, each tremor of each tone, is in its own degree more than a mere passive factor in the music; it is a listener, and also a creator. Wherever there is individuality of form, there is also an individual appreciator and originator. And the more complex the form, the more percipient and active the spirit. Thus in every individual factor within the music, the musical environment of that factor is experienced, vaguely or precisely, erroneously or with greater approximation to truth;

311

and, being experienced, it is admired or loathed, rightly or falsely. And it is influenced. Just as in actual music each theme is in a manner a determination of its forerunners and followers and present accompaniment, so in this vaster music each individual factor is itself a determination of its environment. Also it is a determinant, both of that which precedes and that which follows.

But whether these manifold interdeterminations are after all haphazard, or, as in music, controlled in relation to the beauty of the whole, we know not; nor whether, if this is the case, the beautiful whole of things is the work of some mind; nor yet whether some mind admires it adequately as a whole of beauty.

But this we know: that we ourselves, when the spirit is most awake in us, admire the Real as it is revealed to us, and salute its dark-bright form with joy.

XVI *The Last of Man*

1. SENTENCE OF DEATH

OURS has been essentially a philosophical age, in fact the supreme age of philosophy. But a great practical problem has also concerned us. We have had to prepare for the task of preserving humanity during a most difficult period which was calculated to begin about one hundred million years hence, but might, in certain circumstances, be sprung upon us at very short notice. Long ago the human inhabitants of Venus believed that already in their day the sun was about to enter the 'white dwarf' phase, and that the time would therefore soon come when their world would be frost-bound. This calculation was unduly pessimistic; but we know now that, even allowing for the slight delay caused by the great collision, the solar collapse must begin at some date astronomically not very distant. We had planned that during the comparatively brief period of the actual shrinkage, we would move our planet steadily nearer to the sun, until finally it should settle in the narrowest possible orbit.

Man would then be comfortably placed for a very long period. But in the fullness of time there would come a far more serious crisis. The sun would continue to cool, and at last man would no longer be able to live by means of solar radiation. It would become necessary to annihilate matter to supply the deficiency. The other planets might be used for this purpose, and possibly the sun itself. Or, given the sustenance for so long a voyage, man might boldly project his planet into the neighbourhood of some younger star. Thenceforth, perhaps, he might operate upon a far grander scale. He might explore and colonize all suitable worlds in every corner of the galaxy, and organize himself as a vast community of minded worlds. Even (so we dreamed) he might achieve intercourse with other galaxies. It did not seem impossible that man himself was the germ of the world-soul, which, we still hope, is destined to awake for a while before the universal decline, and to crown the eternal cosmos with its due of knowledge and admiration, fleeting yet eternal. We dared to think that in some far distant epoch the human spirit, clad in all wisdom, power, and delight, might look back upon our primitive age with a certain respect; no doubt with pity also and amusement, but none the less with admiration for the spirit in us, still only half awake, and struggling against great disabilities. In such a mood, half pity, half admiration, we ourselves look back upon the primitive mankinds.

Our prospect has now suddenly and completely changed, for astronomers have made a startling discovery, which assigns to man a speedy end. His existence has ever been precarious. At any stage of his career he might easily have been exterminated by some slight alteration of his chemical environment, by a more than usually malignant microbe, by a radical change of climate, or by the manifold effects of his own folly. Twice already he has been almost destroyed by astronomical events. How easily might it happen that the solar system, now rushing through a somewhat more crowded region of the galaxy, should become entangled with, or actually strike, a major astronomical body, and be destroyed. But fate, as it turns out, has a more surprising end in store for man.

Not long ago an unexpected alteration was observed to be taking place in a near star. Through no discoverable cause, it began to change from white to violet, and increase in brightness. Already it has attained such extravagant brilliance that, though its actual disc remains a mere point in our sky, its dazzling purple radiance illuminates our nocturnal landscapes with hideous beauty. Our astronomers have ascertained that this is no ordinary 'nova', that it is not one of those stars addicted to paroxysms of brilliance. It is something unprecedented, a normal star suffering from a unique disease, a fantastic acceleration of its vital process, a riotous squandering of the energy which should have remained locked within its substance for aeons. At the present rate it will be reduced either to an inert cinder or to actual annihilation in a few thousand years. This extraordinary event may possibly have been produced by unwise tamperings on the part of intelligent beings in the star's neighbourhood. But, indeed, since all matter at very high temperature is in a state of unstable equilibrium, the cause may have been merely some conjunction of natural circumstances.

The event was first regarded simply as an intriguing spectacle. But further study roused a more serious interest. Our own planet, and therefore the sun also, was suffering a continuous and increasing bombardment of etherial vibrations, most of which were of incredibly high frequency, and of unknown potentiality. What would be their effect upon the sun? After some centuries, certain astronomical bodies in the neighbourhood of the deranged star were seen to be infected with its disorder. Their fever increased the splendour of our night sky, but it also confirmed our fears. We still hoped that the sun might prove too distant to be seriously influenced, but careful analysis now showed that this hope must be abandoned. The sun's remoteness might cause a delay of some thousands of years before the cumulative effects of the bombardment could start the disintegration; but sooner or later the sun itself must be infected. Probably within thirty thousand years life will be impossible anywhere within a vast radius of the sun, so vast a radius that it is quite impossible to propel our planet away fast enough to escape before the storm can catch us.

2. BEHAVIOUR OF THE CONDEMNED

The discovery of this doom kindled in us unfamiliar emotions. Hitherto humanity had seemed to be destined for a very long future, and the individual himself had been accustomed to look forward to very many thousands of years of personal life, ending in voluntary sleep. We had of course often conceived, and even savoured in imagination, the sudden destruction of our world. But now we faced it as a fact. Outwardly everyone behaved with perfect serenity, but inwardly every mind was in turmoil. Not that there was any question of our falling into panic or despair, for in this crisis our native detachment stood us in good stead. But inevitably some time passed before our minds became properly adjusted to the new prospect, before we could see our fate outlined clearly and beautifully against the cosmic background.

Presently, however, we learned to contemplate the whole great saga of man as a completed work of art, and to admire it no less for its sudden and tragic end than for the promise in it which was not to be fulfilled. Grief was now transfigured wholly into ecstasy. Defeat, which had oppressed us with a sense of man's impotence and littleness among the stars, brought us into a new sympathy and reverence for all those myriads of beings in the past out of whose obscure strivings we had been born. We saw the most brilliant of our own race and the lowliest of our prehuman fore-runners as essentially spirits of equal excellence, though cast in diverse circumstances. When we looked round on the heavens, and at the violet splendour which was to destroy us, we were filled with awe and pity, awe for the inconceivable potentiality of this bright host, pity for its self-thwarting effort to fulfil itself as the universal spirit.

At this stage it seemed that there was nothing left for us to do but to crowd as much excellence as possible into our remaining life, and meet our end in the noblest manner. But now there came upon us once more the rare experience of racial mentality. For a whole Neptunian year every individual lived in an enraptured trance, in which, as the racial mind, he or she resolved many ancient mysteries and saluted many unexpected beauties. This ineffable experience, lived through under the shadow of death, was the flower of man's whole being. But I can tell nothing of it, save that when it was over we possessed, even as individuals, a new peace, in which, strangely but harmoniously, were blended grief, exaltation, and god-like laughter.

In consequence of this racial experience we found ourselves faced with two tasks which had not before been contemplated. The one referred to the future, the other to the past.

In respect of the future, we are now setting about the forlorn task of disseminating among the stars the seeds of a new humanity. For this purpose we shall make use of the pressure of radiation from the sun, and chiefly the extravagantly potent radiation that will later be available. We are hoping to devise extremely minute electro-magnetic 'wave-systems', akin to normal protons and electrons, which will be individually capable of sailing forward upon the hurricane of solar radiation at a speed not wholly incomparable with the speed of light itself. This is a difficult task. But, further, these units must be so cunningly inter-related that, in favourable conditions, they may tend to combine to form spores of life, and to develop, not indeed into human beings, but into lowly organisms with a definite evolutionary bias toward the essentials of human nature. These objects we shall project from beyond our atmosphere in immense quantities at certain points of our planet's orbit, so that solar radiation may carry them towards the most promising regions of the galaxy. The chance that any of them will survive to reach their destination is small, and still smaller the chance that any of them will find a suitable environment. But if any of this human seed should fall upon good ground, it will embark, we hope, upon a somewhat rapid biological evolution, and produce in due season whatever complex organic forms are possible in its environment. It will have a very real physiological bias toward the evolution of intelligence. Indeed it will have a much greater bias in that direction than occurred on the Earth in those sub-vital atomic groupings from which terrestrial life eventually sprang.

It is just conceivable, then, that by extreme good fortune man may still influence the future of this galaxy, not directly but through his creature. But in the vast music of existence the actual theme of mankind now ceases for ever. Finished, the long reiterations of man's history; defeated, the whole proud enterprise of his maturity. The stored experience of many mankinds must sink into oblivion, and today's wisdom must vanish.

The other task which occupies us, that which relates to the past, is one which may very well seem to you nonsensical.

We have long been able to enter into past minds and participate in their experience. Hitherto we have been passive spectators merely, but recently we have acquired the power of influencing past minds. This seems an impossibility; for a past event is what it is, and how can it conceivably be altered at a subsequent date, even in the minutest respect?

Now it is true that past events are what they are, irrevocably; but in certain cases some feature of a past event may depend on an event in their far future. The past event would never have been as it actually was (and is, eternally), if there had not been going

317

to be a certain future event, which, though not contemporaneous with the past event, influences it directly in the sphere of eternal being. The passage of events is real, and time is the successiveness of passing events; but though events have passage, they have also eternal being. And in certain rare cases mental events far separated in time determine one another directly by way of eternity.

Our own minds have often been profoundly influenced by direct inspection of past minds; and now we find that certain events of certain past minds are determined by present events in our own present minds. No doubt there are some mental events which are what they are by virtue of mental past-processes which we *shall* perform but have not yet performed.

Our historians and psychologists, engaged on direct inspection of past minds, had often complained of certain 'singular' points in past minds, where the ordinary laws of psychology fail to give a full explanation of the course of mental events; where, in fact, some wholly unknown influence seemed to be at work. Later it was found that, in some cases at least, this disturbance of the ordinary principles of psychology corresponded with certain thoughts or desires in the mind of the observer, living in our own age. Of course, only such matters as could have significance to the past mind could influence it at all. Thoughts and desires of ours which have no meaning to the particular past-individual fail to enter into his experience. New ideas and new values are only to be introduced by arranging familiar matter so that it may gain a new significance. Nevertheless we now found ourselves in possession of an amazing power of communicating with the past, and contributing to its thought and action, though of course we could not *alter* it.

But, it may be asked, what if, in respect of a particular 'singularity' in some past mind, we do not, after all, choose to provide the necessary influence to account for it? The question is meaningless. There is no possibility that we should not choose to influence those past minds which are, as a matter of fact, dependent on our influence. For it is in the sphere of eternity (wherein alone we meet past minds), that we really make this free choice. And in the sphere of time, though the choosing has relations with our modern age, and may be said to occur in that age, it also had relations with the past mind, and may be said to have occurred also long ago.

There are in some past minds singularities which are not the product of any influence that we have exerted today. Some of these singularities, no doubt, we shall ourselves produce on some occasion before our destruction. But it may be that some are due to an influence other than ours, perhaps to beings which, by good fortune, may spring long hence from our forlorn seminal enterprise; or they may be due perhaps to the cosmic mind, whose future occurrence and eternal existence we earnestly desire. However that may be, there are a few remarkable minds, scattered up and down past ages and even in the most primitive human races, which suggest an influence other than our own. They are so 'singular' in one respect or another, that we cannot give a perfectly clear psychological account of them in terms of the past only; and yet we ourselves are not the instigators of their singularity. Your Jesus, your Socrates, your Gautama, show traces of this uniqueness. But the most original of all were too eccentric to have any influence on their contemporaries. It is possible that in ourselves also there are 'singularities' which cannot be accounted for wholly in terms of ordinary biological and psychological laws. If we could prove that this is the case, we should have very definite evidence of the occurrence of a high order of mentality somewhere in the future, and therefore of its eternal existence. But hitherto this problem has proved too subtle for us, even in the racial mode. It may be that the mere fact that we have succeeded in attaining racial mentality involves some remote future influence. It is even conceivable that every creative advance that any mind has ever made involves unwitting cooperation with the cosmic mind which, perhaps, will awake at some date before the End.

We have two methods of influencing the past through past individuals; for we can operate either upon minds of great originality and power, or upon any average individual whose circumstances happen to suit our purpose. In original minds we can only suggest some very vague intuition, which is then 'worked up' by the individual himself into some form very different from that which we intended, but very potent as a factor in the culture of his age. Average minds, on the other hand, we can use as passive instruments for the conveyance of detailed ideas. But in such cases the individual is incapable of working up the material into a great and potent form, suited to his age.

But what is it, you may ask, that we seek to contribute to the past? We seek to afford intuitions of truth and of value, which, though easy to us from our point of vantage, would be impossible to the unaided past. We seek to help the past to make the best of itself, just as one man may help another. We seek to direct the attention of past individuals and past races to truths and beauties which, though implicit in their experience, would otherwise be overlooked.

We seek to do this for two reasons. Entering into past minds, we become perfectly acquainted with them, and cannot but love them; and so we desire to help them. By influencing selected individuals, we seek to influence indirectly great multitudes. But our second motive is very different. We see the career of Man in his successive planetary homes as a process of very great beauty. It is far indeed from the perfect; but it is very beautiful, with the beauty of tragic art. Now it turns out that this beautiful thing entails our operation at various points in the past. Therefore we will to operate.

Unfortunately our first inexperienced efforts were disastrous. Many of the fatuities which primitive minds in all ages have been prone to attribute to the influence of disembodied spirits, whether deities, fiends, or the dead, are but the gibberish which resulted from our earliest experiments. And this book, so admirable in our conception, has issued from the brain of the writer, your contemporary, in such disorder as to be mostly rubbish.

We are concerned with the past not only in so far as we make very rare contributions to it, but chiefly in two other manners.

First, we are engaged upon the great enterprise of becoming lovingly acquainted with the past, the human past, in every detail. This is, so to speak, our supreme act of filial piety. When one being comes to know and love another, a new and beautiful thing is created, namely the love. The cosmos is thus far and at that date enhanced. We seek then to know and love every past mind that we can enter. In most cases we can know them with far more understanding than they can know themselves. Not the least of them, not the worst of them, shall be left out of this great work of understanding and admiration.

There is another manner in which we are concerned with the human past. We need its help. For we, who are triumphantly reconciled to our fate, are under obligation to devote our last energies not to ecstatic contemplation but to a forlorn and most uncongenial task, the dissemination. This task is almost intolerably repugnant to us. Gladly would we spend our last days in embellishing our community and our culture, and in pious exploration of the past. But it is incumbent on us, who are by nature artists and philosophers, to direct the whole attention of our world upon the arid labour of designing an artificial human seed, producing it in immense quantities, and projecting it among the stars. If there is to be any possibility of success, we must undertake a very lengthy programme of physical research, and finally organize a world-wide system of manufacture. The work will not be completed until our physical constitution is already being undermined, and the disintegration of our community has already begun. Now we could never fulfil this policy without a zealous conviction of its importance. Here it is that the past can help us. We, who have now learnt so thoroughly the supreme art of ecstatic fatalism, go humbly to the past to learn over again that other supreme achievement of the spirit, loyalty to the forces of life embattled against the forces of death. Wandering among the heroic and often forlorn ventures of the past, we are fired once more with primitive zeal. Thus, when we return to our own world, we are able, even while we preserve in our hearts the peace that passeth understanding, to struggle as though we cared only for victory.

3. EPILOGUE

I am speaking to you now from a period about twenty thousand terrestrial years after the date at which the whole preceding part of this book was communicated. It has become very difficult to reach you, and still more difficult to speak to you; for already the Last Men are not the men they were.

Our two great undertakings are still unfinished. Much of the human past remains imperfectly explored, and the projection of the seed is scarcely begun. That enterprise has proved far more difficult than was expected. Only within the last few years have we succeeded in designing an artificial human dust capable of being carried forward on the sun's radiation, hardy enough to endure the conditions of a trans-galactic voyage of many millions of years, and yet intricate enough to bear the potentiality of life and of spiritual development. We are now preparing to manufacture this seminal matter in great quantities, and to cast it into space at suitable points on the planet's orbit.

Some centuries have now passed since the sun began to show the first symptoms of disintegration, namely a slight change of colour towards the blue, followed by a definite increase of brightness and heat. Today, when he pierces the ever-thickening cloud, he smites us with an intolerable steely brilliance which destroys the sight of anyone foolish enough to face it. Even in the cloudy weather which is now normal, the eye is wounded by the fierce violet glare. Eye-troubles afflict us all, in spite of the special glasses which have been designed to protect us. The mere heat, too, is already destructive. We are forcing our planet outward from its old orbit in an ever-widening spiral; but, do what we will, we cannot prevent the climate from becoming more and more deadly, even at the poles. The intervening regions have already been deserted. Evaporation of the equatorial oceans has thrown the whole atmosphere into tumult, so that even at the poles we are tormented by hot wet hurricanes and incredible electric storms. These have already shattered most of our great buildings, sometimes burying a whole teeming province under an avalanche of tumbled vitreous crags.

Our two polar communities at first managed to maintain radio communication; but it is now some time since we of the south received news of the more distressed north. Even with us the situation is already desperate. We had recently established some hundreds of stations for the dissemination, but less than a score have been able to operate. This failure is due mainly to an increasing lack of personnel. The deluge of fantastic solar radiation has had disastrous effect on the human organism. Epidemics of a malignant tumour, which medical science has failed to conquer, have reduced the southern people to a mere remnant, and this in spite of the migration of the tropical races into the Antarctic. Each of us, moreover, is but the wreckage of his former self. The higher mental functions, attained only in the most developed human species, are already lost or disordered, through the breakdown of their special tissues. Not only has the racial mind vanished, but the sexual groups have lost their mental unity. Three of the sub-sexes have already been exterminated by derangement of their chemical nature. Glandular troubles, indeed, have unhinged many of us with anxieties and loathings which we cannot conquer, though we know them to be unreasonable. Even the normal power of 'telepathic' communication has become so unreliable that we have been compelled to fall back upon the archaic practice of vocal symbolism. Exploration of the past is now confined to specialists, and is a dangerous profession, which may lead to disorders of temporal experience.

Degeneration of the higher neural centres has also brought about in us a far more serious and deep-seated trouble, namely a general spiritual degradation which would formerly have seemed impossible, so confident were we of our integrity. The perfectly dispassionate will had been for many millions of years universal among us, and the corner stone of our whole society and culture. We had almost forgotten that it has a physiological basis, and that if that basis were undermined, we might no longer be capable of rational conduct. But, drenched for some thousands of years by the unique stellar radiation, we have gradually lost not only the ecstasy of dispassionate worship, but even the capacity for normal disinterested behaviour. Everyone is now liable to an irrational bias in favour of himself as a private person, as against his fellows. Personal envy, uncharitableness, even murder and gratuitous cruelty, formerly unknown amongst us, are now becoming common. At first when men began to notice in themselves these archaic impulses, they crushed them with amused contempt. But as the highest nerve centres fell further into decay, the brute in us began to be ever more unruly, and the human more uncertain.

323

Rational conduct was henceforth to be achieved only after an exhausting and degrading 'moral struggle', instead of spontaneously and fluently. Nay, worse, increasingly often the struggle ended not in victory but defeat. Imagine then, the terror and disgust that gripped us when we found ourselves one and all condemned to a desperate struggle against impulses which we had been accustomed to regard as insane. It is distressing enough to know that each one of us might at any moment, merely to help some dear individual or other, betray his supreme duty toward the dissemination; but it is harrowing to discover ourselves sometimes so far sunk as to be incapable even of common loving-kindness toward our neighbours. For a man to favour himself against his friend or beloved, even in the slightest respect, was formerly unknown. But today many of us are haunted by the look of amazed horror and pity in the eyes of an injured friend.

In the early stages of our trouble lunatic asylums were founded, but they soon became over-crowded and a burden on a stricken community. The insane were then killed. But it became clear that by former standards we were all insane. No man now can trust himself to behave reasonably.

And, of course, we cannot trust each other. Partly through the prevalent irrationality of desire, and partly through the misunderstandings which have come with the loss of 'telepathic' communication, we have been plunged into all manner of discords. A political constitution and system of laws had to be devised, but they seem to have increased our troubles. Order of a kind is maintained by an over-worked police force. But this is in the hands of the professional organizers, who have now all the vices of bureaucracy. It was largely through their folly that two of the antarctic nations broke into social revolution, and are now preparing to meet the armament which an insane world-government is devising for their destruction. Meanwhile, through the break-down of the economic order, and the impossibility of reaching the food-factories on Jupiter, starvation is added to our troubles, and has afforded to certain ingenious lunatics the opportunity of trading at the expense of others.

All this folly in a doomed world, and in a community that was yesterday the very flower of a galaxy! Those of us who still care for the life of the spirit are tempted to regret that mankind did not choose decent suicide before ever the putrescence began. But indeed this could not be. The task that was undertaken had to be completed. For the Scattering of the Seed has come to be for every one of us the supreme religious duty. Even those who continually sin against it recognize this as the last office of man. It was for this that we outstayed our time, and must watch ourselves decline from spiritual estate into that brutishness from which man has so seldom freed himself.

Yet why do we persist in the forlorn effort? Even if by good luck the seed should take root somewhere and thrive, there will surely come an end to its adventure, if not swiftly in fire, then in the ultimate battle of life against encroaching frost. Our labour will at best sow for death an ampler harvest. There seems no rational defence of it, unless it be rational to carry out blindly a purpose conceived in a former and more enlightened state.

But we cannot feel sure that we really were more enlightened. We look back now at our former selves, with wonder, but also with incomprehension and misgiving. We try to recall the glory that seemed to be revealed to each of us in the racial mind, but we remember almost nothing of it. We cannot rise even to that more homely beatitude which was once within the reach of the unaided individual, that serenity which, it seemed, should be the spirit's answer to every tragic event. It is gone from us. It is not only impossible but inconceivable. We now see our private distresses and the public calamity as merely hideous. That after so long a struggle into maturity man should be roasted alive like a trapped mouse, for the entertainment of a lunatic! How can any beauty lie in that?

But this is not our last word to you. For though we have fallen, there is still something in us left over from the time that is passed. We have become blind and weak; but the knowledge that we are so has forced us to a great effort. Those of us who have not already sunk too far have formed themselves into a brotherhood for mutual strengthening, so that the true human spirit may be maintained a little longer, until the seed has been well sown, and death be permissible. We call ourselves the Brotherhood of the Condemned. We seek to be faithful to one another, and to our common undertaking, and to the vision which is no longer revealed. We are vowed to the comforting of all distressed persons who are not yet permitted death. We are vowed also to the dissemination. And we are vowed to keep the spirit bright until the end.

Now and again we meet together in little groups or great companies to hearten ourselves with one another's presence. Sometimes on these occasions we can but sit in silence, groping for consolation and for strength. Sometimes, the spoken word flickers hither and thither amongst us, shedding a brief light but little warmth to the soul that lies freezing in a torrid world.

But there is among us one, moving from place to place and company to company, whose voice all long to hear. He is young, the last born of the Last Men; for he was the latest to be conceived before we learned man's doom, and put an end to all conceiving. Being the latest, he is also the noblest. Not him alone, but all his generation, we salute, and look to for strength; but he, the youngest, is different from the rest. In him the spirit, which is but the flesh awakened into spirituality, has power to withstand the tempest of solar energy longer than the rest of us. It is as though the sun itself were eclipsed by this spirit's brightness. It is as though in him at last, and for a day only, man's promise were fulfilled. For though, like others, he suffers in the flesh, he is above his suffering. And though more than the rest of us he feels the suffering of others, he is above his pity. In his comforting there is a strange sweet raillery which can persuade the sufferer to smile at his own pain. When this youngest brother of ours contemplates with us our dying world and the frustration of all man's striving, he is not, like us, dismayed, but quiet. In the presence of such quietness despair wakens into peace. By his reasonable speech, almost by the mere sound of his voice, our eyes are opened, and our hearts mysteriously filled with exultation. Yet often his words are grave.

Let his words, not mine, close this story:

Great are the stars, and man is of no account to them. But man is a fair spirit, whom a star conceived and a star kills. He is greater than those bright blind companies. For though in them there is incalculable potentiality, in him there is achievement, small, but actual. Too soon, seemingly, he comes to his end. But when he is done he will not be nothing, not as though he had never been; for he is eternally a beauty in the eternal form of things.

Man was winged hopefully. He had in him to go further than this short flight, now ending. He proposed even that he should become the Flower of All Things, and that he should learn to be the All-Knowing, the All-Admiring. Instead, he is to be destroyed. He is only a fledgling caught in a bush-fire. He is very small, very simple, very little capable of insight. His knowledge of the great orb of things is but a fledgling's knowledge. His admiration is a nestling's admiration for the things kindly to his own small nature. He delights only in food and the food-announcing call. The music of the spheres passes over him, through him, and is not heard.

Yet it has used him. And now it uses his destruction. Great, and terrible, and very beautiful is the Whole; and for man the best is that the Whole should use him.

But does it really use him? Is the beauty of the Whole really enhanced by our agony? And is the Whole really beautiful? And what is beauty? Throughout all his existence man has been striving to hear the music of the spheres, and has seemed to himself once and again to catch some phrase of it, or even a hint of the whole form of it. Yet he can never be sure that he has truly heard it, nor even that there is any such perfect music at all to be heard. Inevitably so, for if it exists, it is not for him in his littleness.

But one thing is certain. Man himself, at the very least, is music, a brave theme that makes music also of its vast accompaniment, its matrix of storms and stars. Man himself in his degree is eternally a beauty in the eternal form of things. It is very good to have been man. And so we may go forward together with laughter in our hearts, and peace, thankful for the past, and for our own courage. For we shall make after all a fair conclusion to this brief music that is man.

Last Men in London

Contents

Contents

Preface

THOUGH this is a work of fiction, it does not pretend to be a novel. It has no hero but Man. Since its purpose is not the characterization of individual human beings, no effort has been made to endow its few persons with distinctive personalities. There is no plot, except the theme of man's struggle in this awkward age to master himself and to come to terms with the universe. This theme I seek to present by imagining that a member of a much more developed human species, living on Neptune two thousand million years hence, enters into our minds to observe the Terrestrial field through our eyes but with his own intelligence. Using one of us as a mouthpiece, he contrives to tell us something of his findings. The shortcomings of his report must be attributed to the limitations of his Terrestrial instrument.

This book is intelligible without reference to another fantasy, which I produced two years ago, and called *Last and First Men*. But readers of that earlier book will find that *Last Men in London* is complementary to it. In both, the same Neptunian being speaks, formerly to tell the story of man's career between our day and his, now to describe the spiritual drama which, he tells us, underlies the whole confused history of our species, and comes to its crisis today. The present book is supposed to be communicated from a date in Neptunian history later than the body of the earlier book, but before its epilogue.

The last section of the chapter on the War, though it makes use to some extent of personal experience, is none the less fiction.

It will be obvious to many readers that I have been influenced by the very suggestive work of Mr Gerald Heard. I hope he will forgive me for distorting some of his ideas for my own purpose.

My thanks are due once more to Mr E. V. Rieu for many valuable criticisms and suggestions; and to Professor and Mrs L. C. Martin (who read the untidy manuscript) for condemnation and encouragement without which the book would have been much worse than it is. Finally I would thank my wife both for hard labour, and for other help which she is apparently incapable of appreciating.

Let me remind the reader that henceforth and up to the opening of the Epilogue the speaker is a Neptunian man of the very remote future.

September 1932   W. O. S.

Introduction

The Future's Concern with the Past

MEN and women of Earth! Brief Terrestrials, of that moment when the First Human Species hung in the crest of its attainment, wavelike, poised for downfall, I a member of the last Human Species, address you for a second time from an age two thousand million years after your day, from an age as remotely future to you as the Earth's beginning is remotely past.

In my earlier communication I told of the huge flux of events between your day and mine. I told of the rise and fall of many mankinds, of the spirit's long desolations and brief splendours. I told how, again and again, after age-long sleep, man woke to see dimly what he should be doing with himself; how he strove accordingly to master his world and his own nature; and how, each time, circumstances or his own ignorance and impotence flung him back into darkness. I told how he struggled with invaders, and how he was driven from planet to planet, refashioning himself for each new world. I told, not only of his great vicissitudes, but also of the many and diverse modes of mind which he assumed in different epochs. I told how at length, through good fortune and skilled control, there was fashioned a more glorious mankind, the Eighteenth Human Species, my own. I hinted as best I might at the great richness and subtlety, the perfect harmony and felicity, of this last expression of the human spirit. I told of our discovery that our own fair planet must soon be destroyed with all the sun's offspring; and of our exultant acceptance even of this doom. I told of the final endeavours which the coming end imposes on us.

In this my second communication I shall say little of my own world, and less of the ages that lie between us. Instead I shall speak mostly of your world and of yourselves. I shall try to show you yourselves through the eyes of the Last Men. Of myself and my fellow-workers, I shall speak, but chiefly as the link between your world and mine, as pioneering explorers in your world, and secret dwellers in your minds. I shall tell of the difficulties and dangers of our strange exploration of ages that to us are past, and of our still stranger influence upon past minds. But mostly I shall speak of men and women living in Europe in your twentieth Christian century, and of a great crisis that we observe in

335

your world, a great opportunity which you tragically fail to grasp.

In relation to the long drama which I unfolded in my earlier communication it might well seem that even the most urgent and the most far-reaching events of your little sphere are utterly trivial. The rise and fall of your world-moving individuals, the flowering and withering of your nations, and all their blind, plant-like struggle for existence, the slow changes and sudden upheavals of your society, the archaic passions of your religious sects, and quick-changes of your fashionable thought, all seem, in relation to those aeons of history, no more than the ineffective gyrations of flotsam of the great river of humanity, whose direction is determined, not by any such superficial movements, but by the thrust of its own mass and the configuration of the terrain.

In the light of the stars what significance is there in such minute events as the defeat of an army, the issue of a political controversy, the success or failure of a book, the result of a football match? In that cold light even the downfall of a species is a matter of little importance. And the final extinction of man, after his two thousand million years of precarious blundering, is but the cessation of one brief tremulous theme in the great music of the cosmos.

Yet minute events have sometimes remarkable consequences. Again and again this was evident in the great story that I told. And now I am to describe events some of which, though momentary and minute in relation to the whole career of man, are yet in relation to yourselves long-drawn-out and big with destiny. In consequence of these momentary happenings, so near you, yet so obscure, man's career is fated to be the weary succession of disasters and incomplete victories which I described on an earlier occasion.

But the account of these events, though it is in some sense the main theme of this book, is not its sole, not even its chief purpose. I shall say much of your baseness, much of your futility. But all that I say, if I say it well, and if the mind that I have chosen for my mouthpiece serves me adequately, shall be kindled with a sense of that beauty which, in spite of all your follies and treasons, is yours uniquely. For though the whole career of your species is so confused and barren, and though, against the background of the rise and fall of species after species and the destruction of world after world, the life of any individual among you, even the most glorious, seems so completely ineffective and insignificant, yet, in the least member of your or any other species, there lies for the discerning eye a beauty peculiar not only to that one species but to that one individual.

To us the human dawn is precious for its own sake. And it is as creatures of the dawn that we regard you, even in your highest achievement. To us the early human natures and every primitive human individual have a beauty which we ourselves, in spite of all our triumphs, have not; the beauty namely of life's first bewildered venturing upon the wings of the spirit, the beauty of the child with all its innocent brutishness and cruelty. We understand the past better than it can understand itself, and love it better than it can love itself. Seeing it in relation to all things, we see it as it is; and so we can observe even its follies and treasons with reverence, knowing that we ourselves would have behaved so, had we been so placed and so fashioned. The achievements of the past, however precarious and evanescent, we salute with respect, knowing well that to achieve anything at all in such circumstances and with such a nature entailed a faith and fortitude which in those days were miracles. We are therefore moved by filial piety to observe all the past races of men, and if possible every single individual life, with careful precision, so that, before we are destroyed, we may crown those races our equals in glory though not in achievement. Thus we shall contribute to the cosmos a beauty which it would otherwise lack, namely the critical yet admiring love which we bear toward you.

But it is not only as observers that we, who are of man's evening, are concerned with you, children of the dawn. In my earlier message I told how the future might actually influence the past, how beings such as my contemporaries, who have in some degree the freedom of eternity, may from their footing in eternity, reach into past minds and contribute to their experience. For whatever is truly eternal is present equally in all times; and so we, in so far as we are capable of eternity, are influences present in your age. I said that we seek out all those points in past history where our help is entailed for the fulfilment of the past's own nature, and that this work of inspiration has become one of our main tasks. How this can be, I shall explain more fully later. Strange it is indeed that we, who are so closely occupied with the great adventure of racial experience, so closely also with preparations to face the impending ruin of our world, and with research for dissemination of a seed of life in remote regions of the galaxy, should yet also find ourselves under obligation toward the vanished and unalterable past.

No influence of ours can save your species from destruction. Nothing could save it but a profound change in your own nature; and that cannot be. Wandering among you, we move always with fore-knowledge of the doom which your own imperfection imposes on you. Even if we could, we would not change it; for it is a theme required in the strange music of the spheres.

I *The World of the Last Men*

1. HOLIDAY ON NEPTUNE

WHEN I am in your world and your epoch I remember often a certain lonely place in my own world, and in the time that I call present. It is a corner where the land juts out into the sea as a confusion of split rocks, like a herd of monsters crowding into the water. Subterranean forces acting at this point once buckled the planet's crust into a mountain; but it was immediately torn and shattered by gravity, that implacable djin of all great worlds. Nothing is now left of it but these rocks. On Neptune we have no mountains, and the oceans are waveless. The stout sphere holds its watery cloak so tightly to it that even the most violent hurricanes fail to raise more than a ripple.

Scattered among these rocks lies a network of tiny fjords, whose walls and floors are embossed with variegated life. There you may see beneath the crystal water all manner of blobs and knobs and brilliant whorls, all manner of gaudy flowers, that search with their petals, or rhythmically smack their lips, all manner of clotted sea-weeds, green, brown, purple or crimson, from whose depths sometimes a claw reaches after a drowsing sprat, while here and there a worm, fringed with legs, emerges to explore the sandy sunlit bottom.

Among these rocks and fjords I spent my last day of leisure before setting out on one of those lengthy explorations of the past which have made me almost as familiar with your world as with my own. It is my task to tell you of your own race as it appears through the eyes of the far future; but first I must help you to reconstruct in imagination something of the future itself, and of the world from which we regard you. This I can best achieve by describing, first that day of delight, spent where the broken mountain sprawls into the sea, and then a more august event, namely the brief awakening of the Racial Mind, which was appointed for the exaltation of the explorers upon the eve of their departure into the obscure recesses of past aeons. Finally I shall tell you something of my own upbringing and career.

Almost the first moments of that day of recreation afforded me one of those pictures which haunt the memory ever after. The sun had risen over a burning ocean. He was not, as you might expect in our remote world, a small and feeble sun; for between your age and ours a collision had increased his bulk and splendour to a magnitude somewhat greater than that with which you are familiar.

Overhead the sky was blue. But for Neptunian eyes its deep azure was infused with another unique primary colour, which your vision could not have detected. Toward the sunrise, this tincture of the zenith gave place to green, gold, fire-red, purple, and yet another of the hues which elude the primitive eye. Opposite there lay darkness. But low in the darkness gleamed something which you would have taken for a very distant snowy horn, whose base was lost in night, though its crest glowed orange in the morning. A second glance would have revealed it as too precipitous and too geometrical for any mountain. It was in fact one of our great public buildings, many scores of miles distant, and nearly one score in height. In a world where mountains are crushed by their own weight these towering edifices could not stand, were it not for their incredibly rigid materials, wherein artificial atoms play the chief part. The huge crag of masonry now visible was relatively new, but it could compare in age with the younger of your terrestrial mountains.

The shadowed sides of its buttresses and gables, and also the shadowed faces of the near rocks and of every stone, glowed with a purple bloom, the light from a blinding violet star. This portent we call the Mad Star. It is a unique heavenly body, whose energies are being squandered with inconceivable haste, so that it will soon be burnt out. Meanwhile it is already infecting its neighbours with its plague. In a few thousand years our own sun will inevitably run amok in the same manner, and turn all his planets to white-hot gas. But at present, I mean in the age which I call present, the Mad Star is only a brilliant feature of our night sky.

On the morning of which I am speaking there lay full length on the brink of a little cliff, and gazing into the pool beneath her, a woman of my world. To me she is lovely, exquisite, the very embodiment of beauty; to you she would seem a strange half-human monster. To me, as she lay there with her breasts against the rock and one arm reaching down into the water, her whole form expressed the lightness and suppleness of a panther. To you she would have seemed unwieldy, elephantine, and grotesque in every feature. Yet if you were to see her moving in her own world, you would know, I think, why her name in our speech is the equivalent of Panther in yours.

If you or any of your kind were to visit our world, and if by miracle you were to survive for a few moments in our alien atmosphere, gravity would make it almost impossible for you to support yourselves at all. But we, since our bones, like our buildings, are formed largely of artificial atoms, and are far more rigid than steel, since moreover our muscle cells have been most cunningly designed, can run and jump with ease. It is true, however, that in spite of our splendid tissues we have to be more solidly built than the Terrestrials, whose limbs remind us unpleasantly of insects.

The woman on the rock would certainly have surprised you, for she is a member of one of our most recent generations, whose skin and flesh are darkly translucent. Seeing her there, with the sunlight drenching her limbs, you might have taken her for a statue, cut from some wine-dark alabaster, or from carbuncle; save that, with every movement of her arm, sunken gleams of crimson, topaz, and gold-brown rippled the inner night of her shoulder and flank. Her whole substance, within its lovely curves and planes, looked scarcely solid, but rather a volume of obscure flame and smoke poised on the rock. On her head a mass of hair, flame-like, smoke-like, was a reversion to the primitive in respect of which she could never decide whether it was a thing for shame or complacency. It was this pre-historic decoration which first drew me toward her. In a closer view you would have noticed that on her back and the outer sides of her limbs the skin's translucency was complicated by a very faint leopard-like mottling. I also bear that mottling; but I am of the sort whose flesh is opaque, and my bronze-green skin is of a texture somewhat harsher than I should choose. In her, how well I know it, the skin is soft and rich to the exploring hand.

While I watched her, she raised her face from studying the water-dwellers, and looked at me, laughing. It was that look which gave me the brief but strangely significant experience the memory of which was to refresh me so often in your uncouth world. It was not only that her face was lit up with merriment and tenderness; but in that fleeting expression the very spirit of humanity seemed to regard me. I cannot make you realize the potency of that glance, for the faces of your own kind afford almost no hint of such illumination. I can only assert that in our species, facial expression is more developed than in yours. The facial muscles respond to every changing flicker of experience and emotion, as pools respond to every breath of wind with a thousand criss-cross rippling tremors.

The face that now looked at me was unlike terrestrial countenances both in its subtly alien contours and in its dark translucency, which half-revealed the underlying paleness of bone. It was like a stirred and dancing pool of dark but warm-tinted wine, in which the sunlight revelled. But the eyes were bright jewels capable of many phases from sapphire to emerald.

Like others of our kind, this girl bore two additional bright eyes in the back of her head. They sparkled quaintly in the archaic glory of her hair. Like the rest of us, she had on her crown yet another and more important organ of vision which we call the astronomical eye. Normally sunken level with her hair, it could at will be projected upwards like a squat telescope. The exquisite development of this organ in her had determined her career. All of us are in a manner astronomers; but she is an astronomer by profession.

Her whole face, though so brilliantly alive, was unlike any human type known to readers of this book, since it was so much more animal. Her nose was broad and feline, but delicately moulded. Her full lips were subtle at the corners. Her ears moved among her locks like the ears of a lion.

Grotesque, you say, inhuman! No! Beside this the opaque and sluggish faces of your proudest beauties are little better than lumps of clay, or the masks of insects.

But indeed it is impossible for you to see her as I saw her then.

For in that look there seemed to find expression the whole achievement of our race, and the full knowledge of its impending tragedy. At the same time there was in it a half-mischievous piety toward the little simple creatures that she had been watching, and equally, it seemed, toward the stars and man himself.

Smiling, she now spoke to me; if I may call 'speech' the telepathic influence which invaded my brain from hers.

That you may understand the significance of her words, I must explain that in our Neptunian rock-pools there are living things of three very different stocks. The first is rare. One may encounter in some sheltered cranny a vague greenish slime. This is the only relic of primeval Neptunian life, long since outclassed by invaders. The second stock is by far the commonest throughout our world. Nearly all our living types are triumphant descendants of the few animals and plants which men brought, deliberately or by accident, to Neptune from Venus, nearly a thousand million years before my day, and almost as long after the age that you call present. Third, there are also, even in these little fjords, a few descendants of those ancient men themselves. These very remote cousins of my own human species are, of course, fantastically degenerate. Most have long ago ceased to be recognizably human; but in one, whose name in our language you might translate 'Homunculus', nature has achieved a minute and exquisite caricature of humanity. Two splay feet glue him to the rock. From these rises an erect and bulbous belly, wearing on its summit an upturned face. The unpleasantly human mouth keeps opening and shutting. The eyes are mere wrinkles, the nose a wide double trumpet. The ears, deaf but mobile, have become two broad waving fans, that direct a current of water toward the mouth. Beneath each ear is a little wart-like excrescence, all that is left of the human arm and hand.

One of these degenerate human beings, one of these fallen descendants of your own kind, had attracted my companion's attention. Laughing, she said, 'Little Homunculus has got wind of his mate, and he can't unstick his feet to go after her. What a pilgrimage it will be for him after a whole month of standing still!'

She looked down again and cried, 'Quick! Come and see! He's loose, he's moved an inch. He's waddling at breakneck speed.

Now he's got her, and she's willing.' After a pause she exclaimed, 'What a world this pond is! Like the world that you are to plunge into so soon.'

Then she looked up at the fierce star, and the light in her face changed and chilled. She became like your Egyptian Sphinx, which looks across the desert and waits, for something unknown and terrible, but the appointed end.

Suddenly she laughed, sprang to her feet, ran down the rock-edge to the sea, and dived. I followed; and the rest of the morning we spent swimming, either far out in the bay or among the islets and fjords, chasing each other sometimes through submarine rock-arches, or clinging to a sunken tussock of weed to watch some drama of the sea-bottom.

At last, when the sun was high, we returned to the grassy place where we had slept, and took from the pockets of our flying-suits our meal of rich sun-products. Of these, some had been prepared in the photo-synthesis stations on Jupiter, others came from the colonies on Uranus; but we ourselves had gathered the delicacies in our own orchards and gardens.

Having eaten, we lay back on the grass and talked of matters great and small.

I challenged her: 'This has been the best of all our matings.' 'Yes,' she answered, 'because the shortest? Because after the richest experience in separation. And perhaps because of the Star.'

'In spite of all your lovers,' I exulted, 'you come back to me. In spite of your tigers, your bulls, and all your lap-dog lovers, where you squander yourself.'

'Yes, old python, I come back to you, the richer for that squandering. And you in spite of all the primroses and violets and blowsy roses and over-scented lilies that you have plucked and dropped, you come back to me, after your thousand years of roaming.'

'Again and again I shall come back, if I escape from the Terrestrials, and if the Star permits.'

Our conversation, let me repeat, was telepathic. If I were to report all that passed from mind to mind as we lay in the sun that afternoon, I should fill a book; for telepathic communication is incomparably swifter and more subtle than vocal speech. We ranged over all manner of subjects, from the difference between her eyes and mine, which are crimson, to the awakening of the Racial Mind, which we had experienced some thousands of years earlier, and were so soon to experience again. We talked also about the marriage groups to which we severally belonged, and of our own strange irregular yet seemingly permanent union outside our respective groups. We talked about the perplexing but lovely nature of our son, whom she had been allowed to conceive at our last meeting. We spoke also of her work in one of the great observatories. With other astronomers she was trying to discover in some distant region of our galaxy a possible home for the human seed which, it was hoped, would be scattered among the stars before man's destruction. We spoke also of the work on which I am engaged as one of the million specialists who are trying to complete the exploration of the human past by direct participation in it. Inevitably we spoke also of the Star, and of the coming destruction of our world; and of how, if we were both alive in that age we would cling together.

Before sundown we clambered over the rocks and ran inland over the flower-strewn turf. But at last we returned to our grassy nest; and after supper, when darkness had fallen, we were moved to sing, together or each in turn. Sometimes our choice fell upon the latest, wildest, scintillations of rhythm and melody, sometimes on the old songs of her nation or mine, sometimes on the crude chants which we explorers had discovered among the ancient peoples and in extinct worlds. In particular I taught her a Terrestrial song which I myself had found. With difficulty we formed the uncouth syllables and caught the lilt. With difficulty we called up in imagination the dark confusion that gave it birth, the harshness of man to man, and the yearning for a better world. Readers of this book may know the song. *Old Man River* is its name.

While we were still striving with this archaic melody, the colours of the sunset gave place to the profound azure which the Neptunian sky assumes by night for Neptunian eyes. Stars began to appear, first singly and faintly, then in companies and brightly patterned constellations. The wide heaven flashed with them. The Milky Way, flung from horizon to horizon, revealed itself to us, not as a pale cloud-zone, but as an incredibly multitudinous host of lights. Here and there our astronomical eyes could detect even those misty points which are in fact the remote universes. Our singing was now hushed into a murmuring and wordless chant; for this comparatively simple yet overwhelmingly significant percept of the night sky commands us all with a power which might seem to you extravagant. It is, as it were, the visible epitome of our whole thought and feeling. It has for us more than the potency of your most venerated religious symbols. It stirs not only the surface of our being but the ancestral depths, and yet it is relevant to the most modern ventures of our intellect.

While we were still saluting with our voices and our spirits this august and never-too-familiar presentation, the Mad Star rose once more, and scattered its cold steel across the sea. We fell silent, watching. Its dread effulgence extinguished the constellations.

Whether it was the influence of those barbarian melodies that we had been savouring, or a mere flaw in my nature, I know not; but suddenly I heard myself cry out, 'Hideous! That such a world as ours should be burnt, wasted such a world of spirit and sweet flesh!'

She looked quickly in my eyes, with amazed laughter thrusting down dismay. But before she could speak I saw rightly again. 'No!' I said, 'not hideous, but terrible. Strange, how our thoughts can slip back for a moment into the bad old ways, as though we were to lose sight of the great beauty, and be like the blind spirits of the past.'

And she, 'When the end begins, shall we still see the great beauty? Shall we see it even in the fire?'

And I, 'Who knows? But we see it now.'

Silently we watched the Star climb with increasing splendour of violet and ultra-violet illumination. But at last we lay down together in our sheltered grassy nest, and took intimate delight in one another.

At dawn we rose. After a short swim, we put on our flying-suits, those overalls studded with minute sources of sub-atomic energy on the soles of the feet, the palms of the hands, and the whole front surface of the body. It is with these that all lesser flights are performed in our world; and as the action entails much skill and some muscular exertion, it is a delight in itself. Side by side we climbed the air, until the coast was like a map beneath us. We headed inland, first over a wide tract of rock and prairie, marsh and scrub, then over corn and orchard, sprinkled with innumerable homes. Once we passed near a great building, whose crystal precipices towered over us with snow on their cornices. A white cloud covered its upper parts, save for one slender pinnacle, which tiptoed into the sunlight. Sometimes a flying-boat would detach itself from the walls or emerge from the cloud. As we travelled over more densely inhabited regions, sprinkled somewhat more closely with private houses and cottages, a more numerous swarm of these flying-boats continually passed over our heads in all directions from horizon to horizon at so great a speed that they seemed darting insects. We encountered also many fliers like ourselves. Many we saw beneath us, moving from house to house across the intervening tillage. At one point an arm of the sea lay across our route; and there we saw, entering dock, a five-mile long ether-ship, lately returned from Jupiter or Uranus with a cargo of foodstuffs. She was a great fish of stainless metal, studded with windows over her back and flanks. Hidden under water also there would be windows; for this seemingly marine monster could rise like a cormorant, with a great churning of the ocean, to find herself within a few minutes surrounded above and below by stars.

At noon we reached another wild district, and took our meal near a warren of creatures which I can best describe as Neptunian rabbits. The form of these furry descendants of an extinct human species was chiefly determined, as so often with our fauna, by gravity. For support they use, not only their short thick legs, but also their leathern bellies and tails. No sooner had we sat down to eat than these mammalian lizards crowded round us in the hope of titbits. One of them actually made off with a loaf; but before he could reach his earth I captured him, and administered such punishment that henceforth the whole tribe treated us with more respect.

When our meal was over, we took leave of one another. It was a gay, grave parting; for we knew that we might not meet again for thousands of years, perhaps not before the sun, infected by the Mad Star, should already have begun the destruction of our beloved world. When we had looked in one another's eyes for a long moment, we buckled on our flying-suits once more; then, in opposite directions, we climbed the air. By dawn next day we had to be at our appointed stations, far asunder on the great planet's surface, to participate in the Racial Awakening, the sublime event to which every adult person on the planet must needs contribute.

2. MEN AND MAN

When an attempt is to be made to call the Race Mind into being, all adult persons on the planet seek their allotted places near one or other of a number of great towers which are scattered throughout the continents. After a preparatory phase, in which much telepathic intercourse occurs between individuals and between the group minds of various orders which now begin to emerge, there comes a supreme moment, when, if all goes well, every man and woman in the world-wide multitude of multitudes awakes, as it were, to become the single Mind of the Race, possessing the million bodies of all men and women as a man's mind possesses the multitude of his body's cells.

Had you been privileged to watch from the summit of the great needle of masonry round which I and so many others had gathered on that morning, you would have seen far below, at the foot of the twenty-mile high architectural precipice, and stretching to the horizon in every direction, a featureless grey plain, apparently a desert. Had you then used a powerful field-glass, you would have discovered that the plain was in fact minutely stippled with microscopic dots of brown, separated by almost invisible traces of green. Had you then availed yourself of a much more powerful telescope, you would have found, with amazement, that each of these brown dots was in fact a group of persons. The whole plain would have been revealed as no mere desert, but a prodigious host of men and women, gathered into little companies between which the green grass showed. The whole texture of the earth would have appeared almost like some vegetable tissue seen through the microscope, or the cellular flesh of Leviathan. Within each cell you might have counted ninety-six granules, ninety-six minute sub-cellular organs, in fact ninety-six faces of men and women. Of these small marriage groups which are the basis of our society, I have spoken elsewhere, and shall say no more now. Suffice it that you would have found each dot to be not a face, but a group of faces. Everywhere you would have seen faces turned towards the tower, and motionless as grains of sand. Yet this host was one of thousands such, scattered over all the continents.

A still more powerful telescope would have shown that we were all standing, each with a doffed flying-suit hanging over an arm or shoulder. As you moved the telescope hither and thither you would have discovered our great diversity. For though we are all of one species, it is a species far more variable even than your domestic dog; and our minds are no less diverse than our bodies. Nearly all of us, you would have noted, were unclad; but a few were covered with their own velvet fur. The great majority of the Last Men, however, are hairless, their skins brown, or gold, or black, or grey, or striped, or mottled. Though you would recognize our bodies as definitely human, you would at the same time be startled by the diversity of their forms, and by their manifold aberrations from what you regard as the true human type. You would notice in our faces and in the moulding of our limbs a strong suggestion of animal forms; as though here a horse, there a tiger, and there some ancient reptile, had been inspired with a human mind in such a manner that, though now definitely man or woman, it remained reminiscent of its animal past. You would be revolted by this animal character of ours. But we, who are so securely human, need not shrink from being animal too. In you, humanity is precarious; and so, in dread and in shame, you kill the animal in you. And its slaughter poisons you.

Your wandering telescope would have revealed us as one and all in the late spring or full summer of life. Infants had been left behind for the day in the automatic crêches; children were at large in their own houses; the youths and girls were living their wild romantic lives in the Land of the Young. And though the average age of the host gathered below you was many thousands of years, not one of its members would have appeared to you aged. Senility is unknown among us.

Regarding us in the mass, you would have found it hard to
believe that each human atom beneath you was in reality a unique
and highly developed person, who would judge the immature
personality of your own species as you judge your half-human
progenitors. Careful use of the telescope, however, would have
revealed the light of intense and unique consciousness in every
face. For every member of this great host had his peculiar and
subtle character, his rich memories, his loves and aims, and his
special contribution to our incredibly complex society. Farmers
and gardeners, engineers and architects, chemists and sub-atomic
physicists, biologists, psychologists and eugenists, stood together
with creative artists of many kinds, with astronomers, philosophers, historians, explorers of the past, teachers, professional
mothers, and many more whose work has no counterpart in your
world. There would be also, beside the more permanent denizens
of Neptune, a sprinkling of ethereal navigators, whose vessels
happened to be on the home-planet, and even a few pioneers from
the settlements on Uranus and Pluto. The ethereal navigators who
ply between the planets are our only transport-workers. Passenger
traffic on the home-planet takes place entirely in private air-boats or
flying-suits. Freight travels automatically in subterranean tubes,
some of which, suitably refrigerated, take direct routes almost
through the heart of the planet. Industry and commerce, such as you
know, have no representatives among us, for in our world there is
nothing like your industrial system. Our industry has neither
operatives nor magnates. In so far as manufacture is a routine
process, it is performed by machinery which needs no human
influence but the pressing of a button. In so far as it involves innovation, it is the work of scientists and engineers. In so far as it
involves organization, it is controlled by the professional organizers. As for commerce, we have no such thing, because we have no
buying and no selling. Both production and distribution are regulated by the organizers, working under the Supreme College of
Unity. This is in no sense a governing body, since its work is
purely advisory; but owing to our constant telepathic intercourse,
its recommendations are always sane, and always persuasive.
Consequently, though it has no powers of compulsion, it is the
great co-ordinator of our whole communal life. In the crowd

beneath you many members of this Supreme College would be present; but nothing would distinguish them from members of the other and equally honourable professions.

If you had watched us for long enough, you would have noticed, after some hours of stillness, a shimmering change in the grey plain, a universal stirring, which occurred at the moment of the awakening of the Racial Mind throughout the whole population of the planet. The telescope would have revealed that all the faces, formerly placid, were suddenly illuminated with an expression of tense concentration and triumph. For now at last each one of us was in the act of emerging into the higher self-hood, to find himself the single and all-embracing mind of a world.

At that moment, I, Man, perceived, not merely the multitudinous several perceptions of all men and women on the face of the planet, but the single significance of all those perceptions. Through the feet of all individuals I grasped my planet, as a man may hold a ball in his hand. Possessing all the memories of all men and women, not merely as memory but as direct experience of the present, I perceived the whole biography of my generation, nay, of my species, as you perceive a melody, in flux yet all of it 'now'. I perceived the planets whirling round the sun, and even the fixed stars creeping about the sky like insects. But also at will I perceived movements within the atoms, and counted the pulsations of light waves. I possessed also all the emotions and desires of all men and women. I observed them inwardly, as a man may introspect his own delighting and grieving; but I observed them dispassionately. I was present in the loving of all lovers, and the adventuring of all who dare. I savoured all victories and defeats, all imaginings and reasonings. But from all these teeming experiences of my tiny members I held myself in detachment, turning my attention to a sphere remote from these, where I, Man, experienced my own grave desires and fears, and pursued my own high reasoning and contemplation. Of what it was that then occupied me, the Mind of the Race, it is impossible for me, the little individual who is now communicating with you, to say anything definite. For these experiences lie beyond the understanding of any individual. But this at least may be said. Waking into this lofty experience, and looking down upon my individual members as a man may regard the

351

cells of his flesh, I was impressed far more by my littleness than by my greatness. For in relation to the whole of things I saw myself to be a very minute, simple, and helpless being, doomed to swift destruction by the operation of a stellar event whose meaning remained unintelligible to me, even upon my new and lofty plain of understanding. But even the little individual who is now communicating with you can remember that, when I, Man, faced this doom, I was in no manner dismayed by it. I accepted it with exultation, as an evident beauty within the great beauty of the whole. For my whole experience was transfused and glorified by the perception of that all-embracing and terrible beauty. Even on that loftier plane of my being I did but glimpse it; but what I glimpsed I contemplated with an insight and a rapture impossible in my lowlier mode of being.

Had you remained upon the tower until the following morning, you would have seen, shortly after sunrise, the whole plain stir again. We were preparing to go. Presently it would have seemed to you that the surface of the planet was detaching itself and rising, like dust on a wind-swept road, or steam from hot water, or like a valley cloud seen from a mountain-top, and visibly boiling upwards. Higher and higher it would have risen toward you, presently to resolve itself even for the naked eye into a vast smoke of individual men and women. Soon you would have seen them all around you and above you, swimming in the air with outspread arms, circling, soaring, darkening the sky. After a brief spell of random and ecstatic flight, they would have been observed streaming away in all directions to become a mere haze along the horizon. Looking down, you would now have seen that the grey plain had turned to green, fading in the distance into blues and purples.

The dispersal of the gatherings does not put an end to the racial experience. For an indefinite period of months or years each individual, though he goes his own way, living his own life and fulfilling his special function in the community, remains none the less possessed by the race mind. Each perceives, thinks, strives as an individual; but also he is Man, perceiving racially, and thinking in manners wholly impossible in the humbler mode of being. As each cell in a brain lives its own life, yet participates in the experience of the whole brain, so we. But after a while the great being sleeps again.

After the awakening which I have just described the racial mentality endured for many years; but one class of individuals had perforce to refrain from any further participation in it, namely those who were to engage upon exploration of the past. For this work it is necessary, for reasons which I shall explain later, to cut off all telepathic communication with one's fellows, and consequently to leave the telepathic system in which the Race Mind inheres. Yet it was expressly to further our work that this particular awakening had been ordained. It was to strengthen us for our adventures. For my part, as I hastened first to my home and thence through the upper air in my flying-boat toward the Arctic, I felt that I had been kindled with an inextinguishable flame; and that though I must henceforth be exiled from the lofty experience of the Race Mind, I had acquired a new fervour and clarity of vision, which would enable me to observe your world with finer insight than on my earlier visits.

3. BIOGRAPHICAL NOTE

At this point it seems desirable to say a few words about myself, so that you may have some idea of the kind of being who is communicating with you, and the angle from which he is regarding you.

I am at present twenty thousand years old according to your Terrestrial reckoning, and therefore I am still in the spring-time of my life. My parents were chosen for me. They had long been intimate with one another, but the call to have a child arose from the knowledge that there was need of such a being as they together could produce. Recent improvements in man's powers of entering into past minds, together with the new urgency for completing the exploration of the past before our own world should be destroyed, had increased the call for past-explorers. For such a career I was destined even before I was conceived; and while I was still in the womb, the eugenists were still influencing me so as to give me novel powers.

During infancy I remained with my mother. Throughout my life I have retained a closer intimacy with her than is common in my world; for with her tenderness and strange innocent ruthlessness she embodies for me the very spirit of the past and the primitive. And these have enthralled me always. Not that in your eyes she would have seemed primitive; but underlying all her reasonableness and sophistication I detect that savage temperament which, perhaps partly because of my own extreme sophistication, I so enjoy in others.

I spent my thousand years of childhood in the manner characteristic of my race. Mostly I lived in a children's residential club. We managed it with more dash than efficiency; but in intervals between domestic duties, games, quarrels and sentimental attachments, we managed to lay the foundations of our education. Even at this early stage my predisposition toward the primitive and the past was beginning to wake. While others were making toy etherships and model planetary systems, I was digging for fossils, haunting museums, brooding on ancient folklore, and writing histories of imaginary past worlds. In all my recreations and in all my studies this interest was ever apt to insinuate itself.

My second thousand years was spent, as is customary with us, in the reserved continent called the Land of the Young. There our young people sow their wild oats by living as savages and barbarians. During this phase they are definitely juvenile in disposition. They appreciate only such barbarian virtues as were admired even by the most primitive human species. They are capable of loyalty, but only by an uneasy and heroic victory over self-regard. Their loyalties are never easeful, for they have not yet developed the self-detachment of the adult. Further, they care only for the beauties of triumphant individual life. The supernal beauties of the cosmos, which form the main preoccupation of grown men and women, are hidden from these young things. Consequently our adult world lies very largely beyond their comprehension.

For some centuries I gave myself wholly to a 'Red Indian' life, becoming a master of the bow and arrow, and a really brilliant tracker. I remember too that I fell in love with a dangerous young Amazon with golden hair. My first encounter with her was warlike. She escaped, but left her javelin in my shoulder, and her presence in my heart. Long afterwards, when we were both in the adult world, I met her again. She had by now entered upon her career, having been chosen as one of our professional mothers.

Later still, she volunteered to submit to a very dangerous maternity experiment, and was so shattered by it, that the eugenists had finally to put her to death.

I had not been many centuries in the Land of the Young before my master passion began to assert itself. I set about collecting material for a complete history of that juvenile world. For this end I sampled every kind of life in every corner of the continent. I also sharpened my perception, or so I persuaded myself, by intimacy with many resplendent young women. But long before I had completed my history, the work began to be interrupted by visits to the adult world.

There is a party in the Land of the Young who preach that the juvenile world is happier and nobler than the world of the adults. They send missionaries among those whom they know to be turning from the primitive, and seek to persuade them to join a small and pathetic band called the Old Young, who elect to remain in the Land of the Young for ever. These poor arrested beings become the guardians of tradition and morality among the nations of the Young. Like the village idiot, they are despised even while at the same time their sayings are supposed to be pregnant with mysterious truth. I myself, with my taste for the past and the primitive, was persuaded to take the vow of this order. But when I was introduced to one of these bright old things, I was so depressed that I recanted. It came as a revelation to me that my task was not actually to become primitive, but to study the primitive. It was borne in on me that even the past and the primitive can be understood and loved better by the full-grown mind than by the primitive itself.

During their last century in the Land of the Young our boys and girls normally develop beyond the larval stage very rapidly, though not without severe mental agony. For during this period the mind is in bitter conflict with itself. It clings to the primitive, but is at the same time nauseated; it yearns toward the mature, but is at the same time fearful and reluctant. This profound metamorphosis of body and mind continues for some centuries even after the young person has entered the adult world. The simple male or female sexual characters specialize themselves into one or other of the ninety-six sub-sexes. Intelligence soars into a new order of proficiency. New centres of the brain integrate the nervous system so

355

perfectly that henceforth behaviour will be, without exception, and without serious struggle, rational; or, as you would say, moral. At the same time the faculty of telepathic communication appears; and, through the cumulative effect of constant telepathic intercourse, the mind comes into such exact understanding and vivid sympathy with other minds, that the diversity of all serves but to enhance the mental richness of each.

This radical change of nature, which raises the individual in a few centuries to a new plane of experience, was for me the more torturing because of my innate hunger for the primitive. This same characteristic made it difficult for me to reconcile myself to the highly complex adult sexual life of my species, which is based on the marriage group of the ninety-six sub-sexes. My group formed itself with unusual difficulty; but, once constituted, it was maintained without undue emphasis. Only once in a century or so are we moved to come together, and live together, and love together; and then only for about a year. During these periods we take delicate joy in one another, and in ourselves. And though we remain self-conscious individuals, a single group-self emerges in us. We spend much of our time rapt in the perceptions and thoughts which are possible only to the minds of the sexual groups; brooding especially on the subtleties of personality and super-personality, and preparing the ground for the recurrent phases of that far more complex mode of consciousness, the Mind of the Race. Apart from these occasional periods of group-mentality, each of us lives an independent life, and is only obscurely conscious of his group-membership. Nevertheless, much as, after swimming, a freshness may vaguely cheer the body for the rest of the day, or after sun-bathing a tingling beatitude, so for each of us participation in the group affords an enhanced vitality which may endure for many decades.

When I had settled into my sexual group, I was about three thousand years old. My body had attained that youthful maturity which with us is perennial, and my mind had shed all the follies of the Land of the Young. I was apprenticed to work which was perfectly suited to my nature. It was exacting work, for the novel powers with which I was endowed were as yet imperfectly understood. But my working hours would have seemed ridiculously short even in your most ardent trade-unionists. Only for a few years in every century was my mind actually absent from the contemporary world. Only for a decade or two would I devote my mornings to formulating the results of my research. Though inevitably the past, and my study of the past, would be nearly always in my thoughts, the great bulk of my time was occupied with other activities. For decade after decade I would merely watch the manifold operations of our great community, wandering into all countries, seeking intimacy with all sorts of persons, peering through microscopes and astronomical instruments, watching the birth of inventions in other minds, studying the eugenists' plans for new generations, or the latest improvements in etherial navigation. Much of my time was spent in ether-ships, much in the Uranian colonies, much in the interior of the mine-honeycombed Pluto. Sometimes I would go as a guest into the Land of the Young to spend years in comparing our own young things with the primitive races of the past. Occasionally I have been chiefly concerned for a decade at a time with the appreciation or practice of some creative art, most often with our supreme art, which I must reluctantly call 'telepathic verse'. Somewhat as auditory verse uses sound, this most subtle of all arts uses our direct sensitivity to ethereal vibrations for the evocation of rhythms and patterns of sensory images and ideas. Sometimes, on the other hand, I have been absorbed in some special problem of natural science, and have done little but follow the experiments of scientific workers. Much of my time, of course, has been given to cosmology, and much to metaphysics; for in my world these subjects compel the attention of every man and woman. Sometimes for a year or so I would do little but rebuild my house or cultivate my garden; or I would become wholly absorbed in the invention or construction of some toy for a child friend. Sometimes my main preoccupation for several years has been intimacy with some woman, of my own nation or another. It must be confessed that I am more disposed to this kind of refreshment than most of my fellows. But I do not regret it. In these many brief lyrical matings of body and mind I seem to experience in a very special manner that which unites the developed and the primitive. Now and then, like most of my fellows, I spend a decade or so in lonely wandering, giving myself wholly to the sensuous and instinctive life. It was on one of these occasions that I first met the translucent woman whom I have called Panther. Many have I loved; but with her, whom I meet only in the wilderness, I have a very special relation. For whereas my spirit turns ever to the past, hers turns to the future; and each without the other is an empty thing.

This great freedom and variety of life, and this preponderance of leisure over work, are characteristic of my world. The engineer, the chemist, even the agriculturist and the ethereal navigator, spend less time at their own special tasks than in watching the lives of others. Indeed it is only by means of this system of mutual observation, augmented by our constant telepathic intercourse, that we can preserve that understanding of one another which is the life-blood of our community. In your world this perfect accord of minds is impossible. Yet your differences of racial temperament and of acquired bias are as nothing beside the vast diversity of innate disposition which is at once our constant danger and our chief strength.

From the time when I had reached full maturity of mind, and had become expert in my special calling, up to my present age of twenty thousand years, my life has been even, though eventful. I have of course had my difficulties and anxieties, my griefs and my triumphs. I lost my two closest friends in an ether-ship disaster. Another friend, younger than myself, has developed in such a strange manner that, though I do my best to understand him telepathically, I cannot but feel that he is seriously abnormal, and will sooner or later either come to grief or achieve some novel splendour. This has been my most serious anxiety apart from my work.

Work has been by far the most important factor in my life. Peculiarly gifted by inheritance, I have co-operated with the equally gifted fellow-workers of my generation to raise the art of past-exploration to a new range of power. My novitiate was spent in studying one of the earlier Neptunian civilizations. Since then I have acquired considerable first-hand knowledge of every one of the eighteen human species. In addition I have specialized in some detail on the Venetian Flying Men and the Last Terrestrials. But the great bulk of my work has been done among the First Men, and upon the particular crisis which you call present.

Apart from the exigencies of my work, two events have produced profound changes in my life; but they were events of public rather than private significance, and have affected the whole race with equal urgency. One was the first occasion on which we awakened into the racial mentality. The other was the discovery of the Mad Star, and of the doom of our world. For all of us these two great happenings have changed a life of serenely victorious enterprise into something more mysterious, more pregnant, and more tragic.

II *Exploring The Past*

1. THE PORTAL TO THE PAST

IT was with an overwhelming sense of the mystery and formidable beauty of existence that I hastened, after the racial awakening, toward that Arctic settlement which we call the Portal to the Past. Travelling now by flying-boat, I soon reached the icefields; and by noon the great towers which marked my destination stood like bristles on the horizon. Already I encountered many other boats and boatless flyers, bound for the same goal. Presently I arrived, docked my little vessel in her appointed garage, and entered the great white gate of the particular tower which concerned me. Greeting some of my colleagues, I passed through the entrance hall and stepped into one of the many lifts. In a few moments I had sunk a thousand feet below the ground. I then proceeded along a lofty and well-lit passage, in the walls of which were doors, at intervals of a hundred yards. One of these I opened. Within was a comfortable room, in which were chairs, a table, cupboards, and a bed. At the far side of the room was a window, opening from ceiling to ground, and beyond it a delightful sunny garden. How could this be, you wonder, a thousand feet below ground? Had you walked out into the garden, you would have seen that in the luminous blue ceiling there blazed an artificial sun, and you would have felt a refreshing breeze, which issued from among the bushes.

Behind every one of the doors in the many underground passages you would have found similar rooms and gardens, varying only in detail according to the tastes of their occupiers. Such are the apartments where we explorers of the past undertake our strange adventures. You ask, why in the Arctic, why underground? Our work demands that the mind shall be isolated from the contemporary human world; only in a remote land, and beneath its surface, can we escape the telepathic influence of the world-population. Our telepathic intercourse is based on the transmission and reception of ethereal vibrations from brain to brain.

Normally our powers of reception are kept under strict control, so that we receive messages only when we will. But, in the peculiar trance which is our medium for exploring the past, this control fails; so that, unless the explorer is isolated, his mind is lashed like a pond in which torrential rain is falling.

When I had entered my room and shut my door, I went out into my garden and walked up and down for a while, preparing my mind for its adventure. I then brought out from the room a drawer full of rolls of microscopically figured tape, which in my world take the place of books. In normal circumstances these little rolls work by systematically interrupting the radiation of a special instrument. This radiation penetrates the brain of the 'reader', and is interpreted telepathically by the telepathic organ of his brain. But since in the catacombs no radiation other than the normal solar wave-lengths is permitted, we explorers have to learn actually to read the rolls, with the aid of a microscope.

I now spent many hours lying on the turf in the sunshine, reading about the epoch which I was to visit. After a while I re-entered the room and pressed a button in the wall. A tray appeared, bearing an appetizing meal. When I had finished this, and dismissed the tray, I returned to the garden and my studies. For a period equivalent to about ten days I lived in this manner, studying, meditating, eating occasionally, but sleeping not at all. Sometimes I would break off my studies to tend my garden. Frequently I would swim about in the pond among the bushes. But for the most part I merely browsed on my books or on my own records of the past. Toward the end of this period of preparation, I grew desperately sleepy. To keep myself awake, I had to walk up and down more and more, and my dips in the pond became more frequent. It was almost time to be gone. I drew my little bed out into the garden and made it ready to receive me. I pressed another button, which would make day slowly become night. I took a final dip and a final walk, then staggered to my bed and lay down in the twilight.

But even yet I must not sleep. Instead, I concentrated my attention on the recurrent rise and fall of my own breathing, and on the nature of time. This process I had to maintain for about thirty hours, without food or sleep or any respite. Toward the end of this period, had you seen me, you would have said that I was at last falling asleep, and finally you would have declared me to be in a very profound slumber. And so in a manner I was, save that a single organ in my brain, usually dormant, was now intensively active, and preparing to take possession of my whole body as soon as my brain should have been refreshed by its deep sleep. After a couple of days of unconsciousness I did indeed wake, but not to the familiar surroundings.

For months, even years or decades, my body might now remain inert upon its bed, save for periodic risings to perform its natural functions of eating, drinking and excretion. Frequently also it would walk for hours at a time in the garden or bathe in the pond. But these activities would be carried out in complete abstraction, and had any one spoken to me at these times, I should have been unaware. For the higher centres of my brain were wholly possessed by the past. To any one watching me during these routine activities, I should have appeared as a sleep-walker. At these times, no less than during the long periods of quiescence on my bed, the observer would have seen that my face, and sometimes my whole body, was constantly influenced by emotion and thought. For during the whole trance, of course, my brain would be experiencing sequences of events in the remote past, and my whole body would respond to these experiences with my normal emotional reactions. Thus to the observer I should appear to be asleep and dreaming, save that my expressions would be far more definite and systematic than those of a dreamer.

Here I will mention one point of philosophical interest. The duration of the trance has no relation to the duration of the past events observed. Thus I might lie in my comfortable prison for a year, and in that time I might observe many years of past events, or many thousands of years, or even the whole span of man's history. The length of the trance depends only on the complexity of the matter observed. I might for instance spend a year in observing an immense number of simultaneous events which took only a few minutes to occur. Or I might cover the whole life of one individual in far more detail than was afforded by his own consciousness of his life story. Or I might sweep through whole epochs, tracing out only some one simple thread of change. In fact the length of the trance depends simply on the brain's capacity to assimilate, not upon the actual duration of the events observed.

When as much material has been gathered as can be conveniently grasped, the explorer gradually withdraws his attention from the past. He then sinks into an undisturbed sleep which may last for several weeks. During this phase his body shows none of that ceaseless emotional expression which is characteristic of the main trance. It lies inert, as though stunned. Finally the explorer's attention begins to concentrate itself again, and to revert once more to his own body and its surroundings. He wakes, and lies for a while passively accepting the new visual impressions. He then lives in his apartments for months or years recording his experiences in rough notes, to be organized at a later date. Sometimes, when this process is finished, he chooses to return at once, without respite, to the past for further data. Sometimes he leaves his room to confer with other workers. Sometimes he decides to drop his work and return to the contemporary world for refreshment.

2. DIFFICULTIES AND DANGERS

How it comes that at the moment of the onset of the trance the explorer is freed from the limitations of his own date and place I cannot tell you. Suffice it that the process involves both a special organ in the brain and a special technique, which has to be learned through a long apprenticeship. In that moment of awakening the worker has seemingly a confused experience of all the great successive epochal phases of the human spirit, up to his own date. But as the content of that supreme moment almost wholly escapes his memory as soon as it is past, it is impossible to say anything definite about it. He seems, indeed, to see in a flash, as though from another dimension of time, the whole historical order of events. Of course, he sees them only schematically. Their vast complexity of detail cannot be grasped in an instantaneous view. What he experiences can only be described (unintelligibly I fear) as a summation of all happening, of all physical, mental and spiritual flux. One is tempted to say also that he is aware of the human aspect of this flux as a vast slumber of the spirit, punctuated with moments of watchfulness, a vast stagnation troubled here and there with tremors of tense activity. Though all this is seen in an instant, it does not appear static, but alive with real passage and change.

This sublime moment must not be permitted to endure, for it is lethal. Immediately the explorer must begin to select that part of the historical order which he desires to study. To do this he must adopt the fundamental attitude of mind, or temperamental flavour, which he knows to be distinctive of the desired period. This process demands very great skill, and involves a host of uncouth and nerve-racking experiences. As soon as he begins to succeed in assuming the appropriate mental attitude, all the periods save that which he has chosen fade out of his consciousness, and the chosen period becomes increasingly detailed. He has then to specialize his mental attitude still further, so as to select a particular phase or group-culture within his period. And this specialization he may carry further again, till he has brought himself into the mind of some particular individual at a particular moment. Having once gained a footing in the individual mind, he can henceforth follow all its experiences from within; or, if he prefers, he can remain in one moment of that mind, and study its microscopic detail.

Such is the essence of our method. First we have to attain the momentary glimpse of eternity, or, more precisely, to take up for one instant the point of view of eternity. Then by imagination and sympathy we have to re-enter the stream of time by assuming the fundamental form of the minds or the mind that we wish to observe. In this process we have to work by means of a very delicate 'selectivity', not wholly unlike that physical selectivity which you exercise when you pick up ethereal messages on a particular wave-length. But this process of picking up past minds is far more delicate, since the system of basic mental patterns is very much more complex than the one-dimensional series of wave-frequencies.

When our ancestors first acquired the power of 'entering into the point of view of eternity' they suffered many disasters through ignorance of its principles. Very many of the earliest explorers succumbed simply by failing to keep their bodies alive during the trance. Their sleep turned into death. Others fell into such violent convulsions that they damaged themselves irreparably, and were mercifully killed by the superintendents. In other cases the normal trance lasted indefinitely, the body remaining alive but unresponsive for millions of years. A section of the catacombs was until recently filled with these persons, who were looked after by the attendants in the hope that some day they might wake. But a few thousand years ago it was decided to do away with some, and use others for experimental purposes.

Of the early explorers who successfully emerged from 'the point of view of eternity' into some past epoch, many returned insane. Others, though sane when they woke, kept falling into the trance again and again. Others were so embittered by their experiences that they became plague-spots in the community, and had to be requested to stop their hearts. Of these, some few refused, and remained at large, doing so much damage that finally they were put to death. One or two of the pioneers, and one or two of my contemporaries also, have returned from the trance with a peculiar kind of insanity, which suggested that they had actually found their way into the future, and that they still regarded our contemporary world as an episode in the remote past. Unfortunately they could give no account of their experiences; but in one of the earliest cases the recorded ravings seem to refer to the Mad Star, which did not earn its name until long afterwards.

In the early stages of the work few persons were engaged on it, and all that they could do was to collect random incidents from the very recent past. Gradually, however, the technique was greatly improved. It became possible to inspect almost any sequence of events in the history of our own species. This could only be done because the basic mental patterns of all the races of our own species had already been fairly well worked out by our psychologists and historians. Later, however, the psychologists began to formulate a vast theoretical system of possible basic mental patterns; and after some barren experimenting the explorers finally learned to assume certain of these patterns in the trance. The result was startling. Not only did they, as was expected, gain access to many primitive cultures upon Neptune, but also they began to find themselves sometimes in alien worlds, apparently much smaller than their familiar planet. The proportions of common things were all altered. The seas rose into great waves; the lands were often buckled into huge mountain ranges. The native organisms, though unfortified by artificial atoms, were able to attain great size and yet remain slender and agile. And these facts were observed through the medium of human types the existence of which had never been guessed. The very planets which these races inhabited could not be identified. No wonder, since all traces of Earth and Venus had long ago been wiped out by the solar collision that had driven man to Neptune.

This discovery of past worlds was even more exciting to us than the discovery of America to your own ancestors; for it entailed incidentally the overthrow of a well-grounded theory, which traced the evolution of the human race to a primitive Neptunian organism. Interest in the exploration of the past now greatly increased. The technique was developed far beyond the dreams of the early explorers. Little by little the outline of man's whole history on Earth and Venus was plotted, and tract after tract of it was elaborated in some detail.

In observing these extinct species, the explorers found traces of experience very different from their own. Although, of course, the basic mental pattern or temperamental ground-plan was in every case one which the explorer himself had been able to conceive, and even in a manner assume, in order to make contact with these primitive beings at all, yet when the contact had been made, he seemed to enter into a new mental world. For instance, he had to deal with minds whose sensory powers were much more limited than his own. Looking through those primitive eyes, he saw things in much less detail than through his own eyes, so that, though he observed everything with all the precision that his host's crude vision could afford, yet everything seemed to him blurred, and out of focus. The colours of objects, too, were diluted and simplified; for several colours familiar to us are hidden from more primitive eyes. Consequently the world as seen through those eyes appears to us at first strangely drab, almost monochromatic, as though the observer himself had become partially colour-blind. The other senses also are impoverished. For instance, all touched shapes and textures seem curiously vague and muffled. The sensations of sexual intercourse, too, which with us are richly variegated and expressive, are reduced in the primitive to a nauseating sameness and formlessness. It is impossible for you to realize the jarring, maddening effects of this coarseness and emptiness of all the sensory fields, especially to the inexperienced explorer, who has not yet learned to submit his spirit generously to the primitive.

In the sphere of thought, we find all the primitive species of man, however different from one another, equally remote from ourselves. Even the most advanced members of the most advanced primitive species inhabit worlds of thought which to us seem naïve and grotesque. The explorer finds himself condemned to cramp the wings of his mind within the caging of some gimcrack theory or myth, which, if he willed, he could easily shatter. Even in those rare cases in which the ground-plan of some edifice of primitive thought happens to be true to the simplest basic facts of the cosmos, as in your own theory of relativity, the superstructure which it ought to support is wholly absent. The explorer thus has the impression that the cosmos, with himself in it, has been flattened into a two-dimensional map.

In the sphere of desire the explorer has to deal with very unfamiliar and very jarring kinds of experience. In all human species, of course, the most fundamental animal desires are much the same, the desires for safety, food, a mate, and companionship; but the kind of food, the kind of companionship, and so on, which the primitive human mind seeks, are often very foreign and distasteful to us. Take the case of food. Of course the explorer's body, lying in the catacombs on Neptune, does not, if perchance he is inhabiting some primitive glutton of the past, suffer dyspepsia; save occasionally, through the influence of suggestion. But none the less he may experience acute distress, for his brain is forced to accept sensory complexes of overeating which in normal life would disgust him. And they disgust him now. Even when overeating does not occur, the food percepts are often repulsive to our centres of taste and odour. In the matter of personal beauty, too, the explorer is at first repelled by the grotesque caricature of humanity which among primitive species passes for perfection, much as you yourselves may be repelled by the too-human animality of apes. Often, when he is following the growth of some primitive love-sentiment in your epoch, he is nauseated by the adored object, and by the intimacy in which he is reluctantly entangled. It is much as though a part of the mind were to watch the other part entrapped into romantic adoration of a female ape; as if with infinite disgust one

367

were to find himself pressing against those hairy thighs. But indeed in this matter, as in others, since it is not mere animality that disgusts, but the failure to be human, the explorer is far more outraged than if he were compelled to cohabit with an ape. With familiarity, however, these repulsions can be surmounted. Just as your disgust of the ape's approximation to the human is a weakness in you, due to lack of vision and sympathy, so our tendency to a disgust of your own crude approximation to the human is a weakness in us, which we have to learn to transform into a reverent, though often ironical, sympathy. Just as the surgeon may become accustomed to delving among viscera, and may even find beauty in them, so the explorer may and must accustom himself to all these primitive forms, and find beauty in them too. Of course the beauty which he discovers in the adored yet repulsive apewoman is never simply identical with the beauty which delights the adoring ape-man; for it is a beauty which includes within itself both that which delights the primitive and that which disgusts the developed mind.

To all the preoccupations then, and to all the ways of life, and all the ideals, of the early races, the explorer must react with that delight which triumphs over contempt and disgust. Of course there is very much in this sphere which he can whole-heartedly enjoy, since much in primitive life is the unspoiled behaviour of the animal, and much also improves upon the animal. But at a very early stage primitive man begins to torture his own nature into grotesque forms, inadvertently or by intent; much as, inadvertently, he tortures his domestic animals, and by intent he turns his pets into freaks and caricatures. This violation of his own nature increases as he gains power, and reaches its height in primitive industrial communities such as your own. In such phases the individual body and spirit become more and more distorted, impoverished, noisome. The early explorer, studying these phases, was hard put to it to prevent his overwhelming indignation and nausea from spoiling his study. He had, of course, to observe it all as though it were happening to himself, since he observed it through the suffering minds of its victims. And so he was almost in the position of a sick doctor, whose spirit must triumph by delighting in the study of his own disease.

Grotesque sentiments such as the lust of business success or economic power of any kind, and indeed every purely self-regarding passion, from that of the social climber to that of the salvation-seeking ascetic, are experienced by the explorer with something of that shame which the child, emerging into adolescence, may feel toward the still-clinging fascination of his outgrown toys, or with such disgust as the youth may feel when he wakes from some unworthy sexual infatuation. But this shame and disgust the explorer must learn to transcend as the surgeon the disgust of blood. Even the passions of hate and gratuitous cruelty, so widespread in your own and all other primitive species, he must learn to accept with sympathy, in spite of his spontaneous revulsion from them and his well-justified moral condemnation of them.

One great difference between ourselves and most primitive minds is that, while in us all motives are fully conscious, fully open to introspection, in them scarcely any of their more complex motives are ever brought fully to light. Thus when the explorer is following some train of action in a primitive mind, he very often observes an immense discrepancy between the mind's own view of its motives and the real motives which he himself sees to be in fact the source of the activity. To experience all the daily and hourly perversities of a life-long complex, to experience them not merely through clinical observation but in the most intimate manner, puts him to an extremely severe strain. At every turn his own mind is wrenched by the conflict in the mind that he is observing. And in him the conflict is wholly conscious and shattering. Not a few of our early observers became infected by the disorder which they had been studying, so that when they returned to their native world they could no longer behave with perfect sanity, and had to be destroyed.

To sum up, then, the earlier explorers were often desperately fatigued by the monotony of primitive existence and the sameness of primitive minds; and also they fell into disgust, an agony of disgust, with the crudity, insensitivity and folly of the primitive. From the one point of view it might be said that the Neptunian found himself condemned to sift the almost identical sand-grains of a desert, and even to record the minute distinctive features of each grain. From the other point of view, it was as though he had been banished from the adult world to the nursery or the jungle,

369

and was actually imprisoned in the mind of babe or beast. For, once settled in the mind which he has chosen to study, the explorer is indeed a captive until study calls him elsewhere. Though he thinks his own thoughts, he perceives only what the other perceives, and is forced to endure every least sensation, thought, desire and emotion of the other, be it never so banal. Like one who feels within his own mind the beginnings of some mania or obsession which, though he recognizes that it is irrational or base, he cannot control, so the explorer is doomed to experience sympathetically all his subject's thinking and desiring, even while he is nauseated by it. No wonder, then, that many early explorers were tortured by disgust or ennui.

Long before my time, most of these dangers and irks of exploration had been greatly reduced. One serious trouble, however, remains, and has even increased. A great army of workers was of course bred with special aptitudes for supra-temporal experience, and with special insight into the primitive types of mind. These new workers were given also a special enthusiasm and sympathy in respect of the past; and herein lay their danger. In my day every member of the race has something of this enthusiasm and sympathy; and we explorers have them in an extreme degree. So enthralling do we find the past, even in all its monotony and squalor, that many have succumbed to its spell, and lost all footing in the present world. Rapt in some great movement of history, or in some individual life-story, the explorer may lose, little by little, all memory of the future world of which he is a native, may in fact cease to be a future mind inspecting a past mind, and become instead a mere undertone or freakish propensity in the past mind itself, or in many past minds. In time even this may vanish, so that the explorer becomes identical with the explored. If this occurs, his own body, situated in the future and in Neptune, gradually disintegrates and dies.

Certain other troubles hamper even the most modern explorers, in spite of improved technique. The method by which we enter a past epoch is, as I have said, this process of shaping our minds to the basic pattern or ground tone of the epoch to be studied. But when the explorer desires to enter a particular individual, he must try to assume the complex form or temperament which is distinctive of that individual; or else he must seize on one unique desire or thought, which he supposes to be peculiar to that individual at a certain date of his life. Now this process of mental infection or association does not necessarily work in his favour. Often, when he is trying to establish himself in some mind, or even when he has long been established, some chance association in his own thought-process may suddenly snatch him away from the object of his study and fling him into some other mind. Sometimes this other is a contemporary of the recent object of study; but often it is a mind in some different epoch or world. When this happens, not only is the study broken short, but also the explorer may be very seriously damaged. His brain, on Neptune, suffers such a fundamental and rapid readjustment that it is grievously jarred and strained, and may never recover. Even if he does not actually succumb, he may have to take a long holiday for recuperation. Fortunately, however, it is only the more extravagant dislocations that are really dangerous. Occasional jolts into minds of the same basic pattern as the original object of study are more exasperating than harmful.

Often when the explorer is resident in a particular individual he encounters through that individual's perception another individual, who, he thinks, would repay immediate study. He has then to observe this other carefully through the perceptions of the first, so as to discover, if possible, some entry into his mind. This may be very difficult, since one primitive mind's awareness of another is often so erroneous and biased that the perceptions which would make for true understanding of the other fail to occur. Moreover there is always the danger that, when the explorer attempts this 'change of mounts' he may fall between them, and be flung violently once more into his native location in time and space. Or again, he may at the critical moment be snatched by some chance association into some other epoch or world. Such accidents are of course very damaging, and may prove fatal.

Here I may mention that some minds, scattered up and down the ages, defeat all attempts to enter them. They are very rare, only one in millions of millions; but they are such as we should most desire to enter. Each one of these rare beings has caused the ruin of a great company of our most able explorers. They must be in some vital respect alien to us, so that we cannot assume their nature accurately enough to enter them. Possibly they are themselves subject to an influence future even to us. Possibly they are possessed and subtly transformed by minds native to some world in a remote stellar system. Possibly, even, they are under the direct influence of the cosmical mind, which, we hope, will awaken in the most remote of all futures.

Explorers of the past incur one other danger which I may mention. Sometimes the past individual under observation dies suddenly, before the explorer can foresee the death, and free himself. In many cases, of course, he knows the date at which the other's death will occur, and can therefore, having prepared himself for a normal departure, observe the course of events right up to the moment of death, and yet escape before it is too late. But sometimes, especially in pioneering in some unexplored region of history, the explorer is as ignorant of the immediate future as the observed mind itself. In such cases a dagger, a bullet, a flash of lightning, even an unforeseen heart-failure, may fling him back to his own world with a shattering jerk, which may irreparably damage his brain, or even kill him outright. Many of the early observers of your recent European War were caught in this manner. Resident in the mind of some soldier in action, the observer himself was annihilated by the shell that destroyed the observed. If burial were one of our practices, we, like you, might have our war graves of 1914 to 1918, though they would not have been dug till two thousand million years later. Nor would they be decorated by national emblems. Nor would they bear the cross.

3. INFLUENCING PAST MINDS

Our power of taking effect on past minds is much more restricted than our power of passively observing their processes. It is also a much more recent acquisition. To you it seems impossible; for future events, you suppose, have no being whatever until their predecessors have already ceased to exist. I can only repeat that, though future events have indeed no temporal being until their predecessors have ceased to exist with temporal being, all events have also eternal being. This does not mean that time is unreal, but that evanescence is not the whole truth about the passing of events. Now some minds, such as ours, which are to some extent capable of taking up the point of view of eternity, and of experiencing the eternal aspects of past events in other minds, can also to some extent contribute to the experience of those minds in the past. Thus when I am observing your mental processes, my activity of observing is, in one sense, located in the past. Although it is carried out from the point of view of my own experience in the future, it enters the past through the eternal side of past events in your minds. When I act upon your minds, as for instance in inculcating thoughts and images in the writer of this book, that activity of mine is located in your age. Yet it is done, so to speak, from my purchase in the future, and with all my Neptunian experience in view.

From this rare but important action of the future on the past it follows that past events, which themselves cause future events, are in part the product of future events. This may seen unintelligible. But in fact there is no more mystery in it than in the reciprocal interaction of two minds that know one another. The one, which owes its form partly to the other, is itself one factor determining the other's form.

As I said before, the only way in which we can influence a past mind is by suggesting in that mind some idea or desire, or other mental event, which is intelligible to a mind of that particular order, and is capable of being formulated in terms of its own experience. Some minds are much more receptive than others. The great majority are wholly impervious to our influence; and, even among those who are not insensitive, very many are so strictly dominated by their own desires and prejudices that any thought or valuation which we consider worth suggesting to them is at once violently rejected.

There are many complications and difficulties in this strange work. In the first place we may chance to do serious damage to the past mind by unwise influence, for instance by presenting it with ideas which are too disturbing to its nature. For though some ideas are so foreign to a mind that they are simply rejected, others, though alien to the superficial part of its nature, may be incendiary to the submerged part, as sparks falling upon tinder. Thus an idea which to the explorer seems straightforward and harmless may produce in the past mind a self-discrepant experience both of revelation and of horror; and the resulting conflict throughout the mind may lead to catastrophe. Or the idea may so captivate and exalt the unfortunate person that he loses all sense of proportion, is instigated to some fantastic course of action, and finally comes into serious collision with his society.

Another difficulty lies in the fact that our influence is not always voluntary. Thoughts and desires of our own, which we have no intention of transmitting, may sometimes find their way into the mind under observation; and their effect may be disastrous. For instance, a sudden surge of contempt or indignation on the part of an inexperienced explorer, when he observes his 'host' commit some egregious folly or meanness, may flood a hitherto complacent mind with bewildering self-contempt. And this novel experience, coming thus without preparation, may shatter the whole flimsy structure of the mind by destroying its carapace of self-pride. Or again, the explorer's own clear-eyed and ecstatic view of the cosmos, as both tragic and worshipful, may sear the optimistic faith of a primitive religious mind, without being able to raise it to the loftier worship.

Our influence, then, upon the past is a very much more precarious and restricted power than our past-exploration. All that we can do is to offer to a very small minority of minds some vague hint of a truth or of a beauty which would otherwise be missed, or some special precept, or seminal idea, relevant to the mind's particular circumstances. This may be done either by a constant 'tilting' of the mind in a certain general direction, or, much more rarely, by occasional impregnation of the mind with some precise idea or valuation. In very exceptional cases, which number no more than one in many thousands of millions, we can subject the individual to a constant stream of detailed suggestion which he himself can embody in a more or less faithful report. But here we find ourselves on the horns of a dilemma. To undergo this detailed suggestion, the individual must be extremely receptive; but in the main those that are extremely receptive lack originality, so that, in spite of their detailed receptivity, they either entirely miss the true spirit of the communication, or fail to embody it in a manner capable of stirring their fellows. On the other hand the highly original minds, even when they are also very receptive, tend deliberately to ignore the detail of the suggestion. Thus they produce works which, though true to the spirit of the suggestion, are embodied in manners expressive of their own genius.

4. HOVERING OVER TIME

I must now give you a more precise idea of the strange experiences which befall the explorer when he is trying to get a footing in some particular moment of some particular past mind. Each explorer has his own technique, and each adventure its own vicissitudes; but I shall tell simply of my own approach to your world and epoch on that occasion which I have already begun to describe.

Emerging presently from that ineffable moment in which I participated in the eternal view, I was at the outset conscious of a vague restlessness, a most poignant yet indefinite yearning, and along with this a violent and confused agitation of all my senses. Even though this was not my first excursion into these realms, I was overwhelmed with the pathos of man's ever-unsatisfied and blindly fumbling desire, and equally by the tyranny of his rare joys and the torture of his distresses. At the outset this yearning and this sensory tumult were, so to speak, all that there was of me; but with an effort I woke to something more precise. I held the obscure thing away from me, and looked at it calmly. As I did so, it developed under my very eyes, the eyes of my mind, into a surge of specific primitive cravings and passions, which, though I lived them as my own, I also regarded, as it were, from a great height of aloofness. I was now experiencing the summed and confused experiences of all mankind. They came to me with the vagueness of a composite photograph, but also with that sense of multitude, of innumerable individual uniquenesses, which one may sometimes catch in listening to the murmur of a great crowd. Yet all these multitudinous experiences were in a manner mine, and combined into one experience, like the single deliverance of a man's two eyes. I was terrified and longed for safety, hungry and

375

lusted for food. I was enraged against some obscure adversary. I tasted the joy of murder, and equally the final despair of the victim. I was solitary, and my flesh burned with sexual potency; outcast, and my mind hungered for companionship.

Against this vast enduring background of primitive craving I experienced also momentary gleams of loftier desire, rare and faint as voices heard above the storm. I felt the longing and the delight of spiritual intimacy with another mind, the longing and the delight of truth, the longing and the delight and glory of participation in a great community, the longing and the delight of faith. I felt also the terror, the despair, the peace and final ecstasy, which is the way of true worship. But all these illuminations of the spirit were no more than stars piercing for a moment the storm-cloud of the primitive.

While I was undergoing all these obscure impulses, tumultuous messages were also pouring in through all my senses. At first indeed I received such a medley of impressions that I was aware only of a nondescript and distressing commotion. But, as I attended to this, the matter of the various senses began to differentiate itself. Thus at first I seemed to be subjected to a general pressure all over my body; but under scrutiny this developed into a profusion of hardnesses and softnesses, roughnesses and smoothnesses, rotundities and angularities. I felt the pressure of earth under my feet. I felt myself lying on hard ground, and then on a kindly bed. With my hands I felt a multitude of textures, as of stone, tree-trunks, fur, and the incomparable touch of human flesh, in all its repellent and its enticing modes. I felt also a vague warmth and chill, which, by attending to them, I could develop into violent heat and cold, or the bite of fire and frost. Innumerable pains invaded me. At first they seemed to struggle against a sense of physical well-being, a tingling healthiness; but soon pain triumphed; for it had at the outset a compelling poignancy which increased alarmingly under attention. The whole surface of my body, it seemed, was tortured; and my internal organs were all gripped in agony. My brain throbbed and burned, and was stabbed through and through in all directions. But in truth the brain that was thus tormented was not mine, nor the bowels mine, nor the skin. The source of my torture lay in the innumerable bodies of my predecessors. Wrenching my attention from this horror, I noticed a confusion of tastes, fragrances and stenches. And along with these there came sounds. A muffled roar, as of the sea or a distant bombardment, grew as I listened to it into a crashing and shrieking, which reverberated through my whole body. By a special act of attention, a straining of the mind's ear, I could penetrate beyond this uproar, and hear an obscure vocal sound, which, as I listened, became inarticulate lamentation, flecked here and there with laughter.

In the field of vision I experienced at first nothing but a vague brightness above and obscurity below. This was due to the fact that in most minds of all periods, save those in which indoor life predominates over outdoor life, daytime-experience contains in the main a light sky and a darker ground. As soon as I began to attend to the matter of this vision, it revealed itself as being after all rich with detail. First, both in the light and in the dark field, there moved unrecognizable shadowy forms and occasional colours. Then aloft I began to see white clouds sailing in blue sky, then widespread rain-cloud, then thunder-cloud, and then in a moment the broad unbroken blue; then night, obscure, starry, moonlit, and again obscure. Below, I saw sometimes hills, crags, tree-tops, meadows, bright flowers and plumage, sometimes breakers on the shore, sometimes huts, mansions in many styles, or congested towns, sometimes interiors of splendour or comfortable homeliness or squalor. All these forms kept appearing, vanishing, reappearing, invading one another and exterminating one another, like the visions that haunt us between waking and sleeping. I saw also forms of beasts, and human forms of all the species, from hairy pithecanthropus, and your own fantastically clothed half-human kind, to those large and noble beings who were the last Terrestrials, and the bat-like fliers of Venus, and my own immediate ancestors on Neptune. I saw limbs writhing in agony, limbs dancing, limbs straining in toil and sport, fair limbs embracing, limbs grotesque and crippled. Faces also appeared and vanished, singly or in crowds, faces eager and disillusioned, faces twisted by pain, or by rapacity, faces expressionless as pebbles, faces of terror, hate, meanness, faces of peace and of exultation; child faces, faces of maturity all aglow with life, faces grey, wrinkled, sagging, old; and faces of the dead, impassive, sealed against experience.

Along with these visions of humanity, would sometimes come faint sexual sensations, which, when I attended to them, opened out into a whole world of amorous experience, of lyrical first matings and desolate repetitions, of violations, thwarted crises, lonely make-shifts, of the bland unions of long-tried lovers, of senile failures, and the whole gamut of perversions.

Intermingled with these purely perceptual visions, there came to me all manner of experiences of personal relationships. I was flooded with the lovings and hatings, of all men and women, by their co-operations and rivalries, by all the modes of leadership, by all fealties and servitudes. I became a mother toiling for a son whose thought was not of her; I became a son held within the soft, strong meshes of his home. I had a glimpse, as it were both from without and from within their minds, of myriads of the boys and girls of all the species, opening their eyes in amazement upon life, knowing neither what they ought to be doing with it nor even how to wrest from it the simple joys they so vaguely conceived. I glimpsed likewise the myriads of grown men and women, with all their hopes thwarted, and their minds desperately concerned only to keep their bodies alive, or at most their heads above their fellows. And the old.I glimpsed also, with their lives written indelibly into the great story of worlds. Through their eyes I watched the young things rising up all around them and beyond them, like birds that rise and leave their wounded on the ground. It seemed too that I entered into the minds of the innumerable toilers of all the aeons. I felt the ache and the leaden weight of their limbs, the sick ache of their eye-balls, and the hopelessness of their crippled souls. I felt also the calm of spirit, the strenuous peacefulness, of those few who are wholly and gladly possessed by their work.

There poured in upon me also all the thoughts and fantasies and ideals of all men and women in all ages. My mind reeled and staggered in the tide of them, and was swept to and fro upon the great ocean of whimsies and dreams, doctrines and theories. With the pre-human beings, I fashioned imaginatively, step by step, the whole world of perceptual common sense, that tissue of theories and images, so true and so false, which to most human beings of all species appears to be the unquestionable real. I observed, as in my own mind, the flashes of primeval genius that had gone to the making of that great medley of fact and fiction. With the ape-men, too, I projected souls into trees and mountains, storms and stars. And with them also I felt the first painful birth-throes of true intellect. To trap my prey, to beguile my mate, or build my shelter, I reasoned, I put two and two together. But every motion of this reason I distorted with fantasies born of mere desire, and when this hybrid failed me I blamed reason.

All manner of laborious reasonings and intricate bright myths flashed across my mind and vanished. In the twinkling of an eye I savoured cosmology after cosmology, I saw Shiva, Odin, Zeus, Jaweh and his fair offspring Jesus, and innumerable other god-heads, of wrath and righteousness, of wisdom, of power, of love, emanations from the minds of all the races, all the species of man. And with these I tried out a million sciences and philosophies, amongst which, as yet ever so faint and remote, like the voices of two bright confident quarrelling children, that 'materialism' and that 'spiritism' which resound throughout your little play-room world. Theories, theories, myriads upon myriads of them, streamed over me like wind-borne leaves, like the contents of some titanic paper-factory flung aloft by the storm, like dust-clouds in the hurricane advance of the mind. Gasping in this vast whirling aridity, I almost forgot that in every mote of it lay some few spores of the organic truth, most often parched and dead, but sometimes living, pregnant, significant.

5. DESCENT AMONG THE FIRST MEN

During the whole of this early stage of my adventure I was already trying to select from the confusion of experiences something which might serve to bring me nearer to your own particular phase of the human process. My chief method of directing myself toward your age is, as I have already said, to assume imaginatively, and as precisely as possible, first the basic temperamental pattern of your species, and then the particular form of it which is characteristic of your period, and of that unique point and moment of individuality which I desire to study. This work I was already attempting; but it was hampered on this occasion, and on most others, by the prodigious influx of perceptions, thoughts and emotions which I have attempted to describe. I was like a swimmer swept hither and thither by great waves, and scarcely able to make the particular rocky creek which is his haven.

I had first to conceive, and emotionally assume, the general form of all primitive human mentality, so as to exclude from my view the whole of my own species, and also that other, abortive, phase of spiritual maturity, which took place just before man left the earth. I had to become in imagination a bewildered limited being, ignorant of its own nature, ever racked by inner conflicts which eluded its apprehension, ever yearning to be whole, yet ever carried away by momentary cravings which were ludicrous even in its own estimation. With patience I was able to achieve this piece of inner play-acting with such success that I began to have definite but fleeting glimpses of individuals and incidents among the primitive kinds of men, now a winged Venerian, skimming his wild ocean, now a woman of the Third Men, ruddy and lithe, feeding her beasts, now a scarcely human early inhabitant of Neptune. These individuals I perceived, of course, through the eyes of some contemporary; and if ever I troubled to look at 'my own' body during these experiences, I perceived it to be not my familiar body at all, but of the same species as the observed individual. Perceiving through the eyes of past beings, I perceived their bodies as though they were each in turn my own body.

I had now to select that mode of the primitive which is distinctive of your own species, a mode characterized by repressed sexuality, excessive self-regard, and an intelligence which is both rudimentary and in bondage to unruly cravings. Now though all the races of your species in all its stages manifest, in spite of their differences, one unique blend of these factors, yet the process of imaginatively assuming this mode of mentality is dangerous; for there is another species, one of our fore-runners on Neptune, which is strangely like you in this respect. I now found myself, as often before, oscillating painfully between these two phases of man's career. I saw now the hills and tall trees of Earth, now the plains and bushes of Neptune. I assumed now the spidery limbs and jaunty gait of a Terrestrial, now the elephantine legs, kangaroo arms and grave demeanour of an early Neptunian. I listened for a moment to Attic disputation, then suddenly to primitive Neptunian grunts and clicks. It was as though I were listening-in with a radio set of bad selectivity. Or, to change the image, I was a storm-tossed buzzard among the hills, beneath me a dividing range, on either side of it a valley. Into one of these valleys I purposed to descend, but the wind kept thrusting me back over the ridge into the other. At one moment I saw beneath me the desired valley; then, after a vain struggle, the other. At length, however, by a violent effort of attention I succeeded in concentrating upon your species and avoiding the other. Gradually the imagery and thought which flooded in on me came to be entirely derived from the First Men, in one or other of their phases.

But my experience was still chaotic. I had indeed a strong but vague apprehension of your species as a historic whole, of its many long phases of somnolence and its few brief effulgences. And after careful inspection I detected that sense of cosmical tragedy which overwhelmed, or, from your point of view, will overwhelm, the more intelligent of your descendants, when they realize that their species is setting inevitably into decline. But for the most part I had merely a sickening confusion of random samples from all your ages. Thus, at one moment I was an Aurignacian, engraving his cave wall with vivid shapes of deer and bison, while my fellow-hunters peered with admiration through the smoke. Now I was a Chinese citizen of that Americanized world-state which lies future to you; and I was speaking in worn and polluted English to my Soudanese wife. Now I was an Elizabethan dame, tight-laced and plastered with jewellery. Suddenly I flashed many thousands of years ahead into that Patagonian civilization which is the last weary effort of your species. I was a prematurely aged boy, prostrate in a temple before the grotesque image of Power. Not until many more of these visions had appeared, and been dismissed, did I find myself approximately in your age. I was an Indian confronting a topeed, bare-kneed Englishman. Rage was in my heart, fear, contempt and subterfuge, and as little understanding of the other as he had of me.

Fatigued but now more hopeful, I forced myself rigorously into the mentality which is common to most members of a primitive industrialistic community. To you this curious mode of experience is so familiar that you do not suspect its rarity and oddity, though many of you feel that it is neither wholesome nor inevitable. That you may realize the violent effort of imagination and emotional control that was now incumbent on me, I will set down the main features which render the primitive industrial mentality so difficult for the explorer. To revert to the image which I have already used, it is as though the buzzard, having successfully descended into the valley of his choice, were now to enter the ventilation shaft of an old disused mine, and were to sink downwards in the dark through fetid air, with scarcely room to keep his wings outspread. No wonder that he suffers considerable distress and incurs serious dangers, before he finally alights amongst the pale and eyeless fauna of the pit. No wonder that his own eyes take time to accustom themselves to the dim phosphorescence which is the sole illumination of that world. When the explorer seeks to establish himself in your society, he has first to assume that jarred and restless mood which is common to all those whose habitual environment is alien to their native capacities. In particular he must imaginatively produce in himself the lifelong strain of perceiving streets, traffic, and stuffy interiors, instead of the landscapes which originally moulded his capacities. He must also reconstruct in himself the unconscious obsession with matter, or rather with the control of matter by machinery and chemical manipulation. He must conceive also the mind's unwitting obeisance and self-distrust before its robot off-spring. Further, he must subject his own free-roaming spirit to the hideous effects of a narrow specialism, both of body and mind. He must conceive the almost inconceivable ignorance and groping hate of the being whose life is moulded to one narrow round of duties and perceptions. Equally he must conceive the profound unwitting guiltiness of the primitive industrial master, and also of that idle scum that floats on the surface of all primitive industrial societies.

Little by little I reproduced in myself this cramped and ungenerous mode of the mind; and, as I did so, visions of your world came crowding in upon me with increasing vividness. I became a half-naked woman in a coal-mine of your Industrial Revolution. I crept on hands and knees along a low gallery. Tugging at the collar like a beast, I dragged a truck. The trace passed between my legs. I was whimpering, not from any present discomfort, but because I had lost a keepsake. This incident was obviously a century or more too early, but others followed, and more and more of them were of your period. I had now to seek out a particular individual among you, and a particular moment of his life. But in doing so, I nearly suffered catastrophe. On Venus there was once, or rather from your point of view there will be, an industrial phase much like your own in certain respects, although the species which produced it was very different from yours. Into that epoch I was suddenly flung by I know not what detail of identity. A face which was obviously not of the First Men, a pale and blinking frog-like face, with a running sore beneath the left eye and a fantastic hat cocked backwards, slowly grimaced at me. For one anxious moment I feared that I should be trapped in that Venerian phase of man, with my mind still moulded to the mentality of the First Men. But by a desperate effort of concentration upon the Terrestrial mode of experience I managed to disengage myself from this dangerous irrelevance. And with one leap I found myself back again at the desired point of your history.

6. IN THE STREETS OF LONDON

I was in a town. A great red vehicle, roaring and trumpeting, was in the act of swooping upon me. Leaping out of its track, I ran to the pavement where two contrary streams of pedestrians brushed past one another. As the archaic chariot left me, I saw on its flank the English word 'General', in letters of gold. I had already become familiar with this device on my previous visit to your world, and I now knew that I must be in London somewhere between the invention of the motor-omnibus and the socialization of all such vehicles under a metropolitan authority. The clothes of the women pedestrians were of the style worn in 1914. Skirts left the ankle exposed, waists were confined within broad belts of ribbon, hats were large, and poised high on the crown. Clearly I had struck the right period, but who was I, or rather who was my host? I noted with satisfaction that his basic mental pattern fitted very precisely the mood which I had already myself assumed to take me to my chosen object of study. Surely this must be the young man whom I sought. I shall not reveal his name, since with its aid he or his relatives might recognize the portrait, or the setting, which I must give in some detail. I shall therefore refer to him simply as Paul. I had already observed him on an earlier visit, but now I proposed to follow him through the most critical moment of the career of his species.

Paul was gravely agitated. I noticed a visual image looming in the recesses of his mind, an image not open to his own introspection. It was the face of his pet enemy of childhood days, and it was streaming with tears and blood. The child Paul had just put an end to this lad's bullying by defending himself with a table-fork. He now consciously felt once more (though he knew not why) the horror and guilt that he had suffered long ago at the sight of his enemy's damaged cheek. The experience was now accompanied by confused images of khaki, bayonets, and the theme of a patriotic song. Paul was experiencing, and I experienced through him, a distressing conflict of blood-loathing and martial fervour. Evidently I had come upon Paul in the midst of his great crisis. Like so many of his contemporaries, he was faced with the necessity of deciding whether he would or would not fight for king and country and gallant little Belgium. But with Paul the situation was complicated by the fact that ever since his childhood I had been tampering with his mind so as to make him more sensitive to the momentous issues which were at stake.

Had I needed further confirmation that my host was indeed Paul, it was available. He was now passing a shop which bore a panel of mirror between its windows. Such mirrors I had often noticed in your cities, cunning devices for attracting the attention of your amusingly and fatally self-gratulatory species. My host slackened his pace and gazed into the mirror. Indeed he actually halted for a moment. I at once recognized the youthful and anxious face that I had perforce so often observed in the shaving-glass. But I noticed that its habitual expression of watchful self-reserve was now intensified with some kind of suppressed but haunting terror. Neptunian vision detected also, contrasting with this callow distress, a gleam of contemptuous irony, new in Paul.

Only for a moment did Paul regard himself. With a blush and an impatient jerk he turned away, and looked anxiously to see if any one had been watching him. Immediately, with a deeper blush, he faced the mirror again, and pretended to be searching for grit in his eye. Amongst the crowd of passers-by, two figures were approaching, and almost upon us. The young man was in khaki. The girl clung to his arm with demure possessiveness. He did not notice Paul, but she caught Paul's eyes as he was turning toward the mirror. In the fraction of a second that elapsed before his eyes could free themselves, he saw that she dismissed him as no true male, that she thanked God her man was a soldier, and that she was ready to do her bit by yielding herself unconditionally to him. Real tears welled in Paul's eyes to wash out the imaginary grit. I took a hasty glance at the most recent memories of my host, and saw that while he had been walking along the Strand after his lunch he had been subject to several encounters of this sort, real or imaginary. By now he was badly shaken. He turned down a side-street, and wandered along the Embankment. Presently he was calmed by the quietly flowing water, still more, perhaps, by the Obelisk, that proud ancient captive among Lilliputians. To Paul it seemed refreshingly indifferent to their ant-wars. Suddenly his peace was shattered. Half a dozen urchins approached in military formation, accompanied by martial rhythms on an old tin can. As they passed him, one of them struck up on a mouth-organ an excruciating but recognizable version of a catchy song already in vogue among the troops. I felt Paul's mind rear and plunge beneath me like a startled horse. Many times he had heard that tune; many columns of troops he had seen, with full equipment, marching toward the great railway terminus for entrainment toward the coast. But this commonplace little incident stirred him more deeply. It filled him with a desperate longing to be at one with the herd, to forget himself in the herd's emotions. to sacrifice himself heroically to the herd's gods.

A visual image now flashed into his view, a shop-front converted into a recruiting office. The window displayed posters to incite the laggard, 'Your king and country need you', and so on. This image Paul now greeted with a violent assent. On the heels of that swift mental gesture there followed a fleeting tactual image of a hand's pressure on his hand, as though the whole nation were congratulating him on his decision.

Paul hurried away from the river with an almost swaggering gait. He took a short cut by back-streets to the recruiting office that he had so often passed, and as often circumvented so as to avoid its blatant reproaches. Street after street he threaded, and in each succeeding street his resolution was less secure and his swagger less evident. The only clear conviction in his mind, was that, whichever course he finally took, he would regret it, and feel ashamed that he had not taken the other. His perplexity was the outcome not only of the objective moral problem as to what course was in fact the right course, but also of a subjective psychological problem, namely what would his motives really be if he took this course, and what if he took that.

I myself, observing his mind as he hurried along in dangerous abstraction among pedestrians and vehicles, was able to detect in him many motives hidden from his own observation. There is no need to give a complete inventory of the tangled impulses that were pulling him hither and thither in his perplexity, but one point must be made clear because of its significance. Paul's indecision was in fact only superficial, was indeed illusory. To me, though not to Paul himself, it was evident that he had resolved on his course a good month earlier, and that however much he might seem to himself to be vacillating, his will was already fixed. This curious state of affairs was due to the fact that his deciding motive was not clearly apprehended; while at the same time he was very poignantly aware of a conflict between other motives which were not strictly relevant to the problem at all. Thus, he dared not enlist, lest his motive should be merely moral cowardice; he dared not refuse to enlist, lest his motive should be merely physical cowardice or moral pride. Whatever course he chose would almost certainly spring from purely selfish motives. In fact although the decision had indeed really been made long ago, he had ever since been chafing within his illusory cage of morality and selfishness, like a captive beast that rubs itself painfully against its bars without hope of escape.

The same forlorn task was occupying him when at last the recruiting office leapt into view. It was a corner house, diagonally opposite him. He stepped off the pavement, dodged the traffic, and was already half-way across, when his resolution finally vanished.

At the door stood a sergeant with a red, white and blue cockade. He had already sighted Paul, and was preparing to greet him with acquisitive geniality. Paul's legs continued to carry him toward the door, though weakly; but Paul's mind now woke to a surprisingly clear conviction that, whatever the reason, this thing must not be done. He reached the pavement. The sergeant stood aside to let him pass. Paul was almost in the doorway when he suddenly veered and scuttled away. His conviction vanished, but he continued to hurry along the pavement. Tears came to his eyes, and he whimpered to himself, 'Coward, Coward'; with which verdict the sergeant doubtless agreed.

But to me, the detached observer, it was evident that though Paul was on the whole more of a coward than the average, and would have made a very bad soldier, it was not cowardice that had put him to flight. It is difficult to describe the determining though deeply hidden motive which, on this occasion as on others, snatched him away from the recruiting office. It was a motive present also in the majority of his contemporaries, though in few was it able to disturb the operation of more familiar motives. The real determinant of Paul's behaviour was an obscure intuition, which your psychologists mostly fail to recognize as a basic and unanalysable factor in your nature. They fail to recognize it, because in you it is so precarious and so blind. You have no satisfactory name for it, since few of you are at all clearly aware of it. Call it, if you will, loyalty to the enterprise of Life on your planet and among the stars; but realize that, though it is a natural product of age-long events, and though it cannot express itself at all unless it is evoked by education, it becomes, at a certain stage of evolution, a bias as strong and unreasoned as the bias in favour of food or offspring. Indeed these propensities are but gropings toward this more general but equally non-rational bias. This it was that in Paul, partly through my earlier influence, partly through his own constitution, was strong enough to turn him aside on the threshold of the recruiting office. This it was that in the majority of Paul's contemporaries caused, indeed, grave agony of mind, but could not bring them to refuse war.

III *The Child Paul*

1. PAUL AND HIS NEPTUNIAN PARASITE

WHY do I choose Paul for study? Why do I propose to tell you more of him than of any one else in my collection? I have examined in detail at one time and another an immense number of specimens of your kind, not only your contemporaries but many others whose date is earlier than yours, and many who in your day are still to live. I have made myself familiar with every trait and whim, every min- ute episode in the minds of selected individuals from among the Greeks, the Indians, the early Teutons, the ancient Egyptians, the Chinese of all China's phases, and also the still unborn Americans and Patagonians. In fact, there is no race of the First Men that has not yielded me samples; which, as I have grown intimate with them, have so captivated me with their fantastic personalities that I have come to regard them not merely as specimens but, in a manner, as friends. For these beings have yielded me the secrets of their nature to an extent impossible in normal intercourse; and yet they have never communicated with me, and for the most part have never suspected my existence.

If I chose, I could tell you many strange secrets about your famous characters, for instance about your Queen Elizabeth, who is among my collection. Through her eyes I have looked not only on the fair face of Essex, but also on that abnormal formation of her own body which caused her to be so lonely, so insistent on her womanhood, and withal so kingly. And I have tasted her bitter rage against fate, her greedy self-love, her love of England. Leonardo da Vinci also I have inhabited. It was I that tormented him with a thousand ideas in advance of his age. It was the enigma of my influence in him that he embodied in pigment as a smile. Aknahton also I swayed, and in his wife's face my influence conjured another smile. There are moments in my life on Neptune when my beloved specimens crowd in upon my memory and over- whelm me with the infinity of their uniquenesses; when, forgetful

388

of my own Neptunian personality, I seem to be nothing but the theatre in which these many play their parts.

If it is incredible to you that I should have millions of these intimates, remember, not only that the minds of the Last Men are far more agile and far more capacious than your minds, but also that I have spent many thousands of years upon the work, and that in most cases a whole terrestrial lifetime occupies me for no more than a day of my life on Neptune. Of course even my millions of specimens can afford only partial knowledge of your kind. But those of my colleagues who have been working in the same field have worked with no less industry. No doubt all of us together have studied only a minute fraction of your species; but at least we have by now sampled every culture, every local strain, every generation. And your own age, since it is the turning-point of your history, we have sifted again and again with special care.

Why then out of all this collection do I choose Paul as the text and the epitome of what I have to say to you? I choose him because he does epitomize in his character, his circumstances, and his reaction to my influence, the spiritual crisis of your age, and indeed the doom of your species. It would not be true to say that he was an exceptionally average member of his race. Far from it. Though in a sense typical and significant, Paul was not average. Indeed both in character and in circumstance he was rather unusual. Yet he is typical in that he illustrates very clearly the confused nature of his species, and the disorder of its world. In Paul's life there appear with an almost naïve simplicity of outline certain phases of spiritual growth, distorted by the all-pervading blight of his age, nay of his species. In all of you, from the earliest flint-worker, even to the last survivors of Patagonia, the conflict between the primitive simian nature and the genuinely human (or from your point of view the super-human) is present as a fundamental condition of life. In Paul the old simian nature was undisguised and insistent, while the new human nature had defined itself with precision and emphasis. The conflict therefore was clear.

I pride myself somewhat on the discovery of Paul. My crowning research upon the mentality of the First Men and on the crisis of their career demanded a specimen such as I knew would be hard to find. I cannot tell you at all clearly what was necessary, since you are ignorant of the principles of my work. But, to repeat, I had to select an individual both typical and unique, a being of average intelligence, average abilities, average strength of will, but one in whom the simian and the distinctively human were both well developed and delicately balanced. Further, he must be one capable of a degree of self-consciousness abnormal in your species. Many other more subtle requirements I must leave unmentioned. In order to discover this unique creature I had to explore not only your own age but many earlier generations in search of genetic strains favourable to my requirements.

In the Seventeenth Century there was a German family which promised what I wanted; but in them the desirable features were complicated by a musical sensitivity which in many individuals afforded escape from the conflict. I noticed, however, that those members of the clan who most nearly fulfilled my requirements had a subtly characteristic laugh; or rather that, though they laughed in many different styles, the laughter of each had a curious fleeting tremor of bewilderment. Armed with this clue, and certain others more introspective, I continued my search, until in the England of King Alfred I found a similar and even more promising strain. This I followed through the generations hither and thither. One branch of it, the most promising, was exterminated by the Black Death, another became hopelessly contaminated by interbreeding with a strain of defectives, a third produced witches in the Sixteenth Century and mystics in the Seventeenth. Early in the Eighteenth Century a member of this line married into another stock which I had already marked out, and produced a number of more scientifically-minded folk. Throughout the Eighteenth and early Nineteenth Centuries this line suffered social decline, and proliferated in a swarm of poverty-stricken households scattered over the industrial north of England. From one of these sprang Paul's grandmother, who by good fortune married into yet another of my chosen lines. Paul's father also was of a stock that had already interested me.

Having now discovered my unique specimen, I first took a hasty glance at his career, and found to my delight that circumstance was destined to intensify and clarify in him the characteristics which I proposed to study. In that first hasty glance I saw also the quite unmistakable effects of a Neptunian influence, doubtless my own influence which I had not yet exerted. I then proceeded to make a thorough investigation of every line of Paul's ancestry, in order that I might know his nature through and through. Many volumes could be filled with the results of this inquiry, but here I need not elaborate. Incidentally I traced the evolution of Paul's physical appearance, of his nose, eye-brows, hands, and so on. A curious twist of the hair of his left eyebrow, which was a recessive character, and had not appeared in any of his more recent ancestors, came in with a French strain in the Fourteenth Century. A certain scarcely noticeable prominence of the cheek-bones I traced to a Danish invader of the Eighth Century, and beyond him through Swedes and Finns into Central Asia. Another remarkable line of his ancestry, in part responsible for his intellectual curiosity and certain features of his thumb-print, took me via a Dutch merchant of the Seventeenth Century, a Rhenish baron of the Thirteenth, various Swiss herdsmen and Italian farmers to Syracuse, and so to ancient Greece, where one of Paul's ancestors once handed a cup to Socrates. But apart from a dozen or so curious threads of this type, which of course occur in many family trees, Paul's ancestry was the usual tangle of intercrossing lines, stretching back in manifold complexity among the Norse, the Low Germans, the Ancient British, and the Neolithic, and beyond these to the common forefathers of all your races. It would have been useless to trace Paul's ancestry any further in detail, since nothing more that was distinctive of Paul himself remained to be discovered. In the more remote past the genes that were to produce Paul were ancestral also to the mass of his contemporaries. This story was already known to me.

I must now tell you what it was that I intended to do with Paul, and how I carried out my plan. I wished to perform certain delicate experiments on him and observe his reactions. To some of the readers of this book the mental vivisection which I had to practise upon Paul may seem merely brutal. I would remind them first that it was a necessary part of a very lofty task; second, that Paul himself in his best moments would have gladly accepted all and more of my torturing manipulation for the sake of that high enterprise; and lastly that the final result upon

Paul, the individual human being, was a very great spiritual enrichment.

It is difficult to give you any clear idea of my aim beyond saying that, having found this uniquely typical yet also exceptionally self-conscious being, I intended to influence him periodically in such a manner that he should see his world as far as possible from the Neptunian point of view. I should then be able to observe in detail the effect of this vision on his primitive nature. Had he been of the heroic type, this policy would have turned him into some kind of prophet or crank. But he was made of milder stuff, and would never spoil my experiment in that style. Indeed, one effect of my intermittent manipulation of his experience was to inspire him with a dread of showing himself to be different from others. Just because he possessed a whole secret world of his own, and was prone to see the actual world turn farcical or hideous in the light cast by that other world, he became increasingly anxious to maintain a secure footing in the actual world and conform to all the customary modes of behaviour. For in spite of his Neptunian vision he remained essentially a product of his own world. But as my influence extended, he was forced to admit that there was something in him profoundly alien to his environment, something alien even to himself. At times he feared he was going mad; at other times he would persuade himself with immense complacency that he was 'inspired', and that he must indeed be a prophet; but as he was incapable of any such heroism, this delusion was soon shattered. There were moments when he threatened to break into two personalities, one the natural Paul, the other a violent and spasmodic idealist. But I had chosen him carefully; he was too well integrated actually to succumb to this easy solution of his conflict. Instead of disintegrating, he remained one mind, though torn and perplexed.

But as time passed a change came over him. At first he had regarded his native terrestrial mentality as himself, and the Neptunian influence as alien, disturbing, irrational, insane. He was fascinated by it, but he wished to keep it thoroughly suppressed and ineffective. Later, however, it came to seem a divine enlightenment, sane and joyous, still alien to himself but most precious. Then at last he began to try to live according to my influence, and incurred at once the ridicule and hostility of his own world. With horror he now foreswore his 'inner light' which had so misled him. He earnestly tried to become blind to it, and to be like his fellows. But my influence left him no peace. It found something responsive in him, which, as he matured, was emboldened to identify itself wholly with the Neptunian point of view. Little by little he came to think of this Neptunian factor in his mind as truly 'himself', and the normal Terrestrial as 'other', something like an unruly horse which his true self must somehow break in and ride. There followed a period of struggle, which ended in despair; for it became clear that he could not master his Terrestrial nature. Indeed, it seemed to him that he himself was bound and helpless upon the back of this uncontrolled animal; or that while his body and his mundane intelligence went about the world performing all manner of aimless antics, his essential spirit was imprisoned somewhere in his head watching all, but almost wholly impotent. This essential spirit which he regarded as 'himself' was not, of course, merely my influence in him; it was his own best and most human nature, on which my influence was able to work. But this best of his was only the rudimentary best which was characteristic of his species; and though my influence had endowed it with an immense treasure of imagination, it remained almost wholly ineffective, as is usual with your kind. Yet there were times in his life when Paul did succeed in acting in a manner that was really human, and on these occasions my influence played a part. Of these crises I shall presently tell.

2. THE CHILD PAUL

I know Paul perhaps better than I know myself. I have *been* Paul. I have been Paul throughout his life, and watched him to the very moment of his death. The more important passages of his life I have experienced again and again. I know little intimate facts about him, like the feel of the inside of his mouth. I know the feel of Paul slightly drunk, Paul sexually excited, and Paul with one of his bad colds. I know, far better than Paul himself knew it, the obscure tone of his whole body, when through eating too many muffins, he seemed to see the world itself turn foul. I know also, and can hold together for comparison, the feel of Paul the child, Paul the boy, Paul the young man, stiffening into middle age, and Paul awaiting death in helpless senility.

Fortunately there is no need for me to tell you all the details that I know about Paul. I have only to make you realize the main mental themes or motifs of his life. I need not, for instance, tell you much about his birth. It was a normal birth. Several times I have examined the obscure experiences which harassed him during that earliest of his adventures. For it seemed possible that even then something might have occurred to contribute to his idiosyncrasies. But neither in his passage into the outer world nor in his fungoid pre-natal experience (so difficult for the explorer to penetrate) did I find anything significant, save what is common to all his kind. In Paul, whose nature was more sensitive than the average, the shock of exchanging the elysium of the womb for an alien world was serious, and was accentuated somewhat by the clumsiness of the physician. But it caused no unusual damage to his mind, nothing but the common yearning toward a warmer, cosier, less noxious world, which, in so many of you, favours legends of a golden age in the past, or of a golden heaven in the future.

One feature of Paul's experience of birth was indeed significant, and served to confirm my choice of him as a subject of experiment. Like many others, he did not breathe till a smack made him take breath to bellow. I experienced, of course, his bewildered fury at the chastisement. I also experienced his awareness of the cold air that flooded his lungs, and the shock of glee that came with it. In that instant a connexion was registered in Paul's mind for ever after, a connexion between what I may call fate's smiting and the breath of life. In after years Paul was to know himself a coward, yet in spite of his cowardice, he was ever to seek in the harshness of fate for the breath of a new life. Even though, in all his ages, he yearned to creep back into the warm close peace of the womb, he craved also to absorb into his blood the atmosphere of a wider world.

I need not describe Paul's arduous self-education in the cot, the nursery and the garden. Like all organisms he had to learn to cope with his world. Like all animals he had to grapple with the problems of perceiving and acting in a world of space and time. Little by little he learned to observe and to respond to all manner of objects, such as the rotund and fragrant dairy of his mother's breast, and the less delectable bottle. He learned the geography of his own body, mapping it out patiently, unwittingly, day by day, in a surprisingly intricate system of explorations, discovering that all these complex findings fell together beautifully in a three-dimensional system of touch and sight. Many great arts he acquired, first the art of sucking, and of shifting about in bed, then the art of the rattle. Presently he learned how to use his whole body as a vehicle to transport him to and fro in a wider sphere. He mastered the more dangerous arts of crawling and walking, the art of the bouncing ball, and so on. Meanwhile he had distinguished the soothing and indignant tones of the human voice. Also, the intermittent human breasts and arms and laps and voices had fallen into order to make more or less constant systems, each of which might be expected to behave in a distinctive manner. Then at last he discovered that human voices had meanings, and that he himself could use these noises so as to make the great grown-up creatures do his bidding.

This power of controlling the movements of adults was one of Paul's most exciting early triumphs. It was a limited and erratic power. All too often the great creature refused to obey, or actually turned the tables and compelled him to do what he did not want to do. Altogether these adults were a very perplexing fact in Paul's early life. In some ways they were so necessary and reliable, in others so inconsequent and even noxious. Of course, Paul did not consciously make these generalizations, but they were implied in his behaviour. Thus in certain respects, such as physical care and protection, he trusted the adult absolutely, but in others he learned to expect nothing but misunderstanding and ridicule. In yet other respects he himself was so influenced by the prestige suggestion which these mighty beings brought to bear on him, that many of their unintelligible admirations and taboos gradually took root in his own nature. For instance, he slavishly accepted their views about sex. Very early in his childhood he had begun to take an interest in those parts of his body which adults pointedly ignored. He had discovered that a vague pleasure occurred when these organs were touched. But long before he was told that it was wicked and dangerous to take any notice of them, he already profoundly felt that it was so, merely through the awkwardness that beset adults whenever he referred to them. Had Paul been born a young baboon or chimpanzee he would at least have escaped the agony of mind and waste of energy which, as I shall tell later, he, like so many of his kind, incurred through this too ready acceptance of adult standards. Meanwhile it was inevitable that, before sex became an imperious need, Paul should adjust himself to adult standards in this as in so many other respects. Adults were objects which one had to learn to cope with, just as one had to learn to cope with dogs and chairs and fire. Sometimes one failed and suffered for it, but on the whole one succeeded.

I must not, however, dwell on the process by which Paul gradually mastered these earliest problems. In all his adventures, I, his parasite, tasted his success and failure. I suffered all his bumps, scratches and scaldings. I saw beforehand what was impending. I saw both that it was inevitable and that with a little more skill it might have been avoided. Had I chosen, I might have played the mother to him and saved him from many a disaster, but it was better to let him learn. During his earliest years I refrained from any kind of influence, since it was important that he should develop normally up to a certain stage.

Little by little Paul's world crystallized into extensive patterns. No longer a meagre and obscure flux of dream-like forms, it became a more or less reliable world of 'common sense', a house and garden, with surrounding continents made up of other houses and gardens, streets and fields. Gradually also he was able to look backwards not merely into a confused cloud of pastness but along a brief but orderly vista of nights and days.

But with this gradual increase of order in his daylight world, Paul became more and more distressed by that other chaotic world which swallowed him at night. When the light was put out and he was left alone in bed, the whole reliable order vanished. Even if he kept his eyes shut, terrifying shades confronted him with their vague and shifty forms. He saw animal heads and shoulders, and stealthily moving gorilla arms. They kept changing from one thing into another thing. They were unintelligible and therefore terrible.

The Child Paul

Still worse, sometimes the seething confusion of shadows would be dominated by a single staring eye. Paul could not escape it. Wherever he looked, there it was, watching him. Perhaps it was God's eye, seeing right through him, coldly noting all his most secret wickedness. Perhaps God had done away with the world of day because Paul had been so naughty in it. Perhaps there was nothing now but Paul and God and the close dark, with one streak of light pretending to be under the door, to keep up appearances. Somehow the Eye seemed to him both very wise and very stupid, a vindictive clever thing, that intended to kill him just by gazing at him, for no reason but that he did not please the Eye. Sometimes Paul was so terrified that he screamed. Then an exasperated grown-up would appear and ask what on earth was the matter. He could never tell, for grown-ups were somehow blind to the night world, and would think him silly. But to me, Paul's trouble was very real, and also intelligible. To Paul, though he knew it not, the night was the womb. When he was very sleepy, it promised rest and peace; but when he was not sleepy, he regarded it as a well of blackness, stuffiness, formlessness, negation. It threatened to swallow him back from the bright orderly extra-uterine world of day, with its complicated geography, its reliable persons, and its winds that came with obscure messages from still wider spheres.

Throughout Paul's life this contrast of the day world and the night world lay at the back of his thinking and feeling, influencing it, perplexing it. As he grew older, however, the two worlds seemed to interpenetrate more and more, until at last he found that there was a day view of everything and a night view also. But which was the true view? Perhaps the night view of things was in fact just nightmare, a bad dream. But then perhaps it was the other way round. Perhaps the whole day universe was just a foolish dream of the eternal foetus imprisoned in the eternal womb. In early days, of course, Paul never thought of the problem in this way, but I myself could see how the obscure movements of his mind were related to the forgotten experience of birth.

There was one aspect of the night which seemed even to the child Paul very different from the night which imprisoned him in bed, namely the starry sky. He seldom saw it, but even a brief glimpse of it would have lasting effect on him. It gave him a sort of calm elation which fortified him against the terrors of darkness, and would sometimes even last into the next day, soothing his troubles and tempering his joys. This experience, which played an important part in Paul's life, was not simply a spontaneous outcome of his own nature. It was in part due to my presence in his mind, though in part also to his native disposition. Throughout his life, these occasions on which he was able to regard the night sky had a very considerable effect on me, the imprisoned and often fatigued observer of all his experience. They afforded me refreshing glimpses of something common to his world and my own. When I had become too deeply immersed in the minutiae of Paul's behaviour, and was beginning to feel your world more real than mine, the sight of the stars, even through the inefficient eyes of a member of your species, would recall to me with great vividness the Neptunian plains and dwarf jungles, the sky-piercing towers and bland inhabitants of my own far-future world. This vivid recollection would rekindle in me the still, flame-like ardour which is the spirit of our doomed but unperturbed community. And the serene emotion which then surged through me would infect Paul also, lending a tone to his experience, which, though he could never properly account for it, he came in time to recognize as in some manner a gift from a source beyond his mundane nature. I well remember the hush of surprise and gurgle of delight with which the child Paul first greeted the stars. He was in his mother's arms. He stretched out his own fat arms and turned his head slowly from side to side, surveying the heaven. On another occasion, much later, when he was being brought home from a Christmas party, so tired that he could hardly walk, a brilliant night sky overpowered him so that he burst into tears of uncomprehending joy.

As the years advanced, Paul's sense that the starry night was present even by day became an increasing influence in his life. This was partly my doing; for I soon found that by giving him visual images of the night sky in the midst of mundane situations I could help him to regard the affairs of himself and his companions with Uranian detachment. There was an early stage in his development when, through this action of mine, he came to think of the universe as a sandwich made of the upper and nether night, with, between

398

them, the meat of day. Below was the horrible darkness and confusion and closeness which he encountered in his stuffy bedroom. Above was the high mystery of the stars. Between was the world of familiar things.

This middle world had already spread outwards to become a vague expanse of countries, embracing somewhere beyond the familiar streets all kinds of wonders, which were nevertheless definitely day-time wonders. Somewhere there was India, full of tigers, elephants, jewelled princes, and jugglers. Elsewhere lay Iceland, all solid ice, with rivers of fire running down the crystal volcanoes. Then there was France, where they ate frogs and snails and were terribly polite; Germany, where they made cheap copies of English toys, and fought duels; Greece, where they wore no clothes except helmets with clothes-brushes on them; Egypt, all mummies and crocodiles; Fairyland, where magic happened more easily than in England. Yet even in England, magic was not unknown. There was Santa Claus, and dozens of lucky and unlucky things to be sought and avoided.

Over the whole world of countries hung the sky, a blue or cloudy ceiling. Here a discrepancy entered into Paul's universe. If you thought about it from the day-time point of view, you believed that beyond the sky and the stars there was heaven, full of winged angels in nightgowns, their eyes always turned upwards. And above them again was God, whom Paul had somehow come to think of as a huge grown-up, sprawling from horizon to horizon, and looking down precisely at Paul, with eyes that saw even his thoughts. Somehow those eyes were the same as the Eye that stared at him in the nether darkness of his bedroom. When Paul remembered the Eye by day, he would repeat rapidly, 'Oh God, I love you, I love you, I love you.'

But if you thought of things from the point of view of the starry night, God and the angels did not seem to fit in very well. Paul half believed that they were pictures painted on the ceiling of the day world.

In time, of course, Paul's day world ceased to be flat, and became a huge ball. At this stage the universe was more like a dumpling than a sandwich. Vaguely Paul still conceived the three levels of existence. The nether night was deep down within the ball of the day world. The starry night was all around it. On the ball were all the countries except Fairyland, which was nowhere. Many of the countries were British Possessions, and red. At school he learned much about England and the Empire, and became a patriot. The English were – well, English. They had the greatest empire in the world. They were the only people who played fair in games, and were kind to animals, and could govern black people, and fight a losing battle to the end, and rule the seas. And because they were such fine people, God had hidden a lot of coal and iron under their country, so that they could use it for ships and engines and for making thousands of things that other countries were not clever enough to make for themselves. God had also written the Bible in English, because it was the best language, and the angels talked it.

Paul's patriotism was largely an affectation. At this time he had a great longing to be like his fellows, and his fellows made it very obvious that they were patriotic. Also he found in patriotism a source of self-gratulation. Somehow or other, through patriotism, the worm that was the ordinary Paul became one of the lords of the earth. But there was also another factor at work. He had already begun to feel an obscure impulse to devote himself to ends beyond private gratification. Much of this sadly misconceived yearning for lofty ends was expressed in bragging about his school and vilifying other schools; but the Empire afforded it a more imposing object.

3. EARLY EXPERIMENTS ON PAUL

Not until Paul was already at school did I begin to exercise a deliberate influence over him. My aim was to prepare him to attain in early maturity as complete an insight as possible into the Neptunian view of Terrestrial affairs. In his early years I seldom influenced him, but the rare occasions on which I did so had a deep effect on him. They were designed to intensify his consciousness beyond the normal limitations of his species. By goading and delicately controlling his attention I contrived to make him startlingly aware, now and again, of data which commonly lie beyond the apprehension of the First Men. The scope of my early work upon him might be described by saying that I forced him to a more vivid sense of the reality and uniqueness of perceptual objects, of himself, of others as selves, and also of his own underlying unity with others, and of his own participation in the cosmos.

For instance, to deal with the simplest matter first, Paul once found a curious green pebble. He picked it up and examined it intently, noting with delight its veining, its smooth curvature, its rigidity. He turned it about, fingered it, tapped it. Then suddenly I flooded him with a spate of relevant imagery, visual and tactual, so that he seemed to encounter in this one pebble the whole splendour of sight, the whole poignancy of touch. The thing suddenly leapt at him with its unveiled reality. The change in his experience was as impressive as the change from imagery to actual perception, from picturing a friend's face to actually seeing it. It was as though the earlier experience, which at the time seemed normally vivid, had been after all but a shadowy imagination of a pebble, compared with the later experience, which was an actual apprehension of an objective reality. It was over in a moment. Paul dropped the pebble and collapsed on the grass, holding his head in his hands. For a moment he thought some one had thrown a pebble at him and that it had gone right through his head. He opened his eyes. Everything seemed ordinary again. Then he caught sight of the pebble, half-hidden under a dandelion leaf. It was just a little round green thing, but it seemed to look at him meaningly. As they regarded one another, Paul and the pebble, Paul felt the pebble rushing at him again. He covered his eyes and sat for a long while thinking of nothing but his splitting head. He had been rather badly hurt, but also he was intrigued. The effect was something like his forgotten experience of birth, a confusion of shock, pain, brilliant novelty, fear of the unknown, and exhilaration.

Paul spent the next two days in bed with a 'bilious headache'. When he was recovered, he went in search of his pebble. He picked it up almost as though it were a live bomb, but though it raised a vivid memory of the adventure, it gave him no fresh experience.

I repeated this experiment on Paul at rare intervals and in relation to very diverse objects, such as his precious knife, the tolling of a bell, a flying hawk, and his own hand. The last entailed a whole week in bed, for not only had he perceived his hand externally as he had perceived the pebble, he had also perceived it from within; and moreover he had been fascinated by his volitional control of it. It was a little grubby brown hand with black-rimmed nails and many scratches. He turned it about, bending and straightening the fingers, confidently willing it to perform various antics, intensely aware of his own fiat, yet not at all self-conscious in any deeper sense.

Through my influence Paul continued to suffer these experiences throughout his childhood. He became accustomed to them, and to look forward to them with mingled dread and zest. At length I judged him ripe for a different kind of experiment. He had been coveting a minute bronze dog which belonged to one of his companions. He tried to persuade the owner to 'swop' it, but in vain. Paul became more and more obsessed, and finally stole the dog. While he was guiltily playing with it in his own house I played a trick on him. I gave him an intense and detailed visual image of his friend rummaging frantically among his toys for the lost dog. So aggressive did this image become that it blotted out Paul's actual environment. It had, moreover, the intensified reality that he had first encountered in the pebble. Paul's reaction was strange. For a moment he stared at the hallucination, while hatred welled within him. Then, as soon as the vision had faded, he rushed into the street and dropped the little bronze figure down a grid. Henceforth he treated his former friend with shocking spite, mingled with terror.

I did not attempt to influence Paul's slowly dawning awareness of self till he was already well advanced in boyhood. One day, after he had been bathing with his favourite schoolfellow, the two boys, naked, wet, gleaming in the sunlight, had a friendly wrangle over a towel. They tugged in opposite directions, shouting and panting. For a moment they stood still, staring into one another's eyes. Suddenly I re-kindled in Paul all his past groping realizations of the difference between himself and the other, all his past obscure awareness of 'me' and 'you'. I focused, so to speak, the whole vague illumination of this mass of experience upon the present moment. As formerly the pebble and his hand, so now his friend and his own being, impinged upon him with overwhelming reality. It was a reality not alone of visual and tactual form but also of experiencing. Through my manipulation of his imagery he seemed to enter imaginatively into the mind of the other, to have the feel of a different being, in a different body. A fly settled on the other's neck. Paul felt it tickle, and felt the quick contortion that sent it away. Through the other's eyes he seemed to see his own intent face, and his own arms lightly pulling at the towel. He began murmuring to himself, 'I, Paul; you, Dick; I, Dick; you, Paul.' And through Dick's eyes he seemed to see his own lips moving. Through Dick's ears and through his own ears also he heard his own voice. Dick, meanwhile, had seen the sudden intensity of Paul's expression, and was alarmed. Paul saw, and vividly experienced, Dick's alarm. They dropped the towel. Paul reached out a hand and felt Dick's shoulder, as formerly he had felt the pebble. 'Odd!' he said, 'I've waked up. I do sometimes. But never quite this way before.' Dick began to question, but Paul went on, 'I sort-of woke to be really *me*. Then I was *you*. And both of us at once. Did it happen to you too?' Dick shook his head, very perplexed. Then came the headache. Paul dropped, and lay whimpering, with his hands over his eyes.

My next experiment was performed during a violent quarrel between Paul and Dick. Paul had spent a free afternoon making a boat. He was hollowing it with a gouge borrowed from Dick. Dick arrived to demand the gouge, which was long overdue, and was needed for hollowing his own boat. Paul, intent on his work and eager to finish it before tea, refused to surrender the tool. They wrangled, while Paul carried on his work. Dick tried to stop him. At this moment I forced on Paul a vivid apprehension of the other boy, and of his craving to have his tool, and of his rage against Paul. Paul stopped working. Once more he seemed for a moment to *be* Dick, and to see his own ugly scowl through Dick's eyes. For a moment Paul hung paralysed in a mental conflict. Then suddenly he jabbed Dick's hand with the gouge. Both boys screamed with Dick's pain. Paul rushed toward the door, crying, 'Beast, get out of me, you taste horrid.' Before he reached the door he vomited. Then he fled, yelling. He carried off the gouge.

This reaction of Paul's was very typical of his species. His brief insight into the other's point of view merely filled him with resentment. Typical also was his subsequent remorse, which tortured him during his period of illness after this experiment. Dick had been thoroughly frightened. It seemed to him that Paul had gone mad. In time, however, the friendship was restored, and even deepened; for Paul now treated Dick with a gentleness and understanding beyond his years. Occasionally I induced in him the more vivid apprehension of his friend and himself, but I carefully refrained from doing so when their interests were violently opposed.

In this way I produced in Paul a self-insight and insight into others which is very unusual in your species. His rare abnormal experiences now coloured his whole life, and sowed in him the seed of a lifelong conflict between the behaviour natural to his kind and the behaviour which his enhanced insight demanded. When he found himself forced to choose between the two, he almost always acted in the baser way, though afterwards he was bitterly remorseful. Once or twice, however, things turned out differently. I will give one example.

Paul was one of those timid boys who is a constant temptation to the bully. When any bullying was afoot in which Paul himself was not involved, he always took care not to interfere. Sometimes he would actually try to ingratiate himself with the stronger party. One winter day at school, when Paul and a few others of his form were supposed to be doing their 'preparation', the arch bully of the form began tormenting a little Jew whom Paul intensely disliked. The smaller boys, with Paul among them, looked on, applauding now and then with anxious giggles. I chose this moment for an experiment. With dismay Paul felt his cursed imagination beginning to work. He tried to bury himself in his French exercise, but vainly. Do what he would, he could not help entering imaginatively into 'that beastly little Jew'. Then he started being not only the Jew but the bully also. He imagined the big lout feeling the helpless self-disgust which he himself had felt in his one experiment in the art of bullying. I worked up this imagination till he really apprehended the mind of the bully far better than the bully himself. He realized vividly the drowsy, fumbling, vaguely distressed and frightened life that was going on in that hulk of flesh, and was disguised even from itself by the pose of braggartism. Suddenly Paul said aloud in a clear but dreamy voice, 'Chuck it, Williams, you're hurting yourself.' There was a sudden silence of amazement. Paul, terrified at his own voice, bowed over his French book. The bully remarked, 'Your turn next', and then applied himself once more to his victim, who squealed. Paul rose, crossed the floor, laid a hand on the bully's shoulder, and was sent crashing into the hearth. He sat for a moment among the cinders listening to the general laugh. Then slowly he rose, and slowly surveyed his grinning fellow-mortals. Williams gave an extra twist to the Jew's arm, and there followed a yell. Paul, saying quietly, 'Williams, you've got to stop', put his own left hand into the fire and picked out a large completely redhot coal. Ignoring the pain and the smell of his burning flesh, he went over to Williams and said, 'Now, clear out or I'll brand you.' Someone tried to seize Paul's arm. He used his coal with effect, so that the other retired. Then he rushed at Williams. The bully fled. I felt Paul's eyebrows rise and his lips twist in a whimsical smile. He stood dreaming for a moment, then restored the still faintly glowing coal to its place in the fire. Suddenly he caught sight of the charred and smoking mess that was his hand. All along he had been aware of the pain, but he had calmly ignored it. But now that the incident was completed, ignoring was impossible. His strange exaltation vanished. He gave one sharp scream, half for pain, half for surprise, and then fainted.

Paul's hand recovered within a few weeks, though of course it remained scarred for ever. Paul's mind was more deeply affected. He was terrified about himself. He felt that he had been possessed, and he dreaded being let in for even worse scrapes in the future. All the same, he was rather proud of himself, and half-wished he could be like that always.

4. PAUL'S CHANGING WORLD

During his schooldays Paul suffered more than the normal growing pains, for his mind was shooting upward in response not only to normal but to abnormal influences. He was outgrowing not only toys and childish interests; he was outgrowing the world which school life imposed upon him. Like a crab that has become too big for its shell and must struggle out of it, Paul was now too big for his world. It had cracked under the stress of his vital movement, and

405

he was in the act of issuing from it in a soft vulnerable, but flexible and expansible covering, which some day would harden into a new and ampler dwelling-place.

Two conflicting influences dominated him at school, the impulse to assume the stereotyped 'schoolboy' nature and live comfortably in the schoolboy world, and in opposition to this the impulse to find himself and to find reality. He strove to live according to the schoolboy ethic, partly because he genuinely admired it, partly so as to assume the protective colouring of his surroundings. But he could never succeed. The forces at work within him were too strong for him. In his early schooldays Paul never clearly understood that he was trying to live two inconsistent lives at once. He did not know that, while he was so earnestly trying to adjust himself to the school universe, he was also trying to burst that universe apart and grow an entirely new universe to suit the expanding tissues of his mind.

This growth, or rather this profound metamorphosis, was controlled by certain experiences which had an enduring effect on him. They were, so to speak, the centres of reorganization which, little by little, changed the larval Paul into the adult imago. These seminal experiences were of two kinds, though he did not clearly distinguish between them. His attention was arrested, and he was stung into excited admiration by two widespread facts: by the intricacy and relentlessness of physical happenings, and also by biological perfection, or at least functional perfection of every sort.

Paul's sense of the austerity of the physical universe awoke early. Even in the nursery he had conceived an uncomprehending respect for the mechanism of natural events. This spontaneous movement of piety toward 'nature' developed not only into a strong scientific interest, but also into a strangely exultant awe, for which there seemed to be no rational justification.

It was his father who first pointed out to him the crossing wave-trains of a mountain tarn, and by eloquent description made him feel that the whole physical world was in some manner a lake rippled by myriads of such crossing waves, great and small, swift and slow. This little significant experience took place during a holiday spent on the Welsh moors. They were standing on a crag overlooking the grey 'llyn'. They counted five distinct systems of waves, some small and sharp, some broad and faint. There were also occasional brief 'cat's paws' complicating the pattern. Father and son went down to the sheltered side of the lake and contemplated its more peaceful undulations. With a sense almost of sacrilege, Paul stirred the water with his stick, and sent ripple after ripple in widening circles. The father said, 'That is what you are yourself, a stirring up of the water, so that waves spread across the world. When the stirring stops, there will be no more ripples.' As they walked away, they discussed light and sound and the rippled sky, and the sun, great source of ripples. Thus did an imaginative amateur anticipate in a happy guess the 'wave mechanics' which was to prove the crowning achievement of the physics of the First Men. Paul was given to understand that even his own body, whatever else it was, was certainly a turmoil of waves, inconceivably complex but no less orderly than the waves on the tarn. His apprehension of this novel information was confused but dramatic. It gave him a sense of the extreme subtlety and inevitability of existence. That even his own body should be of this nature seemed to him very strange but also very beautiful. Almost at the outset, however, he said, 'If my body is all waves, where do *I* come in? Do I make the waves, or do the waves make me?' To this the father answered, with more confidence than lucidity, 'You are the waves. What stirs is God.'

This experience remained with Paul for ever. It became for him the paradigm of all physical sciences, and at the same time an epitome of the mystery of life. In his maturity he would often, when he came upon still water, pause to disturb its serenity. The little act would seem to him darkly impious yet also creative. He would mutter to himself, 'God stirs the waters.' Sometimes he would take a handful of little stones and throw them into the pond, one after the other in different directions. Then he would stand motionless, watching the intersecting circles spread and fade and die, till at last peace was wholly restored.

Paul's first view of the moon through his father's modest telescope was another memorable experience. He had already seen a ship disappearing below the horizon, and had been told that the earth and the moon were round. But actually to see the rotund moon, no longer as a flat white shilling, but as a distant world covered with mountains, was an experience whose fascination he never outgrew. Throughout his life he was ready to gaze for ten minutes at a time through telescope or field-glass at the bright summits and black valleys along the line between lunar night and day. This vision had a startling power over him which he himself could not rationally justify. It would flash mysteriously upon him with bewildering and even devastating effect in the midst of some schoolboy activity, in the midst of a Latin lesson, or morning prayers, or a game of cricket, or a smutty story. Under the influence of this experience he began to devour popular astronomy books. He looked with new eyes at the first page of the school atlas, which had hitherto meant nothing to him. Rapidly the schoolboy universe ceased to be the whole real universe, and was reduced to a very faulty picture of a tiny corner of a universe which teemed with suns and inhabited worlds. For at this stage he imagined that every star was attended by a dozen or so populous planets.

He was perplexed to find that most adults, though many of them fully believed in some such universe, did nothing with the knowledge. That which to him was so significant was to them either tiresome or terrifying. Even his father, who had helped him to discover the new world, did not seem to appreciate it as it deserved. To the father it did indeed seem wonderful. He called it 'sublime'. But for him it remained merely a sublime irrelevance. It compelled his attention, and in a manner his admiration also; but the tone of his voice, when he was talking of it, suggested a veiled reluctance, almost resentment. He seemed, in spite of all his scientific interest, to be happier and more at home in the world of the Iliad or of the 'Faerie Queene'. The son, on the other hand, though he did his best to appreciate these dream worlds, was never moved by them. But the stars gave him an intense exhilaration, which, when he tried to justify it to his father, turned out to be, or to seem, wholly irrational.

Another overwhelming fact that gradually emerged into the child Paul's ken, partly through the help of his father, partly through his own unaided apprehension, was what he came later to call 'the aliveness of all living things'. His boon companion of early days had been a terrier, with whom he used surreptitiously to share his bread and butter, bite by bite. Of course he believed that this creature had a mind much more like his own mind than was actually the case; but also, by long experience of this animal, he learned to enter into imaginative sympathy with a mind that was not human. This canine friendship drove deep into his own mind and heart both a sense of the kinship of all living things and a sense of their differences. Though Jack could enter into a romp, he could never be induced to play trains. Nor could he be persuaded that rabbits were beings like himself, whose lives should be respected. Paul himself, of course, had to make that discovery; but even in his earliest fly-tormenting and beetle-crushing phase he was already making it. Later there came a stage when this mystery of alien lives was his chief absorption and his chief perplexity. He would watch ants toiling through the grass-jungle with food for the public store, or 'talking' to one another as they met on one of their highways, or fighting to the death in organized battle. Always, of course, he imputed far too much of human intelligence to these strange beings. But even when at a much later date he discovered this error, he remained firm in his sense of their fundamental community with himself. Even worms, exploring the soil with their blind noses, seemed to him infinitely more like himself than the soil they devoured. And when one of them was snapped up by a thrush, Paul suffered an agony of indecision, debating whether to save the worm or let the bird have its dinner in peace. When he saw a cat with a mouse, he rushed indignantly to the rescue; yet somehow, after the event, he fell to wondering if he had merely been meddlesome.

In short, during this phase of his growth he was overwhelmed with what some would call a mystical apprehension of the inner being of all living things, and shocked by their insensitivity to one another, their essential harmfulness to one another. He was troubled by the fact that he himself ate meat and wore leather boots, and amazed that even kind-hearted persons, who doted on their own pets, did likewise without any hesitation. He was still more distressed by a streak of real sadism which survived in himself. At one time he used to catch wasps and cut them in two, so as to observe the strange behaviour of the parts. Worse still was his reaction to stag-hunting. His rare excursions into the world of sport did not occur until he was in his last year at school. They ceased while he was at the University. A well-to-do and much respected friend of his father sometimes invited Paul to spend part of the summer holidays at his house in Devon. He taught Paul to ride, and was determined to make a sportsman of him. When the lad was considered proficient, he was taken out to follow the hounds. With a sickening guiltiness, a sickening sense of his own bad horsemanship, with a sickening blend of adulation and contempt for the rest of the field, he let himself be bumped over moors and through covers, down lanes and through villages, till surprisingly he found himself in at the death. There at last was the stag, chin-deep in a river, or slithering on the roof of some outhouse in a village street, or more majestically at bay in the angle of two hedges. Then Paul exulted, even while he sickened with shame and pity. Why did he do it? he wondered. Why did he stand there watching the great weary beast mauled by the hounds, while the huntsmen tried to grab one of its antlers from behind? And when the knife went home, why did he feel, just for a fraction of a second, a sudden glee and triumph? Why was he so anxiously self-complacent as he stood at his horse's head chewing cake and apples, while the stag was disembowelled and the hounds clamoured for their share? Why did he so desire to be taken for one of these sporting gentry, these overgrown schoolboys? These questions remained for Paul unanswered. Clearly his larval nature was making a desperate effort to reject the more developed mentality that I was forcing on him. In spite of his incompetence, he felt toward the sporting English gentleman not merely respect and envy but a deep kinship. In his revulsion against the primeval hunter and fighter, and aristocrat, he was divided against himself. Essentially the same conflict racked him a few years later when the war forced him to choose once and for all between the two allegiances. But of course in his war-perplexity, the primitive motive was reinforced by much that was by no means primitive.

IV *Paul Comes of Age*

1. PAUL AND SEX

I HAVE now to describe Paul's advance from boyhood to early manhood, which he reached just before the outbreak of the European War. In order to do this I must tell chiefly of his changing reactions to three facts in his experience, namely to sex, to personality, and to the immense impersonal.

As I have already said, Paul discovered early in his childhood that a very special and delectable experience could be obtained from that part of his body on which his elders had conferred a most intriguing mystery. Their dropped voices, their hesitations, their veiled suggestions and warnings, had long ago roused his curiosity and prepared him to feel guilt in his new pleasure. Later, during adolescence, the natural development of his body, combined with the influence of stories and drawings circulated at school, increased his itch of experimentation in this field. His own sensitivity, which had been exaggerated by my influence, made him peculiarly susceptible.

In this new experience Paul found something unique, arresting, mysteriously significant, yet significant of he knew not what. I myself, the observer of these disturbing events, can only describe the character which he seemed to himself to find in them, by calling it an impression of almost mystical fulfilment, or of communion with some presence, or being, or power, wholly beyond the grasp of his intellect. It was as though he had unexpectedly discovered how to reach down and touch the deep, living heart of reality, and as though this contact were to quicken him through and through with an exquisite, though deadly thrill. The experience was all too brief, and after it came a vague fear. In the very act it seemed to be promising more than it could ever give. That fleeting contact with the heart of things was but an earnest, seemingly, of some more profound and lasting penetration, not yet to be achieved.

Now this attainment and this promise were not wholly illusory.

To minds that have passed far beyond your stage of growth, every sensory experience whatever may afford this exquisite, inebriating sense of contact with objective reality. More primitive minds, however, seldom attain this insight. For them it is only when the sensuous has the added glamour of rarity, or of sin and sanctity, that it can deliver its full content. And so the amazed spirit falsely assumes that only through this one particular sensory window can it reach out and touch reality. Among you the sexual experience alone has universally this unique significance and power. For in you, as in the apes, almost alone among mammals, reproductive potency is constant and excessive. And in nearly all your cultures the consequent excessive interest in sex has been thwarted, in most cases very clumsily.

In Paul's case it soon became clear that, unless I intervened, the mystery and horror with which sex was treated would cause in him an obsessive fascination. His plight is well enough expressed in a poem which he wrote at this time, but showed to no one. I should explain that henceforth he was frequently to indulge in what he regarded as poetical expression. I shall occasionally quote from his writings to illustrate his spiritual progress. Note that even at this early stage he was deserting the forms of verse that were still orthodox. Here is the poem.

SIN

I have touched filth.
Only with the finger tip I touched it,
inquisitive of the taste of it.
But it creeps.
It has spread over my body a slime,
and into my soul a stupor.
It is a film over the eyes,
blurring the delicate figuring and ethereal hue of things.
It clogs the ears.
The finer tones of truth are muffled from me.
Beauty has turned her back on me.
I have shamed her, I am desolate.
There is no escape from myself.
And in my loneliness, –
It was because of my mad loneliness, –

I touched again,
I dabbled for a moment in the sweet filth,
and fled back shuddering in the silence.
Presently I shall slink down again and wallow,
for solace in my mad loneliness.

One of the most difficult facts for the Neptunian explorer to grasp about primitive minds is their obsession and their abject guilt and disgust in respect of bodily appetites. In the constitution of the last human species the excess energy of these appetites is very largely sublimated, innately, into the spiritual and intellectual life. On the other hand, whenever they do demand direct satisfaction, they are frankly and zestfully gratified. In Paul's species it was the sexual appetite that caused trouble. Now it did not suit me that Paul should become tangled inextricably in sex. His whole generation, I knew, was going to develop along the lines of sex mania, in revulsion from the prudery of its predecessors. But it was necessary that Paul should maintain a true balance, so that his spirit's energies should be free to direct themselves elsewhere.

The method by which I brought peace to Paul's troubled mind was easy to me, though disturbing to him. Whenever he began to worry himself with guilty fears, I would force upon his imagination scenes from another world, in which not sex but nutrition was the deed of supreme uncleanness and sanctity. Little by little I pieced together in his mind a considerable knowledge of an early Neptunian species whose fantastic culture has many points in common with your own. Let me here tell you briefly of that culture.

On Neptune, then, there once lived, or from your point of view, there will live, a race of human beings which attained a certain affluence and social complexity, but was ever hampered by its morbid interest in nutrition. By what freakish turns of fortune this state of affairs was brought about, I need not pause to describe. Suffice it that physiological changes had produced in this human species an exaggerated mechanism of hunger. This abnormality saddled all its members with a craving for food much in excess of biological need; and from the blundering social repression of this craving there arose a number of strange taboos and perversions. By the time this Neptunian species had attained civil life, the function of nutrition had become as perverse and malignant as the function of reproduction in your own society. No reference might be made to it in public, save to its excretory side, which was regarded as a rite of purification. Eating became a private and vaguely obscene act. While in many social situations sexual intercourse was a recognized means of expression and diversion, and even drinking was permitted in the less puritanical circles so long as it was performed through the nose, eating in the presence of another person was not tolerated. In every home a special privy was set aside for eating. This was stocked during the night by the public food carriers, who constituted the lowest caste of society. In place of your chastity ideal there arose a fiction that to refrain from eating was virtuous, and that the most holy persons could live without eating at all. Even ordinary folk, though pardoned for occasional indulgence, were supposed to refrain from the filthy act as far as possible. Repressed nutrition had by now coloured the whole life of the race. The mouth occupied in its culture much the same position as the phallus with you. A vast and subtle symbolism, like that which in your culture is associated with the sacred and obscene reproductive act, was generated in this case by the sacred and obscene nutritive act. Eating became at once a sin and an epitome of the divine power; for in eating does not the living body gather into itself lifeless matter to organize it, vitalize it? The mouth was, of course, never exposed to view. The awful member was concealed behind a little modesty apron, which was worn below the nose. In prehistoric times the lips had formed the chief visual stimulus to sexual interest, and like the rump of the baboon had developed lavish coloration and turgescence. But very early in the cultural development of the species the modesty apron became universal. Even when the rest of the body was unclad, this garment was retained. And just as in your culture the notorious fig-leaf is vaguely suggestive of that which it conceals, so, in this Neptunian culture, the conventionally decorated covering of the mouth came to mimic furtively the dread orifice itself. Owing to the fact that in polite society no sound might be made which betrayed movement of the lips, speech became distorted and debased. One curious consequence of this obscenity of the mouth was the peculiar status of kissing. Though sexual promiscuity was almost

414

universal, kissing was a deadly sin, except between man and wife. A kiss, bestowed in privacy and darkness, was the true consummation of marriage, and was something infinitely more desirable and more disturbing than the procreative act itself. All lovers longed to be united in a kiss; or, if they were innocents, they looked for some unknown fulfilment, which they vaguely and guiltily felt must be somehow connected with the mouth. Coitus they regarded merely as an innocent and peculiarly delightful caress; but the kiss was the dark, exquisite, sacred, mystically significant, forbidden fruit of all their loving. It was a mutual devouring, the act in which, symbolically, the lover took the substance of the other within his or her own system. Through this connexion with romantic love the kiss gathered to itself all that obscure significance of tender personal relations, of spiritual communion between highly developed personalities, which in your world the same romantic love may confer on coitus. Further, since, like your Trobriand Islanders, the less sophisticated races of this species were often ignorant of the connexion between the sexual act and conception, and since, as with those islanders, sexual intercourse outside the marriage bond often failed to produce offspring, it was commonly believed in the more primitive of these Neptunian societies that the true reproductive act was the kiss. Consequently conception and child-birth came to be endowed with the same mystery, sanctity, and obscenity as nutrition. Sex, on the other hand, remained delightfully uncontaminated. These traditions maintained their power even in civilized societies, which had long ago realized the truth about parenthood. Children were carefully instructed in the hygiene of sex, and encouraged to have blithe sexual relations as soon as they needed that form of expression. But in respect of nutrition they were left in disastrous ignorance. As infants they were suckled, but in strict seclusion. Later they were taken to the food-privy and fed; but they were trained never to mention food in public and of course never to expose their mouths. Obscure and terrifying hints were let fall about the disastrous effects of gustatory self-indulgence. They were told not to go to the privy more than once a day, and not to stay longer than necessary. From their companions they gathered much distorted information about eating; and they were likely to contract diverse kinds of nutritive perversion, such as chewing stones and earth, biting one another or themselves for the taste of blood. Often they contracted such a prurient mania of thumb-sucking, that mouth and thumb would fester. If they escaped these perversions, it was by means of ignorant licentiousness in the food-privy. In consequence of this they were prone to contract serious digestive disorders, which moreover, if discovered, inevitably brought them into contempt. In either case they incurred a shattering sense of guilt, and contracted by auto-suggestion many of the symptoms which rumour attributed to their vice. In maturity they were likely to become either secret gourmets or puritans.

The effect of introducing Paul to this remote world was beneficial in more ways than one. Not only did it lead him gradually to regard his own sexual nature with a new tolerance and a new detachment, so that his mind was no longer tethered to the stake of sex; it also gave him a considerable insight into the mentality of his elders, and opened his eyes precociously to the farcical aspect of his species. Of course, he did not seriously believe his visions. Or rather, as the alien world embodied itself with increasing detail in his mind, he could not entirely disbelieve it, but came to regard it as 'over there', instead of 'here' like his own world. I had, of course, made him picture the Neptunian species. He glimpsed its squat stone cities, thronged with nude and bulky caricatures of his own race. He saw their mouth-aprons, and their secret vices of nutrition. He saw also their frank sexual behaviour, and actually from the study of sex in that remote age and world he learned much about sex in his own race. Not only so, but he learned his first lesson in that general detachment from the purely Terrestrial values, which I needed to produce in him. He learned, too, to scrutinize all prized and all condemned things to discover whether they were prized or condemned for their own sakes or for some other reason. For instance, comparing his fantasy world with the normal world, he saw that sexual activity and nutritive activity were both valued in both worlds, but that in each world one of these activities had gathered a purely accidental and farcical significance. On the other hand, in both worlds, love, the passionate admiration of spirit for spirit, was a genuine experience which lent something of its glory here to sex, there to nutrition.

Paul's mysterious life of imagination gave him an understanding of human nature far beyond his years. Combining with his enhanced self-consciousness, it made him strangely sympathetic yet strangely cynical. His companions regarded him as 'queer'. At most times he behaved as a rather selfish and rather cowardly boy, and he was not incapable of spite. Yet at any moment, it seemed, he might blaze up with what to his companions seemed an almost insane generosity and an entirely self-oblivious courage. At other times he displayed a disconcerting indifference and remoteness. In the middle of some wild game he would suddenly 'fade out', play his part perfunctorily or not at all, and presently be seen watching the action with an interest that was somehow not the interest of a boy.

During his schooldays Paul was generally in love with some other boy or with a girl. His erratic temperament prevented the course of true love from running even as smoothly as it does with normal young human animals. One day he would be terrifyingly earnest, next day entirely uninterested, or, worse, interested in the manner of a scientific observer. One day he would be possessive, touchy, spiteful, the next day devoted and self-oblivious. Consequently his loves were uneasy, brief, and in retrospect bitter. The more he was defeated, the more he longed for a lasting intimacy. The more he longed, the more 'impossible' he became. During the latter part of his school career he grew increasingly aware of and absorbed in human personality. It came to seem to him that the only thing of any account in life was the intimacy of one person with another, in fact with a perfect mate. His whole attention was given to the task of finding for himself the perfect mate. Gradually he began to realize that he would never succeed, and indeed that success was almost impossible. It seemed to him that human beings were doomed to miss for ever the only goal worth seeking, and that in their fated striving for it they must ever lacerate one another.

It was with this conviction that Paul ended his much-prolonged school career and embarked upon an arts course at the University of London. He was very unlike the ordinary 'freshman'. Some years older than the average, cripplingly self-conscious, scholastically backward and erratic, but equipped with a very unusual stock of random knowledge, and of insight into human nature, he seemed to his fellows an amiable but rather tiresome freak.

While he was still at the university Paul met a young woman some years older than himself, whose image was destined to be a permanent influence in his mind. From the Terrestrial point of view she was no doubt a delightful creature, though not a paragon of classical or any other recognized kind of beauty. Even to the Neptunian eye, sufficiently fortified by long Terrestrial experience, she was not without charm. Of course, very little of her was visible. Save for the face and hands, her whole body was covered and insulted by the peculiarly grotesque clothing of her period. But in her face there was something more than the prettiness which attracted the males of her own species and was a source of a certain winsome complacency in herself. There was a vitality in it which to me was elusively reminiscent of the full-blown and fully conscious beauty of women of my own species. In fact, there was a hint of the more fully human and more frankly animal spirit, which the Last Men look for in woman and the Last Woman in man. But in the eyes of her contemporaries, and in her own eyes too, this pervading characteristic of her face, of her slow free gait, and, as I was later to discover, of her body also (about which there was something of the young cart-horse), was but an oddity, a blemish. Now Paul believed that he was attracted only by her conventional prettiness. He did not know that my influence had inadvertently brought him under the spell of a beauty beyond his usual ken. He prided himself on being able, in spite of his adoration, to point out and ridicule her imperfections, and even delight in them. He did not know that these very 'imperfections' of body and mind were the source of her strange spell over him. He recognized, almost apologetically, that they made her for him lovelier, more individual, more real, more peculiarly herself. He did not recognize, though in fact he obscurely felt, that her peculiarity was not a falling short from, but a transcending of, Terrestrial beauty. Mentally she was, he felt, exquisitely complementary to himself, yet basically at one with him. She was able to appreciate and enrich his inner life of fantasy, which hitherto he had never revealed to anyone. She flattered him by regarding him as a 'genius'. He was well content that she should treat him also as a dear simpleton whose dreams were impracticable. Above all, he was strengthened by the knowledge that each had become to the other a most necessary playmate and helpmeet, and that each had already been spiritually enriched by the other for ever after.

This girl, whom I will call Katherine, took delight in 'bringing Paul out of his shell', in helping him to hold his own in social intercourse. She taught him to dance; and, though the physical contact made his head swim, he did her credit. They went to many dances, but the custom of the period forbade them to dance together more than two or three times in an evening. Dancing was at first their only opportunity of close contact; for a strange reason. This fundamentally downright and generous creature had unfortunately been educated in a puritanical tradition. Through loyalty to her father, for whom, as I later discovered, she felt a deep affection, she corseted her nature within the limits of a strict social and moral etiquette. By native constitution strong both in animal zest and in maternal tenderness, by upbringing severely conscientious, she had tried to solve the inevitable conflict between her generous vitality and her moral severity by kindliness toward others and strictness toward herself. Maintaining her own puritan conduct, she took vicarious delight in the peccadilloes of others. It was partly her combination of romantically puritanical idealism with imaginative sympathy that won Paul's respect. Her relation with Paul was at first extremely correct. It had to compensate for the restriction of its physical side by a romantic efflorescence on the mental side. They found many intellectual and aesthetic enthusiasms in common. They also inculcated in one another a common zeal for social service. He swore that in the great cause of making a better world he would 'wear always the armour of her love' so that nothing should strike him down. His own love for her would be his lance. Her beauty would be his inspiration, her sense of beauty his guiding star. Theirs was a union, they told one another, primarily of spirit and spirit. The body should fulfil its minor function, in due season.

It was extremely interesting to see how Paul acted his part during the first weeks of this intimacy. The detachment from Terrestrial values which I had been teaching him, at first enabled him to ridicule and damp down his cravings for a more sexual relationship. Neptunian fantasies helped him here. But soon they began to work on the other side also. He came to see the folly and futility of his romance. Externally he remained for long the tame squire of his beloved; but inwardly, though often he was a selfless admirer of this lovely human animal that had confided in him, sometimes he was sheer greedy sex, chafing within the bonds of decency. At other times, behind his caresses he was ice-cold, or even disgusted, or just an ironical observer, correlating events Terrestrial with events Neptunian. But for long these great inner fluctuations appeared to the beloved only as slight whimsical changes of mood, to which with maternal tact she gladly adjusted herself.

As time passed, however, Paul became more 'difficult'. Hitherto, in spite of his moods, he had seemed to the young woman absolutely safe, absolutely devoted to their common code of decency. His occasional respectful importunity flattered her without seriously disturbing her. But now his normal mood began to be penetrated with rather terrifying moments in which his personality seemed to change to something at once more cynical and more violent, more remote and more animal. Most terrifying was the fact that, to her own amazement, she could not feel disgusted, but only conscientious.

The crisis occurred on a summer evening after a dance. Paul and his beloved, flushed with exertion and mutual delight and exalted by a sense of their own daring unconventionality, escaped through the garden to the bare down that fringed their suburb. Arm in arm they walked, then seated themselves on the grass to watch the rising moon. After the usual discreet caresses, Paul extended a reverent hand and stroked her throat. His finger-tips ventured down to the white expanse of bosom, revealed by her low-cut evening dress. Surprised less by his boldness than by her own sudden delight, she caressed the caressing fingers. He ventured further, feeling his way toward her breasts. Paralysed between desire and anxiety, she allowed him to explore those warm, secret, holy excrescences.

This little tactual event, this marvellous, ecstatic new experience, affected both somewhat violently. For Paul it seemed to constitute an important new stage in that quest which had so long tormented him, the quest for reality. It seemed to fulfil, or almost fulfil, at once his hunger for sexual contact and his yearning for spiritual intimacy. It had about it a quality of home-coming after long absence, as though he had been there before in some forgotten existence. It was indeed as though the starved exile, who had for so long been nourished only on phantoms, and had lost even the memory of his motherland, were to find himself back once more in the bosom of reality, bewildered yet fundamentally at home. In her it roused both sexual warmth and also a poignant tenderness almost as of mother for babe. She was torn between a sudden longing to give herself wholly and a sudden alarm at this unprecedented invasion.

How distressed these two innocents would have been had they known that a third person was witness of this shocking deed, that another human being, a man older than Paul by some thousands of years (though not to be born till long after the earth's destruction) was noting through Paul's eyes the moonlit eyes and features of the girl, was himself caressing, though through Paul's hand, the thrilled Terrestrial breasts, and comparing them with corresponding objects upon Neptune! All these data, and also Paul's own guilty swooning ecstasy, I observed with sympathy born of the most intimate acquaintance, but also with amusement and some impatience, in spite of the detachment and remoteness of two thousand million years.

Even Paul himself was in a manner a detached spectator of his own behaviour. He himself was in a manner standing outside himself and observing these two young courting mammals. This detachment I myself had induced in him. For already at this time of his life I had trained him to be the calm spectator of his own reactions in every fervent experience. In the present case it seemed good to emphasize certain aspects of the matter for him. I therefore began to influence the course of his thoughts. As he savoured the experience, he became increasingly aware of a disturbing and fantastic under-current to his delicious perceptions. He saw with the mind's eye an early Neptunian couple engaged upon an act which to them was one of shocking licentiousness and excruciating delight, but to the Terrestrial eye was merely ridiculous. This guilty pair stood facing one another, their mouth-aprons removed. From mouth to crimson mouth there stretched a curious fruit, not unlike a much-elongated banana. With mobile lips both he and she were drawing this object into the mouth, and eating it progressively. They gazed into one another's kindled eyes, their cheeks aflame.

Clearly they were both enrapt in that exquisite sweet horror which is afforded only by the fruit that is forbidden. Paul watched the banana shrinking, the faces approaching one another. His own hand, feeling the responsive breasts, paused, lay inert. The fruit had vanished. The faces made contact in a long mumbling kiss. The vision faded. Paul was left with an agonized conflict of the sublime and the ridiculous, for it was evident to him that in this farcical scene he had witnessed the exquisite union of two impassioned spirits.

For a moment Paul stayed motionless, wondering whether to an alien eye he and Katherine would seem any less comic. Almost he decided to withdraw his hand. But now that I had forced him in the very act of single-minded zest to take an unsympathetic view, I was able to give him an exaltation which was secure against ridicule because it included ridicule. First I let him suffer in a single flash of insight the stabbing pleasure of those two Neptunians. I then flooded his mind with a spate of visions, such that he seemed to himself to be witnessing in a few seconds the whole pageant of amorous adventure. He seemed to see the earliest mutual devourings of microscopic jellies in the sea, the far-flung pollination of great trees, slow reptilian embraces, the aerial copulations of swallows, the rutting of stags, the apes' more conscious amorousness. He saw human forms, brown, yellow, black or white, in their first adventurous fondlings, or clipped together. He saw them now in caves, now in jungle lairs, now in snow huts, blubber-lit, now in lake dwellings, the water lapping the piles, now in curtained Tudor four-posters, now in jangling iron bedsteads in slums, now between fine linen sheets, now among the bushes of public gardens, furtive, struggling with clothes, now beside moorland tarns, the untrammelled limbs sun-darkened, glossy. Throughout this experience Paul retained a flavour of the earlier ludicrous scene over the forbidden fruit; but he gathered also a new sense of the deep, groping earnestness of sex. And this jerked him into one of his rare moods of heightened consciousness. The little breast and nipple beneath his hand suddenly revealed itself to him in a most poignant vision, and at the same time the individual spirit of the girl (so it seemed) was laid bare dazzlingly to his own spirit's gaze. He saw, moreover, that she wanted what he also wanted.

But now the girl, sensing a change in his mood, and feeling that something ought to be done, first pressed his hand upon her yielding breast, and then tried to extricate it. Paul felt the soft flesh crushed between his fingers. Exulting, he gripped, so vigorously that she gave a little scream. Then suddenly she found herself caught in an embrace that was altogether too frankly sexual to be tolerated. Yet, to her own surprise, she yielded to it for a moment, savouring the new experience. Then it became clear that if she was to preserve any longer that which a virtuous young lady is supposed to cherish more than life itself, she must take immediate action. She struggled, expostulated, then suddenly, greedily, seized Paul's lip between her teeth. The pain shot through him like lightning. His grip relaxed. They separated. While he mopped his bleeding mouth, she arranged her clothing, swore she would never see him again, and then retreated toward the house with all the dignity she could muster.

But they continued to meet, for each had by now become necessary to the other. The intimacy deepened. They became 'engaged', though for financial reasons they had no prospect of marriage. They saw one another every day. The solid basis of their friendship, their mental insight into one another and joy in each other's natures, compelled them to seek one another. But their love was becoming warped by the longing for that final bodily intimacy which both craved, but she dared not permit. To the Neptunian observer it was obvious that for both their sakes she ought to have cut herself away from him once and for all, or else to have yielded fully to her own desire and his. For the former course she had no will. The initial feminine reluctance, the desire to preserve herself intact, had long since given place to the no less feminine hunger to give herself and be merged with her chosen male. But an irregular union would have been intolerable to her self-respect. She was a child of her age, and her age was still in spirit, though not in date, 'nineteenth century'. Though under Paul's influence she had recently begun to modify her puritanism, and now liked to think of herself as 'modern' and unconventional, there was a point beyond which she dared not go.

The months passed. Paul became more and more obsessed. He thought of nothing but love-making and his own unhappy situation. It became neecssary that he should stagnate no longer; for the year 1914 was approaching, in which he must be fully recovered from all the fevers of adolescence. I therefore decided to interfere. Two courses were open to me. Either I could make the girl give herself, or I could remove her. From the Neptunian point of view the obvious course was to let Paul have his way, and gain the little treasure of experience that would thus be added to him. In many ways they would both have benefited. They would have found new health and vigour of body, and for a while new peace and vitality of mind. But I knew that, harmless and invigorating as this culmination would have been for other individuals and in another society, for these two young Terrestrials it would have brought disaster. In the first place, they might have inadvertently produced a new individual of their species; and then both mother and child, and the young father also, would have been persecuted by the barbarian society in which they lived. I judged that such an experience would render Paul unfit for my experiment. It would have tethered his attention for too long to the personal. Secondly, they would have suffered a spiritual disaster, for they themselves both accepted the code which they would have infringed. Had I driven them on to taste their innocuous, pretty, forbidden fruit, they would soon have become a burden to one another. With the inevitable cooling of ardour they would have assumed a false obligation each to the other, and at the same time they would have lapsed into guilty disgust, recriminations and moral degradation. This would have side-tracked Paul's attention for too long a period.

I therefore decided to remove the girl. To do this I had first to enter her mind and discover how I might conveniently effect my purpose. Poor child, she would indeed have been overwhelmed with shame and horror had she known that for several weeks all her most private acts and secret thoughts were observed by a hidden, an indwelling and a male spectator. I was, for instance, present one Saturday night while she lowered her still coltish body into a hot bath, tingling and gasping as the heat devoured her. I detected her mind's quick backward glance at Paul's devouring but unfulfilled embraces. I noted also that she let the hot water flow and the temperature of the bath rise till she was on the verge of agony, before she finally sat up and turned off the tap. I was present also at her dreams, in which so often she let Paul have his way, before she woke and was regretfully thankful it had only been a dream.

A brief study of her personality sufficed to show just which of the young men in her environment would best suit her nature. I turned her attention in his direction; rather roughly, I fear, for I noticed that she began to have doubts of her sanity. In self-pride and in compassion for Paul she clung for a while to the old love, but in vain. She struggled desperately against her fate, bitterly ashamed of her impotence and fickleness. But by a kind of inner hypnotism I forced her to receive into her heart the image of the new love that I had chosen for her. I made her dwell on his admirable and charming qualities, and I blinded her to his somewhat grotesque appearance. Very soon I had made her undertake a vigorous, almost shameless campaign upon him. Much to his surprise and delight, much to the bewilderment of their mutual friends, this unassuming but prosperous young merchant found himself the adored adorer of one who hitherto had treated him merely with calm kindness. I now filled the bemused young woman with immodest haste for the wedding. Within a few weeks the pair did actually enter into a union which, owing to my careful selection, was quite the most successful marriage of their generation. I bore in mind, however, that it would later become desirable to bring her once more into relation with Paul.

While these events were proceeding I was in a sense resident in two minds at once; for when I had done my work upon the girl, I returned to Paul at the very instant in which I had left him. Thus I was able to watch his reactions to the whole drama, and to help him triumph in his defeat.

When first he had begun to suspect that she was turning away from him, he plunged into a more determined suit. But I was now very constantly treating him with visions and meditations of an impersonal kind, which so drenched his wooing that it became less persuasive than disturbing. In fact, by philosophical and poetical extravagances he frightened Katherine into the arms of his rival. When at last he learned of the marriage, he passed, of course, through a phase of self-pitying despair; but within a fortnight he was already, through my influence, no less than through native resilience, beginning to explore a very different field of experience.

425

2. PAUL DEVOUT

When Paul had recovered from the first shock of his misfortune, he emerged to find himself painfully oscillating between two moods. In the one he strove to protect his wounded soul under a bright new armour of cynicism. She was just an animal, and her behaviour was the expression of obscure physiological events. And so, after all, was his own. The love that he so prized had no intrinsic virtue whatever. In the other mood, however, he clung to the faith that though this love of his had foundered, nevertheless love, the mutual insight and worship of one human person for another, was good in itself, and indeed the supreme good of life. All other goods, it seemed, were either negligible, or instrumental to this greatest good. He had recently lived for many weeks on a plane that was formerly beyond him. Now in his loneliness he began to go over again and again the treasure that he had acquired, namely his new and overwhelmingly vivid and delightful apprehension of a particular human being, called Katherine. Bitter as was his loneliness, this treasure could never be taken from him. And the more he pored over it, the more he asked himself whether it was exceptional, or whether it was a fair sample of existence. Hitherto he had increasingly thought of the universe in terms of mechanical intricacies and the huge star-sprinkled darkness, or at best in terms of a vital but impersonal trend of all things toward some goal inconceivable to man. But now he began to regard all this as mere aridity in which there was no abiding place for the one superlative excellence, human personality, love-inspired. It was borne in upon him at last with new significance that love was 'divine'. He began to find a new and lucid meaning for the brave statement, 'God is Love'. It meant, surely, that this best of all things known to man was also present in spheres beyond man's sphere; that human personality and love were not the only nor the highest forms of personality and love; that Love, with a capital L, Love which was not merely a relation between persons but somehow itself a Person, an all-pervading and divine Person, was after all the governing power of the universe. If this were indeed so, as many professed to believe, then all human loves must, in spite of temporary frustration, be secure of eternal fulfilment. Even his love for Katherine and her no less divine, though now distracted, love for him must somehow, 'in eternity', have its fruition.

I must not here describe the struggle that took place in Paul's mind between his cynical and his devotional impulses. It was a fluctuating battle. Wandering along Gower Street, with his hands in the pockets of his grey flannel trousers, and half a dozen books under his arm, he would breathe in cheerfulness with the dilute spring air of London, till, as he pursued his course round Bedford Square, God was once more in his heaven. In Charing Cross Road he would stray into the 'Bomb Shop', and be confronted with new doubts. Walking over the spot where subsequently Nurse Cavell's monument was to proclaim her courage and her country-men's vulgarity, the poor boy would sometimes be infected by a momentary and unintelligible horror, derived from my own fore-seeing mind. Soon the placid bustle of the great railway station would bring comfort once more; but on the journey to his southern suburb he would be flung again into despair by the faces of sheep, cattle, pigs and monkeys that masked the spirits of his fellow-travellers. Then at last, walking bare-headed on the suburban down that overhung his home, Paul might once more, though rather wearily, believe in God.

It seemed to Paul that in his cynical mood he was definitely smaller, meaner and more abject than when he was once more unfurling on the battlements of his own heart the banner of his faith in the God of Love. In many of his contemporaries also much the same fluctuation of mood was occurring, and to them as to Paul it seemed that the issue lay between the old faith, how-ever modernized, and the complete abnegation of human dignity. Yet Paul and his contemporaries were mistaken. It was not in faith but in utter disillusionment and disgust that the human spirit had to triumph, if ever it was to triumph at all.

While he was absorbed in his religious perplexity, Paul was intrigued by a group of fellow-students whose aim it was to solve the troubles of the modern world by making modern men and women into sincere Christians. They introduced him to a young priest, whom the whole group regarded as their spiritual leader. At first this young man's emphatic hand-grip and earnest gaze roused in Paul nothing but a new variant of the disgust and suspicion which, long ago, he had felt toward the ghastly heartiness of the family doctor. He was also repelled by the fact that the elect secretly referred to their master as the Archangel. But as he became better acquainted with the priest, he, like the others, began to fall under his spell. To Paul in his new phase of reverence for human personality, his new revulsion from 'materialism', this man appeared as a spiritual aristocrat, as one who could move about the world without being swallowed up by the world, without so much as dirtying his feet. He was 'other-worldly', not in the sense that he sought to escape from this world, but that he carried round with him an atmosphere which was not this world's atmosphere. Like those water-insects which take down with them into the deep places a bubble of air for breathing, he took down with him into this world a celestial ether to maintain his spiritual life.

So it seemed to Paul. But to his Neptunian guest the matter did not appear in the same light. During Paul's love affair I had of course to put up with much that was tedious and banal, but I had been constantly refreshed by the underlying simplicity and sincerity of the amorous couple. In the new incident, however, I had to watch Paul indulging in a very tiresome self-deception. He allowed his admiration for the person of this young priest to obscure his view of the universe. This aberration was indeed a necessary phase in his growth, a necessary process in the preparation of the experimental culture upon which I was to operate. But it was none the less a tiresome phase for the observer. Not that Paul's new enthusiasm was wholly misguided. Far from it. Even from the Neptunian point of view, this 'Archangel' was indeed in a limited sense a spiritual aristocrat, for undoubtedly he was gifted with a vision and a moral heroism impossible to most of his fellows. But he was an aristocrat debased by circumstance. He had not been able to resist an environment which was spiritually plebeian. Though in his life he faithfully expressed what he called the superhuman humanity of his God, he almost wholly failed to do justice to another and more austere feature of his own vision, a feature which indeed he never dared fully to acknowledge, even to himself, since in terms of his own religious dogma it appeared starkly as a vision of superhuman inhumanity.

Paul saw the Archangel often and in many circumstances, in

public meetings, at the homes of his followers, and at the boys' club which the priest had organized for the young 'rough diamonds' of his dockland parish. He saw him also at his church services. These impressed Paul in a perplexing manner. He noted, at first with some misgiving, the setting in which they took place, the scant and rather smelly congregation, so uncomprehending, but so obviously devoted to the person of the priest; the debased Gothic architecture and strident coloured windows; the music, so historic, so trite, yet to Paul so moving, the surpliced urchins of the choir, furtively sucking sweets, the paraphernalia of the altar, brass and velvet; the muffled noise of traffic in the great thoroughfare outside; and the occasional interruptions by some ship's steam-whistle as she nosed her way through the Thames fog toward China or the Argentine. In the midst of all this stood the tall, white-robed, fair-haired Archangel, intoning with that restrained yet kindling voice of his, which to Paul in his more devout mood made the hackneyed words of the service novel, urgent, significant with a piercing, blinding lucidity. In his rarer cynical mood, however, the same performance seemed no more meaningful than the ritual phrases of a parrot.

The Archangel's influence on Paul was partly physical. The younger man was attracted by the still athletic figure, the delicate firm lips, the finely cut aquiline nose. They seemed to him to embody ages of righteousness. In the priest's manner, too, he found a strong attraction. It soothed him, like a cool hand on the brow. Yet also it gripped him and shook him into life. But chiefly Paul was impressed by the man's sublime confidence, almost arrogance, in his own religious faith and practice, and by his lively bantering affection for the straying sheep of his flock. Paul's faith was weak. His love of his fellow-men was more theoretical than practical. But the Archangel, seemingly, was a real Christian. He practised what he preached. He really did love his fellows, not merely as savable souls but as unique individuals. He really did see something peculiar and beautiful in each person. He accepted others as he found them, and served them with the same spontaneity as a man serves his own needs. Through him Paul began at last to feel a real warmth toward his fellow human animals, and in doing so he felt exultantly that he was definitely rising to an ampler and more

generous life. Because of this he became extremely ready to receive
the metaphysical implications of the Archangel's religion, which
also had been the religion of his own childhood, seldom seriously
contemplated but always absent-mindedly believed.

Paul fancied that he now saw at last, with almost the intuitive
certainty of elementary mathematics, not only that the governing
principle of the universe was love, but that the actual embodiment
of that love was Jesus. Moreover, under the influence of the Archangel, who had been stimulated by Paul's searching questions to
make statements of doubtful orthodoxy, Paul now affirmed that
the universe was celestial through and through, that all things
in it, including Satan, worked together for the perfect expression
of love, the perfect expression of the nature of Jesus. And the
nature of Jesus, Paul learned not from the Bible but from contemplation of the Archangel. For the Archangel was very obviously
sustained from morning till evening by a sense of the presence
of his divine master. All who came near him were infected with
something of this sense. He radiated a conviction of the ultimate
rightness of all things, and at the same time he fired men with a zeal
for putting the apparently wrong things right. Not that he was a
mere stained-glass saint. Paul was proudly, lovingly conscious of
the Archangel's vivid humanity, even of his little weaknesses,
which served greatly to endear him to his admirers. He had, for
instance, a quaint passion for raisins. After a trying day he would
eat them by the handful, almost defiantly. They seemed to have for
him the double attraction of the grape's sacred and profane significance.

Little by little Paul became an earnest Christian. Deep down in his
breast, rather than in his mind, he argued thus, 'Can such a
perfect being as the Archangel be mistaken about God? He is too
wise. Can he be deceiving me? He is too sincere, too loving. If this
man says that God is Love, it is so.' If ever his doubts returned, he
would run to the Archangel to gain strength to abolish them. Once
when this had happened, and the two were talking in the priest's
sitting-room, before a fire that radiated optimism, while the
landlady's cat lay asleep on the hearth-rug, Paul had what he
considered a real religious experience. The Archangel had been
patiently throttling Paul's doubts. 'Hang on to this, Paul,' he said,

'Love alone matters. And whatever is needed in the world for the existence of love is justified. What kind of a world is it that we actually find around us? I don't mean your beloved stars and nebulae and your pettifogging laws of nature. No doubt they are marvellous, and all part of God's house. But they are only the floor-boards. I mean the human world. What do you find there? You find Satan still at large. He always was, and always will be, till time is finished. And why? Because love that has not got to be for ever fighting is no more love than the unborn babe is a man. And so, Paul, we must thank God that, of his great love for us, he made Satan to torment us.' He paused, then continued: 'That's heresy! You see what happens if one thinks too much about these old problems. Think of Christ only. *Feel* his god-head. Can't you feel his presence in this room now?'

The Archangel raised his hand and looked at Paul as though listening to angel choirs. For some moments both remained silent. Gradually it came to seem to Paul that the room was all alive, all aglow, all a-murmur with a presence. Was it the presence of this man? Yes, but surely also it was the presence of Jesus. The room? Nay, the universe. The whole universe, it seemed, was somehow gathered into that room, and the whole of it was manifestly infused with the divine love. Everything was warm and bright, tender and true, or else heroically triumphant over an Evil that was not merely defeated but somehow shown never to have been really evil at all. To the adoring Paul it seemed that the very stars and outer universes came flocking into that little room, like lambs, to be comforted by this Shepherd, this supreme Archangel Jesus. They brought with them their little troubles, their sore feet and their stomachaches, and he, with the magic of his love, cured these little troubles so miraculously that they never had existed at all, save as occasions for his love. Paul and the universes nestled together like little white lambs in the bosom of this Love. Once more it seemed to him that he had made contact with reality, that he had penetrated this time surely to the very heart of the universe. The experience was very wonderful, very strange, yet also mysteriously familiar, with the familiarity of some forgotten existence, an existence so remote that it seemed entirely outside time. It seemed to Paul that an immense energy flooded in upon him. He felt in himself the ancient, the

431

longed-for strength of faith. At last, after all his barren years, he was tense with a new vitality, fully charged, ready to spend himself in a new effulgent life.

The smiling, transfigured Archangel laid a hand on Paul's knee. Paul said, 'At last I feel Jesus.'

Now while Paul and the Archangel were yielding themselves to this glamorous experience, there was indeed a 'presence' with them in the room, though one of a very different nature from that which these two Terrestrial animals themselves had conjured in their imaginations. It was the presence of a man who had seen human species after human species wrest for itself out of chaos some slight amenity and some precarious faith, only to collapse into misery, into despair, often into agony. It was the presence of one who himself looked forward to the impending extinction of Man; who found in this event, and in all existence, overmastering beauty indeed, but for the love-sick human individual no consolation. Strange that it was my presence in Paul's mind, my coldly scrutinizing presence, that had lent actuality to his sense of union with the God of Love! The exhortation of the priest had made him notice in himself an obscure feeling which had already on earlier occasions fleetingly disturbed him with a sense that in some way he was 'possessed'. I now found him peering, as it were, into the recesses of his being in search of the source of this feeling, believing that what he would see would be the love-gaze of Jesus. Had he discovered what it was that actually 'possessed' him, had he come, so to speak, face to face with his Neptunian parasite, his vision would have been shattered, and no doubt he would have taken me for the Devil. But I was at pains to elude detection. Mentally I held my breath, as it were, lest any slight movement of my mind should reveal more of me than that vague 'presence' which he had so fantastically misinterpreted.

It was not easy for me to maintain my immobility, for the spectacle of Paul's fervour stirred me deeply, both toward pity and toward laughter. For what was it that was happening to him? Apart from the complication of my 'presence', which lent a spurious actuality to his vision, his experience was an epitome of the religious history of the First Human Species, a pitiable confusion of factors irrelevant to one another. In the first place Paul, partly through the wealth of cosmic imagery with which I had already drenched him, had indeed come face to face with the majesty of the universe. In the second place he had with Katherine experienced very vividly the great excellence which is called love. But the Christian tradition, working on him through his revered priest, had combined with his own desire so as to persuade him to attribute love to the pitiless universe itself. This confusion was caused partly by a trick played upon him by his own remote past. For the strange familiarity and the delicious consolation and peace which Paul had savoured in this religious moment were after all but an echo of his own obscure yearning for the tenderness of the breast and the elysium of the womb.

Henceforth Paul thought of himself as a soldier of Christ. He undertook a campaign of asceticism and general discipline. For instance, he made rules to limit his eating. When he succeeded in keeping them, the only result was that he rose from every meal with a wolfish craving, and thoughts of food haunted him throughout the day. He tried sleeping on his bedroom floor, but always before the night was over he crept guiltily into bed. His self-discipline was always half-hearted and ineffective, for he had no real faith in its spiritual efficacy. He did it, not with the earnestness of the God-hungry soul, but because earnestly religious persons were supposed to do so, and he wanted to be one of them.

Paul found great satisfaction in doing odd jobs for the Archangel. He took up work at the boys' club. Unfortunately he soon found that he was not much good with boys, having few of the attributes which they admired. He was useless at boxing and billiards, useless at back-chat. And he had no authority, for in his heart he was frightened of the boys. But for the Archangel's sake, and also for self-discipline, he stuck to the club. Finally he took charge of the canteen. He was cheated over halfpence, and at the end of the evening he basely made up the losses out of his own pocket. In intervals of selling coffee and buns he sat behind the counter reading. But this furtive practice caused him much heart-searching; and when the Archangel was about, he put his book away and tried to be genial with the boys.

Paul succeeded in persuading himself that nearly all his actions were expressions of his master-motive, to be a soldier of Christ in the modern world. But as a matter of fact he had many quite independent interests. He lived a varied and often hilarious life with the little band of the Archangel's student admirers. He had also several tentative amorous passages. He worked industriously and with some success. He read much contemporary literature and some popular science. But all his scientific thought he censored rigorously for religion's sake.

Paul's religious fervour expressed itself chiefly not in action but in writing free verse of a quasi-biblical character. He persuaded himself that he had an 'urge' to produce verbal formulations of his spiritual experience, that he was 'inspired'. But to his parasite it was clear that what he produced in this phase was not wrung from him by the intensity of experience. These poems were but literary exercises, imitative in technique, and seldom vitalized by any original imagination. The Archangel applauded these effusions because they were correct in sentiment, but he regarded them as merely play, not as a man's work for God. He could not perceive that though they failed they meant much to Paul. It is worth while to give one example for the light which it throws on Paul's mind at this time.

MEN

Behold the sons of men,
who sin,
whose hearts are divine!
In selfishness they heap misery on one another;
yet for love they die.
They are blown about like dead leaves;
yet for love they stand firm.
For bread they trample one another,
yet for a dream they die.
Scatter gold among them, and they are beasts;
show them God, and they are sons of God.

3. PAUL FACES THE FACTS

Without my help it might have taken Paul some years to outgrow his phase of mental obedience and spiritual confusion. But time was pressing. I needed him to be well-advanced in his next phase at the close of his university career, so that he might be prepared to meet the crisis of 1914 in a significant manner. Therefore, when I had allowed him some months of play in his little Christian nursery, I began once more to exercise my influence upon him. I infiltrated him with images of cosmical majesty and horror, with apprehensions of human weakness and meanness and agony, with doubts and questions intolerable to his religion.

During the previous two years Paul had come across a number of distressing facts about the world, but he had contrived to see them in the rosy light of his religion. These experiences now, through my influence, began to haunt him. At all times of the day and night he was now liable to sinister visual and auditory images, either taken intact from his own past, or reconstructed in still more repugnant forms. It was as though hitherto he had been wandering in a luxuriant but volcanic land in which only now and again he had encountered the blow-holes and sulphurous jets of nether chaos; but now, it seemed, the whole terrain was heaving, cracking, belching under his feet. Over his books in his own comfortable suburban home he would be distressed by visions of the slum-tenement homes that he had visited when he was working for an 'after-care' committee. And somehow they seemed more sordid and overcrowded in imagination than in reality. While he was walking on the down, he would remember with abnormal distinctiveness a brawl that he had once witnessed in the East End. Bottles were thrown. A man's face was cut. A woman was knocked over. Her head came against the kerbstone with an audible crack, like the collision of bowls on a green. While he was reading or eating or walking, and especially while he was lying in bed and not yet asleep, faces would confront him; faces which, when he had encountered them in actuality, had seemed but opaque masks, grey, pinched, flabby, or purplish and bloated, but now in imagination revealed their underlying personalities to him with harrowing expressiveness. For I permitted him to see them as they would have appeared to a Neptunian fresh from the world of the Last Men. He had once been shown over a lunatic asylum. The faces that now haunted him were, he recognized, faces of sane men and women, yet they reminded him distressingly of those imbecile faces. Faces

of all kinds they were, young and old, business men, fashionable
women, unshaven labourers, clerks, young bloods, lawyers; all
pushing themselves forward at him, leering, smirking, whimpering,
impressing, imploring, all so intent, so self-important, so blind.
Somehow they reminded him of cheap ornate lamps, rusty,
shop-soiled, and never lit. The queer phrase 'blind lamps' reiterated itself to him on these occasions. Another image haunted him
in connexion with these faces, and seemed to him to summarize
them all and symbolize the condition of his species. It was an
image which I constructed in his mind in detail and with verisimilitude, and endowed with a sense of familiarity, though in fact it
was not derived from his past but from his future experience during
the war. He seemed to see, lying in mud, a dead mare, already
decaying. From its hindquarters, which were turned towards him,
there projected the hideously comical face of its unborn foal. The
first time he encountered this apparition Paul was at a political
meeting. Before him on the platform sat a company of politicians,
city worthies and their wives. A cabinet minister was perorating.
Suddenly Paul saw the foal, and in a flash recognized its expression
in the speaker, in the ladies and gentlemen on the platform, in the
audience. His gorge rose, he thought he was going to vomit. Stum-
bling over his neighbour's feet, he fled out of the hall. Henceforth
he was very prone to see the foal, at lectures, at dances, in church.
Even in the Archangel's smile he sometimes recognized with
horror that foetal grin.

Another type of imagery and of thought I also forced on Paul
at this time. I first impelled him to read works of contemporary
literature and science which were discountenanced by the Archangel. Furtively he began to return to the interests that had been
roused in him before he came to the university, interests in the intricacy of the physical world, in the types of living things, in the
theory of evolution, in the astronomical immensities. But whereas
formerly these things delighted him, now they terrified him, even
while they fascinated. I took care that they should haunt him with
imagery. He had curious sensations as of sweeping with increasing
speed through space, while the stars streamed past him like harbour
lights. Sometimes it seemed to him that he was dropping into the
tumultuous and incandescent vapours of the sun. Sometimes he

glimpsed spinning worlds, parched and airless, uninhabited, meaningless.

When Paul had been subjected to this violent influence for some weeks, he began, like many of his contemporaries, to find a kind of consolation in the theory of evolution, romantically interpreted. It made worm and ant and man fellow-workers in a great cause. Exactly what they were all working for, he did not know; nor could he justify his strong conviction that, though all had achieved something, man was doing far more than the others, and might yet do infinitely better. Those thrusting imbecile faces that haunted him, and were the faces of his fellow-men and himself, those foal faces, were really not men at all, not what men should be and might be, any more than the grinning and putrefying foal was a horse. Gallantly Paul now began to convince himself that the whole universe was striving toward some supreme expression of life, though blindly in conflict with itself, torturing itself. He wrote a poem in which man appeared as 'the germ of the cosmic egg'. Later he tore it up and wrote another in which the cosmic egg was said to consist entirely of germs, each of which was trying to devour the others and include their substance in its own expanding form. In another he declared that God was 'the Soul of the World, striving to wake'. He put great pains into the making of these verses, and had a sense of vision and achievement such as he had never known before. One short poem I quote, as it shows clearly the rebirth of my influence in him and the quickening of his own imagination.

EVANESCENCE

As a cloud changes,
so changes the earth.
Coasts and valley,
and the deep-rooted hills
fade.
They last but for a little while;
as cloud-tresses among the rocks,
they vanish.
And as a smile gleams and fades.
so for a very little while,
Life rejoices the earth.

> From the beginning fire,
> then frost, endless.
> And between, the swift smile, Life.
> From the beginning fire,
> then frost, endless,
> and between,
> Mind.

Paul ventured to show these poems to the Archangel. The young author was diffident about them, and did not expect them to be taken very seriously; but the manner in which the Archangel received them was something of a shock to him. Gently but also emphatically the priest told him that he was in danger of serious heresy. God could not be the soul of the world, since he had created the world and would survive the world. As for the cosmic egg, still more the evanescence of life in the universe, Paul ought to realize that such bizarre ideas were dangerous, since they obscured the central fact of religion, namely the direct and eternal intercourse between God and man. Surely that amazing fact was far more interesting than these grotesque fancies. Paul was so upset that he turned actually dizzy and faint. No wonder, for here was the being whom he respected above all others and even took to be in some manner divine, condemning ideas which to Paul himself seemed to have very far-reaching and very beautiful significance.

This experience was the beginning of a long period of heart-searching in which Paul became increasingly aware of being torn in two directions, namely, toward the Archangel and toward something which he could not yet at all clearly see. He began to oscillate between two moods. One was a mood of interest in personality and the personal God whom man had rightly or wrongly conceived in his own image. The other was a mood of revulsion from man and his God, and of interest in all that vastness within which man is but a tremulous candle-flame, very soon to be extinguished. He could not integrate these moods in one. Yet whichever was the mood of the day, he felt obscurely but strangely that it was incomplete, that somehow the other was just as necessary, though at the moment he could not feel it. On the one hand was the Archangel, and Jesus, and all the humbler beauties of human persons. On the other was the rippled lake, the stars, the whole vast intricacy of nature. On the one hand was Love, and on the other the more mysteriously beautiful thing, Fate. And Life, how did Life relate itself to this profound dichotomy of the spirit? When he was in what he called the Archangel mood, he could without difficulty extend his interest so as to regard the story of evolution as the story of a great crusade of myriads of spirits freely striving to achieve some glorious end in praise of God, and sacrificing themselves by the way in myriads of casualties. When he was in the mood of the stars, he regarded the same great story as one somewhat intricate system of wave-trains spreading its innumerable undulations in ever-widening, ever-fading circles on the surface of existence, presently to vanish. Strange that, so long as he remained in the mood of the stars, this thought did not outrage him. He accepted it, not with reluctance, but with joy.

It was while he was still only beginning to discover the existence of these two moods in himself that Paul had to decide once and for all what he would do in the world. The Archangel said, 'If your faith is secure, prepare to become a priest of the one God. If it is not secure, find some solid practical work to do in the service of man.' Paul's faith was not secure. On the other hand, he dreaded the thought of being caught up in the mills of business or industry. And he did seriously desire to play some part in the great work of salvation. If it was not for him to turn men's attention to Jesus, at least he might turn the attention of the young to the many lovely features of existence. After much agonized hesitation he finally decided that he must become a teacher. He therefore persuaded his family to let him take a diploma, hoping that a thorough preparation would do away with his proved incompetence with boys. At the outbreak of the European War he was about to take up his first post, in one of the large suburban secondary schools of the Metropolis.

For some months Paul was engaged on what seemed to him a life and death struggle in two entirely different spheres. While he was desperately trying to acquire the art of teaching, he was at the same time, and increasingly, concerned with an unprecedented fact in his world, namely, the European War. Presently this fact gave rise to a new and bewildering personal problem, namely, the problem of his own conduct in a war-racked world.

At the school he had set out to inspire his pupils with the love of 'culture'. In fact he took the work very seriously. He spent many hours in preparation and correction, but was always behindhand, and therefore in class always uncertain. The boys soon found him out, and took delight in tripping him. He became more and more insecure. On the side of discipline also he came to grief, though he had excellent theories on this subject. Discipline, he argued, should be self-imposed, not imposed by others. Unfortunately such discipline is the most difficult to inculcate, especially amongst rebellious young animals who have been brought up on something different. Paul himself had none of that native and unconscious authority which alone could have ensured success in such circumstances. The boys soon found that good sport was to be had by baiting him. He changed his method, and tried to impose order, but could achieve no more than a partial suppression of disorder. The more tyrannous his control, the more gleefully did rebellion raise her hydra heads. Things came to such a pass that one afternoon when the last class was over, and the boys had stampeded away along the corridor, Paul, seated upon his dais, dropped his head forward on his chalk-dusty hands. I felt tears trickle through his fingers on to the desk. The syllables of a desperate prayer formed themselves in his throat and on his lips. 'Oh, God, oh, God,' he cried, 'make me different from what I am.' It seemed to him that he had reached the very rock-bottom of despair. For this despair was more acutely conscious, more precisely formulated than any of his earlier despairs. He was a grown man (so he imagined), and completely incompetent to deal with life. In adolescence his dread had been that he himself would miss fulfilment, that he would 'get stuck', stranded, and never explore the promised lands of life. But now he dreaded far more (so he persuaded himself) that he would never be able to do anything even of the humblest order 'to the glory of God'. This was now his master motive, to pull his weight, to do a man's work, to be able to look his fellows in the eyes and say, 'Of course I am nothing out of the common, but you can see that I am pulling my weight.' He longed to cut adrift and start all over again at something else. But at what? Outside his little

prison there was nothing but the war. The boys were already skil-
fully torturing him about the war. Then why did he not go? He
would make a wretched soldier, but the Government said that
every one was needed. Even if he merely got himself shot, he would
have 'done his bit'. And he would be quit of all this misery.

For some while he continued to lie with his head in one hand,
while the other crumpled the harsh black folds of his gown. To go
and be a soldier. What did it really mean? Military discipline.
Doing stupid things just because you were told to. Pushing
bayonets into straw dummies, and later into live bellies. Feeling
those jagged shell splinters tear through your own flesh and bones.
It was all inconceivably horrible. But apparently it had to be,
since Civilization was in danger. Then surely he *must* go. And how
good to be out of all this fiasco of teaching. Anything was better
than that. How good to surrender one's conscience into the keeping
of the army. That way surely lay peace of mind. Like surrendering
your conscience to the Church. Give it to a general to look after.
Yes, he must not stand aside any longer from the great spiritual
purification and revival that the Archangel said was coming out of
the war. It had begun already. The war was helping people to get
out of themselves, helping them to see Jesus. The Archangel said
so. Yes, he would enlist. Then there would be nothing to do but to
obey, be courageous, relentless. Then all his troubles would be
escaped. Just set your teeth and be a hero. So easy, compared with
this work that was simply beyond him. He looked at his watch.
Late! And he wanted to get his hair cut before catching the train
home. Hurriedly he began to gather up his books.

Then he paused. Once more he bowed over the desk. Must he
really help in their stupid war, their filthy, mad, backward-looking
war, that was wrecking the civilization it was meant to save. It was
like saving a man from death by an operation that was bound to be
fatal. People said war was better than dishonour. But from the
world point of view war *was* dishonour. Nothing was so base as war.
Better far that the Germans should overrun Belgium, France,
England. But no. The Archangel said this was all wrong. He said
Jesus was definitely on our side. What was the truth about it all,
what was the truth? 'Jesus, Jesus, help me, if you ever help any one.
Why am I alive? What is it all for? Why is there this terrible

world? Why are we all so horrible?' Jesus did not answer. Paul lay still, his mind almost blank; then he yawned, raised his head, and rested his chin on his hand. He had no further thoughts. He gazed vacantly at the chalk-grains on the desk.

At this point I undertook a serious intervention in Paul's mind. As he gazed at the minute white points of the chalk, I induced him to regard them as stars in the Milky Way. I then made him blow upon the desk. The whole galaxy shifted, spread outwards, streamed down the sloping board; thousands of stars tumbled into the abyss. Paul watched, fascinated. Then he shuddered and covered his face with his hands. I now flooded his astonished mind with images and ideas. In imagination he still saw the star-dust streaming, whirling. But I made him seize, with miraculous vision, one out of all the myriad suns, round which circled infinitesimal planets. One of these planets his piercing eye regarded minutely. He watched its surface boiling, seething, settling into oceans and continents. Then with supernaturally penetrative eyes, he saw in the tidal waters of the ever-fluctuating, drifting continents the living Scum, our ancestor. He saw it propagate, spread, assume a thousand forms, invade the oceans and the lands. He saw forests creep over the plains; and with his magically piercing vision he detected among the greenery a sparse dust of beasts. Reptiles clambered, ran, took wing, or reached up to crunch the tree-tops. In a twinkling they vanished. Then beneath his eyes a finer and more vital dust, the mammals, was blown into every land. Now the tempo of his vision slowed, slowed. Man, super-simian, sprinkled the valleys with his hovels, the lake-shallows with his huts, the hill-tops with his megaliths. He set fire to the forests, tilled the plains, built cities, temples, palaces, Nilotic pyramids, Acropolis. Along thread-like imperial roads the legionaries percolated, like blood corpuscles. Upon a minute hill, beside a city wall, a minute crowd existed and vanished. Presently there was a rash of churches, then little smoke-clouds of wars and revolutions, then a sudden tissue of steel tracks and murky blotches. And now to Paul's straining eyes there appeared for an instant a little crooked line stretching across Europe. On either side of this line wave-trains drifted, infinitely faint, confused, but unmistakable. Wave-trains of grey, blue, khaki, were seen to advance upon the line from East and West, recoiling in feebler undulation athwart their own advancing successors. They vanished. The tempo of the vision accelerated. Aeons rushed headlong into pastness. The minute continents deformed themselves. The little sun shrank, faded to a red spark; and as it did so the little planet became snowy white, a simple chalk-grain, which presently was lost in obscurity. The sun-spark was snuffed out. Paul's gaze seized upon another sun. This also was snuffed out. One by one, thousand by thousand, all the stars were extinguished, till the whole galaxy had vanished. There was nothing left but darkness. It seemed to Paul that the dark flooded into his mind, wave upon wave. In vain he battled against it. The spirit of night had triumphed. His mind reeled, sickened, sank into unconsciousness. He lay still, with open eyes unseeing. But though he was now profoundly tranced, I, who had worked this change in him, still perceived through all his sense organs. I felt the slight indigestion that had been aggravating his despond. I felt the constriction of his collar, which was rather too small for him. Presently I felt a fly walk across his eyeball. He took no notice. But I, fearing that his trance might break too soon, caused his hand to drive away the intruder, and soothe the irritation. Once more he lay still.

When at length Paul emerged from this swoon, he found himself recalling with strange distinctness the tarn where long ago he had first watched the intersecting waves. In imagination he watched them now, progressing, interlacing, fading, reappearing in varying patterns on every quarter of the lake. On the actual occasion, they had roused in him little more than intellectual curiosity; but now they had acquired such grave significance that every briefest flurry, every ripple, seemed to imprint its form upon his own being. At first he resisted, though vainly. But soon the insistent rhythms calmed him to acquiescence. He let them mould him, re-form him, as they willed; and in this passivity he found peace. Presently he raised his head, sat up, looked round at the desks, the maps, the grey fields of the windows, his chalky hands, the clumsy writing of some 'exercises' awaiting correction. All was as before, yet all was now acceptable, strangely right, even beautiful. Under his breath he whispered 'God! What a fool I was not to see it long ago!'

He looked at his watch, gathered up his things, and hurried

away. In his step I felt a new buoyancy, in the stream of his thoughts a new and bracing freshness. Soon, no doubt, he would return to his former despair, but the memory of this experience would never wholly desert him.

At this point I left Paul, and returned to my own world. My first task was to work up the material which I had gathered from Paul and others, and to make it known to my colleagues. Next I took that holiday which was described at the outset of this book. I also participated in the awakening of the Racial Mind. Then at last I came back to Paul, re-discovering him, not precisely at the date where I had left him, but a few days later. The good that I had worked in him seemed already to have disappeared. I found him, as I have already reported, in an agony of indecision, tortured by little incidents in the streets of London.

It will be necessary to tell how Paul finally tackled his war problem. But for the present we must leave him. My concern with him is incidental to my main theme. He is but an instrument through which I chose to observe your world, and through which I choose to exhibit your world to you. He is also a sample of that world. I have shown the instrument in some detail, and I have displayed the sample; warning you that, though peculiarly significant, it is not an average sample. You have seen that Paul, when he came face to face with the war, was already at grips with certain problems which are in fact the supreme problems of your age. Let me close this chapter by enumerating them. There was the problem of 'the flesh' and 'the spirit', the problem of human personality and evolving Life, the problem of the divinity of love and the austerity of fate. It was with these problems already troubling consciousness or stirring in regions deeper than consciousness, that all the more developed members of your species faced the war.

I now pass on to tell you how your war and your reactions to your war appear to the Last Men.

V *Origins Of The European War*

1. THE NEPTUNIAN ATTITUDE TO THE WAR

IN your Homeric saga the human conflict is observed and swayed by invisible but mighty presences. The achievement of each hero is the issue not simply of his own virtue but of the inspiration and machination of some favouring divinity. The gods and goddesses take sides, some with the Greeks, others with the Trojans.

In the war which I am to describe, the European War, the War to End War, which played so great a part in setting your species toward decline, every turn of events was noted by invisible presences, but these unseen observers were neither divine nor partisan. As on the Trojan plains, so on the plains of Flanders, the hills of Picardy and Champagne and Argonne, Tyrol's wild heights, the bogs and steppes of Russia, so equally in Arabia, Mesopotamia and Salonika, on the sea and in the upper air, in fact, wherever war was present or indirectly felt, there watched invisible and unsuspected presences. These were not gods and goddesses mentally inferior to the humanity that had created them, interested in men only to use them for their own petty though celestial strife; they were actual human minds. They strove not to give victory to one side or the other; they were concerned only to record and relish the ineluctable course of events, and to kindle in such of you as were open to their influence some glimpse of their own high zest.

When first we examined your war, it was not uncommon for us to observe in that epoch features which, inexplicable at the time, suggested that some still future influence of our own must be at work upon them, influences which we had not yet, from the Neptunian point of view, been able to exert. Thus to take the most striking example, in our earliest study we had been perplexed by the fact that the Salonika episode did not develop on the scale that might have been expected. Later in Neptunian time, we discovered that we ourselves were responsible. For it now turned out that certain persons in high military and naval posts were open to our

445

influence. We accordingly swayed them toward inertia, and thus deliberately prevented a sequence of events which would have been far more repugnant to us than those which actually occurred. But such large-scale influence is very seldom possible. Moreover we have become extremely chary of indulging in it; for not infrequently we have come later to regret our meddling.

In our world, as I have said elsewhere, the mature individual has wholly escaped the snares of private egoism. His will is for the racial good. But his heart may still be torn asunder in respect of conflicts between loyalty to the spirit of man and piety toward the actual issue of fate. Even as individuals, but far more clearly as the race mind, we pass beyond the human loyalty which is the spring of all our action, and see in the form of the cosmos a beauty superior to any human triumph.

Now although we regard events in your epoch with complete detachment from your many archaic aims, we do feel with you in your racial struggle to become more fully human. When you fail, or when we fail to help you, we grieve. When we take action in your world, we are often torn by doubt as to whether we shall in fact improve or mar the fortune of the race. But in us pity and doubt are tempered by our intuition that in the highest view the whole, although severe, is excellent. Even as individuals, we have this conviction of the superlative beauty of the cosmos. But in the unique racial experience this insight is far more developed, and has a very curious and beatific effect upon us as individuals. For, if our memory is to be trusted, the race mind, when it looks back on the texture of events accomplished in the past, finds each one of them to be a needed feature in the cosmical beauty. In that supreme experience, seemingly, man looks upon the cosmos with a new discerning vision, and would not have any past event to be other than in fact it is. Thus it seems that, in so far as we ourselves have influenced the course of events, our influence has indeed contributed to the cosmical beauty; yet in so far as we have refrained or failed to achieve what we planned, that inaction and that failure were also for the best, were contributory to that supernal excellence which is clearly seen only by the racial mind.

But do not suppose that, since apparently whatever has occurred is cosmically right, therefore human endeavour is unnecessary.

Only by means of endeavour can the great theme of the cosmos proceed. But also, by some influence which is not revealed to us, the issue of all human endeavour is seemingly controlled so that in its failures no less than in its triumphs it does in fact contribute to the excellent and perfect form of the Whole. I say 'seemingly'; for even to us it is not clear that it *must* be so; although hitherto, the more we have increased in spiritual stature, the more often and the more clearly have we experienced instances of its being in fact so.

Let us now revert to your war. It is perhaps needless to say that, on those rare occasions when we have influenced the course of events in your war, we have never been concerned merely to give victory to one side, or to the other; save when, as has sometimes befallen, an unhappy observer has become so infected by the terrestrial mentality that he has lost completely his Neptunian integrity and understanding. Such disasters are rare. For the most part our observers maintain their sanity and their detachment perfectly.

You may be tempted to suppose that the great concentration of our observers in and around the period of your first world war implies that we are interested in your war for the same reasons as you yourselves are normally interested in it. In this you would be mistaken. We do indeed enter into your feelings in regard to the war. No less fully than you yourselves have felt them, we feel your agony and despair, your glory and shame; for we have participated in them directly. But throughout, we have normally preserved our own detachment. Events which through your minds we have savoured as world-shattering and God-condemning we have seen also in their wider relations, and recognized as but microscopic features in the great whole. And so we have been able to regard your agony and passion with that blend of sympathy and irony which, upon a lowlier plane, the adult feels towards the ardours of children in their games, or the grief of children in their nursery troubles.

The strategy of your generals, for instance, has for us only the kind of interest which your own psychologists have found in watching apes baffled by the simplest problems of intelligence. As chimpanzees, tantalized by fruit which lies beyond their reach, may achieve or miss insight into the potentialities of sticks, packing-cases or ropes, so your commanders painfully achieved, or more often missed, insight into military potentialities which lay all the while patent to every Neptunian intelligence. Time after time we saw these gilt-edged commanders frustrated by problems which even your own brighter minds might well have surmounted. Again and again we saw thousands of lives destroyed, and hard-won military gains abandoned, through the stupidity, or even the mere personal conceit, of some single strategist or tactician. And though this kind of betrayal was the very stuff that we had come to study, and normally we could regard it with equanimity, there have been, for all of us, occasions when such lapses have kindled a certain amused exasperation, or, if we have been too long subjected to the terrestrial mentality, even a momentary rage.

Your war-time politicians, perhaps more clearly than your generals, displayed for us the essential weakness of your kind. We are not greatly interested in the political aspects of your war, save as expressions of factors in your nature much deeper than politics. In the antics of your political leaders, even more clearly than in humbler lives, we saw the insidious, devastating struggle between private interest, patriotism, and that newer, more difficult allegiance which serves before all else the race, or the essential spirit that is man. In the commonalty, public and private interest stood in less dramatic and less momentous conflict than in those who framed national and military policy. It might have been expected that those upon whose acts great issues hung would hold their self-regarding propensity the more firmly under control, that the vast public import of their conduct would induce them constantly to scrutinize their motives with relentless penetration. But no. Decisions which were ostensibly concerned only with the national good were determined in fact by envy, jealousy, or pride. Yet in most cases the agent himself, we discovered, never doubted his own honesty. Similarly, as you yourselves later came to recognize, policies which were expressed in the language of cosmopolitan idealism or of religion, were in fact inspired by nothing but national aggressiveness or fear, or by some even more disreputable private motive. This being so, the diplomatic history of your war period interests us not at all as a record of high policy, but solely as a tangle of psychological data.

With yourselves, interest in your war is often the mere lust of horror, the fascination of bloodshed and destruction. To us, your horrors are unimpressive; for, ranging up and down the aeons of human history, we have observed many more complete and harrowing devastations. We have seen races, civilized beyond your dreams, completely annihilated in swift, or again in long-drawn-out, disaster. We have seen whole populations writhing and shrieking in physical agony. Your restricted and aseptic mutual slaughter, almost homely and kindly in comparison with that which lies a few decades ahead of you, has therefore no horrific interest for us. It has of course the appeal of every human tragedy; but neither in magnitude nor in intensity of suffering is it at all remarkable. Through your minds and your flesh we do, indeed, experience it as unique, world-shattering and world-condemning. We savour very thoroughly the agony of despair which oppressed so many of you in the years of war. Imaginatively we contract our vision within the limits of your war-bound vision, and enter fully into your consequent world-disgust. Indeed, having entered there, we are sometimes shocked that you do not feel more deeply. For even the most sensitive of you is protected from suffering the full agony appropriate to your own short-sighted world-disgust by the mere crudity of his nervous organization, and the consequent obtuseness and callousness of his mentality.

If it was not horror nor yet political or military interest that caused us to flock in thousands to observe your war, what was it? Was it perhaps your acts of individual heroism, your self-transcendence in devotion to a cause? Or was it your rare impulses of generosity toward the enemy, your groping efforts to escape the obsession of nationalism, and to feel the unity of man? We have indeed watched respectfully whatever in your war was truly heroic, devoted. Even when we have been forced to smile at the ends upon which that heroism was squandered, we have recognized that in its degree it was indeed heroism, a virtue which to beings of your stature is precious and difficult. We have also recorded faithfully every occasion on which any of you has transcended nationalism. But we cannot agree with you in regarding your heroism as the very flower of human achievement, or your generosity and your timid cosmopolitanism as sublime triumphs of the spirit. In our world we are accustomed to a completely relentless self-abnegation in all situations which demand it. Any failure in this respect we attribute to insanity. And as for cosmopolitanism, to put the interest of one nation before that of another seems to any member of any of our thousand Neptunian nations no less preposterous than for a man to favour his left eye against his right.

If even your heroism is commonplace to us, seeming no more remarkable than nursery pluck, what is it that we find in your war to attract our interest? The answer can be simply stated, but its full significance needs some further development. We came to see your species face a situation such as it had never hitherto needed to face. We came to see it fail to grapple with that situation in any manner which could have saved it from a fatal spiritual poison, or auto-intoxication. We knew that this failure was inevitable. We had watched your nature evolve and your world situation develop. We had watched these two factors cooperate to produce at a certain date a violent acceleration of world-change, and subsequently a tangle of problems with which you could not cope. We had observed a neck-and-neck race between your developing nature and the developing world, which your nature itself kept stimulating into constant advance. The world won. We had seen far back in your history the first stirrings of a new capacity in you, which, given time, might well have so matured as to master even the kind of world in which you now find yourselves. But your 'modern' world came too soon. In the century before the war it developed with increasing acceleration. You had neither the intelligence nor the moral integrity to cope with your brave new world. When at last in 1914 accident posed you with a crucial choice, you chose wrongly. It was inevitable that you should do so. Being such as you were, you would most certainly choose as you did. But you have only yourselves to blame, for your choice was a considered expression of your own essential nature. The newer kind of behaviour, which alone was really appropriate to the new world-situation, did indeed make here and there a tentative appearance, and no doubt in very many persons there was at least some leaning toward that behaviour; but everywhere a rigorous suppression, both by governmental authority and by the primitive disposition within each individual mind, prevented the more courageous and the only sane behaviour from occurring; save here and there, spasmodically and ineffectively. And so inevitably you took the first step toward disaster.

This was the drama which we came to watch, and not your horrors or your heroics or your strategic prowess or your policies. The actors were the millions of Europeans and Americans. The dramatic conflict took place at first within each mind. It then became a struggle between those many in whom the archaic disposition was victorious, and those few in whom it was defeated. The immediate upshot of your choice was war; but in that choice you set in motion a sequence of causes and effects destined to develop throughout your future. During the war itself we saw your more percipient minds tortured and warped, not only by physical pain and fear, but by the growing though unacknowledged conviction that they had acquiesced in a great and irrevocable treason against the still-slumbering spirit of man; that through blindness or cowardice or both, they had betrayed that which was the only hope of the future. Very often, of course, this betrayal was at the same time itself an heroic transcendence of mere self-regard for the supposed good of a nation; but it was none the less betrayal of that half-formed and nobler nature upon which alone depended man's future well-being. During the war itself the working of this poison, this profound and almost unrecognized shame, was obscured by the urgency of the military situation. But after the war it acted with ever-increasing effect. This effect we have observed in detail, and I shall describe it. When I have told you of the war itself as it appears to us through your eyes, I shall tell how, after the war, a subtle paralysis and despair fastened upon your best minds, and percolated throughout your social organism. I shall tell how both in theory and in affairs you produced a spate of symptoms which your psychologists would call 'defence-mechanisms', designed unwittingly to conceal from yourselves the full realization of your treason and the clear perception of its effects.

That you may appreciate this drama in all its poignancy, I must first report briefly our findings in respect of the nature and the past career of your species, and of the delicate balance of forces which issued inevitably in this betrayal.

2. THE PHILOSOPHICAL LEMURS

Your historians, when they seek to trace the origin of your war, refer only to events which took place within the previous century. They single out such accidents as the murder of an archduke, the ambition of an emperor, the vendetta of two jealous nations, the thrusting growth of a new empire and the resistance of an old, the incompatibility of racial cultures, the debasing effects of materialism, or the inevitable clash of rival economic systems. Each of these factors was in some sense a cause of your war; but to assert that any of them or all of them together constituted the essential cause would be scarcely more profound than to say that the war was brought about by the movement of the pen that signed the first mobilization order. The Neptunian observer, though he duly notes these facts, seeks behind them all for the more general and more profound cause, by virtue of which these lesser causes were able to take effect. He looks further even than the birth of the nations of Europe many centuries before the war. He finds the explanation of your mutual slaughter by regarding it as a crucial incident in the long-drawn-out spiritual drama of your species.

Our observers have traced by direct inspection all the stages in the awakening of man out of his ape-like forerunner. Indeed, as our technique advances we are able to press back our exploration even along the generations of man's pre-simian ancestors. Our most brilliant workers have actually succeeded in entering a few isolated individuals of a much more remote past, when the mammal had not yet emerged from the reptile. They have savoured the sluggish and hide-bound mentality that alone was possible to the cold-blooded forefathers of all men and beasts. They have also savoured by contrast the new warmth and lambent flicker of experience which was kindled when the first tentative mammal began living in a chronic fever. But for the understanding of your war it is unnecessary to go further into the past than the emergence of the ape from the pre-simian.

Even at that early age we observe two themes of mental growth which together constitute the vital motif of the career of the first human species, and the key to your present plight. These themes are the increasing awareness of the external world, and the more tardily increasing insight into the nature of the human spirit itself. The

452

first theme is one of fluctuating but triumphant progress, since it was but the mental aspect of the intelligent mastery of physical nature which brought your species to dominance. The second theme depended on the application of intelligence to another sphere, namely the inner world of desires and fears. Unlike apprehension of the external, it had no survival value, and so its progress was halting. Because this inner wisdom had long ago been outstripped by the outer knowledge, there came at last your war and all its consequences.

Our observers have studied minutely all the crucial events of this age-long drama. Searching even among the dark pre-simian minds, we have singled out in every generation every individual that has been in advance of his kind in respect either of outward prowess and apprehension or of inward self-knowledge. As one may extract any fragments of iron from a heap of rubbish by passing a magnet over its surface, so we, with our minds set to a slightly higher degree of practical intelligence or of self-consciousness than that of the generation under study, have been able to single out from the mass those rare individuals whose minds were definitely in advance of their contemporaries. We find, of course, that of these geniuses some few have succeeded in handing on their achievement to the future, while many more have been defeated by adverse circumstance.

Roaming among the pre-simian minds, we discovered one surprising efflorescence of mentality whose tragic story is significant for the understanding of your own very different fate. Long before the apes appeared, there was a little great-eyed lemur, more developed than the minute tarsier which was ultimately to produce ape and man. Like the tarsier, it was arboreal, and its behaviour was dominated by its stereoscopic and analytic vision. Like the tarsier also, it was gifted with a fund of restless curiosity. But unlike the tarsier, it was prone to spells of quiescence and introversion. Fortune favoured this race. As the years passed in tens of thousands and hundreds of thousands it produced large individuals with much larger brains. It passed rapidly to the anthropoid level of intelligence, and then beyond. Among this race there was once born an individual who was a genius of his kind, remarkable both for practical intelligence and for introspection.

When he reached maturity, he discovered how to use a stick to beat down fruit that was beyond his reach. So delighted was he with this innovation, that often, when he had performed the feat, and his less intelligent fellows were scrambling for the spoils, he would continue to wave his stick for very joy of the art. He savoured both the physical event and his own delight in it. Sometimes he would pinch himself, to get the sharp contrast between his new joy and a familiar pain. Then he would fall into a profound and excited meditation, if such I may call his untheorized tasting of his new mental processes. One evening, while he was thus absorbed, a tree-cat got him. Fortunately this early philosopher left descendants; and from them arose, in due course and by means of a series of happy mutations, a race of large-brained and non-simian creatures whose scanty remains your geologists have yet to unearth, and catalogue as an offshoot of the main line of evolution.

These beings have intrigued our explorers more than anything else in the whole terrestrial field. Their capacity for self-knowledge and mutual insight sprang from the vagaries of mutation, and was at first biologically useless. Yet, merely because in this species it was genetically linked to the practical intelligence which had such great survival value, it developed; until at last it justified itself in an event which from the human point of view seems almost miraculous. At an early stage the new race threatened to break up into a confusion of warring tribes, each jealously preserving its own fruit groves and raiding its neighbours. There was wholesale destruction of fruit. Starvation and mutual slaughter began to tell upon the nerves of this highly strung race. Population declined. Then it was that the miracle occurred. A certain remarkable female, the supreme genius of her race, organized a truce, and a concourse of all the tribes in the trees around a forest glade. Here, with the help of confederates and a heap of fruit, she performed an amazing pantomime, which might be called the forerunner of all sermons and of all propaganda plays. First, by means of dance and ululation, she put the spectators into an hypnoidal state of tense observation. She then evoked in them, by mere gesture and emotive sounds, a fury of tribal passion. At the moment when the companies in the tree-tops seemed about to fling themselves upon one another in battle, she suddenly changed the tone of her pantomime. By sheer histrionic ability she revealed to her bewildered but comprehending fellows her own agony of revulsion from hate, her own heart-searching and self-analysis, her own discovery of profound cravings which had hitherto been ignored. With no medium but the language of gesture and tone which she had in part to improvise, she praised love and beauty, she praised pure cognizance and spiritual peace. The enthralled spectators followed her every movement with unconscious mimicry. Each one of them recognized in his own heart that deeper nature which she was expressing. The result was something like a revivalist meeting, though shorn of the supernatural. In the midst of it the exhausted prophetess, overwhelmed by the emotional strain, succumbed to heart-failure, and thus sealed her gospel with death. The whole incident was miraculous enough, but still more amazing was the issue. Seemingly at one stride, the race passed to a level of self-knowledge and mutual loyalty which the first human species was to seek in vain, and which therefore it is not possible for me to describe to you.

At their height these amiable lemurs attained also a crude material culture. They had wattle dwellings, set in the forks of trees. They used rough wooden tools, and earthenware vessels, which hung from the branches like fruit. They even learned to plant trees so as to extend their forest. They dried their fruits, and stored them in clay-lined baskets. But to our observers this practical ability was less interesting than the precocious inner life with which it was linked. Nature had favoured these animals by setting them in a great luxuriant island. Their sole enemies, the great cats, they trapped to extinction. Unlike their cousins on the mainland, the ancestors of ape and man, these lemurs were neither over-sexed nor over-aggressive. Consequently their population remained limited in numbers, and united in sentiment. They rivalled the ants in sociality; but theirs was an intelligent, self-conscious sociality; whose basis was not blind gregariousness but mutual insight. When they had attained a very modest standard of amenity and a stationary social order, their native genius for self-knowledge and mutual insight combined with their truly aesthetic relish of acrobatics and of visual perception to open up a whole world of refined adventures. They developed song and articulate speech, arboreal dance, and an abstract art based on wicker-work and clay. The flowers of personality and personal intercourse bloomed throughout the race. They began to generalize and speculate, in a naïve but promising manner. By meditation and self-discipline they cultivated mystical experience. It was with amazement, almost with awe, that our earliest observers felt the minds of these tailed, soft-furred arboreals grope toward and even surpass the intuitions of your Socrates and your Jesus. It might be said that these, who flourished millions of years before the Christian era, were the only truly Christian race that ever existed. They were in fact a race of spiritual geniuses, a race which, if only it could have been preserved against the stresses of a savage world, might well have attained a far lovelier mentality than was ever to be attained by the First Men.

This could not be. Nothing but rare good fortune had saved them from extinction throughout the million years of their career. It was by practical intelligence alone that they had won their position, not by self-knowledge, which in the early stages of evolution is indeed rather a hindrance than a help to the battling species. With security and a stereotyped social condition, their practical versatility declined. When at last a submarine upheaval turned their island into a peninsula, the gentle lemurs met their doom. A swarm of the still half-simian ancestors of man invaded the little paradise. Far less percipient than the natives, and less truly intelligent, but larger, more powerful, quarrelsome, and entirely ruthless, these fanged and hirsute brutes overpowered the lemurs by numbers and weight of muscle; by cunning also, for they had a well-established repertoire of foxy tricks. The lemurs had but one weapon, kindliness; and this in the circumstances was ineffective. Moreover they were by now emotionally refined into such fastidiousness that at the sight of blood they fainted. If one of them was caught and slaughtered by the enemy, his horrified companions would drop like ripe fruit from the trees and break their necks. Within a decade the race was extinct.

With the defeat of the lemurs at the hands of a hardier and a more extravert species, it was written in the book of fate that, sooner or later, a world-situation such as your own must occur, and give rise to an epoch of world wars such as you are now to suffer. Between the downfall of the lemurs and your own age there has been a slow, but in the long run triumphant, advance of practical intelligence. That other application of intelligence, namely to the inner life, has developed but spasmodically, as an accidental consequence of the growth of intelligence in action. And so it has happened that man's motives have remained throughout the career of your species almost invariably primitive. Even in your own day, when primitive impulses are intellectually seen to be inadequate, and you struggle pathetically toward loftier desires, your hearts remain the hearts of apes, and your struggle is vain. From the point of view of cosmical perfection, of course, your struggle is not vain at all. By your gallant effort and by your fated downfall also, you fulfil your part well and truly within the drama of existence. But from the point of view of the advancement of the race your struggle is indeed vain, doomed to failure. The profound reorganization of the human will, which you now see to be necessary, cannot be achieved in time to avert disaster. While the world remained primitive, and man's power over physical nature feeble, this paucity of the inner life, though in itself deplorable, did not imperil the survival of the race. But in your day man has gained considerable power. Not only has he made his world so complex and so explosive that it threatens to break from the control of his practical intelligence but further, and more serious, it is now such that the operation of the old blind motives may destroy it. Nothing could save you but a far more radical exercise of those capacities of self-knowledge which in your species have flowered only in rare circumstances, and in your own feverish epoch are more and more crushed out by the routine of industrial society.

3. PREHISTORIC ORIGINS OF THE WAR

In its earliest phase, then, and throughout its career, your species triumphed by means of pertinacity, quarrelsomeness and practical versatility. Little by little, success has strengthened these qualities. In the early conflict of many intelligent half-simian species, one conquered, the most cunning and courageous of all. The rest vanished. By wit and constancy of purpose the one creature made

457

himself at last the veritable king of beasts, attacking even the great flesh-eating cats, till his very smell became dreadful to them. Thus by extravert intelligence did your ancestors come into their kingdom. For savouring their own experience they had neither need nor inclination. They gulped it down, and then sought more. For probing their own hearts they had no capacity. They could never become clearly aware of themselves. Since then, the aptitude for self-knowledge, which in your stock was never great, has not been fostered, save here and there and in a few periods of your history. There came of course a stage when the mere growth of intelligence made man realize that his heart was an unexplored jungle, and forced him to attack it. But this stage came late, too late. The jungle was by then too dense, too well-established.

Our observers have inspected every one of those great strokes of genius by which man came into his power. We have tasted the surprise and glee of him who first smashed his enemy's face with a stone, the triumph of him who first shaped a flint-edge to his liking, of him who secured fire and used it, of him who improved the floating log into a boat with paddles, and the rolling log into a wheel, of him who wrought the first metal tools, of him who made a sail, and so on. We have seen these inventions attained, forgotten sometimes even by the individual discoverers, re-invented, again and again lost and rediscovered, until at last they became the permanent property of the race. In each case we have entered the mind of the innovator, and felt his sudden ecstasy of achievement, his leap into keener being, like the fanned spark's leap into flame. We have watched him subsequently sink back into the old dream-like routine mentality, forgetful of past insight. Again and again, when a primitive man has stared uncomprehendingly at the very stone with which yesterday he triumphantly cracked the marrow-bones, our observer, being himself but human, has longed to remind the poor fool of his past prowess. As the ages advanced, this intelligence, this power of insight into the potentialities of external objects, evolved from a rare flicker to a constant flame, an established habit of mind. It was formerly intermittent, unreliable. It was like the earliest tools, which were but natural clumsy stones, picked up and used occasionally, and then forgotten. In time it became like the wrought and tempered knife, which is kept ever about the person, used at every turn, used often for mere love of using it, toyed with and applied to all manner of objects which seem at first without any practical significance whatever. Sometimes, indeed, as the ages pass, this keen knife of the mind is even applied to the mind itself. The inventor notices his own inventive activity, and tries to dissect it. The hungry man observes his own hunger, the amorous man his own lust. But the process turns out to be rather bewildering, even painful. Also it distracts one from the actual business of living. In the early stages it is therefore shunned.

Nevertheless, as the epochs unfold, the mind of man becomes more capacious, more unified, more active. It is no longer an ephemeral perception, forgetful of the past, or troubled now and then by a mere gleam of memory. Increasingly it carries the past forward with it, and refers to this stored past for light upon the present and the future. Increasingly every moment of its experience becomes interfused by all the rest of its experience. Today gains meaning from yesterday. Nothing can happen to the mind that does not reverberate, faintly or violently, through its whole nature. Every event is interpreted and valued in relation to other events. The man's mind becomes increasingly one mind, not a host of disconnected stupid little minds, awakening one after the other in response to special stimuli. Or so it tends to become. But in fact, it remains, in spite of all advances, very far from unified.

Along with this growing art of comprehending things together and taking more and more into account, comes an increasing discrimination of the actual differences in the world. Eyes distinguish new delicacies of shape, new shades of colour, ears detect new modulations of sound, fingers touch with increasing percipience, manipulate with increasing skill. Thus, age by age, man's experience of his world becomes richer, more coherent. Beasts, trees, one's fellows, become ever more characteristic, recognizable, reckonable. Space enlarges itself, is measured out in paces, leagues, marches; and time in days, months, seasons, years, generations. There looms a past before the clan was founded, a future for grandchildren's grandchildren. Meanwhile things that were formerly mere 'brute facts', shallow, opaque, barren of significance beyond themselves, reveal unexpected depths of meaning, become luminous, pregnant, charged with mysterious power. The sun and moon, darkness, the storm, the seasons, beasts of the chase and hostile beasts, all gather to themselves out of the past a strange, obscure, potent significance,

Meanwhile also another, very different, class of objects is at length gaining precision and significance. The roving curiosity looks sometimes inward. Intelligence is turned more resolutely than of old upon the anatomy of the mind itself. The hunter, in ambush for his prey, is suddenly confronted with his own being. He beholds that strange thing 'himself', with the surprise and awe which he felt when he encountered for the first time some unfamiliar beast of the forest. But this time he has no clear apprehension of the mysterious quarry, only a most tantalizing glimpse, as of a dark form lurking behind the brushwood. He falls into abstraction. He ruminates his own being. 'I – am waiting for the stag. I – want to kill the stag.' The strain of stalking himself gives him a kind of vertigo. It even frightens him. Suddenly he wakes from his novel experience, to find that the physical quarry that he proposed to ambush has appeared and escaped. He has missed his dinner. He vows he will never again be bemused in this way. But on another occasion something similar happens. He is courting his young love, with the great brown eyes and gentle voice. She is ready to be taken. But suddenly two strange things loom into his inner vision, himself and herself, very near to one another, very closely entwined into one another's minds, yet strange to one another, infinitely remote. Once more he falls into abstraction, fascinated, perplexed. 'I – she. I – she'. As he sinks into this meditation, she sees his face change and fade. She seeks to rouse him by winsome tricks, but he remains for a while abstracted. In sudden fear and resentment she breaks from him and flies.

Thus, little by little, men and women grope toward a certain tentative superficial self-knowledge, and knowledge of one another. And, as they proceed, these strange objects, selves, become charged with ever-greater significance. Individuals come to prize themselves as no less gifted creature could ever do. They are proving that they are mighty selves. And, prizing themselves, they learn at the same time to prize other selves. Woman, whom man once saw merely as a thing to covet and embrace and then to ignore, or at most as a vague 'other', agreeable or irksome, now gathers to herself the significance of all past intercourse, all subtle passages of lust and love and hate, and reveals herself at last as a spirit, mysterious, potent, tender, ruthless. So also the man to the woman. Children, once mere objects to tend, defend, fondle, or, as the mood changed, to spurn, now become beings in their own right, rightly demanding service, even to the death. The group, once a vague swarm of fluctuating, discontinuous phantoms, companionable, quarrelsome, tyrannous, crystallizes at length into a system of persons. Close around oneself there is discovered a nucleus of well-tried friends and enemies, each one unique, incomparable. Over the heads of all, remote, mysterious, the old man of the tribe, or the tribal mother, or later the king of the whole land, embodies in his own person the ancient impersonal presence of the group, and later ascends heavenward as the tribal god, finally to become the one God of all tribes and all existence.

But long before this apotheosis there begin to appear here and there among the tribes beings of an intenser self-consciousness and a more insistent egoism, heroes, violent men for whom nothing is respect-worthy but their own exultant spirits. The word 'I' is ever on their lips and in their deeds. Each one of them is poignantly aware of himself as pitted against a huge, base, reptilian universe; and is confident that he will master it. Each lives for the mere zest of mastery. In his triumphant course each is accompanied by a swarm of jackal followers, not of his own kind, but striving to be of his kind. With them he smites the established powers, changing man's life for good or bad, making his mark upon the world, for very lust of scribbling. At the close of it all he confidently expects translation into some Valhalla. Often as not, all trace of him vanishes in a generation, save his name and legend on the lips of bards. If in any other manner his work lasts, it is more or less an accident. For, though aware of the superficies of his individuality in a manner impossible to his fellows, the hero has neither inclination nor time nor courage to penetrate within it and explore it. He accepts the bright superficies of himself at its face-value, and cares nothing for its deeper potentiality. In this respect he is typical of your kind.

Not only so, but the glamour of the hero has helped to make you what you now are. The ideal of personal prowess, which he set, though at first helpful to man's sluggish spirit, became later the curse of your species. With its facile glory it inveigled your forefathers into accepting outworn values, puerile aims. Throughout the whole career of your species the ideal of heroism has dominated you, for good and bad. In the earliest of all human phases, the almost simian mind of man could not yet conceive any ideal whatever, but the hero ideal was none the less already implicit in his behaviour, though unconscious. The best from which man sprang was already self-regarding, quarrelsome, resolute; and his hands were skilled for battle. Since then, epoch by epoch, the glory of innumerable heroes, the spell of innumerable heroic myths have ground the ideal of heroism into men's hearts so deeply that it has become impossible for you 'modern' men, in spite of your growing perception that heroism by itself is futile, to elicit from your hearts any larger ideal. You pay lip-service to other ideals, to love, and social loyalty, and religious possession; but you cannot feel them reverberate in your hearts, as does the ideal of the splendid all-conquering individual. To this ideal alone your hearts have been tuned by age-long hero-worship. No doubt, throughout your career loyalty has played a part. Your triumph, such as it is, rests upon the work of brilliant individuals cooperating in the group's service. But you have never taken the group to your hearts as you have taken the hero. You cannot. Your hearts are strung for the simpler music. They are but one-stringed instruments, incapable of symphonic harmony. Even your groups, even your modern nations, you must needs personify as heroic individuals, vying with one another, brandishing weapons, trumpeting their glory.

Our observers, wandering through the ages which you call prehistoric, have watched your kind spread in successive waves into every habitable corner of your planet, multiplying itself in a thousand diversities of race, diversities of bodily form, or temperament, of tradition, of culture. We have seen these waves, as they spread over the plains and along the coasts and up the valleys, every now and again crash into one another, obliterate one another, augment one another, traverse one another. We have seen the generations succeed one another as the leaves of an evergreen tree. As the leaves of a young tree differ from the leaves of an old tree, the early generations differ from the later in bodily and mental configuration. Yet they remain within the limits of their specific type. And so, inevitably, do you, spiked leaves of the holly.

We have watched all the stages, gradual or sudden, by which the common ancestor, crouched, hairy, and pot-bellied, has given place to the more erect Pithecanthropus, to the still almost simian Neanderthalian, and at last to the taller and more human progenitor of all your races. We have seen the first bare rippled backs, and the first broad upright brows. We have seen woman's breasts form themselves out of the old simian dugs. We have watched the gradual crystallization of your four great racial beauties, white, yellow, brown and black. We have followed in detail many a minor strand of bodily character, and the many facial types within each race, which blend and part and blend again, generation by generation. Similarly we have traced, generation by generation, the infinitely diverse exfoliation of the simian mind into your four great racial temperaments, and all the subtleties of disposition inborn in the many stocks within each race.

There came at length a stage in the career of your species when, through the operation of intelligence, men began vaguely to feel that there was something wrong with their own nature. They had already, here and there, acquired a superficial self-knowledge and mutual insight. They had begun to distinguish, though haltingly, the lesser and the somewhat greater goods of the spirit. From mere sex, mere parenthood, mere gregariousness, they had passed here and there to a kind of love and a kind of loyalty; but they could not maintain any sure footing on this higher plane. They were for ever slipping into the old bad ways. Increasingly they surmised that the purely animal way of life, even when glorified into heroism, was not the best that men and women could attain. Yet when they anxiously peered into their chaotic hearts to discover what was better, they could see nothing clearly, could find no constant illumination. Our observers, studying your early races, report that for each race there came a phase, early or late, poignant or obscure, in which there spread a vague but profound restlessness, a sense of potentialities not exercised, a sense of an insecure new nature struggling to shape itself, but in the main failing to do more than confuse the old brute nature. It is of this phase of your career that I must now speak.

463

4. THE HISTORICAL PERIOD

The action of the drama accelerates. With ever-increasing speed the human intelligence masters its world, brings natural forces more and more under control of the still primitive will, and unwittingly prepares a new world, a man-made world, which is destined to become in your day too intricate for the still unfinished intelligence to master, too precariously balanced to withstand the irresponsible vagaries of a will that is still in essence simian, though equipped with dangerous powers. The ape has awakened into a subtler and more potent cunning. He has attained even a vague perception of what it would be like to be truly human in mind and heart. Ineffectually, intermittently, he strives to behave as a true man would behave; and in rare moments he actually achieves thoughts and actions not unworthy of a man. But for the most part he remains throughout the history of your species, and in your own moment of that history, at heart a monkey, though clothed, housed and armed.

Before we look more closely at your 'modern' world, let us glance at the hundred centuries preceding it. At the outset we see tribes of hunters settling down to till the valleys, especially the valleys of the Nile, the Euphrates, the Indus, the Ganges, the Yangtze. Millennia pass. Mud huts proliferate along the riverbanks, condense into cities, are overhung by megalithic tombs, temples, palaces. The tribes coalesce into kingdoms and empires, and produce the first phases of civilization. Traders score the continents with their tracks. Little ships creep around the coasts, and sometimes venture beyond sight of land. Heroes gather armies and perform mighty evanescent conquests. Hardy barbarians invade the plains, dominate the empires, and are absorbed by the conquered. Daily life becomes steadily more secure, amenable, regular, complex. Triumphantly the intelligent beast finds new ways to gratify its ancient cravings for food, shelter, safety, adventure, for self-display, amorousness, and herd-activity. Yet at heart it remains a beast, disturbed but seldom by an obscure discontent with its own nature and with the world that it has fashioned around it.

With the increase of security a few exceptional minds begin to explore their environment intellectually, and even to probe their own nature. Increasingly the more awakened individuals become aware of their own inner chaos, both of understanding and of will. Here and there, where circumstance is peculiarly favourable to the life of the spirit, men are almost persistent in their self-searching. In India, where the physical cravings are insurgent and irresistible as the jungle, they strive through asceticism to establish the spirit over the flesh. In Greece they seek harmonious fulfilment of body and mind. For the sake of this fulfilment they seek the truth. They pass beyond the rule-of-thumb devices of medicine men, astrologers, builders, navigators, to make guesses about the inner nature of things, about the stars, the shape of the earth, the human body and soul, about number, space, time, and the nature of thinking. Meanwhile in Palestine others conceive a divine law; and in obeying it they expect a heaven of eternal bliss.

Then at length appear, here and there along the centuries, here and there among the peoples, a few supremely penetrating minds. Mostly their careers are cut short by indifferent fate, or by the vindictive herd. But three triumph, Gautama, Socrates, Jesus. Seeing with the mind's eye and feeling with the heart more vividly and more precisely than their fellows, they look round them at the world, and within them at their own nature, as none had done before them. It is a strange world that confronts them, a world of beings superficially like themselves, yet different. So uncomprehending are their fellows, so insensitive, so pitifully weak. In rigorous and ceaseless meditation the three great ones strive to formulate their teeming intuitions in a few great principles, a few great precepts. They live out their precepts in their own lives relentlessly. Gautama said: By self-denial, self-oblivion, seek that annihilation of particular being which is the way to universal being. Socrates said: Let us fulfil ourselves to the uttermost by embodying in ourselves, and in the world that is our city, the true and the good. Jesus said: Love one another; love God; God is love.

From these three greatest of your kind, these three vital germs, issue three vast ramifications of spiritual influence, three widespread endemic infections of the minds of men, passing from generation to generation. The tragedy of your species may be said to lie in its complete failure to embody, rather than merely to mimic, the spirit of these three men.

Our observers, as I have already said, have never been able to establish themselves in any of these three. As the single racial mind of the Last Men we do indeed, if the obscure recollection of that experience is to be trusted, savour and even influence them. But to each individual observer they remain impenetrable. We can, however, study them through their contemporaries, and have done so, very minutely. We have seen those great ones face to face, listened to every word that they have spoken, watched every act they have performed in the presence of any spectator. Through dying eyes we have observed Gautama contemplating death. In the mind of the young Plato we have attended to the quiet ironical voice of Socrates and been confronted by his disturbing gaze. We have heard Jesus preaching on the mount, with dark face kindled. We have stood around the cross and heard him cry out on the God whom he had misconceived.

In such experiences three facts invariably impress us, and fill us with a sense of the pathos of your kind. We are amazed both at the unique genius of these men and at the world-imposed limitation of their genius. We are impressed also by the inability of their fellow-men to grasp even that part of their vision which found expression. For neither their immediate fellows nor you, with all your complacent historical knowledge, can ever understand them. How should you? They themselves strove in vain to comprehend their own profound, unique, intuitions, within terms of their world's naïve beliefs. But though the flame burned brightly in their hearts, they could neither understand it not express it. For neither their conception nor their language was adequate to such a task.

But even if they could have expressed their vision, they would have been misunderstood. For each of these three, though sorely cramped and bewildered by his archaic world, was a veritable man; while his fellows, like the rest of you, were but half-human apes. And so, inevitably, these great ones are misinterpreted even by their own chosen followers. Socrates, who is so much more fortunate in Plato than Jesus in his disciples and Gautama in his interpreters, is seen by us, not only to be more profound in intellect than the great Plato, but to have also a vision, an illumination, perplexing to himself and utterly incommunicable to any of his associates. The lemurs might have understood him. The lemurs might have understood Jesus, and Gautama also. But they, too innocent, could not maintain themselves against the muscle and cunning of man's progenitors.

It is clear to our observers that in your three great minds there occurred an identical insight into the nature of man and of the world. But each interpreted his vision differently, and expressed it differently in action. And from each a very different influence was selected by his followers.

We have traced that influence, that spreading ferment in men's minds. The three proliferations are very diverse. But in the early stages of each, during the first and even the second generation, there occurs a new intensity of experience, an increased though still confused self-knowledge, mutual insight and apprehension of the world. There is also a gloriously increased pertinacity of the will to be man rather than ape. Tidal waves of a new enthusiasm now begin to surge across the peoples, lifting up men's hearts, spreading over the continents. And, spreading, they fade. They multiply into a thousand meandering variations. They are deflected hither and thither, traversing one another again and again. They confuse, annihilate or augment one another. In your day there is not a mind anywhere on your planet which does not pulse, however faintly, to the endlessly wandering reverberations of your three true men.

But long before your day the character of the influence is changed. At first it stormfully resounds in the secret places of men's hearts, and even wrenches their poor ape-hearts into something of the human form. But in the end the simian nature triumphs. Those crude instruments, forced for a while to reverberate in response to a music too subtle and too vast for them, presently relapse into the archaic mode.

The ape nature corrupts the new, precarious, divinely human will, turning it into a lofty egoism, a new heroism,

Here, there is heroism of the intellect, loyal only to the truth-seeking self; there, heroism of the heart, determined to embrace all men in indiscriminate brotherliness, through mere loyalty to the

467

love-proud self; there, heroism of the spirit, domineering over the flesh, proclaiming as the supreme affirmation mere negation.

But there remains a memory, a tradition, a legend, an obscure yearning in the hearts of men for a way of life that is too difficult for them. And so there are formed various mighty associations, whose office is to preserve one aspect or another of the fading illumination. The Christian and the Buddhist churches spread far and wide their hierarchies and their monastic orders. Institutions of learning, schools and universities, are precipitated around the Mediterranean coasts and over the European lands. Indians, Chinese, Arabs, Latins, Franks, thus preserve amongst themselves some smouldering embers. But the flame is vanished.

Yet now and again, once in a few generations, now in this land, now in that, the coals break once more into conflagration. There is a spreading revival of the original ecstasy. Once more, but not for long, the ape-hearts resound obscurely with counterfeit echoes of an experience whose true form they cannot support. Once more it seems to them that they are merged in one another and gathered into God in a mystic communion, that they have pierced behind appearances to the eternal truth, that by self-annihilation they have escaped the limitation of the flesh and individual consciousness, to be gathered into the absolute being. But once more, though the few attain some genuine illumination, the many misunderstand, ignore what is essential and mimic what is accidental; or in frank hostility persecute. Once more, as the insight fades, the institution flourishes, and takes up its place in the established order. Once more the ape triumphs over the man.

Our observers have savoured the minds of the First Men in all these wave-crests of the spirit, these religious revivals, protestations, counter-reformations, these fervours of heart-searching, stampedes of soul-saving, these martyrdoms for an inner light so precious and so misperceived. Everywhere we detect an identical fact. Vaguely aware of his own blindness and incoherence, man yearns toward vision and toward harmony; but he yearns in vain. Vision, indeed, he does now and again achieve, fleetingly, misleadingly; but harmony never. Here and there men see obscurely what they should be doing with themselves, but always their conduct, and their vision also, is distorted by preconceptions and predilections forced upon them by their ape nature. They are confused by phantom lures of immortality, of celestial bliss, of abstract righteousness, of divine love.

Nevertheless men do begin, here and there, to feel stirring within them, striving for expression, some strange new life of the spirit. Did they but know, they are in travail for a twin birth. They are troubled with the first movements of a new piety toward fate and a new loyalty toward man. Of the first they know as yet almost nothing, for whenever they experience it, they confuse it with the old complacent love of a loving God. Of the second, they guess only that they must make the best of man, must seek to know ever more truly both the world and the self, must seek to feel ever more delicately, and to will ever more harmoniously. Obscurely they begin to surmise that the whole active duty of men is to live for men; and that man must be made one, a spirit winged perhaps for enterprise unimaginable in their day. But these two conflicting spirits of cosmical piety and human loyalty remain still deeply hidden in their hearts; and men can neither see into their hearts nor bring forth in action what still is hidden. They cannot obey, they cannot even understand, these two seemingly incompatible divine commandments of the future. Blindly they seek vision; but the knowledge that they would have is for power, not piety. And so they are tricked at every turn by their own cravings. Harmony they seek; but neither within the individual nor in the race of individuals can they attain it. Nor can they find harmony with the universe. In each heart there rages the old conflict between the man and the monkey, and also the obscure new conflict between cosmical piety and human loyalty. In the external world, the quarrelsome apes that fought of old for prey, for mates, for kingship, for hunting-grounds, war now for cornlands, mines, trade, for national glory or security, for fantasies of religion. Armies surge hither and thither. Fields and cities are laid waste; and always in a good cause, whether for some royal master, or some burgher caste, or some nation, or for the glory of God.

While all this is afoot, something else which is new is beginning to happen to mankind. The still unrecognized piety toward fate and fact, and toward the actual course of the world, stirs men to observe the daily features of the world with new interest. At the same time loyalty toward man fires them to master the physical world for man's use, and therefore to understand its working. Some few individuals here and there, fretted by a recrudescence of that curiosity by which the ape had triumphed, begin to pry into the behaviour of physical things. They drop weights from towers, seek new descriptions of planetary motions, peer at the heavens through lenses, observe the workings of flesh and blood, put one stuff with another stuff and watch the issue, brood upon the falling apple, and on the jumping lid of a kettle, devise pistons, cog-wheels, gears, wheels within wheels. Suddenly man puts together a mesh of dangerous little fragments of knowledge, and comes into possession of little dangerous powers. Victoriously the human ape assimilates the teeming influx of new facts. Decade by decade he discovers new features of the intricacy and majesty of the physical universe. Imagination strains to cope with the very great, the very little, the very complex, the very swift, the very long-enduring. Little by little, the familiar universe crumbles away, and a new stupendous universe forces itself on man's reluctant fascinated gaze.

Within this new pattern of things man sees himself as among the very little, the very brief, the very impotent, the wholly mechanical. This discovery, which fills him with indignation and despair, should have been a step in his salvation. It should have taught him to value himself no longer as the immortal, precious, unique child of a God whom his own mind had created, but henceforth as a thread in the fair web of the universe, a theme in the great music, and also as one brief sentient focus of cosmical aspects. But, wholly ignorant of his own interior being, he still cherishes the belief that he is something peculiar, distinct from the physical, something uniquely free, vital, spiritual. And so, when he is forced to regard himself as all of a piece with his world, he feels himself degraded. All that he knows of the physical world is shape, movement, resistance, mechanical sequence of changes. These he takes to be no mere superficies, but the very essence of the physical. And these abstractions he now applies to himself, condemning himself as mere 'matter'. If he knew himself as well as he now begins to know his world, the science of the physical would not dismay him about his own nature, nor remain itself a science of mere appearances. But through inveterate self-blindness the First Men are doomed to misconceive themselves in the light of a physical nature, which, also through self-blindness, they must misconceive. Ignorant of their own interior being, they remain ignorant of the interior being of the world whose gorgeous superficies is now stage by stage terrifyingly revealed.

When the First Men have already firmly grounded their science of the physical world, they begin to direct the same objective study upon their own behaviour. Thus they will acquire in due season a vision of themselves even more devastating, because more precise. They will see themselves at last unambiguously as greedy, self absorbed, vindictive, timorous apes, cunning and powerful up to a point, yet also incredibly weak and stupid. This knowledge, could they but pursue it relentlessly and to the bitter end, should lead them at last up to the locked door behind which is true self-knowledge. Once there, they should be able by biological control to produce a generation capable of penetrating that interior stronghold. Thus should the First Men arrive at last where the lemurs started, and should proceed to surpass those wise innocents in every activity of the spirit. But in the book of fate it is written that this shall not happen. While men are taking the first few halting steps in the new venture, while they are still debating the course, the storm breaks upon them. A world situation arises which demands for its control more intelligence and far more integrity of will than their half-formed nature can achieve.

While man is becoming less and less confident of his own spiritual dignity, he acquires more and more power over his physical world, and sinks further and further into obsession with the material. Steam drives ships across the oceans without care for winds, drives trains across the lands, carrying great loads at incredible speeds. Later comes electricity, and with it the flashing of messages around the planet on wires or on the ether. The age-old dream of flying is at last realized by aeroplane and airship. Meanwhile by machinery and chemical synthesis innumerable materials and utensils are manufactured for comfort, luxury or power.

What is the upshot? From its germ in Europe a new world spreads, devouring the old world. Formerly events happening in one region had seldom any appreciable effect elsewhere. But now, increasingly, each event in every part of the world reverberates within all other events. By means of steam and electricity the human world is becoming one system. Its regions become inter-dependent economically, even in a manner culturally; but not politically, and not socially. The hearts of men are massed against one another in jealous and mistrustful nations. And across this cleavage runs another, the division in all lands between masters and servants, the economically free and the economically en-slaved. The new world should have been a happy and glorious world. But it is not. The new powers should have been organized in service of the human spirit, the one right object of loyalty. But they are not. The First Men can do almost nothing, with their powers, but serve the old ape-cravings for private comfort, safety, self-display and tribal glory.

At the moment of the outbreak of the European War the great majority of mankind are extremely ignorant not only of their own essential nature but of the world. They feel no need that man should be made one, and that all men should cooperate in the supreme racial enterprise. They take the nations to be the true objects of loyalty, and the social classes to be natural elements of the nation. But a minority, mostly in the Western lands, have blindly felt this need of human unity. Their leaders have formulated it obscurely in one manner or another, often discrepantly. But few can take it at all seriously, very few can live for it passionately. In most cases, however bravely they can talk about it, they cannot act for it. If ever they are put to the test, they shy away, affirming that nationalism is 'practical', cosmopolitanism but a remote ideal. Though they see it intellectually, their hearts are not capable of responding to it. If ever the nation is in danger, their cosmo-politanism evaporates, and they stand for the nation in the good old style. Yet intellectually they know that in their modern world this way leads to disaster.

The story of your species is indeed a tragic story, for it closes with desolation. Your part in that story is both to strive and to fail in a unique opportunity, and so to set the current of history toward disaster. But think not therefore that your species has occurred in vain, or that your own individual lives are futile. Whatever any of you has achieved of good is an excellence in

472

itself and a bright thread woven into the texture of the cosmos. In spite of your failure it shall be said of you, had they not striven as they did, the Whole would have been less fair. And yet also it shall be said, even had they triumphed and not suffered their disaster, the Whole would have been less fair.

VI *The War*

1. EUROPE BEFORE THE WAR

I MUST now describe from the Neptunian point of view that moment in the career of the First Men which seemed to those who experienced it an eternity of war.

As the summer of 1914 advanced, our observers crowded in ever-greater numbers into your world, seeking out among you suitable minds in which and from which to observe your coming crisis. As a flock of birds, before settling on a tree, hovers for a moment while each individual selects a convenient twig, so we settled upon your race. The tree knows nothing of its living burden; you were wholly ignorant of your Neptunian guests.

Long before this great company began to arrive, those of us who, like myself, are specialists in your epoch had, of course, already been at work among you, wandering from mind to mind and studying the great movements of human history which were to result in your crisis. But in 1914 an immensely greater company gathered to watch in as much detail as possible your reaction to the unprecedented events of the next four years. In spite of this influx of observers, not every one of you could be directly studied. But a considerable proportion of the total European population harboured within themselves Neptunian visitors. We diligently sought out all those who were significant, not only those in prominent positions but very many obscure persons who seemed to afford peculiarly lucid examples of your nature and of the trend of thought and feeling in your day. Such persons would have been astounded had they known that they were singled out for study along with generals and political leaders; but in truth it was in the masses, rather than in their leaders, that the real drama of the war was taking place. For in the leaders the poignancy and subtlety of experience was in most cases reduced by the necessity of pursuing some official policy.

Throughout the summer of 1914, then, a huge anthropological

expedition, organized on Neptune two thousand million years in the future, was invading your minds in its thousands and its hundreds of thousands. Yet also (to repeat) at the very same time, in the Neptunian sense, other and even greater expeditions were at work upon crises of one or other of the sixteen human species which have their historical location between the First Men and the Last Men. Thus some were studying the fall of the noble Second Men in their long struggle with the cloud-like Martian invaders; others watched the heroic colonization of Venus by the Fifth Men, the last Terrestrials; others, most fortunate, wandered among the lyrical minds of the pygmy Flying Men of Venus, the Seventh species; and many more carried out their devoted work in the field of man's age-long and tortured struggle to take root on Neptune; others again studied the later and happier Neptunian races. But these expeditions I must not now describe, for my concern is with yourselves. In our work upon the First Men we have concentrated our main force in your own crucial age.

In every European capital, in every drab provincial town, in every agricultural district, our observers settled. Had you been gifted with Neptunian vision, you might have seen, whenever you walked in the streets of Berlin, Paris, or London, that the crowd was composed of persons of two kinds. Most of them were uncontaminated members of your species; but about one in twenty (at least in these metropolitan areas) would have appeared to you curiously altered. You would have seen in the expression of their eyes, had you peered closely at them, a fitful gleam, a faint surprise, verging on bewilderment, a queer inwardness combined oddly with an increased intensity of observation and interest, in fact an almost haunted look, which the Neptunian has learned to recognize in such of you as have been singled out by one of his colleagues as a convenient observation-point. It is not surprising that you should manifest some outward symptom when you are thus possessed, as it were, by an all-pervading mental parasite, whose filaments reach into every nook and cranny of your minds. Yet so subtle is this unintentional influence of ours, that the hosts themselves are, as a rule, completely unaware of it, and even their most intimate friends do not notice any alteration in them. Only to Neptunians, using the eyes of other individuals of your species is the 'possessed' look apparent. Sometimes, of course, we deliberately make our presence felt by some act of definite influence, and when such influence is frequent, the host himself may have a sense that he is somehow possessed, or going mad. But the more passive presence of a Neptunian produces only a slight increase of the intensity of consciousness, and especially of self-consciousness.

Conceive then that, before war was declared, Neptunian observers were busy making themselves acquainted with their chosen hosts. That we concentrated in greatest number upon the years of the war and the two decades following, is not to be attributed to any special preference for the mentality of your Twentieth over your Nineteenth Century. As between the generations which, through complacent materialism and sentimentality, brought the war into being, and the generation which, through moral timidity and lack of faith in the human nature of the 'enemy', allowed itself to be herded into the trenches, and again the later generations, which, attaining maturity when the war was over, blamed its predecessors or malicious fate for its own supine laziness and lack of vision, – as between these three groups of persons we have no predilection. To us all alike are 'human', in the manner characteristic of a half-human species. Each is the inevitable product of its predecessors and its world, yet each is in part responsible for its own turpitude. This is, I know, a paradox which must remain insoluble upon your plane of understanding. But to us, there is no paradox. All your generations appear equally culpable, equally pitiable. But since, in the war itself and its consequences, the whole drama of your species finds its climax, it is in the war period and the decades following it that our observers chiefly congregate.

Very thoroughly the pioneers had already sifted your populations for significant individuals, so that when the main expedition arrived it was possible to allocate each new-comer to a suitable host. Most often (but not always) we set our women observers to study Terrestrial women. And as far as possible we contrived to arrange matters so that there should be some kind of temperamental similarity between observer and observed; for thus, we find, the work proceeds most smoothly and effectively. Some of us occupied the minds of the politicians on whose decision so much was to depend, seeking to understand and sympathize with their ingrained political convictions, sorting out the obscure tangle of self-interest and public loyalty which was to determine their behaviour, harking back now and then into their youth or child-hood, or even infancy, to discover the submerged sources of their whims, delusions and prejudices. Others of us familiarized them-selves with the astounding mixture of honest heart-searching and intricate self-deception which was the habitual attitude of your religious leaders to all serious problems, and was so soon to find its most striking expression in the futility of your churches in the face of war. Yet others were savouring the insistent itch of military experts to put their huge lethal toy in action, or the mere boyish braggartism, a relic of the heroic age, which infected your more romantic militarists.

In varying degrees of minuteness we have studied your Asquith and your Grey, your Bethmann-Hollweg, your von Bülow and your Treitschke, your Hindenburg, your Foch, your Clémenceau and your Lloyd George. Each of these, though not one of them is intrinsically of serious interest to us, has called for careful study on account of the momentous results of his actions. Your Lenin, however, we have studied in greater detail; many of my colleagues have had occasion to live through all the phases of that remarkable spirit, in whom, as in no other, we find a most instructive blend of that which might have saved your species with that which was bound to destroy it.

Sometimes we have performed curious experiments by intro-ducing into one mind thoughts and valuations derived from another, as in biological research the experimenter may introduce blood or portions of tissue from one organism to another. Thus it has proved instructive to bewilder statesmen at the council table by momentarily forcing upon them ideas disruptive of their policies and their most cherished faiths. For instance, one of my most brilliant young colleagues, fresh from the revolutionary and exiled Lenin, once contrived that Asquith, the legal-minded premier, in the presence of his cabinet, should sink for a moment into horrified abstraction while a blast of revolutionary schemes and cravings fell on him like a whirlwind. It was indeed instructive to observe how, after the attack the ageing statesman soothed himself by dipping into Carlyle's *French Revolution*, and by slightly changing his attitude to the Welsh thorn in his flesh. Of deeper effects we observed none.

To give another example of this transfusion of thought, Lenin himself, that man of stainless steel, that future Almighty, was once, to his own surprise, so flooded with the timid megalomaniac fantasies of the Czar, that he found himself pitying, even pitifully loving that imperial half-wit. On another occasion, while he was in the act of composing a relentless article on the baseness of an archimandrite, my colleague forced upon him a precise apprehension of the old villain's mind. He suddenly realized in imagination that this profligate priest had once yearned toward the supernal beauty, and that even yet his blind spirit carried out by rote the gesture of prostration before the great lover, Jesus. This incident had a strange and significant effect on the revolutionary. Pent-up springs of mercy and piety welled in him. He experienced, as few Christians have ever experienced, the divinity of Love. Sitting in his hired room in Paris, with the indictment of the priest spread out on the table before him, he whom many were yet to call Anti-Christ, received the divine love into his heart. My young colleague who was in charge of the experiment reports that his host accepted the revelation like any Christian saint, and that for an hour he remained in ecstasy. At the close of that period he whispered in his Russian speech, 'I come not to bring peace, but a sword', and so once more took up his pen.

Not only men of action, but leaders of thought, too, our observers inhabited. In many minds of writers and artists they had detected in the 'pre-war' age the first stirrings of that disillusionment and horror which the war climate was later to foster.

Earlier they had seen the English Tennyson, under the influence of science and a friend's death, face the spectre for a moment, only to cover his eyes and comfortably pray. Carlyle they had seen praise action as a drug for doubt. But now, they saw the writings of Thomas Hardy, formerly neglected, gradually compel men's attention more by their gloomy verisimilitude, than by their obscure conviction of cosmical beauty. In each people our observers heard already, in the midst of the complacency of that age, a whisper of uneasiness, rising here and there to despair. Already the old gods were failing, and no new gods appeared to take their place. The universe, it seemed, was a stupendous machine, grinding for no purpose. Man's mind was but a little friction upon a minor axle, a casual outcome of natural law. He dared not even regard himself as the one divine spark in a waste of brute matter; for he himself was just matter, and his behaviour the expression of his brute nature. Moreover, Freud had spoken, and ripples of horror were already spreading across Europe.

But there was Evolution. Our observers watched Bergson and all those whose faith was given to evolution champion their doctrine of a biological deity with something of the fervour of the old church militant. Their gospel touched few hearts. Disillusionment was already in the air. In laboratories our observers watched great scientists conduct their crucial experiments, and weave their theories, so subtle, so wide-sweeping, so devastating, so true on one plane and so meaningless on another. Again and again we have seen the truth missed when it was hidden only by a film. Again and again we have watched promising enterprises run to waste through the influence of some mad whim or prejudice. In many a study and on many a college lawn we have noted the turn of argument wherein acute minds first began to stray down some blind alley, or first tethered themselves to false assumptions.

But the overwhelming majority of our explorers were concerned with humbler persons. Our pioneers had flitted from mind to mind among artisans, factory hands, dock labourers, peasants, private soldiers, in search of those most significant or most subject to Neptunian influence, so that the main company should be able to settle promptly into posts of vantage for their work. If you incline to commiserate with those of us to whom it was allotted to observe simple minds in obscure positions, you are under a misconception. The difference between your mentally richest and your mentally poorest is negligible to us.

We have sat all day on heaps of road metal in country lanes, wielding a hammer, and savouring humble thoughts in minds not barren but not fortune-favoured. In French peasants we have driven sewage carts over our hectares, estimating the unsown crop, and the cost, and the sowing. In Prussian military messes we have drunk to 'der Tag'. In British foc's'les, homeward bound from

Yokohama and Kobe, we have looked back upon Geisha girls, forward to the wife in Canning Town. In provincial suburbs we have pondered the sententious wisdom of scavengers, while they pushed their hand-carts and condescended to speak with tramps. We have been present with trapped miners, while the flooding water crept up legs and bodies, or lungs were invaded by hostile gases. We have listened to doomed men chanting under the roots of mountains. Some of us, in zeal to observe last acts of piety or panic, have been destroyed in the destruction of their hosts. In factories we have spent our Terrestrial years feeding voracious machines and dreaming impossible triumphs or love idylls. On holidays we have been borne by the released flood of our fellow-workers along esplanades and heaths. Over shop-counters in Bond Street and the rue de Rivoli we have fingered camisoles, stockings, dress pieces. We have pondered, tone by tone, cliché by cliché, the intercourse of customers and shop-girls. We have jostled around buses and down subways, and hurried into city offices. In third-class railway carriages we have read innumerable evening papers through the eyes of clerks and typists, devouring the murders and the sex, skimming the politics. In the discreet dark-ness of picture palaces we have had forbidden tactual intimacies. In jails we have estimated the civilization of Europe through the rage of its outcasts. We have battered impotently on cell doors, counted and recounted the threads of spider-webs, strained to catch sounds of the world's great tide of life, which had left us stranded. We have entered into inmates of lunatic asylums, to gain insight into your mentality by watching its disintegration. We know also what it is to be segregated as mad by a world madder than oneself. In public-houses and Bier Stuben we have escaped for a while from nagging reality through the cheap ecstasy of inebriation. Or, less forlorn, we have found in the applause of our companions false consolation for our defeat in life.

More precisely it was our hosts that had all these experiences, while we, calm scrutinizers, appraised their minds. With the patience of big-game photographers, who endure tropical heat and drought or stand up to the neck in marsh for the sake of one snap of the camera-shutter, we have suffered interminable floods of rhetoric and infantile philosophy, in the hope of confronting one

480

of those rare denizens of the mind's jungle, those most vital and significant mental occurrences, which give insight into the mentality of an alien species.

We have also suffered vicariously the pains, both maternal and filial, of many births. We have watched the clean pages of many infant minds ignorantly scribbled over with indelible fears and loathings. We have experienced in many young things the same hungers and worships that we ourselves have known in our own far-future childhood upon Neptune. But in Terrestrial childhood we find these young healthy lusts and admirations all poisoned, misdirected, blunderingly thwarted or sapped, so that again and again we are reminded that the folly of your generation, as of every generation of your species, is due less to its innate coarseness of fibre than to the disastrous influence of its parents and teachers. Could we but, like your Pied Piper, rescue all your infants from their mothers and fathers, could we but transport them to Neptune, even with their ineradicable simian impulses and their inherited distortions of mind and body, could we but keep them from the contamination of their elders, what a race we could make of them! We could not indeed bring them further than the threshold of true humanity, but within their natural limits they might be made generous, free-minded, zestful, unafraid. Then, if we could but return them to your planet in the first bloom of maturity, how they would remake your world! But instead they must remain unfulfilled, like seeds which, blown into a cave, send forth long pale stems and flaccid leaves, seeking in vain the light.

The many boys and girls whom we have seen, confident at first that life held in store for them some as yet unimaginable treasure or some opportunity of high devotion, already in a few years disillusioned! We have encountered them at first unsullied, equipped by nature to learn prowess of body and mind, to advance from triumph to triumph of skilled and generous living. Then we have seen their bodies hampered, constricted, poisoned by misguided care, and their spirits even more seriously maltreated. Though in physical athletics they have often been patiently trained to habits of free and effective action, in the athletics of the mind and of the spirit they have acquired a cramped style and blind tactics. In the great game of life they never learned to keep their eyes on the ball. For them indeed the ball was invisible. They hit out stiffly or limply at nothing at all, or at hypnotic hallucinations, conjured before them by the exhortations of blind coaches.

Everywhere we have found in the lives of grown men and women a bewildered futility and resentfulness. The men blamed the women for their hobbled lives, the women the men for their servitude. The rich blamed the poor for disloyalty, the poor the rich for tyranny. The young blamed the old for lack of vision, the old the young for rebelliousness. And increasingly, even in that age before the war, men and women, rich and poor, old and young, were beginning to suspect that they were playing their brief game in a madhouse, with no rules and a phantom ball.

No wonder that in our research among the aged of that time we found very prevalent a most tragic condition of the spirit. In-numerable old men and old women, looking back with conscious complacency upon their achievements, and forward with confidence to their reward in heaven, were yet haunted in the recesses of their being with a sense that their lives had been phantasmal, that they had never really lived at all. Most of them were able on the whole to ignore these deep whispers of misgiving, or to drown them with vociferous piety; but many of the more self-conscious old people whom we studied, whether successful business men or members of the 'professions', socially triumphant old ladies or retired matrons of institutions, reviewed their careers with blank dissatisfaction and a nightmare sense that in their moment of living they had missed some great drudgery-redeeming good, simply by looking in the wrong direction. Only those whose lives had been dominated by concrete misfortune or disappointment, or by the demands of some all-absorbing heroic ministration, escaped this universal distaste of all values.

Such was the condition of the First Men as it was revealed to our observers in their survey of the years before the outbreak of the European War. Such were the beings that they studied. On the whole they found themselves forced to be twi-minded about these distressful creatures. From one point of view, as I have said, they could not but regard your species as not yet human; a thing incredibly stupid and insensitive, incredibly distorted and tortured by the fantastic habits, the rudimentary 'culture' which alone distinguished it from the lower beasts; a thing in some ways further removed from true humanity even than ox or tiger, because it had strayed further down the wrong path; a thing incomparably more filthy than the baboon, because, retaining brutality, it had lost innocence and learned to affect righteousness; a thing which was squandering the little powers that it had stumbled upon for ends essentially the same as the ends of monkeys, and in its frantic grabbing, devouring, voiding, had fouled a whole planet.

But from the other point of view our observers were forced to admit, at first reluctantly, that this errant and brutal thing had in it the distinctive essence which is man. Penetrating with difficulty into the minds of tiger and baboon to compare them with your species, they found indeed less brutality, but also less divinity; in fact a greater emptiness. In you they recognized the first blind restlessness of the spirit, which never troubles the mere beast, and wins its beatitude only in the full human estate. In you they found the rudimentary insight of the mind into itself and into others, that insight which lay beyond the reach of all Terrestrial organisms save Homo Sapiens and the Philosophical Lemurs, whose far more brilliant achievement man himself had terminated. In you they found love, though more often hate; in you philosophy though halting and superstitious; in you worship, though for the most part directed on unworthy objects.

All this might have been truly said of your species at any time of its career; but, at the moment which I am now describing, it was balanced on a still finer knife-edge between beast and man. This was due not to any change in its nature but to the pressure of circumstances. Hitherto, though a sensitive minority had been aware that the aims toward which men commonly strove were for the most part puerile, the majority were able to pursue these aims in undisturbed complacency. But in 1914 many forces were combining to shock even minds of average percipience into a sense of the contemptible insufficiency of the extant plan of human life, both individual and social. It is worth while to enumerate these forces. First, then, although the nations and races were still violently opposed to one another in sentiment, the world was already becoming a single economic system. Each section was growing more and more dependent on the healthy life of others.

Secondly, though national and racial cultures were still for the most part mutually unintelligible and repugnant, the seeds of an all-inclusive world culture were already quickening. Third, the battle between doctrinal religion and scientific materialism, in which science had been steadily advancing all along the line, was already beginning to dissolve and crystallize out in a new alignment. For while the old religion was beginning to seem not only intellectually incredible but also spiritually insufficient, the old science was already appearing not only spiritually arid but intellectually naïve. Fourth, man's increasing awareness of his littleness under the stars was combining with his first crude apprehension of the cosmical enterprise of Life to give him a wider horizon, a new humility, and also the first obscure glimpse of a new aim. Unfortunately in 1914 the effect of these forces was nowhere profound; and only in certain regions of the Western Civilization was it at all widespread. It was not strong enough to prevent the outbreak of war. All it produced was a devastating, though mostly unacknowledged, suspicion in all the combatants that human nature had failed.

2. EUROPE CHOOSES WAR

In August 1914 it was said by the more thoughtful among you that a great war in Europe might well cause the 'downfall' of civilization. They expected that the war would lead at once to complete economic and social confusion. In this prophecy they were wrong. They underestimated the recuperative powers of their material civilization. But the war was to cause a disaster more subtle and profound than any which was foreseen in 1914. It was to undermine man's confidence in his own nature. Henceforth your species was to suffer a kind of racial neurosis blended of guilt, horror, inferiority, and hate. Not only civilization was to be undermined, but the integrity of a species.

In the fateful days when ultimatums and declarations of war were being bandied from capital to capital, the population of Europe was wholly unprepared to take the one line which could have saved it. It had neither the courage nor the imagination for a general refusal to fight. On the other hand it could not accept the war innocently, as earlier generations had accepted wars. Hitherto men had fought with a clear conscience, however much they might personally loathe the distresses that war must bring. But, since the last war in Europe, a change had begun to come over men's minds. Though it was not yet possible for the masses to reject war, it was no longer possible for them to accept it without guilt. Few, even of those who suffered no conscious heart-searching, were wholly immune from that unwitting shame and embitterment which was the characteristic mood of your war-tortured populations, and had never occurred at all widely in any earlier war.

It was extremely interesting to observe within minds of various types the different reactions of your species to the novel fact of war. Most were taken completely by surprise. In the manner character-istic of their species they had lived hitherto without serious thought for matters of public concern. The rivalries of national states might indeed rouse in them some sentimental interest, but the life of the race lay almost wholly beyond their grasp. They were fully occupied in keeping themselves and their families afloat in the maelstrom of economic individualism. Inevitably their chief con-cern was private fulfilment, and its essential means, money. National affairs, racial affairs, cosmical events, were of interest to them only in their economic bearing, or at most as occasions of curiosity, wonder or ridicule. They produced and consumed, bought and sold, played ritual games with balls, and transported themselves hither and thither in mechanical vehicles in search of a goal which ever eluded them. They indulged in illicit sexual inter-course; or with public applause they married, propagated, launched their children upon the maelstrom. They put on their best clothes on Sunday, and after church or chapel they walked in the park. Or, with a sense less of moral guilt than of social degrada-tion, they spent their Sundays in old clothes and upon congenial occupations. Almost invariably they applauded the things they had been taught to revile. Or, if they were 'original' and dared to think and feel spontaneously, they found themselves harassed both by their fellows and by their own archaic consciences. They then either recanted or developed into extravagant cranks. But these were few. The overwhelming majority were enslaved by the custom of the herd.

Such were the beings on whom the fate of the Terrestrial spirit now depended. Nowhere was there any clear perception of the issues at stake, nowhere any recognition that the species was faced with the supreme crisis of its career. Scarcely a man or woman in Europe or America, still less in the remote East, realized that the great test of the human animal had come, and come, alas, too soon.

In their reaction to war, Western men and women revealed themselves as falling into a few well-marked types, which nevertheless graded into one another. Indeed, scarcely any individuals could be said to belong wholly to any one type. In almost all there were traces of every kind of war sentiment, and in many there was an almost diurnal fluctuation of mood from one to another. Nevertheless Western Europeans may be significantly classified according to their most characteristic attitude to the war as follows:

First, in every nation there was the incredibly large swarm of persons who, in spite of their vociferous patriotism, were at most times incapable of taking the war seriously in any sense except as a source of possible danger or profit to themselves. Such creatures we found in all classes, from manual labourers to captains of industry and respected statesmen. In the armies also we found many, who had failed to evade their military obligations. They were of all orders of intelligence, from the very stupid to the acute; but even the most brilliant of them lacked the power to see beyond the horizon of private, or at most family, interest. They were nearly always quite unconscious of their own deficiency; yet almost with the unwitting mimicry shown by some insects, they managed to behave, verbally at least, with impeccable correctness. They were seldom suspected of being inhuman. Often have we experimented on these backward animals, striving to introduce into the mind of some munition-profiteer, some popular demagogue, some climbing staff-officer, or some abject shirker in the ranks, glimmers of a self-oblivious view. Most often the experiment has failed completely; but in some cases we have been rewarded by a curious spectacle. The little self, outraged by the incursion of unselfcentred fantasies, has called 'morality' or 'duty' to its assistance. The ambitious general, for instance, troubled for a moment by the sacrifice of life entailed in some brilliant barren attack, has told himself that it is necessary, and could not see that he was caring only for his reputation as a resolute commander.

The second type recorded by our observers was less contemptible, but almost as backward. These were the persons who, though often strong in a kind of social sense, innocently accepted war and the martial code. Their vision was limited to the hero ideal. They saw the war in the good old way as a supreme opportunity of personal courage and devotion. It came, they said, to purge men of the selfishness bred of industrialism and of the softness bred of security. These guiltless champions of the war might personally behave toward it either with cowardice or heroism; but they never questioned it. With complete sincerity they faced it as a god-sent ordeal. For them it was indeed a religious test, an opportunity to enter into communion with some obscurely conceived heroic deity. To speak against it was sacrilege; but a sacrilege so gross and fantastic that it should be regarded as a sign rather of idiocy than of wickedness. Consequently, though they condemned pacifism whole-heartedly, there was no vindictiveness in their condemnation. Again and again our observers, experimenting in these simple minds, have tried to introduce some doubt, some apprehension that there might be another side to the matter. But such doubts as could be introduced appeared to the subject himself as merely an intellectual exercise, not as a live issue. Such images of brutality and disgust as were introduced were accepted simply as tests of fortitude.

Curiously it was among these archaic souls, these happy warriors, that we sometimes came upon a pellucid kind of religious experience. Fortunate innocents, they were exempt from the guilt and torture which wrecked so many of their fellows. For them the issue was a clear issue between self-regard and loyalty to all that they most cherished. And those who had the strength to bear themselves throughout according to their code had the reward of a very sweet and well-deserved beatitude. We attended many a death-agony that was thus redeemed, especially in the earliest phase of the war. Many an old regular thus found his rest. Many a very young subaltern, whose photograph on the parental mantelpiece truthfully commemorated a bright immaculate boy-soldier, found in his last moment that peace which passed his simple understanding. But many more, to whom death came less suddenly or more brutally, could not attain that bliss. Hundreds, thousands of these luckless beings, betrayed by their god, we have watched slipping down into the gulf of death, clutching, screaming, bewildered and indignant, or utterly dehumanized by pain.

More common than the 'happy warriors' was a third type, namely those who, having passed in spirit beyond this knightly innocence, still tried to retain it. These, when the war began, were first shocked and torn asunder by conflicting motives, by loyalty to the old idea of war and by the obscure stirrings of something new which they dared not clearly face. For, in spite of all their regrets and compassion, they very deeply lusted for war. And because this new thing that disturbed them ran counter to this lust and to the familiar code, they strove to ignore it. Or they persuaded themselves that though war was an evil, *this* war was a necessary evil. They elaborated all manner of arguments to convince themselves that their country's cause was the cause of humanity, or that the war, though tragic, would result in a great moral purgation. They eagerly accepted every slander against the enemy, for it was very urgent for these distraught spirits to believe that the enemy peoples were almost sub-human. Only so could they feel confident that the war was right, and indulge their martial zeal with a clear conscience. The pacifists they condemned even more bitterly than the enemy, for in tormenting the pacifists they seemed to be crushing the snake in their own hearts.

The fourth type, though not actually a majority in all lands, had the greatest influence, because in most of the other types the sentiment of this fourth type was present in some considerable degree. These were at the outset little stirred by patriotism, and for them war had but a slight romantic appeal. They thought only of individual lives and happiness, and nearest their hearts were the lives and happiness of their fellow-countrymen. Under the influence of the lying propaganda with which the spirit of each nation was poisoned by its government, they sincerely believed that the enemy government was in the wrong, and was carrying

out a base policy by brutal measures. But they preserved their sanity
so far as to believe that the enemy peoples were on the whole not
very different from themselves. As individuals the enemy were 'just
ordinary decent folk' who, through some lack of resolution, had
been led into a false policy. Consequently (so it was said) the
'group spirit' of these swarms of harmless enemy individuals was
unhealthy. In the mass they were a danger to civilization, and so at
all costs they must be beaten.

Such was the attitude of most men and many women in both the
opposed groups of peoples. They lacked faith in human nature.
And through their lack of faith in it they betrayed it. They might
so easily have risen up in their millions in all lands to say, 'This
war must stop; we will not fight.' Yet of course, though in a sense
so easy, such a refusal was also utterly impossible to them. Because
they were without any perception of man's true end, because they
accepted the world as it stood and human nature as it seemed, they
inevitably missed the great opportunity, and condemned their
species to decline. Pitiable beings, they brought upon their own
heads, and upon the future, deluges of pain, grief, despair, all
through lack of vision, or of courage. They manned a thousand
trenches, endured a thousand days and nights of ennui or horror,
displayed what in your kind is called superb devotion. All this
they did, and all for nothing. They thrust bayonets into one
another's entrails, they suffered nightmares of terror, disgust and
frantic remorse. They were haunted by bloody and filthy memories,
and by prospects of desolation. Those of them who were parents
gave up their sons, those who were women gave up their men, and
all for nothing; or for a hope that was as impossible, as meaningless, as self-contradictory, as a round square, for the mad hope that
war should end war. They believed that from their agony there must
spring a new, fair world. But in fact through their lack of faith in
one another the whole future of their species was overclouded.

The fifth type that we discovered was actually opposed to the
war. There were many kinds of pacifists. A few were those naïve
beings who, loyal to the Christian faith both in the spirit and the
letter, simply accepted the commandment 'Thou shalt not kill',
and thought no further. But the main body of effective pacifists,
even of those who gave as their motive 'religious scruples',

were of a very different water. One and all, though they knew it not, were ruled by that imperious, but still unformulated impulse which I have already noted in the case of Paul, the impulse of loyalty to the dawning spirit of man. But since the real spring of their conduct was still so obscure, they had to rationalize it in various manners. Many supposed themselves to be moved simply by the Christian faith. But indeed in these, so our observers discovered, it was not Chrstianity that had bred pacifism, but pacifism that had given Christianity a new significance. Strong in the intuitive loyalty to the great adventure of the Terrestrial mind, they interpreted that intuition as loyalty to the Christian God. They strove, so they said, to love their fellows as Jesus had bidden them, but also they strove to love Jesus himself even more. And for them Jesus, though they knew it not, was the divine spirit embodied in their groping species.

Others there were, upon whom the basis of the same intuition constructed other rationalizations. Some, believing that they cared only for the happiness of individuals, declared that the misery of war must far outweigh all its good effects. They cared nothing for national honour, nothing for treaty obligations to defend weak peoples, nothing for the propagation of national culture. These, they said, were mere phantoms, for which not one life should be sacrificed. Better for the weak peoples to have their countries occupied peaceably than turned into a battlefield. Let them be defended not by force but by the pressure of world-opinion. As for culture, it was worth nothing if it depended on bayonets and guns. Nothing whatever mattered, so they affirmed, but the happiness of individuals. Yet all the while these hedonistic pacifists unwittingly drew the fervour which made them face tribunals, prison, and in some cases a firing party, not from their liberal individualism but from that deep and obscure intuition that the human race was no mere swarm of happy-unhappy individuals, but a vessel still unfilled, an instrument still roughly fashioned, and some day to be used for cosmical achievement. For this they went to prison, for this they resisted the taunts of their own herd-consciences. For this they died; and because they felt it in their hearts that the Western peoples must now at last dare to say, each to the other, 'Rather than make war, we will let you overrun our lands, sequester our goods, sleep with our wives, educate our children to your way of living. For we are all equal vessels of the one spirit, we and you.'

Such was the composition of Europe when the war began. There was the great host of those who regarded it almost solely from the personal point of view; the smaller company of martial romantics; the conflict-racked enemy-haters and pacifist-baiters; the swarms of unimaginative loyal folk, who accepted the war as the only way to preserve human happiness, but were sorely perplexed by the savagery that was expected of them; the minute band of those who intuited that war between modern civilized men was utter folly and sacrilege, than which there could be no worse alternative.

Of these last the more resolute and the more pugnacious refused absolutely to have any part in the great madness, and were therefore persecuted, imprisoned, or even shot. But others, like Paul, less heroic, less confident of their own opinion, or more sympathetic to the great public agony, could not bring themselves to stand aside inactive. They chose therefore to help the wounded, to expose themselves so far as was permitted, to accept so far as possible on the one hand the great common agony, and on the other the private loneliness of those who cannot share the deepest passions of their fellows.

To Neptunian observers these perplexed beings were the most significant matter for study, for in them the balance between the archaic and the modern was most delicate. The conflict which in most had been violently solved, in one way or the other, was in these ever present and insoluble.

3. EUROPE AT WAR

Viewed from the moon, and with eyes such as yours, your little Great War would have been invisible, save through a powerful telescope, which would have revealed it as a minute and intermittent smoky stain on the dimly green surface of Europe. To the Martians, those intelligent clouds who in the fullness of time were to invade your planet, it was unnoticeable. With optical organs much more powerful than any terrestrial telescope, their astronomers were already observing the Earth as a promised land seen from Pisgah. But what concerned them was your atmosphere, your plentiful water, your vegetation. They sometimes wondered whether the many smears and stipples of cloud which kept appearing and disappearing in your temperate zones were intelligent organisms like themselves. But they guessed that it was not so. They detected normal clouds of vapour, and, much more rarely, clouds of smoke and dust, which they rightly believed to be of volcanic origin. The minute traces produced by your war were assumed to be of the latter type. It did not occur to the Martians that these were artificial smoke-palls, beneath which the proud denizens of Earth were blundering through a great, though a fantastic agony.

Even to the average Terrestrial, your little Great War was a minor and a remote disturbance. A few miles behind the lines one might often find complete rural peace, marred only by distant muttering. Across the English Channel men sometimes heard with awe the sound of the guns; but the widespread sense that the tragedy in France had somehow changed the spirit of peaceful landscapes in Surrey, Cumberland, or the distant Hebrides, was but a projection of war-haunted minds. The psychological reverberations of the war did indeed spread far afield. Few corners of Europe escaped such serious influences as the removal of their young men, the rationing of their food, the over-work of their remaining inhabitants. Throughout the continent there was a sense, illusory but profound, that war had somehow altered the very constitution of the universe; or that it had laid bare the sinister depths of existence, which hitherto had been concealed by the scum, the multi-coloured film, of Nineteenth-century civilization. But elsewhere, over whole continents the military operations were known only as a distant marvel, romantic, magical, scarcely real. Folk tilled and hunted, copulated and bore children, propitiated the gods of rain and storm, trapped marauding beasts and sometimes listened incredulously to travellers' tales of the White Man's War. In more remote parts of the earth, on the upper reaches of the Amazon, in African jungles, and on the Thibetan plateau, there were isolated folk who never heard rumour of your war until after it had ceased.

492

But to most Europeans it did indeed seem that when the war began the whole ground-tone of existence was altered. For a few months many clung to the conviction that this profound change of key was for the good, a transition from the sordid, though safe, to the heroic, though tortured. The Germans pressed forward toward Paris, that mythical city of delight. The French and the British 'gallantly contested every inch', and at last 'miraculously' they held their own. Stories of heroism and horror percolated through Europe, stories of the incredible effects of high-explosive shells, of great buildings collapsing like card-houses, of men's bodies blown to pieces or mown down in hundreds by machine-guns. All this was at first accepted as quite in order, quite as it should be, in the new bewildering heroic universe that had come into being. Amiable bank-clerks and shop-keepers began to spend their leisure in learning to be 'frightful' in the sacred cause, learning to give the right sort of lunge with a bayonet, to stick it success-fully into a belly; learning the right twist to release it. Paul in those early days had bought a little red manual of military training, in which he diligently studied the theory of co-operative slaughter. Here at last, he had told himself, was the grim and heroic reality, the thing that had always lain behind this solid-seeming but, in fact, phantasmal 'civilization'. Yet somehow the little book failed to give him any sense of reality at all. It seemed entirely beside the mark. This killing was after all a laborious, useless, imbecile accomplishment, like learning to play the piano with your toes. Yes, it was a new world that had come into being, and one took some time to get the feel of it. Many people seemed to Paul to unearth a new self to cope with it, a simpler, less doubting, more emotional self, a self that concealed under righteous indignation a terrible glee in the breakdown of old taboos. Even while they inveighed against the enemy's rumoured brutality, these beings of the new world seemed to savour it on the mental palate lingeringly, lustfully. They were trapped hopelessly, these vengeful ones, trapped by the spirit of the archaic animal from which the true spirit of man could not free itself. Talking to such persons, Paul glimpsed images of the half-born foal, which, through my influence, had so long haunted him.

493

Last Men in London

Gradually the romantic early phase of your war was succeeded by something very different. It almost seemed that man, in origin arboreal and subsequently terrestrial, was to end his career as the greatest and most noxious of burrowing vermin. The armies dug themselves in. They constructed immensely elongated and complex warrens, and settled down to a subterranean life of tedium punctuated by horrors formerly unimagined. It became evident to the combatants, and gradually to the home populations also, that the war was not going to be what it ought to have been. It was not a gentlemanly war. It was ruthless in a way that made the wars of the history books seem temperate. It was a life-and-death struggle in which rules were all abandoned. And it was mechanized. The spirit of it was indeed a strange blend of the machine, with its regularity and large-scale effectiveness, and the brute at bay. It was an affair of stop-watches, mathematical calculations, weight and frequency of projectiles, mechanical transport, railway co-ordination; but also it was an affair of mud, dust, blood, knives, even teeth. Everything that happened in it had two sides, a mechanical and a brutal, at the one end the exquisite designing, making, emplacing and sighting of the great gun, at the other, the shattering of human bodies, the agony of human minds. At one end the hum of munition factories, at the other the corpse-laden mud of No-man's-land, and the scream of tortured men out on the wire, imploring, inaccessible. Machinery, that creature of human imagination, had seemingly turned upon its creator, and was not only tearing up his body, but reducing his mind to the brute level from which it had emerged. For strange and disturbing things were now happening in civilized Europe. There were still, of course, plentiful stories of heroism; human nature was said to be showing itself capable of unexpected devotion and fortitude. But also there were whispers of something less reputable. The bravest and most trusted, it seemed, might be suddenly converted into panic-stricken cattle, trampling one another under foot. The most level-headed might suddenly run mad. The most generous might suddenly indulge in brutality or meanness. There were stories also of tragic muddle and betrayal of duty, stories of British shells falling in British trenches, of troops sent up to certain destruction through a staff-officer's blunder, of supplies misdirected, of whole forlorn

494

offensives launched for no reason but to satisfy the pride of some general or politician.

There is no need for me to enlarge upon these matters. They have been well enough recorded by your own scribes, and are, on the other hand, of little interest to the Neptunian observers of your great folly. Though more than ordinarily disastrous, they were but typical of the blend of organization and chaos, which is the outstanding character of your whole world-order. The Neptunian, studying that order, is inevitably reminded of the fortuitous, unplanned organization, and the blindly apt, but precarious behaviour of an ant colony. But though your massed stupidity afforded us little interest, we found in the lives of individual soldiers, and in their diverse adjustments to the war, much to arrest our attention.

For the majority, adjustment consisted in acquiring the technique of a new life, in learning to make good use of cover, to contrive some slight animal comfort for oneself even in the trenches, to make the best of minute pleasures, savouring them, drop by drop, to live upon the hope of strawberry jam, or a parcel from home, or a letter in a well-known hand, or a visit to some woman behind the lines; or, failing these ecstasies, to make the best of plum jam, of a rum-ration, or of sex without woman; to 'wangle' small privileges out of the great military machine, to be expert in 'système D'; and at the same time to take deep into one's heart the soldier's morality of faithful obedience to superiors, faithful loyalty to comrades, and complete irresponsibility in respect of all things further afield; to live within the moment and within the visible horizon; to shut the eyes of the spirit against disgust, and stop the ears of the spirit against horror, against self-pity, against doubt.

It is true that to many spiritually undeveloped beings the war-life was a tonic. Many of those who had been nurtured in prosperity, or at least in ease, who had never faced distress, and never been tortured by compassion, were now roughly awakened. Generously they gave themselves, and in the giving they found themselves. But others of their kind were broken by the ordeal. The awakening came too late, or to natures incapable of generosity.

But it was not in these, either the made or the marred, that our

observers were interested. We were concerned rather to watch the
adjustments of those in whom there was at work a force alien to
the simple soldier ideal. Many such have I myself inhabited. At the
outset they have gone forth with a sense that the heavens applauded
them, that there was a God whom they were serving, and who
would recompense them for their huge sacrifice with the inestim-
able prize of his approval. But, soon or late, their faith has been
destroyed by the ugly facts of war.

Let me tell of one case, unique, yet typical of thousands on both
sides of the line. From the Terrestrial point of view, the events
which I am about to relate were contemporary with the story of
Paul, already partially recounted; and they culminated in 1917,
when the war was far advanced, and Paul had already been more
than two years in France. But from the Neptunian point of view
my exploration of these events took place some time before I had
made the acquaintance of Paul. The specimen case that I shall now
report is one of my most interesting treasures. Also, it nearly cost
me my life.

He was a young German, a native of Neustadt in the Black
Forest, and he had been trained for the care of trees. His hands
were skilled in tending the baby pines in their crowded nurseries,
and in planting them out in the greater world of the forest. When
he wielded the axe or the saw, the deed was done with precision,
and also with a deep sense of fate. The resinous odour of the forest
and of fresh-cut wood, the ever-present vision of towering shafts
and swaying branches, the occasional glimpse of a deer, – these
things he valued lightly while he was yet with them; but when he
was removed from them he longed for them.

Now this young man, whom I will call Hans, had been selected
for study because, though he became a good soldier, he was more
than a good soldier. During his career as a forester I had found in
him a very unusual feeling for individual trees, and for the
massed ranks of the forest. He could not help regarding them as
each one a unique spirit, living according to the laws of its own
being, and striving toward perfection of life. In his capacity of
woodman, tender in nurturing, relentless in the final execution, he
persuaded himself that, though to the trees themselves the goal
seemed to be merely endless enlargement in girth and stature, he,

in his lethal ministration, afforded them in spite of themselves a nobler destiny, a fuller achievement. Sometimes when he regarded a score or so of the great felled trunks, laid flank to flank, with the resin still oozing from their clean-sawn wounds, he would say to the standing forest, 'Do not pity them, for they have gloriously attained their destiny.' Then with reverence, almost it seemed with envy of this beatitude, he would lay his hand on the rough and tawny skin of some prone giant, in a last salute. For the great communal being of the forest, reclining so grandly on its many hills, he had a feeling compounded of benevolence and awe. It was for him a spirit, one of God's nobler creatures. When it began to be depleted for the war he was distressed. But even the forest, he admitted, must be sacrificed for that even nobler forest, the Fatherland.

He was a good son of the Fatherland, and also a good Catholic. They told him that the English and the French were servants of Satan, who wanted to harm the Fatherland. He went to the war filled with a sense of glorious adventure in a great cause. He was very proud of his new life. He cared for his rifle as he cared for his axe, and became as deadly a shot as he was precise a sawyer. When he killed his first man, with a bullet through the forehead, he had that sense of fate, and of calm almost loving execution, which he had known in felling the beloved trees in their ripeness. His next man he overcame in savage hand-to-hand struggle in the dark. For the Fatherland and in defence of his own life he did it; but there was no joy in it. Little by little he earned a reputation for coolness and resolution. He volunteered for a number of dangerous tasks and carried them out with distinction. When steel helmets were issued, he was proud to wear one. Its noble curves suggested the mythical heroes of his race. Its weight on his head crowned him.

At first Hans thought of the war in terms of his forest-born philosophy. He and his comrades were trees, who sought one destiny but were to find another, less easeful but more fulfilling to the spirit. But little by little it began to appear to him that this war, nay this world, was no well-tended forest but a terrible primeval jungle in which everything was crippled by everything else, and all things were useless. He strove to put away this thought by drugging himself with war propaganda, or with duties, or with pleasures. But it would not leave him. So greatly did it disturb him that everything began to seem changed and sinister to him. Common objects looked at him meaningfully, tauntingly. Empty tins and trampled cigarette-ends would leer at him like little devils, deriding him for being trapped. His own hands in their ordinary actions seemed somehow to reproach him for putting them to serve the Devil. He had an overwhelming sense of betrayal. But whether it was that he himself was betrayed, or that he had betrayed something else, was never quite clear. Emblems of his religion, encountered in shattered churches or shrines, sometimes reproached him with his irrevocable treason; sometimes on the other hand they confessed themselves mere jests perpetrated by the universal diabolic power which had masqueraded as the God of Love. He began to think about the men he had killed, and to see them again, especially at night, especially a French corporal whose face he had smashed with a hand grenade. His rifle now took on a snake-like coldness in his hands, so that he shuddered. His helmet pressed on his forehead vindictively. Over all things there was a kind of darkness, which was the worse because he knew it was not 'real'. In his ears there began to be a distant wailing as of wind, which when the great guns roared and crashed, was yet heard screaming above them.

In fact, Hans was on the way to breakdown. Now Neptunian observers found amongst you two kinds of breakdown, very different in origin. Both types are of great interest to us, because the more effectively integrated minds of our own species afford the psychologist no such opportunity of study, even under the most severe strain. One type of Terrestrial disorder, the commoner, was due to the conflict between primitive biological impulses of self-preservation and the behaviour imposed by military obligation. The other, which was more interesting to us, sprang from the conflict between military obligation and the still unrecognized impulse of loyalty to the striving Terrestrial spirit. This was the conflict which was most seriously undermining Hans, though the other also was of course adding to his distress. He himself lacked the self-knowledge to understand his trouble. He thought it was simply a trouble of the more primitive kind, and was bitterly ashamed. He determined not to give way, but to pull himself together. Both loyalty and self-pride demanded it.

In the case of Hans and a small minority of his fellow-men this ruinous mental conflict was complicated by another and even less understood division of the mind, namely by the fundamental and insoluble problem of your species, the discord between loyalty to the adventuring spirit of Man and on the other hand the ecstatic admiration of fate even when tragic. Although deep in his heart Hans was coming to realize that to fight for the Fatherland or any nation was treason to Man, and that this war was diabolic, he had also a vivid though unintelligible apprehension of the whole great hideous tumult as somehow an expression of super-human, in-human, beauty. His mind was therefore torn by a three-cornered conflict, between old tribal loyalty, the new loyalty to Man, and the zest of tragic existence.

It was with dreadful satisfaction that Hans found himself involved once more in the centre of a great offensive. I, his in-dwelling companion, knew that within the next few days he would meet his death; but I did not know precisely when it would occur. I had therefore to prepare myself to leave him by partially reverting my attention to my own world. But at the same time it was neces-sary to observe him closely, for the moments of his life which would be of supreme interest to me were now at hand. I had also to keep a wary eye upon his circumstances, lest I should be entangled with him in his death.

All this happened at a time when I had been rather too constantly engaged on work in your world, and was so soaked in your mental-ity that I could not at all easily disengage myself from it. Moreover I found myself extremely reluctant to do so. Not only was I desirous to follow Hans through to his last moment, and if possible to afford his tortured spirit something of the Neptunian serenity, but also I was by now trapped by an overwhelming affection for your tragic world. It was therefore both with difficulty and with a strangely violent regret that I set myself to recapture in imagina-tion the wider horizons and the crystalline titanic edifices of Neptune, the great limbs and eloquent features of my own race. My regret alarmed me; for it was a sure sign that I had stayed in your world much longer than was wholesome. Like one lost in the snow, who has an overwhelming desire to lie down and sleep, but knows that if he does he will never rise again, and never complete his work, so I now realized that a great effort was necessary. I began to goad myself by thinking of all the precious fruits of my exploration, which, if I were to succumb, would never be delivered to my own world.

Meanwhile the hour of the offensive was approaching. From the felt tone of Hans's body, it was evident that he was going sick; but he would not admit it to himself. He developed a distressing colic and diarrhoea, but he clung to his post. He was seized also by a strong premonition of death, an infection from my own awareness that this was indeed his last battle. While he and his comrades were awaiting the order to attack, Hans experienced a sudden increase of mental lucidity. In desperate haste he reviewed his whole life, his whole experience of existence. He was terrified at the contrast, not the physical but the spiritual contrast, between his forest years and the present. Then, there was a bland rightness about everything. Now, everything, even generous and gallant action, was somehow evil, tainted by an all-pervading shame. He said to himself, 'We have simply walked all together into Hell.'

It was almost the moment of attack. I knew that he would survive the storming of the enemy first-line trench; for I had previously learned from a Neptunian colleague, who had already observed this action through the eyes of another individual, that Hans was to be seen alive in the trench. Therefore I felt secure enough to watch my man minutely for a while, and to prepare his mind to meet death with peace, instead of the rage and despair that had hitherto possessed him. While he was still waiting inactive, Hans was very near to breaking-point. It seemed possible that he would not obey the order to advance. But when the word came, he clambered up with the rest; and as he pounded across the tract of shell-torn earth and tangled wire, he suddenly blazed up with maniac hate of the universe and all its denizens. In those moments it mattered not at all to him whether his bayonet should pierce a blue or a grey uniform. Nothing mattered, but that he should void the hate that was in him. I felt a bullet tear one of his ears. He did not notice it. A near shell killed the man on his right, and half-buried Hans himself. He picked himself up and stumbled on.

It now became clear that I was far more dangerously entangled in your world than I had thought; for at this moment, as I watched the desperate plight of this blind half-human spirit, I found myself suddenly undermined by doubt of my own Neptunian vision. Here was a mind blessed neither with the insensitivity of the beast nor with the all-redeeming vision of my own species, a mind deranged by the horror and guilt of three years of war, and now overwhelmingly nauseated by its own being and by the satanic universe which had spawned it only to devour it, a mind which looked forward to nothing but horror and annihilation for itself, and futility for its world. It suddenly appeared to me that a universe in which such torture could occur must be utterly vile, and that the Neptunian complacency was heartless. This apostasy I noted with dismay; but by now I was in no mood to withdraw myself into spiritual safety. More important it seemed to stay with Hans, and afford him at all costs at least an illusory consolation.

While he was covering the last few paces to the enemy trench, I was somewhat anxiously engaged in two very different undertakings. The first was to thrust upon the mind of Hans an image of the forest, which might serve as the starting-point for a spiritual change. The second, which I undertook at first with reluctance, was to prepare myself for a sudden exit from your world. I successfully established in him the vision of lofty trunks and sombre foliage. As he plunged into the trench with his bayonet in the neck of an enemy, this image took possession of the deeper region of his mind. I then began to think more conscientiously of my own safety, and to steady myself in earnest for the leap to Neptune. I pictured my own far future body, lying asleep in my subterranean garden. I dwelt upon the translucent features of the woman called Panther. I reminded myself of the Mad Star and of the supreme disaster which we, the Last Men, await undismayed. Contemplating this the last scene of the tragedy of Man, I began once more to see your little war in its true proportions. Presently the cramped and unwholesome feel of the young German's body began to fade from me. The racket of battle, the tumbled and bleeding human forms, began to seem as a dream when one is all but wakened, a dream of being entangled in the insensate feuds of wild animals.

But now something happened which recalled my attention wholly to your sphere. A savage tussle was taking place in the trench, and the invaders were becoming masters of the situation. Hans, however, was playing no part in the fight. He was standing aside watching it, as though it were a dog-fight. In his mind was a vast confusion, caused by a sudden enlightenment. Not only had the forest-image started a change in him, but also he had been infected by my own reversion to the Neptunian mentality, so that in those moments he too experienced a kind of awakening. Suddenly he flung away his rifle and rushed with a huge laugh into the melée. Seizing one of his countrymen by the collar and the seat of the trousers, he tugged him away, crying, 'No more brawling.' An officer, seeing that Hans was out of his mind and causing trouble, shot him through the head.

Fortunately I had caught sight of the muzzle of the weapon out of the corner of Hans's eye. Desperately, with a wild leap of the mind, I disengaged myself from your world.

I awoke to find myself in bed in my garden. I could not remember what had happened, but I had a violent pain in my head, and several of my colleagues were standing round me. They had heard me scream, they said, and had come running to my assistance. A few minutes later, apparently, I lost consciousness again and fell into convulsions. I remember nothing further till six weeks later, when I awoke to find myself in the tree-girt hospital where shattered explorers are nursed back to health.

4. PAUL IN THE WAR

While I was studying Hans, I was of course also, in the very same span of Terrestrial duration, resident in Paul. Yet from the Neptunian point of view, let me repeat, my operations upon Hans took place before I had even discovered Paul. Consequently while I was in Hans I knew nothing about Paul and my work upon him, but while I was in Paul I remembered my experiences in Hans. This fact, as I shall tell in due season, had in one respect a curious effect on Paul.

Meanwhile I must revert to Paul's career at the point where I first introduced him into this survey. It will be remembered that he was suffering an agony of indecision about the war, that he hurried to a recruiting office, and then fled away from it. We left him slinking through the streets of London.

During the next few days Paul was frequently troubled by his waking nightmare, the mare that was dead, with her strangled foal. Sometimes it seemed to him that he himself was the foal, unable to free himself from the restriction of an outgrown mentality. Sometimes the whole human race was the foal. Sometimes on the other hand, the foal was just his unborn martial self, throttled by his most unmartial past.

A few days later Paul heard of a curious semi-religious ambulance organization, which, while professing pacifism, undertook voluntary succour of the wounded at the front. It was controlled and largely manned by a certain old-established and much-respected religious sect which adhered strictly to the commandment 'Thou shalt not kill', and to its own unique tradition of good works and quietism. Some members of this sect preached a rigorous pacifism which very soon brought them into conflict with authority; but others, who tempered pacifism with a craving to take some part in the great public ordeal, created this anomalous organization, whose spirit was an amazing blend of the religious, the military, the pacific, the purely adventurous, and the cynical. This 'Ambulance Unit' lasted throughout the war. It was formed in the first instance as an outlet for the adventurousness of the younger sectarians, who very naturally chafed at their exclusion from the tremendous adventure and agony of their contemporaries. Throughout its career it contained many such, normal young men eager for ardours and endeavours, who, though they had no very serious pacifist convictions, remained loyal to the tradition of their fathers, and refused to bear arms. Others there were, both within and without the sectarian fold, who, though they profoundly felt that to make war in modern Europe under any circumstances whatever was treason against something more sacred than nationalism, had yet not the heart to wash their hands of the world's distresses.

Such were the pioneers of this strange organization; but as time passed it gathered to itself a very diverse swarm of persons who were driven from their civil occupations either by public opinion or their own consciences, or finally by legal compulsion. A few, very few, were narrow-hearted beings whose chief motive was simply to avoid what they regarded as the spiritual defilement of a soldier's work. There was also a sprinkling of artists and intellectuals whose main concern was neither religion nor pacifism, but the adventures of the mind in novel circumstances. Among those who were admitted into the Unit after conscription had been introduced into England, some were serious pacifists who had been loyal to their civilian duties as long as possible; and a few, whose pacifism was only skin deep, chose the Unit as the line of least resistance, simply because they had no stomach either for the trenches or for prison.

To the military authorities this fantastic organization was a minute and negligible excrescence on the military machine. The dignitaries of the armies, if ever they came across it at all, regarded it at first as something to be kept at arm's length until it had been brought under proper military control. It was a God-sent butt for ridicule. On the other hand it proved to have its uses; and often it earned a kind of incredulous respect, even affection.

To Neptunian observers this uncomfortable medley of cranks and commonplace individuals appeared, surprising as it may seem, as one of the most interesting phenomena of your whole war. It was not the mere pacifism of these beings that concerned us, for at home and later in the prisons there were pacifists more logical and more heroic. What interested us was the heart-searching bewilderment of minds which could not find harmony either with the great mass of their warring fellows or with the more relentless pacifists. We are interested too in the reactions which these unclassified beings aroused in any ordinary persons who happened to come across them. For they were neither fish, flesh, fowl, nor good red herring. They claimed to be pacifists, but obviously they were 'helping to win the war' by releasing others for more arduous military duties. Surely, then, they were either fools or shirkers. Surely, said the martial-minded, they ought all to be in the trenches, or put in prison, or, better still, shot. But others, the majority, gave them a contemptuous toleration.

To Paul it seemed that by joining this body he would be both taking part in the war and registering his protest against it. In fact, as he ruefully admitted, he would both have his cake and eat it. But what else could he do? He was convinced at last that some mysterious thing inside him would always prevent him from enlisting. But if he could not fight, neither must he shirk. That he was moved at all by the will to avoid the extremity of danger and agony he did not admit; for he pictured himself as a stretcher-bearer rescuing the wounded under fire, or as a motor-ambulance driver trundling his car where the fight was hottest. So little did he yet know of 'modern' warfare.

Paul joined the Unit. With surprise and with shame-faced delight, he learned that he must dress as a British officer, though with certain distinguishing signs. On his left arm he must wear a red-cross brassard, stamped with a kind of postage mark. His hat also bore a red cross on a huge white square. Neptunian observers have been much indebted to this uniform. Nothing could have better symbolized the mental discord of Paul and his like. Nothing could have been more nicely calculated to intensify that discord. One side of Paul clung to the delusion that since he was to be dressed as an officer he must be after all, in spirit, a member of that gallant fraternity. The other side of him recognized that this could not be. He became in fact an object of ridicule, sometimes of indignant scorn. Wherever he went, he felt people wondering what on earth he was, and how he dared to caricature his betters. Pacifists, on the other hand, raised their eyebrows at his military colouring. One day while he was still painfully conscious of his uniform, he met Katherine in the street. Her husband was already in the trenches. She gazed at Paul for a moment in amazement, suppressed a smile, was smitten by Paul's distress, and became blunderingly tactful.

In France Paul was less conscious of his uniform. There were others of his kind, and anyhow no one seemed to mind. Moreover he had work to do. Having had some slight acquaintance with a motor-bicycle, he was set to help in the repair of broken-down cars at the headquarters of the Unit. A few weeks later he became an orderly on a motor ambulance. He made innumerable journeys between the advanced stations and the hospitals, working entirely for the French army. For the first time he dealt with the wounded, with sitting-cases mostly cheerful at their release, and stretcher-cases in all phases of distress and weakness. Paul was at first deeply disturbed by compassion for these much-bandaged blue-clad figures, many of whom moaned and lamented at every jerk of the car. He was also bitterly ashamed before them, because he was whole and full of life. Yet there was another part of him which reacted in a less orthodox manner, and one which Paul himself at first regarded as disreputable, even Satanic. It was almost like the glee of the scientist watching a successful experiment, or of the artist apprehending some high, intricate, inevitable form. Paul tried hard not to feel in this way, or not to know that he felt so. But he could not help it; and he was abashed at his own brutality. It was I who caused this feeling in him, I, working upon his own rudimentary impulses. He need not have been ashamed.

In these days the main concern of Paul's life, apart from the overwhelming wounded themselves, was to get to the end of each journey without a mishap, and to escape night work. There was also an increasing sense that, after all, this was not good enough, not the sort of thing he wanted for his conscience' sake. Occasionally he saw a shell burst in the sand-dunes, or knock off the corner of a house. But as for stretcher-bearing in the front line, there was not to be anything of the sort. None of the armies were going to let irresponsible volunteers do work which demanded strict military discipline. One day, however, a gay young member of the party was killed by a shell. Paul found himself torn between regret for the dead boy and selfish satisfaction that, after all, this work was not entirely sheltered.

The weeks and months passed, weeks made up of sultry day-driving and pitch-black night-driving, of blood-stained blankets, packs, overcoats, of occasional alarms, of letters written and received, of bathes in the sea, not far from the steel entanglements which crossed the beach at the end of the line. Then there were talks, talks with those who shared the dilemma of Paul himself, and talks with the utterly different beings who accepted the war with a shrug; laborious, joking conversations with innumerable *poilus*, and still more laborious smutty jests, sometimes with Algerians and Moroccans.

506

Some months after the beginning of his war career, Paul, who had learnt to drive, was put in charge of a motor ambulance on a new convoy, which was to go far away south to a part of the line beyond the British front. His companions, some forty in all, constituted a fair sample of the Unit. There were sons of rich and religious manufacturers, and there were very small traders. There were printer's apprentices, social workers, mechanics, students, clerks, teachers, shop assistants, artists. There were devout sectarians, less devout sectarians, and those who in revulsion from piety were at pains to shock the devout with cynicism and ribaldry. There were careless young Irishmen seeking adventure without military discipline. There were kindly and earnest products of sectarian schools, and others who had emerged from the same schools with a no less earnest, no less kindly, frivolity. There were grizzled men who secretly cared nothing for pacifism, but sought the quickest way of seeing the spectacle of war. Here I may mention, too, the colourless but useful creature whom I have chosen as my mouthpiece for communicating with you. He has served me well in the past for the recounting of events in which he played no part; but now that it is necessary to dwell for a moment on microscopic occurrences of which he himself was a witness, I find him less manageable. It is not always possible to prevent him from dwelling unduly on the insignificant hardships and dangers in which he participated. Such were the companions of Paul, the unique being whom I had so carefully prepared for this experience.

With a sense that at last the test was coming, the Convoy lumbered south. It left behind it all traces of the British Army, which it so envied, respected, and obscurely feared. Presently it found itself established in a town beside an old royal hunting forest. And there for months it stayed, finding much hard work, but none of the ardours which it sought. In time even the work decreased, to a steady routine. In the earliest and more disorderly phase of the war the pioneers of this 'Ambulance Unit' had found ample opportunity to show that pacifism was not incompatible with courage and endurance; and even now, other Convoys of the Unit, it was said, were being of real use, and suffering real danger and hardship. But this Convoy, it seemed, was fated to idleness. There grew up a general restlessness, a tendency to quarrel over nothing,

a disposition to walk violently along the geometrically ruled
'allées' of that prim forest. Paul conceived a sentimental passion
for the forest. He withdrew as far as possible from his companions,
and tried to think of himself as some kind of a fawn trapped into a
human way of life. He found a deep satisfaction in sleeping on a
stretcher under the stars and branches. I contrived that the forest
should increasingly take possession of him, for I wished to perform a minor experiment on him. Reconstructing in my own mind
the personality of Hans, who was at this time sniping Frenchmen
further down the line, I brought Paul also under the young
forester's influence. Paul began to feel toward this neat French
forest almost as Hans toward his grander German one. He spent
all his spare time in it, laying bare his spirit, so he thought, to the
presence of the trees. He began to write verses again, in his own
groping technique. Here is one of them.

TIMBER

Stroke of the Axe! The trunk shivers and gapes.
Stroke on stroke! The chips fly.
'Oh year upon year upon year I grew,
since I woke in the seed.'
Stroke of the axe!
Raw, wounded wood, and the heart laid bare.
'Oh sun, and wind, and rain!
Oh leafing, and the fall of leaves!
Oh flower, love, and love's fruit!'
Fierce bite of the axe!
Staggering, crying timber.
Down!
The twigs and the little branches are shattered
on the ground.
The woodman stands,
measuring.

After some months of futility, the Convoy became so restless
that its leaders persuaded the army authorities to give it a change.
Henceforth it was to be attached permanently to one of the
divisions of the French army. Once more the dark-green vehicles,
plastered with red and white emblems of mercy, lumbered through

France in search of a dreaded and a longed-for goal. The Convoy joined its Division in 'Lousy Champagne', whose barren hills were now snowclad. This was during the Great Cold. The bread crystallized, the ration wine froze. The radiators of the cars, boiling at the top, froze at the bottom. At night Paul, shivering in his sleeping-bag under a pile of blankets in his canvas-sided car, thought of the trenches and was abashed.

The weeks rolled by. In quiet times Paul and his friends played rugger with the Division, or walked over the down-like hills which were already beginning to stipple themselves with flowers. It grew warm, hot. They bathed in the stream, their white bodies rejoicing in freedom from stiff military clothes. On one of these occasions Paul, dozing naked in the sun before his dip, dreamed about my seaside holiday with the woman, Panther. This dream had an interesting effect on him. He woke with a sense of the shadowy unreality of all Terrestrial events beyond the immediate reach of his senses; but the bright meadow, the willow-shaded stream, the delicious aliveness of his own sun-kindled body, had gained from his dream a more intense reality, an added spiritual significance. He thought of Katherine, whose breasts at least he had known. His flesh stirred. In sudden exasperation at his own futility and the world's perversity, he dived.

Sometimes the young Englishmen went into the little town behind the lines to take wine or coffee, omelettes or *gauffres*; or to talk to the daughter of the *patron*. By the cynics it was maliciously suggested that this grey-eyed Athene had relations other than conventional with certain members of the Convoy. But to the devout this horror was incredible. Paul at least confessed to himself that he would have gladly lain with her, for he was hungry for woman, and she found her way into his dreams. But, however she treated others, to Paul she remained sweetly unapproachable. His failure with her intensified his discontent with the whole life of the Convoy. He wanted to prove himself a man, to have a share in the world's burden, even if the world was a fool to bear it. To the Neptunian it was very interesting to observe in the Convoy this growing obsession with the need to vindicate pacifism by physical courage. At this time some who had hot blood and little care for pacifism went home to join the fighting forces. Others went home not to enlist but to go to prison for their pacifism. New hands came from headquarters to replenish the Convoy. Now that conscription was in force there was no lack of personnel.

Paul himself, whenever he went home on leave, had thoughts of joining the army. But he knew that these thoughts sprang only from his loneliness in a land intent on war, not from conviction of duty. On leave he was always cowed. He felt himself an outcast. He felt the women flaunting their soldiers at him. And the soldiers, though they let him alone, put him to shame. People at home judged him according to their own natures, as an impossible idealist, a fool, or a common shirker. All arguments closed with the same formula, 'But we *must* fight, to keep the Germans out.' When Paul dared to say 'Would it really matter so *very* much if they came?' he was silenced by stories of atrocities which in his heart he could not believe.

Once when he was on leave he met the Archangel, who was now an army chaplain, and had been wounded. They dined together at a railway restaurant among officers and women. Paul, homeward bound, was shabby. His tunic had a torn pocket, mended clumsily by his own hands. Those hands, which he had scrubbed till they seemed unusually clean, now turned out after all to be ingrained with engine oil; and his nails were ragged. He felt as though, for his ungentlemanly conduct in refusing to fight, he had been degraded from his own social class. This sense of loss of caste was intensified by the fact that he was wearing a closed collar; for since conscription had come in, the Unit had been made to give up the secretly cherished open collar of the officer's tunic. The Archangel was friendly, sympathetic even. Yet in his very sympathy, so at least it seemed to Paul, condemnation was implied. Over coffee Paul suddenly asked, not without malice, 'What would Jesus have done?' While the priest was looking at the tablecloth for an answer, Paul, to his own horror, said in a clear loud voice, 'Jesus would have shot the politicians and the war lords and started a European revolution.' There was a silence in the restaurant. The pained Archangel murmured, 'Strange talk from a pacifist, isn't it?' Then at last quite suddenly Paul's pacifism defined itself in his mind, assumed a precise and limiting outline. To the Archangel he said, not too loud, but with conviction, 'To fight for one's nation

against other nations in a world insane with nationalism, is an
offence against the spirit, like fighting for a religious sect in a world
insane with sectarianism. But to fight for revolution and a new
world-order *might* become necessary.' Paul was surprised at himself for making this statement. How it would grieve his pacifist
friends! Was it true, he wondered. One conviction at least became
clear in his mind. Whatever was needed to bring about a right
world-order was itself right. But national wars could never do
this, and were utterly wrong. Perhaps the only thing that could
bring about a right world-order was not violence but a very great
change in the hearts of ordinary people. But could that change
ever occur? Somehow, it must.

Such were the thoughts that occupied Paul during the pause
that followed the Archangel's protest.

It was always with mingled despair and relief that Paul went
back from leave. On leave he was haunted by the foal-image.
When he was in the war area he felt there was some life in the
creature yet; it was struggling though doomed. But at home it
seemed already dead, mere horsemeat, never to be the friend of
Man.

Life on the familiar sector was in the main too humdrum to be
very repugnant. Sometimes for a day or two there would be activity.
The roads would be seriously shelled, and the loaded cars would
have to run the gauntlet. It was unpleasant, even nerve-racking,
but it was soon over. And always one knew that this was but child's
play, not the real thing. During one of these minor disturbances,
while Paul was returning to the front with an empty car, and shells
were dropping close around him, he saw a figure lying at the road-
side, its head badly smashed. Obviously the man was dead, so
Paul drove on. But the next car stopped to pick him up, and he was
still alive. For months Paul was haunted by that incident, going over
it again and again in an agony of shame. It became to him the
nadir of his existence. It increased his ludicrous obsession over
physical courage.

The Division liked its 'Section Sanitaire Anglaise'. It had come
to regard these strayed English no longer with suspicion, but with
affection tempered by incredulity. It excused their pacifism as one
might excuse a Mohammedan for not eating pork. No doubt in

both cases there was some equally remote and fantastic historical explanation. To Frenchmen it was apparently inconceivable that anyone should take pacifism seriously unless it happened to be an element of his religious orthodoxy. For Frenchmen themselves, so the Convoy had long ago discovered, the only serious religion was France, the only orthodoxy uncompromising loyalty to France. If any one suggested that some policy beneficial to France might not be acceptable to other peoples, these amiable, lucid, but strangely unimaginative Latin children would no doubt charmingly express regret, but would also point out that if the policy was necessary for France, they must support it. The extermination of wild animals by the march of civilization is to be regretted, but no sane man would suggest that civilization should be restricted in order to save them. As to pacifism, anyhow, it was no more practicable in Europe than in the jungle. Thus talked the considerate and very gallant officers of the Division, so respect-worthy in sky-blue and gold. Thus talked the amiable *poilus*, so devoted to their distant families and the land they should be tilling. And, indeed, all that the troops said about pacifism was true. They and their like *made* it impossible. Once more, the foal.

One Frenchman indeed did show some understanding of these English cranks. He was one of the two priests attached to the Division. His colleague, a red-bearded lover of wine, wore military uniform, and was a hearty friend of the troops; but M. l'Abbé himself wore his black cassock, tramped the whole sector with his finger in a little volume of St. Thomas, and was revered. He would talk long with the English over meals in dug-outs, for he was interested in their sect and their ideas. Of their pacifism he would repeat, 'Ah, mes chers messieurs, si tout le monde pouvait sentir comme vous!' One day he was caught by a shell, which broke his leg. Members of the Convoy visited him in hospital, where his clean body was making a quick recovery. Then, through some muddle over a change of staff, he was neglected, and died. In the commemorative address given by his colleague, the abbot's death was laid to the account of the God-hating enemy. To Paul it seemed to be due to more complex causes.

In most Frenchmen's eyes the pacifism of these English merely gave an added and farcical piquancy to a body that had already earned respect for its efficiency. For these pacifists were extremely conscientious in their work, as is indeed to be expected where consciences suffer from chronic irritation. The Division also admired, and politely ridiculed, the extravagant cleanliness of the Convoy. In quiet times the paintwork of its cars was sleek with paraffin. Lamps, fittings, even crank-cases were kept bright with metal polish. Some of the members grumbled, but all acquiesced. Thus did the Convoy pay tribute to the great British Army, which in spite of antimilitarism it so faithfully admired.

Cleanliness did not interfere with efficiency. What the Convoy undertook to do, it invariably did. On the other hand, from the Division's point of view, the conscientiousness of these English sometimes went too far, as when they flatly refused to transport rifles and ammunition to the front in their red-cross cars. The General was indignant, and threatened to get rid of this pack of lunatics. But an artist member of the Convoy was at that time painting his portrait, so the matter was dropped.

By now this little speck of Englishmen in an ocean of Latins had acquired a strong group-spirit. Though internally it was generally at loggerheads with itself, all its jarring elements were in accord in maintaining the prestige of the Convoy. If any one indulged in some minor lapse, public opinion was emphatically against him. On the other hand, if the officers of the Convoy sought to introduce customs which to the rank and file seemed unnecessary or obnoxious, the cry of 'militarism' was raised; and the long-suffering officers, though they had behind them the whole power of the British and French armies, patiently argued the matter out with the rebels. Punishment was unknown in the Convoy.

This little group of two score persons was ever in a state of internal strain, either between the officers and the rest, or between one clique and another. Thus the earnestly devout would outrage the earnestly frivolous by organizing religious meetings. The frivolous would conscientiously get mildly drunk on ration wine. The earnestly philistine talked sex and sport, motors and war, to maintain their integrity against the earnestly intellectual, who talked art, politics, pacifism, and what they thought was philosophy. Yet all alike, or nearly all, received something from the strange corporate being of the Convoy. All were intensely conscious of their nationality, and of the need to impress these foreigners with British excellence. Yet all were outcasts from their nation, and deeply ashamed; even though also they consciously despised nationalism, and vehemently prophesied cosmopolitanism.

At last the test came. The Division moved to a part of the line beside the Montagne de Rheims. On the way the Convoy was caught up in a continuous stream of traffic making for the front, a stream of troops, guns, limbers, troops, motor-lorries, tanks, troops, ambulance sections. There was indescribable congestion, long waits, snail progress. Ahead a ceaseless roar of guns. On this journey I found in Paul a ludicrous blend of thankfulness and fright. His body was continuously in a state of suppressed tremor. Now and then he fetched a huge sigh, which he carefully turned into a yawn, lest his companion should guess that he was not looking forward to this offensive with the enthusiasm affected by all true members of the Convoy. Paul kept saying to himself, 'This is the real thing, this is reality.' But sometimes what he said was, 'Reality? It's just a bloody farce.'

The Convoy reached its destination and took over its duties. For a few days there was normal work, save that the roads were fairly steadily shelled. One shell Paul had reason to remember. He was in the courtyard that served the Convoy as a parking-ground. A score of blue figures tramped past the gateway singing, exchanging pleasantries with the English. They marched on, and disappeared behind the wall. Then there was a shattering explosion, followed by dead silence. The English rushed out into the road. There lay the twenty blue figures, one of them slowly moving the stump of an arm. Blood trickled down the camber of the road, licking up the dust. It flowed along the gutters. Paul and his mates got stretchers and carried away those who were not dead, shouting instructions to one another, for the shelling continued. During this operation Paul had one of those strange fits of heightened per-cipience which my influence sometimes brought upon him. Every-thing seemed to be stamped upon his senses with a novel and exquisite sharpness, the limpness of the unconscious bodies that he lifted, a blood-stained letter protruding from a torn pocket, a steel helmet lying in the road, with a fragment of some one's scalp in it, bloody and lousy. Paul's legs were trembling with fright and nausea, while the compassionate part of him insisted that these unhappy fellow mortals must be succoured. For some might live. That letter might yet after all be answered. It seemed to Paul now imperative that this *poilu* and his *maraine* should communicate once more. Yet at the same time that deep mysterious alien part of him, which he was gradually coming to accept and even value, laughed delicately, laughed as one may laugh with tenderness at the delicious gaucherie of a child.

It seemed to say to the other Paul, and to the stricken men also, 'You dear, stupid children, to hurt yourselves like this, and to be so upset about it! Babes will be babes; and monkeys, monkeys.'

When Paul was off duty he went up into the forest-clad mountains and looked down at the line of dense smoke which marked the front, overhung at regular intervals by the two rows of captive balloons, stretching indefinitely into the south-east. An enemy 'plane, harassed at first by white points of shrapnel, attacked a French balloon, which burst into flame. A scarcely visible parachute sank earthward from it. Paul went further into the forest. Here there was a kind of peace in spite of the roaring guns. Under my influence the spirit of Hans came on him again, so that he had a perplexing sense that, in the presence of his brothers the trees, he was brought mysteriously into touch also with his brothers the enemy.

The offensive began. Henceforth there was continuous work, with rare meals and no sleep. French and German wounded came flooding in. Hundreds who could find no place in the cars had to stagger all the way down to the chateau where the gaily-clad doctors grew more and more flustered. Slowly, uncertainly, these walking wounded swarmed along the road, their blue and their grey clothes sometimes indistinguishable for dust and blood. The roads now began to be impossible with shell-holes, and choked with wreckage. At one time Paul, hurrying along under shell-fire with a full load of sorrowing creatures shaken together in his reeling car, found himself behind a galloping artillery wagon. At the cross-roads, where some one, for reasons unknown, had propped a dead sergeant against the sign-post, a shell fell on the front of the wagon. The two men and one of the rear horses were killed. Its fellow floundered with broken legs, then died. The leaders stampeded. The road was now completely blocked. French and English dragged the dead horses and the limber to the ditch, tugging frantically at harness and splintered wood, while the wounded in the waiting cars, supposing themselves deserted under fire, cried out for help.

At night things were worse. Cars slipped into ditches, plunged into shell-holes. Paul, with a full load of stretcher-cases, almost drove off a broken bridge into the river. All the cars were damaged by shell-fire. Some were put out of action. One, going up empty to the front, suddenly found itself in a covey of bursting shells. The driver and orderly tumbled hurriedly into a ditch, and a shell burst on the driving-seat. The petrol went up in a huge column of flame and soon nothing remained of the car, but scrap iron and pools of aluminium on the road. Later, a line of tanks, going up, met a line of ambulances, coming down, where there was no room to pass. Confusion and altercations. A tank was hit; once more a column of flame, dwarfing the other, afforded a beacon for enemy guns.

Two or three days and nights of this kind of thing severely strained the Convoy. One or two members had already been wounded, and others had been badly shaken. Nerves developed here and there. Some one began to behave oddly, wandering about delivering meaningless messages. He was taken away. Paul himself was in a queer state; for his head was splitting, his mouth foul, his limbs curiously stiff and heavy. His stomach seemed to have collapsed. Worse, his driving was becoming erratic, and he sometimes said things he did not intend to say. He was continuously scared, and also scared of being found out by his calmer colleagues. His bogy, the foal, began to haunt him again. Somehow it was all mixed up with another vision, a bloodstained letter protruding from a torn pocket; and with yet another, a cow so flattened in the mud by the wheels of lorries and the feet of troops that nothing of it remained three-dimensional except its head in the gutter, and one broken horn. The thought that, after all, this ambulance life was mere child's play compared with what was afoot elsewhere, hurt him so badly that inwardly he whined. For if things grew much worse than this he would certainly crack; and yet 'this' was nothing. Superficially he had maintained thus far something like the appearance of calm. He even contrived an occasional stammering joke. But inwardly he was by now going faint with terror. And this welling terror was beginning to spoil his affected calm. People were beginning to look at him anxiously. Paul found himself reviewing his case in this manner once while he was crouching in a ditch waiting for a lull in the shelling, and for a load of wounded. Yes, inwardly he was by now not far from cracking.

Yet more inwardly still, so he remarked to himself, he was quite calm. That was the odd part of it all. His silly body, or animal nature, as he put it, might very well crack, or run away howling, and yet he, Paul, would have no part in it. He, Paul, the rider of this quivering animal, was unperturbed, interested, amused. The beast might run away with him or throw him. It was proving a rather worthless sort of beast, and he had his work cut out to force it to the jumps. He would damned well master it if he could; but if he could not, well, it was all in the game, the extremely interesting game of being a human thing, half god, half beast. He knew quite well it didn't seriously *matter* if he was killed, or even if he was horribly wounded. It didn't *really* matter even if he cracked, though he must hang on if he could. He had a strange conviction, there in the ditch, that whichever *did* happen would be just the right thing; that even if he cracked, it would somehow be part of the 'music of the spheres'. Even the foal unborn was part of the music. Even this war, this bloody awful farce, was part of the music. If you couldn't be anything but a vibrating, a tortured string in the orchestra, you didn't like it. But if you had ears to listen, it was – great. These wounded – if only they could somehow hear, even through their own pain, the music of the spheres! If he himself were to be caught by the next shell, would he still keep hold of the music? Not he! He would be a mere tortured animal. Well, what matter? The music would still be there, even if he could not hear it, even if no man heard it. That was nonsense. Yet profoundly he knew that it was true.

Presently, for no apparent reason, the sector quietened down. The offensive, it seemed, had been a failure. The advance, which was to have swept the Germans out of France, never began. The Division, moreover, was in a state of mutiny, sensing mismanagement, declaring that thousands of lives had been lightly thrown away. It was withdrawn. The Convoy travelled with it into a flowery region far behind the lines. Tin hats were discarded.

Then occurred a little incident very significant to the Neptunian observer. The Convoy, having borne itself well, was cited in the orders of the Corps d'Armée. It was therefore entitled to have the Croix de Guerre painted on its cars. The artists undertook this task. The bronze cross, with its red and green ribbon, was earned also by certain individual members of the Convoy. Should they accept it, should they wear the ribbon? To refuse would be insulting to the French army. But that pacifists should display military decorations was too ridiculous. There was some debate, but the thing was done. Thus did these pacifists, hypnotized for so long by the prestige and glamour of the military, bring themselves to devour the crumbs of glory that fell from the master's table.

There is no need to dwell upon the subsequent adventures of this war-scarred and war-decorated group of pacifists. The being whose brain I use in communicating with you would gladly tell of them in detail, for in his memory they have a false glamour and significance. But already I have allowed him too much rein. The life of his Convoy is indeed significant to the student of your species; but the events on which he seeks to dwell are minute with an even more microscopic minuteness than the Great War, which to the Neptunian observer, searching for your War through past ages, is so easily to be overlooked. The significance of the war itself, lies partly in its fatal results, partly in that it reveals so clearly the limits of a half-developed mind. The importance of the ulto-microscopic events that I have allowed my instrument to enlarge upon in this section, is that they show how, even in the less conventional minds of your race, the archaic impulses caused devastating perplexity.

When the Convoy had rested, it wandered from sector to sector, till at last it found itself once more near the vine-clad and forest-crowned Mountain of Rheims, and once more destined for a great offensive. Once more the din of the troops, guns, lorries. Once more torn-up roads, smashed cars, night-driving in blurred and suffocating gas-masks. Once more the in-flooding wounded, and now and again a member of the little group itself wounded or killed. This time the offensive went on and on. Car after car was put out of action. Half the personnel were laid low, some by gas, some seemingly by bad water.

One day, as Paul was turning his car round before loading, a shell caught his companion, who was directing him from the road. This was a lad with whom Paul had often worked, and often amicably wrangled about art and life, a boy full of promise, and of the will to make his mark. Now, he lay crumpled on the road. Paul and others rushed to him. The lower part of his body had been terribly smashed, but he was still conscious. His eyes turned to Paul, and his lips moved. Paul bent to listen, and seemed to hear a faint gasping reiteration of one phrase, 'Won't die yet.' With difficulty they got the boy on to a stretcher, his face twisted with added pain. As they carried him away, he stirred feebly, then suddenly went limp, his head rolling loosely with the motion of the bearers. An arm slipped off the stretcher, and dangled. They put him down again and bent over him. A French *broncardier*, who was helping, stood up with a shrug and a sigh. ' C'est déjà fini,' he said. Looking down at the smooth face, he added, 'Oui, mon pauvre, c'est fini. Mort pour la patrie! Ah, les sales Boches!'

Paul gazed at the tanned bloodless features, the curiously changed eyes, the sagging mouth. This was the moment for me to undertake an operation which I had long contemplated. Bringing all my strength to bear on Paul I lashed him into a degree of self-consciousness and other-consciousness which I had not hitherto produced in him. With this heightened sensitivity, he was overwhelmed by vivid apprehension of the life that had been cut short, the intricacy and delicate organization of the spirit which he had known so well, and had now seen extinguished, with all its young ambitions, fears, admirations, loves, all its little whims and lusts and laughters. The experience came on him in a flash, so that he let slip a quick sharp scream of surprise and compassion. He stared fascinated at a smear of blood on the cheek, seeing as it were right through the present death-mask into the boy's whole living past, retaining it in one imaginative grasp, as music may be retained in the mind's ear after it has been interrupted; may still be heard, gathering strength, proliferating, and suddenly broken across with the breaking of the instrument. Paul heard, indeed, what the boy himself did not hear, the terrible snap and silence of the end. This was but the first stage of my operation on Paul. I also contrived that, with his hypersensitive vision, he should seem to see, beyond this one dead boy, the countless hosts of the prematurely dead, not the dead of your war only, but of all the ages, the whole massed horror of young and vital spirits snuffed out before their time. Paul's mind reeled and collapsed; but not before he had glimpsed in all this horror a brilliant, and insupportable, an inhuman, beauty. The operation had been completed, and in due season I should observe the results. He fell, and was carried away in one of the ambulances.

In a few days, however, he recovered, and was able to take part in a new phase of the war, the advance of the Allies. It was a swarming advance along unspeakable roads, over pontoon bridges, through burning villages.

During this final advance Paul one day perceived in a field by the road the mare and unborn foal whose image had so long haunted him. The unexpected but all too familiar sight shocked him deeply. Volume by volume it corresponded with his image, but there was an added stench. How came it, he wondered, that for years he had 'remembered' this thing before ever he had seen it?

One symbolical aspect of his foal was still hidden from him. When at last the armistice came, so longed for, so incredible, Paul did not yet know that the peace ensuing on the world's four years' travail was to be the peace, not of accomplished birth but of strangulation.

The following curious poem, which Paul devised shortly before the end of the war, expresses his sense of the futility and pettiness of all human activity.

> If God has not noticed us?
> He is so occupied
> with the crowded cycle of nature.
>
> The sea's breath,
> by drenching the hills
> and descending along the meadow brooklets
> (whose backwaters
> are playgrounds of busy insect populations),

returns seaward
to rise again.
Water-beetles
skating on the stagnant skin of a backwater.
we get rumour of Oceanus,
of storm-driven worlds and island universes.
And we would annex them!
We would dignify the fiery currents of the Cosmos
by spawning in them!
But the minnow, death, he snaps us;
and presently some inconsiderable spate
will scour the cranny clean of us.

Long after man, the stars
will continually evaporate in radiant energy
to recondense as nebulae,
and again stars;
till here and there some new planet
will harbour again
insect populations.

VII *After The War*

1. THE NEW HOPE

YOUR little Great War reached its ignominious end. During the four years of misery and waste, the short-lived combatants felt that the war area, fringed with the remote and insubstantial lands of peace, was the whole of space, and that time itself was but the endless Duration of the War. But to Neptunian observers, ranging over the considerable span occupied by human history, the events of those four years appeared but as an instantaneous flicker of pain in the still embryonic life of Man. The full-grown Spirit of Man, the Race Mind of the Eighteenth Human Species may be said to use the great company of individual Neptunian observers as a kind of psychical and supra-temporal microscope for the study of its own prenatal career. Peering down that strange instrument, it searches upon the slide for the little point of life which is to become in due season Man himself. The thing is discovered. It is seen to reach that stage of its history when for the first time it begins to master its little Terrestrial environment. Then is to be detected by the quick eye of mature Man the faint and instantaneous flicker, your Great War. Henceforth the minute creature slowly retracts its adventuring pseudopodia, enters into itself, shrinks, and lapses into a state of suspended animation, until at last, after some ten million years, it is ripe for its second phase of adventure, wholly forgetful of its first. It becomes, in fact, the Second Human Species.

When your Great War ended, it seemed to the soldiers of all the nations that a new and happier age had dawned. The veterans prepared to take up once more the threads that war had cut; the young prepared for the beginning of real life. All alike looked forward to security, to freedom from military discipline, to the amusements of civilized society, to woman. Those who had been long under restraint found it almost incredible that they would soon be able to go wherever they pleased without seeking permission, that they

522

would be able to lie in bed in the morning, that they might wear civilian clothes, that they would never again be under the eye of a sergeant, or a captain, or some more exalted officer, and never again take part in an offensive.

For the majority these anticipations were enough. If they could but secure a livelihood, capture some charming and adoring woman, keep a family in comfort, enjoy life, or return to some engrossing work, they would be happy. And a grateful country would surely see to it that they were at least thus rewarded for their years of heroism.

But there were many who demanded of the peace something more than personal contentment. They demanded, and indeed confidently looked for, the beginnings of a better world. The universe, which during the war years, had been progressively revealed as more and more diabolical, was now transfused with a new hope, a new or a refurbished divinity. The armies of the Allies had been fighting for justice and for democracy; or so at least they had been told. They had won. Justice and democracy would henceforth flourish everywhere. On the other hand the armies of the Central Powers had believed that they had been fighting for the Fatherland or for Culture. They had been beaten; but after a gallant fight, and because their starved and exhausted peoples could no longer support them. To those hard-pressed peoples the end of war came not indeed as a bright dawn, as to the Allies, but none the less as the end of unspeakable things, and with the promise of a new day. Henceforth there would at least be food. The pinched and ailing children of Central Europe, whom the Allies had so successfully, so heroically stricken by their blockade, might now perhaps be nursed into precarious health. The beaten nations, trusting to the high-sounding protestations of the victors, not only surrendered, but appealed for help in the desperate task of re-establishing society. President Wilson prophesied a new world, a Brotherhood of Nations, and pronounced his Fourteen Points. Henceforth there would be no more wars, because this last and most bitter war had expunged militarism from the hearts of all the peoples; and had made all men feel, as never before, the difference between the things that were essential and the things that were trivial in the life of mankind. What mattered (men now vehemently

523

asserted) was the fellowship of man, Christian charity, the co-operation of all men in the making of a happier world. The war had occurred because the fundamental kindliness of the peoples towards one another had been poisoned by the diplomats. Henceforth the peoples would come into direct contact with one another. The old diplomacy must go.

These sentiments were tactfully applauded by the diplomats of all nations, and were embalmed, suitably trimmed and tempered, in a new charter of human brotherhood, the Peace Treaty of Versailles.

To Neptunian observers, estimating the deepest and most obscure mental reactions of thousands of demobilized soldiers and of the civilian populations that welcomed them, it was clear that the First Human Species had not yet begun to realize the extent of the disaster which it had brought upon itself. All the belligerent peoples were, of course, war-weary. It was natural that after the four years of strain they should experience a serious lassitude, that after responding so magnificently (as was said) to the call for sacrifice, they should be more than usually prone to take the easy course. But our observers, comparing minutely the minds of 1914 with the same minds of 1918, noted a widespread, subtle, and in the main unconscious change. Not a few minds, indeed, had been completely shattered by the experience of those four years, succumbing either to the conflict between personal fear and tribal loyalty or to that rarer conflict between tribal loyalty and the groping loyalty to Man. But also, even in the great mass of men, who had escaped this obvious ruin, there had occurred a general coarsening and softening of the mental fibre, such that they were henceforth poor stuff for the making of a new world.

The slight but gravely significant lassitude which we now observed in all the Western peoples had its roots not merely in fatigue, but in self-distrust and disillusionment. At first obscured by the new hope which peace had gendered, this profound moral disheartenment was destined to increase, not dwindle, as the years advanced. In those early months of peace scarcely any man was aware of it, but to our observers it was evident as a faint odour of corruption in almost every mind. It was the universal though unacknowledged sense of war-guilt, the sense that the high moral and patriotic fervours of 1914 had somehow obscured a deeper and more serious issue. Western Man had blundered into a grave act of treason against the spirit that had but recently and precariously been conceived in him. Few could see that it was so; and yet in almost every mind we found an all-pervading shame, unwitting but most hurtful. Knowing not that they did so, all men blamed themselves and their fellow-men for a treason which they did not know they had committed, against a spirit that was almost completely beyond their ken. Neptunian observers did not blame them. For these unhappy primitives had but acted according to their lights. They could not know that another and a purer light had been eclipsed in them before they could recognize it.

In many thousands of minds we have watched this subtle guilt at work. Sometimes it expressed itself as a touchy conscientiousness in familiar moral issues, combined with a laxity in matters less stereotyped. Sometimes it became a tendency to blame others unduly, or to mortify the self. More often it gave rise to a lazy cynicism, a comfortable contempt of human nature, and disgust with all existence. Its issue was a widespread, slight loosening of responsibility, both toward society and toward particular individuals. Western men were to be henceforth on the whole less trustworthy, less firm with themselves, less workmanlike, less rigorous in abstract thought, less fastidious in all spheres, more avid of pleasure, more prone to heartlessness, to brutality, to murder. And, when, later, it began to be realized that this deterioration had taken place, the realization itself, by suggestion, increased the deterioration.

But the effects of the war were by no means wholly bad. In the great majority of minds observed by Neptunians after the war, there was detected a very interesting conflict between the forces of decay and the forces of rebirth. The hope of a new world was not entirely ungrounded. The war had stripped men of many hampering illusions; and, for those that had eyes to see, it had underlined in blood the things that really mattered. For the most clear-sighted it was henceforth evident that only two things mattered, the daily happiness of individual human beings and the advancement of the human spirit in its gallant cosmical adventure. To the great majority of those who took serious interest in public affairs the happiness of men and women throughout the world became henceforth the one goal of social action. Only a few admitted that the supreme care of all the peoples should be the adventure of the Terrestrial spirit. Because so few recognized this cosmical aspect of human endeavour, even the obvious goal of world-happiness became unrealizable. For if happiness alone is the goal, one man's happiness is as good as another's, and no one will feel obligation to make the supreme sacrifice. But if the true goal is of another order, those who recognize it may gladly die for it.

In the Western World, during the decades that followed the war we encountered far and wide among the hearts of men the beginnings of a true rebirth, an emphatic rejection of the outworn ideals of conduct and of world policy, and a desperate quest for something better, something to fire men's imaginations and command their allegiance even to the death; something above suspicion, above ridicule, above criticism. Far and wide, among many peoples, the new ideal began to stir for birth, but men's spirits had been subtly poisoned by the war. What should have become a world-wide religious experience beside which all earlier revivals would have seemed mere tentative and ineffectual gropings, became only a revolutionary social policy, became in fact the wholly admirable but unfinished ideal of a happy world. The muscles which should have thrust the new creature into the light were flaccid. The birth was checked. The young thing, half-born, struggled for a while, then died, assuming the fixed grin of Paul's nightmare foal.

In Russia alone, and only for a few decades, did there seem to be the possibility of complete rebirth. In that great people of mixed Western and Eastern temperament the poison of war had not worked so disastrously. The great mass of Russians had not regarded the war as *their* war, but as the war of their archaic government. And as the suffering bred of war increased beyond the limit of endurance, they rose and overthrew their government. The revolutionists who heroically accomplished this change were troubled by no war-shame, for the blood which they shed was truly split in the birth throes of a new world. They were indeed fighting for the spirit, though they would have laughed indignantly had they been told so. For to them 'spirit' was but an invention of the oppressors, and 'matter' alone was real. They fought, so they believed, for the free physiological functioning of human animals. They fought, that is, for the fulfilling of whatever capacities those animals might discover in themselves. And in fighting thus they fought unwittingly for the human spirit in its cosmical adventure. When their fight was won, and they had come into power, they began to discipline their people to lead a world-wide crusade. Each man, they said, must regard himself as but an instrument of something greater than himself, must live for that something, and if necessary die for it. This devotion that they preached and practised was indeed the very breath of the spirit within them. Little by little a new hope, a new pride, a new energy, spread among the Russian people. Little by little they fashioned for themselves a new community, such as had never before occurred on the planet. And because they allowed no one to hold power through riches, they became the horror of the Western World.

To the thousands of our observers stationed in Russian minds it was evident even at the outset that this promise of new birth would never be fulfilled. The ardour of revolution and the devotion of community-building could not suffice alone for ever. There must come a time when the revolution was won, the main structure of the new community completed, when the goal of a happy world, though not in fact attained, would no longer fire men, no longer suffice as the 'something' for which they would gladly live or die; when the spirit so obscurely conceived in men would need more nourishment than social loyalty. Then the only hope of the world would be that Russian men and women should look more closely into their hearts, and discover there the cosmical and spiritual significance of human life, which their creed denied. But this could not be. In few of them did we find a capacity for insight strong enough to apprehend what man is, and what the world, and the exquisite relation of them. And being without that vision, they would have nothing to strengthen them against the infection of the decaying Western civilization. Feared and hated by their neighbours, they themselves would succumb to nationalistic fear and hate. Craving material power for their defence, they would betray themselves for power, security, prosperity.

In short, the new hope which the European War had occasioned, especially in Russia, was destined, sooner or later, to be destroyed by the virus which war itself had generated in the guilty Western peoples. While that new hope, still quick and bright, was travelling hither and thither over Asia like a smouldering fire, this dank effluence also was spreading, damping the fibre of men's hearts with disillusionment about human nature and the universe. And so, that which should have become a world-wide spiritual conflagration was doomed never to achieve more than revolutionary propaganda, and smoke.

2. PAUL GATHERS UP THE THREADS

It is my task to show your world in its 'post-war' phase as it seemed to one of your own kind who had been infected with something of the Neptunian mood. First, however, I must recall how Paul faced his own private 'post-war' problems, and emerged at last as a perfected instrument for my purpose.

Crossing the Channel for the last time in uniform, Paul looked behind and forward with mixed feelings. Behind lay the dead, with their thousands upon thousands of wooden crosses; and also (for Paul's imagination) the wounded, grey, blue and khaki, bloody, with splintered bones. Behind, but indelible, lay all that horror, that waste, that idiocy; yet also behind lay, as he was forced to admit to himself, an exquisite, an inhuman, an indefensible, an intolerable beauty. Forward lay life, and a new hope. Yet looking toward the future he felt misgivings both for himself and for the world. For himself he feared, because he had no part in the common emotion of his fellow-countrymen, in the thankfulness that the war had been nobly won. For the world he feared, because of a growing sense that man's circumstances were rapidly passing beyond man's control. They demanded more intelligence and more integrity than he possessed.

Thus Paul on his homeward journey could not conjure in himself the pure thankfulness of his fellows. Yet, looking behind and forward, with the wind chanting in his ears and the salt spray on his lips, he savoured zestfully the bitter and taunting taste of existence. Comparing his present self with the self of his first war-time crossing, he smiled at the poor half-conscious thing that he had been, and said, 'At least, I have come awake.' Then he thought again of those thousands under the crosses, who would not wake ever. He remembered the boy whom he had known so well, and had watched dying; who should have wakened so splendidly. And then once more he savoured that mysterious, indefensible beauty which he had seen emerge in all this horror.

I chose this moment of comparatively deep self-consciousness and world-consciousness to force upon Paul with a new clarity the problem with which I intended henceforth to haunt him. This task was made easier by the circumstances of the voyage. The sea was boisterous. Paul greatly enjoyed a boisterous sea and the plunging of a ship, but his pleasure was complicated by a feeling of sea-sickness. He fought against his nausea and against its depressing influence. He wanted to go on enjoying the wind and the spray and the motion and the white-veined sea, but he could not. Presently, however, he very heartily vomited; and then once more he could enjoy things, and even think about the world. His thinking was coloured both by his nausea and by his zest in the salt air. Resolutely blowing his nose, meditatively wiping his mouth, he continued to lean on the rail and watch the desecrated but all-unsullied waves. He formulated his problem to himself, 'How can things be so wrong, so meaningless, so filthy; and yet also so right, so overwhelmingly significant, so exquisite?' How wrong things were, and how exquisite, neither Paul nor any man had yet fully discovered. But the problem was formulated. I promised myself that I should watch with minute attention the efforts of this specially treated member of your kind to come to terms with the universe.

Paul returned to his native suburb, and was welcomed into the bosom of the home. It was good to be at home. For a while he was content to enjoy the prospect of an endless leave, lazing in flannel trousers and an old tweed coat. At home, where he was not expected to explain himself, he was at peace; but elsewhere, even when he was dressed as others, he felt an alien. He attributed his sense of isolation to his pacifism, not knowing how far opinion had moved since the beginning of the war. This loneliness of his was in fact due much more to my clarifying influence in him, to his having been as it were impregnated with seminal ideas gendered in another species and another world. He found his mind working differently from other minds, yet he could not detect where the difference lay. This distressed him. He hated to be different. He longed to become an indistinguishable member of the herd, of his own social class. He began to take great pains to dress correctly, and to use the slang of the moment. He tried to play bridge, but could never keep awake. He tried to play golf, but his muscles seemed to play tricks on him at the critical moment. The truth was that he did not really want to do these things at all. He wanted to do 'the done thing'.

There was another trouble. He had not been at home more than a fortnight before he realized with distress that his relations with his parents were not what they had been. In the old days he used to say, 'I have been lucky in my choice of parents. Of course they don't really know me very well, but they understand as much as is necessary. They are both endlessly kind, sympathetic, helpful, and they have the sense to leave me alone.' Now, he began to see that in the old days they really had understood him far more than he supposed, but that the thing that he had since become was incomprehensible to them. Even at the beginning of the war they had lost touch with him over his pacifism, accepting it thankfully as a means of saving him from the trenches, but never taking it seriously. Now, they were more out of touch than ever. It seemed to him that they were living in a kind of mental Flat Land, without acquaintance with the third dimension. They were so sensible, so kind, so anxious to be tolerant. He could see eye to eye with them in so many things, in all those respects in which Flat Land was in accord with Solid Land. But every now and then intercourse would break down. They would argue with him patiently for a while in vain; then fall silent, regarding him with an expression in which he seemed to see, blended together, love, pity and horror. He would then shrug his shoulders, and wonder whether in earlier times the gulf between the generations had ever been so wide. They, for their part, sadly told one another that his war experience (or was it his pacifism?) had so twisted his mind that he was 'not quite, not absolutely, sane'.

After a few weeks Paul went back to his old post in the big suburban secondary school. He was surprised that they took him, in spite of his pacifism and his incompetence. Later he discovered that his father knew the Chairman of the Council. Ought he to resign? Probably, but he would not. He was by now well established as one of the less brilliant but not impossible members of the staff; and though the work never came easily to him, it was no longer the torture that it had formerly been. He was older, and less easily flustered. And he must have money. After all, he found, he rather liked boys, so long as he could keep on the right side of them. If you got wrong with them, they were hell; but if you kept right, they were much more tolerable than most adults. The work was respectable useful work. Indeed, it was in a way the most important of all work, if it was done properly. Moreover, it was the only work he could do. And he must have money; not much, but enough to make him independent.

His aim at this time was to live an easy and uneventful life. He told himself that he did want to pull his weight, but he was not prepared to overstrain himself. He must have time to enjoy himself. He proposed to enjoy himself in two ways, and both together. He wanted to win his spurs in the endless tournament of sex; for his virginity filled him with self-doubt, and disturbed his judgements about life. At the same time he promised himself a good deal of what he called 'intellectual sight-seeing' or 'spiritual touring'. Comfortably, if not with a first-class ticket, at least with a second-class one, he would explore all the well-exploited travel-routes of all the continents of the mind. Sometimes he might even venture into the untracked wild, but not dangerously. Never again, if he could help it, would he lose touch with civilization, with the comfortable mental structure of his fellows, as he had done through pacifism. Thus did this war-weary young Terrestrial propose. Much of his plan suited my purpose admirably, but by no means the whole of it.

So Paul settled down to teach history, geography, English and 'scripture'. He taught whatever he was told to teach, and for mere pity's sake, he made the stuff as palatable as he could. On the whole the boys liked him. He seemed to regard the business much as they did themselves, as a tiresome necessary grind, which must

531

be done efficiently but might be alleviated by jokes and stories. Even discipline, formerly such a trouble to Paul, now seemed to work automatically. This was partly because he did not worry about it, having outgrown the notion that he must preserve his 'dignity', and partly because in the critical first days of his new school career I influenced his mood and his bearing so that he gave an impression of friendliness combined with careless firmness. Paul himself was surprised and thankful that the self-discipline of his classes relieved him of a dreadful burden. He used to say to visitors, in front of the class, 'You see, we have not a dictator, but a chairman.' All the same, he secretly took credit for his achievement.

By thus helping Paul to establish himself in a tolerable routine, I enabled him to keep his mind free and sensitive for other matters. The boys themselves knew that there was another side to him. Occasionally in class the lesson would go astray completely, and he would talk astoundingly about things interesting to himself, things outside the curriculum, and sometimes of very doubtful orthodoxy. He would dwell upon the age and number of the stars, the localization of functions in the brain, the abstractness of science and mathematics, the kinds of insanity, the truth about Soviet Russia, the theatre and the cinema, the cellular structure of the body, the supposed electronic structure of the atom, death and old age, cosmopolitanism, sun-bathing, the crawl stroke, Samuel Butler, coitus and the birth of babies. To these floods of language the boys reacted according to their diverse natures. The stupid slipped thankfully into torpor, the industrious revised their home-work. The shrewd masticated whatever in the harangue seemed to have a practical value, and spat out the rest. The intellectually curious listened aloofly. The main mass fluctuated between amusement, enthusiastic support, and boredom. A few sensitive ones took Paul as their prophet. After these outbursts Paul became unusually reticent and cautious. Sometimes he even told the boys they 'had better forget it all' because he was 'a bit mad then'. He was obviously anxious that rumour of his wildness should not go beyond the class-room door. The sense of secrecy appealed to the boys. Whatever their diverse opinions of the stuff, all could enjoy a conspiracy. Paul's own class began to regard itself as something between a band of disciples (or even prophets), a secret revolutionary society, and a pirate crew.

3. PAUL COMES TO TERMS WITH WOMAN

For some months Paul was so busy becoming an efficient schoolmaster that he had little time for those 'other matters' which I required him to undertake. But when he had established his technique and could look around him, he began to ask himself, 'What next?' His intention was to see life safely, to observe all its varieties and nuances, to read it in comfort as one might enjoy a novel of passion and agony without being upset by it. What was the field to be covered? There was woman. Until he had explored that field he could never give his attention to others. There was art, literature, music. There was science. There was the intricate spectacle of the universe, including the little peep-show, man. There were certain philosophical questions which had formed themselves in his mind without producing their answers. There was religion. Was there anything in it at all? But here, as also in the sphere of woman, one must be careful. One might so easily find oneself too deeply entangled. For the post-war Paul, entanglement, becoming part of the drama instead of a spectator, was to be avoided at all costs. But could he avoid it? Could he preserve in all circumstances this new snug aloofness, which had come to him with the end of war's long torment of pity and shame and indignation? He knew very well that there were strange forces in him which might wreck his plans. He must be very careful, but the risk must be taken. His sheer curiosity, and his cold passion for savouring the drama of the world, must be satisfied.

Paul now began to lead a double life. In school-hours he tried to be the correct schoolmaster, and save for his lapses he succeeded. Out of school he inspected the universe. With cold judgement he decided that the first aspect of the universe to be inspected was woman. But how? There was Katherine. She alone, he felt, could be for him the perfect mate. But she was obviously happy with her returned soldier and her two children. He met her now and again. She was gentle with him, and distressingly anxious that he should

533

like her husband. Strangely enough, he did like the man, as a man. He was intellectually unexciting, but he had an interested and open mind, and could readily be enticed out of Flat Land. Paul, however, disliked the sense that Katherine wanted to hold the two of them in one embrace. No, he must look elsewhere for woman, for the woman that was to show him the deep cosmical significance of womanhood.

The girls of his suburb were no good. In his thwarted, virginal state, they often stirred him, but he could not get anywhere with them. He lacked the right touch. Sometimes he would take one of them on the river or to a dance, or to the pictures, but nothing came of it. They found him queer, a little ridiculous, sometimes alarming. When he should have been audacious, he was diffident. His voice went husky and his hand trembled. When he should have been gentle, he was rough. With one of them, indeed, he got so far as to realize that to go further would be disastrous; for though she was a 'dear' she was dull. Moreover, she would expect to be married. And for marriage he had neither means nor inclination.

Of course there were prostitutes. They would sell him something that he wanted. But he wanted much more than they could sell. He wanted, along with full physical union, that depth of intimacy which he had known with Katherine. Once in Paris while he was coming home on leave, a girl in the street had said to him 'Venez faire l'amour avec moi', and he had stopped. But there was something about her, some trace of a repugnance long since outworn, that made his cherished maleness contemptible in his own eyes. He hurried away, telling himself she was too unattractive. Henceforth all prostitutes reminded him of her. They made him dislike himself.

What other hope was there for him? He once found himself alone with a little dusky creature in a railway carriage. She reminded him of a marmoset. Might he smoke, he asked. Certainly. Would she smoke too? Well, yes, since there was no one else there. They talked about the cinema. They arranged to meet again. He took her to a dance, and to picture shows, and for walks. She told him she was unhappy at home. Things advanced to such an extent that one day he put a protecting arm round her, with his hand under her breast; and he kissed her. She began to trust him, rely on him. Suddenly he felt an utter cad, and determined to give her up. But when he said he would never see her again, she wept like a child and clung to him. He told her what a beast he was, and how he had intended merely to get what he wanted from her, and take no responsibility. As for marrying her, he was not the marrying sort. She said she didn't care. She didn't want marriage, she wanted him, just now and again. Yet somehow he couldn't do it. Was it fear of the consequences? No, not fear, shame. She was only a child, after all, and he found himself feeling responsible for her. Damn it, why couldn't he go through with it? It wouldn't hurt her really. It would all be experience. But he couldn't do it. Yet he had not the heart to keep away from her. Hell! Then why not marry her and go through with it that way? No, that would be certain hell for both of them. The affair began to get on his nerves. His teaching was affected; for in class he was haunted by images of the little marmoset, of her great wide black eyes, or of the feel of her hair on his cheek. Obviously he must put an end to it all. He wrote her a strange muddled letter, saying he loved her too much to go on, or too little; that in fact he did not really love her at all, and she must make the best of it; that he was desperately in love with her and would be miserable for ever without her; that the upshot anyhow was that he could never see her again. He kept to his resolve. In spite of a number of beseeching letters, he never saw her or wrote to her again.

Paul thanked his stars he had escaped from that trap. But his problem remained completely unsolved. How was he to come to terms with this huge factor in the universe, woman? For in his present state he could not but regard sex as something fundamental to the universe. He was desperate. He could not keep his mind off woman. Every train of thought brought him to the same dead end, woman, and how he was to cope with her. He spent hours wandering in the streets of the metropolis, watching all the slender figures, the silken ankles, the faces. Even in his present thwarted and obsessed mood, in which every well-formed girl seemed to him desirable, his interest was in part disinterested, impersonal. Behind his personal problem lay the universal problem. What was the cosmical significance of this perennial effloresence of femininity, this host of 'other' beings, ranging from the commonplace to the exquisite? Many of them were just female animals, some so brutish as to stir him little more than a bitch baboon; some though merely animal, were animals of his kind, and they roused in him a frankly animal but none the less divine desire. So at least he told himself. Many, on the other hand, he felt were more than animal, and the worse for it. They were the marred and vulgar products of a vulgar civilization. But many also, so it seemed to him, were divinely human and more than human. They eloquently manifested the woman-spirit, the female mode of the cosmic spirit. They had but to move a hand or turn the head or lean ever so slightly, ever so tenderly toward a lover, and Paul was smitten with a hushed, a religious, wonder. What was the meaning of it all? The man-spirit in himself, he said, demanded communion with one of these divine manifestations. The thing must be done. It was a sacred trust that he must fulfil. But how?

He made the acquaintance of a young actress whom he had often admired from the auditorium. He took her out a good deal. He spent more money on her than he could afford. But this relationship, like the other, came to nothing. It developed into a kind of brother-sister affection, though spiced with a sexual piquancy. Whenever he tried to bring in a more sensual element, she was distressed, and he was torn between resentment and self-reproach.

There were others. But nothing came of any of them, except a ceaseless expenditure on dance tickets, theatre tickets, chocolates, suppers, gifts. There was also a more ruinous and no less barren, expense of spirit, and a perennial sense of frustration. The girls that he really cared for he was afraid of hurting. Of course, he might marry one of them, if he could find one willing. But he felt sure he would be a bad husband, that he would be sick to death of the relationship within a month. And anyhow he could not afford a wife. On the other hand, the girls toward whom he felt no responsibility, he feared for his own sake, lest they should entangle him. Meanwhile he was becoming more and more entangled in his own obsession. The intellectual touring which he had proposed for himself, and was even now, in a desultory manner, undertaking, was becoming a labour instead of a delight, because he could not free his mind from woman. In bed at night he would writhe and mutter self-pityingly, 'God, give me a woman!'

At last he decided to go with a prostitute. On the way with her he was like a starved dog ready to eat anything. But when he was alone with her, it suddenly came over him with a flood of shame and self-ridicule, that here was a girl, at bottom a 'good sort' too, who did not want him at all, and yet had to put up with him. It must be like having to make your living by hiring out your toothbrush to strangers. How she must despise him! His hunger vanished. She tried to rouse him, using well-practised arts. But it was no good. He saw himself through her eyes. He felt his own body as she would feel it, clinging, repugnant. Stammering that he was ill, he put down his money, and fled.

From the point of view of my work with Paul the situation was very unsatisfactory. It was time to free his mind for the wider life that I required of him. I decided that the most thorough cure could be obtained only by means of Katherine, who was by now a superb young wife and mother. I therefore entered her once more, and found that by a careful use of my most delicate arts I might persuade her to serve my purpose. Five years of exceptionally happy marriage had deepened her spirit and enlarged her outlook. The colt had grown into a noble mare, the anxious young suburban miss into a mature and zestful woman, whose mind was surprisingly untrammelled. I found her still comfortably in love with the husband that I had given her, and the constant friend of her children. But also I found, on deeper inspection, a core of peaceful aloofness, of detachment from all the joys and anxieties of her busy life; of detachment, as yet unwitting, even from the moral conventions which hitherto she had had no cause to question. I found, too, a lively interest in her renewed acquaintance with Paul. She saw clearly that he was in distress, that he was 'sexually dead-ended'. Such was the phrase she used to describe Paul's condition to her husband. She felt responsible for his trouble. Also, before I began to work on her, she had already recognized in herself a tender echo of her old love for Paul. But without my help she would never have taken the course toward which I now began to lead her. For long she brooded over Paul and his trouble and her own new restlessness. Little by little I made her see that Paul would be for ever thwarted unless she let herself be taken. I also forced her to admit to herself that she wanted him to take her. At first she

537

saw the situation conventionally, and was terrified lest Paul should ruin all her happiness. For a while she shunned him. But Paul himself was being drawn irresistibly under her spell; and when at last she forbade him to come near her, he was so downcast and so acquiescent, that she shed tears for him. He duly kept away, and she increasingly wanted him.

But presently, looking into her own heart with my help, she realized a great and comforting truth about herself, and another truth about Paul. She did not want him for ever, but only for sometimes. For ever, she wanted her husband, with whom she had already woven an intricate and lovely pattern of life, not yet completed, scarcely more than begun. But with Paul also she had begun to weave a pattern long ago; and now she would complete it, not as was first intended, but in another and less intricate style. It would re-vitalize her, enrich her, give her a new bloom and fragrance for her husband's taking. And Paul, she knew, would find new life. With all the art at her command she would be woman for him, and crown his manhood, and set him free from his crippling obsession, free to do all the fine things which in old days he had talked of doing. For this was the truth that she had realized about Paul, that he also had another life to lead, independent of her, that for him, too, their union must be not an end but a refreshment.

But what about her husband? If only he could be made to feel that there was no danger of his losing her, or of his ceasing to be spiritually her husband, he ought surely to see the sanity of her madness. The thought of talking to him about it all made her recognize how mad she really was, how wicked, too. But somehow the recognition did not dismay her, for I kept her plied with clear thoughts and frank desires, which somehow robbed the conventions of their sanctity.

Katherine I had dealt with successfully. But there remained the more difficult task of persuading her husband, Richard. I had at the outset chosen him carefully; but now, when I took up my position in his mind, I was more interested in my experiment than hopeful of its success. It would have been easy to infatuate him with some woman, and so render him indifferent to his wife's conduct. But if tolerance had to rest merely on indifference, this marriage, in which I took some pride, would have been spoiled. I had decided, moreover, that Richard's predicament would afford me the opportunity of a crucial piece of research upon your species. I was curious to know whether it would be possible so to influence him that he should regard the whole matter with Neptunian sanity.

I took some pains to prepare him, leading his mind to ruminate in unfamiliar fields. I did nothing to dim in any way his desire for his wife; on the contrary, I produced in him a very detailed and exquisite apprehension of her. And when at last she found courage to tell him of her plan, I used all my skill to give him full imaginative insight into her love for Paul and her different love for himself. It was very interesting to watch his reaction. For a few minutes he sat gazing at his wife in silence. Then he said that of course she must do what seemed best to her, but he asked her to give him time to think. For a whole day he acted to himself the part of the devoted and discarded husband, biting through a pipe-stem in the course of his tortured meditations. He conceived a dozen plans for preventing the disaster, and dismissed them all. Already on the second day, however, he saw the situation more calmly, even with something like Neptunian detachment; and on the third he recognized with my help that it did not concern him at all in any serious manner how Katherine should spend her holiday, provided that she should come back to him gladly, and with enhanced vitality.

Paul and Katherine took a tent and went off together for three weeks. They pitched beside a little bay on the rocky and seal-haunted coast of Pembroke. In this choice they had been unwittingly influenced by me. Thoughts of my recent (and remotely future) holiday on a Neptunian coast infected them with a desire for rocks and the sea. In this holiday of theirs I myself found real refreshment. Through the primitive mind of Paul I rejoiced in the primitive body and primitive spirit of Katherine.

She was already well practised in the art of love, at least in the unsubtle Terrestrial mode. Paul was a novice. But now he surprised himself, and Katherine also, by the fire, the assurance, the gentleness, the sweet banter of his wooing. Well might he, for I who am not inexperienced even according to Neptunian standards, prompted him at every turn of his dalliance. Not only was I determined, for my work's sake, to afford these two children full enrichment of one another, but also I myself, by now so well adapted to the Terrestrial sphere, was deeply stirred by this 'almost woman', this doe of a half-human species. Her real beauty, interwoven with the reptilian clumsiness of an immature type, smote me with a savage delight of the flesh, and yet also with a vast remoteness which issued in grave tenderness and reverence.

They lay long in the mornings, with the sun pouring in at the open end of the tent. They swam together in the bay, pretending to be seals. They cooked and washed up, and shopped in the neighbouring village. They scrambled over the rocks and the heather. And they made love. In the night, and also naked on the sunlit beach, they drank one another in through eye and ear and tactile flesh. Of many things they spoke together, sitting in the evening in the opening of the tent. One night there was a storm. The tent was blown down, and their bedding was wet. They dressed under the floundering canvas, and having made things secure, for the rest of the night they walked in the rain, reeling with sleep. Next day they repaired the tent, spread out their blankets in the sun, and on the sunny grass they lay down to sleep. Paul murmured, 'We could have been man and wife so well.' But Katherine roused herself to say, 'No, no! Richard has me for keeps, and you for sometimes. I should hate you for a husband, you'd be too tiring, and probably no good with children. Paul, if I have a baby, it will count as Richard's.'

For three weeks Paul basked in intimacy with the bland Katherine. This, then, was woman, this intricacy of lovely volumes and movements, of lovely resistances and yieldings, of play, laughter and quietness. She was just animal made perfect, and as such she was unfathomable spirit at once utterly dependable and utterly incalculable, mysterious. Paul knew, even in his present huge content, that there was much more of woman than was revealed to him, more which could only be known through long intimacy, in fact in the stress and long-suffering and intricate concrescence of marriage. This, Richard had, but he himself had not, perhaps would never have. The thought saddened him; but it did not bite into him poisonously, as his virginity had done. Fundamentally, he was to be henceforth in respect of woman at peace. Her beauties would no longer taunt him and waylay him and tether him. Henceforth he would have strength of her, not weakness.

In these expectations Paul was justified. His retarded spirit, starved hitherto of women, now burgeoned. I could detect in him day by day, almost hour by hour, new buds and growing points of sensitivity, of percipience, hitherto suppressed by the long winter of his frustration. Even during the rapturous holiday itself, when his whole interest was centred on the one being and on his love-play with her, he was at the same time exfoliating into a new and vital cognizance of more remote spheres. On their last day he wrote this poem:

> Last night,
> walking on the heath,
> she and I,
> alive,
> condescended toward the stars.
>
> For then we knew
> quite surely
> that all the pother of the universe
> was but a prelude to that summer night
> and our uniting,
> and all the ages to come
> but a cadence
> after our loving.
>
> Nestled down into the heather,
> we laughed,
> and took joy of one another,
> justifying the cosmic enterprise for ever
> by the moments of our caressing,
> while the simple stars
> watched
> unseeing.
>
> Thus lovers, nations, worlds, nay galaxies,
> conceive themselves the crest of all that is.

4. LONDON AND THE SPIRIT

Paul spent the last fortnight of his summer holiday at home, preparing for the next term, and feeling the influence of Katherine spread deeply into his being. When he returned to work, he found that he looked about him with fresh interest. Walking in the streets of London, he now saw something besides stray flowers of femininity adrift on the stream of mere humanity. He saw the stream itself, to which, after all, the women were not alien but integral. And just as woman had been a challenge to him, so now the great human flood was a challenge to him, something which he must come to terms with, comprehend.

The time had come for me to attempt my most delicate piece of work on Paul, the experiment which was to lead me to a more inward and sympathetic apprehension of your kind than anything that had hitherto been possible; the deep and subtle manipulation which incidentally would give Paul a treasure of experience beyond the normal reach of the first Men. It was my aim to complete in him the propaedeutic influence with which I had occasionally disturbed him in childhood. I therefore set about to induce in him such an awakened state that he should see in all things, and with some constancy, the dazzling intensity of being, the depth beyond depth of significance, which even in childhood he had glimpsed, though rarely. With this heightened percipience he must assess his own mature and deeper self and the far wider and more fearsome world which he now inhabited. Then should I be able to observe how far and with what idiosyncrasies the mentality of your kind, thus aided, could endure the truth and praise it.

It was chiefly in the streets and in the class-room that Paul found his challenge, but also, as had ever been the case with him, under the stars. Their frosty glance had now for him a more cruel, a more wounding significance than formerly, a significance which drew poignancy not only from echoes of the street, and the class-room, and from the sunned flesh of Katherine, but also from the war.

Paul had promised himself that when he had come to terms with woman he would devote his leisure to that intellectual touring in which he had never yet been able seriously to indulge. But even now, it seemed, he was not to carry out his plan, or at least not with the comfort and safety which he desired. What was meant to be a tour of well-marked and well-guided routes of the mind, threatened to become in fact a desperate adventure in lonely altitudes of the spirit. It was as though by some inner compulsion he were enticed to travel not through but above all the mental cities and dominions, not on foot but in the air; as though he who had no skill for flight were to find himself perilously exploring the currents and whirl-pools, the invisible cliffs and chasms, of an element far other than the earth; which, however, now displayed to his miraculous vision a detailed inwardness opaque to the pedestrian observer.

Even in the class-room, expounding to reluctant urchins the structure of sentences, the provisions of Magna Carta, the pro-ducts of South America, Paul constantly struggled for balance in that remote ethereal sphere. Sometimes he would even fall into complete abstraction, gazing with disconcerting intensity at some boy or other, while the particular juvenile spirit took form in his imagination, conjured by my skill. He would begin by probing behind the defensive eyes into the vast tangled order of blood-vessels and nerve fibres. He would seem to watch the drift of blood corpuscles, the very movements of atoms from molecule to molecule. He would narrow his eyes in breathless search for he knew not what. Then suddenly, not out there but somehow in the depth of his own being, the immature somnolent spirit of the child would confront him. He would intimately savour those little lusts and fears, those little joys and unwilling efforts, all those quick eager movements of a life whose very earnestness was but the earnestness of a dream. With the boy's hand in the boy's pocket he would finger pennies and sixpences, or a precious knife or toy. He would look into all the crannies of that mind, noting here a promise to be fulfilled, there a blank insensitivity, here some passion unexpressed and festering. Rapt in this contemplation, he would fall blind to everything but this unique particular being, this featured monad. Or he would hold it up in contrast with him-self, as one might hold for comparison in the palm of the hand two little crystals, or in the field of the telescope a double star. Some-times it would seem to him that the boy and himself were indeed two great spheres of light hugely present to one another, yet held eternally distinct from one another by the movement, the swing,

543

of their diverse individualities. Then, like a memory from some forgotten life, there would come to him the thought, 'This is just Jackson Minor, a boy whom I must teach.' And then, 'Teach what?' And the answer, more apt than explicit, 'Teach to put forth an ever brighter effulgence of the spirit.'

While Paul was thus rapt, some movement would recall the class to him, and he would realize with a kind of eager terror that not only one but many of these huge presences were in the room with him. It was as though by some miracle a company of majestic and angelic beings was crowded upon this pin-point floor. And yet he knew that they were just a bunch of lads, just a collection of young and ephemeral human animals, who almost in the twinkle of a star would become black-coated citizens, parents, grandparents and discreetly laid-out corpses. Between then and now, what would they do? What were they for? They would do geography and scripture, they would make money or fail to make money, they would take young women to the pictures, they would do the done thing, and say the said thing. Then one day they would realize that they were growing old. Some of them would scream that they had not yet begun to live, others would shrug and drift heavily gravewards. So it would be, but why?

In the lunch hour, or when the school day was over, or in the evening when he was waiting to go to some show, he would let himself glide on the street flood to watch the faces, the action, to speculate on the significance of this gesture and that.

Sometimes he would walk unperturbed through street after street, carelessly turning the pages of the great picture book, dwelling lightly for a moment on this or that, on this comicality or elegance, on that figure of defeat or of complacency. Straying up Regent Street, he would amuse himself by sorting out the natives from the provincial visitors, and the foreign nationals from one another. He would surmise whether that painted duchess knew how desolate she looked, or that Lancashire holiday-maker how conscious that he was a stranger here, or whether the sweeper, with slouch hat and broom, felt, as he looked, more real than the rest. Odours would assail him: odour of dust and horse-dung, odour of exhaust fumes, rubber and tar, odour of cosmetics precariously triumphing over female sweat. Sounds would assail him: footsteps, leather-hard and rubber-soft, the hum and roar of motors, the expostulation of their horns; voices also of human animals, some oddly revealing, others a mere mask of sound, a carapace of standard tone, revealing nothing. Above all, forms and colours would assail him with their depths of significance. Well-tailored young women, discreet of glance; others more blowsy, not so discreet. Young men, vacantly correct, or betraying in some movement of the hand or restlessness of the eye an undercurrent of self-doubt. Old men, daughter-attended, tremblingly holding around their withered flesh the toga of seniority, bath-wrap-wise. Women of a past decade, backward leaning for weight of bosom, bullock-eyed, uncomprehending, backward straining under the impending pole-axe. After the smooth drift of Regent Street, he would find himself in the rapids of Oxford Street, buffeted, whirled hither and thither by successive vortices of humanity, of tweed-clad men, and women of artificial silk, of children toffee-smeared, of parents piloting their families, of messenger boys, soldiers, sailors, Indian students, and everywhere the constant flood of indistinguishable humanity, neither rich nor poor, neither beautiful nor ugly, neither happy nor sad, but restless, obscurely anxious, like a dog shivering before a dying fire.

At some point or other of his easeful wandering a change would probably happen to Paul. He would suddenly feel himself oppressed and borne down by the on-coming flood of his fellows. He would realize that he himself was but one indistinguishable drop in this huge continuum; that everything most unique and characteristic in him he had from It; that nothing whatever was himself, not even this craving for discrete existence; that the contours of his body and his mind had no more originality than one ripple in a wave-train. But with a violent movement of self-affirmation he would inwardly cry out, 'I am I, and not another.' Then in a flash he would feel his reality, and believe himself to be a substantial spirit, and eternal. For a moment all these others would seem to him but as moving pictures in the panorama of his own all-embracing self. But almost immediately some passing voice-tone in the crowd, some passing gesture, would stab him, shame him into realization of others. It would be as in the class-room. He would be overwhelmed not by the featureless drops of an ocean, but by a great company of unique and diverse spirits. Behind each on-coming pair of eyes he would glimpse a whole universe, intricate as his own, but different; similar in its basic order, but different in detail, and permeated through and through by a different mood, a different ground-tone or timbre. Each of them was like a ship forging toward him, moving beside him and beyond, and trailing a great spreading wake of past life, past intercourse with the world. He himself, it seemed, was tossed like a cork upon the inter-crossing trains of many past careers. Looking at them one by one as they came upon him, he seemed to see with his miraculous vision the teeming experiences of each mind, as with a telescope one may see on the decks of a passing liner a great company of men and women, suddenly made real and intimate, though inaccessible. The ship's bow rises to the slow waves, and droops, in sad reiteration, as she thrusts her way forward, oxlike, obedient to some will above her but not of her. And so, seemingly, those wayfarers blindly thrust forward on their courses, in hand-to-mouth fulfilment of their mechanism, ignorant of the helmsman's touch, the owner's instructions. Here, bearing down upon him, would appear perhaps a tall woman with nose like a liner's stem, and fo'c'sle brows. Then perhaps an old gentleman with the white wave of his moutache curling under his prow. Then a rakish young girl. Then a bulky freighter. Thus Paul would entertain himself with fantasies, till sooner or later a bleak familiar thought would strike him. Each of these vessels of the spirit (this was the phrase he used) had indeed a helmsman, keeping her to some course or other; had even a master, who worked out the details of navigation and set the course; but of owner's instructions he was in most cases completely ignorant. And so these many ships ploughed hither and thither on the high seas vainly, not fulfilling, but forlornly seeking, instructions. And because the mechanism of these vessels was not of insensitive steel but of desires and loathings, passions and admirations, Paul was filled with a great pity for them, and for himself as one of them, a pity for their half-awakened state between awareness and unawareness.

After such experiences in the heart of the city, Paul, in the train for his southern suburb, would already change his mood. Even while the train crossed the river the alteration would come. He would note, perhaps, the sunset reflected in the water. Though so unfashionable, it was after all alluring. The barges and tugs, jewelled with port and starboard and mast-head lights, the vague and cliffy rank of buildings, the trailing smoke, all these the sunset dignified. Of course it was nothing but a flutter of ether waves and shifting atoms, glorified by sentimental associations. Yet it compelled attention and an irrational worship. Sometimes Paul withdrew himself from it into his evening paper, resentful of this insidious romanticism. Sometimes he yielded to it, excusing himself in the name of Whitehead.

If it was a night-time crossing, with the dim stars beyond the smoke and glow of London, Paul would experience that tremor of recognition, of unreasoning expectation, which through my influence the stars had ever given him, and now gave him again, tinctured with a new dread, a new solemnity.

And when at last he was at home, and, as was his custom, walking for a few minutes on the Down before going to bed, he would feel, if it were a jewelled night, the overwhelming presence of the Cosmos. It was on these occasions that I could most completely master him, and even lift him precariously to the Neptunian plane. First he would have a powerful apprehension of the earth's rotundity, of the continents and oceans spreading beneath him and meeting under his feet. Then would I, using my best skill on the many keyboards of his brain, conjure in him a compelling perception of physical immensity, of the immensity first of the galactic universe, with its intermingling streams of stars, its gulfs of darkness; and then the huger immensity of the whole cosmos. With the eye of imagination he would perceive the scores, the millions, of other universes, drifting outwards in all directions like the fire-spray of a rocket. Then, fastening his attention once more on the stray atom earth, he would seem to see it forging through time, trailing its long wake of aeons, thrusting forward into its vaster, its more tempestuous future. I would let him glimpse that future. I would pour into the overflowing cup of his mind a torrent of visions. He would conceive and sensuously experience (as it were tropical rain descending on his bare head) the age-long but not everlasting downpour of human generations. Strange human-inhuman faces would glimmer before him and vanish.

By a simple device I made these glimpsed beings intimate to
him; for I permitted him ever and again to see in them something of
Katherine, though mysteriously transposed. And in the strange
aspirations, strange fears, strange modes of the spirit that would
impose themselves upon his tortured but exultant mind I took
care that he should feel the strange intimate remoteness that
he knew in Katherine. With my best art I would sometimes thrash
the strings of his mind to echoes of man's last, most glorious
achievement. And here again I would kindle this high theme with
Katherine. Along with all this richness and splendour of human
efflorescence I established in him an enduring emotional certainty
that in the end is downfall and agony, then silence. This he had felt
already as implicit in the nature of his own species, his own
movement of the symphony; but now through my influence he
knew with an absolute conviction that such must be the end also
of all things human.

Often he would cry out against this fate, inwardly screaming
like a child dropped from supporting arms. But little by little, as the
months and years passed over him, he learned to accept this issue,
to accept it at least in the deepest solitude of his own being, but not
always to conduct himself in the world according to the final
discipline of this acceptance.

At last there came a night when Paul, striding alone through the
rough grass of the Down, facing the Pole Star and the far glow of
London, wakened to a much clearer insight. One of Katherine's
children had recently been knocked over by a car and seriously
hurt. Paul saw Katherine for a few moments after the accident.
With shock he saw her, for she was changed. Her mouth had
withered. Her eyes looked at him like the eyes of some animal
drowning in a well. It was upon the evening of that day that Paul
took this most memorable of all his walks upon the Down. I
plied him, as so often before, with images of cosmical pain and
grief, and over all of them he saw the changed face of Katherine.
Suddenly the horror, the cruelty of existence burst upon him with
a new and insupportable violence, so that he cried out, stumbled,
and fell. It seemed to him in his agony of compassion that if only
the pain of the world were his own pain it might become endurable;
but it was the pain of others, and therefore he could never master

548

it with that strange joy which he knew was sometimes his. If all pain could be made his own only, he could surely grasp it firmly and put it in its place in the exquisite pattern of things. Yet could he? He remembered that mostly he was a coward, that he could not endure pain even as well as others, that it undermined him, and left him abject. But sometimes he had indeed been able to accept its very painfulness with a strange, quiet joy.

He thought of a thing to do. He would have a careful look at this thing, pain. And so, sitting up in the grass, he took out his pocket-knife, opened the big blade, and forced the point through the palm of his left hand. Looking fixedly at the Pole Star, he twisted the blade about, while the warm blood spread over his hand and trickled on to the grass. With the first shock his body had leapt, and now it writhed. The muscles of his face twisted, he set his teeth lest he should scream. His forehead was wet and cold, and faintness surged over him; but still he looked at Polaris, and moved the knife.

Beneath the Star spread the glow of London, a pale glory overarching the many lives. On his moist face, the wind. In his hand, grasped in the palm of his hand, the thing, pain. In his mind's eye the face of Katherine, symbol of all compassion. And, surging through him, induced by my power in him, apprehensions of cosmical austerity.

Then it was that Paul experienced the illumination which was henceforth to rule his life. In a sudden blaze of insight he saw more deeply into his own nature and the world's than had ever before been possible to him. While the vision lasted, he sat quietly on the grass staunching his wounded hand and contemplating in turn the many facets of his new experience. Lest he should afterwards fail to recapture what was now so exquisitely clear, he put his findings into words, which however seemed incapable of expressing more than the surrounding glow of his experience, leaving the bright central truth unspoken.

'This pain in my hand', he said, 'is painful because of the interruption that has been caused in the harmonious living of my flesh. All pain is hateful in that it is an interruption, a discord, an infringement of some theme of living, whether lowly or exalted. This pain in my hand, which is an infringement of my body's

549

lowly living, is not, it so happens, an infringement also of my spirit. No. Entering into my spirit, this pain is a feature of beauty. My spirit? What do I really mean by that? There is first I, the minded body, or the embodied mind; and there is also my spirit. What is it? Surely it is no substantial thing. It is the music rather, which I, the instrument, may produce, and may also appreciate. My glory is, not to preserve myself, but to create upon the strings of myself the music that is spirit, in whatever degree of excellence I may; and to appreciate the music in myself and others, and in the massed splendours of the cosmos, with whatever insight I can muster. Formerly I was dismayed by the knowledge that pain's evil was intrinsic to pain. But now I see clearly that though this is so, though pain's evil to the pain-blinded creature is an absolute fact in the universe, yet the very evil itself may have a place in the music which spirit is. There is no music without the torture of the strings. Even the over-straining, the slow wearing out, the sudden shattering of instruments may be demanded for the full harmony of this dread music. Nay, more. In this high music of the spheres, even the heartless betrayals, the mean insufficiencies of will, common to all human instruments, unwittingly contribute by their very foulness to the intolerable, the inhuman, beauty of the music.'

By now Paul, having bound up his hand, having wiped his knife and put it away, had risen to his feet, and was walking towards home with trembling knees, pursuing his argument.

'To make the music that spirit is, that, I now see, is the end for which all living things exist, from the humblest to the most exalted. In two ways they make it: gloriously, purposefully, in their loyal strivings, but also shamefully, unwittingly, in their betrayals. Without Satan, with God only, how poor a universe, how trite a music! Purposefully to contribute to the music that spirit is, this is the great beatitude. It is permitted only to the elect. But the damned also, even they, contribute, though unwittingly. Purposefully to contribute upon the strings of one's own being, and also to respond with ecstasy to the great cosmic theme inflooding from all other instruments, this is indeed the sum of duty, and of beatitude. Though in my own conduct I were to betray the music which is spirit, and in my own heart dishonour it, yet seemingly it is not in reality sullied; for it dare avail itself alike of Christ and Judas. Yet must I not betray it, not dishonour it. Yet if I do, it will not be sullied. Mystery! Purposefully to make the music that spirit is, and to delight in it! The delighting and suffering of all minded beings are within the music. Even this very profound, very still delight, this ecstasy, with which I now contemplate my hand's pain and Katherine's distress and the long effort and agony of the worlds, this also is a contribution to the music which it contemplates. Why am I thus chosen? I do not know. But it is irrelevant that this instrument rather than that should sound this theme and not another, create this ecstasy and not that agony. What matters is the music, that it should unfold itself through the ages, and be fulfilled in whatever end is fitting, and crowned with admiration, worship. But if it should never be rightly fulfilled, and never meetly crowned? I have indeed a very clear conviction that over the head of time the whole music of the cosmos is all the while a fulfilled perfection, the eternal outcome of the past, the present and the future. But if I am mistaken? Then if it is not perfected, it is at least very excellent. For this much my eyes have seen.'

He was now coming down the slope toward the street lamps and lighted windows. On the other side of the little valley the water-tower of the lunatic asylum rose black against the sky. He stood for a while. At that moment a faint sound came to him from across the valley. Was it a cat? Or had a dog been run over? Or was it a human sound between laughter and horror? To Paul it came as the asylum's comment on his meditation. Or was it the comment of the whole modern age? For a while, he kept silent, then said aloud, 'Yes, you may be right. Perhaps it is I that am mad. But if so this madness is better than sanity. Better, and more sane.'

On the following day Paul wrote a poem. It reveals the blend of intuitive exaltation and metaphysical perplexity in which he now found himself.

> When a man salutes the perfection of reality,
> peace invades him,
> as though upon the completion of some high duty,
> as though his life's task were achieved in this act of loyalty.
> Was the task illusory?
> Is this beatitude but the complacency of self-expansion?
> Or does the real, perfect formally,

yet claim for its justification and fulfilment
admiration?
As a man's love transmutes a woman,
kindling her features with an inner radiance,
does mind's worship
transfigure the world?

VIII *The Modern World*

1. PAUL UNDERTAKES HIS TASK

WITH this spiritual achievement solidly accomplished, Paul was
ready to observe London and the world with new eyes. In fact he
was now well fitted to carry out the main work that I had purposed
for him. He himself would have been content simply to carry on his
teaching with new vitality and conscientiousness, and for the rest
to pursue with deeper understanding his leisurely tour of the
countries of the mind. But he was soon to discover that more was
demanded of him, and that he who had so lately learned the lesson
of quietness, must now embark on a life more active, more resolute, than anything that he had formerly attempted.

His new purpose dawned on him slowly, and as it became clear
to him and formidable, he both lusted in it and feared it. His final
and precise apprehension of it flashed upon him as he was waiting
on the top of a stationary and throbbing motor-omnibus outside
the great railway terminus of Cannon Street, watching the streams
of bowlered or soft-hatted business men, hurrying to their offices.
There surged through him suddenly a violent hunger, or was it a
sacred call, to apprehend precisely and with understanding the
whole phenomenon of the modern world, to see it in relation to his
recent vision, to discover its deeper significance. So insistent was
this new craving that he had to restrain himself from descending
there and then into the street to ask each of the crowd in turn what
he was really doing with his life, and why.

Paul was frightened by the violence of his own desire, and by its
quality of freakishness, even of insanity. He pulled himself
together and argued against it. It would interfere with his own
work, and with his peace of mind. He was not fitted for any such
world-study. Moreover, he ought not to give up his life to merely
apprehending; he must do, must serve. However well he should
understand, the world would be none the better.

As the days passed, however, this new craving took firmer hold of him. He felt it growing into an irresistible, an insane obsession. So violently did he strive to exorcize it, that he was threatened with breakdown. Clearly, if he were forced to pursue my purpose against this desperate reluctance, he would pursue it ill. I therefore decided that, in order to gain his willing co-operation, I must attempt to give him a frank and precise explanation of my relations with him. This would be a difficult undertaking, and one which would have been impossible to carry out on any but a carefully selected and prepared individual.

One night, as Paul was lying in bed, I constructed in his imagination a detailed image of myself as I should have appeared to his eyes. He saw me as a great grey human monolith, snake-eyed. I then spoke to him, through his own imagination. I explained that I was a human being of the remote future, living upon Neptune, and that it was my task to study the Terrestrial ages of Man. For this work, I said, I had chosen him as my instrument. If necessary I could by an inner compulsion force him to work for me, but the work would fare better if he would enter into it willingly. I explained that, by helping me to render something of Terrestrial history into the consciousness of my own species, which, I said, was mentally far more advanced than his own, he would be serving not only me but his own kind. ,

Next morning Paul recalled the night's experience with amazement, but dismissed it as a dream. On succeeding nights I influenced him again, giving him more detail of my world and my power over himself. I referred him, moreover, to two books. One of these, already published, was *An Experiment with Time*, by J. W. Dunne, This work, I told him, though to the Neptunian mind it was philosophically naïve, might help him to understand the incursion of future events into the present. The other book, which would be called *Last and First Men*, had yet to appear.

When Paul encountered the first of these books, he was profoundly disturbed, and still more so when, some months later, he read the other in manuscript. He now became convinced of the reality of my intercourse with him. For a while he was terrified and revolted at the knowledge that another human mind had access to his every thought, and could even induce him to think and desire as it was not in his own nature to think and desire. That his character should be largely the product of another mind seemed to him at first an intolerable violation of his privacy, nay, of his identity. I had therefore to remind him, patiently and night by night, that even apart from my power over him he was an expression of influences other than himself, that whatever was distinctive of him was not truly his at all. 'You forget', I said, 'that your nature is the product of an infinite mesh of causes; of evolution, of the hither-thither turmoil of human history, and finally of your parents, of Katherine, of the war, and of your boys. Will you then rebel because yet another influence, hitherto unsuspected, is discovered to have part in you, an influence, too, which has very greatly increased your spiritual stature? If so, your recent illumination on the Down was less deep than it should have been. You have not realized in your heart that the bare private individuality is a negligible thing, that what is glorious or base is the form which circumstance imposes on it. I myself am in the same case with you. I am the product of a vast web of circumstance, and my mind is probably open to the critical inspection and even the influence of I know not what beings superior to myself. Compared with you I am indeed of a higher order of mentality, but no credit is due to me for this greater richness and significance of my nature. As well might the concluding chord of a symphony take credit for the significance poured into it by all its predecessors. There is of course in both of us, and in all men, and all living things, and all sub-vital beings, the one universal miracle of spontaneous doing, which is the essential life of all existence. Through the aid or the limitation of circumstance some may do much, others little. What matter which of us does which? All the tones of the music are needed for the music's perfection. And it is the music alone that matters, not the glorification of this instrument or that.'

In a few days Paul was reconciled to his fate to such an extent that he began eagerly to debate with himself how he should gratify the new passion which hitherto he had only with difficulty restrained. The fervour with which he embarked on his task combined the lusty hunger of an appetite with the exaltation of a sacred duty.

I further prepared him by making him realize that his recent experience on the Down was the vital spark lacking to all typical modern thought, the missing and all-relevant word without which its jumble of verbiage could never make sense, the still small voice which alone, working in each heart, could ever bring peace to the modern world. Paul knew, of course, that this experience of his was by no means unique. Other ages had more profoundly entered into it. Even in his own age it sometimes occurred. But it had played little part in the common life of the mind; the few who had known it had nearly always withdrawn into their inner fortress. Disengaging themselves from the dross which confuses modern thought, they had at the same time unwittingly rejected a treasure which had never before come within man's reach. Contenting themselves with vain repetitions of old truths, they were deaf to the new truth which was as yet but stammeringly expressing itself in men's minds. They could see very clearly the central error of the modern spirit, namely, the belief that reality is wholly included in the world of sense. Revolting from this folly, they erroneously declared this world a phantom and a snare, and naïvely conceived that in their ecstasy the soul, escaping from illusion, found herself at last untrammelled and immortal. I was at pains to make Paul see unmistakably that, for those who have entered superficially into the life of the spirit, this is the most insidious, the most lethal of all snares.

On the day after his illumination upon the Down, Paul had told himself that he had escaped from the foundering vessel of himself. The swarms of his fellow men and women all over the world could do nothing but labour incessantly from wave to wave of the maelstrom, pausing only now and then on some crest to look around them and realize that they were ploughing a waste of waters; and that one and all must sink. Paul saw them tormented by self-prizing; though also more nobly tortured and exalted by personal love, and by the intensified pain of watching the beloved's pain. This it was, indeed, that chiefly dignified them above the beasts. But this also it was that tethered them to the waste of waters, like foundering may-flies. Their interest was almost wholly personal, either in self-regard, or hate, or love; but increasingly they saw that in the waste of existence there could be no lasting home for personal spirits anywhere, and so no permanency of comfort for any one's beloved. Each of them, and each beloved, must settle heavily down into old age, like leaky vessels. If only they could have sunk in battle array fighting for some great cause! But their sailing orders had not come through to them, or had been so mutilated that they found no clear direction.

Thus Paul had figured things out on the day after his illumination. By some miracle he himself, seemingly, had escaped from the foundering vessel of himself. He had escaped simply by a leap of the imagination, a soaring flight into the upper air; whence, selfless, he could watch the shipwreck of himself and all selves with a strange, still compassion, but without revolt. Yet subsequently, under my continued influence, he saw that this image was false and dangerous. He had not escaped. No self could escape. And now at last he realized that escape was not desirable. For he had seen something of the beauty for which all selves, if they could but see it, would suffer gladly, and gladly be annihilated.

Paul now once more turned his attention to the world that it was his task to observe. Suddenly a truth, which he had long vaguely known, but had never before clearly stated to himself, became both clear and urgent. At last he saw the situation of his species unambiguously from the cosmical point of view. He saw what it was that he and his contemporaries should be doing with their world. Fate had given them an opportunity which had been withheld from every early age. They had stumbled on the power of controlling the destiny of the human race. They had already gained some mastery over physical nature, and a far greater mastery was seemingly in store for them. Already their world had become one world, as it had never been before. Moreover, they must some day learn how to remake human nature itself, for good or for ill. If they could begin to outgrow their limitations of will, if they could feel beyond their self-regard, their tribal jealousies and their constant puerile obsessions, then they could begin not only to construct a Utopia of happy individuals, but to make of their planet a single and most potent instrument of the spirit, capable of music hitherto unconceived.

What humanity should do with itself in the far future, no one could tell; but one conviction now stood out with certainty in Paul's mind, namely, that over all the trivial and inconsistent purposes that kept the tribes of men in conflict with one another, there was one purpose which should be the supreme and inviolate purpose of all men today, namely, to evoke in every extant human being the fullest possible aliveness, and to enable all men to work together harmoniously for the making of a nobler, a more alive human nature.

Some such purpose as this was obscurely dawning in many minds throughout the Western and even the Eastern world. But though they were many, they were a minute proportion of the whole; and their vision was unclear, their will unsure. Opposed to them were many violent powers, and the dead-weight of custom, not only in the world but in themselves also. What chance was there that these few groping minds would wrench the great world into a new way of living? Paul now with eager interest, nay with passion, with awe, with grim zest, took up his task of watching and assessing the intense little drama of your age.

Lest he should lose sight of the wider bearings of that drama, Paul first meditated on the cosmical significance of human endeavour, which now for the first time was beginning to be tentatively apprehended by man himself. The immediate outcome of his meditation was this poem:

> Is man a disease
> that the blood of a senile star
> cannot resist?
> And when the constellations regard us,
> is it fear, disgust, horror,
> (at a plague-stricken brother
> derelict from beauty),
> that stares yonder
> so sharply?
>
> Gas the stars are.
> They regard us not,
> they judge us not,
> they care for nothing.
> We are alone in the hollow sky.
>
> Then ours, though out of reach, those trinkets,
> withheld,
> unspoiled;

ours the sleeping and uncommanded genii
of those old lamps;
ours by right of mentality;
by right of agony,
by right of long heart-searching,
by right of all we must do with them
when our day comes,
when we have outlived our childishness,
when we have outgrown
the recurrent insanity of senility.
Then surely at last man,
and not bickering monkeys,
shall occupy the universe.

2. THE RESEARCH

Paul now devoted all his leisure to his great exploration. He began tentatively, by reading much modern literature, and talking politics and philosophy with his friends. Both these occupations were of course familiar to him; but whereas formerly they had been pursued in the spirit of the tourist, a rather bewildered tourist, now they were carried out with passion and an assurance which to Paul himself seemed miraculous. This beginning led him on to make a careful study of the mentality of the whole teaching profession, both in schools and universities; and this in turn developed into a wide and profound research into all manner of mental types and occupations from road-menders to cabinet ministers. With my constant help, and to his own surprise, the silent and retiring young schoolmaster, who had always been so painfully conscious of the barrier between himself and his kind, began actively to seek out whatever contacts promised to be significant for his task. With amazement he discovered in himself a talent for devising inoffensive methods of making acquaintance with all sorts of persons whom he needed for his collection. Indeed, he pursued his work very much in the spirit of a collector in love with his specimens, and eager to discover by wealth of instances the laws of their being. If one day he happened to conceive that such and such a well-known personage or humble neighbour could give him light, he would be

559

tormented by a violent, almost sexual, craving to meet the chosen one, and would leave no stone unturned until he had achieved his end.

Under my influence he also developed a captivating power of social intercourse, which, however, would only come into action in special circumstances. In the ordinary trivial social occasions he remained as a rule clumsy, diffident and tiresome; but in any situation which was relevant to his task, he seemed to come alive, to be a different person, and one that he thoroughly delighted to be. It was not merely that he discovered a gift of conversation. Sometimes he would say almost nothing. But what he did say would have a startling effect on his hearer, drawing him out, compelling him to get a clear view of his own work and aims, forcing him to unburden himself in a confession, such that at the close of it he would perhaps declare, 'Yes, that is really how I face the world, though till today I hardly thought of it that way.' Sometimes, however, Paul himself would be almost voluble, commenting with a strangely modest assurance on the other's function. Often he would find himself assuming for the occasion an appropriate personality, a mask peculiarly suited to appear intelligent and sympathetic to this particular man or woman. Paul was sometimes shocked at the insincerity of this histrionic behaviour; though he pursued it, for the sake of its extraordinary effectiveness. And indeed it was not really insincere, for it was but the natural result of his new and intense imaginative insight into other minds. Sometimes when he was in the presence of two very different individuals whom he had previously encountered apart, he would be hard put to it to assume for each the right mask without rousing the other's indignation. Thus, to give a rather crude example of this kind of predicament, having on Monday won the confidence of a member of the Communist Party, and on Tuesday the benevolence of a British Patriot, he happened on Wednesday to come upon them both together in violent altercation. Both at first greeted him as an ally, but before he fled he had been reviled by each in turn.

One curious limitation of Paul's talent he found very distressing. Brilliant as he was at evoking in others a clearer consciousness of their own deeper thoughts and desires, he was incapable of impressing them with his own ideas. Strong in his own recent spiritual experiences, and in his increasing grasp of the contemporary world, he yet failed completely to express himself on these subjects. This was but natural, for he was no genius, still less a prophet; and, save in the office in which I needed him and inspired him, he remained inarticulate. This incapacity disturbed him increasingly as the months and years passed. For increasingly he became convinced that the modern world was heading toward a huge disaster, and that nothing could save it but the awakening of the mass of men into a new mood and greater insight. More and more clearly he saw in his own meditations just what this awakening must be. Yet he could never make it clear to others, for as soon as he tried to express himself, he fell stammering or mute. The trouble lay partly in his incompetence, but partly also in the fact that through my help he had seen both sides of a truth which to his fellows was almost never revealed thus in the solid. Paul's interlocutor, therefore, was sure to be blind either to one or to the other aspect of Paul's central conviction; either to his sense of obligation in the heroic and cosmically urgent enterprise of man upon his planet, or to his seemingly inconsistent perception of the finished, the inhuman, beauty of the cosmos.

Most painfully when he was with members of the 'intelligentsia' did his mental paralysis seize him. He made contact with many writers and artists. Each of these brilliant beings he treated at first with doglike respect, believing that at last he had come into the presence of one who had broken into new truth. But somehow he never went very far with any of them. For a while he delighted them, because he stimulated them to apprehend their own vision with a new clarity. But since their visions were not as a rule very profound, they and he soon saw all there was to see in them. At this point Paul's talent invariably disappeared, and henceforth they thought him dull, bourgeois, not worth knowing. He could no longer hold their attention. He had not the necessary flow of personal tittle-tattle to carry him through when deeper interests flagged. On the other hand, if ever he dared to tell them his own views, he merely made a fool of himself, and was treated either with kindly ridicule or with inattention. Thus, though he came to know his way about the intellectual life of London, he was never taken into any circle or school. Most circles had at one time or other tolerated him on their fringes; yet he remained unknown, for no one ever bothered to mention him to any one else. Thus it happened that he was always apart, always able to look on without pledging his faith to any creed, his intellect to any theory. Every creed, every theory, he secretly tested and sooner or later rejected in the light of his own recent illumination. In this manner Paul served my purpose admirably. As a tissue-section, to be studied under the microscope, may be stained to bring out details of structure that would otherwise have remained invisible, so Paul, whom I had treated with a tincture of Neptunian vision, revealed in exquisite detail the primitive organs of his mind, some of which took the stain and others not. Obviously it is impossible to reveal the whole issue of the experiment to readers of this book, since they themselves suffer from Paul's limitations.

Throughout these crowded years Paul still carried on his daily work at the school, though inevitably as his attention became more and more occupied, his teaching suffered. All his free time, all his holidays, he now spent on his task of exploration. It was a strange life, so rich in human intercourse, and yet so lonely; for he dared not tell any one of the real purpose of his activities, of their Neptunian aspect, lest he should be thought insane. To his friends he appeared to have been bitten by some queer bug of curiosity, which, they said, had filled him with a quite aimless mania for inquiry, and was ruining his work.

To aid his project he undertook a number of enterprises, none of which he did well, since at heart he regarded them only as means of the pursuit of his secret purpose. He worked for a political party, lectured to classes organized by the Workers' Educational Association, collaborated in a social survey of a poor district. Also he haunted certain public-houses, attended revivalist meetings, became intimate with burglars, swindlers, and one or two uncaught murderers, who, he found, were extremely thankful for the opportunity of unburdening themselves under the spell of his mysteriously aloof sympathy and understanding. He made contact with many prostitutes and keepers of brothels. He respectfully explored the minds of homosexuals, and others whose hungers did not conform to the lusts of their fellows. He found his way into many chambers of suffering, and was present at many death-beds.

562

He was welcomed in mining villages, and in slum tenements. He discussed revolution in the homes of artisans. Equally he was received in the houses of bank managers, of ship-owners, of great industrial employers. He conferred with bishops, and also with the dignitaries of science, but no less eagerly with vagabonds; over stolen delicacies, seated behind hedges. Part of one summer he spent as a dock labourer, and part of another as a harvest hand in the West of England. He travelled steerage on an emigrant ship, and worked his passage on a tramp steamer along the Baltic coasts. He made a brief but crowded pilgrimage to Russia, and came home a Communist, with a difference. He tramped and bicycled in Western Europe; and in England he made contact with many visitors from the East. Yet also he found time to keep abreast of contemporary literature, to haunt studios, to discuss epistemology and ethics with bright young Cambridge philosophers.

In all this work he found that he was constantly and sometimes sternly guided by an inner power, which, though I never again openly communicated with him, he knew to spring from me. Thus he was endowed with an infallible gift of selection and of detective inquiry. Through my help he covered in a few years the whole field of modern life, yet he never wasted his strength on vain explorations. With the precision of a hawk he descended upon the significant individual, the significant movement; and with a hawk's assurance he neglected the irrelevant. Sometimes his own impulses would run counter to my guidance. Then he would find himself directed by a mysterious, an inner and hypnotic, impulsion, either to give up what he had planned to do, or to embark on some adventure for which his own nature had no inclination.

Month by month, year by year, there took shape in Paul's mind a new and lucid image of his world, an image at once terrible and exquisite, tragic and farcical. It is difficult to give an idea of this new vision of Paul's, for its power depended largely on the immense intricacy and diversity of his recent experience; on his sense of the hosts of individuals swarming upon the planet, here sparsely scattered, there congested into great clusters and lumps of humanity, here machine-ridden, there ground into the earth from which they sucked their scanty livelihood. Speaking in ten thousand mutually incomprehensible dialects, living in manners reprehensible or ludicrous to one another, thinking by concepts unintelligible to one another, they worshipped in modes repugnant to one another. This new sense of the mere bulk and variety of men was deepened in Paul's mind by his enhanced apprehension of individuality in himself and others, his awed realization that each single unit in all these earth-devastating locust armies carried about with it a whole cognized universe, was the plangent instrument of an intense and self-important theme of mind. For Paul had by now learned very thoroughly to perceive the reality of all human beings and of the world with that penetrating insight which I had first elicited from him in childhood. On the other hand, since he was never wholly forgetful of the stars, the shock between his sense of human littleness in the cosmos and his new sense of man's physical bulk and spiritual intensity increased his wonder. Thus in spite of his perception of the indefeasible reality of everyday things, he had also an overwhelming conviction that the whole fabric of common experience, nay the whole agreed universe of human and biological and astronomical fact, though real, concealed some vaster reality.

It must not be forgotten that throughout his exploration Paul was jealously mindful of my presence within him, and that his sense of an ulterior, a concealed, reality, was derived partly from the knowledge that within himself, or above himself, there was concealed a more exalted being. He knew that I was ever behind his eyes, ever attentive in his ears, ever pondering and sifting the currents of his brain. Yet, save when I swayed him with unaccountable cravings and reluctances, my presence was wholly unperceived.

It must be remembered that I used Paul in two manners, both as a transparent instrument of observation, and as a sample of your mentality. I was interested not only in the external facts which he recorded, but in his reaction to them, in the contrast between his appraisement of them and my own. That contrast I may express by saying that whereas I myself regarded the Terrestrial sphere primarily with detachment, though with detachment which held within itself a passion of imaginative sympathy, Paul regarded all things primarily from the human point of view, though he was able also by a continuous effort to maintain himself upon the loftier plane. For me it was a triumph of imagination that I could enter so fully into your remote and fantastic world. For Paul it was a triumph that in spite of his fervent humanity, his compassion and indignation, he could now regard his world with celestial aloofness. Thus the two of us together were like two different musical instruments playing against one another in two different tempos to produce a single intricacy of rhythm.

To the Neptunian intelligence, however, there was a slightly nauseating pathos even in Paul's most chastened enthusiasm. Only through the secret and ironical influence of my presence within him could he avoid taking the fate of his world too much to heart. The mind that has but lately received a commanding revelation which exalts it above the pettiness of daily life is very prone to a certain extravagance, a certain farcical pomp, in its devotion. The Neptunian mind, on the other hand, born into the faith and needing no sententious conversion, was sometimes impelled by Paul's solemnity to wonder whether even the final tragedy of man on Neptune called most for grief or for laughter.

3. FRUITS OF THE RESEARCH

Paul had already made it clear in his own mind what the human aim should be. Man should be striving into ever-increasing richness of personality. He should be preparing his planet and his many races of persons to embody the great theme of spirit which was as yet so dimly, so reluctantly, conceived. In fact man should be preparing to fulfil his office as a centre in which the cosmos might rejoice in itself, and whence it might exfoliate into ever more brilliant being. Paul found also in his heart a conviction, calm, though humanly reluctant, that in the end must come downfall; and that though man must strive with all his strength and constancy of purpose, he must yet continually create in his heart the peace, the acceptance, the cold bright star of cognizance which if we name it we misname.

In his exploration Paul sought to discover what progress man was making in this twofold venture. He found a world in which, far from perceiving the cosmical aspect of humanity, men were for the most part insensitive even to the purely human aspect, the need to make a world of full-blown and joyful human individuals. Men lived together in close proximity, yet with scarcely more knowledge of one another than jungle trees, which blindly jostle and choke, each striving only to raise its head above its neighbours. Beings with so little perception of their fellows had but a vague apprehension of the human forest as a whole, and almost none of its potentialities. Some confused and dreamlike awareness of man's cosmical function no doubt there was. As a very faint breeze, it spread among the waiting tree-tops. But what was to come of it?

In such a world there was one kind of work which seemed to Paul, not indeed the most important, for many operations were equally important, but the most directly productive work of all, namely, education. Among the teachers, as in all walks of life, Paul found that, though some were indeed pioneers of the new world-order, many were almost entirely blind to the deeper meaning of their task. Even those few who had eyes to see could do but little. Their pupils had at all costs to be fitted for life in a world careless of the spirit, careless of the true ends of living, and thoughtful only for the means. They must be equipped for the economic struggle. They must become good business men, good engineers and chemists, good typists and secretaries, good husband-catchers, even if the process prevented them irrevocably from becoming fully alive human beings. And so the population of the Western world was made up for the most part of strange thwarted creatures, skilled in this or that economic activity, but blind to the hope and the plight of the human race. For them the sum of duty was to play the economic game shrewdly and according to rule, to keep their wives in comfort and respectability, their husbands well fed and contented, to make their offspring into quick and relentless little gladiators for the arena of world-prices. One and all they ignored that the arena was not merely the market or the stock exchange, but the sand-multitudinous waste of stars.

Of the innumerable constructors, the engineers, architects, chemists, many were using their powers merely for gladiatorial victory. Even those who were sincere workers had but the vaguest notion of their function in the world. For them it was enough to serve faithfully some imposing individual, some firm, or at best some national State. They conceived the goal of corporate human endeavour in terms of comfort, efficiency, and power, in terms of manufactures, oil, electricity, sewage disposal, town-planning, aeroplanes and big guns. When they were not at work, they killed time by motor-touring, the cinema, games, domesticity or sexual adventures. Now and then they registered a political vote, without having any serious knowledge of the matters at stake. Yet within the limits of their own work they truly lived; their creative minds were zestfully obedient to the laws of the materials in which they worked, to the strength and elasticity of metals, the forms of cantilevers, the affinities of atoms.

Of much the same mentality, though dealing with a different material, were the doctors and surgeons; for whom men and women were precariously adjusted machines, walking bags of intestines, boxes of telephone nerves, chemical factories liable to go wrong at any minute, fields for exploration and fee-making, possible seats of pain, the great evil, and of death, which, though often preferable, was never to be encouraged. They were familiar equally with death, and birth, conception and contraception, and all the basic agonies and pities. They protected themselves against the intolerable dead-weight of human suffering, sometimes by callousness of imagination, sometimes by drink or sport or private felicity, sometimes by myths of compensation in eternity. A few faced the bleak truth unflinchingly yet also with unquenched compassion. But nearly all, though loyal to the militant life in human bodies, were too hard pressed to be familiar with the uncouth exploratory ventures of human minds. And so, through very loyalty to life, they were for the most part blind to the other, the supernal, beauty.

Even more insulated, those very different servants of human vitality, the agriculturists, whose minds were fashioned to the soil they worked on, lived richly within the limits of their work, yet were but obscurely, delusively, conscious of the world beyond their acres. In the straightness of their furrows, and the fullness of their crops, in their sleek bulls and stallions, they knew the joy of the maker; and they knew beauty. But what else had they? They had to thrust and heave from morning till night. They had to feed their beasts. Brooding over their crops, dreading floods and droughts, they had not time for the world. Yet they enviously despised the town-dwellers. They censured all newfangled ways, they condescended to teach their sons the lore of their grandfathers, and they guarded their daughters as prize heifers. They put on black clothes for chapel, to pray for good weather. They believed themselves the essential roots of the State. They measured national greatness in terms of wheat and yeoman muscle. The younger ones, town-infected with their motor-bicycles, their wireless, their artificial silks, their political views, their newfangled morals, revolted against enslavement to the soil. Both young and old alike were vaguely unquiet, disorientated, sensing even in their fields the futility of existence.

Most typical of your isolation from one another were the seamen, who, imprisoned nine parts of their lives in a heaving box of steel, looked out complainingly upon a world of oceans and coasts. They despised the landsmen, but they were ever in search of a shore job. Monastic, by turns celibate and polygamous, they were childlike in their unworldly innocence, brutelike in their mental blindness, godlike (to Paul's estimation) in their patience and courage. They loved the flag as no landsman could love it. They were exclusively British (or German or what not) but loyal also to the universal brotherhood of the sea (or disloyal), and faithful to the owners (or unfaithful). Day after day they toiled, shirked, slandered, threatened one another with knives; but in face of the typhoon they could discover amongst themselves a deep, an inviolable communion. They measured all persons by seamanship, crew-discipline, and all things by seaworthiness and shipshapeliness. They took the stars for signposts and timepieces, and on Sundays for the lamps of angels. Contemptuous of democracy, innocent of communism, careless of evolution, they ignored that the liquid beneath their keels was but a film between the solid earth and the void, but a passing phenomenon between the volcanic confusion of yesterday and the all-gripping ice-fields of tomorrow.

Seemingly very different, yet at bottom the same, was the case

of the industrial workers of all occupations and ranks, whose
dreams echoed with the roar of machinery. For the mass of them,
work was but a slavery, and the height of bliss was to be well paid
in idleness. They loudly despised the wealthy, yet in their hearts
they desired only to mimic them, to display expensive pleasures, to
have powers of swift locomotion. What else could they look for,
with their stunted minds? Many were unemployed, and spiritually
dying of mere futility. Some, dole-shamed, fought for self-esteem,
cursing the world that had no use for them; others, dole-contented,
were eager to plunder the society that had outlawed them. But
many there were among the industrial workers who waited only to
be wrought and disciplined to become the storm troops of a new
order. Many there were who earnestly willed to make a new world
and not merely to destroy an old one. But what world? Who could
seize this half-fashioned instrument, temper it, and use it? Who
had both the courage and the cunning to do so? Seemingly only
those who had been themselves so tempered and hardened by
persecution that they could not conceive any final beatitude for
man beyond regimentation in a proletarian or a fascist State.

Certainly the politicians could never seize that weapon. They
climbed by their tongues; and when they reached the tree-top, they
could do nothing but chatter like squirrels, while the storm cracked
the branches, and the roots parted.

The journalists? Was it they who could fertilize the waiting seed
of the new world? Little seekers after copy, they made their living
by the sale of habit-forming drugs. They had their loyalties, like the
rest of men; but they trusted that in preserving the tradition of the
Press, or in serving some great journal, they served well enough.
They ignored that in the main their journals spread poison, lies,
the mentality of society's baser parts. They made sex obscene,
war noble, and patriotism the height of virtue. A few there were of
another kind, who sought to bring to light what the authorities
would keep dark, whose aim it was to make men think by offering
them sugared pills of wisdom, spiced problems of state-craft,
peepshows of remote lands and lives, glimpses of the whole of
things. They were indeed possible trumpeters of a new order,
though not world-builders. But they were few and hobbled, for at
every turn they must please or go under. And the thought which

they so devotedly spread was of necessity over-simplified and vulgarized, to suit the spirit of the times.

The civil servants, could they remake the world? Wrought and tempered to a great tradition of loyalty, they were devoted only to the smooth-running and just-functioning and minor improvement of the social machine.

The social workers, so formidable with eye-witnessed facts, so indignant with the machine, so kindly-firm with 'cases', so loyal to the social gospel, and to the fulfilling of personality, so contemptuous of cosmical irrelevances, and morally outraged by those who, even in a foundering world, have an eye for beauty! They had their part to play, but they were repairers, physicians, not procreators of a new world.

The religious folk, who should have been society's red blood-corpuscles, transfusing their spiritual treasure into all its tissues, had settled down to become a huge proliferating parasite. Mostly of the middle class, they projected their business interests into another world by regular payments of premiums on an eternal-life assurance policy; or they compensated for this world's unkindness by conceiving themselves each as the sole beloved in the arms of Jesus, or at least as a life member in the very select celestial club. But some, teased by a half-seen vision, by a conviction of majesty, of beauty they knew not whereabouts nor of what kind, were persuaded to explain their bewildered ecstasy by ancient myths and fantasies. For the sake of their bright, featureless, guiding star, they believed what was no longer credible and desired what it was now base to desire.

The scientists, so pious toward physical facts, so arch-priestly to their fellow-men, were indeed a noble army of miners after truths; but they were imprisoned in deep galleries, isolated even from each other in their thousand saps. Daily they opened up new veins of the precious metal; and sent the bright ingots aloft, to be mortised into the golden temple of knowledge, with its great thronged halls of physics, astronomy and chemistry, biology and psychology; or to be put to commercial use, whether for the increase of happiness, or for killing, or for spiritual debasement, or to be instrumental in one way or another to the achievement of pure cognizance. Two kinds of scientists Paul found. Some were but eyeless cave-reptiles, or moles who came reluctantly into the upper world, nosing across men's path, concealing their bewilderment under dust-clouds of pronouncements. Some, though innocent of philosophy, ventured to set up metaphysical edifices, in which they repeated all the structural defects of the old systems, or were sent toppling by the dizzying of their own unschooled desires, whether for the supremacy of mind, or for the immortality of the individual. The public, tricked by the same unschooled desires, applauded their acrobatic feats, and was blind to their disaster. Others, more cautious, knew that all scientific knowledge was of numbers only, yet that with the incantation of numbers new worlds might be made. They were preparing to take charge of mankind, to make the planet into a single well-planned estate, and to re-orientate human nature. But what kind of a world would they desire to make, whose knowledge was only of numbers?

But the philosophers themselves were scarcely more helpful. Some still hoped to reach up to reality (which the scientists had missed) by tiptoeing on a precarious scaffold of words. Others, preening their intellectual consciences, abjured all such adventures. They were content merely to melt down and remodel the truth ingots of the scientists, and to build them together upon the high, the ever-unfinished tower of the golden temple. Some were so in love with particularity that they ignored the universal, others so impressed by the unity of all things that they overlooked discreteness. Yet doubtless by exchange of findings and by mutual devastation they were year by year approaching, corporately, irresistibly, but asymptotically, toward a central truth; which lay ever at hand, yet infinitely remote, because eternally beyond the comprehension of half-human minds. For, like their fellows, the philosophers of the species had a blind spot in the centre of the mind's vision, so that what they looked at directly they could never see. Like archaeologists who lovingly study and classify the script of a forgotten language but have found no key to its meaning, the philosophers were wise chiefly in knowing that whoever claims to interpret the rigmarole of half-human experience is either a fool or a charlatan.

There were the artists, despisers of the mere analytical intelligence. What hope lay with them? Microcosmic creators, for whom love and hate and life itself were but the matter of art, in their view the whole meaning of human existence seemed to lie solely in the apprehension of forms intrinsically 'significant', and in the embodiment of visions without irrelevance. Athletes of the spirit, by the very intensity of their single aesthetic achievement they were prone to cut themselves off from the still-living, though desperately imperilled world.

There were others, artists and half-artists, who were leaders of thought in Paul's day, publicists, novelists, playwrights, even poets. Some still preached the Utopia of individuals, the private man's heaven on earth, ignorant that this ideal had lost its spell, that it must be sought not as an end but as a means, that it must borrow fervour from some deeper fire. Some affirmed, pontifically or with the licence of a jester, that all human endeavour expresses unwittingly the urge of some cryptic, evolving, deity, which tries out this and that organic form, this and that human purpose, in pursuit of an end hidden even from itself. Some, ridiculing all superstition, declared existence to be nothing but electrons, protons, ethereal undulations, and superstitiously asserted that cognizance, passion and will are identical with certain electrical disturbances in nerve fibres or muscles. Some, zestfully proclaiming the futility of the cosmos and the impotence of man, cherished their own calm or heroic emotions, and deployed their cloak of fortitude and flowing rhetoric, mannequins even on the steps of the scaffold. Some, whose sole care was to avoid the taunt of credulity, and the taunt of emotionalism, fastidiously, elegantly, shook off from their fingers the dust of belief, the uncleanness of enthusiasm. Some, because reason (jockeyed and overpressed by so many riders) had failed to take her fences, condemned her as a jade fit only for the knackers; and led out in her stead a dark horse, a gift horse whose mouth must not be inspected, a wooden horse, bellyful of trouble. Some, gleefully discovering that the hated righteousness of their fathers drew its fervour from disreputable and unacknowledged cravings, preached therefore that primeval lusts alone directed all human activities. Some, because their puritan mothers dared not receive the revelation of the senses, themselves wallowed in the sacred wine till their minds drowned. Some were so tangled in the love of mother, and the discord of mother and mate, that they received from woman not nourishment, not strength, but a sweet and torturing poison, without which they could not live, by which their minds were corroded. Some, exquisitely discriminating the myriad flavours and perfumes of experience, cared only to refine the palate to the precision of a wine-taster; but registered all their subtle apprehensions with a desolate or with a defiant conviction of futility, a sense of some huge omission in the nature of things or in man's percipience. Some cognized their modern world but as flotsam gyrating on the cosmical flux, a film or ordure in which men and women swam spluttering, among disintegrated cigarette-ends, clattering cans, banana skins, toffee papers, and other disused sheathings. For them filth was the more excruciating by reason of their intuitions of purity violated, of austerity desecrated. Others there were, no less excruciated, who nevertheless by natatory prowess reached the mud-flats of old doctrine, where at last they thankfully reclined, 'wrapped in the old miasmal mist', and surrounded by the rising tide.

What was the upshot of Paul's whole exploration? For me there issued in my own mind the pure, the delighted cognizance, both of Paul's world and of Paul himself, the appraising organ that I had chosen. For Paul the upshot was a sense of horror and of exaltation, a sense that he was participating in a torrent of momentous happenings whose final issue he could but vaguely guess, but whose immediate direction was toward ruin.

He saw clearly that man, the most successful of all Terrestrial animals, who had mastered all rivals and taken the whole planet as his hunting-ground, could not master himself, could not even decide what to do with himself. All over the West man was visibly in decline. The great wave of European energy, which gave him mastery over nature, which carried the European peoples into every continent, which lent them for a while unprecedented intellectual vision and moral sensitivity, now visibly failed. And what had come of it? The Black Country and its counterpart in all Western lands, mechanized life, rival imperialisms, aerial bombardment, poison gas; for the mind, a deep and deadly self-disgust, a numbing and unacknowledged shame, a sense of huge opportunities missed, of a unique trust betrayed, and therewith a vast resentment against earlier generations, against human nature, against fate, against the universe. What more? An attempt to cover up guilt and futility by mechanical triumphs, business hustle, and the sound of a hundred million gramophones and radio-sets.

Paul asked himself, 'How has all this happened?' And he answered, 'Because we cannot look into our minds and see what really affords lasting satisfaction, and what is merely reputed to do so; because our individuality is a dimensionless point, because our personalities are but masks with nothing behind them. But in the East, where they say man is less superficial, what is happening? There, presumably, men have seen truths which the West has missed. But they stared at their truths till they fell into a hypnotic trance which lasted for centuries. They made it an excuse for shunning the world and all its claims, for gratifying themselves in private beatitude. And now, when at the hands of the West the world is forced on them irresistibly, they fall into the very same errors that they condemn in us. And the Russians? Socially they are the hope of the world. But have they as individual beings any more reality, any more percipience, than the rest of us?'

Over this despair, this disgust of human futility, Paul triumphed by taking both a longer and a wider view.

'We shall win through,' he told himself. 'We must. Little by little, year by year, aeon by aeon, and in spite of long dark ages, man will master himself, will gain deeper insight, will make a better world. And if not man, then surely some other will in the end fulfil his office as the cosmical eye and heart and hand. If in our little moment he is in regression, what matter? The great music must not always be triumphant music. There are other songs beside the songs of victory. And all songs must find their singers.'

Shortly after the final meditation in which he summed up the whole issue of his inquiry, Paul wrote a poem in which he made it clear to himself, though with a certain bitterness, that he cared more for the music which is spirit than for the human or any other instrument. In the final couplet there appears the self-conscious disillusionment which is characteristic of your age.

> If man encounter
> on his proud adventure
> other intelligence?

574

If mind more able,
ranging among the galaxies,
noose this colt and break him
to be a beast of draught and burden
for ends beyond him?
If man's aim and his passion be ludicrous,
and the flight of Pegasus
but a mulish caper?

Dobbin! Pull your weight!
Better be the donkey of the Lord,
whacked on beauty's errand,
than the wild ass of the desert
without destination.

Vision! From star to star the human donkey
transports God's old street organ and his monkey.

4. PAUL SETTLES DOWN

Paul had by now almost fulfilled the task that I had demanded of him. Not only had he collected for me an immense store of facts about the crisis of his species, facts the significance of which he himself often entirely failed to see, but also in his own experience he had already afforded me a very precise insight into the capacity of his kind. He had shown me, through years of inner turmoil, the aspirations and reluctances of a primitive being haunted by visions from a higher sphere. In particular he had shown me the limits of your intelligence and of your will. There were innumerable problems which Paul even with my patient help could never understand. There were austerities of beauty which even with my most earnest illumination he could not admire. But one test at least Paul had triumphantly passed. He had shown that it was possible for the average mentality of the First Men, under careful tuition, to apprehend without any doubt whatever the two supreme and seemingly discordant offices of the individual mind, namely, loyalty to man and worship of fate. To the Last Men these offices are displayed as organic to one another; but to the First Men, they are for ever discrepant. Paul's intellect at least saw this discrepancy, and refused to be put off with false solutions of the problem. For the rest, though he so clearly recognized that all human purposes should be subordinated to these two supreme ends, he himself, like the rest of his kind, was but a frail vessel.

Since I had no further use for Paul as a visual and auditory instrument through which to examine your world, I now ceased to trouble him with the insatiable lust of inquiry which had mastered him since the conclusion of the war. Hitherto he had pursued his task indefatigably, but now his energy began to flag. This was due partly to the withdrawal of my stimulation, partly to the fact that his uncapacious brain was already charged to the full and could bear no more, partly also to the long physical strain of the double life which he had led. For Paul had indeed been wearing himself out. Katherine, with whom he still spent an occasional week, had declared that he was withering before his time, that his arms and legs were sticks and his ribs an old rat-trap. Privately she had noted also that his embraces had lost their vigour. She had urged him to 'take things easy for a while'. And now at last he discovered that he had in fact neither the energy nor the inclination to pursue the old racketing way of life.

I made it clear to him that I required no more work of him, but that I should continue to be with him to observe the movements of his mind during his normal career. For, though I had no further use for him as an exploratory instrument, it was my intention to watch the way in which his Neptunian tincture would influence him in middle age and senility. At this juncture Paul displayed rather interestingly the weakness of his kind by futile rebellion, and an attempt to pursue a heroic career for which he was unsuited. I must not dwell upon this incident, but it may be briefly recorded for the light which it throws upon your nature. He had already, it will be remembered, become convinced that his race was heading for a huge disaster, from which nothing could save it but an impossible change of heart, of native capacity. In spite of the current 'world-economic crisis', he had no serious expectation of a sudden catastrophe; but he had come to believe in a long-drawn-out spiritual decline, masked by a revival of material prosperity. He looked forward to centuries, perhaps millennia, of stagnation, in which the half-awakened mind of man would have sunk back once more into stupor. But he saw this phase as but a momentary episode in the life of the planet. And he saw the little huge tragedy of the modern world as, after all, acceptable, a feature of cosmical beauty. He knew, moreover, not clearly but yet with conviction, that he himself had played some small part in apprehending the drama of his age for the cognizance of the mature and final human mind. He knew also that without my continuous support he had no outstanding ability. Yet, though fundamentally he had accepted all this, and was indeed profoundly at peace, he could not express this acceptance and this peace in conduct. He could not bring himself to participate in the tragedy without making efforts to avert it, efforts which he knew must be futile, because in the first place he himself was not made of the stuff of prophets, and because in the second place the nature of his species was inadequate. Though he knew it was so, an irrational fury of partisanship now seized him. Instead of continuing the work which he could do tolerably well, instead of striving by his school-teaching to elicit in certain young minds an enhanced percipience and delight, he must needs take it upon himself to become the prophet of a new social and spiritual order.

It is no part of my purpose to tell in detail how Paul, after earnestly seeking excuses for a project which he knew to be ridiculous, gave up his post in the school; how he devoted himself to writing and speaking, in fact to preaching the new truth that he supposed himself to possess; how he tried to gather round him a group of collaborators, whom secretly he regarded as disciples; how he made contact once more with his old acquaintance the author of *Last and First Men*, hailed that timid and comfort-loving creature as a fellow-prophet, and was hastily dismissed for a lunatic; how, subsequently, his literary products proved even to himself their inability to find their way into print, and his efforts at vocal prophecy earned him the reputation of a crank and a bore; how he tried to persuade the Communists that he knew their mind better than they did themselves; how he was expelled from the Communist Party as an incorrigible bourgeois; how the communistically inclined editor of a well-known literary journal, who at first hoped to bring Paul within his own circle, was soon very thankful to get rid of him; how after several disorderly scenes in

Hyde Park, Paul was eventually marched off by the police, from whose care he finally escaped only to take up his abode in the Lunatic Asylum near his suburban home; how after some months of enforced meditation he was at last released, thoroughly cured of his disease; how, finally, but not until many far-reaching wires had been pulled in his interest, he was re-established in his old school. These facts I record chiefly so that I may also record another. Throughout this fantastic phase of his life, Paul remained inwardly the calm, the compassionately amused spectator of his own madness.

Of his subsequent career I need only say that within a year he had settled himself firmly into harness once more, with the determination never again to see the inside of a lunatic asylum. He became indeed an admirable schoolmaster of the more advanced and sympathetic type, bent upon reform, but cautious. In consequence of my influence during his youth he was now able to earn a reputation for daring ideas, yet also for patience, tact and extreme conscientiousness. In due season he married, begat children, became a head master, and introduced far-reaching novelties into his school, in respect of curriculum, teaching methods, and dress. From the point of view of readers of this book, the tense of this last sentence should have been future, for up to the date of publication, Paul remains a bachelor. Nevertheless I have already observed his future career, and can report that, when the time comes for him to retire, he will look back on his work with thankfulness and modest pride; that, having earlier determined to commit suicide soon after his retirement, he will change his mind and allow himself a year or two to re-assess his life and his world in the mellow light of a peaceful old age; that during this period he will afford me much further knowledge of the senescent phase of your individuality, with its strange blend of wisdom and puerility, its increased potentiality of insight, progressively thwarted by neural decay; that when there is no further reason for him to remain alive, Paul will no longer have the resolution to kill himself, and will be trapped in the quagmire of senility.

IX *On Earth and on Neptune*

1. SUBMERGED SUPERMEN

I HAVE been describing a situation in which, had the intelligence and the integrity of average men and women been slightly more robust, your world might have passed almost at a leap from chaos to organization, from incipient dissolution to a new order of vitality. Many minds were clearly aware that they were puppets in a huge and tragic farce, though none were able to put an end to it. I have now to tell of a different and much less imposing pattern of events, which was enacted in your midst without revealing its significance to any man. In this case disaster was brought about, not by any lack of native intelligence or of native integrity, but by the action of a savage environment on minds too gifted for your world.

While our observers were watching the forlorn efforts of your species to cope with problems beyond its powers, they detected also in many regions of your planet the promise of a new and more human species. The tragic fate of these more brilliant beings is amongst the most remarkable incidents in the whole history of Man. Here it is impossible to do more than outline this amazing story.

Throughout the career of your species, biological forces have now and then thrown up individuals in whom there was some promise of a higher type. Nearly always this promise was frustrated simply by the physiological instability of the new mutation. The new brain forms were associated either with actual distortions of body, or at best with normal structures which were inadequate to bear the novel strain. During the great ferment of industrial revolution in Europe and America, these biological mutations became much more numerous. Thus was afforded a serious possibility of the emergence somewhere or other of a type which should combine superior mentality with a physique capable of supporting the new cerebral organs.

579

When the earliest phase of industrialism was passed and conditions had improved somewhat, it became less difficult for abnormal beings to preserve themselves. The growth of humanitarianism, moreover, tended to foster these crippled supernormals along with the subnormals for whom they were invariably mistaken. Toward the end of the Nineteenth and the beginning of the Twentieth Centuries, we found here and there in the cities and industrial areas of the Western World, and later in industrial Asia, many hundreds of these individuals. They were of diverse biological constitution, but similar in respect of the factors which, with good fortune, should produce supernormal intelligence and supernormal integrity. Many of them, however, were tormented by gross bodily malformation; some, though more or less like their fellows in general anatomy, were no less hampered by biochemical maladjustments; some, though otherwise normal, were crippled by excessive weight of brain. But a few, sprung from stock of exceptionally tough fibre and ample proportions, were able to support and nourish their not excessively large heads without undue strain, at least in favourable conditions.

Now it might have been expected that these individuals, potentially far more brilliant than the most gifted of the normal kind, would have risen very rapidly to positions of power; and that, at the same time, they would have successfully established their type by propagation. Within a few generations, surely, they would have completely dominated the earlier and inferior species. But this was not to be. Even among the very small minority who combined mental superiority with bodily health, circumstance was fatally and ironically hostile. With regard to propagation, to take the simpler matter first, most of these superior beings, even those who were healthy and sexually potent, were strongly repellent to normal members of the opposite sex. They did not conform to any recognized pattern of sexual beauty. They were neither of the classical nor of the negroid nor of the mongolian styles, which alone were favoured by the 'cinema'. Indeed they were definitely grotesque. Their heads, in most cases, looked too big for their bodies, and they were apt to have bull necks. In many of them, moreover, there was a disturbing uncouthness of facial expression, which to the normal eye seemed sometimes insane, sometimes infantile, sometimes diabolic. Consequently it was almost impossible for them to find mates.

More interesting to our observers was the failure of these potentially superior beings to assert themselves in a world of inferiors. Though they were biologically very diverse, springing in fact from entirely independent mutations, these beings were alike in one respect, namely their very prolonged childhood and adolescence. The new and more complex brain organization could not develop successfully unless it was associated with an abnormally slow rate of growth. Therefore such of these beings as were able to survive were always 'backward' not only in appearance, but in some respects, mentally also. Thus a boy of ten years would look like a child of six; and mentally, though in some respects already more developed than his parents, he would seem to them to be hopelessly incompetent. Judged by similar standards, the normal human child would appear hopelessly backward in comparison with the baby ape, although in reality he would be far more intelligent and promising. Similarly, these superior children were invariably considered by their parents and guardians as distressingly inferior.

This backwardness of the new individual was due, not solely to the slowness of physiological growth, but also to the fact that with more delicate percipience he found in the experiences of childhood far more to delight and intrigue him than the normal child could gather. These beings remained so long in the phase of perceptual and motor experimentation, and later so long in the phase of play, partly because for them these fields were so crowded with interest. Similarly, when at length they attained adolescence, the dawn of self-consciousness and other-consciousness was for them so brilliant and overwhelming that they had inevitably to take many years to adjust themselves to it.

So great was this seeming backwardness that they were often regarded by their elders, and by their own generation also, not merely as inferior, but as seriously deficient. Often they were actually treated as insane. Thus in spite of their superiority they grew up with a devastating sense of their own incapacity, which increased as they became increasingly aware of the difference between themselves and others. This illusion of inferiority was

aggravated by their slow sexual development; for at twenty they
were sexually equivalent to a normal child of thirteen. But, it may
be asked, if these beings were really so brilliant, how could they
be so deceived about themselves? The answer is given partly by
their serious physiological backwardness, but partly also by the
overwhelming prestige of the inferior culture into which they were
born. At thirty they had still the immaturity of the normal youth
of eighteen; and finding a fundamental discrepancy between their
own way of thinking and the thought of the whole world, they were
forced to conclude that the world was right. It must be remembered,
moreover, that they were isolated individuals, that no one of them
would be likely ever to come across another of his kind. Further,
owing to the precarious balance of their vital economy, they were
all short-lived. Hardly any survived beyond forty-five, the age
at which they should have been upon the brink of mental maturity.

One characteristic of their childhood was, as I said, a seeming
backwardness of interest, which was taken to be a symptom of
mental limitation. Now with the passage of years this limitation
seemed to become more pronounced. At an age when the normal
young man would be dominated by the will to make his mark in
the world by eclipsing his fellows, these strange beings seemed
quite incapable of 'taking themselves seriously'. At school and
college they could never be induced to apply themselves resolutely
to matters which concerned only private advancement. While
admitting that for the community's sake it was necessary that
individuals should 'look after themselves', so as not to be a burden,
they could never be made to see the importance of personal
triumph over others in the great game of life, the great gladiatorial
display of personal prowess, which was ever the main preoccupation of the First Men. Consequently they could never conjure up
the necessary forcefulness, the relentlessness, the singleminded
pushfulness which alone can advance a man. Their minds, it
seemed, were so limited that they could not form a really effective
sentiment of self-regard.

There were other respects in which the interest of these beings
seemed to be pitiably limited. Even those few who enjoyed physical
health and delighted in bodily activity, could never be persuaded
to concentrate their attention earnestly upon athletics, still less to

give up all their leisure to the pursuit of the ball. To the football-playing and football-watching population these lonely beings seemed almost criminally lax. Further, while enjoying occasionally the spectacle of a horse race, they could raise no interest whatever in betting. Blood sports they heartily loathed, yet without hate of those who practised them; for they had no blood lust secretly at work within themselves. They seemed also to be incapable of appreciating military glory and national prestige. Though in some ways extremely social, they could not pin their loyalty to one particular group rather than another. Moral sensitivity, too, seemed either absent or so distorted as to be unrecognizable. Not only did they break the sabbath without shame, even in districts where sabbatarianism was unquestioned, but also in respect of sex they were a source of grave offence; for they seemed wholly incapable of feeling that sex was unclean. Both in word and act they were shameless. Nothing but their sexual unattractiveness restricted their licentious tendencies. Persuasion was entirely ineffective, calling from them only a spate of arguments which, though of course fantastic, were very difficult to refute. Compulsion alone could restrain them; but unfortunately, though these beings were so lacking in self-pride and personal rivalry, any attempt to prevent them from behaving as seemed good to them was apt to call forth a fanatical resistance, in pursuance of which they would readily suffer even the extremes of agony without flinching. This capacity for diabolic heroism was almost the only character that earned them any respect from their fellows; but since it was generally used in service of ends which their neighbours could not appreciate, respect was outweighed by ridicule or indignation. Only when this heroism was exercised to succour some suffering fellow-mortal could the normal mind fully appreciate it. Sometimes they would perform acts of superb gallantry to rescue people from fire, from drowning, from maltreatment. But on another occasion the very individual who had formerly gone to almost certain death to rescue a fellow-citizen or a child, might refuse even a slight risk when some popular or important personage was in danger. The former hero would scoff at all appeals, merely remarking that he was worth more than the other, and must not risk his life for an inferior being.

Though capable of earnest devotion, these god-forsaken creatures were thought to be too deficient to appreciate religion. In church they showed no more percipience than a cat or dog. Attempts by parents and guardians to make them feel the fundamental religious truths merely puzzled or bored them. Yet Neptunian observers, stationed in these sorely perplexed but sensitive young minds, found them often violently disturbed and exalted by the two fundamental religious experiences, namely by militant love of all living things and by the calm fervour of resignation. Far more than the normal species, and in spite of their own racked bodies, they were able to relish the spectacle of human existence.

Most of them, both male and female, showed a very lively curiosity, which in one or two cases was successfully directed towards a scientific training. Generally, however, they made no headway at all in science, because at the outset of their studies they could not see the validity of the assumptions and method of the sciences. One or two of them did, indeed, have the enterprise to go through with their training, acquiring with remarkable ease an immense mass of facts, arguments and theories. But they proved incapable of making use of their knowledge. They seemed to regard all their scientific work as a game that had little to do with reality, a rather childish game of skill in which the arbitrary rules failed to develop the true spirit of the game with rigorous consistency. Moreover, the further they explored the corpus of any science, the more frivolously they regarded it, being apparently unable to appreciate the subtleties of specialized technique and theory. Not only in science, but in all intellectual spheres, they were, in fact, constantly hampered by a lucidity of insight which seemed to the normal mind merely obtuseness. In philosophy, for instance, whither their natural curiosity often led them, they could not make head or tail even of principles agreed upon or unconsciously assumed by all schools alike. Their teachers were invariably forced to condemn them as entirely without metaphysical sense; save in one respect, for it was often noticed that they were capable of remarkable insight into the errors of theories with which their teachers themselves disagreed. The truth was that at the base of every intellectual edifice these beings found assumptions which they could not accept, or in which they could find no clear meaning; while throughout the structure they encountered arguments in which they could not see a logical connexion.

There was one sphere in which several of these beings did earnestly try to make themselves felt, namely in politics and social improvement. But here they were even more ineffective than elsewhere. They could never see the importance of the accepted political aims or the validity of the recognized party maxims. When politicians demonstrated the inevitable results of this policy or that, these unhappy misfits could only deplore their own stupidity in not being able to follow the argument. When they themselves confessed how they would deal with some problem or other, they were either cursed for their lack of true feeling or derided for their childish idealism. In either case they were charged with being ignorant of human nature; and this charge was, in a manner, just, for they had seldom any conception of the gulf between themselves and the members of the older species.

I have been speaking of those few who were educated so far as to be able to take thought for matters of theoretical interest or public concern. But the great majority never attained this level. Those who were born into comfortable circumstances generally came into conflict with the taboos of their society, and were ostracized; so that they sank into the underworld. Those also who were born into poor families were frequently outlawed by their fellows; and being entirely unfit to make their way in the huge dog-fight of industrialism, they nearly always subsided into the humblest occupations. They became dock-labourers, charwomen, agricultural labourers, clerks of the lowest order, very small shop-keepers, and especially vagrants. It was remarkable that they received on the whole more sympathy and understanding in the lower than in the higher reaches of society. This was because in the simpler, less sophisticated, manner of life their native intelligence and integrity did not come into obvious conflict with the proud but crude culture of more 'educated' folk. Indeed, those whose lot fell among the 'lower' classes of society were generally treated by their peers with a strange blend of contempt and respect. Though they were regarded as ineffective cranks or freaks, as children whose development had somehow been arrested, as 'daft', 'fey', 'mental', they were also credited with an odd kind of impracticable wisdom that was too good for this world. Not only so, but even in practical matters their advice was often sought; for they seemed to combine a divine innocence and self-disregard with a shrewdness, a cunning, which, though it was never used for self-advancement, struck the normal mind as diabolic.

The kind of life into which these abortive supermen gravitated most frequently was a life of wandering and contemplation. Often they became tramps, drifting from one big town to another, trekking through agricultural districts, tinkering, sharpening scissors, mending crockery, poaching, stealing, breaking stones, harvesting. A few became postmen, others drivers of motor vans or buses; but though, whatever their occupations, they worked with incredible efficiency, seldom could they remain for long in posts which entailed subordination to members of the normal species. The women were more unfortunate than the men, for vagrancy was less easily practised by women. Some became seamstresses. A few, protected by sexual unattractiveness, faced the difficulties and dangers of the road. Others, blessed with more or less normal looks, chose prostitution as the least repugnant way of earning a livelihood.

Our observers, whenever they studied these unfulfilled approximations to a new species, found invariably a mental pattern definitely far superior to the normal, but also one which was much less developed than that of the Second Men, whose career was destined to begin some ten million years after your day. These superior contemporaries of yours had indeed, for beings whose heads were not much larger than your own, remarkable intelligence. They were remarkable also in respect of the organization and unity of their minds. Where the normal personality, torn by conflicts of desire and loyalty, would split into two or more incomplete systems imperfectly related to one another, these preserved their integrity, and chose that action which did in fact offer the greatest good possible in the circumstances. They were almost entirely without selfishness, for they had a capacity for self-insight definitely more penetrating than that of the normal species. Like the Second Men, they had also an innate interest in the higher mental activities, a craving for intellectual exercise and aesthetic delight no less imperious than the simple needs for food and drink. But unfortunately, since they were isolated individuals overwhelmed in childhood by a world of inferior calibre, they were unable to satisfy these cravings wholesomely. They were like potential athletes trained from birth to use certain muscles in grotesque and cramping actions, and the rest of their bodies not at all. Thus they never developed their powers, and were haunted by a sense of falsity and futility in all their mental life. They were beings, moreover, in whom we found a vigorous and lucid innate loyalty toward the supreme adventure of the awakening spirit in man, and in the cosmos. They were very ready to regard themselves and others as vessels, instruments of a great corporate endeavour. But, unfortunately, in their terrible spiritual isolation from their neighbours, they could never whole-heartedly give themselves to the communal life. In spite of the contempt with which they were treated, in spite of their own confusion of mind, those of them who survived beyond the age of twenty-five or thirty could not but observe that the minds of their fellow-men were woven upon a different pattern from their own, a pattern at once cruder and more confused, less intricate yet more discrepant. Moreover, they soon found reason to suspect that they themselves alone had the cause of the spirit at heart, and that the rest of the world was frivolous. Each of them was like an isolated human child brought up by apes in the jungle. When at last he had begun to realize the gulf between himself and others, he realized also that he had been damaged past repair by his simian upbringing. In these circumstances he would, as a rule, content himself with a life of personal kindliness and humour, which was ever rooted in the strength of his own unshakable ecstasy of contemplation.

2. PAUL AND HUMPTY

It so happened that one of these rare beings was sent by his parents to the school where Paul was head master. In appearance he was a great lout rather like a grotesque child of eight seen through a magnifying-glass. His thick neck and immense, almost bald head, was very repulsive to the normal eye. Only the hinder part of his head bore hair, which was sparse, wiry, and in colour like grey sand. The bare and lumpy dome of his cranium overhung two pale brown eyes, so large that they seemed to occupy the whole middle region of his face. Beneath an inconspicuous nose was a huge and clear-cut mouth. So small was the lower jaw that the chin, though well moulded, seemed but another nose under the great lips. The head was held erect in the attitude of one supporting a pitcher on his crown. This carriage gave to the face a farcical dignity which the alert and cautious eyes rendered at times malignant. The thick-set body and great restless hands made women shudder.

No wonder that this unfortunate child, who received the nick-name Humpty, was persecuted by his schoolfellows. In class his laziness was relieved now and then by fits of activity, and by un-couth remarks which roused derision among the boys, but which to Paul were sometimes very disturbing. The form master at first reported that Humpty was stupid and incorrigibly indolent; but later it appeared that he was perpetually active either in remote meditations or in observing and criticizing everything save the work in hand. Puzzled by the lad's seeming alternation between stupidity and brilliance, Paul contrived to give the whole class a series of intelligence tests. Humpty's performance defeated analy-sis. Some of the simplest tests floored him, yet some of those intended for 'superior adults' he solved without hesitation. Inquiring into the failures in the low-grade tests, Paul found that they were always due to some subtle ambiguity in the problem. The psychologists were not intelligent enough to test this unique boy.

Paul tried to win Humpty's confidence. He took him out to tea, and walked with him occasionally at week-ends. Paul had long been in the habit of taking parties of boys into the country and on the river, and in the summer he organized camping holidays and trips on the Continent. At first he had hoped to fit Humpty into this communal activity, but very soon he realized that nothing could be done with the strange creature in the presence of his contemporaries. He therefore devoted some time to treating the boy separately. Humpty was at first hostile, then politely reticent. When he found that Paul (with my aid) realized the gulf that lay between him and his fellows, he became cautiously well-disposed.

Conversation was at first extremely difficult. Paul's old gift of adopting a *persona* suited to his companions was now invaluable, but failed to produce the sudden and easy intimacy which he desired. The trouble was that Humpty did not belong to any known type. It was impossible to get in touch with him on the assumption that he was a normal adolescent; yet in spite of his infantile traits he could not be successfully treated as a child, for in some ways his interests were already those of an adult. On the other hand, Paul's well-tried policy of speaking to his boys 'as man to man' was in this case unsuccessful, because Humpty seemed to be without the normal craving to be a member of the adult fraternity. With patience, however, and with a sense that he was exploring a mentality more remote than anything he had discovered in earlier adventures. Paul plotted out some of the main landmarks of Humpty's nature. Gradually an important principle emerged in this study. In so far as Humpty was infantile, his attention was arrested by aspects of infantile experience which the normal child would miss. Sometimes, for instance, before a swim he would lie naked on the bank twiddling his toes for a solid quarter of an hour, like a baby in its cot, untouched by Paul's bright talk, or his suggestions that it was time to take the plunge. This conduct filled Paul with despair, till he discovered that what fascinated the boy was the difference between his control of his toes and his control of his fingers. Moreover, Paul had reason to suspect that there was some other more recondite aspect of the situation, which either could not be expressed in the English language, or was too subtle for Paul's apprehension.

When Paul first made the acquaintance of Humpty, he found the boy in a state of morbid diffidence punctuated now and then by flashes of contempt for his fellows. But under the influence of Paul's sympathy and insight Humpty began to realize that he was not, after all, merely an inferior being. As his mind developed, and as he came to understand that he was made on a different pattern from his fellows, it was borne in on him that in many ways he was superior, that he was basically more intelligent, more capable of coherent behaviour, less beset by atavistic impulses, and above all that there were certain aspects of his experience (in some cases the most delectable) to which none but the most sensitive of his fellow human beings had any access whatever.

A year after his first contact with Humpty, Paul began to feel that the tables had been turned, that he who had formerly played the part of the superior was being forced step by step to yield precedence. The change began one day when Paul had been trying to rouse Humpty to work harder at school by appealing to his competitive self-regard. When the sermon was over, the boy looked at him with a wonder tinged with dismay. Then he gave out a single bark of laughter, and said, 'But why on earth should I *want* to beat Johnson Minor and the rest?' This was not a very remarkable question, but coming from Humpty it seemed to have a peculiar significance. And Paul felt that somehow in his error of tactics he had displayed a gross vulgarity of feeling.

Somewhat later Paul discovered with dismay that he had been quite seriously asking Humpty's advice about certain matters of school policy. It was his custom to ask his boys for advice, so as to give them a sense of responsibility; but this time he was perturbed to find that he actually wanted the advice, and intended to use it. By now Humpty had sized up the mentality of his fellow-mortals very shrewdly; and in spheres of which he had experience, such as the school, he displayed a cold and often a cynical intelligence.

After another year had passed, the indolent Humpty surprised Paul by settling down to work, and making up for lost ground so successfully that he soon became the school's most brilliant, but most difficult, pupil. He gave his teachers the impression that in all his work he was but playing a game, or that he was learning the mental tricks of the human race without believing in them or approving of them. It was impossible to avoid thinking of him as a naturalist in the jungle studying the mentality of apes. After six months his fame as a prodigy of scholarship had spread over the whole country. This change in Humpty gratified Paul, but there was another change which was both incomprehensible and distressing. Hitherto he had seemed to Paul to be dangerously lacking in self-regard. Amongst the boys his generosity over toys, sweets and money had caused him to be mercilessly plundered, while in his work it was inveterate carelessness of self (so Paul thought) that had made him so ineffective. But now, along with his fever of work he developed a propensity for sacrificing the pleasure or well-being of others to his own interests. In most respects he retained his normal and unselfish nature though tinged with a contemptuousness that made him cast favours about him as one might fling refuse to the dogs; but in matters in which he felt a serious concern he was now a relentless self-seeker. It took Paul some months to discover the cause of this extraordinary change, and of the boy's increasing reticence and frigidity. At last, however, Humpty, during a walk on Leith Hill, announced that he would take his head master into his confidence, because he must have the help of some intelligent adult. Paul was then given a lengthy account of the boy's conclusions about himself, about the world which he had the misfortune to inhabit, and about his future. Paul had a sense that the tables had indeed been turned with a vengeance, and that the grotesque youth was treating him with the confident superiority with which normally a grown man condescends toward a child; while the head master himself involuntarily adopted the respectfulness of one of his own prefects receiving instructions. Yet according to all sane standards Humpty's plans were preposterous.

After careful psychological and biological inquiry, so Humpty said, he had discovered that he was profoundly different from the normal human being, and indeed very superior in mental calibre. Unfortunately his nature had been seriously distorted by his barbarous upbringing, 'Though', he added, 'you yourself have certainly treated me with sympathy, and with as much comprehension as can be expected of your kind. Indeed it is to you I owe it that I was not completely ruined during my adolescent phase.' Having made this contemptuous acknowledgement, the formidable boy declared that, in spite of Paul's care, he was probably by now too much damaged to win through in the enterprise which he must attempt. However, he would triumph or die fighting. Here Paul unwisely interrupted to say how glad he was that Humpty was at last determined to show his ability, and that undoubtedly he would make a mark in the world whatever career he chose. The boy stood still and faced his head master, gazing at him with a quizzing expression under which Paul found it hard to preserve his self-respect.

Presently Humpty remarked, with all the assurance and quietness of one who says he must buy cigarettes, or change his clothes, 'What I must do is to make a new world. I am not sure yet whether I shall have to destroy it and produce another.' Paul, with immense relief, burst into laughter. But the other said only, 'I thought you had more intelligence. In fact I know you have. Think! I mean what I say.' With dismay Paul realized that Humpty did mean what he said; and with bewilderment he realized further that something in his own mind applauded. However, he reminded himself that this would-be builder of worlds was merely an eccentric boy; and he set himself to persuade Humpty that he was making a fool of himself, that no single individual, no matter how superior, could achieve such a task. The boy replied, 'What you say is sound common sense, the kind of sense by which your species has hitherto triumphed. But an alien mentality such as mine can see very clearly that common sense is also your undoing, and that, as a species, you have neither the intelligence nor the virtue to save yourselves in your present plight. A superior mind may perhaps be able to discipline you, or to afford you a merciful extinction. With regard to myself, you are right that I shall almost certainly fail. Your world is not easy to move, or to destroy; and I have been terribly mutilated by early contact with an insensitive, a brutish, species. But I must make the attempt. And for a few years I shall need your help. Think the matter over for a few weeks, and you will see that I am right, and that unless you would betray your own highest ideals you must henceforth subordinate everything else to my service.'

Once more Paul earnestly protested against this folly; but to humour the lad he listened during the rest of the walk to his amazing plans. First, Humpty declared he would assimilate all the cultures of the human race. He was convinced that this would not take him long; for, having discovered his own superiority, he had also gained unique insight into the weakness and the limited but solid achievement of the best human minds. Having made himself the master of all man's wisdom, he would proceed to correct it by his own finer percipience and intelligence. Much that he would thus produce would be beyond the comprehension of his fellows, but he would publish simplified versions of all his work, based on his thorough knowledge of the inferior mentality. When this preliminary, easy, and purely theoretical, task was completed, he would set about the practical reform of the world. He was confident that by the time he had reached maturity, his superior tact and the unique power of his personality would enable him to deal with normal individuals much as a shepherd deals with his sheep; but he did not disguise from himself the fact that he would have to cope not only with sheep but with wolves, and that very grave difficulties would arise when the time came to break down the great atavistic organizations and vested interests of the world. This task, he admitted, would need all his skill, and would probably defeat him. Meanwhile, however, he would have taken steps to produce other individuals of superior type. Possibly, if his sexual development turned out normally, some of these would be his own offspring. Possibly he would have encountered other unique beings scattered up and down the world. Possibly he would be able to use his finer understanding of biology and physiology to produce superior men and women from normal ova. Anyhow, by one means or another, if the worst came to the worst, and the normal species proved incorrigible, he would found a small colony of supermen in some remote part of the world. This would become the germ of a new human species and a new world-order. Little by little it would gain control of the whole planet, and would either exterminate the inferior species, or more probably domesticate such members of the subhuman hordes as it required for its own uses.

At the close of this announcement of policy Humpty paused, then began again in a voice which betrayed an unexpected hesitation and distress. 'This programme,' he said, 'sounds to you fantastic, but it should be possible to one of my powers in a world of inferiors. I am no paragon. There should some day be minds incomparably finer than mine. Yet even I, if my health can stand the strain, should prove fit for the task, but for the severe mutilation which I have already received at the hands of your species. Till now I have never told you of my most serious trouble. I must bring myself to lay bare my secret, since you must help me to make myself whole for the work which I am to do.'

Humpty now told Paul that his sufferings during childhood had filled him with a violent hate of whatever passed as morality amongst his fellows. Things had come to such a pitch that, whenever any conduct seemed likely to earn general approval, he conceived an irresistible desire to take the opposite course. In his recent burst of hard work, for instance, public commendation had almost forced him to plunge back into indolence. Only by reminding himself that the real aim of his work was to destroy the so-called morality of the inferior species could he keep himself in hand. His increasing contempt for the well-being of others, though it found its excuse in his self-dedication to a great duty, drew its vigour from the sense that he was earning the condemnation of his fellows. There was also a more serious, or at least more dramatic, way in which his revulsion from the stink of moralism threatened to undo him. He was sometimes seized with an ungovernable, an insane, impulse to violate public decency in whatever manner would seem at the time most outrageous. He himself was sexually backward, but the awe and shame with which his elders regarded sex had in early days intimidated him; and when at last he came to realize the folly and abject superstitiousness of his countrymen in this matter, he conceived a violent craving to shock them.

Having forced himself to broach the subject, Humpty was carried away by his passion. He poured out on the bewildered head master a torrent of grotesque and mostly obscene fantasies ranging from schoolboy smut to acts of brutal sexual aggression. Of the most horrible of these gruesome titbits he said, after a hushed, almost it seemed a reverent, laugh, 'That ought to be done on the island in Piccadilly Circus, if you could catch the right woman there, one of those who look like princesses. But could I do it before they got at me?'

Paul felt with relief that leadership had once more come into his hands. He reasoned with the unhappy boy, and promised to help him. Subsequently he took Humpty to a psycho-analyst who had often dealt successfully with difficult cases in the school. But this time the expert was defeated. It was impossible to cure Humpty by bringing to life his unconscious cravings, for in this strange mind everything was fully conscious. Humpty knew himself through and through. Suggestion and hypnotism proved equally impossible. After a few meetings the analyst began to be ill at ease, for Humpty was taking a malicious pleasure in forcing him step by step to a most unflattering self-knowledge. Not only did the unhappy man begin to realize that his skill was mostly blind guesswork, and that his wisdom left out of account far more than it embraced, but also to his horror he discovered that he was dominated by secret desires and loyalties of a religious type which he had never had the courage to recognize. When Humpty appeared for the fifteenth meeting he was told that the analyst was missing. Later it turned out that the distracted man had suffered a religious conversion, and had fled away into solitude to meditate. Like so many of his profession, he was at bottom a simple soul; and when he found in himself needs that could be satisfied by religion but not by the doctrines of Freud, he could discover nothing better to do than to leap from the frying-pan of one orthodoxy into the fire of another. Within a few weeks he had joined a monastic order, and was studying the psychological principles of St Thomas.

The crippled mind of Humpty seemed now to go from bad to worse. The more clearly he realized the damage that had been inflicted on him in childhood, the more he succumbed to hatred, not of his fellow-men, but of their false righteousness.

In sane periods he told himself that his passion was fantastic; that when the mood was on him he lusted merely to violate and smash, and would harm what was precious no less than what was contemptible; that his obsession was ruining his mind, and making him unfit for his great task; that he must not let himself be dragged down to the level of the unhappy and unseeing beasts who surrounded him.

Paul, watching from day to day the desperate struggle of his protégé, was overawed by the sense of a momentous biological tragedy. For he could not but surmise that, if this lonely and potent being had not been mutilated, he might indeed have founded a new mankind. Humpty had already fallen into several minor scrapes, from which Paul had with difficulty extricated him. The head master now lived in dread of the final catastrophe which would ruin

Humpty and incidentally disgrace the school. But the school was, after all, spared the extreme disaster. One morning Paul received a letter in which Humpty declared that, realizing that he was defeated, and that at any moment he might do grievous harm to some innocent person, he had decided to die. It was his last wish that his body should be given to a certain world-famous neurologist for dissection. Inquiry proved that Humpty had indeed ceased to live, though the cause of his death was never determined. Needless to say, though he had always been the black sheep of his family, his parents secured for him a decent Christian burial.

Thus ended one of Nature's blundering attempts to improve upon her first, experimental, humanity. One other superior and much more fortunate individual was destined almost to succeed in the task that Humpty had merely imagined. Of this other, of the utopian colony which he founded, and of its destruction by a jealous world, I may tell on another occasion.

3. BACK TO NEPTUNE

My task is almost completed. My mind is stored with an immense treasure, which I have gathered, bee-like, in your world, and with which I must now return to the great and fair hive whence I came. The other side of my task also is drawing to a close. I have almost finished this my second message to my own remote ancestors, the First Men.

Very soon I shall be free to leave your world of sorrow and vain hope, of horror and of promise unfulfilled. Presently I shall return to an age long after the destruction of your planet, and not long before the more tragic destruction of my own more delectable world. Only with difficulty and danger can the explorer, after close work in the past, revert once more to his own world. With difficulty and reluctance also, I shall now begin to put off your mental pattern from my mind, as one may put off a mask. As the grown man who has been long with children, living in their games, grieving with them in their childish sorrows, is torn with regret when at last he must leave them, and half-persuades himself that their nature and their ways are better than his own, so I now with reluctance leave your world, with its childish, its so easily to be avoided yet utterly inescapable, its farcical and yet most tragic, disaster. But even as, when at last the grown man is once more at grips with the world of men, his childishness falls from him, so, when I earnestly revert in imagination to my own world, my assumed primitiveness falls from me.

It is time to recall myself to myself. I have been dwelling in your little world, not as one of you, but in order that I might bring to the racial mind of the Last Men matter for delighting cognizance; in order, also, that your world may find its crown of glory, not indeed in the way that was hoped, but in being exquisitely savoured, life by life, event by event, in the racial mind of the Last Men.

I recall myself to myself. The great world to which I am native has long ago outgrown the myths, the toys, the bogies of your infant world. There, one lives without the fear of death and pain, though there one dies and suffers. There, one knows no lust to triumph over other men, no fear of being enslaved. There one loves without craving to possess, worships without thought of salvation, contemplates without pride of spirit. There one is free as none in your world is free, yet obedient as none of you is obedient.

I recall myself to myself. The most lovely community of which I am a member, the most excellently fulfilled Spirit of Man, within which my mind is organic, must very soon be destroyed. The madness of the Sun is already hideously at work upon my world. There lies before my contemporaries an age of incalculable horror and disintegration. From that horror we must not escape by means of the racial suicide which alone could save us; for our two supreme acts of piety are not yet accomplished. We have not yet succeeded in impregnating the remote regions of this galaxy with the seed of a new mankind. We have not yet completed our devoted survey of the past. Therefore we may not yet put an end to ourselves. We must be loyal to the past and to the future.

I recall myself to myself. Presently I shall wake in my Arctic and subterranean garden. Once more I shall see with precision and with full colour through my own eyes, not through the obscuring organs of the First Men. I shall recognize the familiar forms of Neptunian leaves and flowers, swaying in the subterranean breeze. I shall feel the large easefulness of my own body. I shall yawn and stretch and rise. I shall swim luxuriously in my pool. I shall enter my apartment and ring for food. Then, before I see any of my colleagues, I shall begin to review my exploration; I shall record it, and critically edit it. For now at last I shall have recovered full Neptunian mentality. I shall see with new insight not only your world but my own self as I was during my long immersion in your world. Probably I shall smile at my recent earth-infected thoughts and feelings. I shall smile when I remember this book, this strange hybrid sprung from the intercourse of a purely Terrestrial mind and a Neptunian mind, earth-infected. I shall know that, even when I most strained the understanding of my poor collaborator, I was not really giving him the full wisdom of the Last Men, but something far less profound, something that was already earth-dimmed, already three-parts Terrestrial even at its source in my own mind.

With a great thankfulness I shall recognize my own complete reversion to lucidity. With a new awe and zest I shall lay myself open once more to the inflooding richness and subtlety of my well-loved world.

After many weeks of labour I shall have completed my report, and then I shall leave my apartment and meet many of my colleagues, to exchange findings with them.

But, since in the Catacombs telepathic intercourse may not occur, we shall soon travel south to live together for a while in a great crystal pylon where we may pursue our collaboration telepathically. And when we have made of our combined findings a single, living, apprehension of your species, we shall broadcast our great treasure telepathically over the whole world; so that all the million million minds of our fellows may be enriched by it, so that when the time comes for the next awakening of the single mind of the race, that great spirit also, which is not other than each of us fully awakened, may avail itself of our findings, for its meditation and ecstasy.

When all this is done I shall call up telepathically the ever dear companion of my holdiays, with whom, before my last exploration, I played and slept, where the broken mountain lies spread out into the sea. There once more we shall meet and play, watching the populations of the rock pools, and the risings and settings of the Mad Star. There once more we shall wander over the turfy hillocks and swim, seal-like, in the bay, and make for ourselves nests in the long grass, where we may lie together in the night. There perhaps I shall tell her how, in another world, seemingly in another universe, I myself, striving in the numb, the half-human flesh of Paul, lay with the half-human Katherine. There we shall contemplate the strange beauties of the past and of the dread future. There we shall savour lingeringly the present.

When our holiday is over I shall return with her to her place of work, where they prepare for the spreading of the seed. And when she has shown me how the task is progressing, I shall go wandering about the world for a very long time, absorbing its intricate beauty, watching its many and diverse operations, having intercourse with the great population of my intimate friends, playing my part in the life of my marriage group, visiting the Land of the Young, voyaging in ether-ships among the planets, wandering alone in the wild places of the home planet, idling or meditating in my garden or working among my fruit trees, or watching the most distant universes from some great observatory, or studying with the help of astronomers the slow but fatal progress of the sun's disease.

It may be that before it is time for me to go once more into the past, there will occur again a supreme awakening of the racial mind. It may be that after the unique day of the awakening I shall for a long time move about the world entranced like my fellows, rapt in the ineffable experiences of the single Spirit of Man, contemplating perhaps at last the supernal entities which it is man's chief glory to strive to worship. Sooner or later, however, I shall return once more to my work in the past, either to the First Men or to some other primitive species. I shall bring back with me more treasure of living history, and deliver it into the world of the Last Men. And again I shall play, and again I shall participate in the rich life of my world, and again I shall return to the past. And so on for I know not how many times.

But each time, when I leave the present for the past, there will have been a change in my world, a slight deterioration, sometimes perhaps imperceptible. The climate will have grown hotter and more unwholesome. The inescapable rays of the mad sun will have done more harm to eyes and brains. Society will perhaps no longer be perfect, rational conduct no longer invariable, telepathy perhaps already difficult; and very probably the racial mentality will have already become impossible. But also the exploration of the past will be advancing toward completion, though with increasing difficulty; and the dissemination of the seed of life will be at last begun.

The Last Men can look forward without dismay to the inevitable deterioration of all that they cherish most, to the death of their fair community, and to the extinction of the human spirit. We have only one desire, namely that our two tasks may be accomplished; and that happily they may be accomplished before our deterioration is so far advanced as to make us incapable of choosing to put an end to ourselves when at last we are free to do so. For the thought is somewhat repugnant to us that we should slowly sink into barbarism, into the sub-human, into blind and whimpering agony, that the last of Man should be a whine.

This may well happen, but even by such a prospect we are not seriously dismayed. If it does occur, it will doubtless seem intolerable to our degraded spirits. But today, we are fully possessed of ourselves. Even as individuals, even apart from the exaltation of racial mentality, we can accept with resignation, nay with a surprising fervour of appreciation, even the moral downfall of our world. For we have gone far. We have drunk deeply of beauty. And to the spirit that has drunk deeply of the grave beauty of the cosmos, even the ultimate horror is acceptable.

4. EPILOGUE BY THE TERRESTRIAL AUTHOR OF THIS BOOK

Readers of my earlier book, *Last and First Men*, may remember that it closed with an epilogue which my Neptunian controller claimed to have transmitted to me from a date in Neptunian history many thousands of years after the communication of the body of the book. The present book was obviously originated at a Neptunian date shortly after the transmission of the main part of the earlier book, but very long before its epilogue. Now I have reason to believe that at some date long after the communication of that former epilogue itself, my controller attempted to give me an epilogue to the present volume, but that owing to the serious disintegration of the most delicate brain tracts of the Last Men, and the gradual break-up of their world society, the result has been extremely confused and fragmentary.

I shall now attempt to piece together the random thoughts and passions, and occasional definite statements, which have come into my mind seemingly from my Neptunian controller. By supplementing them with a careful use of my own imagination, I shall try to construct a picture of the state of affairs on Neptune when the disaster was already far advanced.

From the vague flood of intimations that has come through to me I gather that the hope of disseminating a seed of life abroad among the stars, before the disaster should have extinguished man's powers, was not fulfilled. The dissemination had indeed actually been begun, when it was discovered that the vital seed was all the while being destroyed in the process of scattering. This trouble, and other unexpected difficulties, which occurred seemingly at some date after the communicating of the earlier epilogue, not merely delayed the enterprise, but even led to its abandonment for some thousands of years. Then some new discovery in psychophysics raised a hope of achieving the Dissemination by an entirely new method. A vast new enterprise was therefore set on foot; but was seriously hampered by the increasingly cruel climate, the steady deterioration of mental calibre, the ceaseless national wars and civil confusion. It would seem, though the inference is by no means certain, that at the date of this final and intermittent communication, the Dissemination had already ceased for ever; whether because it had been successfully accomplished or because it was no longer physically possible, or because the will to pursue it had already been broken, I cannot ascertain. Probably the work was now beyond the powers of a degenerate and disorganized world-community.

The other great task which the doomed population had undertaken to complete before its final downfall, the Exploration of the Human Past, seems to have been in a manner finished, though in less detail than was originally planned. Several communications suggest that such workers as remained able and willing to enter into the past were trying to concentrate their failing powers on certain critical points of Man's career, so as to reconstruct at least these moments in full minuteness. But as the racial mode of mentality had already become impossible, and as the individual explorers had evidently very seriously deteriorated, it seems clear that such data as were still being collected would never be incorporated in the single racial consciousness, in the aesthetic apprehension of the Cosmos by the fully awakened Spirit of Man. In fact the continuation of the work of exploring the past seems to have become as automatic and irrational as the aimless researches of some of our Terrestrial historians.

In the epilogue to the earlier book it was reported that, as the higher and more recent brain-tracts were corroded by the fury of ultra-violet solar radiation, the surviving members of the community suffered a harrowing struggle between their nobler and their baser natures, a struggle which issued inevitably in the defeat of all that was most excellent in them. At the date of the epilogue to the present book, the race seems to have been reduced to a remnant of distraught and almost sub-human beings clustering round the South Pole, which, one may suppose, was the only region of the planet still capable of supporting human existence at all. The life of this remnant must have been completely aimless and abject. It apparently consisted of half-hearted agriculture, occasional hunting expeditions against the wild creatures that had been driven south by the heat, and frequent predatory raids of neighbouring groups to capture one another's food and women.

The population was evidently obsessed by the terror of death, of starvation, and above all of insanity. The death-rate must have been very high, but there was also a huge birthrate. Conception was no longer controlled. Invalid children seem to have composed a large proportion of the population. Parenthood and sex evidently bulked very largely in the popular mind. There were wild sexual orgies, which apparently had acquired some religious significance; and there was a vast ritual of superstitious taboos, most of which seem to have been intended to purify the soul and prepare it for eternal life. Apparently some divinity, referred to as the God of Man, was expected to destroy the world by fire, but to snatch into eternal bliss those who had kept all the taboos. His Younger Brother, it seems, had already appeared on Neptune, but had been killed by his enemies. This legend should, perhaps, be connected in some way or other with the superior being who, in the epilogue to the previous book is referred to as 'this younger brother of ours'.

Not every one succumbed to these superstitions. My controller himself rejected them, and retained a pathetic loyalty to the ancient wisdom, some shreds of which he now and then remembered. But I have reason to believe that very often his memory of them was but a verbal formula, without insight.

Clearly, for those who, like my controller, had kept alive in themselves something of the former purpose of the race, there was now no longer any reason to refrain from racial suicide. The two enterprises for which euthanasia had been postponed could no longer be usefully continued. But the unhappy members of what had once been the noblest of all human communities had no longer the courage or the common sense to destroy themselves. Those who accepted the popular superstitions declared that the God had forbidden men to seek death before their time. Those who rejected the doctrine of salvation persuaded themselves that they refrained from suicide because to flee was cowardly.

At this point I will report a verbal fragment of communication which is typical of most that I have received, and seems to bear out many of the foregoing inferences.

'Vain to live. Yet Life insists. Work insists. Too many thousands of men, of women, of crawling children with eyes festering. Too little food. Blue sun piercing the deep cloud-zone, parching the fields. Child meat in the flesh pots. Eat the mad, who come to grief. The many mad. Mad men with knives. Mad women with smiles, with skull-faces. (And I remember beauty.) Too many labours and fears. Too hot. Hateful proximity of men hot. Love one another? With sweat between! Love best in the water, the cooling water, that makes the body lighter. The pools, the rains, the house-uprooting storms, the everlasting cloud, blinding purple. God will come soon, they say it. To burn the world, to take away his friends. The God-dream. Too good, too cheap. Radiation the one God, all pervading, cruel. To die quickly, to sleep and not wake! But life insists, work insists. Vain work insists. Yet why? The old far days, Godless, beautiful. The glorious world. The fair world of men and women and of the single awareness. Eye of the cosmos. Heart of the cosmos. Cunning hand. Then, we faced all things gaily. Even this corruption, when we foresaw it, we called "a fair end to the brief music that is man". This! The strings all awry, screaming out of tune, a fair end!'

This passage is typical, though more coherent than most. There are others more striking, but so repugnant to the taste of my contemporaries that I dare not repeat them, passages describing the prevailing brutishness of sexual relations in a population that had already so far degenerated that neither sex could interest the other save in the crudest manner. This impoverishment of sexual life was due to the fact that physical health and beauty had been undermined, that apprehension of the more delicate, aesthetic and spiritual aspects of experience had become almost impossible, that the realization of other individuals as living personalities was very uncommon. Nearly all behaviour was the impulsive behaviour of beasts, though of beasts in whose nature were incorporated many tricks derived from a forgotten humanity.

Some men and women there still were who had not permanently sunk to this brutish level. Several communications make it clear that, although the culture and the actual mental capacity of the Last Men were by now so degenerate, some few, a scattered and dwindling aristocracy, were still capable, at least intermittently, of personal love, and even of perplexed loyalty to certain ideals of conduct. The evidence for this lies in such passages as the following, which with its fleeting recovery of the earlier intelligence, and its bewildered groping after a forgotten ecstasy, affords perhaps the right conclusion to this book.

'She lies motionless in the shallow water. The waves, fingering the hot sand, recoil steaming. Her flesh, translucent formerly, now is filmed and grey, blind like her filmed eyes. We have taken of each other very deeply. The heat tricks us sometimes into intolerance each of the other's unyouthful body, unpliant mind; yet each is the other's needed air for breathing. We have ranged in our work very far apart, she into the astronomical spaces, I into the pre-historical times. But now we will remain together until the end. There is nothing more for us to do but to remember, to tolerate, to find strength together, to keep the spirit clear so long as may be.

The many aeons of man! The many million, million selves; ephemeridae, each to itself, the universe's one quick point, the crux of all cosmical endeavour. And all defeated! The single, the very seldom achieved, spirit! We two, now so confused, participated once in man's clearest elucidation. It is forgotten. It leaves only a darkness, deepened by blind recollection of past light. Soon, a greater darkness! Man, a moth sucked into a furnace, vanishes; and then the furnace also, since it is but a spark islanded in the wide, the everlasting darkness. If there is a meaning, it is no human meaning. Yet one thing in all this welter stands apart, unassailable, fair, the blind recollection of past light.'

MORE ABOUT PENGUINS

Penguinews, which appears every month, contains details of all the new books issued by Penguins as they are published. From time to time it is supplemented by *Penguins in Print*, which is a complete list of all available books published by Penguins. (There are well over four thousand of these.)

A specimen copy of *Penguinews* will be sent to you free on request, and you can become a subscriber for the price of the postage. For a year's issues (including the complete lists) please send 30p if you live in the United Kingdom, or 60p if you live elsewhere. Just write to Dept EP, Penguin Books Ltd, Harmondsworth, Middlesex, enclosing a cheque or postal order, and your name will be added to the mailing list.

Note: *Penguinews* and *Penguins in Print* are not available in the U.S.A. or Canada

Also by Olaf Stapledon

SIRIUS

For years Thomas Trelone had tried to breed a superman by injecting hormones into various mammals. Sirius was the end-product, a viable puppy with the senses, instinct and physique of an Alsatian-Collie cross, but with the brain capacity of a human being.

Brought up with Thomas's daughter, Plaxy, Sirius learns to speak an intelligible language and shares lessons with her. Child and puppy develop an intense understanding of each other.

Out of the inevitable conflict between the instincts of a dog and the mind of a man, and its effects on a human girl, Olaf Stapledon wove a Science Fiction story which, for its immense and tragic pathos, compares with *Last and First Men*.

NOT FOR SALE IN THE U.S.A.

STAR MAKER

One moment a man sits on a suburban hill. The next, he is whirling through the firmament. Street lamps become blinding stars and rushing grains swell into planets.

Like H. G. Wells's Time Traveller, he visits many worlds, often at times of political and social crisis. Like the 'Other Earth' from which he escapes with the quasi-human Bvalltu just before techno-logical change sweeps and annihilates the planet. Like the worlds of the Nautiloids, men-cum-fish-cum-boats, and the Plant Men, vast mobile herbs . . .

As they search up and down time and space for the Star Maker behind the cosmos, the two travellers are joined by others, to develop into a strange mental community, both 'I' and 'We', reacting multi-dimensionally to a mind-spinning range of ex-periences.

NOT FOR SALE IN THE U.S.A.